THEY
DREAM
IN
Gold

Title Artwork To Come

THEY DREAM IN

A NOVEL

MAI SENNAAR

Title Artwork To Come

PICADOR

First published 2024 by SJP Lit, an imprint of Zando

First published in the UK 2024 by Picador
an imprint of Pan Macmillan
The Smithson, 6 Briset Street, London EC1M 5NR
EU representative: Macmillan Publishers Ireland Ltd, 1st Floor,
The Liffey Trust Centre, 117–126 Sheriff Street Upper,
Dublin 1, D01 YC43
Associated companies throughout the world
www.panmacmillan.com

ISBN 978-1-0350-3370-6 HB
ISBN 978-1-0350-3373-7 TPB

1 3 5 7 9 8 6 4 2

A CIP catalogue record for this book is available from the British Library.

Printed and bound by CPI Group (UK) Ltd, Croydon, CR0 4YY

Visit **www.picador.com** to read more about all our books
and to buy them. You will also find features, author interviews and
news of any author events, and you can sign up for e-newsletters
so that you're always first to hear about our new releases.

To A. D. and Diana

For your dreams and the dreams they've begotten

Stay close to any sounds that make

you glad you are alive.

HAFIZ

CONTENTS

AUTHOR'S NOTE

On the day the second draft of this novel was due, a dust storm from the Sahara Desert traveled west, sprinkling cars with African dust and tinting the evening sky gold in parts of the UK and Ireland. Such a storm occurs at least once a year and illustrates a truth that otherwise remains amorphous: the reality that our world is but one place.

I wanted to write a novel that could do what the dust storm does: say a great deal about our shared experience in an organic, tangible way, and from this intention, *They Dream in Gold* came about. Rather than centering the external racial pressures that often drive narratives around Blackness and Black identity, I wanted to reckon with another important reality: the questions that arise and the transformation that occurs when different cultures *within* a diaspora are intimately engaged with one another.

Like the storm, the exploration of these ideas in fiction revealed to me the blurriness of the lines that divide us. How the cultures we all claim such rigid and separate allegiance to are perhaps necessarily and inherently enmeshed. That origin is not only a long established point in the annals of our history, but also an internal, living place to which we all are constantly returning, in our lifelong struggle to be and know who we are.

PART
ONE

I.

THE INGREDIENTS

Switzerland, 1969

1. **HIS PILLOW RUPTURES** between her knees. Feathers plucked from the breasts of live geese burst into the darkness of the room. She watches them by the flashes of the storm's lightning. Some descend into the gaps of the floorboards; others wilt between the poles of the hot water pipes. They land in her palms, along her pregnant stomach, and on the meeting of her thighs.

August, the third month since his departure, begins today and Mansour and his musicians have still not returned from their three-week tour of Spain. The last of her American cash has now been converted into francs, then tokens, and emptied into the phone booth around the corner. She's memorized the flat note of the dial tone. Having not reached him since May, she is finally imagining the worst.

Frantic, swollen, urinating often, she goes about naked beneath her nightgown as the night ends. For several days, she has found calm in smoking out of her small attic window and watching the summer storm rage through Switzerland. And though the storm has not left, this morning, fondling the nightstand as the sun rises, she discovers that her last cigarette is gone.

With the dawn, a mix of frying tomatoes, couscous, and dehydrated fish rises from the kitchen below. Beside it, the living room downstairs houses the restaurant of Mansour's mother, Eva, and the grand opening is two days away.

In feverish preparation, Mama Eva and her three sisters become the enemy of all rest. There has been the clattering of clay dishes; the destruction of garlic, shallots, and pepper grains with mortars and pestles; the pounding of cassava; the rise and fall of the women's frantic voices. But then, always, comes the good thing—the music they play: the fiery blare of the horns, the contrary percussion.

Whenever Bonnie needs to let more in, to get closer to the sound, there is a loose floorboard she can shift in the middle of her large, empty attic that will send it through.

It is Cuban music, but the singers don't sing in Spanish. They sing in Wolof, Bambara, Peule, Kikongo. She once read that the founders of the genre were Afro-Cubans whose records first came out on Victrolas some forty years before. Records recorded in brothels and steaming kitchens; harmonies perfected on the wet earth between shacks. Records the recorded never saw a penny from. The Second World War helped carry those same albums to the Congo, where the people made the sound their own, a first stop before it then made its way across the continent.

Bonnie's favorite record is also Mama's favorite. It has been played so often that there is a scratch right before the second chorus. Bonnie chuckles when, just like the day before, the record skips and the women lose their place in the backup vocals, their cacophony briefly quieting down to a disappointed silence.

Some of us are helpless before melodies, our great plans for our lives escalated or abandoned with a singer's choice to wail or wait. This is Bonnie's nature. Her mother's too. Growing up in Paris with Claudine—a Black American who'd come to dance with an Allied ballet troupe during the Second World War—Bonnie's family of two had no traditions, no holidays, few visitors. She knew nothing of the place in the world she and her mother came from, and as a child she believed that they had come from sound.

The spines of albums stuck out from the cabinets where food should have been. Some albums lived in the bathtub, so they took to taking showers. She addressed her diary entries to Ella Fitzgerald and Johnny Hartman, swearing them to secrecy in each.

Please do not tell my mother that I am keeping the gutter cat in the closet. Do not tell her that I made friends with the girl downstairs. Do not tell my mother that my new friend brings me boiled eggs when she forgets to make me dinner.

Her childhood was marked by hunger. Dinner could be stewed leeks and chicken thighs, or the gray dust on the cabinetry when her mother disappeared for days at a time. Twice it was the tulips on the windowsill (first the petals, then the leaves, then the stems). Often famished, Bonnie slept and woke throughout the day, never truly leaving either state. So sleep and wakefulness were her first toys: the balls she juggled, the paints she mixed, as she explored the limits of consciousness. At six, she dreamed of levitation and learned how to change the course of her nightmares by breathing through her nose (inhale and hold), a fading dream reignited by tightening her fists. And by seven, she could bring Sarah Vaughan from a dream and onto the Paris apartment floor to sing beside her. The pensive singer smelled like roads, humming gently until Bonnie's inevitable exhalation made her disappear.

Her memories of childhood are like this: wispy mixes of dreams and reality, of days alone turning into weeks. His absence has brought those days to mind again.

The night before Mansour set off for Spain, she had whispered her fondest memory of levitation into his ear: her and her mother slow dancing to Nat Cole, just a few inches above ground. He had lifted her up and they danced in the silence.

2. **BONNIE DOES NOT** usually eat with Mama and her sisters. She had retreated after suffering through the questions his mother asked her the first time they dined on the patio: *Her father's name? Her grandfather's name? Her mother's address?* Simple questions she could not answer. Questions that introduced her to a shame she had not felt before. Black American, for his mother, seemed to be an incomplete self-definition. She seemed to be asking something else, for something greater, when she asked Bonnie where her people were from.

Bonnie has since kept her distance, so even after months in the house, she is still treated like a guest: her food brought to the attic door on a tray under cloth napkins. But today Mansour will appear on television, his first televised interview, and she heads downstairs to catch it. The only television is in the living room, among the women.

She clutches the banister on her way down; each rickety step is slick with grease from the kitchen to the right of the landing. She is trying to remember if the living room is up ahead or behind the grand staircase. She has mostly stayed to herself in the attic since his departure, and the path of the house remains unmemorized. Even more so now as the restaurant's ingredients begin to crowd and obscure the large foyer. She steps over sacks of corn—the silk spilling over onto the floor—bags of flour, industrial cans of tomato paste that are stacked like pyramids.

That she booked him on television still seems a great feat, though the appearance fee was barely enough to cover the prenatal doctor's appointment, where they discovered that she was prediabetic, or maintenance on the used Vespa that was now banished to the garage shed after hardly surviving its first ride onto the sprawling estate grounds. They had both thought that his mother was exaggerating over the phone, had ignored her advice to come before sundown. Arriving at night at the high cobblestone gate of the driveway, they had descended from the Vespa in stunned silence at the forest that surrounded them, the dark so thick they could only see the other's eyes and teeth. The music, a faint Fela Kuti, helped them find the front yard.

There, Bonnie had seen a striking sight: a low yellow moon waning beside a towering stone mansion, half in ruin, half in repair. She'd started to count the windows but quickly failed. Old ivy had wed with most of the upstairs shutters, pulling them sideways so that they clung to the windows by one hinge, and down in the front yard, tangled brown vines whispered of a garden that neglect and time had long killed. The lone figure working there to restore it, by the light of two lanterns, was his mother. Mama Eva, a woman whose name he did not speak of with warmth. Her feet bare, a loose golden dress slipped off her shiny dark shoulder, her long cornrows, ending below her shoulder blades. She was pulling up weeds, and turned around at their footsteps. Her brow unfurling, the wrinkles falling from her kaftan. She had stood, a towering height, to meet Mansour as he approached proudly, with Bonnie by the hand.

Today, the women wait on the sunken couch for his interview. At the top of the hour, they were silent and still, but the barrage of preceding guests and commercial breaks have loosened the atmosphere and now they are talking over the television about silverware orders and napkin rings, coming and going from the kitchen as they await Mansour's appearance.

Mama has not moved. In the corner of her eye, Bonnie clocks her blank stare at the television, full fingers fondling her wooden prayer beads, her hair covered by a shawl. Bonnie sits beside Marie, the first of his relatives Bonnie had met, and the closest to her in age. Marie manipulates the antennae by the long foil cord she's constructed, and the women lean forward, finally seeing a picture.

The host emerges. Shiny salt-and-pepper hair. The tight, brooding mouth of a smoker. He tugs his tie before he speaks, his voice waning with the slinking pixels as Marie struggles to straighten the picture. The static competes with the sound of hissing oil from the open kitchen door.

Our last guest tonight is a friend to the show: Mr. Ezra Olivier . . .

The TV audience applauds as Bonnie and the women sit in quizzical silence.

"Are you sure this is the right show?" one of the women says.

"This is it, right?" Marie asks Bonnie, confused. Bonnie looks at Mama, seeing the panic in her eyes.

"Yes, this is it," she says finally.

"Maybe he'll come on later," Marie replies, hesitant.

"No, that's it . . . that's the last guest . . . ," Bonnie says and swallows, her heartbreak pulsing in her cheek.

Marie's hands go slack, releasing the antennae, letting the picture fizzle out, the static roaring loudly.

"Excuse me," Bonnie whispers, racing from the room.

She rushes into the attic bathroom, vomiting. When she can stand on both feet, still dizzy, she pulls their bedroom apart, digging for tokens for the pay phone, but can only find American quarters. There's a knock at the door.

"Yeah," she says, and the door opens slowly to Marie, smoking in the doorway.

"I thought you were up here balling," she jokes, easing the mood, and Bonnie sits on the bed, reaching for the cigarette. Marie brings it to her, and she inhales and closes her eyes. She exhales, feeling worse again.

"Not exactly."

"I'm sure he's fine. You know how he is. Just letting life carry him." Marie winks at Bonnie.

It was true. He had always been that way. She sits now on the serape blanket he had returned with after disappearing for two days in Los Cabos. He'd returned renewed, melting her rage in seconds, as he recanted his forty-eight-hour adventure with a Mexican sextet. He'd held his hands very close together to demonstrate, a tiny bit of space in between.

The harmonies . . . they're so dangerous. Right on the edge, right on the edge, but they never clash. Always perfect.

"No one has reached him in months, Eva!" An argument grows fierce downstairs, bringing Bonnie back, out of the safety and comfort of her dreams.

"Anyway," Marie says, covering her terror, talking over their row with a forced nonchalance that cannot hide her voice's trembling. "I'll leave you to your princess thing up here, but if you need anything, you know where to find me."

"Actually, there is something." Bonnie suddenly remembers why she came upstairs. "Do you have a pay phone token?"

Blinking rain out of her eyes, Bonnie goes to the phone booth a block away. The homeless man inside treats her knocks like an alarm clock, pulling his jacket over his ears like a pillow, making a great display of being disturbed.

When she finally gets inside, she reaches the show's producer, but all the woman knows is the obvious: that he did not show. Then she calls the Spanish police and gives the officer on the line the date she last heard from Mansour; the letters of his name, which the man repeats back incorrectly every time; a physical description; and the phone number to call if they discover anything.

In broken French, the man tells her that these details and his tour schedule are not enough. He will need more dates, times, places. She argues with him, growing desperate, loud, and more afraid as thunder begins to drown him out.

Then, a golden line appears. Lightning that moves with the grace of fire as it races atop the trees and glides along phone lines. Bonnie freezes; it's approaching her in the booth. Thunder cracks. The town blackens. The call drops. The line of lightning sizzles out in the drooping leaves of a tree before her, the sound of a steak searing. She opens the door where lightning has left the smell of a busted light bulb in the air.

Bonnie places the phone on the hook and marches back out into the rain. Her feet slip as the sloped road carries a current. She rolls her jeans up to her knees and walks on toes in her sandals through the water's flow, following the path back to Mama Eva's, her thoughts turning dark as the sky.

3. **AT HOME IN DAKAR**, it is a week before the country's busiest holiday. The sheep to be slaughtered will be heard braying in the distance. The roar of a thousand sewing machines and the gossip of seamstresses toiling through the night. But this evening, as she gazes at across the serene Swiss countryside from the foyer window, waiting and watching for Bonnie's return, it occurs to Mama that Mansour's child may only know this silence.

And yet—silence was always the sound between her and Mansour. She knew so little of what went on in his mind. As she'd tried to explain to his Aunt Sohkna earlier tonight, Mansour had disappeared to America this same way three years ago. Called to inform her of his whereabouts on a muffled line from overseas, two months later. It was only the way he'd been with the girl that makes Mama question if he meant to stay away so long this time.

There was a rawness, an ease to them, that Mama had never seen between a man and a woman before. They were quick to tug and tickle and pull one another around the house, maneuvering limbs without words, like the body of one belonged to the other. Life had convinced her early on that the deepest bonds were born from pain. What dark thing had they weathered together to grow so close in so little time?

The night before his departure for Spain, when he entered her room, Mama had observed him closely. He was as slender as he'd been when he ran off to America three years before and still had that walk—the footsteps of a thief, she always thought: weightless, soundless, gone before you noticed—but his presence had tripled in size. It exaggerated the silence of her bedroom, breeding that uneasiness they could not navigate.

Unsure of where to begin, in this last moment together, Mama had thrown incense cloves into her pot and asked about the girl.

"Ndax mu ngi nelaw?" *Is she sleeping?* "Waaw." *Yes.* Mansour had said and rested his arms on his knees. Though they spoke in Wolof, there was a new rigidity to his tongue; it refused to be loose in the ways their language required. And as she listened to him speak, a strange panic brewed in her. Yes, you should never look an elder too intently in the eye, but on this night, she'd wished that he would.

For years, it felt like Mama had been watching Mansour from the back or the side. On the floor with the record player or walking out the door on his way to another town, or continent. Just gone for three years and leaving again in some hours, there seemed to be no way to bring him closer to her.

In the room, Mansour's eyes had stayed on the floor, his back straight against the wall, committed to keeping his distance, it seemed. Had it been obligation or a show of appreciation, the money he handed her? When he left the room, she'd cried. For his generosity—with that money, he had finally granted her dream of starting her restaurant, the only dream she'd ever had for her life—but in mourning too. The money felt like the end of something, a way, perhaps, to say thank you and goodbye.

Please take care of her, he'd said as he left, along with a stream of warnings. Bonnie was not going to do the traditional things: to curtsy before Mama (though she'd done so the first time they'd met, her left hand still holding Mansour's when she gave Mama her right, like she needed his support for this simple gesture); to greet her first thing in the morning; to sweep and tend to pots and pans without being asked.

It was a cultural thing but, he swore, she meant no harm. And the more that he talked, worried about the girl's doctors' appointments, high blood pressure, and the resulting medication that she couldn't keep down, the more girlish Mama had felt. Impending fatherhood had made the eighteen years between them suddenly worth no more than a few minutes.

Mama had wanted to chastise Mansour, for failing to marry the girl and expecting her to pick up the pieces, and yet she was frustrated with herself: Why did she always find it so difficult to be pleased with him?

The following day, at a chicken farm not far from the estate, the storm has cleared. Mama is prepared to haggle for a good forty minutes for chickens and feed, but the man concedes to her price within ten. He tries hard not to seem eager, but she can tell that her business is a godsend. The place is falling apart: the tin ceiling so cracked that she could see plenty of the sky, a floor practically made of chicken turds. She walks cautiously, her face tied with a scarf, the off-white feathers in the air an endless snowfall. The man gruffly instructs her on how many times a day to feed her chickens, how much the chicks will cost her over their lifetimes, and where they should be stored.

As the man speaks, Mama's eyes move to the chicks closest to her. A trio, just born. Their skin is translucent and gray, and loose along their necks. Their breaks look soft. Mama touches one, and the chick collapses. She recoils, and the man looks at her in a way no one has in a while—like she's delicate.

"Chicks die all the time," the man says. "By the hundreds, the thousands. You sure you want to get into this business?" The man is sweating. He hacks a dry cough, and feathers come out of his nose and mouth.

Mama counts out the money in front of him and then waits by her car while he assembles the cages. She listens to the chicks chirping.

They are a chorus of distressed fervor, a sound as menacing as the heat. She thinks of the money again, contemplates the man's warning. What if they all die?

Buying the property had been expensive enough. Perhaps owning a farm and raising her own chickens is now reaching too far. But Mansour left her plenty of money before he went to Spain, and now that he's making a name for himself, she tells herself not to worry. He'll return with more.

When the man is gone, Mama rearranges the chickens in the trunk so that the grown ones are next to the chicks, comforting and quietening them. But while the chicks scream, the mother hens remain somber and indifferent. They are so still and sunken that she wonders for a moment if they are male.

Fifty chicks, sixty cartons of eggs, and twelve full-grown hens. She heads home.

4. **THAT NIGHT,** to keep from blowing power, the women must choose between ceiling lights and the record player as they prepare the food. There is no contest. The music wins, so they light a pack of candles. A Cuban record plays as the living room becomes a night market. Bonnie watches them again from the stairs, an outsider once more. She observes their rhythm as the women count and cut ninety-eight yams, stem amaranth leaves, peel one hundred garlic cloves, and fuss over the twenty-eight malformed cassavas grown in their own yard. The sun is rising as they finish with the vegetables, and Bonnie retreats upstairs. But there is more work to be done.

The women venture outside. Bonnie watches from the attic window as they toil in a misty rain, venturing far deeper into the forest than what she had first imagined they owned.

Clearing a road and parking lot for the restaurant's future patrons, the Africans axe down the forest's silver firs and Napoleon oaks with high, triumphant grunts. With the trees goes the shade the local elders rely on while tending to their gardens and flocks. But this is the doctrine of conquest: anything the conqueror cannot see—the invisible order of a people and a place—does not exist.

The land's only true aborigines—the bearded vultures—land at the women's feet in protest, curiously tilting their heads at all the dark bodies and braids. Then they take to the air, circling, beating their enormous wings until the women are petrified, shooing them with boots and headwraps and rocks.

The women move on to the willows.

Bonnie looks away, slipping down under the sheets. Under those trees, now golden in the early morning sun, there is spray paint on the grass from where she and Mansour marked the staging for his Spanish shows. It is where they had walked off her nightmares in the days before he left, bare toes parting the knee-high grass. And, after time spent together in cities, there under the willows is where she also saw his true complexion for the first time. There were no streetlights, no fumes of industry to temper the strength of the moonlight and the emerald green hiding in his shade of brown.

5. **THE RADIO ANNOUNCES:** *A black man was found dead in Geneva.*

Twenty, maybe even forty-something. He was bloated from the water so they couldn't tell his exact age.

It is a week into the opening and the best night they've had. The news plays quietly beneath the chatter of their diners.

Covered in layers of dark soil from the Arve river's shore.

There is the pattering of dancing feet, the squeaking of the front door as more people enter.

Six foot three . . . No ID . . . A single silver bracelet corroding on his wrist.

The story is heard by each woman at a different moment as they work the crowded dining room floor.

Their panic moves through the room without the patrons noticing, like a stench overpowered by a stream of good aromas. The mountain dwellers are busy letting their guards down, smearing tomato jam and garlic on bread that is fresh, while more of it rises under checkered towels over the raging hearth. This is all to say that they wouldn't have noticed a thing if Bonnie had not screamed.

The African women crack jokes to keep the diners cool. They migrate to the kitchen slowly but all at once, bumping into each other along the way. Sokhna spills yassa on a baby's bald head, the dishwasher scorches the town's banker with palm oil, a carafe of bissap smashes on the floor.

They find Bonnie in the kitchen, desperately twisting the dials on the radio for a clearer sound. Her frantic tuning only makes for more static, blurring out the report. Sokhna snatches the radio from her, tries her hand at tuning to no avail.

"Get Mama's radio! Go!" Sokhna shouts at the dishwasher girl, who runs across the hall to retrieve it. Marie notes how Bonnie shakes and tries to be gentle with her, pulling her to a bench against the wall. Bonnie flinches with each buzz of static, her arms wrapped tight around her body as she tries hard to breathe.

The women huddle around the radio, still trying to make out the report. They shush one another and shut the windows to block out the noise of diners driving in and out of the yard. Their ears are so close to the tiny speakers that they are skin to skin, and, in feeling the heat of each other's flesh, the fear and sweat, they all become more afraid. The chatter in the crowded dining room only seems to get louder, the laughter reaching a high-pitched shrill that makes Marie throw the kitchen door open. She yells into the dining room.

"*Shut up! Please!*"

Before the door swings closed again, Bonnie notices a bread roll fall from a woman's mouth, stunned stiff by Marie's command.

"Marie!" Mama exclaims, entering the kitchen last, hands holding an empty tray and streaked with peanut sauce from an order of maafe. She puts everything down and grabs her by her ear.

"Foog naa ne Mansour lañuy wax." *I think they're talking about Mansour*, Sokhna warns Mama.

Mama releases Marie. The dishwasher girl finally returns with the good radio, her head down.

"It's over," she says sullenly.

The women watch Mama for a cue, a directive on what to do next. But Mama will not meet their eyes. She wanders to the pot of frying fish, uncovers it, muttering quietly that they should know better, that covering the fish while it fries will make it soggy. When two of the women start sniffling, it gives the others permission, and soon the room is heavy with sobbing and moans of despair.

"Put your hands in cold water when you're chopping onions," Mama says to no one in particular, as if that is the cause of their tears.

The only place for peace in this house is out in the horse shed. Mama goes there most mornings to empty her mind. This evening, after calming down the women and ending the night's service, she goes out to feel the chill of the night air. As she settles herself, Mama thinks a familiar thought: *This house will fall down. And I will go with it.*

She said it every time a doorknob dropped to the floor or when another light bulb burned out; when the carrots choked the pipes out in the yard and the sink water turned orange; when mice invaded the rice bags in the basement and dropped dead from *Bacillus cereus* a week later.

The first step toward disaster had been the arrival of Bonnie. Prior to this, all Mama knew of Black Americans was what she'd gathered from dubbed episodes of *Amos 'n' Andy*, *American Bandstand*, or sometimes a news program. She knew that women marched beside their men in a fight for rights. Some were good singers. Some were ignorant, others glamorous, others were lewd. Once or twice, she'd seen her own face mirrored in Aretha Franklin's, but she said and thought no more about it.

What surprised her most about Bonnie was the way she thought the world of herself. Mansour thought the world of her too. Mama had yet to discover why. Bonnie seemed to be such a strange choice.

He'd had many girls around before. Mama had loved Amalia, his last girlfriend, most of all. She was the one she'd thought he should marry. A broad-legged, beaming Italian girl he'd met in Paris, who knew to take off her shoes at the front door and who could rattle off four hundred years of her ancestry in the time it took to plait her hair. *All blood is ancient, handed down, borrowed for a lifetime. Nobody's blood is new, nobody's life is their own*, Amalia had said in response to Mansour's passionate soliloquy about individuality.

Amalia knew where her blood had come from, all the way back to the beginning of things. She was pure nobility, just like Mama. So they talked heritage. Long nights swatting away the smoke drifting off Mama's grill, the noise of the streets drifting in, swapping stories of forebearers, men and women long gone, who'd made buildings and dug wells and gave wisdom that was still at work in the world.

Mansour had found another noble, an equal, in Amalia, so why did he now want to be with a ghost?

Still, Mama has worried about Bonnie incessantly. Lately she's been thinking that the old roof will surely collapse into the attic and strike the girl and unborn child. Half of the mansion's thirteen rooms are uninhabitable due to fallen ceilings and mold and God knows what else. She can't imagine a time when she'll have the means to restore it all. In the meantime, she's deemed more than half of the house officially off-limits.

She had no choice after the dishwasher girl wandered out to the east wing and found a man squatting there. A wood-carver. He'd done a beautiful job with the mantle and bedposts of the room he'd chosen. He tried to bargain with them, first with labor and then with good Catholic prayers, promising them that as a former Latin scholar, he was privy to special words that could get them into heaven even though they didn't have souls—a conclusion he'd likely come to from the propaganda defaming the Black soldiers moving about Europe in the Second World War. These pamphlets, for many of the elder villagers, showed the only Black faces they'd ever seen, before now.

Even here in the horse shed, Mama can see that the beams are rotting and liable to collapse. She grips her knees and notices the lightness of her skin, worries again that she is losing the pigmentation on her hands, even though the doctor told her that she was perfectly healthy, that her skin was only adjusting to the years she's spent on a colder continent. She works hard to think of anything but Mansour.

In the end, I didn't save him. Coming here didn't save him.

But they cannot call the police. It could reveal Mama's illegal status: a sponsorship from a job she'd been fired from over a decade before, the immigration applications she'd filed but that had been lost in bureaucratic wastelands. The rules of permanent citizenship seem to change with the seasons, and her temporary status—which, in her first few years in Europe had been a tremendous source of anxiety—soon faded into the background. She'd long learned to live beside impending disaster. Life meant daily triumph or defeat. She stayed alert and ready to move.

Mama had once been a twin, her sister disappearing in the wake of a storm. The day she lost her, Mama started a story in her mind, a life for her twin that ran parallel to her own. The story was now almost two decades old. In Mama's mind, Kiné was married and had children. She owned her own restaurant (not as nice as Mama's) in a small but lovely building in Dakar. Her restaurant was shrouded by bushes of limes—her favorite seasoning—and she sold soursop juice in glass bottles. Kiné had witnessed the independence of their country; she had watched the French run out of the Presidential Palace.

Those first years in Europe, Mama had written her sister letters, asking after these imagined life events as if they were true. She wrote in cursive, asking Kiné to tell her what revolution and childbirth felt like.

It's been ten years since her last letter. The letters she drafted and redrafted until there were no blotches or marks, letters for which she walked the five miles to the post office, pretending to mail them. Pretending so much so that she believed her own lie.

Tonight, there is pen and paper in the horse shed. And there is news that Kiné must know: Mansour is missing. And though she will write this letter because she cannot not bear this news alone, Mama tells herself that she is only writing this because Kiné, Mansour's real mother, deserves to know.

II.

THE TWINS

Senegal, 1949

6. **AT SEVENTEEN,** Mama and Kiné were the best cooks of their sisters. They had a talent for market shopping; lugging home the best fermented fish, tomato paste, cassava, garlic, cabbage, onions; layering sauces. For their talents, their mother and their father's second wife favored them and allowed them more freedom than the five others. Their father lived farther south with his third and youngest wife, returning home infrequently.

With money saved from their aggressive deals with vendors, Mama and Kiné sometimes took a cab into town to go dancing. One such night, a dance partner, someone finally tall enough to seduce Mama's six-foot frame, emerged.

Adnan. His French was sharper than Mama's, without melody. Like the radio personalities. She asked him if he was a government official's son. He nodded.

"A child of the opposition, I'm afraid," he said.

After three consecutive dances, the longest time that Mama had ever spent with a boy, they retreated against the half-finished tin wall that enclosed the party. Immersed in their conversation, Mama lost sight of Kiné in the crowd. She imagined her shy sister patiently waiting for her, nursing a Coke at the back of the room.

Wind raised the warm sand high. Every time Mama and Adnan laughed, they could feel it on their tongues. It crunched between their teeth. When it was time to say goodbye, Adnan kissed her neck instead.

The party dwindled around midnight. The speakers were tied down to a horse-drawn wagon, the glass Coke bottles clinking as they were gathered by a shopkeeper. Begrudging the end of the night, the young crowd strolled in the direction of home together for as long as they could. By the third mile, Mama and Kiné were alone. The sky was black, infinite, free from the glare of any buildings. The girls walked ahead blindly, navigating their way by a few stray stars.

Mama was saving up her story. Her anticipation of Kiné's reaction excited her more than the experience itself—but she had to wait for Kiné to ask. It hadn't been a real kiss. Adnan's lips had only grazed her neck, but even that, Mama knew, would floor Kiné, who could not even look the neighborhood coal man in the eye.

But Kiné didn't ask. She seemed to be in a world of her own.

Arriving home, Mama and Kiné noticed that their traditional clothes were no longer in the soursop tree where they'd hid them. Their headscarves were gone too. Mama scolded Kiné. Why hadn't she chosen a better hiding place?

They spotted their father, waiting for them in the courtyard, sitting in his iron chair with a long wooden cane in his right hand.

Mama stepped forward first. Her father examined her. She hadn't seen his face in several months, and, in defiance of customs, she snuck glances. He'd lost weight. His hair was thinning to a gray fuzz, and one of his eyes was covered by a patch. Once a sturdy brigadier general with a perfect eye for shooting, her father had become so sad looking that she wanted to cry. When he grabbed her arm, his skeletal hands shaking and struggling to get a firm grip, she realized she pitied him.

But when he hit her, the force of the blow was a shock. Kiné flinched from several feet away, but Mama stood firm—she didn't feel any shame.

Her father took his stick to Mama's rear.

"Why do you encourage Kiné to do such horrible things?"

After a few strikes, she learned the rhythm of her father's stick, making it easier to stand his blows. Until he stopped. Only then did she feel the enormous pain along her lower back.

He then moved toward Kiné, who screamed as he approached, but he only walked past her to go back inside.

Mama stood on damp bricks in the outhouse, poured cool water over her body. The pain dissipated as she watched ants march out into the patch of moonlight that illuminated her toes from beneath the wooden door, realizing then that she'd grown too big for her own world.

She dried off her skin in her mother's bedroom. Kiné sat across from her sullenly, still weeping.

"He didn't even touch you," Mama said. "Why are you crying?"

Mama thought it might be a perfect time to tell Kiné her story about Adnan and lift their moods, but Kiné had a story of her own.

A short walk from the party, the building that Kiné and the shop-keeper came upon was made of clay. It trapped the torrid heat from the day into night, never releasing the sun. He propped her body into the hot crevice between two walls. Once sweat made her supple, her naked back chafed against the coarse grit.

In the beginning, she could only feel him. His scaly tongue moved in straight lines, heating and cooling the sides of her neck in turn, making her laugh. Her chuckle echoed against the ceiling and floor and came back to her tenfold, making her laugh even more. Making love was hilarious—much funnier than the way it sounded to Kiné in French novels: a sacred, silent ritual where the man held the woman's gaze and hands and dared her to speak. But once Kiné's eyes adjusted to the darkness, she saw him racing. Her ample flesh, spilling over his hands. He snarled and panted like she puzzled him. She wanted to tell him that there was time, to slow down. But there wasn't time. He held her tight and still, forcing all of her enigmatic parts into one tangible thing, and came inside.

7 TWO YEARS AFTER THAT PARTY, and seven hours after her twin sister is pronounced dead, Mama showers in the outhouse. She is rinsing sand and salt and dried tears from her skin. The air is humid, any hint of breeze stifling and warm. It grates her tongue, already raw and white from screaming at the police, the elders, and God. She'd tried (and failed) to dispel the myth the town had decided on to explain away her twin sister's disappearance.

When the tides defied the moon, they said, *Mama's twin was taken by the waves. The billion grains of sand beneath her feet rushed away, sliding her into the swallow of the ocean.*

That day, a couple of weeks ago, Kiné had been hunched over, rinsing sand from her sandals. The tides had been low, the waves mild, but when Mama had looked up a moment later, Kiné was gone.

For Mama, Kiné cannot be dead. Death does not come that way, silently in broad daylight, and her sister's body has yet to be found.

Orphaned by her twin when she vanished, Mansour has been placed in Mama's charge. Now, as she washes herself, she distracts him by sitting him in the soursop garden. It seems to Mama that his craving for the fruit followed him out of the womb. His hunger still lingers after handfuls of the fruit's rich, creamy flesh, and he's taken to picking up the stray cats' leftovers around the courtyard. To Mama, he seems content. Seems to have done all his crying and screaming the day Kiné disappeared and, in a mere week, forgotten her.

He is occupied by the sticky fruit until he hears the family's chanting crescendo. A note in unison, sending prayers on Kiné's soul. From the outhouse doorway, Mama sees Mansour turn toward the noise, urgently, like someone has called his name. On his hands, he drags himself toward it as if he's regressed to crawling, and listens, unmoving. He stays this way, and after a moment Mama returns to showering, until she hears him moaning. She realizes that he's straining to make something like the sordid sound he hears.

That night, Mansour bites Mama's breast, startling her out of sleep. Wide-eyed, he claws for her, scratching her neck and cheek. She jumps away, covering herself with her nightgown. From the edge of the bed, she trembles as she watches him flail alone. Mama remembers her mother's words when she'd put the child in her charge: *A semblance of a mother is better than no mother at all.*

Mama had laid awake that first night, terrorized, her arms tight around her body, thinking through a plan to rid herself of him. The following day, she'd told Mansour, a shy two-year-old, to sit on a little wooden bench in the marketplace while she shopped. She'd ducked under the dusty maze of a multicolored awning, eager for him to lose sight of her in the crowd.

Out of their father's three wives, Mama and Kiné were their mother's only children. Their hierarchy, the ranking of the wives and children in their father's eyes, was never discussed but always demonstrated in subtle ways: the siblings who went to private school, while Mama and

Kiné did not; the siblings who were driven to school by the family driver, while Mama and Kiné walked, hardly ever seeing the inside of that car. Everything implicit became explicit when Mama and Kiné were pulled out of school entirely to pay for the college fees of their half-brother.

On the day of her father's wedding to his third wife, Mama loathed that her mother had consented to appear, loathed her silence. She'd taken her sister by the hand and walked them far away to the dust road, so that they could not hear the singing nor see the whirling dancers. She'd wiped Kiné's tears with the back of her back and vowed to take charge. She decided thereafter to be the one to dictate their future, the one to forge the careful path that would be their salvation in the wake of their father's neglect.

Kiné had strayed from this path and now she was possibly dead. And in having failed to give her sister the protection and guidance she'd promised her, Mama could not tell what she was, or why she was, or what in her own life should come next.

In the market, Mama had watched while Mansour waited for her patiently. His trust in Mama endeared her to him. In this moment, he'd reminded her of the parts of Kiné that she missed the most: her love, her loyalty. When she'd returned to him, he'd showed no anger. Only reached up for her to take him.

The next evening, it happens again. Mansour's sleep breaks and he's scratching at the darkness, squirming on the hot bed. This time, his panic is deeper: soundless, breathless, his tiny chest pumping up and down like it might explode. He reaches out for her.

Pitying him, Mama opens her nightgown to the child's mouth. Indifferent to her fear and the dryness of her breast, Mansour latches on. His wet eyes flicker but stay on hers as a calmness overtakes him. And his calmness loops back, slowing her heartbeat too. Though she wonders, and perhaps will always wonder, if he is really seeing her or seeing Kiné, Mama, seeking anchoring and purpose, breathes in his need for her, his wanting, like a perfume.

8. IN PREPARATION FOR Kiné's funeral, Mama's elder female relatives take their time cleaning the house, creating room for the barrage of guests. Everything else happens quickly. Their father arrives in Tivaouane. He discusses funeral preparations with his two elder wives. The town where Kiné disappeared builds fences at the entrance to Petit Mbao beach and runs a radio story about her. It results in ugly signs, handwritten by the lowest echelon of government officials, being staked at the entrance to the ocean and announcing that the beach is restricted.

No one goes back to look for Kiné again. That would require an unraveling of things: wrestling with divine decree, a bold-faced quest for disaster.

Neighbors pray loudly and quickly, not for Mama's sister, but for their own children, for sense and order to remain in their own lives. For days, Mama speaks to no one. Her only comfort is the radio as the funeral preparations carry on.

Fula cousins bring sympathy to Tivaouane in the frothy milk of horned cattle. Overflowing the worn brims of handmade wooden bowls, it spills and settles on the plastic table in the hallway, attracting elderly neighbors and flies. Perfected over centuries, the vibrating cry of the mourners rocks the bowls, spilling more of the fluid with every song for the soul of the girl who Mama knows isn't dead. *She's missing,*

Mama insists. But with sympathetic eyes, Mama's father again refuses her plea to return to Petit Mbao with another search party.

Now, she is under the plastic table on her hands and knees. She mops the sticky puddles of milk with an old rag. The flies are too satiated to fight. They let their bodies drown in the heavily powdered soap and water. As she sops up the last of the milk from the floor, Mama is reminded of the steady drip of milk from her sister's breasts in the mornings after Mansour was born.

Mama had traveled a full week during Ramadan to reach Kiné in Kedougou. She'd traveled with loaves of French bread and two outfits for Kiné that she had washed by hand. She'd traveled secretly, without the blessing of her family, who had meant for Kiné to birth Mansour out of sight. The first bus left Tivaouane in the early morning, cramped with fasting people, sucking on miswak, chanting prayers in a hypnotic unison that lulled Mama to sleep.

She'd hitched a ride on the broken wagon of a Tuareg nomad. In and out of sleep, Mama watched the slight green-eyed woman, whose skeletal hands never left the hunched cow's reins. She didn't know how long they traveled for, but the henna on the nomad's nails seemed to fade as time went by. By the time they'd arrived, it was the palest orange, nearly gone.

Mama had walked another day and night to reach her nephew's place of birth.

In Tambacounda, country people guided her, waving their grass fans in the direction of the right, the right, the right . . . until when? Until she could see the water.

Through the dusty wind, she'd only seen more brown, more cracked ground and elegant trees. Women bent to the ground, making their homes by their own hands, their task a plea and bargain with nature.

The deeper into the desert Mama went, the animals changed. Lizards became grotesque reptiles that moved slower and held Mama's gaze with confidence. On her journey's final night, she had passed a wedding celebration, people roasting meat, whole cows and goats blackened over fires. That night, Mama had warmed her hands by the flames. She'd put the goat meat into her mouth and sighed—so tender and hot, it melted on her tongue.

The following morning, an elderly stranger insisted she stop and pray Fajr. After, Mama asked the old woman where to find the pond. She'd been told along the way to look for water, and a pond was all she could imagine, having grown up in a desert. But the woman laughed.

"In Kedougou, there are only waterfalls." She said.

Soon the ground changed colors. A richer hue, a solid surface without cracks. Then she'd seen grass for the first time. The air had been different too, reeking of wet earth, a place so fertile that it almost smelled rotten. And finally, she'd come across a waterfall fed by a narrow stream of white water, on whose banks lay a pale Mansour, ten days old.

She had long missed the birth.

Kiné sat nearby, at the mouth of the stream. Naked and huddled on the ground, the murky fluid seeping from her breasts ran down her body like tears.

Of course, there is no body for the burial. The absence of a body to bury has stumped the imam, who is seated in the grandest chair in the courtyard, deep in the pageantry of meditation. He rhythmically fondles his black prayer beads, his long feet outstretched. Flies, fattened and drunk from the Fula milk, settle in the large gaps between his toes.

Though the other children of the household have been taken to a relative's home for the duration of the funeral, Mansour has been left behind. In twos and threes, curious relatives sneak down the hall to see Kiné's sin. Up from a long sleep, Mansour sits on Yaye's bed, trying to fit his foot into his mouth.

Mama has been instructed to cook the funeral's repass. The salted palm oil scorches the few hairs left on the shank of the senile ram: Mama gags at his smell and the act of cooking him. She pulls his browned thigh from the boiling pot of grease. Once it's stuffed with pepper cloves and parsley, she drowns it in a pan of tomato and onion sauce. In a better mood, she would have seduced herself with the warmth and aroma of the bubbling fluid.

When it's time for dessert, Mama carries a tray of fluffy, hot thierré and seasoned cow's milk into the room of the male elders. There, the men debate the meaning of her sister's life. Smiling like children, the town's officials make loose, mushy balls of her food and suck their fingers. The imam has eaten so much that he can hardly sit up. He rests his weight on his side and laughs. He's discarded his prayer beads now. The string of beads is tangled in the pile of shoes near the door. Mama imagines poisoning these men with her food, standing in the doorway and watching their laughter melt into scratching and sores.

When she brings the calabash of fresh water and holds it before each man to wash his hands, she listens. They have shifted from the subject of Kiné's lost virtue and the country's overdue independence to talk of Mansour. He should be sent to the Saint to join the talibé order, one clergyman suggests. Mama looks to her father, who is silent on the matter. That he does not immediately reject this suggestion frightens her. The talibés wear no shoes. They sing prayers and beg for change and rice. They roam the streets with old canisters around their necks. They eat with the goats and rams. A fate for Kiné's son she cannot bear to imagine.

She lies awake that night, plotting a way to keep him home, though she knows it is ultimately her father's decision.

Well into the morning, the sound of the maid scrubbing the ram's blood from the courtyard tiles wakes her. She goes to her father's room to plead her case, but the maid tells her that he has already gone. The imam has summoned everyone to the mosque for prayers.

The maid tells Mama that her father wants her to bring Mansour to meet the Saint. To delay the inevitable, Mama pretends to be dissatisfied with the maid's job and begins cleaning the courtyard a second time. She slowly sweeps a few stray feathers and ram fur into a corner, Mansour tied to her back so that no one else can take him. Some hours later, when she still hasn't shown up, a young talibé is sent from the mosque to the house to fetch Mama and Mansour. Mama notices the boy's foot, hanging loose and limp like a tail, and the thin wooden cane he maneuvers from under his sleeve. But when he speaks his voice is firm, and he moves swiftly along the unpaved road as she anxiously follows him the two blocks to the mosque, heeding her father's command.

Inside, incense cloves roast over crackling coals in the corner, and a green felt rug lines the tile floor. The first room they enter has a high ceiling, squares carved out of the cement walls that stand for windows, and painted murals of ornate Arabic calligraphy. The young talibé guides her to an open doorway. In the musalla's center, her father and the imam are seated at the feet of the Saint.

Cloaked in a white cloth, the Saint's face is not visible—only his hands are, outstretched and curved upward. The imam gestures for her to place Mansour before him. Slowly untying the toddler from her back and bringing him into her arms, she studies the Saint's long fingers and nails, his stacks of gold and brass rings. She hears someone begin to incant the call to prayer on the mosque's loudspeaker. The vibrato in his voice reaches Mama in her spine, a jolt that awakens her willingness to fight for Kiné's son. She holds Mansour to her hip, tightening her grip.

"Mama," her father says sternly. "Give the child to the Saint."

Mama stands, defiantly, head down, holding on to Mansour.

"Is this the child's mother?" asks the Saint, his voice softer and sweeter than most women's.

"Yes. Yes, I am," Mama replies, surrendering to the title for the first time.

The Saint turns to her father, perplexed, and states, "If this is his mother, she must have a say."

Her father struggles to his feet. "This child's mother is dead."

III.

THE SEARCH FOR MANSOUR

Switzerland, 1969

9. **AS BONNIE ENTERS** the kitchen from the hallway, she lets in the sound of the hall clock chiming midnight and a breeze that stirs a clashing tone from the clean pots and pans that swing overhead. Bonnie turns up her nose as Marie tips a pot of burnt rice in her direction.

"Want some?"

"Hell no."

"Your loss." Marie retorts, eating a spoonful.

The lights of the prairie are extinguished by a sudden gust of wind.

The storm is relentless. The kind that warms the river until it's rancid and ruins harvests, washing away settled seeds and buds that were already green. The village elders have named her Sheba. She is, they say, a curse that these dark women have brought with them, corrupting Swiss land that had been fruitful and blessed for generations with the spirit of whatever country they have run from.

Meanwhile, the younger Swiss folks patronize the restaurant a third, a fourth, a fifth time. For whoever does go, it seems, cannot go only once. They return home potbellied and bewitched, without words when asked to describe what they've tasted.

Bonnie knots the belt on her polka-dotted raincoat and ties a matching nylon scarf under her chin. She opens the back door, losing some nerve at the sight of the lightning. When it flashes, it reveals how the earth has turned soupy, that the ground is a gargling brown river.

She puts a foot in, and the warmth of the water is a surprise. Something in the air smells good, vaguely of vanilla, thyme, and mud. She takes another step. Underwater, a wire or a branch tears her shin. She trips and falls where the storm has eroded the ground. Armpit deep, with nothing around to grip, she cannot think enough to stand. She is frozen and sputtering. Marie calling her from the kitchen doorway breaks her trance, and she begins to fight and kick.

"Where are you going? It's dangerous!"

Bonnie grips the iron fence that's now in reach, pulling herself up. Wading, she reaches the door of Mama's Peugeot, and, battling against the strong wind, she grips and opens the driver's side door.

Inside the car she shivers, fumbling around for the keys in the glove compartment, on the door, under the seat. She stops at the sight of the rain on the car's front window: the world is damn near underwater. It is impossible to see.

"Why are you doing this to me, man?" she says, to Mansour, aloud.

Lost in her thoughts, Bonnie jumps at the sound of the passenger door opening, half-expecting Mansour to hop in, soaking wet, his eyelids sunk low from the long road home. That scent on his scalp and hands after worrying or running, like warm milk and electricity. Kissing her before the door is fully closed, letting in the rain . . . but Marie hops in shotgun. It's painful for a moment, and then a relief to see her.

"OK," Marie says, anchoring her mind by planting her hands on the dashboard. "I wasn't interested in a suicide mission."

"Maybe it'll ease up," Bonnie says, staring at the water that pounds the front window, still seeing Mansour.

"I'm not talking about the *storm*," Marie continues. "I'm talking about stealing Mama Eva Ndoye's Peugeot.

"I don't know why all of you are so scared of her."

"Please. You don't even talk to her."

"Why would I unless I have to? Doesn't mean I'm scared of her."

"You should be terrified of her!"

"Why's that?"

"Well, for one, she doesn't have sex! A woman in her condition is liable to do anything."

Bonnie chuckles at the depth of her own longing and then falls silent, eyes back on the storm.

"Before I give you these"—Marie holds up the keys—"I need to know your plan."

Bonnie inhales.

"To get to Geneva, and make sure that body's not him."

"Then what?"

"Keep going until we find him."

Bonnie gestures for the keys. Marie drops them in her hand. Her voice is quiet beneath the sputtering engine as the car starts.

"And what if it is him?"

Bonnie looks at her. "It's not," she says simply, and speeds ahead, cutting a path through the water.

PART
TWO

I.

THE GEEKS OF MULBERRY HIGH

New York, 1967

10. **THERE WAS SOMETHING** strange about 1967 for the other geeks of Mulberry High; '66 was the last of the summers they spent happily abstinent. Content with decoding glances and walks from a safe distance around the skate park. Content with getting splashed at the pool, or dunked, dragged in by the arm and made to scream and curse and play pissed. Maybe meeting a crush later on in some hiding place, under trees in Central Park North or the car-shop lot where the few Black Columbia kids performed Shakespeare plays, braids still wet from what the boys had done. The brave among them might kiss with their eyes closed and their hands to themselves.

But in the summer of '67, an urgency descended, a yearning for more. Bonnie watched the other geeks as they approached the boys carefully, in pin-curled and cornrowed ones and twos. The notorious lunch rabble of twelve loud virgins became something quieter, more self-conscious, as the end of senior year approached.

Bonnie observed her classmates carefully and listened closely, keeping her eyes on the drawings of her hovercraft in her lap. She always drew in her lap, was protective of the talent that was her only connection to her past. The one thing about her that only her mother knew.

When Bonnie first revealed a talent for drawing, in the Paris summer of '55, Claudine panicked. It was not dance, her own noose, but it was still an art form: a reliable predictor of another generation of chaos.

Claudine did not speak a single word when presented with the thirty portraits of her that Bonnie presented for her birthday. She'd rendered her mother in every available medium from an upstairs neighbor's stash: charcoal, watercolor, pencil, crayon. She'd drawn her dressed in tatty robes and torn dresses; in jeans and in the nude; fresh from the bathtub. Her breasts low, her waistline as crooked as her scoliosis had turned it, her face just as gaunt and tired as it looked in the mirror.

Claudine was Bonnie's only subject, and she'd captured her in each portrait with an exactness that felt vengeful. True in a way that felt cruel to someone that took great pains to never see themselves clearly. And though Claudine knew the child meant no harm, had meant in fact to express her love, shame drove her to tear each rendering into tiny pieces. Pieces she never meant for the child to find in the very bottom of the trash can. But Bonnie did.

In the cafeteria, Bonnie added dimension to the hovercraft, layering and layering until the pencil blackened her fingertips, bringing it to life as she listened to the geeks tell their stories of virginities lost.

Berniece returned to lunch after the weekend it happened, silent, fiddling with cold fries. Her icy coke turned to bubbleless black water before she finally sipped. Pearl returned singing high as Minnie Riperton's first note on "Completeness," suddenly in possession of a rare octave that drew Mrs. Walton from the teacher's lounge to pressure her to sing in chorus.

By the summertime, everyone thought that Bonnie had left the geeks because she was getting too pretty, but the truth was, she was embarrassed. Any day now, the time would come for her to tell her story, and she knew she wouldn't have anything to say.

Bonnie finds a summer job at a sunny deli on Prince Street. Her first job. The only time she is allowed out of the house, let alone in SoHo, without prompting panic from her grandmother, Sylvia. *I lost both of my children to this world.* Another lecture on the darkness and danger of America beyond their yard.

The deli owner lets Bonnie bring her albums to work. She plays Oscar Peterson all day on the loudspeaker and finds herself asking for customers' orders in the rhythms that he plays, swaying, dancing, marking his high C in the air with her fingertips. She doesn't even notice that she's doing this until a person ordering a pastrami sandwich flashes her a self-conscious smile. "Sorry," she mutters. But Oscar once again owns the rhythm of her hands as she counts the man's change.

Her first job was strategically chosen, a place right across from a crowded basketball court where she can watch boys play for hours in the netless hoops. She isn't ready to approach (or be approached), but she watches for boys the way her grandmother told her boys watch for girls. And when the boys come from the basketball court to the deli's counter, very rarely, but sometimes, she feels them in her bones something like the way she feels music.

But nobody knows. She masks any moments of enchantment with a gruffness that becomes legendary. Young people wandering the block or grown folks on their way back from church crowd the deli on sweaty summer weekends to see her cut boys down. The whole place cackles at her quick retorts to one-liners, catcalls, and unsolicited phone numbers. Some turn venomous as they stumble, shamed out the door.

"Ugly-ass bitch."

Others get more persistent, crowding the deli counter with flowers until the owner begs her to give one of the young men a chance.

"He's a good kid. For God's sake, who are you waitin' for?"

Then there is the man in a sports car, a soap actor every other person in the deli recognizes. They tell her that he appeared on *Days of Our Lives.* He waits patiently at the back of the line. When it's his turn, he doesn't pretend to want food, just tells a story of seeing Bonnie in the window as he was driving by.

"Let me take you to dinner," he says. The roar of the car pours in from the street, the glass door still wide open from his wild pull. The deli is silent, waiting.

"Is that your car?" she says, eyes on the bread she's buttering.

"Sure is, sweetness."

"Then your vehicle is parked illegally. Please move it." She turns her back to hide her smile as she slips the bread into the toaster. The people howl.

"You are stone cold, young lady! *Stone cold*. Don't ever change," an old Black woman says as she takes her brisket and goes out the door.

———

Friendless that summer after breaking it off with the geeks, Bonnie confides more and more in her coworker from the night shift, a Black Panther who's done some time and still has the scent of prison (wet bricks, blood, plaster, a hint of madness) on her body. In the breezy Manhattan evenings, the woman walks with her to the bus, the subway, always telling her she shouldn't be alone so much.

"Be careful out here, sis. You got a mouth on you, but I can tell you can't fight."

They prepare a corporate catering order by a single overhead light after the shop is closed to the public. As always, Oscar Peterson plays quietly beneath them. Bonnie describes what she imagines love would be like, or at least what she hopes for. The woman laughs a little.

"So, if you never find some boy that makes you feel like Cinderella, you never gon' be with *nobody*?"

Bonnie shrugs, slicing bell peppers. Bonnie finally asks the question she can't ask anyone else.

"What does it feel like?"

"With men?" The woman asks in a quieter voice, understanding Bonnie's question. Bonnie nods. The woman takes a moment before answering, "It's cool. But women . . . women do something different. We bring our souls to it."

The woman seems to be happily married, speaks often of her husband and son, but Bonnie watches some longing pass over her face as she speaks.

"Do you really wanna be with him forever?"

"My husband? Yeah, that's my husband," the woman says, biting the fresh mozzarella she's supposed to put on a sandwich.

"But what if there's more? What if you could feel more with somebody else?" Bonnie asks, earnestly, relieved to get out the questions she's been holding in for years. But the woman looks back at her, a motherly exhaustion.

"You too deep, sis. Way too deep. And look how you makin' that sandwich . . . the olive oil and sautéed onions. One twist of pepper, two twists of salt. Wiping off the knife between the mustard and the mayonnaise. I'm through twenty of these and you barely got five. How you gon' keep that up for every single one?"

11. **THEIR SUPER CALLS THE DELI.** Bonnie's grand-mother is at Mount Sinai Hospital. She hails a cab and sits on the edge of her seat, trembling with the road the whole way to Brooklyn.

She runs down hallway of the skylit atrium, dodging the aides pushing wheelchairs in both directions. Blinds block the view into her grand-mother's room, so she pounds on the glass. A nurse opens the door to reveal Sylvia lying down, her eyes open, knees up in bed, a meditative figure before a crowd of white coats. She seems overly cool (excessively medicated?), in a separate realm altogether. It is a teaching hospital and the crowd of doctors is not so much tending to her as they are observing her, leaning close and away again, taking notes, speaking over her and to one another. Lights flash from several machines, as if a roll of photographs is being shot in rapid succession.

The crowd soon dissipates, and Bonnie recognizes one of the doc-tors. Emmanuel Alvi has a mother living in the same senior commu-nity as Sylvia, one of her dear friends, so he's been to their apartment from time to time to pick her up, replace a fan, or bring a rug back from the cleaners. Her grandmother knows him well, but Bonnie only knows him in passing.

He stands before her now. She notes the dark hair on his chest, peeking out from his scrubs, the way he only smells sterile, his natural scent erased by his profession.

Outside the room, they chat about her grandmother, and he doesn't seem worried by the initial observations, so she relaxes, accepting his invitation to lunch in the hospital cafeteria. He's invited her to lunch before, in fact, and to dinner often. She's always said *sure*—the kind of agreement they both know lives comfortably between a no and a yes— but she's never showed up.

So, this time, when she says, "Sure," he asks her: "Is that really a yes? The cafeteria is right downstairs."

He gestures to a sign five steps in front of them with an arrow pointing downward. This morning has disrupted her routine, forced her into an uncommon sense of freedom, so she accepts this man's invitation. He says, "Cool," before disappearing.

Before going, she peeks into her grandmother's room again. She is awake but Bonnie doesn't want to enter, doesn't want to disturb her. A nurse is combing Sylvia's long silver hair, plaiting a section of it in that underhanded pattern that Bonnie had always found so difficult to grasp. Bonnie watches intently, needing to know, all of sudden, what her grandmother's hair feels like.

As a child, after she left Paris and came to New York to live with her grandmother, Bonnie looked for holes in women. Her grandmother had none. The woman seemed self-sufficient, and stoic to a fault, so Bonnie looked to their neighbors in the assisted living facility. She looked for loneliness, for those with children who did not visit or call.

Misunderstood women who accrued unwanted gifts: large baskets of expensive things they did not eat, clothes they did not like. She looked for those whose children called with rounds of fast questions without waiting for answers, the women's speech stumbling from excitement to dishonesty as they spewed the short answers that would appease their busy children. *Yes, yes, fine, fine.* She looked for dreamers, intellectual women who were called antisocial, uncooperative, insane. Women who were grandmothers and not grandmas, whose silent natures intimidated their attendants and were punished in turn with no eye contact and harsh handling, their breasts lifted to scrub under and then dropped hard. She looked for overthinkers, worriers, strategists who'd borne children and married to give their lives meaning but, now alone in old age, found their passion, their ambition, ever present and unsatisfied.

She learned from these women how the world worked, that she had to know what she wanted out of life in order to move through it. Inaction and ambivalence, it seemed, had given these women their holes.

She climbed into them. Succeeded at almost replacing children, husbands, pets, friendships. She did their grocery shopping, discussed their pains, snuck them chocolate and whiskey after hours. They were mostly white New England women who delighted in her beauty, good diction, quick wit, and poise. She mistook their admiration for affection.

Ms. Mallory, a neighbor with Alzheimer's, once called Bonnie by her daughter's name. At first Bonnie corrected her. But still, every time the woman woke up from a nap during Bonnie's visit, she would call her Delilah.

For about a month, Bonnie enjoyed Ms. Mallory's attention as she passed for her daughter. It came in loving gazes she would catch from the woman. A smile that was a language unto itself, a deep happiness she seemed to evoke in Ms. Mallory by simply being. It was the wanting to know what Bonnie's day had been like, listening to the details with such attention that the two of them breathed in tandem, Bonnie's dream of knowing and being known fulfilled.

But one day the real Delilah visited. Bonnie watched Ms. Mallory and her daughter together, the woman's love going back to where it rightly belonged, and not long after, when she visited Ms. Mallory again, the woman opened the door and stared too long. She asked Bonnie what her name was and told her that children were not allowed in the assisted-living facility unaccompanied.

Then Bonnie found herself running from the door. Racing without knowing why, down the long hallway, only stopping, finally, at the parking lot. Panting with her hands on her knees. A man worked quietly on a car alone, his palms black with grease. She watched, imagining that was the color, the texture, of her insides. And with that thought came a calm and strangely numbing feeling.

Her soul vowed to keep its distance from people. A boundary, now as she ages, that strangles more than it comforts. She wonders if it might be possible to break free of it, to overcome this feeling and get back into the world—or if, maybe, she will one day run into something, someone, who can take it away.

12. THEY MEET IN THE empty café of the hospital. Aides and doctors rush around the gray room, clutching paper bags of day-old bagels with the desperation of the homeless. Emmanuel is already seated, his head hanging forward as if he's taking a nap.

"Hi, Bonnie," he says, not lifting his head.

He makes small talk, strange small talk, as he opens the folder of X-rays and diagnoses that he has yet to look at and spreads the papers across the table.

Bonnie feels exposed when he asks her what she had for breakfast. Had she eaten? Did she want anything? A bagel, toasted maybe? Hiding herself, she says no.

"Are you seeing anyone?" he asks suddenly, and then seems to hold his breath.

She has seen Emmanuel's wife at holiday parties in the senior facility. Always coming through briefly in that way important people do. Busy, stylish, childless.

All she knows is that she works in the music industry, a detail from her grandmother that makes the woman even more intriguing. She remembers his wife's musky perfume, her damp raincoat brushing against Bonnie's arm in the building hallway. The woman was polite. *Excuse me*, she'd said.

"Are you seeing anyone?" he asks again, now impatient, irritated, as if she is depriving him of something he needs immediately, like a key to the bathroom. She still doesn't answer him, wanting to see what more he'll do to get an answer.

She notices SYLVIA KING in cursive poking out in the pile of X-rays. She holds it up to the cafeteria's dim light.

Her grandmother's leaning skeleton. It is strange to see her from the inside. Even her bones make a pose that means business. Through the light, her lungs look like a sky full of too many stars. There is dark matter here, more toward her abdomen.

"No one told me about this," she says.

"Bonnie, I'm sure she's fine," he assures her. Pockets of air, a little gas, anything. The ward's primary doctors will be looking into it. No one was concerned about her lungs. But at Bonnie's insistence, they go to his office to examine the image more carefully.

"My timing must be terrible," his voice echoes as they stand in his cold office with the lights off, the door closed, her grandmother's X-ray perched on the lit board. "I just didn't know when else I'd have time alone with you."

He turns to the X-ray. She watches his face turn slack.

After a few minutes: "It's blood."

Shame—or fear—in his voice. The blood and chafed bone have likely been floating around Sylvia's chest for a few years, maybe more. Emmanuel orders more X-rays, calls his subordinates and superiors.

They discover within hours that her grandmother's ribs have punctured her lungs. The miniscule specs of blood have been overlooked by specialists who have been monitoring her dementia, anemia, back spasms, sluggish heart rate—everything except her lungs.

"How could they miss this?" Bonnie asks Emmanuel hours later in his office. Her back against the wall, her head tilted to the ground.

"I'm going to take care of it, Bonnie," he says. She watches as he pours over the files. A decade of X-rays, blood work, and charts spread across his table. The lights are on now. He comes and goes from the room, returning with nurses, specialists, and administrative staff. Bonnie curls up like a snail and falls asleep on the couch in the far corner of his office, sweating cold, waking hours later to hear the quiet words of the doctor's, the words that begin to change things.

The following morning, back at home, she calls Emmanuel. She asks him if the coma Sylvia slipped into is related to the lung puncture.

"It could be," he says.

"So . . . so she's dead," Bonnie says, not a question, the word made certain under its weight. She clears her voice, hoarse from a lack of sleep, takes another bite from her Snickers.

"Are you OK?"

"Is she dead." It happens again. Bonnie can't make it a question.

"She could still wake up. It happens."

Bonnie lies on the floor of her grandmother's kitchen, feeling the cracks in the tiles, places shaped by Sylvia's feet over the years she walked these tiles, over the years she integrated this place, its first Black resident. Bonnie shivers: malnutrition, dehydration, sleep deprivation. Her heart can't settle, can't tell if it is time to love harder or let go.

Still on the phone, she can hear Emmanuel's wife in the background, speaking to him in Urdu.

"There's too much noise," Bonnie mumbles bitterly.

"I said, Miss Sylvia hasn't been out long. She could wake up."

The wife says something else.

"Hold on," he says to Bonnie.

The line goes quiet for what feels like a long time. Too long. Her tired eyes wander around the room. To the mail on the floor that she'd searched and then thrown on the ground. Nothing from her mother, as usual. She's written to an old Detroit address, the only address she could find among her grandmother's things. She thinks—hopes—the coma will be the excuse, the drama needed, maybe, to finally get her mother to reply, after years without a word from her.

He calls her back many hours later, after midnight. She tells him what she overheard the doctors saying. About sixty-eight years being more than enough life for her grandmother, dismissing their neglect. He begins to apologize but she interrupts.

"I want to see you," she says. She hangs up the phone quickly.

A day later, Emmanuel drives from Brooklyn to Little Italy, where they eat at three different restaurants on the same street. Antipasto after antipasto after antipasto. It's what she wants. Shucking oysters under dusty awnings, slipping sideways through the sticky bodies of a crowded street fair. She spends fifteen dollars buying mugs, compasses, a small porcelain doll, beads for cornrows she's planning to have done (now that her grandmother's not around to stop her), wares from around the world, she has never had this kind of freedom, has never roamed around New York City just for kicks.

And on this excursion in the city, she discovers that she can pretend to be in a universe in which her grandmother is home drinking sherry, sorting her card deck on the veranda, beating Bonnie's ass at spades and talking politics. All the things Malcolm had done right (*He was such a good-looking kid*), and what the hell was wrong with that girl Nina Simone (*Her hair!*)?

What's your plan? What's your plan? Sylvia would say, looking over Bonnie's shoulder, assessing the quality of her hand. *Start light. What's your plan, little girl? You have to win in your mind before you start.*

On this street in Little Italy, licking gelato, Bonnie's grandmother is not in a coma, she is neither dead nor undead, and Bonnie's terrors can go unstirred for a few hours.

She stops at a table of antique handmade globes. She plays with one, watching countries and oceans spin into a blur.

"I want to leave here. I want to travel the world," Bonnie whispers to herself. She walks on ahead of Emmanuel and says no more. They walk down a cobblestone street in lower Manhattan. Fire escapes hang above their heads from the sides of a giant warehouse. When he reaches for her hand, she pulls away and puts it in her pocket.

13. **AS THE WEEKS GO ON,** Emmanuel begins to express frustration with the hospital, with his life as an ER doctor and departmental manager. He makes a confession he's made to no one else—that for almost a decade, he has wanted to return to Pakistan, a country he only lived in for the first six years of his life and has, given its own unrest, probably romanticized. Still, he desperately wants to go back. This they share: a nagging feeling that America is not quite home. And for this and her obvious isolation, Bonnie seems an ideal vessel for Emmanuel's secrets: a solitary life no one else enters and exits, a place where his most private feelings are safe.

He's long given up on distinguishing himself in a profession that is, after seven years, essentially clerical: filing, writing, inputting data while his patients seldom recover.

His wife, Rabia, sleeps alone, has slept alone for most of their marriage. He prefers the couch in the living room and eventually, the one in his office. He thought, at first, that it was only a matter of convenience. But he soon realized that the problem was her. Rabia's body heat, imprinted on the mattress beside him when she rose for work, had become a cypher of death: what remains when his patient dies. For him, the warmth a body leaves behind is not a comfort, it is the final evidence of life. Sharing a bed feels like endless mourning.

Still, he feels guilty about the life he's given her, about the law school classes he refused to pay for, afraid, he says, of losing her to her ambition.. In the end, after working first as an aide at the hospital and then as a secretary at a day care center, his wife saved enough money to put herself through law school. She is now the first female head of Artists & Repertoire for a small Manhattan record label. Once he says all this, Bonnie looks away from where they sit on a park bench to the swings across the way in the park. She's staring intently at the empty swing the wind pushes the hardest, its chains whine loudly in the breeze.

"I've never done it before." She says, squinting against the sun.

"Swing? Never?"

"No. I told you. My grandmother's paranoid. I didn't go to parks. I didn't go anywhere." She looks down at the dirt, drawing a circle with her shoe. When she looks back at him, Bonnie tells him that he can kiss her if he wants to. She offers it bluntly, her elbow on the park table, holding up her chin as she examines him. A look that could suggest anything from arousal to the possibility that he has something in his teeth. No matter how he tries, she is impossible to read.

"You feel that bad for me, huh?"

"Yeah, you're pretty pathetic," she says easily, earnestly, in a way that somehow doesn't sting. She has the gift, or maybe the curse, of a frank nature.

When he kisses her, he tells her breathlessly that it's like pressing his lips to a spring. Her lips are thick—she knew this and liked them on her own terms, but the way he says it makes her smile. So different from his wife's. It makes him wonder how everything else would feel with her. He leans in again.

That's how it begins.

14. **MONTHS PASS** and the coma persists. Bonnie wanders around the Alvis' apartment every morning before heading to work, Emmanuel's wife always already gone for the day. Bonnie's saddle oxfords squeak on the hardwood as she stops and looks at the wall of records, organized in alphabetical order. She feels his eyes on her moisturized legs.

She'd offered Emmanuel her grandmother's ticket to her high school graduation, an invitation to see her present at the closing ceremony of the Science Honors Society. But he'd been busy. His reaction to her admission to Yale ("How'd you pull that off?") bothered her too. She'd forfeited the acceptance anyway, never mailing the letter to confirm her enrollment, through with being one of two, three Black girls in her class. Yale was just another Mulberry High.

Now he asks if she's been to the hospital to check up on her grandmother, and she lies.

She peruses the record collection closely. He has many of the albums she grew up on. In a tone akin to accusing him of theft, she asks why. *Why do you have all this Black music?* She is jealous, deeply possessive of Sarah Vaughan, of Ella Fitzgerald, of Ray Charles, the members of her imagined family.

"Everybody loves them. They're the standard," he says, perplexed and excited by the strength of her reaction. As they discuss these albums, she seduces him with the nuance of her analysis. *Mingus shouldn't play Mingus. Mingus is better in softer hands.*

Her sense of what music means, of how it feels, is complex and prodigious. He tells her that his wife is hiring for small jobs at the label. He mentions it in passing—a mistake, as he is quickly exhausted by how relentless and persistent her follow-up questions are. But soon, he's committed to getting her an interview at Onyx Records for a proofreading position. She'll have to wait, though. The position won't officially be open until the spring.

As she walks, inventing a longer route to delay seeing Sylvia at the hospital, Bonnie returns again and again to Emmanuel's words. So Black music can belong to him too It was hard to process an identity that seemed to both have no gatekeepers—its roots breeding, building, breaking under everything America was—while also kept from claiming any of its parts for itself. She'd taken her mother's words literally, and she thought again of them now. Who was she if the sound of her people belonged to the world?

Back when Bonnie and Claudine still lived in Paris, there was a fight in the apartment below them. A couple at war, screaming and launching everything they owned at each other. Bonnie remembers this moment because her mother was holding her, a rare and cherished thing. She spoke into her ear, explaining conflict. The cause of most trouble between people wasn't difference, but twinhood. *On the inside, everybody has a sound*, Claudine had said. Some people are crying all the time. Some are always sighing. The sound of yourself, she'd said, is whatever you can't stand to hear from other people. And whatever you look like to yourself is what you can't stand to see.

At the hospital, the darkness and coolness of Sylvia's room makes it easy, easier than she thought it would be, to come close. She dares to touch her grandmother's hair. Feeling it for the first time. Cotton-soft strands, too fine to resist static. Just as she'd hoped it would be, it is her mother's hair. She closes her eyes, savoring this feeling of belonging, of being part of at least two other people in the world. And as if to say that she belongs to her too, Sylvia's breathing grows fiercer. Breaths that are deep, loud, harder than those of anybody Bonnie knows among the living.

The nurse peeks in, sees hope in Bonnie's eyes. As gently as she can, the woman says, "She does that," pulling the edge of the blanket over the unconscious woman's whitening feet before disappearing again.

But Bonnie has never heard a breath more determined. It is strange to Bonnie that a woman who lived her last decades so quietly, sleeping her years away behind the shady oaks of a senior home, wants to die so outrageously loud. Bonnie considers for the first time that there was once more to this woman than she knows. That perhaps it is not the quiet, not the folding of fitted sheets, the snapping of rollers into hair, but this sound, this defiance, that is truly hers.

WHEN SYLVIA WENT SOUTH TO DEFEND
THE WIDOWS OF THE LYNCHED

Alabama, 1927

15. **SYLVIA AND HER FATHER,** Carlyle, reach Gee's Bend shivering in total darkness. They are stranded by faulty kerosene lamps and a useless moon that hardly does more than display clouds that look like the foam in the mouth of a rabid dog. The files for the case warm their knees.

When their boat docks, the scattered lights in the distant woods don't feel kind. Sylvia asks her father if they can go another way, but his warm palm only guides her forward.

They hike through sloped back roads to reach the widows in the woods. The tent where they pray for their murdered husbands towers above them, and the leaves of weeping willows brush its sides, making a sound like sighing. The tent: handmade, somebody tells her, over three nights by forty quilters. Scraps from worn-out jeans and cotton tablecloths unified in a faultless pattern.

The raucous wailing from within strikes Sylvia between the eyes like a punch as she stares up at the stitching in the ceiling. Remembered and passed down through centuries, the vibrating cry of the mourners stands out from all of the others. Distinct from sadness, it is a skillful weeping, a sound that will transform all the mourning in the room into power.

Sweating, Sylvia rips off her silk gloves, but fear has turned her hands numb. Four small wooden boxes crowd the dais. So small and slender, they could only be caskets for cats.

Carlyle is a civil rights lawyer; his name is known. To protect Sylvia, they stay in separate places. Across town, he prepares arguments by candlelight under the hind legs of cured pigs in the local butcher shop. She revises his opening statement by lantern in the house of one of the widows. She will interview the others in a few days for the case. In the house, they keep the lights off and the moon gives the rooms a blue darkness that Sylvia worries is too shallow to keep her safe.

―――――

At the breakfast table (cheese grits, smoked sausage, coffee), some numbness has dwindled. Sylvia's right hand can clasp a fork and her left hand has feeling in three fingers again. In the evening, she learns from the widow that the caskets are small because the husbands inside are in pieces.

―――――

The morning after, both of Sylvia's hands turn numb again, so numb that Sylvia can pick off the skin around her nails without feeling anything. She cannot stop thinking of the caskets.

―――――

That day, more widows arrive. After telling Sylvia the stories of where and how they found the bodies of their husbands, some become slack, saying they need a good chair to hold them up, a feeling like their own bodies are suddenly without bones. Some hold on to the widow, changing positions to do the holding and be held. Others stay in the tub for hours, long after the water turns cold. Some get under covers with their shoes and coats and hats still on and sweat. Some force their faces into pillows to muffle their cries. Sylvia watches one woman part the shutters on the front windows and scream.

On the morning of the trial, in the car on the way to court, Sylvia's body finally demands rest. She drifts off, waking up seven times to a sky that is still the color of fresh water. Her father practices his arguments with the windows down. She's written most of them, and even half-awake she can decipher the terrible changes that he insisted on. Changes that soften the women's stories and bend the truth. She keeps her hands hidden from him in her white gloves. She has peeled and picked at the skin around her nailbeds so deeply that the flesh shows.

They are not welcomed at the nearest rest stop, so he holds up the plaid tablecloth that has been their picnic blanket and faces the woods while she pees. Two fingers wrapped around the trigger on the handgun inside his breast pocket.

They arrive, but their protection—a procession of Black and white journalists—has not. Looking out at the empty road where the journalists should have been, Sylvia finds it hard to steady herself. She walks wide, as though each marble step to the courthouse were a seesaw.

It is difficult to breathe inside the courtroom, a place full of the dust from blinding sunlight and old antebellum curtains, beaten daily but never washed.

"Our case is not with Mr. Lawrence, nor his hounds and cousins. It is with the state of Alabama for its failure, it's consistent failure, to offer Negroes equal protection under the law . . ."

As her lips move to her father's voice, speaking the words she's written, Sylvia looks around the courtroom for signs of danger. Are they the subject of the whispers a couple of pews behind her? Her own scent, a whiff of the foulest sweat, shoots up her nostrils and she forces herself to be calm. She closes her eyes.

They lose the case on the grounds that there are no witnesses. In what is left of their time in Alabama, a foggy early evening, Sylvia can hardly make out more than their clients' silhouettes. The widows wrap themselves around her and hold on. Her tears seem to spring out from the tightness of their grip on her body. Their words keep her from breaking. They are praising her courage, praising her tongue.

On the road, her father works hard to avoid her eyes. She doesn't look his way either. She can feel the rage steaming from him; it's like a gust of warm air on the side of her body. It soothes her own.

Sylvia hears it first. A sound like treading water. A little ripple of cold wind into her right ear. Something cracks the glass on the front window. Then there's nothing but deafness that comes and leaves within the same ten seconds. Then it seems for a moment that nothing at all has happened. But then there's something about the way her father's head is hanging, swinging loosely on his neck, that tells Sylvia he's dead. She feels the car drifting off the road and grips the steering wheel, pulling it toward her.

The scent of her father's blood resurfaces days later. It wakes Sylvia out of sleep on the train home to Boston. It does not dissipate with time. The scent grows and grows in presence and forever becomes a part of her. That and the screech of the tires, when they'd started to drift from the road.

III.

THE SEARCH FOR MANSOUR
(PART TWO)

Switzerland, 1969

16. **THE CAR GLIDES** until the earth slopes deeper. It buoys like a boat as the tires squeal and tread and then lock. Bonnie and Marie don't hear the car stop; they hear instead what emerges in the motor's absence: the loud squeak of a flapping tin roof, foxes tearing open farm fences, then lunging headfirst into rabbits and hogs.

They are trapped in a ditch. A sheep body deep in the water beside them seems human around the panicked eyes as it struggles to keep its head above water. Bonnie presses hard on the accelerator, but the car won't go.

"Come on," Marie says, opening the door.

Bonnie hesitates at first, opening the door and freezing. "Get out here and push!" Marie screams over the wind.

She leaves the car on. Both women get behind it and shove all their weight into it. They cry from the strain, slicing their knees and knuckles, but the car finally moves forward again. Inch by inch, they get it back on the wet road.

They reach the road that leads to Geneva before sunrise. Feverish, the chilly twilight breeze feels damp on Bonnie's skin. The chill has worsened the tenderness of her breasts, a sting in sync with her pulse. Though the rain has quieted to a patter, abandoned cars and toppled trees block the path forward. There is no other person, no other living thing, on the road. The concrete is wet and the wheels have been slipping. They pull over and agree to wait until the rain stops entirely.

"Whatever happened to that cute white boy?" Marie breaks the silence, almost mocking the dystopian mood of the landscape with her ease as she crosses her legs on the dashboard, ashen white from the mud. "Wouldn't he know something?"

Bonnie looks out the window. "You're always talking about some white boy," she chides.

"Liam!" Marie snaps her fingers as she remembers. "They were like glue. He probably knows everything."

"I've tried. I can't get him on the phone," Bonnie replies.

She takes off her glasses to wipe away the sludge. Then the light of the sky is visible. It shows some lingering clouds that seem close enough to touch.

Marie speaks: "After Geneva, maybe we should pay him a visit."

IV.

THE FIRST ALBUM

New York, 1968

17. **WHEN LIAM THINKS** of that first album, he tries to only recall the good things, the way it all began: the used Hammond B3 they pushed up three flights of stairs to their walk-up and the way their voices, in strained unison, had called each lift like a football play. Their elation after getting the electric organ upright in the middle of the attic. How when the floorboards began to creak, their reaction had been to whisper as if their voices added weight to the room.

The album's first practice session took place there, with a borrowed drum set they muffled with blankets, the landlord's cat pruning the keyboard wires like yarn until Mansour clocked her with a shoe. They started with a gulp of whiskey, prayers in two religions, and a meatball sandwich with everything on it.

Upon arriving in America, something neither of them could name—maybe fear, maybe foreignness—had fused Mansour and Liam in a solid bond. During their time living in that attic apartment above the flower shop (rented to them by Liam's uncle for next to nothing), every note, chord, or lick that one brother offered struck the other as a perfect suggestion, a divine directive that must be honored as they lived this answer to their childhood prayers. They had been planning this moment since they first met in Catholic school ten years ago in Switzerland, and they felt that they'd finally arrived.

But that night in late January, their first rehearsal after finally signing with Onyx Records, quickly descended into purgatory. Every note hummed or played was questioned, Liam repeating the label's suggestions like a mantra. Mansour obsessively examining every musical idea for originality, flavor. At any hint of nostalgia or sameness to their idols, whole pages of sheet music were struck out, scrunched, doused in vodka, set on fire, flung from the window. *You're dead weight*, Mansour accused Liam.

———

Ever since their arrival in New York, Liam's aunt had refused to speak directly to Mansour. So he had quickly begun calling her the wrong name as payback. Her body would stiffen, her mouth releasing a huff or two, but due to some personal vow not to speak to him, she never had any words at her disposal. But over time, living in the same building softened their posture, and they soon found themselves engaged in a toothless quarrel, a kind of flirting, most of the time.

She was the opposite of Mansour's aunt, Sokhna. Sokhna had introduced Mansour and Liam to American music, sneaking Four Tops and Temptations records into the school at the bottom of baskets of socks and jams. For Liam specifically, Sokhna had bought good guitar strings, finally, a full steel set of six. She was the first of many women they would share a crush on. They'd idolized her to the point of myth, their teenaged admiration giving her a good laugh as she drove them across cities and farm towns for their first gigs. They'd started off playing acoustic covers of Motown in little barns that hosted dances for village youth. Mansour would sing in happy gibberish, mimicking Eddie Kendricks, routinely butchering the English lyrics until Liam—a proud Irishman—intervened. Through the lyrics, Liam taught Mansour English, but he still avoided speaking the language, always avoided things he couldn't do perfectly.

When Mansour and Liam had dreamed of America, they dreamed of it through these songs. Restless in the night, feigning for life, they'd studied the river that traveled through the school backyard, imagining it to be the river Sam Cooke was born beside: a blue and rolling thing, glistening like it carried gems.

One day, while she was visiting them, Sokhna had sent Mansour to bring her car around and pulled Liam aside. She'd adjusted Liam's collar and looked back to Mansour. Excited to drive her car, even just around the bend, he was happily jogging away.

"Take care of him," she'd said to Liam. She rested her hand on his shoulder and held it, giving him time to feel the weight of her grip, and words, before letting go.

He wouldn't understand her plea until their first gig a few months later.

18.

MANSOUR HAD BEEN taking too long to join him onstage. Behind their two spectators (a drunk, a bartender), a broken beer tap had dripped into a bucket, making the only sound in the room. After several minutes of waiting, Liam had walked offstage and gone around back to see what had become of Mansour. He'd knocked hard on the bathroom door, before opening it and seeing that no one was inside. He'd gone next into the supply room. With its rotting floor planks and mildewed couch, it's where they'd been told they could stack their few things. There, Liam had found Mansour face down on the couch, grunting quietly. His arms were straight and stiff at his side. When Liam had rolled him over, spittle rolled down the left corners of Mansour's mouth. Liam had gotten him on his back and watched him. Panting, slower and slower, until his chest settled and he dosed off.

When he'd sat up sometime later, insisting he only needed five minutes to go onstage, worried, Liam had fought him, throwing him from the door with both hands, wrestling him with all his might. But Mansour had pulled off the shirt crusted with his spittle and persisted until he fought his way to the stage. He went out alone.

Liam heard the first note from the back—a cappella, wobbly, flat—and Mansour had held it this way, loud and wrong, until it brought itself, naturally, beautifully, into tune. His voice behaved like a bass string that had been plucked with excessive might and left to quake until it stilled itself. Relief. Liam heard it, and it made him exhale, like the relief was his own. And his brother went on this way, singing a cappella to the audience of two. A lot of humming, stopping and starting, trying things; he was singing for himself.

They had only been fourteen and fifteen, and would spend a week on suspension for fleeing the school grounds, but Liam would say that *that* was the day he first met his brother Mansour, a man at war with his terror, forever squirming from the clutches of his own fate.

19. **ON THE NIGHT** they'd arrived, Manhattan advertised its chaos the way the Swiss and Senegalese belabored their civility, and Mansour had known then that his flightiness—his inability to focus for the length of a television program, eat sitting down, or choose a god—would be welcomed here.

When their plane touched down in 1966, Mansour and Liam had fled their choir's Christmas concert at Carnegie Hall and hopped on the subway to Brooklyn, carrying out their plan. From that night to today, a year and half later, Mansour has not seized, and, wide awake around 4:00 a.m. in Bay Ridge, he is rummaging through a table of things he believes to be the reason.

The table contains every kind of remedy. Western: some prescription pills (half bummed, half legitimate). Eastern: Chinese teas. Spiritual: some tonic procured from a séance in the Bronx. *America cured me*, Mansour mumbles to a half-awake Liam, lighting the cigarette in his mouth.

———

Liam's aunt tells him that for what they're paying, they can't use the lights after midnight, so the young men argue over transitions, over bridges and lyrics, by the flashing red lights of the twenty-four-hour

Irish-only (they learned this the hard way) strip club across the street. They throw one another from the grimy wall to the grimy couch.

Their shot with Onyx Records has come with extreme conditions: a signing of sorts (renewal contingent upon satisfactory album sales), payment from said album sales and gigs only (no advance), seven hours of professional studio time allotted for the whole record, and only a few weeks to bring it all together. This means that they must come to the first recording session prepared to lay things down. And given that the session is in two days and there is only a track and a half that the men agree on, they know better than to sleep.

They wait for five in the morning so they can flush the toilet, use the shower. If the aunt hears the water a second earlier, they will be fined five dollars, as they had been the week before, indicated by a note stuck with gum to the bedroom door. The aunt's redeeming quality, in their eyes, is that she can cook: beef stews so rich with bones that chilling them always reveals several layers of fat, potatoes roasted in butter and rosemary, tiered cakes filled with fruit and soaked for nights in dark spirits. And the food, unlike her towels, her sheets, her soap, her liquor, her kindness, is given freely.

Mansour and Liam's first meeting with a musician for the album—a keyboardist from the Onyx roster—isn't until 9:00 a.m., but they head out around seven. For Mansour's sake, it is better to get out of the neighborhood early, before the streets begin to stir. He is the only dark-skinned person around and even at this quieter hour will still be called a nigger twice before they are on the subway. It's something he pretends not to hear. Instead, he whistles the horn section, the bass line, the background, everything but the melody, of Martha and the Vandellas' "Dancing in the Street," pulling his hoodie down on his head, his passion for living seemingly indestructible.

Liam, who knows Mansour as well as anyone could, still doesn't know how it burns him. The way it disorients him. Not the word itself, for which he has no former knowledge or cultural precedent, but its

aftermath: the cyphers of unbelonging that range in passion from curious gawks to physical blows and drag him so far out of his daydream-
ing it is becoming harder to fight his way back in. But Mansour knows
to expect some estrangement in a foreign city, and New York, for all its
strangeness, is delivering on its promises of manifesting dreams.

As they ride to Manhattan from Bay Ridge for the meeting, Mansour
finds the city familiar. He is no longer shocked by the jolting of the
subway, the sound like the sharpening of knives the train car makes on
the tracks. Nor the homeless man brazenly gawking at their exchange
in rapid French. As the gray sky turns white with daylight, the men's
yearning for the warmth of their beds finally leaves them.

They make it to the café where they are scheduled to meet the keyboardist—but he never shows.

They talk through the label's other referrals and make their way to
a phone booth on West Fourth Street, where they start making calls.
Liam's accent is no help on the phone, and Mansour's limited English
makes him too shy to help. He's staring into the alley, trying to tell the
difference between the rats and squirrels. Liam presses on.

The first on their list of musicians is woken up by the call.

"How you get this number?" Click.

The next is flattered but can't do the gig for what they're offering.

"I've got kids, man."

Their momentum begins to drain out with their sweat on the
crowded street. Dodging the misty rain, they stand under the checkered awning of a restaurant, briefly seduced by fried mozzarella and
steaks grilled at a thousand degrees. They are starving but know they
ought to wait to get home and save what little money they have.

"We have to find our own people," Mansour says. "Ask the girl
about the clubs around here." He gestures to a pretty waitress looking
bored in the corner.

"No way, on y va," Liam says. He is terrified of pretty women.
Mansour pushes him in the girl's direction.

Liam walks briskly toward the subway instead. Hoping, though not really expecting, Mansour to follow, he turns to see him approach the waitress, trying his hand at English.

"Uhhh, excuse me . . ."

"Yeah?"

"We are music peoples?"

"I'm sorry?"

"We are to . . . go see the music where?"

"What?"

Mansour can hear Liam laughing, loud and cruel. He turns, laughing at himself as he curses Liam in French, then begs him to save his ass.

"Alors, tu vas m'aider ou quoi?!"

The woman has some suggestions. She uses a coffee-stained city map, circling with a pen the areas where they can find what they seek. The nearest thing will be jazz music, though the clubs won't be open for another few hours. But she tells them to take their chances.

The door is wide open at the Blue Note. A jazz trio is in rehearsal. Mansour is transfixed. The Irishman watches the African approach the stage as if under a spell, sliding down the back wall into a squat without blinking.

Even now, when Liam remembers that day, he still wonders why they were not questioned, not immediately thrown out. It was the first place in the world that they, the orphaned misfits, seemed to simply belong.

20.

LATER THAT EVENING, after their first set, Liam catches up to the drummer. The man is easygoing and kind. In his early sixties, he walks awkwardly on tiny feet that seem ill-suited to his large frame. He tells Liam to walk with him as he makes his way to the bar, where a milkshake waits for him on the counter.

"This vanilla?" the drummer asks the bartender.

"Yessir."

"Well, you plan on puttin' any ice cream in it? Add a couple more scoops in there."

"I'm sorry, sir, right away."

The bartender pulls back the glass, and the drummer keeps his eyes on the milkshake as the man drops in the new scoops. Then he turns his attention to Liam. His eyes are small and tired. He picks up a napkin and swipes sweat from his face.

"Go on, sid'down."

Liam takes the seat beside him.

"When's the session?"

Liam is shocked that this man, who has drawn a crowd that is already wrapping around the building for the second set, is actually considering his request.

"It's tomorrow night."

The man shakes his head. "I'll be trapped here all week." He sips on his new milkshake, lets out a sigh of relief. "That cold's so good," he says, observing the glass with reverence.

"What do you really need? Somebody to keep time, or somebody who can really play?"

"Really play."

"Really play, yeah." He fiddles with his ear. "I'm thinking of somebody."

A young white man approaches from behind, tells the drummer to get ready for the next performance.

The drummer stands, puts his hat on. "Carl Keifer," he says to Liam. "He's not easy to get along with, but he's damn good."

The man walks away, milkshake in hand. Liam stammers, thanking the man profusely, but the old man only throws a hand behind his back as he walks on, as if to say, it's nothing.

Liam calls after him, "Where do I find him?"

"Uptown somewhere. He's shootin' a movie. One of those karate things. And tell him . . . tell him Gil sent you."

He says this without turning around.

"Karate thing" is the hint that leads them to Harlem, a place where Mansour keeps looking over his shoulder. He hasn't seen this many Black folks in one place since he left Senegal as a child.

Certain details pull his attention. It is the way a man on Lenox Avenue stands against a streetlight with one leg crossed over the other, and a newspaper in his hand, staring out into the chaos of the road with a smile, like he is seeing another scene entirely. A throwback to Mansour's grandfather, leaning against their courtyard door. His grandfather was the first daydreamer Mansour had ever known, a

man with a mind like his: ever elsewhere, ever imagining more beauty
from the world than what it was willing to give.

They were breathless, reeking with sweat, but once they got to St.
Nicholas Avenue it was finally easy. Under an early evening sky, tinted
the color of mud from the smog, the Harlem folks guided them, stepping down from dominos games on their brownstone stoops to point
their fans in the direction of the bridge. *To the left, to the left.* Until
when? Until they could see the river.

The shooting location is a Shotokan school near the Harlem River.
As they approach the water, the breeze gets strong and cold against
Mansour's scalp. Inspired by his once-cited resemblance to Jimi
Hendrix (*If Hendrix were darker and prettier*, his first favorable review
had begun), he feels the world differently since he got his hair conked.
Not just the cool air, but everything—even sounds seem closer, and his
mind seems to be thinking fewer thoughts, as if the conk has simplified
him and destroyed some barrier between him and the world.

In front of the dojo doors, Mansour stumbles on a cord, thick as
snakes at his feet. His throat itches from the smoke of the haze
machines. A small group of men are filming, the set is quiet, he swallows the pain. A brunette in glasses approaches the chatty men and
grabs Liam by the edge of his shirt with one hand, a red fingernail
pressed to her lips with the other, silencing them.

"Who are you?" she mouths.

"Musicians. We're—" Liam begins.

"Go that way," she mouths and points toward an open basement
door, releasing Liam with a wink. He looks back over his shoulder, but
she swiftly disappears.

As they descend the steps, a little jazz club of fifteen tables (made
for the movie) reveals itself by a few dim ceiling lights. A hi-fi system,

the kind of model Liam dreams about, is mounted on the wall. It plays Judy Garland with an uncanny fidelity, capturing, even, her gasps for breath between notes. A Black woman in her sixties, seemingly still in character, smokes and polishes glasses behind the counter, and a young white man, a member of the film crew by his casual jeans and torn T-shirt, sits at the far end of the bar playing Checkers alone.

The crew member looks up from his Checkers game and speaks to Liam like a savior, the only white man he's seen in hours.

"Is it finally over? Are we wrapping for the day?"

"I couldn't tell you. We're just musicians," Liam says.

"*More* musicians?" Overhearing Liam, a man interjects from the stage at the center of the room. "So what the hell are we doin' here? We've been waiting for the director to come shoot this damn scene for *seven hours*, man!"

Balancing a trumpet on his bouncing knee, he is the largest of four black men in expensive suits on the stage. Behind a drum set, a shiny Baldwin, and a towering double bass, they have wilted into weary poses. Liam and Mansour study the men, trying to decide which one is Carl Keifer.

"May as well dip out of here then," the large man continues.

"Don't you leave, Aristotle. Don't give them any reason to play with your check," the actress warns, shaking the glass in her hand.

The musicians groan, but they turn over again in their seats, shifting their tired bodies and staying put.

"Who y'all with?" Aristotle asks Mansour, who's understood the question but is too timid to fumble around in English with all these eyes in his direction.

Liam answers, "Nobody, we're a duo."

Aristotle mimics his thick accent. "*We're a duo.* That's Irish-Irish. When'd you get here, man?"

The other men onstage begin to laugh passively. Liam yells their mimicry, his voice loud and firm. It echoes.

"We were told that we could find Carl Keifer here."

"Sure thing, he's right there." Aristotle points out the young brown man sitting silently at the piano. Distinctively gaunt, the brim of his hat casts a dark shadow over the silhouette of his pointy nose and full lips. He's playing different triads, moody, dark things that illustrate the room's atmosphere. He's pretending to mind his business while listening to all the banter with a careful ear.

"You play drums?" Liam asks, cutting into the pianist's chords. The men snicker.

"That's Carl Keifer, fool. Talkin' about *does he play drums?* You really did just get here, didn't you?" the actress answers for him. Liam wonders why the room seems to revere this man, seems to be protecting him. It makes him push harder. He approaches the stage. Keifer's using the piano peddle now, making the sound louder, more robust. Liam shouts over Keifer's playing.

"Carl, we have a deal with Onyx Records—we have a recording session tomorrow night, me and my friend over there—and Mr. Gil thought you might be available to play drums for us."

"Oh, Gil sent you," the man scoffs, without looking up, but he stops playing.

Liam continues, "We hardly have any time to record, and the music isn't easy—"

"There's nothing but musicians in this town—"

"But we really need somebody of your caliber, so if you name your price—"

"Mais arrêtes de le supplier comme ça." *Stop begging him*, Mansour chastises from across the room with a bitterness, a brashness that makes the men perk up and look in his direction.

"Wha'd he say?" Carl Keifer asks.

"Let's go, man," Mansour says in French, firm and exhausted as he moves toward the door. And the two of them continue in French as Keifer and the others watch quizzically.

"Mansour! We're out of time!" Liam explodes. "We have to talk to him!"

"They all think they're better than us! Let's just go."

Keifer stands. "Wha'd he say?"

"That you think you're better than us," Liam replies, resigned.

Keifer speaks directly to Mansour. "Am I wrong?"

The Black men exchange a glance, their frustration—though for different reasons—equal in measure. They recognize this and feel a passing kinship before turning again, in opposite directions. Mansour has reached the door by the time Keifer speaks again.

"Let me hear you, let me hear the music," he says.

Liam picks up the idle guitar on the stage and starts the chords of "Mende," the only track they've agreed on. Mansour walks back toward him.

He sings the room silent. Awed, the eyes of his audience change in the way that Mansour's change when he sings: sparkling, widened, suspended in space. The performance earns them the respect of the actress, and her referral to a regular weekly gig at a nearby club.

But most importantly, on the platform of the 1 train, Keifer agrees to join them on the record, under certain conditions.

"Three things," Keifer says, not raising his voice to accommodate the noise of the train. "One: I'm not playing drums. I'll get you a drummer, but I'm playing piano. Two: We can't record yet. We need to work on it for a while with the band." Mansour and Liam nod. "And three: Don't ever mention Gil Rodney again."

Maybe because he sees the strange look on Liam's face, Keifer elaborates.

"Just don't bring him around what we're doing here—not around me, the band. Just steer clear of him." They can hear the downtown train approaching. "See you at rehearsal." He speaks eye to eye with Mansour but shakes both their hands.

Had they seen the smile on Keifer's face all the way down from 153rd to 135th, through the stop at the bodega, and the brisk walk home to 139th, the look of reverence that lingered after showering, the joy that still stirred in him, still hearing their song, "Mende," in his ears, after tucking in his stepdaughters and snuggling up to his wife, Mansour and Liam might have envisioned a glint of everything that followed.

V.

MENDE

New York, 1968

21. **BONNIE WAITS OUTSIDE** Mrs. Alvi's office for her interview, still contemplating the very last scene in *Planet of the Apes*.

Was that already a week ago? The last time she saw Emmanuel. At the Brooklyn theater doors, she'd pretended to feel shy as he pulled her close. She'd rested her head on his chest, watching the street from the side, a place still restless since Dr. King's murder. During the long walk to her building, he'd suggested a detour to the hotel they'd passed on the street, but when she didn't smile, he'd covered it quickly with a loud laugh, sputtering that he was only joking. He'd apologized profusely when they arrived at her door.

He'd keep waiting if she wanted to wait. He hadn't meant to make her feel cheap. In the corner of the hallway, they'd shared a kiss, sour from his nerves. She'd stepped away first. Suddenly tired, she said, "I'm kind of drained," and she squatted down. She was seeing his holes, feeling them too. That and guilt for holding back, for she knew what it took to live with open wounds. She was discovering, finally, her own holes.

Whatever you fed them, they swallowed down without chewing, never savoring, never showing mercy. But every time they'd get lost in rich arguments about the harms of radiology, or Ossie Davis versus

Sidney Poitier as Walter Lee Younger, the tactics of the student organizers in Lahore versus those in Montgomery, she'd see a glimpse of
the real him, and wonder, for a moment, what it might be like to truly
know Emmanuel. How they might be, if they were not in shackles,
feeding each other to their own monsters to spare themselves.

Sylvia's bedroom door is still closed. Almost year later, Bonnie hasn't
been inside. The things returned to her by the coroner—her grandmother's tweed suit, stockings, wedding ring—remain in a laundry
bag hanging on the brass knob of the door.

And today, sitting outside Mrs. Emmanuel Alvi's office, Bonnie
cannot piece a coherent thought together, even though she spent the
night in preparation, fogging up the bathroom mirror, practicing solil-
oquies on the label's history. The glass door is ajar but the interview is
now nearly an hour behind schedule. Bonnie's beginning to wonder if
the woman is deliberately making her wait, perhaps in retribution.

The elevator operator is a Black man who will not make eye contact
with her. Every time the doors open, the portable fan he keeps inside
the elevator expands Bonnie's hair, her first attempt at a press-n-curl.
She wishes again that she knew how to braid.

When she finally gets inside the office, the job interview is a rapid
fire of questions, mostly asked by a secretary. Emmanuel's wife, Rabia,
continues her other tasks as she listens. Taking notes, crunching numbers on a loud calculator. Bonnie watches a receipt recording losses on
an album crawl down the side of the desk, until it is low enough for
her to kick under the table.

After what seems like a half hour, Rabia looks up.

"Do you have any questions for us?" Rabia asks, removing her
glasses. She looks like a sleepy Sophia Loren.

"I'm not sure what you mean?"

"About the company, the role? It's important to take these opportunities to learn."

"So this was just some learning opportunity? You're not actually considering me?"

Rabia leans back in her chair and exchanges a glance with the secretary. The woman hands Rabia her page of notes and disappears.

"You're direct."

"I try to be," Bonnie says, feeling defensive. But there is something warm in the older woman's gaze, and Bonnie hates the way she responds to expressions like a child. The mood of perfect strangers, pulling her up and down. Even now, despite herself, she's softening, a little guilt creeping in too.

"I take it that you've never been to a job interview before," the woman says gently. Bonnie shakes her head, and Rabia studies her for a moment too long, with a look too close to pity.

She looks over Rabia's head. Right above her is an album signed by Miles Davis. To the right is a black-and-white photograph of Rabia and Emmanuel on their wedding day. They're young, teenagers or in their early twenties, both of their necks stacked in layers of garlands, their striking beauty tempered by huge, goofy smiles.

"Ask me a question. Anything," the woman says, coaching her.

"What's your favorite album?" Bonnie asks.

Rabia sits with this question, her reverence for music widening her eyes, and Bonnie knows, right then, that Emmanuel once truly loved her. They felt music in the same way.

"That's an impossible question," Rabia says, alive, "but I can tell you what I've been listening to all weekend. *Sketches of Spain*. He's really at the pinnacle of his talent. His greatest work yet."

"I like it too, but I almost feel like it should be played backward. 'Solea' is the best track. It should've gone first."

The woman smiles. "You have good taste."

She gathers the paper on her desk.

"Bonnie, don't be late. You're the first woman to have a job in the editing department." She extends her hand.

Bonnie, genuinely grateful, shakes it as hard as she can. She stands to leave.

"And about your grandmother . . . I'm so sorry."

Bonnie nods, trying to feel appreciative of her words. Trying hard to feel any way about them at all.

She can hardly remember the death. And though she's lived alone these past ten months, in some ways, she still does not believe it happened. The funeral, a dignified ceremony in the stuffy assisted-living chapel, was filled to standing room. Two of the sixty people who hugged her claimed to be her cousins, well-dressed brothers from Poughkeepsie in their forties. Tall men shaped like teapots, smelling of mall perfume, without wives or children.

"She has the mole," one said to the other. The family mole. The mole under the left eye that went back at least a hundred years. The mole that did in a runaway ancestor ten miles from the Mason-Dixon Line, forever dividing the family history. It was the ultimate signifier of twinhood with her mother, so Bonnie had tried to scrub it off with Ajax when she was nine. But even after bleach, Ajax, and a night in the ER, the mole remained. Instead, she scarred her iris (a permanent discoloration; her "cat eye," Mansour later called it), which blurred the vision in her left eye and meant she would always need glasses to see farther than her hand.

Otherwise in attendance were a senator's son—handsome, white, with gray hair—who hugged Bonnie like she was a long-lost grandchild, and a congressman who retreated from the mic with sobs, letting the organ take over after he failed to say more than "This woman . . ." The local news covered the event, as did *Ebony* magazine and the *Amsterdam News*. Of course, as she scanned the pews and the parking lot, the one person she had hoped to see, her mother, never arrived.

Emmanuel's mother cried throughout the two-hour ceremony, her sobbing at times loud enough to drown out the sermon of the shy preacher. But Bonnie didn't cry, her brow perpetually furrowed, like a driver in a snowstorm struggling to see the road.

———

Without a college degree in music (without a college degree in anything), Bonnie is an assistant to the assistant editor of liner notes at Onyx Records. Just one last pair of eyes on the one-, two-, sometimes three-page documents that are stapled crooked and stacked on her desk. Her real work is gathering the documents, organizing them by date, and carrying them upstairs to the art department, where they can be typeset. Every Friday, she takes the papers upstairs in a humiliating cart, the loud squeak of the wheels, the way they stick and move against the grain, make her struggle with the thing at an angle, a terrible feat in heels and a pencil skirt.

She works at a small round desk in the basement, sharing the space with two men. One is a tall father in his early thirties. On her first day of work, he entered the room with a hairpin in his mouth, sat at the bureau across from her, and secured his yarmulke. That one gesture gave her the courage to keep her front bang in a curler until she was at her seat. It was a choice that would've horrified her grandmother, but it is the only way she knows how to keep her hairstyle for at least the first few hours of work. The other is a stocky Korean man closer to her age who wears crisp Brooks Brothers suits and is always the first to arrive at the office.

Both men give her assignments, approaching her desk up to nine times a day with liner notes that need proofing. In the case of the Jewish man, this is done with great apology, as he continues to add more articles to the tipping pile on her desk. The Korean, however, has no remorse.

One day, she is deep into the copy for the first album of a duo named Mansour & Liam, sometimes Liam & Mansour in the document. She's speeding through, looking for typos, but stops when the title of the first track catches her eye. Paris was one thing, but she'd never crossed paths with another living person who knew where Mende was: the creepy, quiet place in Southern France where she was born. She slips off her shoes and sits on her feet, eager to dive into the singer's notes. Farther down, he explains that while he'd grown up in Paris, he had always preferred Mende, a province that, somehow, shared the name of an ethnic group in Sierra Leone.

Bonnie smiles at the transcript, charmed by the singer's nerdiness as he rambles on: *And the city goes back to 200 BC, and the world is very small, so, you know, maybe there's a connection.*

When she turns back to the liner notes, the writing is sloppy, difficult for Bonnie to edit because she can barely decipher what's written in the first place. The last sentence reads: *These ambitious and tender folk selections are a gift to fans of John Coltrane and Louis Armstrong.*

"What?" she says out loud.

She takes the article back to the Korean, nervous as she nears him. He is bent over, plowing through documents at the speed of an assembly-line worker. His stacks are far higher than hers: enough papers to obscure most of her view of him. He stops, looks up at her before she speaks.

"What?"

"I can't edit this. It just doesn't make much sense. Coltrane and Armstrong in the same sentence? Coltrane and Armstrong as *folk* music?" She slides the paper across the desk, stopping herself before she says more. He picks it up with both hands, holding it close to his eyes. She feels a sudden solidarity with him—the darkness of the room and the incessant reading is taking her eyes from challenged to nearly blind.

He huffs and scoffs at this messy paper, his enemy in a race against time. He strikes out lines, circles others, and slides it back across the table to Bonnie.

"Here. Blue pile."

She hesitates but ultimately follows his orders, placing it with the things she'll take upstairs for printing on Friday afternoon.

"Do you read liner notes?" she asks Emmanuel at lunch, stirring her iced tea with a straw.

He shrugs, busy with a stubborn steak. "Sometimes."

"Do they make you wanna buy the record more?"

"If I don't know the artist, I'd say the cover matters more."

He tears a slice of sourdough bread in half and submerges it in dark olive oil. Bonnie turns pensive.

"What?" he says, taking in the pout on her face. "Disillusioned already? Has it even been a month?"

"You should tell her," Bonnie says. They never refer to his wife by name to each other. An unspoken agreement.

"Tell her what?" he replies carefully.

"That the writers don't care. That they skirt their way through 90 percent of the liner notes—unless it's for the famous artists—and could be costing these people their careers."

"Most of them are going to fail for other reasons, Bonnie."

"Like what?"

He shakes his head, swallowing the olive from his cocktail. "A million things." He reaches across the table, flicks crumbs from the corner of her mouth with his fingertips. "I don't think there's much she can do."

She can see his green scrubs under his open raincoat, and what he's just said reminds her of the doctors at his hospital. The way they framed her grandmother's unnecessary death as some acceptable expression of fate.

Emmanuel sees her sadness settling, a shadow wide enough to cast over him too.

"Let's get you home," he says in a tone striving for distance.

They are silent as they walk against the warm wind. When they reach the door of her grandmother's building, she feels him hesitate. Though he visited Sylvia here over the years, he hasn't been inside since Bonnie's lived alone. But tonight, Bonnie cannot bear her empty house, she bangs the glass until he turns around.

Fully clothed, she mounts him on her grandmother's Persian rug, doing finally what he wants, moving quickly before her mind intercedes. Strips him of his scarf and jacket and shirt and climaxes from the friction of their bodies before they have even undressed. Surprising convulsions that suspend her mourning, comforting her for seconds in a pleasure as taut and private as a womb. After some time, he whispers that this has to stop. That they have to be over. He says this before she feels strong enough to begin her life completely alone.

———

When Emmanuel is gone and she can finally feel the house (still, empty), feel that there is no one there (the breathing, all her own), can see that her grandmother, her only real kin, has died, Bonnie waits again to feel something more. She picks out her hair until she can't see any curls. She folds clothes and watches *The Flintstones* and cuts bananas and throws them out and cuts some more and throws those out until the garbage is full. And waits, still, to feel something more.

On the street people are starting to gather, faints screams that she imagines have something to do with Dr. King's murder. She listens. She sits out on the terrace and smokes and counts. She counts the times she hears the splash of a new fire hydrant being opened. She counts the cracks of bottles as young folks gather down the street. She pokes holes in the sofa with the steel end of her rat-tail comb.

When she still feels nothing, she goes out and riots.

22.

SHE WALKS WITH a blank mind, obeying her body without question. She follows some noise, like a hailstorm, out to an empty street. Down the road are a dozen slender silhouettes, scattered, from a wide distance. Bodies colored and shaped like the trio of wooden sculptures from Benin joined in cobwebs on her grandmother's windowsill: hardly a torso, mostly legs and arms. When she arrives, she encounters a dreamy, serene scene. They could all be sleepwalking. There is no fire. Just a parade of young people wandering, calling one another what they are called at home, filling the American air with their nicknames, asserting that America is their home too, before some begin to pass around liquor. And the ones who partake get louder, drowning in Colt 45s and laughter.

The second time, she walks until a single window breaks and the crowd scurries. A boy tries to walk Bonnie home. Asks her to his senior prom in a whisper.

This time—the third time—she wants to engage. It takes all of her courage, but she approaches a trio of Black girls her age and size, who are standing in the middle of the sidewalk wearing bathrobes and rollers, watching the car they'd just set on fire roast in flames. One holds the hand of a younger boy, maybe her brother. He jumps from side to side and plays tag with his shadow.

"I like your braids," Bonnie says to the girl, admiring the white beads clanking at her shoulders. The girl smiles, revealing a gap.

"Thanks. My Mama did it." She looks around, taking in the night. "She's gonna kill me," she adds, as they return to the fire.

Some of the girls make Molotov cocktails. Bonnie grabs a bottle from the ground, still half-filled with cheap liquor, and tosses it at the burning car. She's enlivened by the fire's immediate flare. Terrified as its edges approach the phone lines and trees.

She hears the siren, the patter of feet running.

"Girl, come on!" the braided girl screams at her.

She makes it inside her pitch-black apartment, humid and silent. The highest leaf of the wilting snake plant waves a tired hello. Her sweat stings her eyes; her feet bleed through her slippers, where miles of broken glass has punctured her soles.

Instead of sleeping, she counts down the minutes until the office opens. At 4:30 a.m., she rolls over on her stomach to get on her feet, and sees her grandmother's robe hanging on the bathroom door. She vomits into the sink. Turns on the faucets and the bathtub, letting all the water run, her thoughts drowned out by the sound. She washes her hair. Giving up on wearing it straight, she puts it in a puffy bun.

She sees the braided girl at the bus stop on her way to work. The girl is in a school uniform, still holding the hand of the younger boy, her socks over her knees. They exchange a smile but do not speak. It's like encountering a person from a dream.

23. **THE CART IS STACKED** high with this Friday's delivery of liner notes for the art department. The liner notes for *Mansour & Liam*, pawed and read a few more times, are now stained black with the soot that's still under her nails. She is curious about what this record sounds like, wonders if she might be able to adjust the liner notes and submit them later if she could only hear the music herself.

Every time she enters the art department, she is struck by the atmosphere. The enormous room of large windows and hardwood floors would be mistaken for a record store were it not for the handwritten stickers marking every album "Not For Sale." Bonnie senses that the people up here are a little closer to the music, nourished by a feeling that doesn't reach the lower floors.

There is a visual artist working in the corner. White, forty-something, knobby knees angled toward his canvas. His mouth a little tight with a problem that excites him. Bonnie takes in his work, an abstraction of a body with too many limbs, a gorgeous green monochromatic piece. She recognizes the same of the artist: Celia.

"Are you new?" Bonnie jumps at the sound of his voice. She hadn't realized that she'd come so close, her nose almost at the canvas. He's speaking but hasn't stopped working, his pencil still making tiny strokes, so subtle and gentle. She stumbles back a few steps, adjusts her glasses.

"I started a few weeks ago."

"Well, don't let Cobb see you standing around." He tips his head to indicate that the art director is on the other side of the room.

She pulls the wrinkled paper for *Mansour & Liam* from her pile, wipes it on her knee to smear off some of the tar. She shows it to the man, putting it between his face and his canvas. She asks her question quietly.

"Do you know what the cover is for this one?"

The artist examines it for a moment, then sort of gestures to the side of him.

"Right there."

Bonnie looks: a stencil of a coffee mug emitting steam.

"*This?*"

"*Yes,*" the man replies, returning her sharp tone.

She goes back in the evening under the guise of dropping off a few more liner notes. At this late hour, she's startled when she feels the rumble of footsteps beneath her, the elevator gate clanking loudly as she makes her way up to retrieve Mansour & Liam's record. She moves fast, parsing through the demo albums stored in thin white sleeves. She finally finds it toward the back, fishes it from the crate, and scurries out of the room.

At home, she lifts the dust cover off the record player and takes off Ray Charles's *Yes Indeed!*, the last album her grandmother played. Bonnie pulls *Mansour & Liam* from the sleeve and sets the needle in the first groove. She sits on her feet in grandmother's chair, watching as the record spins on the record player. A man's voice counts off the beat, "One, two, three," and a pianist begins a trill. The singer believes in patience, in silence. He starts and stops a hum like he's testing the air to make sure it can hold him. Then a low note that clashes and melds with the instruments until it all produces a perfect sonic marriage.

The low note he holds stirs up a feeling in Bonnie's crown. A wet heat like the blood's moving there, like it's turning warm. It moves on, leaking down her spine, dripping, like a sap. Soon the feeling embraces the full breadth of her silhouette, and the long hairs on her arms lift, reaching for the dim room's few sources of light. She slides from her chair to the ground, where she breaks and finally weeps.

She plays Mansour & Liam's record into the night, but never the whole way through. She keeps drawing it back to the second track, "Mende."

It was a town where people kept their heads down, any great hopes quickly hidden under brooms, in pots, and in soil. A meditative place of hymns and Gregorian chants that shimmered with a peace that did not penetrate their door. At home, sometimes, there was a feeling of being hunted. By what or who, Bonnie didn't know. She gathered what she could, her mother's memories of the war only slipping out after dark liquor or sleepiness:

When the bombs exploded, the girls, the dancers, their dresses, their bodies were flying. And, Bonnie, I remember, I remember, the explosion rocked me so hard that I couldn't feel my body. I couldn't feel anything, and I remember that I looked down just to see if I still had legs. And when I saw my legs, this joy came over me, so strong it was almost madness, so powerful that I screamed. She laughed.

The happiest I'd ever been was about my feet. Until I had you.

She finishes the cover art on the 6 train. A Yoruba priestess, all in white, watches it come together over her shoulder. She attaches the sketch to the album sleeve with paper clips and goes straight to the room of records, greeting the operator with a confident nod. She slips it into the crate. She goes down to the basement and sits at her desk. She wonders what the boy who loved Mende will think of his cover. She wonders if it will ever reach Claudine.

VI.

THE DEATH OF CARL KEIFER

New York, 1968

24. **IT SEEMS TO COME FROM** the chords Keifer chooses—this thing that flows between him and Mansour. Liam has been watching them from the upholstered nook of the large brownstone window, waiting for the other musicians to arrive for their rehearsal. He rolls up his shirt so that his sweaty arms might catch the breeze. At its size and depth, Keifer's house was usually cool, but the sun is relentless this morning. Liam's studying them, trying to understand what it is about their new dynamic that makes him feel shut out. The only way he can describe it is that it's like the two men are remembering a secret. With each chord Keifer strikes, each run Mansour improvises, more and more of this tale is recalled, their recollection insulates them, and they move farther away from Liam, into a place where only they reside.

Whenever Keifer plays a chord, Mansour closes his eyes and laughs. Leans into the deep sway of the baby grand in the center of the living room, letting his head drop back and belting out an array of notes that make Keifer shoot up from where he sits at the keys.

Today, as they rehearse, Keifer's wife, Vanessa, calls to them from the kitchen.

"Is that Mansour cookin' like that?"

"You better believe it, baby!" Keifer replies.

It is strange to Liam how close, how in sync, Keifer and Mansour
are when it comes to the music. Keifer has even gotten Mansour to
speak English, something that has given them another means to carry
on without him.

When the backup musicians arrive, Mansour is revising the drum
parts with a pencil. Today, the drummer Keifer's been promising will
finally arrive.

Mansour had spent yesterday morning notating the parts under
the kitchen table. He'd been dragged into a game of hide-and-seek
by Keifer's youngest stepdaughter, Poinciana, and while he waited
for her to find him, the rhythms had come to him. He'd sat under the
table in one of those effortless, rushed, artistic fits that was difficult to
keep pace with. He'd sung aloud to capture it all as he charted the
drum sequence for the first track in the margins of the *Amsterdam
News*.

The girl found him twenty minutes later, passed out. When he came
to, he could tell from the sour taste of metal that it had finally happened. Manhattan and its medications, its tonics, its chaos, had not
made a difference. He'd seized. He was cursing under his breath, but
the little girl's fear made him force a smile to comfort her.

"Did you die?" she'd asked, offering him her jelly-stained blue-eyed
doll for comfort.

Today, in this chaotic rehearsal, Mansour cannot focus, the never-
ending battle with his body still on his mind. A sourness emits from
the kitchen (Vanessa and her obsession with vinegar), and Keifer's
daughters and their little friends are involved in some game of leaping
over the living room furniture. Their obstacle course includes the
men's music stands and instrument cases. It tickles Mansour that
Keifer, for all his strictness with the musicians, is so soft and easy with

the girls. He cannot tell them to stop running without breaking into laughter. It is his wife's firm yell from the kitchen that finally gets the children to plop down into the dining room chairs and stare at the television in silence. Watching it all, Mansour wonders what his home might feel like. And if kids would one day soften him too.

The drummer, Davis, finally arrives. He comes and sits beside Mansour. The scent of his hair gel convinces Mansour that it must be the same one Sokhna uses. The man's silky black hair is slick, his nose too flat to hold up his glasses. His skin is darker than Mansour's, but a different kind of darkness, more maroon, that Mansour will only see again some years later in Mexico, when he finally succeeds at teaching Bonnie how to float. It is the skin tone of the man who will wander the beach and sell him an overpriced shawl that Bonnie will keep at the foot of her bed in the attic every day that he's gone.

Mansour is still writing, adjusting the drum notations, when the man snatches the page from him.

"I don't need you to spell it out for me, man. You from the goddamn Philharmonic?"

The man runs his hands over his hair in frustration, wriggling and shifting the carton of orange juice between his knees. "I know what to do here."

Mansour only makes out half of what the man has said. He doesn't have the language to respond, probably wouldn't even if he did know what to say. His quest to understand Black Americans is ongoing.

Mansour tried to explain these feelings to Liam once but couldn't.

"It's the culture. It's different here," he'd said, and shrugged, with indifference. "What do you expect from Blacks anyway?" he'd asked, and Mansour had stayed silent.

Liam had been short with Mansour ever since he'd moved into Keifer's house. Keifer had told Mansour that he could stay with him, that he didn't have to endure the hostility of Liam's Irish neighborhood in the wake of the city's unrest.

But now, in Harlem, it is strange to Mansour to live in a place with so many Black folks again and to dismiss any likeness of affinity as a matter of circumstance and nothing more.

When the rehearsal's over, Keifer leaps across the room and grips Mansour by his shoulders. He shakes him until he smiles.

"We gotta name you Gutter, you bring the gutter, man. Goddamn. You got people in your voice, man. A hundred of 'em."

The trumpeter reaches out, shaking Mansour's hand. "Well done." He's a large, quiet man from Chicago who they'd met briefly on that film set months ago. He shares Liam's addiction to beef jerky. This afternoon, the bag slipped between them during moments of panic. When the riots came on television, and others moved to share cigarettes, the men's eyes met, and the trumpeter whispered to Liam, "Say, man, you got that jerky?"

The sax player also shakes Mansour's hand, but the drummer only sips on his orange juice, combs his hair again.

"What are we gonna do about the lyrics?" Davis asks Keifer as the other men gather their things. "He can't be singing in whatever that is."

"It's Wolof," Mansour says from across the room, his eyes narrowed on Davis.

"Nobody even knows what that is. People are gonna think we're losing it, man." Davis looks to Keifer, who remains silent, his head in a scroll of Charles Mingus sheet music. A score he's been studying since their work on the album began.

"Keifer? Keifer, you got me on this, right?"

"Huh?" Keifer is pretending not to hear him.

"The words are gonna put people off. It's hard enough to get folks to come out as it is."

"It ain't hard to get folks to see me," Keifer says, serious and shifting the jubilant mood of the room. "It's different. The people need something different."

"You sure about that?" Davis mutters.

"Say what?"

"Nothin', man."

"What'd you say?"

"I said, are you sure you can pack a house without Gil Rodney? Man, if Gil was *my* dad, you couldn't catch me dead backing up some singer."

Keifer says nothing to this, but Mansour sees a darkness settle around him. It makes Keifer seem as wounded as he is dangerous, like a dethroned king. And now Mansour realizes what Keifer's trouble is: He is not the king. Gil is. But why did Keifer insist on waging war with Gil's magnificence? Drowning in his father's shadow instead of just floating in it peacefully? Mansour wonders, but he doesn't say more.

Across the room, the men gossip in subtle murmurs, nervously packing up their instruments.

"I gotta get up out of here, man," the trumpeter says, and the others agree, grabbing binders and zipping up jackets, exaggerating impending encounters with horny wives and girlfriends. Davis and the others stagger out of the room.

When the room clears, Mansour picks up his dinner plate from the table, famished. Leftovers from earlier: corn dogs and coleslaw. A shot of cheap vodka. When he empties the glass, his eyes are red.

"Your drinks here? They're shit," he says in English to Keifer.

"Well, *we* didn't come here for the drinks," Keifer says, speaking of America. He crosses into the kitchen and disappears for the rest of the night.

Mansour is lying in bed, face down, when it occurs to him that Liam was absent for the latter half of today's rehearsal. No one else seemed to notice either. The song they'd been working on had gone on just fine without bass.

They are scheduled to finally begin recording the next morning, so Mansour spends the night awake, worrying. As the album progresses, as their date to debut at the downtown club approaches, even since it happened again, the fear of seizing onstage engulfs him.

He's been in America for almost two years now, but when he's this nervous, he sleeps and wakes on Swiss time. The other dwellers in the home are used to his peculiar hours and hardly stir when they hear him untangling the chain on the front door to venture out into the dark. They gossip over breakfast about it being an African ritual.

"That nigga be out there, howlin' at the moon and shit," Keifer mutters as he dumps cornflakes into a bowl, Vanessa muffling husky laughter with the thick sleeve of her robe.

It is the tail end of winter, and Mansour walks through the hours it takes for night to become day. There is another Black man on 137th, moving exactly as he does. Gangly, a long stride that flaunts oversized shoulders another would work hard to hide. When they are face-to-face, or close enough to be, Mansour is afraid to look, certain that he will see himself.

He finds his spot. Some stack of bricks, where he crouches and smokes in the alley. A space between a new movie theater and a Chinese-takeout spot. The streetlights, curving down with the shame- less flare of the Harlem Renaissance, lord over him. They pulsate a perfectly amber light. His sweaty stomach cooling off in the twilight breeze, his head propped back against the wall, a cigarette sweet in his mouth, and then he knows why he keeps returning here.

These few square feet of Harlem conjure the mood of the place where he first heard his own sound. He was maybe five, maybe six, in Saint-Louis, Senegal, sitting under streetlights like these, with only the talibé boy-beggars like him on the street.

He'd been sent into the talibé order by his grandfather, a man looking to protect his noble lineage from an illegitimate child. Mansour had had Kiné until she drowned, Mama until she left him for Paris, and then aunts, nameless now. He remembers them most for the way they fed him constantly: he wasn't used to not having a warm bed and women's arms to curl up in. Once with the talibés, he'd been in search of a way to soothe himself and had found it in the streets.

All the children, incanting prayers, each one praying alone. Boys barefoot, dressed in white smocks or blue jeans, five or fifteen raucous in worship, facing the wall, the sky, the ground, the river. The street emptied of anyone but them. A night wind full of harmony. The people kept their windows and doors open to let in the sound. Mansour can still hear them, can feel it all again tonight.

Some of the boys would be in ecstasy, rocking back and forth. Others dogmatically monotone, ready, already, for another long night of their lives to be over with. This is the place where he discovered himself. That his upper register could lift his spirit, his forehead soon tingling, his mind livelier, as if he'd had a taste of citrus. Low notes and rounding the mouth cooled the body down and filled his gut almost as well as rice. And his vibrato was like fingertips. So close to Kiné's tickle, the only facet of her touch that he remembers.

Tonight in Harlem, he watches the Chinese women across the street begin their day, descending from a gray van and click-clacking through the alleyway in stilettos and men's coats. The back door to the restaurant is always cracked open. He eavesdrops, hearing his aunts in the rhythm of their water and knives. They carry vats by the twos, pouring black grease into the weeds. The first signs of spring foliage seem to feast on it, the weeds turning greener every morning he returns.

25. **MANSOUR IS SURPRISED** to see Liam already inside the studio, biting his nails in the doorway of the booth, losing a debate on sound levels with the engineer. Liam gestures for Mansour and then walks ahead quickly, leading them to the privacy of a narrow carpeted hallway with a lamp so dim it hardly lights the table it sits on. The cacophony of the band's warm-up glides beneath Liam's guttural voice.

"I can't believe you let those motherfuckers kill three—*three*—of my songs! After I've been your mouth and your eyes and your ears all this time. You're finally in with them, huh? So you let them take what's ours?"

Mansour feels Liam testing his loyalty. The feeling is merciless and burdensome, their bond at stake. It is too much to face. He sighs and plays it off. But Liam goes on, getting louder.

"Have you considered that he's using us? That he's using this album to break away from Gil and start his own career?"

Mansour doubles down, refusing to hear this. He turns away.

"You're so paranoid."

"You can't hear that?" He's gesturing to the men in the booth. "Listen to that! He's made this into a *jazz* album. Do you want to make a jazz album?"

Mansour gets louder, "It's not about the genre, it's about making the best album that we can and—"

"*Jesus* man, could you please, *please*, fill me in on your criteria for the best record we can make? Or should I just ask Keifer?"

The African and the Irishman are silent, but it is not a standoff. They would rather speak, but neither of them have the words. They do not know the language for the place they've entered. After a decade of an indestructible bond, this rupture is foreign to them. They cannot even name or understand its true cause. Liam steps back.

"I'll play my parts . . . I'll play my parts and then I'm going home," he says.

Liam's eyes move back toward the studio, where the trumpeter and saxophonist have begun their embouchure, where Davis is tightening his cymbals and Keifer stands behind the piano in the center of the room, preparing to conduct. The sheet music stretches across two music stands before him. Mansour's eyes follow.

"*That* is supposed to be you," Liam says, pointing to Keifer.

He storms back into the studio. Mansour watches Liam strap up his bass. He keeps his head down, disappearing into his own groove.

As the session progresses, Keifer tightens control over the musicians, driving them harder. They are twelve takes in on the third track before Liam cracks, yanking off his headset.

"Hey, Keifer . . . Keifer! We gotta play. We're running out of money!"

When Keifer speaks, his voice is muffled by the glass of the booth. "Liam. Don't do that. You're throwing me off. Let's go back to bar sixteen."

"Non, non! Ça suffit!" *That's enough*, Liam shouts. "*Ça suffit!*" He rushes out of the booth. The studio door slams behind him.

They play on with Liam gone. Keifer lays down the bass himself.
Mansour's voice turns frail in Liam's absence, his high notes cracking.
He spits over and over into the garbage can at his feet, his mouth dry.
Keifer tells him to take five.

Then a merciless three hours more. A foul vibe. The horn players
finish sweetening and then rush out, relieved. They leave Mansour,
Davis, and Keifer alone in the booth to start track four, a vocalese
blues. With the others gone, Keifer zeroes in on Mansour, cuing the
engineer to pause the recording after every phrase the African sings.
Pushing him for more grit:

"More like field hollers."

"This is that revival shit."

"Muddy. Muddy!"

"Mississippi, nigger."

"Like you on a dirt road, nigger."

"*Black*."

"*Black*."

"Come on, man."

Keifer stands up from the piano.

"You want a playback of that?" the engineer asks.

"Naw, scrap it," Keifer says, cutting his eyes at Mansour.

Mansour smokes in the bathroom, waiting for the others to leave, cursing out Manhattan in his mind. The New World was supposed to
make him feel invincible, enormous. Not smallness.

He makes it two blocks before he's lost. The city looks different at night.

He finds a different subway entrance, jumps the turnstile as he's seen others do, and waits for the train with the small group of twilight passengers. A homeless man walks up and down the platform on the other side, bellowing "Ave Maria." A perfect alto. Mansour envies his control. He yells out and harmonizes with him, indifferent to the shocked crowd. When he finally makes it to Strivers' Row, he curses, walks past Keifer's, and heads down the quiet block of towering brownstones and their twinkling lights. He sleeps on his jacket on a bench in Central Park North, stretched wide under huddled stars.

A few months ago, before he moved into Keifer's house, Mansour had already begun and ended his first love affair on American soil: a fiery eighty-seven days with a slender Haitian janitor with his complexion. An aspiring professor who was too busy learning Twi, raising a parrot, and acing physics at SUNY Purchase to convince him that she cared. He wanted her, she wanted Africa, so when she asked him what he knew about the orishas ("The what?" "Oh, come *on*, Mansour. Yemayah! Oshun!"), and he told her to stop playing Nigerian, she threw him out—with a sheet, for she was averse to public nudity—onto the twenty-sixth-floor fire escape and shut the window.

He didn't realize he had loved her until he saw her again, waiting far ahead of him in line at a Jamaican restaurant they'd frequented as a couple. It was the closest thing to his aunts' cooking that he'd found in the New World—closer than the few Senegalese restaurants he judged too harshly: no yitt, weak roff. He'd followed her for half a block from a distance. Ultimately deciding against approaching her, trying again, he crossed the avenue and went his own way. The memory of her strut forever tangled with the scent of Scotch bonnets and allspice, a memory like camera footage he plays over and over to get through the sexless Harlem days and nights. It takes another tryst and some time alone before he can finally release her.

Now, in the spring, he cuts his hair, learns the subway lines, and retreats from Keifer's family into the wilderness of his own manhood. He gets a job stocking shelves, learns Spanish (far easier than English) in the early mornings at a thriving bodega. He doesn't think of himself as homeless, though he sleeps almost every night in the park, still stopping by Keifer's after recording to shower, rehearse, or catch the latest news on the riots.

He and Liam still do not speak. Mansour continues to stay with Keifer. And there, at Keifer's house, there are some days when they are family.

After rehearsal one such night, the two men sit in lawn chairs in the brownstone's backyard, seeking refuge from the heat of the small house. Keifer is still shaking his right hand, shaking off carpal tunnel from the fast playing—chasing Mansour's adlibs. A song they named *The Chase*.

"So, your people. They're all singers too?" Keifer asks.

Mansour shakes his head. They sit under a drooping clothesline and an evening sky the color of lava. Damp socks swing above their heads. "No way, my family's very religious."

"Now I get it." Keifer sits up, smiling. "That's why you're so free— you don't have any shoes to fill."

Mansour shakes his head, unfamiliar with the expression.

"I mean, you're not carrying somebody's else's legacy on your back. You get to start fresh. You're free to be you." Keifer's eyes open in a new way, look distant, so Mansour finally asks,

"What's with you and Gil?"

"Don't go there, man," Keifer mutters, quietly.

"I don't know my father's name. I've never even seen his face. You're not gonna tell me anything worse than that." Mansour drops his cigarette, stomps it out. He looks down for a long time to make sure it's dead.

Keifer sighs, sitting back in his chair.

"Alright. I'll tell you." He says.

The great Gil Rodney was a protégé of Louis Armstrong. Keifer speaks of an old Hollywood movie he won't name. A film where his father played an eye-bucking trumpeter who sat on the back of a bus and made music for the film's climactic scene. He'd returned to Harlem from Los Angeles strange and quiet. Leaving the room when the film was mentioned, telling his wife that they would not be attending the premiere.

But whatever words he had for the film's director would, in drunken moments, be directed toward his son. Once, while drunk, he'd told Keifer the story. The director, dissatisfied with his refusal to portray the character as instructed (bulging eyes, licked lips, singsong voice), made him shoot seventy-two takes of the same scene. The producer, annoyed at the wasted money, came down from his office. Then they both were shouting at Gil, demanding he do as told, until, on take eighty-one, Gil broke. The crew watched. The director nodded, finally satisfied.

The night after he told Keifer this story, Gil, drunk again, had aimed a .22 pistol at Keifer for stepping on his foot. A decades-old memory that still brings Keifer to tears, a memory his father vehemently denies, his mother too.

As they spend more time together, Mansour learns more and more about what it takes to *sound* Black, the kind of Black that Keifer means: leaning into his guttural voice, always staying ahead of the listener with creative choices. An approach to singing that challenges Mansour's mind even more than his voice.

Other days he is a foreigner, a stranger only passing as Black who cannot be trusted. The music had once given their brotherhood the weight of a decade without the roots. There is nothing else truly holding them together, and as the recording process draws to a close, their bond is fractured often and easily.

Though he likes the sound he produces, singing in the way that Keifer demands requires self-exploitation for Mansour, a constant unearthing of pain. Some of it was his own, buried longings for home this style of singing drew out of him, but the other pain he felt belonged to the sound itself. Chattel slavery, Keifer warned him, had made jazz. Mansour drinks sometimes after the session is done. But sober, the feeling returns and is sometimes too much to bear. When he does not emote, is not willing to tear himself completely open, he has to stomach Keifer's disapproval. Soon Mansour begins to ignore Keifer, finding his own way into the sound, a way without suffering. Keifer backs off some, but their minds never quite meet, and the two men war and dance, war and dance, tugging at the spirit of the music until the end.

Months late and well over budget, the record—*Carl Keifer Presents . . . mansour & liam*—is submitted to the label in late April. The men go to their corners of the city and wait.

26. **MID-SPRING AND THE** rehearsals are long over, the album submitted long ago, and they've heard nothing from the label. Liam returns to Harlem to retrieve from Mansour the spare key to his uncle's apartment, his amp, and a pocket watch he plans to pawn for rent at his own place. Vanessa answers the door, Poinciana asleep in her arms.

"Hey, Liam," she whispers.

Another girl, the older daughter, begins crying on the stairs. She asks why he has come without Mansour, why Mansour has to sleep in the park.

"I guess he just needs some space, honey," Vanessa consoles, but the girl whines on.

"But why does he have to be homeless, Mama?"

Liam decides that the girl has a point, that despite their fallout, it might be a good idea to catch up with him.

"He's with the Cubans these days," is all Vanessa knows.

Liam mounts the hills and crosses the bridge into Central Park North, passing the homeless, searching their faces to no avail. Walking faster, he calls his brother's name. He can hear the Cuban drummers but can't tell where the sound comes from. When he walks to the left, it seems to come from the right. When he walks to the right, the sound swells left and then divides, seeming to come from every direction.

Finally, in a love song, some men are chanting to the Yoruba deities, and Liam hears Mansour's sound. Expansive, circular, a note stretched and held until it changes tone.

By the time Liam finds them, the drum circle is past the point of no return. The groove slows Liam down. Calms his nerves, calling him to hope. Mansour sits in the center of the circle, eyes shut, lost in song. Liam sits on the bench nearest to him. He does not understand, has never understood, where this music or the work with Keifer takes Mansour. But he can see Mansour's joy, and that, at least in this moment, is enough.

Mansour breaks, sweat running down his face. He catches his brother's eye, too used to his presence to be surprised by his being here, and tells him with a pearly smile: "I've seen the album—the cover—in a dream. It's coming."

27. **IT ONLY TAKES** three boxes before Onyx Records' head of A&R, Rabia Alvi, stops again and sits on the edge of the U-Haul. Her red toes dangle over the hot asphalt as she worries that she has not sufficiently considered her husband's side of things before initiating this separation. After all, she cannot bear children and had anticipated long ago that that would end in some kind of punishment. Emmanuel loves children. He mentors across the city in underfunded programs, teaches biochem for free at a public high school in Jamaica, Queens, not too far from their building. He's particularly fond of Black children, telling her that as immigrants, they are indebted to the Black struggle for justice. He regularly derailed already-awkward dinner parties with the few Pakistani neighbors she could stand, drunkenly belaboring the role of the civil rights movement in their own success in America. It was a point Rabia respected but did not consider worth the disruption it always caused.

She'd wanted to believe that his general regard for young people was the cause of his closeness with Bonnie. That Emmanuel's mother and Bonnie's grandmother had been fast friends had made it easier too. They had met for the first time in the assisted-living dining hall in 1959. The only two people to rush to the chickpeas, each brown, high-cheekboned woman had mistaken the other for her ethnicity. After confirming Lahore and Boston's South End as their respective places of origin, they laughed at their miscalculations and remained, until Sylvia's death, the best of girlfriends. Knowing this story, Rabia tried to see the girl as family, no matter how unsettling her presence was. She could have persisted in this, at least for a while longer, if it were not for a comment Emmanuel made one evening after the girl had gone home. Rabia had remarked about Bonnie's appearance, the rate at which she was growing up in the wake of her grandmother's passing.

"She's really into makeup now. I didn't even recognize her today," Rabia had said in Urdu, poking at her salad, the sound of her fork too loud on the plate. "The little mark she's made under her eye."

She noticed how Emmanuel started to twist his glass of dark wine by the stem, a slow turn while he studied the liquid inside. "It's a mole," he said, and took a long sip.

The look in his eye, the confidence of his voice, turned Rabia cold. Her appetite was gone. She took her plate to the kitchen and gripped the sink to stay standing. The following morning, he woke her before sunrise, mumbling about the torment of inertia, how they had to move in or out of one another's lives. Whichever way she wanted. But they had to move. Then he broke down and confessed to the affair.

Though she only takes a week of summer vacation to move out of the apartment (while other executives take two, even four), Rabia knows she will be blamed for the slew of departmental mishaps that have overtaken the label in her absence. Several albums are running over budget, several more delayed; most of them are accounts of the new A&R executives. She knows what has to be done to reestablish order.

She calls the first young executive on her list into her office and fires him. He does not expect this, has just come from lunch, the grease of beef empanadas glossing his lips. He calls her a Guinea bitch (the wrong slur), slamming her door so hard that the Miles Davis record framed on the wall behind her crashes to the ground, shards of glass narrowly missing her head. The firings take all week, leaving several over-budget albums shelved, fledging artists dropped. Her assistant works overtime to draft cancellation letters, make good with producers and recording studios with overdue bills. Rabia is so overwhelmed by the chaos of the week that she forgets that Bonnie works at the label. But one evening, she sees the large shadow of a tall woman filling the atrium as Bonnie makes her way out of the double doors. The girl's shadow is so gangly, so youthful, so awkward, it seems impossible that it belongs to the person who has turned Rabia's life upside down.

It feels like the work of a ghost when Rabia sees the debut album for Mansour & Liam on her desk. The striking image of a Black woman peeking between her fingers. Rabia immediately calls the art department to inquire how a shelved project received a cover, let alone a full printing. She's told that the project was submitted for printing several weeks ago, that if she has any concerns she should call the publicity department before the album's release the following weekend. Perplexed, she puts the album aside for a few days while she puts out other fires.

She takes the demo copy home to her new apartment and listens to the first track before she pulls up the stylus. She doesn't need to hear any more. It is marvelous, the kind of record she's been eager for the label to produce. She paces the room as she stares at the cover. She knows the work of the art director, has seen at least a hundred images come from his department, and has never known him to render a Black figure. It's a financial risk, and he knows better. He's always opted for images of coffee mugs, beach landscapes, or typographic abstractions. Never a Black face. Rabia reads the art credits again; it is exclusively attributed to him, as per usual.

She looks at the album again the next morning, the intensity of the portrait's detail magnified in the daylight. It stalls her on her way out the door to work. She drops her keys when she notices the mole beneath the woman's left eye.

A week later, Rabia files for divorce, the first step in a process that she discovers, much to her annoyance, will take time and require further interaction between them. But what, her mother-in-law insisted, had he even really *done* with the girl? Bonnie, a sweetheart, she claimed, had just needed someone to lean on as she grieved.

"What about the others?" Rabia had responded.

There were indeed others. Girls from his tennis club. Biochem students. A PhD student from NYU. He was on her dissertation committee. Rabia was beginning, at least, to see a pattern. Tall like Bonnie. Smart like Bonnie. He had a type.

And now, at Onyx, she finds herself callous, unable to feel the music, unable to offer valuable critiques of the records on her desk. At the next departmental meeting, a young executive shares the date for the release party for *Mansour & Liam*. She is already exhausted, just imagining the feedback of the instruments.

"Where is it?" she asks.

"The place you wanted, just past the bridge," the executive says.

There are six copies of the album on the boardroom table. Rabia turns to Bonnie, her eyes fixated on the album cover. Glued to the image that resembles her. Rabia studies Bonnie's gaze closely, knowing what she cannot prove.

"Add a ticket for Miss Bonnie King. She will attend in my place," Rabia says, getting up from the table and adjourning the meeting.

28. **ON THE NIGHT** of the release party, Bonnie arrives at the venue. And then there, crossing the street, indifferent to the short stop he's caused, is the singer. He wears white wide-legged pants that remind her of a zoot suit without the jacket, sandals, a loose blouse—mostly open. What looks to her to be a stack of necklaces bearing little leather books (talismans) swing at his chest. Bracelets stacked on his right wrist. He laughs at something a woman behind her in line has said at the sight of him ("You gon have a hard time leavin' here without me"). Just passing by, he wields the same power over Bonnie that he had on wax.

Standing on the stage in the packed silent room, Mansour is supposed to lead the band in with a hard bellow, a B-flat held long and loud enough for the bass and piano to trinkle in under it, just like the record—but he is silent, staring out at the sizeable audience in a daze. Suddenly, the fear of seizing stunts him.

Liam jumps in to fill the silence, beginning the bass line. Keifer follows Liam with another chord, and finally the B-flat pours out of Mansour, a sound so raw that the reviewers will write in the morning that it seemed like more an end than a beginning.

The drummer comes in, and the audience locks in.

Once they're in flight, Mansour backs off the mic, laughing out loud at the sudden joy that overtakes him. A portal opens within him, a new suggestion of how living can feel, and it makes him leap and move about the stage in a clumsy trance. The music gets ahead of him, flowing from his voice without intention. His mind is, at best, an observer in this experience; at worst, a foe that might dare interrupt this first taste of true love. As he ascends, he turns to look at the band, confirming that Keifer too is overcome: all hunched shoulders, closed eyes, and loose neck, for they have all been ravaged, made senseless and drunk by this feeling.

Mansour has never come this far out of himself before, and he fears what going further into joy will do. He considers returning to the safety of Keifer's melancholy melody but cannot bear the fall. The band resists with him. Begging one another in every note and every grunt not to move from here. No one, not even Liam, will break the groove to wind things down, but Mansour is feeling more and more that he is losing control of his body, and the refrain is the only means to land. And so, Mansour cues it, releasing this new American freedom with regret.

————

It baffles Mansour that the others can socialize, can find their way back into the world so easily after the moments they had onstage. With the house lights back up, Mansour finds the room's ecstatic brightness assaulting, the crowd's English dizzying and frenetic, like a bad dream.

He retreats to the dark dressing room, alone with its smell of sweat and the weeks-old photographs of Sammy Davis Jr. on the stage he's just left. His hand trembles as he grips the watery beer a short-necked waitress has slipped behind the curtain.

"Wow." Her one sound at the sight of him. It means *yes* in Wolof; he wonders what it means here.

Like the vodka and the whiskey, the beer in America is terrible. He still hasn't gotten used to it. But now he drinks as much of it as he can before a sudden spell of chills makes him put it down. Relief spreads through him. He did not seize. And he could feel that the people—the label and the audience—were satisfied.

And yet, he himself is not. Splayed flat and shirtless on the concrete floor of the dressing room, with the lights off, he groans, desperate for the last vestiges of this wild, uncontrollable thing to leave his body but terrified that he'll never taste it again. How could he have let it go so soon? Something so otherworldly and precious, a flavor that a thousand prayers in two religions have never left on his tongue.

29. **BONNIE DOES NOT** see the singer in the crowd. But his band members are signing their names on her work. She trembles at the way they are passing a piece of her around the room in exchange for balled-up cash and postdated checks. Her mother's face has become an object. Some hold the album in the air, waving it to grab the attention of friends or to harass a slow waiter. Others use it as they mack, jotting down phone numbers in the negative space. Some rest their shot glasses on it, her mother's face divided by olive seeds and cocktail umbrellas.

Earlier that week, when Bonnie confirmed that her cover art had been credited to the art director, she was relieved. The image is out in the world, where her mother might find it—but her hands are clean. And because the art director is a man she can only recall from the back—the roundness of his shoulders, an excessive gravity to his frame that reminds her of a gnome—they don't know one another, and so perhaps there will be no repercussions in the end.

If she socialized at all at the office, she would've learned that the biggest controversy about the cover art had been its likeness to Miles Davis's *Sorcerer*.

"It's a magnificent portrait." Bonnie is standing behind a white woman, gray-haired with a Barnard sweater knotted at her neck, speaking to the only white musician from the band. When asked, he leans closer to tell the woman that his name is Liam and, yes, he's from Ireland. Which part? Galway. Bonnie wants to tell them that she's been there. At five or six years old. They stopped on the road to her mother's audition (what hadn't they seen on their way to make her mother's auditions?), captivated by the sight of sheep being shorn by the hundreds. Bonnie had held the wool in her hands and felt the grease. Her mother beside her, her tongue put out with disgust, both of them giggling at the gross gamey smell that made such beautiful sweaters.

Bonnie is irked when Liam signs the record, his sloppy signature obscuring Claudine's beautiful face. He pulls his cigarette from his lips to thank the woman very much for praising the cover.

"I hope the rest of the music stands up to it."

Bonnie appreciates this distinction; it is her first compliment.

Nervous when it's her turn, she begins to walk away, but Liam greets her first.

"Thank you for coming, miss." She notes the fair brown of his eyes, his full lips, the lone long pinky nail for plucking the guitar. "Can I sign that for you?" He points to the record in her hands.

She takes his pen and signs her own name in the lower corner, before handing her record back to him.

"I'm actually the artist."

He examines the record, looking between her and the art, seeing it anew.

"You are," he says, with wonder. "You're fantastic. It's a stunning picture."

"Thank you."

A smile breaks across his face. "Would you wait—right here?"

Liam barely gives Bonnie time to answer before he dashes away. His excitement makes Bonnie wonder if she shouldn't have told him; she can feel the comfort of her anonymity making way for something more uncertain.

He pops back over. She smells his sweat more powerfully now. He reeks of ginger beer.

"What shall I call you?"

"Bonnie."

"Miss Bonnie—just one minute," and he disappears again behind the backstage door. She twists her mouth, trying hard not to smile at his strange charm.

It takes all his effort, but Liam drags Mansour from the floor to the bench, and from the bench through the door, telling him he has to meet the artist. Liam speaks in English, Mansour in sleepy French.

"You dreamed of the cover! And she made the cover! You have to talk to her."

Mansour shakes his head, tired and disbelieving. "You really think she made it?"

"Who would claim something like that for the hell of it? You're out of excuses, man, let's go!"

Mansour is halfway out the door from Liam's pushing and his shirt is hardly on.

"But what about my English?"

"What about it?"

"It's gone out of my mind . . . it happens all the time."

"Well, maybe she speaks French."

Liam lugs him through the crowd where, every few paces, a new person stops Mansour for an autograph, to ask for a photo, to compliment his cheekbones.

They get to the center of the room, and by then he's starting to get into it, scoping the women in the room.

"Which one is she?" Mansour asks Liam.

"She's . . . she's gone."

30. RABIA CALLS BONNIE to her office the following Friday. On her way up, Bonnie takes the latest liner notes to the art department as usual and then takes the elevator even higher up to the executive floor. She leaves the cart for the liner notes outside the executive bathroom, where she gathers herself and tries to outwit time. Then Bonnie knocks softly on Rabia's door, hoping she won't hear.

"Yes," she replies instantly.

Bonnie moves into the office, sits in the same chair from her first day, and waits.

"How was the launch party?" Rabia doesn't look up from where she signs a stack of contracts, all turned to the same page for her signature.

"Thank you for sending me. I think they're wonderful."

"Yes. I know you do."

Rabia removes her glasses. She puts the album on the table between them, staring down at Claudine's face.

"Is this . . . a self-portrait?"

"No."

"Is it a relative?"

Bonnie looks at the ground.

Her voice is missing, a sound with no tone. "It's my mother."

Rabia leans back in her chair.

"Well, she's very beautiful. Was she . . . I don't remember meeting her at Ms. Sylvia's funeral?"

"She wasn't there."

"Why wasn't she? Is she all right?"

Bonnie feels a pain rising in her gut, so she tunes into the street noise below, where a record store blasts one of Dr. King's speeches in mourning. The wind distorts King's timbre, mixing him with Cantonese from the bookstore below, and the whiny cranes, and an uptown breeze carrying steel drums, until he fully dissolves and becomes a part of everything. Was that what it meant to die?

"Here, here. Take this." Rabia is speaking, and Bonnie brings her mind back to the room, where the woman has pushed over a pile of tissues. It's only then she realizes she's crying. Bonnie smears the mucus off her upper lip. When she looks up again, Rabia's face is sullen.

"It seems an impossible thing to miss your mother's funeral. I'm sure your mother had her reasons."

"Like what?" Bonnie hears herself say, loud and clear. But Rabia stares and says nothing, seeming not to have heard.

When she speaks again, there is a sullen tone to her voice; she is conceding some kind of defeat. A release of something very old and worn. Rabia exhales.

"You're very, very talented, Bonnie. It seems like you could do almost anything in life that you choose. But this wasn't work you had the right to do. It wasn't your place."

Bonnie hears the quiet rage cutting through the formality of her tone.

"Today will be your last day. Do you understand?"

Bonnie's tears flow while a stoic expression hardens on her face.

"Yes, Mrs. Alvi."

"Then please . . . please go," the woman says and turns her chair away. She's crying too.

31. **THERE IS NOTHING** to take from her desk but her colored pencils and a handful of fried-trout receipts. She leaves the office and walks from midtown Manhattan to the Village, eventually finding what she'd never admit to herself to be looking for: a poster of Mansour and Liam on a downtown club marquee. The album is in an adjoining record-store window, for sale next to Joni Mitchell's latest.

Their set starts soon. She joins the sizable line, feeling a vague mix of pride and terror. The marquee advertises a signing after the show. She is the only person in line without the record bearing her mother's face under their arm.

This early evening set is good, but the sound is imbalanced. When Mansour belts, Bonnie feels it in her teeth. He keeps cupping his ear, wincing at the feedback. For his part, the drummer solos for too long. So long that Mansour gets visibly pissed.

Looking for holes, for flaws, she finally finds his: transparency. Everything shows on his face. She can tell when Mansour misses a cue. When the drummer has gone off script.

The pianist yells something to the horns and the musicians all go with it, and as if lit by a fire, the singer dances across the stage. Head up, head down. It would be a Jackson 5 kind of thing if it weren't for the exotic flavor of the movement. Mansour yells something in Spanish, and a conga player who'd been going easy, sort of backing up the drummer, takes control. The music switches again. Mansour sings in another language now, in a style and a rhythm foreign to her ears.

Bonnie's mind searches for something to do with the sounds she hears, but her body is already in motion. Beside her, a woman's head flops up and down and she screams, already inside the portal that is sucking Bonnie in. She lets it take her.

32. **HE CAN'T GET** a second more than the time it takes to introduce himself to her before he's distracted. Then he steals another moment to lean down for her to repeat her name into his ear. Determined to speak with her about the cover, Mansour keeps Bonnie by the hand as he conquers the room: cheek-kissing concertgoers in that French way, signing albums, throwing back spiked Earl Grey, cornering Davis over the protracted solo, promising her he'll just be a minute more. This goes on for almost an hour, but he never lets go and she never pulls away.

Between these interruptions, he leans close to ask her other questions, gathering her review of the concert piece by piece. Her first critique stings—a thing he already knows and struggles with. *You shouldn't close your eyes so much onstage.* Then the sound. He agrees that it was horrible, promises her he'll fire the soundman (and he does, the first of Keifer's friends he cuts). Within the hour they have inside jokes, have offended each other and apologized, have traded home remedies for both their migraines, tricks to avoid the perpetual construction on the 4 line. In this single summer night, they are intimately familiar, as if they've known each other for years.

They have many of the same records, have memorized the same time stamps on *Hugh Masekela Is Alive and Well at the Whisky* for drowning out loud neighbors, for making a day move at a faster pace.

How, Mansour says, could Otis Redding know him on the inside like that? What did a man from Dawson, Georgia, know about the peanut fields in Senegal? How did he know just the right notes to take Mansour's mind to such a personal time and place? Nine or ten again, kneeling in a heap of rotten peanuts with blistered hands. And when he looks up from telling Bonnie this, palms open, like he means to show her blisters that have long healed, he looks shy, as if he's mistakenly made some confession, remembering that they are strangers.

She stands with crossed arms in the brick-walled backstage hallway, waiting for him to wash up. He told her that needs to wet his face and hair and arms between every set, releasing the electric charge of the body, so she stands there and meets the other men. Though Mansour introduces her as the cover artist, Keifer starts the rumor that she's the fine-ass girlfriend he's been hiding all along. ("And for good reason. Did you see that sister? Goddamn.") Keifer tips his hat to her at the door.

Once the crowd is gone, they go back out to the stage from the greenroom. Mansour sits on the edge of the stage in the empty club. She sits on the table across from him, letting her legs swing.

He wipes his face with a towel, picks up a copy of the album from the edge of the stage beside him. Displaying it before her, he says with a furrowed brow:

"So how does this happen?"

"I don't know. I'm not even sure if I believe you . . . but it's a great line."

He moves his cigarette in the air as he searches for the words in English and, coming up blank, watches the smoke dance.

"You mean, like, uh, to, uh—"

"A pickup line. Yeah."

He smiles a gorgeous, full smile, scratches his facial hair.

"I don't use lines," he says, holding her gaze.

She drops her eyes first, shy.

"I saw it, I swear I saw your cover, in my dream . . . I wouldn't lie to you."

"Sure you wouldn't," she says with a smirk.

"Liam," Mansour shouts across the room, his eyes still on her.

"Yeah?"

"Tu as trouvé ma femme." *You've found my wife.*

Liam laughs loudly from the back. Bonne smiles at his antics, shakes her head.

"Oh, please. Je ne suis pas ta femme." *I'm not your wife.* She says this firmly, parading her perfect French accent to startle him.

Mansour tilts his head in disbelief at her French.

He reaches out, to give her a pound.

"Ma soeur." *My sister.*

She breaks into laughter as they bump fists.

He takes her to a rooftop party in the village, but they grow weary of a crowded dance floor, of loud music that makes it hard to have a conversation. She tells him that she's just been fired, that all she really wants to do is get salty food and go to bed. So now they stand in line at the greasy counter of a Chinese takeout spot in the theater district, yelling in French over the clamor of industrial pots, the banter of the Chinese cooks, the Manhattan street noise from the open door. She fans herself with a takeout menu.

"How does this supposed dream start?" She asks.

"I see nothing but this woman, just the woman."

"You see the picture?" she says drily.

"No, she's moving. She comes to the chair, sits, moves into the pose you painted."

Bonnie looks at him with narrowed eyes.

"Does she talk to you?"

He shakes his head, lights a new cigarette.

"Anything else?"

He's silent for a moment.

"Her feet are bruised. Really badly," he says. "Was she injured?"

Bonnie's studying him. A look of shock.

"Next!" The man at the counter bangs it for the second time, breaking her spell. She keeps her eyes on Mansour as she orders.

Mansour mocks her enormous order: three different kinds of chicken, two kinds of beef rice, and lo mein.

"You got what? Six kids at home?" he says.

"Ten. All boys."

They stroll toward the R train, delaying the steps that will take them their separate ways.

At the station entrance, Mansour stands square in front of her, his hands in his pockets. Several thoughts pass through his mind before he finally speaks.

"Where'd you learn all that pretty French?" he asks, moving the fuzzy curls from in front of her eyes.

She looks away into the deserted street, seemingly wrestling with something that has awakened within her.

"From the woman in your dream," she says.

VII

CLAUDINE

France and North America, 1956–1968

33. **THEIR EARLY NIGHTS** of homelessness were spent in a classic Mercedes-Benz. It had been purchased after a West End gig that toured seven cities, the kind of job, the kind of money, they hadn't seen in years. The car, Bonnie imagines now, is what allowed her and her mother, Claudine, to park and sleep in good neighborhoods undisturbed. Quiet cobblestone blocks in the sixth arrondissement, where they watched well-dressed white Parisians and their North African maids march in and out of empty shops that had yet to resume their prewar glory. For the year that they went without housing, they discovered the car was also an ideal observatory for stars. They savored the Paris twilight, watching the airborne tumbleweeds of silk scraps. They floated out from the open shutters of the textile shops, orbiting the car's windows like planets and hypnotizing the stray dogs enough to keep them at bay.

Bonnie slept with her mother's dark legs across her body. Legs that were hairless, the skin taut and cold-smooth. The feet were permanently stained by deep-blue bruises from a past Bonnie knew almost nothing about. The color always looked beautiful to her, a beautiful addition to her darkness.

Claudine had promised to take Bonnie to Marseille for the jazz festival once her military pension arrived. Everything, it seemed, would happen once her military pension arrived. There would be a house with a yard and a real oven, a private school and proper winter clothes.

One day, after a fruitless search about town for a pitying landlord, they visited an old friend. The walk from the front door of Madame Prevert's apartment to her dining room was a museum tour. A corridor lined with stale, sparkling costumes in glass cases; headless mannequins draped in three or four layers of tulle; stacks on stacks of yellowing pamphlets; posters announcing ballets and operas from another century. Hats made of grass were pinned to the ceiling. Two flappers from the twenties, nude but for socks, kissed on the mantle. Everything was ancient. Bonnie scarfed down Madame Prevert's nutted cheese, eager to continue her exploration of the house. In a hallway, she discovered photos of her mother, standing far left in a row of white ballerinas, all of them dressed in stiff tutus. Her mother was immediately recognizable; her face and frail frame had not changed. For the first time, Bonnie imagined her mother as young and vulnerable, a feeling that made her worry until she heard the shrill of her mother's laughter. A rare sound. She rushed back to see Claudine clasping the table, smoke rolling off her long white tongue.

"That's why she's gonna be a scientist," Claudine said, gathering herself, reaching to straighten Bonnie's skirt and yank her matted plaits as she returned to her mother's side.

"A couple of ballet solos ... a couple of standing ovations ... I wanted to dance *so much*. But it wasn't worth it. This isn't a life," she said, breaking a dry biscuit with two shaky hands. "Would you say it was worth it?"

"Of course!" the woman replied, before sipping from her glass of wine. "Who else can say that their legs ended the war?" The women roared as their glasses clanked, toasting to their pain. To all the promises that life, in the end, had not fulfilled.

Her mother seemed to be a different person in the house of this old dancer. She was eager to share, eager to speak. But before long, the women's conversation turned sour, an argument that Bonnie has since forgotten, but for a single sentence that burned into her memory:

"I don't know about you staying here again, Claudine. You already been here once. Is this a pattern with you?"

As Madame Prevert had surmised, there was indeed a pattern to Claudine's decisions, though it wouldn't be fair to attribute it to Claudine alone: it ran in the family. The handing over of children to strangers without much hesitation, without a wild contest of emotion, had been common among her kin for generations. Such a tradition probably began several centuries earlier in West Africa, where children in certain classes and ethnic groups were given to other relatives— grandmothers, distant barren aunts, and cousins in infancy—to strengthen family ties or to end rivalries. But no one remembered that now. And anyway, thinking of anything that way always bred more confusion and insecurity than anything else. Connecting Africa to American Blackness in the 1940s, or any decade for that matter, was like staring at your own reflection in a bowl of water and waiting for another face to show.

This pattern, though ancestral, took on another flavor after the events of 1927, when Sylvia King journeyed south with her father for a case and returned home to Boston with his dead body.

After that, Sylvia's blood moved differently, more slowly, some days depriving her brain of enough sustenance to stand, and by the time it was her turn, it made her first a tired mother, then a bedridden one, next a suicidal one, then a mother called other things. (When asked, *Is that your mother?* Claudine would answer, *She had me.*)

At the end of their visit, Claudine left Bonnie at Madame Prevert's house. Her mother was always chasing work, following rumors of gigs in other cities, so Bonnie wasn't worried until one day turned into three. Madame Prevert did not visit her in her room, did not call her down for dinner, but when Bonnie wandered through the dark house and found the woman—reading, writing, drinking alone—she was always kind and courteous and answered Bonnie's questions.

"Your mother has gone to a city office, to arrange for the payment of her pension."

"Do you think they'll really give it to her this time?" Bonnie asked, climbing into the rocking chair across from the woman. The woman seemed surprised by her candor.

"They must. It's payment for her military service."

Bonnie stared blankly, so the woman went on.

"We both danced in a ballet troupe for the French army during the Second World War . . . she never told you any of this?"

Bonnie shook her head.

The woman went back to her book.

Bonnie spent most of her time in the woman's house in her room. She slept on a futon next to a stack of novels.

Time was lost in difficult books, snacking on olives, sitting inside the small square of sunlight that spread slowly, like honey, on the parquet floors of an otherwise dark room. She read *Cendrillon* (the French Cinderella) three times, and when she finished all she could read of a French translation of *Faust*, she curled up in the sunspot beside her olive pits and yearned for her mother.

Madame Prevert woke her up on the fourth morning, a dry, cold hand on her bare neck.

"Your mother is waiting for you."

<hr />

The car ride to the airport is silent. Madame Prevert speeds through the empty highway in her stick-shift. She parks, grabs Bonnie's suitcase, and rushes ahead into the heavy doors. Bonnie struggles to keep up, a bit drowsy and lightheaded—weak from strange hours of sleeping and sporadic eating. Madame Prevert dashes through the endless walkways; she shows Bonnie's passport and cuts lines. She looks over her shoulder every few minutes to confirm that the child is behind her. Bonnie runs, gripping her large backpack in her hand as it slips off her shoulder. She drags her sweater along the ground, holding her teddy bear under her arm.

Bonnie hears the plane before she sees it. The loud whir of the engine. As Bonnie approaches, she struggles to walk against the wind that the giant propellers push in her direction. She sees Claudine standing by the plane's stairs. She rushes to her mother, stopping for a moment to turn to Madame Prevert, who's waving goodbye. Her mother is dressed beautifully, her dark pleated skirt flaring in the heavy wind. Her hands reach for Bonnie, and she holds her to her body for a long time. Claudine is speaking but her voice cannot be heard over the engine. She helps Bonnie mount the steps of the plane, and a smiling flight attendant takes her by the hand. Claudine gathers the things that Bonnie has dropped: her sweater, coloring book. The flight attendant reaches to take Bonnie's things, but Claudine hesitates, bringing the sweater to her nose, breathing it in.

Bonnie turns, reaching for her mother, but she is walking across the tarmac. Bonnie calls for her, but Claudine continues steadily toward the terminal doors, never looking back.

Bonnie will always remember the walk: slow, mechanical, as if she were in another dimension. Her screaming makes no difference, a wall immediately erected between her and Claudine. And then there is the flight attendant who restrains her, a restraint that morphs into a loving hug. The flight attendant sits in the seat beside her on the plane to New York, holding on until they both are no longer in tears.

34. **ABOUT THREE YEARS** to the day after she sent Bonnie to live with her mother in New York and checked herself into rehab in Paris, Claudine gets a call from the US. It's Sylvia. Finally, after at least twenty unanswered calls made earlier that year, several more letters sent. She never gets her mother to acknowledge this, and after they've had enough of one another, Sylvia finally puts the girl on the phone.

It is mostly small talk. The girl is polite and guarded. Her voice has dropped an octave, already deep enough to make a good alto, and her words are incredibly fast. It's hard to keep pace with her mind as she darts from the Olympics to nail polish, pimples to the sordid origin of picnics, never revealing anything personal but sharing so many thoughts. Claudine can't believe she's already so smart.

"I want her back," Claudine says to her mother. She knows, as she wipes her eyes with her paper napkin, that she sounds like a child.

"You clean up and get her a decent place to live, and we'll see."

"Put her back on."

"That's enough now."

"One question. Please."

Sylvia curses under her breath but returns Bonnie to the phone. "Yes?" she says.

"Where would you like to live?"

The girl is quietly umming, and Claudine can tell that she's trying not to hurt her, or herself.

Claudine rephrases the question. "I mean, what sort of place do you dream of living in?"

"Oh. I like brownstones a whole lot. I like the houses in Park Slope," she says. "They have gargoyles, and flower gardens, and terraces, and—I'm sorry, Grandma's calling me."

"That's all right. We'll talk soon."

"OK. bye, Mama."

For a while, the calls continue, Sylvia comforted by Bonnie's new joy. But in the end, what Sylvia has always been most afraid of happens. Claudine cannot deliver on her promise of moving, a series of excuses that Sylvia refuses to believe. Of course, she could not confess her ill-confidence, the simple truth that she needed a moment to earn back, at least, her own respect. The following spring, when Claudine next calls, Sylvia does not answer. And when she does finally pick up, Sylvia won't let her speak to the child, the girl apparently asleep.

Months pass, until, one day, Claudine watches from the TV as America burns. A story on Philly. Vacant houses abandoned in the midst of the riots that resulted from years of tension with police. She calls an old acquaintance from a pay phone, and, within twenty-four hours, she has a quote on a Philly brownstone for an unreasonably low price. Seven floors, ten rooms, six fireplaces, and a dumbwaiter. In need of much repair and in a terrible neighborhood, but the owner wants out. She wires the down payment that night, knowing she'll have to wait a little while and earn the money back before she can fly home.

35. **WITHIN AN HOUR** of arriving in Philly in 1964, Claudine is squatting below the parlor windows in her underwear, smothering a hissing cocktail bomb with her only dress. When her eyes finally adjust to the smoke, she gets a better look at the thing that was hurled through the glass of her window.

It is a pitiful little thing, more like some homemade fireworks than a weapon. She tastes its liquid on her fingertip: What was the vinegar for? She knows then that the perpetrators are even younger than they sound. That they believe the recipes in the funnies or on the Johnny Carson show. She retreats to the room's center, away from the windows.

Their silhouettes hover at her corner of her block for what seems to be hours. Plotting in whispers but never moving an inch. Whenever she returns to the window for a little peek, there they are, standing still and far enough apart that their shadows resemble a group of ghosts that are too shy to slow dance and are waiting for the music to change. She wonders if she should show herself, to let them know that she, a Black woman, is the new owner of this house. Before she turns away again, she hears one speak.

"This one's for Odessa Bradford, motherfucker!" they shout as another Corona-bottle-wannabe-bomb comes flying through her window. This time she's ready, has her dress opened like a tarp to catch it.

She launches it back at them and crouches, waiting to hear it explode. Then she hears laughter.

"You betta teach 'em! *Goddamn*, woman! Where the hell you come from rollin' like that?" The voice of a man, sitting just outside her shattered window. She knows, from the place inside herself that war helped her hone, that the man is not dangerous. He's just drunk. She carries on.

The gossipy Italian realtor said that brownstone's previous owner, the neighborhood's last white resident, ran from the house the night before she arrived—scrambling out of the service entrance, half-dressed, cradling a wheelchair-bound son, demanding that they leave with whatever they could fit in the Volkswagen. Many things have been left behind. Claudine finds a gun in the drawer of the master bedroom. The bed is unmade, and the comforters, thick and red, lie there in a cool heap.

That night, for some reason, she relapses. Just as she'd done the night before and the night before that, she drinks rum straight until she feels calm.

A quake on the fifth floor rouses her. Emptiness, her favorite symptom of drunkenness, vanishes in a single second, like a heavy blanket has been snatched from her legs. She follows the sound with the gun in hand. She could be dreaming, but she can't always tell the difference, and trying to is the only time she feels as crazy as she's been told she is.

She hadn't felt like this before the war, true. The war, her doctor warned her, is what attracted her to chaos, violence. To the bottle. To images of these riots on television. What has driven her to return to America and move into a house right in the thick of it. *You're reliving your trauma*, he said. *It's not about your daughter. You told me yourself that you never wanted her. Don't you remember?* She'd hung up the phone.

Months later, as she dresses to go to Sylvia's assisted-living facility, she does remember saying that. She remembers the rape that brought her Bonnie too. It's why she can't finish the flower garden in the backyard of the brownstone.

The smell of earth. He'd held her face to the ground.

Her new boyfriend, Daniel (Cuban, twenty years her junior, her carpenter turned dance partner—a story for another time) drives her to meet her daughter. Claudine buys a new dress for the occasion. White with a thick black belt. It's the first thing she's worn in years that doesn't make her body look oblong. She chews through a pack of gum on the highway, trying to erase the smell of rum on her breath, and her guilt.

Her first thought when they arrive is that it doesn't look like Brooklyn, not the Brooklyn she remembers from a decade ago. Claudine walks up the hill toward the entrance to the facility, expecting to have time to gather herself, but her mother is outside on this day, sitting in a lawn chair, waiting for her. Her mother is still beautiful, a little wrinkled, and much, much smaller, half the size Claudine remembers. Her white hat is enormous, further dwarfing her demure frame.

Claudine isn't surprised when she doesn't see Bonnie. She'd expected to have to fight her way past the dragon. At least the dragon has shrunk.

36.

"YOU LOOK SO DIFFERENT," Sylvia says. "My God." She extends her hand, and Claudine leans forward. Her mother touches her face.

"Want some lemonade?"

"Water. Please."

Sylvia pours her a glass, hands it to her. Claudine places the cup on the table with a shaky hand.

Sylvia giggles to herself. She's staring straight ahead, not looking at Claudine.

"You write like you never set foot in Howard. Good Lord. That last letter was terrible," she says.

Claudine scoffs, shaking her head.

"So you read them?" she asks.

"Read what, dear?"

"My letters."

"Some of them, yes." Sylvia sips lemonade, steady. "But I'm very busy with the girl. She takes everything out of me. These aren't supposed to be the parenting years, you know."

They are silent.

"I brought this for my daughter."

Claudine places a teddy bear on the table between them.

"I know you did, dear," Sylvia mutters with a hint of pity. "But she's not the age she was when you sent her here. She's got a mind that could build a city. She doesn't need toys anymore."

As soon as she says this, Sylvia, sensing Claudine's breakdown, grabs her wrist. Claudine begins to cry. Sylvia goes on.

"It's natural, dear. We always want to keep them young. Same way I wanted to with you. But you were so talented, I couldn't hold you back. I'm sorry it all . . . wasn't what you'd hoped for."

Sylvia releases Claudine, pats her leg carefully, and pulls her hands back into her own lap, watching the hills ahead again. She hums to herself.

"Mother, I bought a house. In Philadelphia. I'm ready. I wanna take Bonnie home with me. Today."

Sylvia leans closer and lifts her sunglasses.

"I smell it on you, dear. And I will not let that sweet girl think that *this* is an option."

Claudine retorts in her mind: *Hey, Mother, remember when me and Dad visited you in the psych ward? Remember when you tried to burn the house down with me in it? Remember when you believed that people were watching you in the shower?*

Claudine cannot say any of these words without taking things from bad to worse and further delaying her reunion with her child. So she stands up and takes her bear, walks down the hill, and gets back into her boyfriend's car, berating his driving all the way home.

37. **FOR EVERYONE BUT CLAUDINE,** the last straw was a rumor about a New York hotel booting Sammy Davis Jr. from his penthouse suite over a bounced check. Everyone was perplexed because he'd just appeared on the *Playboy* show with his voice and performance as smooth as they'd ever been.

After that, Claudine watched the other dancers around town lose their morale and humble themselves. If Sammy wasn't working, they didn't have a chance. The clubs didn't want them. The theaters didn't either. No one had seen a marquee advertising a tap act in at least a decade. And the marquees that did pop up around town were sloppy, handwritten without care, nailed illegally to lampposts in the night.

It seemed to the others that it was time to accept that they'd been replaced, by television and, more offensively, an endless supply of singing groups (*That damn Motown*). To retell the slander something like it was said: country-ass choir members, gyrating through terrible arrangements of the same harmonies, hair grease and hand gestures of the acts that had preceded them.

Claudine saw her best friends—talented tappers—straight up wrestle the police and preachers in bitter rivalries over sidewalks and street corners. Even during remarkably treacherous winters, dancers could be seen at 5:00 a.m., sprinkling the concrete with sawdust and shuffling for victory in tap battles that were understood less and less by anyone among the living. They were battling not for the hot dog change the tourists dropped into their cups but for their place in their own cities, in their own world. They didn't mean to inspire the B-boys or the jazz musicians (who took their club jobs) in rhythm. But that happened too.

Ultimately, most of them accepted that the culture had moved on, desired to express itself in other ways. But Claudine refused.

She had to work. She had to earn her daughter back from Sylvia.

———

She fought the tide of the times with whatever was at her disposal. Her legs still called attention everywhere they went, and so she wore them proudly to crowded theater parties, to rancid Subway stations, to an audition for an abandoned revival of *In Dahomey*, quitting on the spot when the young Austrian director came to the edge of the stage and offered to lick her calves.

On this June morning of 1968, she doesn't even remember whose idea it had been to try some other cities. It was so humid that Claudine kept her hair in pins the whole time she rowed a canoe across a stagnant, smelly green swamp to a Miami beachfront club seeking talent while still under construction. Though she'd toured Europe, though she'd danced in the world's finest opera houses before the war, she agreed to start her tap routine a *fifth* time for the club owner, who was busy counting the mosquitos he'd smashed into her headshot. She shuffled hard on wooden planks while twelve-year-old Negro boys in prison stripes catcalled louder than she could tap as they worked the grounds.

The club owner said no.

But she didn't stop.

That same week, she was the only middle-aged colored woman costumed in polka dots and sequins, trying to cut the endless open-call line on a smoky Hollywood lot, her tap shoes softening on the kettle-hot asphalt, when she bumped into the Texan that became her manager.

The gigs had been flowing ever since.

She'd been in love with Daniel for a while, but they remained unmarried. They did not want any more children, nor to live any farther than within a fifteen-mile radius of a theater of some kind, maintaining a diet mostly of vegetables. From the day she returned to America, Claudine had taken great pains to remain in the dancer's life however she could: ushering at Lincoln Center while her house in Philly was being repaired; acting, for five weeks, for a tenement-based community theater where the playwright-directors required talent to memorize the Ten-Point Program and learn to shoot a gun.

She was forty-something by the time she ended up on Broadway for ten months, and so today, after two months in LA shooting a pilot that was not picked up and teaching a tap class at the Negro Ensemble Company, on the way to catch a train back to Philadelphia, Claudine collapses in the middle of Fourteenth Street.

Her fall is slow. She gives up at least two chances to break it, wills it in a way that is impossible for even her to understand. Upon falling, she lets herself lie in the street for several seconds. If cars are honking, she doesn't hear them, and if she does, it makes no difference. In a desperate effort to steady herself, she pulled down a young white girl with her. The girl is sympathetic and, with the help of a drag queen, carries Claudine to the sidewalk. She sits on the curb, eye level with the tires of a bus that, once it pulls off, reveals ads for goat cheese and adoption across the street.

All of the working, the hard-earned sobriety, and the mansion she bought with cash and renovated has not been enough to regain custody of Bonnie. Nothing has made a difference to Sylvia. She has long stopped replying to letters. For being abandoned and having abandoned, Claudine's pain remains strong, undiluted by time.

Even though she's long stopped claiming the identity of *mother*, in conversations with young dancers and actresses with whom she shares dressing rooms, complaining about their own children, and the back talk, the slacking in school, she cannot be free of this desperate feeling. And after years of resistance, it has once again consumed her. Last July signaled the end of possibility. It was the month in which the child turned eighteen, and thus was officially emancipated from Claudine and impossible to locate.

Her battle with alcohol; the voluntary relinquishing of her child to her mother, Sylvia; an attempt to regain custody that ended in her mother threatening to call the police before she got to see the child: it now makes the street move in waves beneath her feet. A loud ring starts in her ears.

She begins to walk again. Taking her time, gripping the streetlight poles on every block along the way. She feels better as she gets closer to Penn Station. They are side by side, so she makes herself go into the record store instead of the liquor store.

Immediately she spots an album in the contemporary-jazz section with her face on it. She is indifferent to the gawks of others as she crouches down on the floor, staring at the record while the world around her grows dark and quiet.

She would recognize the style anywhere. It's Bonnie's hand. Her left hand: steady, impressionistic. On the cover, Claudine looks ethereal and ecstatic, thin braids over her face, her hand at her mouth with the fingers stretched wide. The features that mother and daughter share have been exaggerated: the lips, the eyes, the mole. It looks like Claudine, yes, but it *feels* so much like her: pride and shame wedded in her eyes. The belief that she'd been born worthless, that she was nothing and absolutely everything at the same time. And how strange, that in spite of her mother's best efforts, the years and distance between them, that Bonnie had, in the end, seen Claudine for exactly who she was.

She buys several copies of the record, asks the store clerk what he knows about the album, the artist, the label, and where she can catch them in concert. He tells her she's got the worst luck.

All their shows in town have been canceled as of last week.

"What on earth happened?"

"One of the band members died," he says.

She takes the albums home, reading the liner notes, the credits, the lyrics, the bios, never seeing Bonnie's name. When she sleeps, she dreams of Mansour. Her sleep is steady and rich. For she knows that she is finally very, very close.

VIII.

THE DEATH OF CARL KEIFER
(PART TWO)

New York, 1968

38. **THE ALBUM SELLS ENOUGH** copies to require another small printing, but the money finds its way to the men slowly, and this intensifies the strain between them. Liam and Mansour, who've never lost touch with Gil Rodney, invite him to their East Elmhurst show in a week's time. He doesn't say yes, but, for the first time, he doesn't say no either.

They never tell Keifer that they are mentees of his father, that since they met him back in January, they've spent Sundays in Gil's basement on Long Island, coughing on his imported cigars, now taking his advice on navigating their new success, with nods and cheeks full of sunflower seeds. He tells them not to take any of it seriously, tells Mansour to work on his nervousness ("That'll take you out") and to never, ever read reviews ("The writers aren't even musicians"). To protect themselves from the impending roller-coaster ride of a working artist's life with a fanatical devotion to their craft. To stop smiling so goddamn much. To get married young. To have plenty of babies. To be faithful most of the time but that it can be necessary to stray on occasion. It helps you keep the music first.

When he asks about his son and daughter-in-law, they answer with redacted, glossy stories to bring the man as close to smiling as they can. They hide their distrust of Keifer, the disputes and competing tastes that have kept each concert and rehearsal rife with tension. Rodney is generous with recommendations, referrals to good venues (half their gig roster), and his time. He is also full of anecdotes, vague and ominous warnings about the dangers of America, especially in the wake of King's death, that go over the European men's heads:

"Y'all be careful rollin' together around here like a couple of happy little girls. This ain't Paris."

They laugh, but Rodney doesn't, his eyes red and wet with the perpetual sadness he never speaks of.

En route to a show in Bay Ridge, Liam and Mansour tell Rodney to drop them at the corner store near his place so they can grab some cigarettes. Liam keeps prying Mansour to tell him more about Bonnie. Mansour only smiles.

The A&P's storefront window is so completely shattered that at first glance it appears to still be in place. The woman at the counter sees Liam and Mansour gawking and ushers them in.

"Oh, man," Liam mutters, observing the damage.

The woman gathers her sandy hair into a huge clip. With it out of her face, the men can tell she is spooked.

"You know what's funny?" she says while reaching, without looking, into the exact place where the cigarettes are propped under the glass, knowing what they've come in for without having to ask. "They didn't take anything but tube socks." She scoffs, pulls one cigarette for herself before handing them the pack. "You don't mind, do you?" Liam shakes his head. She always does this. The woman looks at Mansour wearily as she lights it, sucks hard, then says, "Thing is, I would've just given them the socks." She's looking at him, like this involves him somehow.

"I'm really sorry about this," he offers.

She shrugs it off, but she's studying him like she's trying to decide if he and his people are worthy of her forgiveness.

"You guys want anything else?" she says, looking at Liam now.

"You got any jerky?"

She smiles. "You with the goddamn jerky. Sure. You?"

Mansour shakes his head, still processing the damage to the store. He looks up at the television, reporting riots in Baltimore. His eyes travel to the Frigidaire, where the rioters have damaged the cord, and the weary machine croaks, sounding like frogs in Dakar at sundown in the rainy season.

While Liam settles up, Mansour wanders out of the door and waits on the block, hands in his pockets, surveying passersby. He'd forgotten what it was like to live on this side of town. The Irish boys stare as they walk past him; most drop their eyes when he stares back in response. But some keep looking at him, and once their eyes meet, their faces open. A look that drifts from a hard leer to one of heartbreak. Like Mansour is a thief, someone who has taken too much from a place that already had far too little to give.

At the sound of Liam's voice, Mansour turns back to the store. Liam's face has reddened and he's arguing with a young man standing by the counter. Mansour approaches the doorway, watching to see if it is going to get physical, if he needs to intervene. The woman has turned away so that only her back is facing them. The stranger sees Mansour through the broken window and spits on the ground. He retreats to the back of the store, ending the row. Liam storms out.

"He's seen you here a hundred times. What's the difference tonight?" Liam says, shaking as he walks ahead of Mansour. It's not the first time that Mansour's presence has brought Liam trouble. He throws an arm around him.

They wait for a baseball game to break so they can cross the street. In an accent so thick that Mansour can barely unravel it, the tallest player, a teenager with his rib cage poking through his skin and the ball in his hand, yells to Liam:

"Why do you keep bringing them to our neighborhood?"

He pretends not to hear, and they walk on.

39. **MANSOUR EXPECTED** to survive longer than four games in the chess tournament Bonnie's brought him to in Washington Square Park. But distracted by what's playing in his head from their conversation on the subway—the death of her grandmother, their shared connection to Mende—in the end, he's bested by a kid from Yonkers, who's wearing rain boots (on a day when there's no sign of rain) and a combat helmet. He leers at Mansour through hair that hangs down in long sandy ringlets.

"Good game," he says, before Mansour even realizes that in just three moves, the boy has won.

Wandering, Mansour expects Bonnie to be on the grass where the other defeated have migrated to, but she's not there. He joins a small crowd and finds that she is the attraction. Sitting on her feet, deep into a speed game. Her white-haired opponent grunts and groans, but she makes no sound, sucking on an unlit cigarette, the strength of focus showing in the tension of her mouth. Thickened and kinkier from sweat since he last saw her an hour before, her hair is pushed up high into a puff. She has a tick: each time she hits the timer, she swivels to the left, then the right, the body rock of a rapper in the zone. Mansour moves with her subconsciously. She looks up, catching him doing this dance. Sheer joy takes over her focus, making her giggle alone and loudly like a little kid, indifferent to the crowd.

They are yelling over the traffic and he's pulling her by the hand as they hustle toward the subway station that will take him to Queens.

"You distracted me. You cost me that game!" she says.

"Maybe he's just a better player than you," he teases.

"Why are we running?"

"My gig's in forty minutes!" he says.

"What?" she yells over a bus.

"Forty minutes!"

He begins his pre-show ritual on the sunny street. A perfect mimic, he's making the sound of a siren. He imitates the purr of the pigeons. It is New York City, so no one pays him any mind. He vocalizes loudly, going high—something close to a screech—and winces at his own sound. "Annnd . . . We won't be goin' up there tonight, kids," he says, as Johnny Carson. By the time they arrive at the station, she is in tears from laughter, holding her stomach, and clasping his arm to stay standing.

"I gotta get away from you," she says, and he's grinning at her giggles. Losing track of the time again, he slips an arm around her waist, pulling her in.

"You're late," she says, but she keeps her eyes on him, a smile with closed lips and a cautious glare. She steps back, brushing hands with him as she slips out of his grasp and jogs across the street for a train home to Brooklyn.

Halfway home on the R train, Bonnie is still thinking of, still feeling, his hands. Hands that are all skin and veins, and remind her of that feely map in her homeroom class back at Mulberry High on which the blue tributaries of the Mississippi river raised up off the wood. *This is where we ran,* Bonnie had thought once as she felt the river, wondering how many with her blood drowned on their journeys out of hell and how many survived. She imagines where Mansour's hands might take her.

40. **ON HIS WAY** to their show in East Elmhurst, Liam crosses the street with his bass strapped across his body. It fits tighter than usual. He's starting to feel the weight he's gained since landing a steady girlfriend of his own: an Italian American carpenter's apprentice, who lives on the first floor of his building. At the gate of the train, he feels a warm breath on the back of his neck, the sharp prick of a knife at his side. He stiffens.

"The watch," a vaguely familiar voice says. Liam fumbles for his wrist, suddenly dumb with fear. He yanks the watch off, feels a clammy hand gather it from his palm. He doesn't dare turn around.

"Where's your nigger?" the voice hisses, and then it disappears.

When he can move again, Liam bolts back up the subway-station steps. Still trembling, he goes into the nearest hardware store and buys the first handgun the old man pulls from the display case. When Liam tells the salesman that he's never used a gun before, the man shoots out the naked light bulb to warn Liam about its power.

Over the course of their set, the audience dwindles to a third of its original size. Keifer's insistence on a jazz treatment is beginning to cost them in the folk venues Liam and Mansour had done well in as a duo. As they bow to disparate applause, Liam tries to hide his trembling. His teeth slam uncontrollably. He hasn't stopped shaking since the moment the knife was in his side.

Mansour storms off the stage before the applause ends. Keifer follows him onto the street, also angry and shouting, furious at Mansour's betrayal—as the crowd parted, he'd seen his father. Their voices, loud and insistent, carry as Liam and the other musicians follow the men outside.

"What part of 'don't bring him around' don't you understand?!"

"I didn't bring him here! He came on his own!"

"Yeah! For you! Congratulations."

By the time Liam reaches them, the trumpeter is pulling Keifer off Mansour. Davis stands to the side, unusually silent, his back at the brick wall. Mansour charges at Keifer again, but the trumpeter blocks him. Mansour throws him out of the way, gripping the pianist once more. They are equal in power, taking it in turns to throw each other to the ground.

"Carl Rodney! Get off that boy!" Keifer releases Mansour at the sound of his father's voice. His fiery eyes turn on Gil.

"What are you doin' here?" he asks, almost desperate.

"I came to see you," Gil says, and he takes a cautious step or two forward.

"You mean you came to see *him*." Keifer turns back to Mansour, who's now off the ground, gaining his bearings. "I told you to stay away from my family," Keifer says, pointing at Mansour. "*This* is my family!"

Keifer is shaking his head, speaking to Mansour again, but now like a brother who's betrayed him. "I told you, man, I can't be around Gil, man. I told you *everything*. I told you things I never told my wife . . . I told you what he did."

"Talk to me," Gil cuts in, louder. "I'm right here, son. Talk to me."

"And say what?!" Keifer screams at Gil. He stands, walks toward the club, but stops, facing Gil again. And when he does, he's finally calm.

"You throwin' him gigs. You comin' out here in your big car to hear him sing. I've been playin' in this city for ten *years*. You ain't never come anywhere to see me!"

Gil is silent, and Keifer finally turns away, heading back into the club. The band follows him. The steel back door shuts.

Mansour and Liam accept a ride from Gil back to Liam's place in Bay Ridge.

"He told me to stay out his way," Gil says to himself and shakes his head, watching the road as he drives. "There's no pleasing him. No pleasing him. He was always that way."

Mansour lays awake on the dusty couch at Liam's. He's shaking his head, Keifer's voice still ringing in his ears. Liam had suggested that he come by in the morning once everyone had cooled down, but Keifer insisted. He wants his money tonight.

The buzzer goes off, and Liam grabs his jacket, stuffing the cash in his pocket.

"Stay here," Liam instructs Mansour wearily. "We don't need any more trouble tonight."

He goes to meet Keifer downstairs.

The front door whines loudly when it shuts. In the silence of the sweltering apartment, Mansour can feel that it is over. Not only the band, which is mostly made up of Keifer's friends, but, more significantly, his sonhood with Gil Rodney and his (turbulent) brotherhood with Keifer. Keifer had set his three rules—and meant them.

Mansour tries to ignore it, but the loss cuts deep. It has triggered a memory of the first time a father was lost. And now some hibernating terror in him is suddenly alive again, pumping an old wound with fresh blood.

IX.

MORNING. BLACK. FIRE.

France, 1955

41. **ON THE WINDY NIGHT** an eight-year-old Mansour arrived in Paris, an albino woman gave him his first hot bath. He was terrified by the blonde of her eyelashes, the way her whole body was the color of his palms. The scent of burnt leather in her blonde braids lured his mind back to the world he'd run from, to the car shop across the street from the talibé orphanage.

Mansour had often gone to the car shop, sometimes to steal water, most times to bring them bottles of the potion the Marabout made to cause accidents on the road and give the shop business. Mansour would place the bottles on the ground, one in each corner of the sand. (For the rest of his life, every time he hears a car skid, he will imagine the work of the gris gris that totaled sixteen Mercedes but looked like nothing more than urine.)

The albino woman's circular cornrows dizzied him, lulling him away from his memories and back to the hot bathwater that was waking his wounds. He had thought the browning of the water, which came from the blood and dirt crusted on his skin, was simply his melanin depositing itself, the way kinkiliba tea leaves turned water brown. He watched the woman's hands, thinking also that touching him might give her color too. The woman muttered to herself as she scrubbed his arm. He picked out the words from her rapid French that he could understand: *Morning. Black. Fire.*

She'd just come home from her night job cleaning toilets at Louis Vuitton and was complaining, Mama would tell him later that evening, about the three hundred purses they burned that night. Tossing the thousand-dollar wares into the flames like dirty rags instead of selling them at a price people like her could afford.

"C'est dingue. C'est tellement dingue ce monde." *This is a crazy world*, she said.

When it was over, Mansour wheezed at the stale European air, shocked by the amount of water the woman drained from the bathtub, freezing and trembling in a knockoff Louis Vuitton shawl in the bedroom of a crowded Paris apartment.

Marie was the little girl on a naked box spring mattress beside him, the albino woman's daughter, holding her father's ruler as she calculated the dimensions of various stains based on their approximate likeness to squares, circles, hexagons. She did this with a furrowed brow and feverish precision, sucking her index and middle fingers. A brainy, merciless child who read the newspaper at four years old, adults knew to avoid her when they were tired, but Mansour listened as a six-year-old Marie reported these dimensions with the conviction of a government official.

"Bon," she began, "158; 38; 1,023; 159. Comprends-nga?" *Do you understand?* she asked, and when he nodded, she kissed him. His first kiss: a garlicky, slimy welcome to the Western world.

42. **WHEN THEY MOVED** into their own place, Olu came night after night and waited for Mama to finish her shift, parking in the back alley of the noisy French restaurant where Mama worked. She earned just enough for a studio apartment in Roubaix that had hot water once a week and a radio with three stations. It was the building where they first moved after leaving Marie-Antoinette's parents' place across town. Mansour will always remember their building for the door that would swell so wide it couldn't be shut when it rained; where a diabetic trafficked boy from the floor above ran Mama's errands in exchange for a homemade lunch and asked Mansour to squeeze and pray over his fingers whenever he couldn't feel his hands.

Over the building's battling radios, the fish ever frying in Mama's pan, Olu read Mansour children's books. Mama watched him from the couch as he sat the mute boy on his knee, congratulating him on each small improvement. Mansour looked away less and less and started to smile. Before long, Olu was spending most of his time with Mansour, bringing balls for his mouth to help him enunciate and those choral recordings of French nursery rhymes.

Since arriving in Paris and reuniting with Mama, deeply introverted, Mansour often found it safer not to speak. A habit of protective silence, but one that made her think he was mute. It was the songs that finally got him to again. Olu, an orphan, saw himself in the boy and encouraged Mansour as he strove to mimic the sound of other children's voices, the words starting to form naturally. But he came to mimic so well, while still conversing so little, that it was difficult to tell if he truly understood what the words meant.

Sometimes, on weekends, Olu came over in the morning. One morning, Mama set him a place alone at the breakfast table. She put a white cloth over the scuffed wood, a glass of plastic flowers at the center, polished his plate before placing it before his seat, and made him a cloth napkin from an old bedsheet. She completed the breakfast, then carefully placed the perfectly folded napkin over it and busied herself with other things until he came into the kitchen.

She faced away, washing dishes that were already clean, feigning indifference to his reaction. She heard a sound of delight come from him as he approached the table, and she struggled to control her grin.

Olu became perplexed, and his food became cold, as he waited for Mama and Mansour to join him at the table.

He left the table in search of them and found Mansour first, alone in his bedroom, eating his breakfast on a little stool at a little table.

"Hey," Olu whispered. "Are you in prison?" The boy smiled. He'd always enjoyed his table and bench, a birthday present from Mama. *You are a real man now with your own place to eat*, she'd said.

Once Olu retrieved Mansour from the bedroom, he went and found Mama in the living room, eating her breakfast on the couch while she browsed the paper, reading with her finger to the line as she was taught in school.

"Why have you punished me?" he said. "Your table is beautiful. But it would be even more so with your presence."

And though she was not used to this arrangement of the man eating with the family, a custom she'd become familiar with from television but could never imagine for herself, with time, she came to appreciate the informality.

Within a month, Mansour was going to the Catholic church's day school. He was the oldest child there, but he was finally speaking. Mama was quietly surprised, but Olu was beaming.

Olu asked Mama to marry him on a snowy night in the back seat of his car.

"Will you marry me?" he asked nervously, repeating the question when she was slow to answer.

"Will you marry me . . . and accept Jesus Christ?"

Jesus would not be a problem. Over time, she could bring Olu around to Islam. She had convinced herself, just as he'd convinced himself that he could pull her his way. But there was more. She had seen it already, what a life with him might entail, for everything she wanted to feel, she watched him give away to Mansour. He rocked the boy; he whispered to him. He wiped his eyes when he cried. He took him by the hand on Sundays and introduced him to the world gently, one word, one park, one street at a time. And she saw the boy change. She saw Mansour speak, use his diapers less and less. And laugh—like his mother, a laugh that made the face look mean and put the whole body in a groove. The sight of Kiné in the boy's face was too much. It put her in bed with a headache for nights at a time. It was painful for Mama to feel her so close.

Back home, Olu followed her to the living room and asked Mama again if she would marry him. She pulled her blanket on the sofa up to her nose and inhaled the stale scent of the old quilt, a gift from the landlord. She still said nothing.

"Why don't you think it over while I take Mansour to town with me tomorrow?"

"But there's no church school tomorrow," she protested.

"There's a choir in town from Switzerland. I met the director at church, and I told him about the boy's voice. If he gets into that school, they would take care of everything. And he could catch up with boys his age. Let him try, Eva."

She sighed and turned away.

"You have to pick him up before seven," she said, her voice gruff and muffled by the couch pillow. Olu grabbed her, holding on until she laughed.

43. **THERE MUST HAVE BEEN** other children, but Mansour only remembers hiding under Olu's arm, nestling in the silk lining of his wool coat, turning a small hole into a big one when he attempted to climb inside of it. The man smelled of wine, made him think of Sokhna. It was a comfort. But just as he dozed off to sleep in the pews, the choir director finally approached, telling Olu that it was Mansour's turn to audition.

The director had to drag Mansour by the arm. He whined all the way from where he'd sat with Olu, down the cold central hall, where the flooring changed to cobblestone and the walls to wood panels. The choir director pushed him up the steps of the main stage, where the accompanist—an incredibly strong yet gaunt elderly woman—held Mansour in place and warned him not to move.

"We won't have any more of that!" she said. And he believed her.

As he stood there, Mansour became distracted by the life-size glossy portraits of actors in medieval costumes that hung on the walls. All of them flaunting generous dark hair and olive skin, seeming to be real people, frozen in clownish poses. Each one made immortal just to entertain.

And on the stage, as he skimmed the room, Mansour locked eyes with the man who smelled like wine and felt a familiar feeling he had not long escaped in Senegal with the talibé: the power and the dread of performance.

From the back wall, Olu smiled and mimed things to make Mansour laugh. Mansour finally began to sing "O filii et filiae," producing a sound so high and pure that the director's face grew hot with tears and he dried his skin with the sleeve of his robe. He told Olu on the spot that Mansour was accepted.

"What a wonderful, wonderful find!" he said, with a muscular hand squeezing Olu's shoulder.

They talked as the man ushered Olu back out into the entryway.

"I think he'd be more suited to the orphanage than the day school. That will give us more time to work with him," the man said.

"But, Father, he's not an orphan. His mother works in town."

The man's face soured. He turned to go back inside, walking quickly. Olu pursued him.

"Father, I don't understand. We're happy for the boy to join the choir, but he will live with his mother—as the other boys do."

"No, he needs to be here. He needs real training."

"I don't want to take him from his mother. They've been separated before—"

"He can be the absolute best singer this choir has ever produced. But he needs to live here."

Olu saw the man's eyes brighten, felt himself being seduced. The man continued.

"How much do you want for him?"

In the car home, Olu was mostly silent. That moment and for the hours that followed, every time he looked at Mansour, Olu had a strange, stubborn look on his face.

Soon came the day that Mansour would see him for the last time.

44.

RAISED VOICES BRING Mansour from his bed. He stands in the open sliver of his bedroom door to watch them in the living room.

"Eva! It is a place for orphans! Don't you want your son to stay with you?"

"I work all hours. Who will bring him home every day?"

"I will!"

"And take him back? *Every day?* It's hours away."

Olu nods, and Mama's gaze hardens.

"What about when you get tired of him? Yes, you will tire of taking care of a mute boy who will never repay you!"

"Don't speak about him that way!"

"I thought that you trusted the church? Isn't that why you took him there?"

"I took him there for the school, to give *your* son an opportunity. I did not take him there to become a ward of the state!"

"What does it matter?" Mama chupses.

Olu takes a step back, looking at her in a way that makes her want to take back her words. He speaks softly now, almost whispering.

"Why would you want to rid yourself of your own child?"

"He's not my child," she whispers back. "My sister died."

Mansour shrinks into the darkness of the bedroom. Wonders what has happened to the aunt who wrote to his grandfather, asking for him. Wonders how that woman is the same one that he's been brought to.

Mansour sees Mama disappear from view as she goes to the kitchen. Olu follows her, and Mansour steps out just enough to see them.

Mama is pulling garbage together for disposal. She knots the bags as she sniffles and drags her left hand across her nose. She pulls on her coat and leans beside the bags, against the dingy wallpaper of the old apartment.

"I thought I could earn enough to take care of him. I really thought I could give him..." She stops herself, stifling her emotions. "It's good." She wipes her eyes. "It will be good for him. They will give him food and clothes. It's no less than what I have done."

She gazes up at Olu. Her eyes look like they have been emptied of something, are now as fresh as they are cold. Then she opens the door and closes it behind her.

When she is gone, Olu stands in the dark and looks around the apartment as if he's just arrived. He paces the dirty rug, squats on it, and feels the fibers with a large gentle hand.

"Mansour," he calls, perceiving the boy from the corner of his eye. He turns to face him.

"Listen to me. The schoolmaster tried to buy you. He asked me what I would charge for you." Olu looks at the boy, who stares back, unmoving. "They are not all bad people. But the man in charge there is not good. Do you understand?"

Mansour does not speak, and Olu stands from where he's been squatting, and Mansour watches the man's enormous shoes print the pattern of his soles onto the rug. He watches the man pick up Mama's glass of water from the armrest of the plastic-covered sofa. The man drinks it down and stands at the window with his hands half in his pockets and elbows outturned. All the wrinkles seem to fall from his clothes, and he seems to be whole and perfect again.

Anticipating something that he cannot bear to see, Mansour closes his eyes, savoring the man for the last time.

He goes to put his fingers to his ears but finds that he wants to hear. He wants to remember this moment, these sounds: The leather briefcase squeaking as it's lifted from the plastic sofa cover. The man's hand cupping his cheek. Then the sound of footsteps moving away . . . steady and then unsteady, steady and then unsteady, steady and gone.

45. FOR THE FIRST TIME since they'd become a family with Olu, Mansour wakes up to the scent of the incense pot. The smoke of thiouraye is thick enough to make him wonder if he's dreaming. The traffic outside seems particularly loud, and more light than usual is coming through the windows, revealing fingerprints on the dirty glass and browning leaves on the houseplants. He realizes that he and Mama are usually not home at this time of day.

She's set a place for Mansour to eat alone at the couch as she used to do before Olu arrived in their lives and insisted that they all eat together. This is when Mansour begins to mourn, knowing for certain that life has reverted to what it had been before.

Sitting in Olu's chair, Mama's prayer beads move rapidly through her fingers as her lips silently mutter a name of God. She is looking right into Mansour's eyes, but he can tell from the awe in them that it is not him she sees. Mansour watches her eyes return to him—the look she always gives him: expectation, as her spiritual ecstasy comes down.

Olu's leftover newspapers remain on the breakfast table and there's a half-eaten plate of breakfast that Mama hasn't finished. Her head tips downward and her breathing becomes heavy.

Mama snaps her fingers, pointing to the plate of food that waits for him. He sits, eating alone, and he feels his lips quivering as he raises the omelet to them. When he tries to open his mouth, he wants to wail, so he closes it as tightly as he can again, presses his lips together until he goes numb.

At the French restaurant, where Mansour goes back to spending many hours now that Olu is not there to look after him at home, the cook who gives him madeleines tells him that fasting makes dreams stronger. It brings the mind closer to the mysteries of the universe.

Mansour stands for forty minutes in the crowded shop of a popular seamstress while Mama sits near the storefront window trying on gloves she can't afford. He struggles to keep his tired arms outstretched as the woman measures him for the fitting of a jacket.

"You're a most lucky boy."

Her cross necklace rests on his head as she bends over him to complete the measurements.

"Nobody gets to sing for that choir."

Once the measurements are taken, Mama takes him next door to the barber.

"Is this how you want it to be?" the barber says to Mama, perplexed by his own work when he's finished with Mansour's head. It's something between a lopsided Afro and a Mohawk. Mama holds her chin at the mess with squinted eyes. Then she takes the clippers from the man's hand and shaves Mansour's head herself.

His head is cold then, so she buys him a hat and they head home.

The next day, they begin their long journey to the Catholic school. Mama drives her car to the train station, and Mansour watches the

sun change places, lets all the heat and light sting him sweetly in the
eyes.

When they arrive, she shakes the whole way from the street to the
cathedral's enormous front doors and hesitates before them. Facing a
failure so complete. She is giving him away. The very thing she'd
begged her father not to do. The very thing she's come to Europe to
impede. And to a church. When they were through with him, what
would he believe about himself? About God? Or her? She looks back
at the boy, who is some paces behind, his mouth tight, his eyes carefully
blank and swollen. It seems that he heard something of her words with
Olu, has been wary of her ever since, and she wonders how much he
remembers Kiné. But in his silence, in the blankness of his expression,
she cannot tell what he has understood. They'd been different, not as
close, when he finally arrived in Europe. But Mama thought that
maybe, over time, they might be close once more. But she knows now,
with this decision, that he will never see her as he once did, that he will
never again prefer her arms to anyone else's.

X.

THE DEATH OF CARL KEIFER
(PART THREE)

New York, 1968

46. **MANSOUR'S VOICE TEARS** as he screams down to Keifer from Liam's window: "*You're costing us gigs!*"

"*Nigger, I put you on! Get out of here, I put you on—*"

"Keep it down out here!" Liam's interjection does no good.

"You put on *you*! All this jazz, jazz, jazz. It was never jazz, that was never our sound!"

"You're not hearing me! I brought you around my wife—my family!—and the one thing I asked you to do, the only thing I asked you to do, was to never bring Gil Rodney—"

First there is the sound.

A startling pop that competes with the passing train in volume. Did a basketball explode? Was a firecracker lit? Liam peers at the dark for a clue until Keifer gasps like he's caught a chill in his spine. One small sigh. Baby-innocent, like a sneeze. And then, as if pushed into a cartwheel by a ghost, he collapses sideways. He's been shot.

Reflexively, Liam fires with a shaky hand into the direction of the shooter: a shadow with gray eyes. Liam goes mad with adrenaline shooting, shooting, shooting thrice, the fired gun scorching his palm.

Mansour flies down the building's winding staircase, fighting through the screaming tenants as they flood the steps.

But he freezes on the sidewalk, at the sight of Liam backing away from Keifer's body. Liam pulls Mansour with him, but the African resists and waits with the dying man.

Because of his stillness, his silence, Liam cannot tell if the African is mourning the American or waiting to be certain that he truly is no more.

Mansour takes the train uptown to Vanessa and stands outside the house, unable to enter. Keifer would have been twenty-seven in six days.

Mansour looks up at the house from the street. There are lights flashing through the stained-glass windows, projecting a rainbow onto the black night, and he knows that Keifer's stepdaughters have snuck downstairs to watch cartoons.

Carl Keifer. His second brother. Who called him *nigger* out of love. Who made a bed for him in his great-grandfather's house on Strivers' Row.

After Keifer's body is taken, Gil Rodney sits on the bed in Liam's apartment. Mansour stands against the front door, his arms still bearing the weight of Vanessa's body. He lets himself slide to the ground.

He'd knocked on the side door to the house so the girls wouldn't hear, and when he told Vanessa, she gritted her teeth, gripping his forearms deeply enough to draw blood.

"Don't let me fall," she'd muttered. "Don't let me fall." And he'd held her up. She didn't make a sound, shaking violently in his arms, and then, abruptly, turning so stiff that he'd shouted her name. She'd forced a hand against his mouth to spare the children.

He'd cradled her on the ground, her eyes even, gazing at him with a look that was not peace but had peace's stillness. She'd asked him what was taking the sun so long.

Now, the three men sit in silence with the lights off.

"It was the same guy who stuck me up at the subway. Same guy at the store. I think he wanted *you*," he says to Mansour. "He must've thought Keifer was you." There is stunned silence again.

"Did you kill him?" Gil asks, eying their apartment door.

"I don't know . . ." Liam shakes his head, near tears. "I saw him on the gurney . . . he was bloody . . . he was so bloody . . . I don't know." Liam put his head in his hands.

Gil moves to the door of the apartment and slides the lock shut, listening closely to the voices from down below, in the streets. There is a crowd growing louder. He knows from experience how fast this night can turn even worse.

He looks at Mansour.

"You gotta go," Gil says. Mansour looks up at Gil, sees his face wet from tears. "Get a plane to Paris soon as you can. This town isn't safe for you."

"Paris?" Liam says.

"And you gotta find somewhere else to be tonight. They'll be looking for you." Gil watches the crowd gathering in the street from the window, the young Irish American men patrolling the sidewalk with their baseball bats in hand.

Gil ignores the brothers' bewilderment. This isn't the time to explain America again.

"You can't stay by me, but I'll take you where you're goin'."

"We don't have anywhere else to go," Liam says helplessly.

"Find somewhere!" Gil yells. "I'll be in the alley. You got ten minutes."

He shuts the door after himself.

Liam looks at Mansour. It takes Mansour a second to catch on.

"No. Not her."

"We don't have a choice!"

They pack their few possessions in the dark. Under streetlights, Mansour and Liam rush into the alley, their duffle bags over their shoulders, but Gil Rodney has already pulled off. They chase the silver car for half a block, banging the trunk when it's finally in reach. Rodney stops short, and the men climb inside, panting. Gil turns down his headlights.

"So what's it gonna be?"

"His girlfriend lives at the old folks' home in Fort Greene," Liam says, out of breath. Mansour shoots him a look.

"I'm sorry. Do you have someone else in mind?" Liam snaps.

47. **ONCE THEY'VE SETTLED IN,** Liam asks after the food they can smell in Bonnie's warm apartment: mustard greens with onion, roasted potatoes and trout, black-eyed peas and basmati rice. Lazier versions of her grandmother's recipes that Bonnie's prepared for herself, cooking again for the first time since Sylvia's passing. Mansour had been by once before. And as soon as he'd entered, she'd felt like a stranger in her own house. His presence made everywhere feel bigger and more playful. A freshness that still lingers about the place and has been renewed with his return.

She warms the food for them but tells them they'll have to clean up. Mansour does not eat much, quickly going out the front door and staying away for a while. Long enough to make Liam and Bonnie uneasy. Liam seems fine at first; they debate the outcome of the *Perry Mason* episode while he completes his assigned chore of sweeping up. But soon, he cannot hide the way his hands are shaking, so violently that he cannot grip the broom.

She helps him to the guest-room bed. When she asks him what is wrong, all he can manage, still shaking, is, "Our pianist is dead."

Now she is relieved to hear him snoring peacefully, loudly enough that the sound reaches her in the living room. But Liam's disposition only heightens her worry for Mansour.

When he finally returns, hours later, Bonnie is still sitting on the living room couch. She is not sprawled but sitting up and tight on her feet like the Sphinx. The room is dark, lit only by the street and a weird glow from the television. She will not look at him.

"The dishes are waiting for you," she says and adds nothing more. He moves into the kitchen, quiet.

After listening to him for a while, trying to come up with a way to make him talk, she goes in and sits on the counter across from Mansour, watching him dry the last bowls, hoping he'll speak first.

He dries her bowls so expertly, in steady circles, the dish towel flung across his shoulder in between wipes. He's organizing her sloppy cabinets in the process, fitting everything in size order.

"I'm impressed. I expected you to fail miserably at this," she says.

"At washing dishes?" he answers without turning around, wiping down the sink.

"You really know your way around a kitchen. Do African men cook or something?"

Mansour laughs at this question, one *ha* and turns to face her, crosses his arms, studying her for a while.

"Why are you looking at me like that?" she says.

"How am I looking at you?"

"I don't know, like I'm the one who came to your door at 4:00 a.m. and never said a word more about it."

Mansour's eyes drop. He fidgets with the dishcloth over his shoulder.

She whispers, "Liam's a wreck."

"He told you?"

"All he said was that your pianist died. Mansour, just tell me. What happened?"

"Our pianist was murdered. And we're not safe here anymore. We gotta go."

"Go where?"

"Home," he says, wiping the counter again but already miles away.

His new coldness feels spiteful, like he's punishing her for something and she is supposed to guess what she's done. But it is strange, the way he looks at Bonnie, a desperate, weightless expression, like he might collapse on the ground or float up to the ceiling in perfect peace.

"And what are you gonna do?" he says, wiping the clean counter again, jittery. "You told me you got fired. What are you gonna do?"

She doesn't answer the question, gives him a piece of his own medicine. She pulls his bracelet off her wrist, extends it to him. "I forgot I was still wearing this."

"Keep it."

She shakes her head, keeps her arm outstretched.

He approaches her, and she feels a jolt, a little hiccup, when he stands between her legs.

"Just keep it."

Under the merciless, off-brand bulbs of the kitchen fixtures, he appears more hardened to Bonnie than he seemed before. The muscles along his face look firm and tense. He seems to have lived a lot more life than her though they are close in years. She can tell that he's high. And that he has erected a boundary between them. And she worries now that she has never seen him beyond his stage performance. That they've shared nothing more than the circumstantial banter that might occur between two strangers. How, she wonders, do people manage to truly get close?

He still won't take the bracelet back, so she puts it on the counter and hops down, heading for the door. When he blocks her, she closes her eyes, and it feels even worse in her chest than she'd anticipated when she whispers for him to move. Head down, he does. She tells him that there's a blanket for him on the couch. He thanks her and smiles a little smile. And then, though she doesn't know why, she tells him to turn out the kitchen lights. Or why she rests on the wall, waiting for him to come closer. Soon an arm on the wall on either side of her. But why, instead of kissing him, does she whisper for him to keep the TV low if he intends to watch it before bed? His hot hands finding her waist in the dark as she whispers for him to double-check the lock on the front door before lying down to sleep. Grazing his arms with the backs of her hands, then the front while he watches, silently. Then she is the silent one, watching him slide his cold bracelet back on her right wrist, before she crosses out of the kitchen door, she locks herself in her bedroom, watching Mansour's shadow give and take, give and take, give and take light from her room as it moves beneath her door.

48. THE EVENING BEFORE their flight, and two days
after his murder, Carl Keifer Rodney is buried beside
his grandfather. Vanessa asked Mansour to sing "Amazing Grace,"
but he cannot move beyond the very edge of the burial grounds. He
holds himself up on the thick limbs of the evergreens, his head tilted
toward the earth as he listens to the music of the funeral: only horns,
six of them, performing a medley composed by Gil that replaced any
need for speeches. The four movements titled "Birth," "Boyhood,"
"Fatherhood," "Divinity."

As he walks with Liam through the mud back to the car, Mansour
hears Gil scream. The sound never leaves him. It births his new musical direction.

In the twilight hours before they leave for their flight, Liam and
Mansour return to gather their things. Bonnie lets both of them in but
only speaks to Liam, and she turns sullen when Liam knocks on her
bedroom door at two in the morning and says what she knew was
coming.

"You should lock up. We're heading out."

It had been nice to have them around. The company, even at a distance, made the apartment more tenable. Despite her troubles with Mansour, she follows them out onto the Brooklyn street. In their haste to leave, they have no real luggage, just duffle bags (it perplexes her how men can wear the same things all the time), waiting for a cab they called that's running late.

She's standing on the steps of her building in her bathrobe, waiting with them like they're children.

The cab pulls up, and Mansour gets in without saying a word to her. She swallows it down, hugs Liam goodbye, and walks back up the steps.

Back inside, she lets the morning news keep her distracted. But that old feeling she's known so well is growing wide and loud. Even as she's focused, and determined not to be overcome, staring away from it with all her might, that ravenous emptiness calls her away from life, from people, claiming her always for itself.

The door opens and she jumps. She hadn't locked it. She feels the weight of his footsteps as he approaches the couch. He's breathing hard, like he's about to sing.

"Come with me," Mansour says.

There's something she needs to do before they leave. The taxi runs the meter while she packs.

"I have to go in there," she says very quietly, staring at the door across from them. She leans back into Mansour, her ear close enough to kiss. He whispers into it.

"Was that her room?"

She nods, and he takes her hand. With his grip firm, he walks them forward. Her hand shakes as Mansour guides it to the knob and, together, they twist open the door to Sylvia's room.

Without turning on the light, she touches everything, lets her hand slide across the teacup wallpaper, peeling off the dust that has gathered on Richard Wright and Alexandre Dumas on the bookshelf, her grandmother's sweaters and suits, the dead plants, Sylvia's dolls, the tall mahogany bedposts, the curtains with no lace. She sits on the bed in the dark and notices that the room has no scent but dust, but dirt, but decay. Life does end. So completely.

In a strange way, she feels relief. That her grandmother is not a ghost, not stuck in the ether, not trapped between worlds, in a scent, or hair strands, or fingerprints.

It is all just dust. And it is up to Bonnie to inhale it or blow it away.

PART
THREE

I.

REPATRIATED EXPATRIATES

France, 1968

49. **THEY LAND AT** Charles de Gaulle a little before midnight. A hard landing that makes the plane lights flicker and some overhead luggage tumble, the passengers' cussing quickly turning into applause as the plane hits ground. Bonnie yanks her seatbelt off, standing while the plane parks. She searches the bowed heads of the passengers until she finds Mansour toward the rear. Liam, some seats behind him, has somehow slept through the landing, his head resting forward on the seat before him. Bonnie raises her hand to catch Mansour's attention.

He calls to her across the plane. "Bienvenue chez moi."

She tries to smile back, but her last time in Paris is on her mind.

She loses Mansour and Liam at the crowded baggage claim, distracted by the sound of a roaring plane engine, the sight of people boarding, and the memories this scene awakens: the texture of her mother's skin, soft and slippery from a mix of sweat and powder. The kiss that Bonnie didn't know was a goodbye. Her mother walking down the tarmac away from her. Mansour finds her a half hour later sitting in the middle of the airport floor. When he comes down on the ground beside her and asks what's wrong, she tells him that the flight made her motion sick.

And then, as they leave the airport, as she and Mansour say goodbye to Liam and go their own way across town, she watches from the metro-car window and feels herself being pulled back in time. A return to Claudine's burnt pots of rice, her absence for days at a time from their apartment, liquor bottles clinking in the trash, the living room covered in stacks of thick paper. If it was not city forms and files, it was newspapers; if it was not newspapers, it was coupons she was planning to clip; if it was not coupons, it was tissue paper, paper bags, and old gloves she intended to repurpose.

The past keeps flooding her mind, so when Mansour closes the door to this apartment he's subletting from an old friend and she hears it shut, she isn't sure if she wants to stay.

"Water?" he asks her. She doesn't answer, but he fills a cup anyway, after splashing his own head and face at the sink. She wanders over to the living room window and pushes back the lace curtain, heavy from grease. It reveals a pale night, metro tracks, telephone poles, and wires.

She watches from the wall with crossed arms. Mansour moves quickly about the place. He's already barefoot, pulling a couch into the center of the floor, scraping dried food from the furniture, discarding the old baby clothes that someone left in the kitchen sink. He lights a cigarette, turns a toy truck upside down for an ashtray. In seconds, it seems, he has made the place his own. "May I?" he says, and when she nods with a slight smile, he unpacks her record player from its case at the door, setting it on the coffee table. From his own collection, she watches him pull Sly Stone from the sleeve, the cigarette flickering between his lips.

They dance until they're dizzy, sweaty, falling back on the couch as the record ends. She lifts the stylus, slides the record gingerly back into the sleeve.

She's out of breath. "That's all you got?"

"What?" he pants.

"You peter out quick."

"The record's over"

"There's still the B-side," she teases.

Slouching on the couch with a knee up, he watches with a quiet chuckle as she treats the record with the tenderness one might show to a small child. She wipes the space before she places it carefully on the empty shelf, then throws her handkerchief over the record player.

He invites her to sit beside him by banging the sofa twice. She plops down. They smoke, watching the room from opposite ends, losing themselves in the darkness.

The building is eerily quiet above and below, not even the sound of a floorboard bending, not a kettle's whistle or a radio. The silence reveals the mystery between them. It occurs to her that she's traveled across the world with someone she hardly knows.

"You don't like this city," he says. "I can tell."

She shrugs. "Do *you*?"

"I *know* it, anyway," he says.

"Why not Senegal? Don't you know it better?"

He shakes his head. She is desperately curious about the continent but hesitant to ask him more, doesn't want him to close up again.

"Tell me about Senegal." She dares to pry again, gathering cigarette ashes on the tip of her tongue.

He is silent so long that she's surprised when he answers.

"There's a lot of rice." His brow furrows as if the memory is vague. "*Rice?*"

"Yeah, rice. That's what I remember most." He observes the surprise on her face and playfully rubs her hair, fuzzing up the pin curls she'd been so proud of. He gets up from the couch, and she doesn't see him again until morning.

SOKHNA AND THE TALIBÉ

Senegal, 1955

50. **THE RICE MAKES** a mountain well above his head. And were it not for the pile's utter enormity, Mansour's hunger would've only been hunger; it would have never become rage at the plenty, and certainly not the kind that made him think of running away, a third time, after everything that had happened before. He's walking better now. His foot is still twisted at the ankle from the Marabout's grip—but at least the man's tooth is missing from his left hook. And seven-year-old Mansour's tears turned to laughter when an older talibé told him that teeth do not grow back, that the Marabout's smile would look like a messed-over corn cob for the rest of his life.

Mansour takes the canister full of rice and cubed sugar from around his neck, pouring his day's work onto the pile, but not before he sneaks a fist full of the raw rice into his mouth, looking over his shoulder, quickly brushing the crumbs across his torn shorts before the Marabout or the other talibés arrive.

Maybe he'll work later tonight with his best friend, a savant who memorized the Qur'an at the age of six, or maybe even with one of the older talibés with broken limbs who are harmless but good for protection. Otherwise, Mansour doesn't like to beg in groups. His voice always yields the best tips, the most rice, the most sugar, and some of the older boys keep him by his shirt, dragging him from corner to corner, until their pockets are full of change and they can be guaranteed a

night without a beating. He is still small, short for his age, and seldom
the one to best the others in the fights over cash and rice. He's learned
to become discreet. The talibés do not go beyond the Catholic church
that divides the white and Black sides of Saint-Louis, but between the
seamshops, the canopied marketplaces, and the taxi ports, they still
have plenty of room to roam.

His feet are still pulsing, sandy and raw from begging barefoot on the
hot asphalt. Outside of the outhouse, he waits for a girl-orphan to bring
him a pail of water to bathe in. She is walking proudly, in that rhythm
girls have as if time ought to be glad to wait for them. She stops short
before she reaches him.

"Ndox amul." *There is no water*, she says.

He tells her that she's lying. He saw a line of children bathe not long
before. But the girl leans on her leg, pointing to the pump.

"Pompu ndox mi dafa yàqu" *It's broken*, she says, and she walks
away. When he tries his hand at the pump himself, and hears from the
pathetic squeak that the well is indeed dry, he knows he has no choice
but to try and steal some water, at least a cup to drink, from the broken
faucet outside of the mechanic shop next door.

Mansour takes his chances, slipping expertly through the sliver of
the spaced-out fence made of rusty slabs of iron. He rushes to the
mechanic's pump. For some reason, the flow, typically a stingy drip, is
for once a steady drizzle. In his excitement, he puts his mouth over the
faucet, savoring a whole mouthful of tepid water.

Then he must get back on the street, incanting prayers for whoever
will pay, until the bats begin to congregate in the trees. How he envies
them, the way they sleep so comfortably, smiling blue-black faces poking out from the cotton budding on the trees. He once knew what it
meant to feel that way, nestling in the mahogany bed at his grandfather's house.

When Mama Eva left for Paris, he had been folded back into the rhythm of his grandfather's house easily, finding his peers—a dozen cousins, and neighbors around his age. Running with them through the home's large courtyard, going with them to the beach. Remembering Kiné, he would not go near the water, but he loved getting under the hot sand, letting his playmates stack it on his body until only his head was poking out.

Home life as a child of the house—loved, and cared for at a distance—had gone on well until the tutor arrived. The tutor was a tall man, only eighteen. He had been commissioned by Mansour's grandfather to teach the science of reciting prayers—Tajwid—to the teenagers of the house. Mansour was only four years old, but on overhearing teacher's instructions, he would rush into the house and stand in the doorway. Face sandy from a game of tag, he imitated the sounds he was hearing, completely oblivious to the unusual quality of his voice. It had a rare richness that prompted the admiration of the tutor and a report to his boss, the Marabout. When approached now, a second time, about sending Mansour to join the order—a gift through which to derive blessings—his grandfather agreed.

He's running late now, but he doesn't want The Lady to see him dirty, so he takes the time to rinse his shirt under the faucet and put it back on wet.

She's his favorite new patron, and he tries to see her first, right after bathing, hoping that one day she might finally ask him to stay with her. The pretty woman has only been in town for a little more than a week, which, from the long days he keeps, feels like a month; in that time, he's gone by her room every day. Sometimes he returns to her at the end of the day too.

When he first spotted her, he knew to slip into a gap between the buildings, under the guise of peeing, so that the others would not follow him. He waited until the other talibés had wandered on and crossed the street. On her is where he smelled alcohol for the first time—a nauseating scent—so when she turned and he saw her beauty, he felt for the first time that his mind had betrayed his senses.

"Sarax ngri Yàlla." *Please give unto God*, he'd said, approaching her in the store. The woman took his hands and pushed them up to the counter. She'd slid her change into them. He noted the red on her nails. The shiny fabric of her pencil skirt. It reminded him of the way colors looked when he closed his eyes and let the sun heat his eyelids.

He'd heard the other talibés before he saw them enter. They prayed raucously, talking over one another, their extended hands overlapping in a pile before the woman, who was soon overwhelmed, digging deeply in her purse as the man behind the counter rolled his eyes.

"If you keep giving, they're gonna keep coming."

That was a week ago, and as he walks to where she's staying (a third-floor suite at the pilot hotel across the road), he wishes that he could stay there all day, that he didn't have to beg until dark.

He knocks on the door. This time, the white man answers. It is the first time Mansour has seen him on his feet. He is short. Up close, his gray lifeless complexion scares Mansour, so he stands back. Mansour looks to the side of the man for The Lady.

"Sarax ngri Yàlla," he says.

"That boy's here again," the man says before leaving the door open and slowly climbing back into the large bed. Mansour wants to press on the mattress, to feel its softness after years of not having a bed of his own. As the man steps away, Mansour sees The Lady across the room. She knots a cloth belt at the waist of her fitted yellow dress with green flowers, her lips bright red.

"Salam Alaikum," she says, "jigesil, duggal." *Enter*, and he does. She gestures for him to come closer.

Having seen the man's illness for the first time, Mansour finally understands the cause for her welcoming of him. She's needs his prayers; she has not taken a personal interest in him after all. He swallows his disappointment and begins to recite the Fatiha. The man motions for him to stop.

"Just pay him so he'll go," he says wearily. "There's no point." The woman caresses his back. The man's body flattens, his breathing deepens, he groans.

"Ngóor si, yaa ngi woy ne malaaka." *You have the voice of an angel, young man.* The man says in Wolof, perfect Wolof, surprising Mansour, who's never spoken to a white person before. "But I'm holding off on hearing that sound for as long as I can," the man continues. "I used to be more fun, believe me," he laughs into a cough as The Lady smiles softly, first at him and then Mansour. Her hands continue to rub his back in a circle.

Mansour is eager to leave, but The Lady whispers to him, "Wait."

The man on the bed coughs again. His body quakes afterward like a sounding gong. The woman unties the yellow scarf from her neck and puts it on her head, knots it at her chin, and puts her hands together in prayer.

"What harm could it do?" she says as her husband watches her.

"Muslims open their hands, Sokhna," is all he says before turning over again. So she opens her hands.

51. **ON THIS STRANGE** anniversary, hours from their home in Dakar, a week and a half in Saint-Louis, the place where they first met nearly fifteen years ago, there is evidence that Sokhna's husband, who has been mostly bedridden, has finally gone out, though not far: the trail of muddy footprints from the shower to the bed, maps of Saint-Louis unfolded on the table and sprinkled with flakes of chocolate croissants. The morning had been a good morning. Ever since the talibé's prayers the night before, for the first time in eight months, they'd been intimate again.

They've already spent three days in the room together, bewildering housekeeping with the curtains drawn. She needed her body to herself for a while, and she hopes that perhaps, since he's feeling better, they can spend the day about the city.

Sokhna finds Claude at the estuary, shivering in the pleasant morning weather. He's watching flamingos sink their jaws into the sand for sardines and come up empty.

"They'll fly away soon," he says, taking her hand, tickling the inside of her palm. "There's no food here."

She is taller than him, so she can kiss the smooth middle of his head. The pale veins swell when her lips press against them. His veins are bluer, skin grayer, turning transparent. She closes her eyes against the salty air, erasing these changes from her mind.

They take a tour of the old French quarter on a horse-drawn carriage. The young man giving the tour cannot get a word in as Claude comes alive, identifying the stores and shops they pass. He brings their guide to a dumb, adolescent silence. "This old man once lived in a world they could only imagine," Claude says. Back in the true colonial days, when the town was also the capital of Mauritania. "When it sparkled with the promise of what Africa could be," he says.

"This was a bar. A good bar too," he says, his eyes glistening by the lights of the crowded street. They pass a bodega, where a woman in an unraveling hijab roasts peanuts on the front step.

Claude asks the driver to get them some.

"Do you want some peanuts, love?" he asks Sokhna, as he always asks her things, in a way that isn't really a question. She knows that she doesn't need to answer. She only smiles and wipes a trace of her lipstick from his cheek.

The carriage driver calls to the woman selling peanuts, and her price is low, so Claude asks for an extra pound.

"He wants more!" the carriage driver calls over.

"I hope they're not rotten for that price," Claude says.

"They're the best nuts in the city," the young man retorts.

"Let's have a look first," Claude says. Sokhna follows him to the woman's stand. When he reaches into the roasted peanuts, the woman pushes him back.

"Ay yo lanla?!" *What's the matter with you?!*

"I'm checking the quality!"

Two men approach and stand in between Claude and the woman, defending her.

"C'est quoi le problème, monsieur?"

"I want to check the quality of her peanuts. The price is too low."

Claude goes to put his hand in again, and one of the young men pushes it away, just as the woman had before, but his force is stronger and Claude shuffles backward, nearly falling to the ground.

Sokhna is facing away from them all, taking a swig from her flask, looking into the street, where the lights of the bridge have caught her attention. The carriage driver calls out from the front seat.

He hops down from the carriage, going over to break up the commotion.

Sokhna looks over to where her husband has now overturned the woman's first batch of peanuts onto the ground. Claude recedes from the small angry crowd.

"White man, you are a guest here. *Go home!*" a woman shouts.

Claude immediately retorts, "I was born here! This is my country too!"

Sokhna grabs her husband by the arm, dragging him away. He's out of breath, spent, by the time they return to the carriage.

He rests his head in Sokhna's narrow lap. His eyes are on the blackening sky. She can feel his whole body vibrating. Their driver returns, and the tour continues.

They are a ways away from the peanut stand before Claude stills. As the sky grows darker, his gray eyes become brighter. They seem to Sokhna like two perfect full moons.

"It was all planes then," he says. "Do you remember the plane ride we took?"

"Yes, love. I remember."

They are back in Saint-Louis for the first time since her father's funeral three years ago, and as the carriage driver turns the corner, he passes the church where it took place. Sokhna grips Claude's hand harder. He gently presses her fingers open and tickles her palm until she smiles.

Sohkna's father and Claude had become good friends over the years. Perhaps too good. When Sokhna sat, one summer night, in the kitchen of her mother's bakery, watching the baguettes rise and brown in the open hearth, her mother blamed Claude for her divorce earlier that year.

"He'd rather be anywhere else than home ... first with that plane and now with Toubab." She sucked her teeth.

As his illness progressed, her father had insisted that he did not intend to die in the hospital, that he wanted to live whatever remained of his life free, so one day Claude drove him out to the countryside, Sokhna in the passenger seat. Sokhna knew how much her father delighted in the dynamic between her and Claude. The way Claude listened to her tangents. The way he didn't dismiss or indulge her.

Some miles from Louga, they pulled off the road into the desolate, arid landscape to rest. It had no water for miles, an open terrain divided only by the occasional baobabs, often ninety feet tall—the heights of Adam and Eve, according to local residents. For some reason, her father fell in love with the place at first sight. She watched him take in, with great inspiration, what looked to her like nothing but infertile earth.

Sokhna, in search of whatever was delighting him, began to wander the land too. That's when she spotted a family of rhinos. The baby waddled clumsily, colliding with the mother's flank. Sokhna didn't realize how deep into the bush she'd gone until she heard her father's voice, so small, calling to her from across the way:

"Perhaps you should ask your husband for permission before running about the world," he'd teased. Sokhna turned and saw Claude, who was close enough to hear, turning even redder than the African sun had already burned him.

Over the last years of her father's life, he and Claude built two long, sable-colored mansions on this arid land. The houses began as towering alien structures on either side of the same dirt road. A corner store, roadwork, and a water system followed, and within a decade, several families arrived. When they were drunk, the two men liked to argue about which one of them had founded the town, about whether or not their homes would be finished before the country descended into the chaos of independence from France.

Tonight, fifteen years later, Claude asks to see it again.

And the carriage driver, who is renting his horse from the local Marabout and is not supposed to take it more than a fifteen-mile radius from the French quarter, looks back at Sokhna in disbelief.

She shrugs and mouths, "Please."

They agree upon a price for the young man to take them overnight through three towns to the village to see their homes.

As they leave the city for the bush, the terrain quiets and Claude drifts off to sleep. The loudest sounds are his wheezing and the bluesy rhythm of the stallion's stride. Sokhna peels open the collar of Claude's shirt, hoping to cool him down, but closes it quickly when she sees the grayness of his skin. Death whispering. The plane fuel, the inhalation of the fumes day in and day out, had given him and her father the same cancer. Why them and not her? She examines her eyes all the time for the yellowing her father suffered. The fear that she too has been poisoned keeps her restless. She panics when she has no appetite or cannot recall simple things.

The driver's voice interrupts her thoughts.

"He's your . . . employer?" he asks.

"My husband," she replies fiercely, insulted by the insinuation.

The carriage vibrates as they cross rockier ground. It reminds her of when Claude would come to see her at her mother's house. As he landed his plane, it rattled the china in the cupboards, lifted the pages of the books from her lap, and, her favorite part, made her tutor wait for Claude to hit the ground before continuing the physics lecture.

"I think we're here," the driver announces the next morning, but Sokhna, still half asleep, isn't sure.

There is so much development, the town so full of life, that it's difficult to spot their properties. Children in blue uniforms, filing through an unpainted concrete gate into a school; women behind wooden tables, selling breakfast to construction workers.

"There they are!" Claude says, somehow immediately spotting the buildings. He pulls her along as he rushes inside.

They have no keys with them, so he breaks the glass of a side window. The air of the house is stale, the floors and furniture are browned with several layers of dust, but everything, even two unfinished cups of scotch, are still where Claude and her father left them three years ago.

Later, she hears Claude's voice calling from the bedroom. It has no door—just a curtain, holding place for the handcrafted one from Bamako that never arrived.

"What's taking you so long? Come here, love." His voice sputters into a husky cough. "Come here . . ."

She sits beside him and reaches for his cheek, hoping for softness (a cheek must be soft). But the illness his conquered there too, leaving it leathery and hard. No place on his body is safe. Everywhere is an echo of death. She takes her hands away, keeping them safe in her lap. And he, from the look in his eyes, heartbroken but wise, understands. He touches her instead. But soon, in his weakness, her flesh is too smooth to grip. He's apologizing for far more than his weakness as he lets her slide through his hands.

She lies beside Claude, watching him sleep. Then she stands up from the bed in a sudden panic and stares, looking down between him and the dust. Claude and the dust. He is sprawled wide and peaceful. Not a sneeze or a cough. She considers for the first time that he might be done with living. Happier with the earth.

52. **AFTER YEARS WITHOUT USE,** the bathroom faucet spits out a roach before clear water flows. Dressed in Claude's shirt and jeans after bathing, she steps out into the night with wet braids. Letting the clay wall of their house warm her back, watching the frogs hop high from puddle to puddle, she stumbles on a thought that comforts her: her talibé. His words had been the only thing that made a difference. She believes this, even though she would never say it aloud. Doctors had done them no good, but after the boy had incanted whatever he'd incanted, for the nights that followed, she'd become blind to the changes in her husband's skin; her passion and peace had been briefly restored. And though today the spell has expired, the protective blindness has dissipated, and death seems omnipresent, she is hopeful that the peace could be summoned again. Even if Claude is through wrestling death, fighting its grip on their lives, she is not.

―――――

The next day, Sokhna returns to Saint-Louis alone in search of the talibé. Claude, possessed by some strange solace, refuses to leave their dirty village house. The maid Sokhna has hired is overwhelmed within an hour. The weight of the dust from the bedroom alone has warped and ruined her broom.

Sokhna does not know where to find the boy (where do talibés live?), knows only that his name is Mansour. She knew it as the name of a Persian mystic who was known for spontaneous spiritual trances, who was said to have lit four hundred oil lamps in Jerusalem with the touch of his thumb.

She cannot remember Mansour's face exactly, but as she looks at the boys outside the boutique where she first met him, she knows that he is not here. She spends the afternoon in the lobby of the Pilot Hotel, where he visited her and Claude, but he never shows. Around sunset, under the fans at the hotel bar, she wearily watches the street for him, the scraps of her hope leaking out now with her sweat. Her head rests sideways on the counter between her two empty wine glasses. She is staring at a building across the way that looks like a jail. It was once the force-feeding chambers for the Atlantic-bound enslaved who protested their fate through self-imposed starvation. When the bartender comes by, announcing, again, the dinner specials, she waves him away.

From the bar, she hears the Adhan called from the local mosque, announcing Maghrib. For its overwhelming volume, it is a sound so common that it would not have pulled her attention, save for the voice incanting it. She knows it is the boy. She gets back on the street, cooler as the sun sets, and, having run, she is there when he, small and barefoot, emerges from the grand white mosque's enormous arch.

For some time, they meet daily. A meal for a prayer at the river. He teaches her the Fatiha's seven verses over seven nights: carving the Arabic letters around the shells steeping in the hot sand. They work a few feet away from the flamingoes that sleep standing on the water. The single leg they stand on is so slender that their fuchsia bodies seem suspended in air. By their third meeting, though he does not ask about Claude, though he hardly says anything, she finds herself reporting to the little boy like a doctor. She tells him when Claude has a spell of energy, racing her around the house. She tells him when Claude takes her out dancing, so renewed, that she is the first to need to sit. But soon, her reports shift. She tells him when Claude can no longer walk the distance from the bedroom to the kitchen without help; she tells him on the day that Claude calls for her from the tub, now needing help to wash himself. She tells him, one day, that Claude will not recover; that day is the day that she tells him everything that happened before.

III.

THE FIRST TIME SHE FLEW A PLANE, SOKHNA WAS THIRTEEN

Senegal, 1940

53. **IT WAS THE AFTERNOON** that she finally con-fronted her father about his illness. It was something she'd overheard her mother discussing on the phone with the doctor the night before.

"I am not sick, Sokhna," he said, his glasses at the bridge of his nose, his mouth full of grilled chicken and rice. "Your mother exaggerates." But his eyes could not meet her eyes, so she knew he was lying.

"Just tell me," she said.

He sighed.

"Just tell me what's going on, Père. I'm strong."

"I know . . . ," he said, looking sadly at his thirteen-year-old daughter and taking his glasses from his nose, placing them down on the table, picking them up again, as if surprised by their weight.

"I know that you are strong. Perhaps it's me." He rubbed his face with both hands and returned his glasses to his nose. "And I was having such a good lunch," he said. She was already weeping, facing the door so that he couldn't see.

Sokhna ran out onto the tarmac where the planes were parked. The men were about painting and repairing planes, and the ground was slick from fuel and water.

From the age of five, and with great protest from her mother, Sokhna would climb into her father's lap and accompany him while he tested commercial and private planes for routine maintenance at the Saint-Louis airport. The rides were usually short, and sometimes, to excite her, he'd do tricks: twisting and rolling the planes in the bright orange sky of the early evenings—military tactics he'd never had a chance to use in combat.

When she could no longer fit with him in the pilot's seat, she sat beside him. She'd gotten used to talking over the engine, venting to him about fickle schoolboys and difficult professors, her mother's strictness and high-pitched voice, and her mother's kitten heels, her mother's hot bakery in the city. She hated dough.

She'd kick off her shoes, pulling her feet into her lap, waiting silently for her favorite moment in the plane ride: when the image of Saint-Louis—a sight ever-softened with red dust, of white and black folks, cars and horses moving slowly through crowded streets—would give way to the Atlantic Ocean, a sparkling, flat jewel that belonged to her and her father alone.

"Be patient with the world, Sokhna. We are not all as swift as you," he would tell her.

And so, on the day that she fled her father's office in tears, upon reaching the tarmac, she instinctively opened the door to his favorite jet: a sparkling Breguet. She kicked off the brake, pulling the small plane out into the open lot. The handle was wet; it still reeked of those chemicals in the yellow buckets the men threw over the planes in the mornings. She lifted the loose, gear and it took her straight into the air, an easy, faultless lift; all the time of watching her father fly had made aviation second nature to her. She was surprised to find herself aboveground so quickly. Then she felt fear.

It was dreary afternoon, and the fog hadn't cleared. The cockpit quickly grew cold, and she became blinded by the thickness of the clouds. She took her hands from the wheel. They were trembling.

Her father had told her once before that the plane could go some ways away.

"How far?" she'd asked.

He'd hesitated to answer. "Not too far."

"How about to Paris?"

"Not unless the pilot was very, very foolish," he'd said, suspecting her.

Now up in the air, on her own for the first time, there was nothing above or below but a piercing whiteness that led to more whiteness, a huge tunnel of loose, whirling clouds that looked to be made from smoke rather than air.

The plane plunged downward, throwing her through the layers of the atmosphere. When the sun pierced through the whiteness, she saw the edge of Mauritania. She knew it by the strip of scant trees that separated it from Senegal. She saw the sparkle of the water as she descended rapidly toward it. She turned the wheel to the left, holding it in place with all her might.

She strained and grunted, keeping the wheel to the left until the plane followed.

When it steadied in the air again, she laughed with relief.

As she landed, she smiled at her father, who was standing with two men on the tarmac.

She opened the door and put her foot to the ground, dizzy, feeling the earth's motion. She laughed again in awe of herself.

Before she could reach for her father, a security man had her by the arm.

"Come with us, miss."

"Where are you taking me? Père!" she screamed.

"You're under arrest, miss," the man said, dragging her inside.

By her father's request, Sokhna was locked into one of the unused offices. The room was dark. There was only a desk and chair and old colonial maps, handwritten and heavily doodled on and edited, zones retraced, extracted, redefined as the country approached independence.

At first, she was too in awe of her feat to contemplate the realities of jail, but then worry settled in. By the time her father entered, claiming that he'd bailed her out on the condition she commit to attending flight school, she agreed.

As her father's condition worsens, Sokhna spends more and more time at the airport. Her mother begrudgingly allows her to forgo most of her sophomore year at Catholic school to complete her flight-school courses.

Each Friday, as soon as her classes are over, she meets him at his office.

"Let's go flying, Père."

One day they go, for what turns out to be the last time, through the clouds. There is very little turbulence, not even any birds about, but her father struggles to bring the plane to an even balance in the sky. They are both silent as he struggles, as if speaking will reveal what both of them can already see.

He turns the plane around well before they reach the water, cutting the journey to half of its usual time. When he lands, they still don't speak. She opens her door and descends. But when she is far away from the plane, she turns back and catches him banging the yoke hard enough to break it, her father's screams muted by the plane's steel body.

54. **THE WORK IN PILOT SCHOOL** doesn't come nearly as easily to her as her high school classes. She studies incessantly to pass the first two courses, Aerodynamics I and II, usually staying up until 4:00 a.m., when she goes into the kitchen to watch her mother and her six bakers separate two hundred eggs in time with the tick of the broken Swiss grandfather clock that her mother keeps around for its beauty. They slice up cold butter into enough cubes to fill a bathtub. Occasionally stirring a pot of ganache, or testing the icing for the correct stiffness, her mother mostly supervises the bakers and completes paperwork at the breakfast table.

Sokhna opens the shuttered window and sits on the deep mahogany ledge, watching from over her mother's shoulder as she checks off inventory in the old thick P&L notebook for the bakery. It's filled with pages of her perfect cursive, without one scratch or blotch of ink. Sokhna's mother, a Martiniquais with her same chestnut complexion, hums old plantation songs that she remembers her own mother humming back in Fort-de-France.

They are songs the enslaved once sung about deliverance. Songs about sky and sun. But the sky and sun are places Sokhna goes to almost every day. She's stared into their infinity, and it bothers her that the songs of the enslaved put so much stock in reaching the sky:

a place no safer, no more welcoming for humankind, no more forgiving than earth.

Still, when neither of them can bear to hear her father vomiting upstairs or coughing through another morning, they hum together to drown out the sound. The maids, two slight Jola women from Thiès who quietly wipe up behind the bakers, have never heard such a sour song. They have never heard of slaves or slavery. They smile and wait for the terrible tune to end.

After she passes her first two courses, Sokhna starts to lose interest in pilot school, her mind drifting again and again to her father, who is stuck in his office across the hall, a senior pilot unable to fly his plane. Every time she hears another engine start outside on the ground, her heart breaks, knowing that it couldn't be him. She spends her bathroom breaks passing his door, looking through the keyhole to make sure he's still alive. Most times he seems like himself, listening to the radio, reading documents. But sometimes she finds him staring straight ahead at nothing. She tries not to overthink, to not read into his recent mood swings, his vomiting, his disinterest in her mother's cooking, as signs that he's slipping away, but sitting in class she can think of nothing else.

Sometimes she falls asleep in class. Other times she calls out answers to every question with a sarcastic response. She turns in assignments early, or not at all, and the instructor is losing patience.

———

The instructor, in his early twenties, has not long returned to Saint-Louis from Paris. Just getting from his apartment—a mosquito-infested bedroom at the top floor of a municipal building—through the unmitigated traffic of the city each morning exhausts him.

He'd been shocked to see Sokhna when he looked out on the first day: a young dark girl in the back row of his class. A class exclusively of men who were at least eighteen: three of them biracial, one of them as dark as her, the rest white.

"Sir, she's quite ... disruptive," the instructor finally says to her father when he meets him one evening.

"Disruptive ..." Sokhna's father could think of no better word to describe the instructor himself, a white man—no—a white *boy*, named Claude, who'd been flown in by the mother country overnight to take his job. He'd expected to be replaced as his symptoms worsened, but he'd hoped to pass the position on to one of the other Wolof men he'd trained for years. Not Claude.

Still, it is his responsibility to mentor the Frenchman, so he does.

"Actually, sir," Claude corrects him the next day as they walk out toward the plane lot, "I'm from Saint-Louis. I was born here."

"My apologies," her father says, with a smirk across his lips, though it was true that Claude's ancestors had first arrived at the town's coast on the *Méduse* in 1816, surviving the shipwreck that killed almost half of the passengers.

Sokhna's father and Claude hear an engine start.

Their eyes go to Sokhna, who is sitting in her father's old plane.

"*Stop! Hey, stop!*" Claude yells.

She doesn't understand that her father has been officially stripped of all flying privileges, nor why, while she sits in his plane, the white man has something to say about it. She doesn't even know that he's talking to her.

"Père, come on!" she calls from the open window. Her father smiles back, but his eyes are empty with sadness. He shakes his head.

"Go with her," he shouts to Claude. The young man turns around, and his gray eyes widen. "Don't worry," her father continues. "She's a far better pilot than you."

Claude approaches the plane, cursing to himself, remembering the warnings of his university roommates in Paris, their anxieties over the chain of African revolutions. "They're taking over now," one had said. "They've lost their heads."

He pounds on Sokhna's window, but she ignores him. He bangs louder, screaming over the engine.

"I have to come with you!"

"*What?*"

"*I have to go with you!*"

She looks at him: wiry and short, a heavy brown bang obscuring his eyes. She turns her attention back to the gears.

He opens the passenger-side door in a huff, slams it shut.

"How's the fuel?"

"Why are you here?" she replies, without looking at him, flicking on the lights.

"Because . . . because I've made a terrible mistake," he says, thinking over his life decisions. "Now check your fuel."

Sokhna looks up.

"Release the—"

"I know, I know," she says, dismissing him.

He's forcing his back against his seat, his shoulders stiff and high at his ears.

But despite himself, he is taken with her. An intense admiration as she, at thirteen, tilts the plane into the air, steering them up into the sky with ease and confidence. A smoother takeoff than he could manage half the time. He's never seen anything like her before. The round wooden beads at the ends of her braids clank on her shoulders as she turns her head to the left and the right, taking in the sky.

She flashes her full smile and says, "Don't look down if you're afraid."

IV.

THE PEOPLE OF THE CAVE

Senegal, 1955

55. **MANSOUR WAS PETRIFIED.** He reeked like the nightly stampedes of stray goats, like the parking lot around the corner where the neighborhood's broken lamps and radios buzzed like a swarm of flies when it rained. He lay awake, side by side with the other talibés, shoulder to shoulder on a plastic mat the length and width of the roofless room. To his right was his friend, the Wolof savant, who'd whispered for hours, trying to talk Mansour out of his plan to run, until he'd exhausted himself and fallen asleep.

Mansour could feel an intense heat at the backs of his eyeballs, his lips moving as he rehearsed his way out of their room, past the Marabout's bedroom, up the cement wall, over the barbed wire, and into the road. With his bag containing a couple of letters from Mama he took from his grandfather's house, his shorts, and a single can of tuna, he didn't know where he was going, only that he was leaving for good.

His meetings with The Lady, who he now thought of as Aunt Sokhna, had given him courage. The Marabout had caught him twice on his way to see her. The first time, the man gave him a verbal warning about being on the road at night, but the second time, the beating gave him his first seizure. When he came to, lying on the ground and feeling the world return to him first with sound, then with sight, Mansour was emboldened. He'd experienced the man's worst and had survived. Recalling a holy story, he prayed for the cloak of night. *Lord, veil me from the world, and veil the world from me. Make me like the people of the cave*, he said in his mind.

In Saint-Louis, on the road home to her village house, as the carriage driver slows and the boy approaches the light, Sokhna knows for certain that that is indeed her talibé sneaking with careful footsteps, his back sliding along the wall of a half-finished building. He is barefoot, without the shoes she'd given him. She calls out, whispering at first and then louder, and, without looking to see who the sound came from, the boy dashes into the street, colliding with their nervous horse. The animal leaps, kicking high up in the air and throwing their carriage off the road. Sokhna screams as the horse bucks, trying to break free of his reins.

Sokhna jumps out of the carriage and rushes to her talibé, where he moans on the ground. It is the first sound without a melody that Sokhna has ever heard him make. She is surprised by the depth of his voice, reminiscent of her father's last days: a patient wail, a sweet, easy limpness to the limbs and the head, a palpable tiredness with living. Stricken, the boy lets some of what he's running from show on his face, and she vows silently to protect him.

Something in the body of the carriage has broken, and it rocks wildly from side to side along the ground, like a boat on turbulent waters. The horse whines and hardly budges when the driver taps his flank for a faster pace. The boy, who seemed just fine at first, is now moving in and out of consciousness. Sokhna curses; tells God, *Work harder*; and smacks the talibé's bloody cheek.

"Wake up! Wake up!"

The boy's eyes flicker. Sokhna exhales, gripping his chin.

The driver tries the boy again. "Who is your Marabout, child?"

"We will *not* take him back there!" Sokhna cuts her eyes at the driver. "What is your father's name, boy? Tell me," she says, holding his face by the chin.

Mansour is silent, his face stiff as if in a trance. Sokhna cradles him and though he does not embrace her, she feels him relax, transferring more of his weight to her body. She hopes she will not have to watch his suffering as she'd done once with her father and, again, with Claude.

The coachman looks over his shoulder, asks Sokhna, "Did he speak?"

"He will. He just needs time," she whispers.

In the dark living room of their village home, by candlelight, Sokhna sits across from Mansour. Claude lies down on the couch under sheets. His eyelids are low, but he's watching Mansour just as dotingly as Sokhna. Mansour is wrapped in an old suit jacket of her father's that had been lying over the couch's armrest. His right eye is navy blue from the square kick of the horse.

When she asks him where he'd like to go, he hands her his single sack. She gingerly opens the red bag—blackened with car oil and dirt—and pulls out the can of tuna. Beneath it, the soiled and tattered letters from Mama to her father from a year before. Two letters he'd taken with him when he was sent into the talibé order.

Sokhna opens one. It seems to her like the penmanship of a child. The ink is splotchy, the paper wrinkled, but she spreads it flat and reads.

"Who is this from?" she asks him, and he says nothing, though he's staring at her intently, a kind excitement stirring from him. She reads on patiently, capturing the gist of Mama's letter to her father—and its request for Mansour to come and live with her. But Sokhna is suspicious. The letter is dated from two years before, and the child is nearly mute, won't offer any information. She hands the letter to Claude, unsure of what to do. He reads it quickly, holding it under the glow of the kerosene lamp beside him.

"Ndax foofu nga bëggóona dem?" "*Is this where you would like to go?*" He asks Mansour frankly, and Mansour finally speaks.

"Yes," he says, in a voice far more determined than Sokhna or Claude expected.

———

Sokhna pushes aside the mosquito net at the bedroom doorway, looking out to Mansour, who, dressed in one of Claude's shirts, sleeps soundly on the living room couch. It is nearly impossible to corroborate the boy's story—and the letters, only two of them, years old. This relative could be anywhere now, and how could Sokhna be certain that he was really wanted there? He'd already been discarded by this same family. Still, the boy seemed certain. There was likely a better life for him there than here.

A few nights later, with Mansour still staying at their home, Sokhna calls the man who presided over her father's funeral, a veteran fighter pilot from the Second World War named Monsieur Sarr. He wakes up out of a lovely sleep in his four-poster bed to answer the phone.

The story pours out of her, including the address in the letter. When she is done, he sighs, then asks simply, "Is he ready to leave?"

"Yes."

"Then bring him to the airport at 6:00 a.m. tomorrow. Don't speak to anyone. Just meet me there at my old office . . . You haven't changed at all, I see." He hangs up the phone.

Sokhna taps Claude in his sleep to tell him about what Monsieur Sarr has arranged for Mansour. She kisses his ear, and his eyes open, his head turning to her.

"Go with him," he says.

"Claude, no. He . . ."

"Go," he says again. "There's nothing here to see."

He kisses her then, long and slow, for the last time.

V.

THE SEARCH FOR MANSOUR
(PART THREE)

Switzerland, 1969

56. **MARIE AND BONNIE** walk into the precinct barefoot. The sun has dried their clothes, but their limbs are still numb. Until she sees her reflection in the glass, Bonnie doesn't know why people are staring. She grabs her hair, pulling it out, pushing it down, rushing to fix her appearance as they approach the busy woman at the front desk.

"You're making it worse," Marie says, pushing Bonnie's hands away from picking at herself. Marie's black cornucopia of braids has fallen but somehow, after all the water, and wind, the cornrows are still glossy and fresh.

Marie pulls Bonnie down into a seat. A few people look over their shoulders as Marie grabs a pin from her hair and parts Bonnie's down the middle to begin two big cornrows.

"What are you doing? Ow, Jesus!"

"I'm trying to make you look human."

"Good luck." Bonnie's examining the woman at the desk, who's just broken quick, suspicious eye contact with her. "What do we even say to her?"

"It doesn't matter. It *isn't* him anyway, remember?" Marie looks down into Bonnie's face. "The dead cat isn't him." Marie repeats the mantra.

Bonnie nods, agreeing again to believe what they have to believe.

"OK, let's go," Marie says when she's content with her work. As Bonnie approaches the front desk again, she sees herself in the round mirror above the woman's head and can't believe how Marie has transformed her.

"We've come to see . . . the body, please."

The woman looks at her blankly.

"The dead Black guy," Marie says for the white woman.

The morgue director is a little too thrilled to see them. Says that he was the one who pushed for the radio story, that he didn't want this black body to have the fate of the last one: unidentified, transferred to a community gravesite to be bagged and tossed on top of the homeless, the forgotten, the ones nobody claimed.

"They may not have any family here, but these people often worked hard to send every penny home to a family somewhere else," the man says in the meditative room of teal lights, pulling open a few drawers of bagged bodies until he finds the right one. "Here we are."

He unsentimentally zips it down to the chest. Looks at the women. The women look at each other; neither of them approach.

"Come on, he won't bite."

He tells them to observe carefully, that the bloating may have altered his appearance. Bonnie steps forward, contemplating some way to look without looking. She starts with a strange place, staring just at the tip of the nose, then moving to the concentration of flesh above the upper lip. Then she gets bolder, willing to see a cheek, the shape of the ear, the hairline.

And the hairline is Mansour's.

She thinks back to his soccer matches, crowded dusk affairs in Goutte d'Or in Paris, where she watched from their seventh-story window as he weaved through the Afroed Algerian boys, seeming to trace the circular pattern of her breaths along the cobblestones. Then she's seeing the accordions of sheet music that outgrew the closet space and that lay beside them on the bed. And how seriously he took breakfast, standing in line at the bakery when it first opened, a meal she hadn't bothered with since the fifth grade.

Marie is yanking her arm, dragging her back to the world.

"Bonnie"—her breath is hot on Bonnie's nose—"it's not him."

As they walk back to the car (still barefoot) they chatter, calling each other punk asses for avoiding the body.

"At least I looked!" Bonnie says.

"No, you didn't. You blacked out! I touched it!"

"You did not!"

"I did, and his bracelet was fake. That's how I knew. Mansour would never wear that fake shit."

Their laughter is a force, a sound they push out into the world from their guts. Their hands pressed firmly to their stomachs, as if they mean to rid themselves of every ounce of it. They shut the doors of the car, sighing a final time as they look over the quiet city that's just beginning to stir. Their peace becomes a nervous silence.

"So where are you?" Bonnie says aloud to him.

Marie looks at Bonnie, points at her wrists stacked with bracelets.

"Did he give those to you?"

Bonnie nods. Marie gives them an affectionate touch.

They both look at the bakery across the street at the same time.

"Do you have money?" Marie asks. Bonnie shakes her head, sheepish.

"You didn't bring *money*?"

"It was in my pocket when I got out to push the car."

"So?" Marie says, her scratchy voice speaking with harmonies.

"So, it's gone," Bonnie replies.

Marie sucks her teeth.

"We have to go back anyway."

"To Mama's?"

"Yes, we don't even have clothes."

Marie does the cross across her chest. "I lived a good life, Jesus," she says.

Bonnie scoffs.

Then she does a double take, looking again at her lap, seeing something sticky caked on her left thigh. It looks like mud. Maybe from the muddy water, but that was hours ago, and it looks fresh. She runs her hand up and down her leg in a panic.

"I think I cut myself," she says, but there is no wound and now she feels the wetness coming out from her body.

"Let me see," Marie says, pushing Bonnie back, seeing how she's bleeding out.

Bonnie heeds Marie's instruction for her to get in the back and lie down flat on the seats.

"Has this happened before?" Marie says.

"No, never," Bonnie lies. It had once before, but that is not a story that she is ready to tell. She hears the strangeness of her own voice, how the sound seems to come from outside herself. She swallows, trying to pop her ears, but it does not change. She stares up at the buckling ceiling of the car as Marie speeds down the road. The cold of the leather beneath her body, the woozy feeling softening her vision and amplifying with the jolts and twists of the car, reminds Bonnie of when she first arrived in New York. That moment of matching her grandmother's face with the photograph in her hand.

Sylvia had fussed over her crooked collar and uncombed hair as they moved through the crowded line. "Long Tall Sally" played quietly over the airport speakers.

"Go on in," Sylvia had said when she helped Bonnie into the back seat of her old Volvo outside the airport. The leather was cold against her bare thighs. Bonnie felt the coldness of her grandmother's rings, smelled the scent of her floral perfume as Sylvia had put her black shawl across Bonnie's bare legs like a blanket, chastising under her breath.

"Did your mother remember that you were coming to *New York?* In the *winter?*" Bonnie felt a pang of something sour in her chest, her first taste of loyalty. The woman had insulted her mother.

"How are you, honey?" said a voice from the front passenger's seat. Bonnie hadn't noticed the other woman in the car: young, probably in her twenties, with long dark hair in waves from pin curls. The woman turned back to Sylvia.

"I think we need to get her some food."

"No, no more stopping," Sylvia had said. Then quieter: "She looks sick with God knows what as it is. We need to get her home."

"That's what I'm sayin'. She's sick! She needs some food."

"Oh, please. *You* want something," her grandmother had protested. The passenger laughed, then turned around to face Bonnie. "I'm Laura, your grandma's slave."

"Hush!" Sylvia shouted.

"We've been in this game a long time together."

"Laura is my nurse and a dear friend."

When Bonnie didn't say more, Sylvia had asked: "Do you speak much English?" Bonnie shook her head no.

Laura turned up her nose. "Well, what she speak then?"

"French," Sylvia said.

Laura's eyes had widened with curiosity.

When they'd finally arrived, Laura opened the door to Sylvia's apartment. She turned on a lamp that was too dim to give a full impression of the room. What Bonnie could see was congested elegance: four antique lamps stuffed into a corner, cardboard boxes on a fine marble table, mismatched upholstered sofa chairs that were too large for the space. An old gray dog with no room to roam was stretched flat, and Bonnie had mistaken him for a rug on the hardwood. Laura took Bonnie to the bathroom to brush her teeth. The light in there was too bright, and Bonnie's eyes took a while to adjust. She hadn't recognized herself in the mirror, as if, in traveling around the world, some part of her had yet to arrive. The bathtub was full of paintings, enormous portraits with thick gold frames. The one closest to Bonnie's fingertips was of Claudine. She wore a white dress, her hair rolled and pinned tightly. She appeared to be nine or ten, around Bonnie's age—but Claudine's face was the same as it had been the last time Bonnie saw her: long, calm, unsmiling. A wheelchair and a pile of other things blocked the toilet, and she struggled against a tower of *Architectural Digest*s to reach the seat. She knocked them over.

Laura knocked. "You all right? Let me know if you need anything."

Bonnie had waited until she was certain that the woman was gone. Then she'd climbed the stack of magazines to access the small window. The ledge was covered with spiderwebs that she peeled away with both of her hands to get a glimpse of the world outside. Brooklyn was dark, complicated, sure of itself. There was no place in its perfect maze for her questions. So she kept them inside and let them erase her hunger. In bed that night, she settled into a blackness so complete that her eyes, wide open, never graduated to discerning shapes. Over time, the sleepless hours lent themselves to a sort of swimming, another kind of levitating. In their invisibility, the walls began to disappear. Soon the levitation was deliberate flight. She rose into the Brooklyn night sky. It was no surprise that she met stars, or that they, after all, as merely dust, could not be held in her hand. Her mother's legs were in the sky, her stockings a shimmery black.

The next morning, Laura moved her to a new room, and Bonnie knew from first glance at the patterned curtains and ugly glass box of plastic fish and glittering lampshade that this new place would not lend itself to such nightly travels. Laura parted the curtains, and daylight flooded in. She stood over her, mixing a white powder into a glass with a spoon. Bonnie swallowed it down, and the darkness that came was pale in comparison to previous medicines. The medicine, whatever it contained, ended her nightly travels.

She'd needed to discover a new way to fly, so she turned to the record player. A familiar egress from unbearable things. The first question she asked her grandmother in that apartment, her French accent still thick, was "Can I play this?" Her grandmother sat up, straight. The child had finally come out of her room and was talking to her. The little girl was pointing to Billie Holiday. "Could I play this, please?" she said again.

Her grandmother had sighed. "Billie's in a lot of pain. You sure you want to start with her?"

Bonnie nodded, her own pain evident.

"All right. Go ahead," Sylvia had said. "Good Morning Heartache" filled the house. And Bonnie could fly again.

—————

Though her understanding of her childhood did little to ease the pain of her own mother's relinquishing, now that she was due to be a mother in four months, Bonnie could see some wisdom in the family pattern. The truth was that just because somebody had a child, it did not mean they were the most suitable to raise them. Turns out it's what she meant when she'd once said to Emmanuel that Mingus shouldn't play Mingus, that his music, his creation, was better served by softer hands.

57. **THE NEAREST PLACE** is the men's bathroom at a gas station, and Marie blocks the entry with her foot as Bonnie cleans her thighs. The wooziness has passed, Bonnie claims. But she can't stand up without leaning on the wall and Marie says again that they should go to the hospital. Bonnie shushes her, a sound far louder than Marie's voice, a sound she keeps making even after Marie falls silent, shushing her body as if it were the baby itself. For a moment, she manages to restore her own peace, but the sticky blood along her thigh, no matter how hard she wipes, won't move. She gives up, dropping her long arms to her sides.

"He promised," she says, and she throws the stained tissue in the toilet. It expands in the water, tinting it pink like a rose. Bonnie reaches for the floor, sliding down, and Marie comes to her, helping her to the ground.

Bonnie whispers, her eyes on the tile floor, "He promised me I wouldn't have to do this alone."

Marie goes to the sink and wets toilet paper under the cloudy water. She wipes the blood from Bonnie's hands. Then from her arms, then from her thighs, as Bonnie stays slack and sullen, letting her.

After a long wait, they do not see a doctor, but a Polish second-year medical student—a former classmate of Marie's—examines Bonnie in a parking lot at the University of Geneva. She's on a break from DJing at the student radio station and still has huge headphones around her neck. The sun is beaming and the contrast of students strolling easily around campus while Bonnie lies back in the dirty Peugeot with her legs in the air, chewing gum with her designer sunglasses on, makes Marie laugh. She doesn't know what else to do. With no credentials and no cash, this is their doctor's office.

"I should've gone to Yale, like my grandmother wanted," Bonnie whines wearily, hearing her carefree peers mingle about the campus from the car's open window. A college girl squeals the way she'd squeal when Mansour, out of nowhere, would sneak up behind her and lift her off the ground.

"You look fine," the woman says, finally sitting up from between Bonnie's legs.

Bonnie, who will not remove her sunglasses, mutters, "Told you," to Marie.

"Did you really get in there good?" Marie teases.

Bonnie rolls her eyes, dropping her legs as the Polish girl stands. The young woman observes Bonnie with a new curiosity.

"It's a wonder you didn't do more damage to yourself. Did you really drive through that storm?"

The woman doesn't wait for an answer as she packs her tools and removes her gloves.

"I saw him sing once, in Paris. And you know, I might've driven through a storm or two for that," she says, observing a swollen, bruised Bonnie with envy—and the tiniest smile.

58. BONNIE AND MARIE walk toward the house, through the mangled herb garden of the backyard. The back door that leads to the kitchen is cracked. Malian music pours out with the low light from the oven's hood.

Bonnie and Marie exchange a glance, bracing themselves for the encounter with Mama.

The dishwasher girl has left a rack of dishes to dry on the counter, and she's bent forward, with both hands and bare feet moving backward, as she swipes a dry towel across the sparkling floor.

"Where's Eva?" Bonnie asks.

"Mama's in her room," the girl answers without looking up. "But she says to tell you that the Peugeot will cost you. And that work starts at 6:00 a.m."

Bonnie looks at Marie.

"Welcome to the family business." Marie shakes Bonnie's hand and leaves the kitchen chuckling. "Mama never loses out."

Of all of the ways to exact vengeance, Bonnie never expected that she'd have to work in Mama's restaurant.

On her way to Mama's room, Bonnie steps over a diner's sleeping dog
and a forgotten sack of red onions. She squeezes through the tightly
arranged tables, through the loose clouds of cigar smoke, bay leaf–
scented steam, and eager diners. The overcast has left the dining room
unusually humid for the season; the wet heat makes Bonnie dizzy.
More than once, she steps unwittingly on the foot of a stranger. The
room is too crowded. For the first time, she's feeling her weight in a
new way. Her arms want to fall off her shoulders. Her knees need to
buckle. She has to lift her heavy feet from her hips.

She reaches the hallway of bedrooms and hesitates before knocking
on Mama's door. She's never been in her room.

"Sokhna?" Mama says. Bonnie becomes nervous then, anticipating
her chastisement.

"C'est moi."

"Kann?" *Who?*

As usual, the woman toggles between two languages without ever
helping Bonnie along. Mansour never taught Bonnie Wolof, hardly
ever spoke it around her. So around Mama, for this and other reasons
she doesn't understand, Bonnie perpetually feels apologetic and dumb,
a giant step behind.

"C'est moi. C'est Bonnie," she says.

"Entrez."

Bonnie opens the door. The room is white with haze and she
struggles to see through the smoke, to discern the powder-blue walls,
the huge photograph of a Senegalese saint on the wall. A black-and-
white television on mute is stacked with magazines, opened boxes of
new dishes, opened boxes of old dishes, tablecloths, and shoes. In the
center of everything is a large photograph of Mansour. He is a gangly, petrified version of himself, maybe fourteen, in a shirt and tie.

His expression further weakens her. She cannot bear to imagine him so afraid.

Bonnie's eyes find Mama as the smoke breaks. She appears to be on a cloud. The woman's purple-black skin glistens. She wears a multicolored piece of cloth around her large body like a towel, her thin hair sectioned while she wraps a piece at the front in thread. Bonnie's never seen anyone do this to their hair before. She's staring.

"What do you want?" Mama says in French, plainly, without heat, then goes on wrapping her hair.

"I can just pay you the money."

"Huh?" Mama leans forward, dropping more balls of black incense into the pot at the foot of the bed that's filling the room with this haze. It starts up again, smoking out the already-smoky place. It's Mansour's scent, a woody aroma. He never burned that stuff, but whatever it was, it must have seeped into his skin over the years.

"I can just pay you for the car, instead of working."

"Working is better for me," Mama says, rubbing some lotion into her arm. "Come down at 5:40 a.m. tomorrow."

Bonnie is silent. This woman is indeed intimidating. She gives up on pressing further.

"It wasn't him."

"Tu dis quoi?"

"The body in Geneva. It wasn't him," Bonnie says, and she closes the door behind herself.

———

Her final obstacle to the staircase is the cluster of four tables that have been pushed together for what looks to be someone's birthday. The local police chief lords over the hungry pack, reenacting last week's murder with an empty bottle of wine—not quite empty—and when he raises the bottle like an axe coming down on wood, some wine spills, splashing a freckled woman at the next table in the face. Maybe because he is the chief, the woman laughs, licking around her mouth to savor the splash of his sour rosy liquid.

Bonnie sits on the ninth step, well away from the people but not quite in the attic, watching the African women carry trays to and from the packed dining room, watching couples yell over one another to finish jokes, eager children reaching across the table to steal from one another's plates. She watches the ease and cacophony of family life as if it were a film and puts a cold hand to her stomach, wondering again if it could ever be hers.

When Bonnie is gone, Mama cups her hands and bows her head.

"Alhamdulillah." *Kiné, it wasn't your boy. He is still out there, some-where, alive.*

59. **MAMA'S GAZE SETTLES** on the police chief. On weeknights like this, he usually comes with his mistress, but tonight he dines alone. As she recalls, there have been two women, maybe three, each one younger than the last by a decade, just like her father. She watches him eat heartily at one of the tables at the back and then arrange his fish skeletons on his plate so that all the heads face away from him.

She *knew* the police chief, and he knew her. Maybe, she thought, if some detail of her illegal status were to be revealed in helping her find Mansour, he would overlook it. Maybe they could even laugh about it one day. She'd catered his mother's eightieth birthday party a few weeks ago, had walked the old woman arm in arm to the car afterward. She remembers pulling the hat over the old woman's head and her hair being so slick and flat that it slid right off again. She remembers the rumors that his wife or his latest mistress left him—she can't remember which—but she surmises that this is the cause for his sullen disposition.

She approaches him.

"The new girl, she doesn't chatter much. Just straight to the menu. All business," he says, watching the dishwasher across the dining room.

"Yes, she's very shy," Mama replies.

"You should know that that sort of thing can be mistaken for arrogance. Tell her to get me another brandy as an apology," he says bitterly, staring down into his glass.

"I'll get it myself."

"No, I would like her to."

"I'll get it for you, sir."

Mama quickly crosses to the bar. Her hands shake as she pours his drink. Bringing up Mansour will be harder than she thought. The chief is the sort of man she loathes, and it's hard to pretend otherwise, but she knows him more than any other town official, and so she has no choice but to try.

When she spots him leaving about an hour later, she has summoned her courage. She follows him to the door.

"Eh! Henri! Henri!" she calls. She follows the police chief outside.

The man stops but doesn't turn to face her. Mama puts her hands in her coat pockets, noting that he has not come in the police buggy as he usually does. She can tell, without asking, that he has no intention of going home, that he will spend a drunken night probably sleeping at a bar or wandering through the village until he's due back at work right before sunrise. She walks around him so that they are face-to-face.

"Are you all right?" he says, and she's mortified that her worries are showing on her face. She's lived her whole life this way: feeling one thing but showing another. Now is not the time to crack.

"Yes. How's your mother?" she asks. She watches three separate thoughts move through his mind at once.

"Mothers," he says with a shrug. "She stopped talking a week ago."

"I'm sorry to hear that."

"Just stopped talking out of nowhere. I don't think I've known anything more terrifying. She just . . . looks around. No voice. Not a sound."

"I'm very sorry," Mama says, and she is. And the man feels her sincerity, so he softens.

"How's your son?" he asks in turn.

Her stomach flips; her heart is in her throat.

"He's . . . well. Very well." She fakes a smile.

"I haven't seen him around."

"He's . . . still touring."

"Oh, very good. I hope the, uh," he gestures to his own stomach, "baby won't come as a surprise when he gets home." He laughs, moving past her toward his car. "She seems like the type."

He laughs again, the sound echoing as he moves deeper into the dark woods. Mama listens; the insects in the trees grow louder. Were they mocking her cowardice too?

VI

THE LAW OF CONSERVATION OF ENERGY

Senegal, 1947

60. **THE DAY MANSOUR WAS BORN**, Kiné had a song in her head. A piano tune that traveled the full breadth of the instrument. Something like Ahmad Jamal, an artist Mansour would play for Mama many years later, but certainly not a song Kiné would ever have heard, in that place, in that time. Nonetheless, it found her, a sound she heard in her mind. It persisted as she went about her morning, squatting before the little fire she'd made for morning tea. She'd been bedridden for a couple of days and was grateful that she could get on her feet and help out Mame, the hundred-something-year-old relative who lived in the village and was hosting her birth when no one else would. Mame still ran and swam and cooked her own meals but hadn't spoken a word since the passing of her daughter some thirty years before. As Kiné observed the woman, she began to admire the freedom that her muteness had begotten: the way she was and wasn't in the world.

Even before she was shamed for her pregnancy, Kiné often thought of disappearing. Not in the way of dying, of disappearing forever, but in the way of merging with her twin. She had early memories of playing a hiding game with neighborhood children and never losing because she pretended to be the other.

"If they catch you, just say you're me," her sister would say, and so when Kiné was caught, which didn't take long, Kiné would give

Mama's name and keep playing. Kiné never took her own beatings or made her own friends. And as she matured, she was unsettled by the truth that certain features distinguished her. She had a beautiful singing voice and a calm, easy manner that made her more popular with boys, and, by and by, without any effort, Kiné eased into the spotlight. Mama, who was surprised but not resentful, embraced the new distance between them, but Kiné couldn't cope with her independence. She needed her twin, needed the comfort of becoming her. Kiné began to suffer.

That's when her fantasies about dying began. Soft, calming thoughts, far more soothing than sleep. They called her away from the house. Called her to trail off at night. Called her to come barefoot, to come alone, to the cool, quiet desert where the sand was dense and faultless. Called her to the fetid edge of the bush, where the entangled, thorny vines and the cracked shells of freshly devoured birds warned her that she'd arrived. And then there was her summoner: a tall lion, a pride male, approaching her through the sandy wind. His large head moved in a circle, and the wind spread open his mane, making his head alone nearly the scale of her body. He spoke in her mind, a whisper, the way he'd done every time before, telling her to come closer. She listened. The bush was tingling, her hands were tingling, the sand at her feet felt like pins. And then she heard the song—the Ahmad Jamal melody. It dizzied her, tickling her up and down like a feather was being dragged from her forehead to her soles, a gentle seizure that made the desert night turn green.

When she awoke from swooning, the lion was smiling like a dog; his eyes revealed his youth. He was guarding her, resting at her feet.

———

Kiné's family soon sought the help of the Marabout. He had medicine, but his medicine was not pure. He could take away illnesses, but he could not destroy them. He could only transfer them to a different vessel, so he placed them, without her knowledge, into her womb. There was no child at the time, but the darkness was patient.

About a year later, like a cloud, made dark as earth by holding in a year of rain and needing to release itself, the darkness forced its vessel, Mansour, into the world three months before he was due. As she stood at the stream gathering water for Mame's bath, Kiné heard the song again. She collapsed and wailed as the child entered the world. Kiné's darkness—which Mansour would learn to call seizures—entered the world with him.

After washing Mansour one day in the stream, Kiné and Mama started back to Mame's. Kiné stumbled, her legs weak, struggling to walk under the blazing sun. The heat was visible: a thick white haze in the air like a laser. It gave the world a violent, crackling brightness that made Kiné want to close her eyes.

"Take him," she said, holding up Mansour's bright-red body as she struggled to stay on her feet. Mama carried the baby home.

Kiné tried to leave Mansour with Mama as much as she could, but Mama started to catch on.

"Kiné Ndoye! Is this not your child?"

Mame snapped her fingers all day and night, pointing toward the baby, whom Kiné, overwhelmed by his presence, tended to leave on the tables and stools like a pillow.

Mama laughed. "Ay Kiné!"

When the child cried, the sound was in tune and sort of pleasant. It was a cry like a howl, solemn and steady. A sound that you could sleep through if you tried hard enough. The rooms stayed dark and cool, but Mama always woke up covered in sweat, rushing to him. Sometimes, for a moment she'd stare up at the intricate pattern of the woven grass ceiling, waiting and hoping that Kiné would stir, but she never did.

Mame wanted Mama to step back and let Kiné care for her own child. But Mama knew that Kiné needed the help. Mama held a sleeping Mansour to her chest as the old woman walked in the direction of her room and gave a glance that beckoned Mama to follow. Once inside, Mame untied a knot of black cloth to reveal a small calabash. Mama sat on the edge of the mat in the center of the room, respectfully. Mame took the contents of the calabash out and placed them on the ground beside her one by one. The last thing she pulled was a small linen pouch. It was white but had oxidized over many years to a pale yellow, and when Mama went to open it, Mame shook her finger no. The old woman helped Mama put Mansour down and grabbed both of Mama's hands into her own, a firm, strong hold, and shook them.

She pointed to Mama's chest. *You*, she mimed. *Take this*. She put the pouch in Mama's hands and held them closed. *Be free*. She threw her hand up into the air, and Mama was stunned by the quicksilver sparkle that flickered in the woman's eyes.

LIKE CLAUDINE, MAMA WAS A WOMAN
WHO TRAVELED THE WORLD ALONE

France, 1955

61. **MAMA COULD'VE DONE** many things better, but the fall of 1955 was the first time that the hotel restaurant docked her for her offenses: sloppy plates with sauce around the edges, broken teacups, fingerprints on glasses, two missing orders, slowness, heavily accented French, sloppy posture, dirty apron, messy hair, looking patrons in the eye, not looking patrons in the eye, singed pans, wasting butter, eating off the serving spoon, not smiling at the patrons, smiling at the patrons, not letting the guests call her by the wrong name. As he looked up from this list of offenses, the maître d' explained that these were the reasons she could not be promoted to a full-time waitress, why she had to stay part-time in the kitchen, and why her pay would be less than the standard. He had one more thing to say as she felt the cold knob of the front door:

"Just be Eva," his hand moving when he said Eva as if to highlight the deliciousness of the sound.

"But my name is Mama Eva," she said.

He shook his head. "You want everybody to think that you're a mother or something? That's nothing to be proud of with no husband. You'll learn that here in France."

She froze, bit down, and felt blood gush from her lip. She slammed the front door behind herself. But his loose old neck had jiggled when he spoke, and she knew from sitting across from him on the metro that he didn't live too far from her and likely didn't make much more than she did. This all gave Mama something to chuckle about as she walked down the hall.

At least he hadn't noticed that she'd started taking things from the restaurant's downstairs closet. It had begun with a bar of soap, just a handful of Wockenfuss candies. But soon Mama had found herself rearranging the contents on the shelves, filling in the gaps her quiet habit was making. And though no one had initially suspected her, the closet's emergence as a subject of conversation was enough to make her stop. That is, until she met her first winter. She'd never known a cold so precise. It stung in places on her body she'd hardly ever even thought of: the dimple in her elbows, the edges of her teeth. When she slept, she nearly smothered herself, all her towels and wrap skirts—and sheets and blankets, even one of the rugs, piled on top of her. She'd crawl out from under it all into the violent chill of the morning. Sweating profusely, her wetness made the cold stickier.

So that day, when she discovered that her docked pay wouldn't stretch far enough for rent and winter clothes, she returned to the restaurant's closet.

Instinct told her to pick the cheap-looking coat. Dirty and mauve. But the sleeves would be too short, and the middle button likely wouldn't close. She yearned instead for the gray one. A man's coat that would reach her ankles. When she lifted the arm and released it, she felt the wool's enormous weight. She rolled it into her bag and waited until she'd descended the metro stairs to slip inside it. The warmth made her grin. In the reflection of the metro car's window, she could see that it fit well too. But her palpitations started as soon the train moved. She couldn't escape the stench of the owner's cologne in the collar, and its weight began to feel like a measure of what she'd done.

Twice before, an albino woman with a child about the same age as Mansour had approached her on the train, noticing how she was always alone, asking if she had any family in town. Mama didn't trust the woman. Her appearance had bothered her, and Mama's pride had made it easy to decline her offers. But that day, when the woman greeted her, Mama returned the greeting, reaching over and shaking her hand. She was relieved once they arrived at the Blacker side of town and the car flooded with the Cameroonians and the Senegalese, a swarm of faces to hide in.

The gusts of the winds for some reason seemed stronger in France, but Mama was too numb to truly feel the cold. And soon a strange weight folded over her. She saw the white hands fitting a crochet blanket around her shoulders. She looked up into the albino women's pale pupils. The little girl the woman was always with pressed her small hand on Mama's thigh to help herself climb into the seat beside her.

"*Mon dieu*," the little girl said. "Your leg is like ice." She shook her hand in the air as if to shake off the cold from it.

"Come with me. We get off at the next stop," the albino woman said.

"Tu t'apelles comment?" *What is your name?*

"Oumou," the woman said.

"Foo o jogé?" *Where are you from?* Mama said, but the woman just shook her head with a smile.

"I don't,speak Wolof," she replied, explaining that she was from Bamako. Then the women switched to French again—the language they had in common.

In the room beside the kitchen at the Malian woman's house, Mama stood at the wall, feeling Paris differently. Her shoulders dropped, and she wondered, for the first time, where she could go dancing in this city. Where she'd find a good place to get her hair done. Where she would find good work; how she could sustain her right to stay and work in France now that she couldn't be at the hotel full-time.

She climbed into bed in the quiet room, but before drifting off to sleep, she fished her diary from her purse. It was where she planned her dream restaurant, one of the few things she'd grabbed when she ran from her Paris apartment. Every evening, she thought of something new to add to the thirty-page menu, so that night, she dreamed up a soursop-pomegranate sauce over skewered shrimp, guava Jell-O over frozen madd, toasted baguette slices slathered with anchovy and palm oil paste.

Months ago, she'd started sneaking home restaurant scraps and testing recipes in her kitchen. She had worked by moonlight with the radio on low to keep her company. At that hour, they'd only played classical music. So she'd discovered a love for Schumann and Chopin, Debussy and Brahms.

In the quiet at Oumou's, Mama began to feel the severity of her situation, that the bud of a life she'd managed to find here was at risk. Her mistakes flooded her mind. A thousand avoidable things that had gone wrong, well before this night.

For example, she could've stayed in the airport line back in Senegal after the kind woman agreed to let Mansour fly, even though Mama had only gotten one ticket, thinking a child his age could fly for free.

She could've stayed in line instead of trying to satiate his appetite and stepping outside to the woman selling mangoes and egg sandwiches across the street. She'd ordered Mansour a bag of mango chunks, but the woman had no change for her bill. Mama had looked to the man in uniform not far from where they stood.

She asked if he had change as she held up one of the crisp bills from Mame—change from her plane ticket. The man had approached, produced spare coins.

As they'd strolled back toward departures, he'd asked her about her travels.

"Where is your husband?" he'd said. Tired as she was, she forgot to lie and she'd told him the truth: that she had no husband, that the child was her nephew, the son of a sister who'd gone missing.

"Who are you going to see in Paris? Do you have family there?"

She'd shaken her head no.

She didn't process what she'd done until the man asked her and Mansour to follow him into his office. Their argument had ended with him writing down her address and calling the officials in Tivaouane, instructing them to alert her family of her intended departure. Though he cautioned her against traveling to a foreign land without a husband, he'd admitted that he could not stop her from leaving. He would, however, stop her from taking the child, whom she had no legal authority to take from Senegal without his family's consent.

Within an hour, the call had been made and Mama was informed that her eldest sister would be arriving soon to retrieve Mansour. Meanwhile, the line for her flight had gathered before the doors. She'd remembered Mame's warning years ago, telling her to choose herself, to be free.

The doors had opened, revealing the bright white plane, letting a warm wind into the terminal.

On the plane, Mama had slumped down low in her seat. She'd kept the boy close to her chest. He had been silent, mirroring her alertness with wide eyes and a tight jaw. She'd kept looking down the aisle, wincing every time another passenger strolled by. Then a flight attendant had announced that the plane could not move, as the authorities had a matter to resolve.

Mama had heard her eldest sister's voice before she saw her. The woman's salt-and-pepper hair had been slicked into a neat bun, the slit in her wrap skirt just high enough for her to swivel down the aisle in her heels.

When she spotted Mama, she'd hurried down the aisle, twisting around the luggage of passengers. Every soul on the flight had watched the scene.

"Have you lost your mind, Mama Ndoye? Yo lai wax!" *I'm talking to you!*

She'd snatched the boy from Mama's arms—slapping her hard in the face when she'd protested. Her eldest sister's eyes had been wild with fury and hurt. She'd put Mansour on her hip and told Mama to stand up.

"Juggal, ay cha!!" She'd told Mama again to get up so they could leave. Mama had begun to cry as her sister started to tug at her overhead luggage, Mansour wailing on her hip. When her sister had gone to hit Mama again, the passengers around her intervened.

"Have mercy on the child!" one exclaimed.

"Listen to your elder!" others chastised Mama as she had stayed seated, still protesting, even as she wept.

An older man, dressed in a suit and kufi, had called across the plane, "If she wants to go, let her go!"

"She doesn't know anybody in Paris!" her older sister had shouted back, firmly clutching a squirming Mansour, who was slipping down from her arms.

"Paris *is* Senegal," a man had said. Some had laughed at his comment, and the tension eased. It was true. France was the mother country. And whether in the realm of dreams or nightmares, it lived in the consciousness of everyone that Mama knew. The man continued.

"There are Senegalese everywhere. She'll be fine."

We can all help her, someone else had said from the rear.

"I'm leaving Senegal," Mama had finally said, more to herself than anyone else. She'd wiped her tears with both hands and sat up, defiantly adjusting her seatbelt. Helplessness had descended over her sister's face like a shadow. Her fellow passengers fell silent as the flight attendant approached the aisle impatiently.

"We have to leave now," she'd said, in Wolof this time instead of French.

Mama's eldest sister had gripped the seat beside her to keep from falling as the plane's breaks shifted beneath them. She'd tried to comfort Mansour as he wailed, bouncing him on her hip.

"Write to Yaye when you land," she'd said, stern. She reached the plane's open door. With the high wind engulfing them, stirring up their clothes, Mansour and her eldest sister had appeared to be entering a separate world.

"Kiné's death was already too much; I don't know how your mother will recover from this. Whatever happens next is on you."

"*Kiné is not dead!*" Mama had yelled over the sound of the ignited engine.

Mansour, who'd been squirming and whining with discomfort in his eldest aunt's arms, had stopped moving. He'd locked eyes with Mama, seeming to know what would happen next. When his eldest aunt had begun to step down from the plane, he'd shrieked, a terrible sound, the same sound he'd made on the afternoon Kiné drowned. A sound Mama had not heard from him since. As they'd descended the plane, the last Mama had seen of them were his small hands, still reaching for her. When the door closed, she'd kept her head down, her own tears dropping into her lap, disappearing into the dark blue of her Bazan skirt.

She had still been awake by the time they passed Algeria. The emptiness of her arms, the absence of Mansour, who she had become so accustomed to cradling, kept her from peace. The Sahara and the early moonlight had stained the sky an ink-violet, a color so stunning that she had felt weary and closed the window curtain. But there had been something so magical about traveling to another place. Even if the only gift of arriving there would be that she could believe, in peace, that her sister was alive.

Mama had landed with indigestion, cradling herself in a cloth on the airport floor as her mind adjusted to CET. The Senegalese passengers did as they had promised her sister, leaving her with phone numbers and pocket money. Addresses to their homes, invitations to dinner. They were mostly men, and she trusted the one in the kufi the most; he was the elder, the most paternal.

"Who are you staying with here?" he'd said. She'd produced her offer letter from the hotel. The letter contained a recommendation for housing.

"I don't live far from there," the man had assured her.

They'd ridden the metro together, and Mama rested her cheek on her suitcase, watching Parisian townhouses from the window as they passed through the city. As the ride went on, Mama kept looking at the man in the kufi to see when he would stand for the next stop, but when they finally arrived, it was he who shook her out of sleep.

Their suitcases rolled loudly on the gravel as they'd approached the neighborhood. There had been nothing there but large complexes. No homes like the ones she'd seen on the metro, or the ones she'd lived in herself in Senegal. Only dark, strange buildings, the size and depth of which she had never seen before.

As they'd approached her building, the man stopped walking. Mama did too.

"Il faut faire attention ici, ma fille," the man said, looking at her like a father. "There's nothing but men here," he warned again. "You're very brave."

He'd watched for her until she was inside the building, and she had looked back at him from inside, a little bit afraid inside the cagey hallway when he disappeared from her sight. She learned that night why there were towels and sheets under her front door when she arrived and squealed at the mice.

She had been eager for morning, for her first day of work to begin. She had been alone in a house before but could not sleep, comforted by recalling that she'd only be alone there for a week, that an Algerian man would be coming to rent the other room. She was shocked by Paris's accommodations: that the toilet had to be flushed by filling the trash can with water from the kitchen sink and pouring it down. That the windows were in such desperate need of a wash, just like the floors and the walls. She was not used to living like this. But a part of her had been excited to live without the surveillance of parents or a maid who was really a parent's second pair of eyes, more of a snitch than a servant.

She began her first letter home to her father. By the time she was done, it was poetry. Full of lies, full of reasons for Mansour to come and be with her very soon.

Mama could not pay Oumou any rent, so she helped with lunch and dinner. Cooking meals for, she soon discovers, a house full of expat boarders. A parade of voyagers, transitioning between countries, between life paths, between marriages. The man in the bedroom across from her was from Benin; he ate her meals gluttonously. There was a woman from Mauritania who left her things to dry in the community bathroom—undergarments and big shawls crowding the pole of the shower curtain. She messed over Mama's food, pulling out the meat, leaving the rice.

Working out of Oumou's kitchen, Mama made more catering African holidays and naming ceremonies than she ever had at the hotel. Years went by that way: living under the radar, building a potato soup under the kitchen window, and filling a notebook with her dreams for her restaurant—a thing that felt more and more attainable by the day.

Until the day that Mansour had finally come.

VIII.

CHICKS DIE ALL THE TIME

Switzerland, 1969

62. **BY THE TENS**, the hundreds. Mama knows by how the room sounds. The chaotic chirps quieting down to a gentle purr. The dishwasher girl blames the neighborhood children she'd chased out of the barn a few times: their dirty nails grating at the fur of the chicks. It wasn't the foxes; she promised Mama that she'd locked the barn door. But one could never be certain. Viruses came all the time, with the weather or the air or from nowhere at all. Today, Mama ties her face with an old T-shirt and gathers the dead chicks.

The first time this happened it seemed sacrilegious, heartless, to not gather them one by one, but today she scoops them up with the shovel, dumping them all into the old metal can. As she empties her shovel, Mama notices one that is still alive. He chirps, wobbling into her hand. She pets him with her thumb, his slender dark eyes narrowing at her touch. But she can tell from his dreamy disposition that he is sick. To send him peacefully, she squeezes him, and he does not even resist her. Nestling into the warmth of her palm, surrendering his life for her touch.

There will come a time when even our children will have gray hair and will lose most of their power. This September dawn, from the time she showers, tasting metal in the cold water, to the time she walks through the barn, injecting the surviving chicks with antibiotics, she thinks of brokenhearted Olu's words. Perhaps she'd let him go too easily.

She'd once thought of children indifferently, trusting life to bring them about, the way she trusted a harvest to arrive in season. She'd once thought of men that way too: a thing available in excess, a thing that came from life itself. But with Mansour's child arriving soon, she is beginning to see time, to feel the years that she lost raising him. When she'd first arrived in Paris, she wanted nothing more than to have him with her, but by the time he arrived, he shifted her life's balance, changing her momentum—pushing them in the direction of another path.

She knows now that something is wrong, that he should be home. But she is holding fast to her belief in his strength. She is still trying, and failing, to conceive of a way to take action, a way of finding him that won't pull the trigger on her whole life. Too much has been built. Too many wars have been won.

She gets into her car to take a ride across her land, to gather the modest harvest of herbs and cassavas.

Out on the land, as Mama pulls up vegetables and weeds, she stops for a moment and watches her own shadow, stretched across several rows of infant cabbages. *You lie about him being safe, same way you lied about Kiné being alive. Still can't say it, can you? Still can't say she's dead.*

She is startled by her silhouette. It looks like it should belong to someone else. Her body is beautiful, far firmer and stronger than it has become in her mind. She is newly forty, has never married, and feels sometimes that her life still hasn't begun. If she were to die overnight, the restaurant would be the only evidence that she'd existed, the one thing on earth that had truly been hers. And if she succumbs to her fears for Mansour, and risks everything in search of him, will the time ever truly come, for her own life to begin?

PART
FOUR

I.

A DROP OF GOLD

France, 1968

63. **GIL RODNEY'S SCREAM** gets between them: the piercing note that followed Carl Keifer into his grave. Within days of arriving in Paris, memories of the scream wrestle Bonnie and Mansour from hopeful lovers into housemates. Most times, the scream is hardly louder than a hum in Mansour's head, but it seldom hushes. Then it colonizes Otis, Sly, and Aretha like a virus, expressing itself through their mouths, turning their records into toxins. He tells her none of this, so Bonnie decides she's the cause when he abruptly trails away. For Mansour, what makes Gil's sound so menacing, so unforgettable, is the surprise in it. It is a sound that makes Mansour see a man falling backward, falling where he thought there was ground.

In the humid Olympique, Mansour can't stand beside Bonnie for long. A young and old crowd presses into each other to see Umm Kulthum. At this concert of his favorite singer, Mansour thought he'd be safe, but soon comes Rodney's scream out from Umm's lower register, overpowering her, like a background singer who didn't know their place. So he eases his way out of the venue and pretends not to hear Bonnie calling his name.

Out on the street, with relief, Mansour savors the noises of the city. The dying transmission of a white-wheeled cab, a telephone line overhead that buzzes in the rhythm of a waltz. And Umm's applause. Her applause follows him like a devoted sprite, keeping pace with him for

a whole block, before he finally gives into it and lets himself feel the
warmth of the people. It convinces him that he needs to get back on a
stage if he is going to survive. But so far in Paris, work has been harder
to come by than he'd expected. In the three weeks since they landed,
there has been one gig, and Liam blew it. He played like he was in and
out of sleep, stopping and starting, a palpable stage fright that was not
characteristic of him. They talked it out on the phone some days later,
Liam saying vaguely that he needed a break. *A break from me?* Mansour
had joked, but he felt the sting of his own words when Liam didn't
answer.

Mansour is beginning to suspect that he is going to have to do this
without Liam. He is going to have to navigate the music alone. It is a
thought that makes the city vaster; he doesn't know where to start. He
keeps walking. A woman coming down the street alone gathers her
jacket at the collar as if the summer night were chilly and walks harder,
averting her eyes as they near each other. *Women fear the wrong men*, he
thinks, a thought he's had before, and then he remembers that he's left
Bonnie at the club alone.

When he returns, he pushes and shoves through the ravenous standing ovation, calling her name. But Bonnie is gone. He panics a little, as
he asks after her, but people shake their heads: no one's noticed a
woman that tall leaving the venue.

Soon he's wandering around the surrounding cobblestone blocks at
a feverish pace. When he gets nowhere, he decides to try home. He
arrives at the landing of their floor panting, and he exhales when he
sees the light spilling out from beneath the apartment door. Once
inside, he can tell from the slight crack of the bathroom door (it swells
from the steam of hot water and is never fully closed) and the complete
stillness of the house that she's in the bathtub. She always does her
reading in the tub, stays there for hours in silent concentration. Her
clothes are flung across the couch as usual. (She'd pretended to be as
neat as he was for about a week.) Angry with her for scaring him, he

goes to the bathroom door and knocks, making a sound that comes out a little too honest in its loudness and meanness.

"What?" she says, stirring loudly in the water, startled. The force of his knock has opened the door.

He leans against the hallway wall so he can't be accused of trying to see her without her clothes on—a boundary they haven't crossed. If he speaks, the panic that still lingers from searching for her will spill out. And if not the panic, she will certainly hear his yearning.

"Bonne nuit" is what he says, and nothing more.

Their busy summer days in Goutte d'Or grow out of sync, and soon they are coming and going from the apartment at different times.

Her, first looking for work at the city's music labels, but, after offers of nothing more than clerical positions, she decides to wait for something in A&R. In the meantime, she works at a textile shop right there in the eighteenth arrondissement, a job she keeps for the smell of rayon. (It takes her back to sleeping in the car with her mother near a seamshop, a thing she won't realize until after she has quit.)

She is full of stories like this. Stories of the cotton sheets that warble from the ceiling to the dirty floor and whip up a wind for the window-less room of sleepy workers. And the pay isn't really worth it, *you know?* So maybe she will take Khadijah—the fellow left-handed girl who works across from her—up on her offer to apprentice at an uphol-stery shop and learn to repair Persian rugs. In the rare moments their paths cross, Mansour loves to hear her stories, the joy she finds in the quotidian, the scent from her body when she comes home sweaty that reminds him of dishwater, a cypher of the rawness in her that he finds irresistible.

But every time he catches her eye, shame calls him inward, and he wonders again what she knows about Keifer's death and if he, in her mind, is to blame. *Grief* and *mourning* are not words he'd use. He only knows that his appetite for life is milder. He only knows that he, lately, prefers evenings to daytime, that he still must be careful what records he plays to keep Gil at bay. And that, despite his wanting, something in him wants also to push Bonnie away.

When he isn't running errands for the bakery—biking for ten hours a day on local streets, where all the shop names are in Arabic (street signs he can actually read)—he is auditioning, backing up a singer here and there. Since the May riots in Paris, a student protest that had grown into a citywide upheaval, the police seem to patrol the clubs that dig his sound the most: those catering to the immigrants, the intellectuals. So the work is slow.

His steadiest gig becomes a solo one in the basement of a bank-turned-apartment building in Barbès, not far from the metro station. In the building's basement, the youth of the neighborhood have established their own nightclub. Promoting their gig roster exclusively by word of mouth, on college campuses and in ghetto tenements, they run a thriving midnight world at the bottom of a steep marble staircase that's invisible to anyone who isn't in the know. It is not an entirely legal enterprise, but it goes on just the same. They call the place Goutte d'Or, "A Drop of Gold," after the name of their neighborhood.

The basement club's founders are also Mansour's weekend futbol mates: sunset games where he and all the other brown boys from the Caribbean, from Africa's North and West, lord over the streets, frustrating traffic and drawing a crowd, the game's goalposts marked with kids standing guard and the poles of defunct streetlights. The police want no part in the neighborhood, so most nights they play for hours and hours in peace. He really plays for fun, but he plays harder around the time Bonnie walks up the block from work. One time, she'd stopped, watching him play with a gaze so penetrative that he was the first to drop his eyes.

The food at the Goutte d'Or club is Moroccan some nights, Syrian other nights, Belgian a few times. Always abundant, all payments in cash. They don't sell much more than water in the way of drinks, but somebody always finds Mansour some hard liquor: the only item on his radar. The place is filled with miniature postcolonial flags, sketches of North African and Parisian protest slogans on napkins, handwritten tributes to murdered mothers and uncles hiding in water glasses with straws and toothpicks. A crowd as determined for revolution as they were for romance, the request is always for love songs.

Bonnie comes some nights, but less and less as August nears. He has felt her drifting from him, a thing he knows he is causing but can't help. He isn't sure how far he's pushed her away until she turns up at the club one evening with a man. While the drummer solos, Mansour spots them entering. He usually is a master at playing it cool, but he feels weightless, caught off guard by the sight of them together, as if the heaviest part of him has already leapt from the stage. But he's in the middle of a good show, with an audience he respects: a distraction from his worst instincts. As the drummer solos, Mansour assesses her companion: Moroccan; grass-blade thin; likely a Marxist, judging by the pained expression on his face; and, considering his slacks and glasses, a college boy.

College boy guides Bonnie to a table near the stage, a bit of a forceful tug by the hand, as though he meant to indicate to the room that she belongs to him. Mansour knows then that this is only maybe a second week out together at the most. The boy doesn't know Bonnie at all. (If he did, he'd know that forcefulness wasn't going to work in his favor.) And then Mansour composes himself enough to look at her finally. He is expecting guilt or some look of defiance—it would have been easier to accept—but she smiles and waves at him like a friend.

She is staring up at him with that mix of awe and coyness, the way she's always looked at him. But he clearly sees longing, a somberness in her gaze, like she's missed him.

Somebody shouts from the corner: "Are you gonna sing?"

The band is staring at him, the people too. He laughs a little, at how completely she's undone him.

"Come on, are you gonna sing?" the man says again.

"I'm gonna try," Mansour says. He closes his eyes. Opens them again. Looks right at her.

"What do you need?" he says.

She is startled, put on the spot in front of the quiet room. But she smiles her anti-smile, tightening her mouth like she's fighting to keep it in.

"Maybe something slow."

He turns to the keyboardist, asks in French for a blues.

Unhooking the mic, he starts to walk the stage, beginning to vocalize, testing notes, as the musicians build the sound. He sings for her, a sound warning her about the way he loves (he needs something slow too): a thing with pauses, with play and trepidation. Each note is careful, a brave step forward in the dark. And there, standing between the crooked posters of Elvis and Sam Cooke, Mansour sings and sings and sings Gil Rodney away too. When the evening ends around three or four in the morning, and the tables have been wiped and stacked with chairs, the collective pays Mansour a third of whatever they made on the door, cash collected in a woven grass basket a Congolese grad student donated for some fundraiser or another. By the time he wraps his set, Bonnie and the Moroccan have long left their seats, like the rest of the crowd. But on his way out to leave, Mansour finds Bonnie slumped, sleeping in the corner, waiting for him near the coatrack at the front door.

At the club's back alley, in the twilight, they dash through the misty rain. And soon there is no one but them, walking up into their shadows, as the streetlights paint each raindrop golden for a moment on its way to the ground.

64. **BONNIE DROPS THE** stylus onto Sarah Vaughan's record, her hands still damp from the rain.

In the dark, beside their records, Mansour undresses her by the flashes of the storm's lightning: dropping her silk blouse onto *A Love Supreme,* her black slip onto *The Modern Sound of Betty Carter.* Then she's shivering in the hot room, a nervousness in her body that her mind doesn't share.

"What do you think I'm gonna do to you?" He whispers with a smile, teasing her.

"Whatever I've done to you, hopefully," she says, teasing back as she observes him, his hunger.

Mansour lifts her by the thighs, walking her to the bedroom's open doorway, shocking her with the ease of his handling. When he slides inside her, his rhythm splits Sarah Vaughan's notes into fourths, then sixths, then eighths in her ears: the guts of some future J Dilla beat. Her body chases his rhythm, drifting from her mind's control. The panic, the excitement of this enlivens her; a blinding heat rises in her as she changes their pace, starting to use her hips.

Then they focus, forehead to forehead. Patiently aligning, until there is nothing between them but skin. Bonnie catches a glimpse of inside Mansour: a flash of bright emerald that briefly obscures her vision. And what she cannot see any more of this first time, Bonnie feels. Mansour is endless. Open, maybe broken.

His arms weaken under her thighs as Bonnie rests her chin on his head and holds Mansour to her body. Coolness covers them and they breathe and stop.

65. **LIFE IS A COMPULSIVE GOSSIP,** always whispering what's to come. Some months before they landed in Paris, the Sahara sneezed west. Then sand crossed time zones like streets, fertilizing the tangled abundance of the Amazon, sending a light sprinkle of dust over Western Europe. This Afro-Brazilian dust arrives in Goutte d'Or in September and presents itself modestly: a subtle amber muting to the sky that keeps a dawn feeling through the hours. But this strange sight, this strange color, burrows so far into the subconscious minds of the people that for a few nights, they dream in gold. Daily life in the streets loses some of its gravity, as they reckon with this rare evidence that the world is one.

Peeling her eyes from the strange sky, Bonnie pulls the last of their things—a fitted sheet—from the communal clothesline and it cracks in the cool air, throwing microscopic traces of the Sahara between her toes. She keeps looking for her childhood in this terrain, in this place. There is maybe some hint of Claudine at the counters of convenience shops, when brown little girls in buckled shoes get on tiptoes to be eye level with their mother's hands, or in the racing silhouettes of those same young mothers, chasing buses at sundown with their daughters on their hips—but that is all. Bonnie's early life didn't have a single witness, and it seems these days to be a thing imagined.

Now that she quit the textile factory (out of boredom), she is home most days, where she and Mansour play incessantly, like children. Their carrying on has incurred some pounding on the ceiling from the family above them, chastisements in Arabic from the floor below. But when he goes off to work at the bakery or the club, the neighborhood feels sordid again. Some of the houses seem to be made in jest—sheets and shawls for windows, a slab of wood for a door.

This morning, Bonnie returns from the clothesline surprised to see that Mansour hasn't left for work. He is on his hands and knees in the living room, drawing a map of Europe across their warm wooden floor with white chalk. He's made mountains where there are mountains, rivers where there are rivers. Numbers and names are scribbled on countries. His body scurries after his left hand as he tallies prospective money and mileage. Without turning around, he speaks, startling her with the richness of his morning voice.

"It's looking pretty apocalyptic out there," he says.

"Lil bit. Aren't you supposed to be at work?"

"Yusef sent everybody home. He thinks the sky's a bad omen."

"Black people think everything's an omen," she says, and he laughs a little. She climbs between his legs, leaning back into him. She observes his expression carefully as he studies his drawing on the floor.

"Too much?" she says, quietly.

"Is what too much?" He says, his eyes still on his map.

"Am I crowding you lately?"

"Yes, woman! Get away from me!" He says, a perfect mimic of an American superhero. He squeezes hard, his arms tight around her, kissing her face until she's squirming away, squinting and squealing.

"OK, OK! I got it. Jesus." She laughs.

Her eyes drift across the floor, observing his map wordlessly as she leans back, snuggling into him comfortably.

"There's nothing for the UK," she says.

He rests his chin on her shoulder from behind. "I'm aware of that."

"You worried about those English, aren't you?" she teases. He cuts his eyes as she giggles.

"I can help, you know," she says. He leans back, peering at her suspiciously.

"I'm serious."

"How good's *your* English?"

She scoffs.

"What?" he says. "I need *English*. Not American."

His plan is simple, if ambitious: Six countries in eight weeks. Enough money and press to start over. She will make the calls to English-speaking promoters. He will teach her what Gil taught him ("You can't just be an *artist*, you got to know the business side of things too—unless you out to be a slave all your goddamn life"): to say she's from a company, to lead with his credits, to get past the secretary by asking for the decision-maker by name. She can find the names in the paper—which he's hoarded for months, same way her grandmother hoarded the *Afro-American* newspaper. She'll say her client opened for Bob Dylan; *The Guardian* called him the African James Brown. The first part is a lie, the second is true. All deals are closed that way, he tells her, just as Gil told him.

He coaches her like a film director. She plays the part of a tempera-mental American manager. He watches her performance while he sits at her feet, his arms tight around her shins, a pencil between his teeth, listening to her interrogate British promoters.

Her client needs a room with a good view, thirteen pieces of bak-lava, a pianist familiar with the work of Nana Caymmi.

"Who?" Mansour hears a man shout back over the phone.

"*Nana Caymmi!*" she screams, playing her part.

"Who is Nana Caymmi again?" she asks Mansour quietly, a hand over the receiver.

Artist-minded, he is modest in his financial asks. Lowballing. A number that, she points out, hardly leaves a profit after transportation and the band.

"It's more than what we played for in the States," he yells with a mouth full of toothpaste from behind the bathroom door.

"Well, as Malcolm would say, you've been had!" she yells back.

After the first two days of carefully studying his tactics, she starts to riff with her own variations. Bonnie discovers she has a way of syncing up with people, of matching their tone, mirroring them until she seems like a part of them, thus inspiring their full surrender. She tries a few different accents, discerning in the first few seconds of a call whether it's better to seem American or European, Black or white. When negotiating, she oscillates between being girlish and someone ruthless who will end phone calls midsentence.

"You can't hang up on people," he says.

"Why not? They didn't have the money."

She sees him stop midstroke while painting the living room wall when he hears her throw out a figure far higher than what they'd discussed, the look on his face caught between horror and admiration. She has the timing, the sensibility, of the kind of drummer he still can't find. It's all in the way she uses silence. Tiny pauses—just enough time for adjusting her glasses, for scratching behind her ear—to create pressure. The start of an invisible clock. *Did they want her wares or not?* He asks her what planet she comes from and she laughs. But her penchant for negotiation has been inherited from a long line of Black attorneys who had saved Black people, kept them safe and free, with their tongues.

Later, he leans in the bathroom doorway, staring for a long time as she pin-curls her hair.

"What?" she asks coyly, matching his leer in the mirror.

"You're mean," he says. An epiphany.

She grins her cocky grin. A perplexing combination of innocence and wisdom. A rigorous mind that works a problem until it cracks.

66. **THAT EVENING,** as they're discussing the terrible exchange rate, the weakness of their dollars abroad, he smells tar. It congests him, cutting through the candied yams Bonnie's left simmering on the stove while they lick stamps, packaging demos for southern Europe. And then he feels it coming on. That delicate aura that tunes the room to a disturbing precision: her hair strands are suddenly so important to his mind that he can see where they sprout from swollen follicles. Then the silence of the room drops an octave in tone, as if they've been sucked underground. And then he's certain.

He goes and hides out in the bathroom. There, he locks the door and turns on the tub faucet for an alibi. Defeated, he slides to the floor and waits.

By the time Bonnie knocks, announcing a burnt dinner with a giggle ("oh Lord, this is a mess") and humming Laura Nyro, he's come to, tasting pennies as always. He cannot tell how much time has passed until he feels the wetness along his back where he's splayed on the floor; the bathtub is running over. She's pounding on the locked door, trying to break in, calling his name.

When he can get to his feet and unlock the door, it takes all his power not to collapse into her arms.

"What happened?"

"I'm OK. I swear."

"What *happened*?"

"Just got a little dizzy."

Holding himself up with his hands on her shoulders, they waddle, as if drunk dancing, to the edge of the tub, where, under his weight and despite the water, they plop down—until he, unable to sit up for long, slides to the ground again. She turns off the tub faucet, the silence now so piercing that it creates a pain in his head. A silence like that crowd he couldn't charm the night before at Goutte d'Or.

"What do you mean 'just dizzy'? Dizzy from what?"

He is silent for a moment, as he always is when she asks her many questions. The pause is always his chance to decide whether or not to tell her the truth. He kisses her thigh, sweaty and salty beside his face, says nothing more. His heart is still convulsing out of rhythm, like a little sticky-fingered demon had reached into his chest while he was seizing and tangled the veins. Bonnie puts her hand there, pushing down a little, like she could press it back into its standard time signature. This kind of touch, the tenderness of it, is new from her. He's staring at her hand, surprised.

"I think you drink too much," she says, and he wants to laugh a sullen laugh. *If only*, he thinks to himself.

67. **HIS GIGS AT** the local club start to attract a larger and larger crowd. He continues with his job biking deliveries, and Bonnie continues to take the lead on his bookings. Now when he returns from the club in the evenings, the kitchen table and walls, the living room floors and couch, are all covered with poster paper filled with venue names with checks and *x*'s beside them. More than once, he carries her from the living room floor to the bed, prying the phone out of her sleeping hand. Then he takes over, calling overseas until his eyes won't stay open. Then he wakes before her to make his calls before work. Their lives begin to take on a rhythm.

While he's at work one day, the landlord calls for the rent. Twice. Bonnie doesn't know the state of things until she takes the call.

She dips into her grandmother's account for the first time, has the money wired to a bank in Paris. But when she hands it to Mansour, he asks her what it's for, then tells her to keep the money, that he'll find a way.

"How? With what?"

They argue for the first time. Their voices loud and raw, testing one another, as she follows him from the bedroom to the kitchen. She needs

to learn how to live with a man, he yells as he violently scrambles eggs.
She slams the bedroom door.

As the bookings from further afield continue to come in slowly, Bonnie
feels like a failure. Mansour assures her that this happens all the time.
But instead of feeling comforted, it amplifies her fear of losing him. If
she can't help, she thinks, what does he need her for? The possibility of
separation—or, more so, the perceived impossibility of ever simply
belonging anywhere, with anyone—resurfaces. She makes more calls.

At night, they turn into chain-smoking postal workers, addressing
and packaging copies of the first album with press kits to be shipped
off to hundreds of promoters. That's when she discovers that he cannot
write in French. His call notes, even the phone numbers, are in ornate
Arabic. When she expresses fascination with his handwriting, he jokes
that the only European language he learned to read and write in with
any dexterity is musical notation. He tries to teach her the Arabic
alphabet: *alif, ba, ta* . . . but she doesn't get very far before he lays flat on
the floor, holding his head at the American accent she cannot shake.

"Don't use your nose like that. It's not ah-leef; it's *ah-leef*."

"Mansour," she says, eyes closed, exasperated. "That's the same
exact thing."

"It's not the same at all! You speak two languages. How can you not
hear that?" he says, sitting up on his elbows, assessing her with genuine
curiosity, his eyes squinted. Throughout their lesson, all of the windows are open, the broken ones propped high with dictionaries and
serving spoons, but they are still drenched in sweat. By the end of the
night, she's begging him to forget it.

Beyond the music—the records, the work—as a man he is still,
mostly, a mystery to her. Attempts to venture any deeper into his story
still produce a wall, a thing that she resents as they become more and

more enmeshed. But Bonnie learns that the easiest way to get Mansour to talk about his past is to get him to talk about music. One day she put on Otis Redding, and when he is singing along—a fidelity to the singer that is uncanny—she asks about some memory he vaguely mentioned when they first met, and when the record dies down, and they've done their packaging for the day, without prompting, he'll usually tell her more: Otis makes him see the Casamance peanut fields.

Otis's grit brings to mind the terrain: a sharp deep-brown gravel that spikes your heels, a dust so fine and hot that it billows through the air like steam. When Otis goes high, Mansour feels the relief he felt at the day's end: when his rounded arms, still soft with childhood, released the last harvest of peanuts into an enormous truck bed. And along the road home, he will smell nothing but peanuts, the scent all through the air; the other Talibé children beside him on the road. . He'll stop there, saying no more, and both of them will lie in the living room's peaceful silence, each seeing their own version of his past.

As they make headway, shipping off fifty packages, closing in on a hundred phone calls, he suddenly seems conflicted. He is moody, picking fights with her after one too many nights of seeing Keifer's name across the top of each record they ship out. After fifty more have been packaged and are waiting at the door, he tells her to stop.

"We're not gonna sound like this anymore," he says. "We can't send these."

"I'm sorry, *what*?" And from the way she's leaning forward, it is clear another argument has begun. Soon, he is gone every morning and most nights, scrambling to find studio time in the city. He has a demo for her some weeks later.

"How much did this cost?" she says. He won't give a straight answer, but she figures it out when the lights go out around nine at night, and she finds him sitting on the floor in the living room, in a dark corner, dressed only in jeans, and with his back against the wall. His elbows are on his knees; he's humming something somber. For the first time he seems unsure of himself. And when unsure of himself, he has a way, she learns, of disappearing. His senses drift elsewhere.

She lights a twelve pack of candles, illuminating every corner until the whole place glows like a church. The wobbly refractions of the amber flames are enough to draw by, so she does. She is in just the right mood—mirroring his: pensiveness, melancholy, not quite sadness.

She likes being in the room with him, though they are not speaking and at opposite ends. But after a while he comes closer, and she lets him see. She's drawing a woman. "Who is that?" he asks. "I have no idea," she says, shaping the soft jawline, the gap in the teeth. He won't go away, so she gives her pencils to him to sharpen.

68. AS THE WINTER APPROACHES, they lose a third of their prospective bookings to budget cuts and ghosters. She blames the new demo but doesn't tell him so. She thinks back. When they were still in America, in the spring before they left for Paris, lying in Washington Square Park, he'd explained his musical taste to her, his vision for the next project. Thinking back on that fusion—Pavarotti, Malian and Cuban music—she wonders, who would understand this combination of sounds? Will anyone? She worries now.

For several days, she disappears from morning till evening, leaving well before he's awake. Taking the train into the city on her own dime, she bogarts the promoters who won't answer her calls. Then she goes further. In cities across Europe, using her hardly tapped inheritance, she ambushes club owners after performances. If she finds them at the kitchen door, she'll jump in to take the tray in their hand to the crowd. If she finds them moving chairs, she'll grab one too, following them to the back in her heels. This gives her time for her thirty-second pitch. And she learns when to push and when to recede. She moves quickly: fifteen, sometimes twenty venues in a day. She knows when she has a buyer, and now, she never leaves without something written down, selling gigs on the spot. "Could we put this on paper?" she'll say with a smile. Mansour had brought that smile out of her. He's a smiler, regardless of his mood, and it's sometimes a way, she discovers, of keeping people at a distance, a way of diverting attention from your true feelings.

She gets signatures on bar napkins, on the backs of sticky drink menus, throwing back strains of Vodka she can't pronounce to prove that she can hang. She learns to hold in her cough until she is out in the snow, racing to a phone booth to report the victory to Mansour. But she doesn't tell him everything.

She doesn't tell him that some men leave their personal numbers with their signatures. That while they peruse her contract, discussing the deal points, they slip in matters about their personal lives too. Their problems are always the same: that they are aging, that their wives are inattentive, that they have too much money in the bank.

They are comfortable touching her even if she squirms. Even if she laughs nervously and shifts in her seat, they slap their hands on her thigh with greasy, defiant grips. They want to tell her what they think of her body, in more and more explicit terms as the conversation progresses and the alcohol flows.

She replays these events in her mind afterward and is ashamed of how often she resorts to laughter, to stepping back and back until there is nowhere else to go. Ignoring their hands, while she repeats the deal points, pretending somehow that the hand that is caressing her shoulder, that the foot bringing her chair closer, does not belong to the man she is speaking to.

He never confesses that these long trips disturb him. That while she's gone, he imagines that there are other men. He has never recovered from the shock of seeing her walk into Goutte d'Or with that Moroccan, one of many things they moved passed by not discussing. When he watches her with the phone to her ear, looking over her shoulder to gives a thumbs-up for another deal that has been closed for him, he can't say more. It feels foolish to belabor old pains, when she seems to be devoted to him in so many ways.

When she gets back to the apartment in the early mornings, Mansour is seldom home. He has taken a new, additional job on the metro tracks, joining a campaign to extend the city lines. He knows that he shouldn't work on the road, that the fumes could trigger his condition. But he lies to the manager and starts work as soon as he's hired. Observing the group, he gathers that the other two Senegalese men do not speak French. As the boss runs through security measures, Mansour watches the men stare blankly; he finds them later in the lunch line, trying to repeat the instructions to them in Wolof. He is surprised when the words do not flow easily, that his native language is almost something forgotten. It makes him think that maybe his past could be shed in its entirety, that maybe there was a way of stepping into a new life, a different path, with her.

69. **BONNIE WAITS FOR** Mansour on the street. They have spent the evening at a Paris nightclub owned by Mansour's gypsy friend. The club owner is twenty-one, energetic, and slender. He banged the table defiantly when Mansour explained that America is nothing more than smelly convenience stores and bad traffic.

Mansour, a delight for the gypsies. His friend's great-grandmother, the club's original owner, comes down the steps from her apartment sideways, one by one, to see him. The bartender tells Bonnie that the woman hasn't been to the club in months, that her arrival now is an event. The patrons applaud her entrance, standing until she's seated. Mansour breaks his song to applaud too. When she is comfortable in her seat, which has been brought onto the stage not far from Mansour at her request, he and the pianist resume.

The woman is frozen, her face gazing upward at him like a light. Between songs, she reaches for him, and when he comes close, he brings his head down to meet her. She kisses him. She says to him, in a language that he cannot understand, *You are my soul. You are my soul.* She says it again and again. And for the first and the last time, Bonnie sees him cry.

It is the same when they go to Livorno. A weekend trip they take (unbeknownst to her) to evade their fuming landlord in Goutte d'Or. Mansour introduces her to more of his friends, men and women who are just as in love with him as she is, several of them more so. The place is crawling with his ex-girlfriends, or lovers at least. Bonnie would call them white girls; they'd call themselves Syrian, Egyptian, Toulousian, Italian.

The club's owner in Livorno is a five-foot-tall, fast-talking, drink-making, table-wiping, mic-setting woman with full hips named Amal. She hugs Bonnie first, then Mansour. Mansour and Amal hold on to each other too long, nose to nose, so close that Bonnie is certain that they will kiss, right in front of her.

"You don't look well," Amal says in Italian, a hand to his cheek. She pats it playfully until he smiles. He remembers enough of the Italian the thick-legged woman taught him to say that he's fine.

Bonnie is focused on Amal's body. There is so much of her, a frame that fills Mansour's hands in a way that hers never will. When the club lights dim and he takes the stage, Amal slips in beside Bonnie, asking with warm breath and a hand on her hand to see to it that he stays well.

"It's very difficult, isn't it?" Amal says to Bonnie while staring straight ahead at Mansour. When Bonnie doesn't respond, Amal looks right at her. There's wisdom on her face, a knowing of something, maybe herself, maybe Mansour, that Bonnie envies. "He's very difficult."

"He isn't with me," Bonnie says.

Amal smiles at the competition in Bonnie's voice.

"Have the dreams started?" she says.

Bonnie says nothing, fighting the urge to know more. Amal sighs, taps Bonnie's hand lightly, and heads back to the bar.

Mansour sings that night for free. Had insisted on it. When his set is over, his rejuvenation, his renewed freedom, is palpable. He kisses Bonnie so hard he almost knocks her back. Out on the street, Amal's brother chases him up the block with the cash in hand. Bonnie is relieved to see the money, but then Mansour tucks it back in the man's pocket before hugging him goodbye.

70.
IT IS DECEMBER, and he still cannot tell her with words. So instead, as they walk through the neighborhood, he points at the motifs in the Turkish rugs, some beaten good as new, hanging from the walls of half-finished buildings, others dividing the stations of spices in the tiny mazes of the city's miniature souks. The patterns of the rugs hanging in front symbolize marriage, he says, hoping she'll take a hint. But she just smiles. They have watched the snow silence Paris, the unpaved roads turn soupy and slick with dirty ice, the scarce trees still harboring leaves that are too weightless to shed. And though he knows that it is not quite the time, he's worried that there is no sign at all that she wants more too.

———

In the middle of December, the underground club in Goutte d'Or shuts down, making money even tighter. Bonnie tallies their final earnings on a calculator and is devastated by the outcome, holding in the news all day until the lights are off and Mansour cannot see her. She sees him illuminated by the low light of the window. Just home from the metro tracks, he faces away from her as he undoes his boots, sitting on the edge of the bed, his arms on his knees, leaning forward, exhausted. When she tells him the figures, he says nothing. Crosses to the bathroom. She hears the water start. She slips into bed. The tears gather under her chin.

She goes south on the weekend, trying to see how it feels to be alone again. She agrees to meet a promoter for dinner in Toulouse. Over the course of their three phone conversations, it has become clear that the meeting is personal. And on the phone, for some reason, it is easy to agree, but when she gets off at the train station and sees the handsome gray-haired man waiting for her on the empty platform, she cannot approach him.

She goes instead to the train café and waits for a night train to Mende. In the early morning light, she walks the town's quiet quarters, its dirt roads and moss comforting her. She stops at the corner where the house she was born and raised in is, almost walking past it. The property, like the others on the block, is now marked as an administrative building for the local water-filtration system. Surprisingly, staring at the brown-bricked, red-shuttered house where she lived on the top floor with her mother is like staring at any house on the block. There are no answers here. No feelings. There is no lost part of her to find.

When her cab from the metro station drops her home, she walks five blocks past their residence, avoiding entering for as long as she can. She doesn't want to face him. She doesn't want to hear him say it. She doesn't want to have to say it first. When she eventually does go in, she's relieved that he isn't home. She starts packing, puts her things by the door. It would be easier to just go. She could call him later from wherever she ends up. In the end, she decides that she cares too much to leave him suddenly. She decides to wait.

He comes through the door minutes later, a baguette in his hand, soccer ball under his arm. Before his keys are out of the lock, he notes her bags. She stands awkwardly in the middle of the room in her good coat, her hands in her pockets.

"I'm sorry," she says.

"Tu vas où? Qu'est-ce qui se passe?" *Where are you going? What's going on?* he says, dropping everything on the table.

"I don't think . . . You don't need me here." She gazes around as if she's just arrived.

"What's going on?"

"I really tried."

"Tried what?" he says, approaching.

"I tried to get the gigs. I . . ." She can't speak. He takes her face into his hands. His grip is firm, assuring. She begins to cry. She tries to pull his hands away but he resists, and she ends up holding on to them. But she will not look at him.

"I really did try. I'm sorry," she says through the tears.

"Is that why you're . . . you're *leaving*? Bonnie look at me."

She finally does.

"Fuck the gigs," he says quietly, but stern, grounding her. Her face is still in his hands. He tips it up to meet his. "It's supposed to be hard. We'll just keep trying, or maybe take a break from all that for a while. Cool?"

"Yeah, OK," she says, her voice almost making it a question. She is baffled as she considers being wanted for her own sake.

He is watching her in turn, waiting for her to fully rejoin the world before he lets his hands fall from her face to her shoulders.

"You weren't gonna get away from me that easily," he jokes quietly, and kisses her, she smiles for him as much as she can.

She takes a few steps backward, sits on the coffee table, and watches him go to the front door and take her bags back into the bedroom. By the time he returns to the living room, her body has calmed. She breathes deeper than she has in years. Love in abundance? At least well within her reach? Mansour is watching her; she looks away from the shock on his face.

The phone rings. She goes to it, picks it up.

"Allo? Oui . . . oui."

Mansour lies back flat on the floor, trembling a little, in shock. Across the room, Bonnie scribbles something on the notepad near the phone. She hangs up and begins to laugh—a deep belly laugh that makes him sit up, worrying again, just as she comes over and lies beside him. She laughs and laughs, the tears streaming down.

"That was . . ." She tries to gather herself, speaking slowly, savoring the words. "That was *Brazil*. Apologizing for the short notice. Milton Nascimento dropped out. And they wanted to know if this—" she holds up the figure she's scribbled down on a piece of paper, "is a suitable fee for you to replace the headliner's opening act for the World Music Festival."

She laughs harder as he screams, pulling her up to her feet. She smiles down from the window as he runs out the front door, his footsteps echoing on their stairs until she sees him bolt onto the streets of Goutte d'Or, leaping up at the sky. They are days from the New Year, only a year away from a new decade, and, for the first time, this has meaning. Bonnie is convinced, finally, that life does change.

MAMA'S DREAM

Switzerland, 1969

71. **ONCE THEY RECEIVE** the deposit from the Brazilian festival, Mansour finally has real money to send to Mama in Switzerland. She pays off a good chunk of her debts and prepares to close on the estate where she will open her restaurant. She buys the first sets of tablecloths and dishes but delays her excitement. She knows that money doesn't solve everything. She's tried this once before.

After Mansour left for New York, Mama had started to save for her restaurant more seriously. She'd gone to the Swiss countryside, where she'd heard rent was cheaper and the visa paperwork didn't take too long. Working in restaurants during the day, she'd made dinners to sell at night, staying up late in the kitchen of the boarding house she lived in with her sisters and the dishwasher girl who she'd just sent for. She'd wrap meals in dish towels and carry them to neighbors, people she'd consider kind so long as they were willing to pay for her product at the price she'd set. She convinced herself that she didn't care if she had to leave food on the back steps or pass it through a narrow slit in the back door, only seeing the pale hand of the purchaser. Her cooking gave her a decent living and kept her out of domestic work, which was

paramount, because with a father of noble lineage, domestic work was
something that she had vowed never to do.

With her savings, she was soon able to rent the lobby of their boarding house every Wednesday night for three hours, which gave her
enough room to serve twenty guests at a time. She'd been ecstatic to
design a menu of her favorite homemade dishes: soupou kanje, thie-
boudienne. She would make simple versions for her European patrons,
ensuring that most of the spices could be locally supplied. She'd called
the lobby Les Mercredis de Mama Ndoye, which she wrote across the
tops of the handwritten menus, crafted with expensive pens and pretty
translucent paper. She'd watched over the dishwasher as she folded
and refolded napkins that first night.

"You're a boss now, Mama," the girl said.

Mama had done her makeup for the first time in years. She'd worn
a pair of black capris she'd bought for the occasion. She'd even bought
a hair relaxer and painted her nails red.

In the weeks prior, she'd made invitations—sixty or so—and sent
them to the neighbors, who had always eaten her dinners, pinning
them to the dishcloths that covered their meals. That night, she'd
waited by the banister. Her sisters roamed the room, looking back at
her every few minutes to share in her nervousness and excitement.

The first hour, they'd had no customers. Mama had snuck under the
stairs and cried. She'd hidden there until she heard her sister speaking
to someone unfamiliar and crept out to see three diners spread cautiously across the room. No one else had come.

After hours, once the sisters had sullenly migrated back to their
room, Mama had gone out to the backyard of the boarding house alone
and broken the three diners' dishes. The three china bowls and three
plates had spread across the rocky ground of the back alley, each shatter a sound that she'd found pathetic, unsatisfying.

From where she'd stood, she could see a black silhouette in the window of a nearby house, one belonging to a family that she'd invited.

The woman, Emma, had been buying Mama's dinners twice, some-times three times, a week. Mama supposed it was her in the window. The light around her figure was golden, the candle close enough to the curtain to show the details of her hair. After a moment, she had blown the flame out and disappeared.

The next day, Mama had soaked her eyes with the juice of a white onion, worried that their heavy redness signified something greater than a consequence of crying through the night. God, she thought, had given her a mouth sore overnight: whenever she thought of confront-ing those she'd invited and had not seen the night before, she'd just bite the sore and cause herself enough pain to keep quiet.

Winter in the mountains could not be avoided with tricks of any kind. It changed daily life, complete with unhurried and giant sheets of cold wet air hovering over the ground. But this year, Mama had not noticed the arrival of the cold. In preparation for her Wednesday din-ners, she'd forgotten to buy herself proper shoes. The morning after her failure, she slipped and fell on the way to deliver her evening meal to Emma's house.

She'd been angry enough, at first, to walk straight to the front door, but she thought of the mouth sore, the pain of which had actually begun to numb because of the cold, and it was in forbearance, in obedience, that she'd chosen to walk around to the back. There she'd encountered a wide and glistening patch of ice and collapsed onto the ground.

She'd lain on her back. The plates of food, which now rested on her stomach, had been luckily spared from the fall. She winced, the back of her head throbbing and hot on the ice. She lay there for a while, watch-ing the snow thicken around her. It had been hard to see her hand, which she lifted up in front of her eyes as the moving white settled around her, separating her from the rest of the world. She'd sat up, found her footing, and finally marched up to the front door.

"I'm coming," Emma had called from another room, deep in the house.

When she'd opened the door, she had her baby on her hip, and her hair was tied down with a rag. Both women waited.

Mama had swallowed. She could taste blood above her lip, felt it dripping down from her nose.

"Your food, ma'am." She'd lifted the wrapped dinner, holding it up high to Emma's face so that their eyes might meet. Face-to-face, hand-to-hand, for the first time.

"Just leave it on the steps," Emma said, closing the door in Mama's face.

Stunned, Mama knocked again.

"Just leave it there," Emma had shouted from inside the house, firm this time.

Mama had knocked still. She'd knocked and knocked until others could hear.

An old man yelled at her from outside a house nearby. "Get away from there before I call the police."

"Just shoot her!" another woman shouted through an open window.

Mama wiped the salty blood coming from her nostrils with her sleeve and kept pounding, her frozen knuckles unable to feel how hard she was hitting the door, the splinters sliding into her skin.

She'd heard a shot, then a whisper, as a bullet pierced the icy air above her. She couldn't see it, but she saw the way it parted the fog. It had brought her back to her senses, gave her a clearer picture of things. She could see something of the narrow street. The fur-shrouded pale faces of the small gathering crowd. The streak of her blood on Emma's door.

She'd retreated, walking down the steps backward, her whole body shaking as if her legs were melting into the cold. The ice seemed thicker on the ground than it had been before, and she'd struggled to walk.

A policeman and the crowd of onlookers watched her slow steps down the ice patch.

Mama had walked the two blocks home and rested in the living room alone, until the landlady came and covered her with a blanket and called the dishwasher girl down to get her.

The night before closing on the estate, this memory comes back to Mama, in all of its detail, and she cries even more than she'd cried before. She vows to leave the past behind her, as she's left so many other painful things behind, and she promises herself that this time will be different. That with a place of her own, life will be new.

III.

SALVADOR DE BAHIA

France, 1969

72. **MANSOUR AND BONNIE** cash the Brazilian check and take the train back to Goutte d'Or in guarded silence, like hand-to-mouth Parisians might detect their money and pounce if they so much as breathe. Home, they spread the francs on the bed and marvel at the dirty paper like it's a child just born. The first thing they've accomplished together.

The news spreads fast. Neither of them know who is telling people, but that night, there begins a stream of quiet knocks by a neighbor, then two, then three, offering congratulations, and before long their apartment is combustible with dancing and glee, and the Goutte d'Or nightclub is briefly reincarnated in Mansour and Bonnie's living room until the light of the morning finally convinces the crowd that it's time to go home.

With all the jubilation, the anticipation, the sudden wealth and resulting anxiety, it should have come as no surprise to Mansour that he seizes. Something fast and noisy and nauseating, mostly in his sleep. In between fits, he looks to his side, thankful she's not there. And maybe because of Bonnie's absence (she is still smiling in her sleep, curled up in a ball in the living room where she passed out on the floor), he lets the thing ride him, hoping it will take its course and soon be gone. When he feels well enough, when he feels that he can breathe and the worst of it has passed, it is because he's in a familiar dream.

A startling cold rises from his heels and moves up to his head. When the cold reaches his mouth, it starts to taste like water, salty. He sputters as his sight returns. He is underwater, in the ocean. A hand pulls him farther in. As the tide withdraws, lowering the water to his waist, it reveals Kiné, her braids flattened to her face by the water. She blocks the sun, but all the light in the world spills in from either side of her. She looks at him with a troubled gaze and then he is suddenly small and she puts him on her hip, gazing out into the horizon. He touches her face. Her skin is slick. Her heartbeat pulses against him like an amplifier, the warmth of her breath on his face.

"Mama!" she calls over her shoulder. "Do you have Mansour's medicine?"

Mama calls back, "Let me go look for it."

They are now on sand, and Kiné places Mansour on the ground. He whines and reaches for her leg, but she turns around and walks back toward the water.

He sees a wave coming. He freezes.

Kiné leaps inside.

The very edge of the wave absorbs him and he floats for a while beneath the surface of the water. Underwater, he sees his mother drifting before the force of the water slams him into a rock and he tastes the blood gushing from his broken nose. A hard pull yanks him from the water. Mama is pulling him above the surface.

He coughs as she screams for his mother, a scream that stretches from the shore to the horizon.

On the day of their flight to Rio (the only way to Bahia) for the World Music Festival, the band meets for lunch in Paris. A little bit drunk,

Mansour tells a rambling story about Liam's only prospective adoptee as a child.

"Is that supposed to be funny?" the drummer, Davis, asks in a Brooklyn accent that makes Bonnie smile to herself. It's been too long. He's flown in for the festival, one of two old band members to reunite with them. The trumpeter, after much back-and-forth, is planning to meet them in Brazil. The significance of the gig has brought Liam and Mansour back together.

"It wasn't funny then," Liam says.

"Come on, man," Mansour retorts, speaking now to the group. "Listen, he was born *into* the system—he'd been in the system for fifteen years! And who adopts him?" Mansour's eyes glaze over with laughing tears, and he grips the Irishman's shoulder as he laughs. "A pedophile! He waits his whole life for parents, and he gets a pedophile."

The Irishman is looking down at his toast. He starts to smirk, and then the rest of the table feels permission to break.

"I said: 'My man, you have the worst luck. You have African luck, brother.'" They're all laughing now, and the Irishman shakes his head with closed eyes and a smile.

Mansour continues, "So I say: 'What do you want me to do?' We had a little gig somewhere that night—where were we, man?"

"It was in Copenhagen," Liam chimes in drily, repeating the obvious, a thing he's already said.

"*Copenhagen!* Yes. I said: 'What do you want to do?' And he says to me: 'Nothing. I just want to run away.'" Mansour turns sullen. "Man, some kids shouldn't come into this world. They just got the worst luck."

Bonnie's glare startles him when he meets it across the table. She is seeing through his laughter. Seeing him down to the bones. Looking at him with her head titled and her heart open, like he's wounded. That way she had of prying too far into him. A thing he felt but couldn't ever quite put into words. Sometimes she does it with language, but mostly with her eyes and her touch.

THE RIO AIRPORT IS ONE BODY

Brazil, 1969

73. **BREATHING, REEKING, SWEARING** in thirty tongues. There, in the middle of Carnival season, there is no such thing as space between people. Bonnie keeps her grip tight on Mansour's arm, letting him drag her forward through the airport as the body of the crowd starts to move.

She thought they came early. Mansour doesn't perform until Thursday, so she'd assumed that arriving by Monday would be enough to avoid all this chaos. He is a quick replacement for the headliner's opening act, so there had not been much lead time anyway. Their shot arrived (as shots do) as one of those quick yes-or-no moments, and of course they'd said yes without thinking about what was to follow.

"Can you see any of the guys?" Bonnie's yelling to Mansour, who, for all his aural gifts, for his tantrums over the flatness of the phone ring in their apartment, cannot hear a word she says over the moving crowd.

On the plane, Mansour had sat with her in silence for a while. But then he'd lifted the armrest, wanting her closer, and even on the plane she'd managed to encircle him tightly, like she needed to get inside of his skin. The passengers were sleeping, the turbulence had settled, the lights had dimmed.

"What do you dream about? I heard you again last night."

For the first time, he does not hesitate. "My mother. She drowned herself when I was small."

He was testing himself and her, but his words had passed between them easily. But the absence of her hot breath on his stomach made him look down. She was holding her breath, and when she let it out and finally spoke, her eyes were glazed over, like she'd turned blind.

"That doesn't have to mean you have bad luck," she'd said quietly, more to herself than him.

———

Bonnie has a photograph of the man who is supposed to meet them outside the terminal in her pocket. But the bodies are so tight around her that she cannot reach into her jeans. Then the line picks up pace, and she's being pushed into Mansour, then into a short man with a swayback. In the movement, there is a little gap and she takes this chance to slide her hand into her pocket. She holds the now-crumpled photograph of their guide: a curly-haired man who grins like a toothpaste model.

She's been standing for so long, she feels certain she will soon swoon. All of a sudden, Mansour has their things, and they finally hurry out of the doors. There at arrivals, Bonnie looks from the crumpled picture to the room-deep lineup of sweaty people welcoming disoriented travelers with signs. She looks for Mansour's name and is surprised when she sees her own instead. The man holding it is most certainly not the toothpaste model in the picture. This one looks like he works under cars all day, maybe sleeps under them too. Having barely survived their journey through the airport, and having already tasted the rigor of Brazil, Bonnie decides that she prefers it this way. She'd rather be in this rugged man's hands.

When the man speaks, she remembers his voice from the phone call in Paris that changed their lives. He is kind, so full of excitement about

Mansour's demo that Bonnie feels embarrassed to ask, but she does. Out in the parking lot in the dark humid night, she peels open the photograph.

"This is not you ... ," she says gently as the man looks up from handing off their luggage to the Black driver.

"No, that's my assistant. He reels 'em in. But I kill 'em." He smiles, so she finds a way to do the same. It baffles her that *this* man is the promoter. She'd expected someone more debonair.

Just as she goes to get in the car, just as she's imagining a smooth and fast ride to their hotel so that they can sleep and regain the power of speech before their flight to Bahia the following evening, the man takes a deep breath. She braces herself.

"So, we have a small, small problem," he says.

"Yes?" she says, impatiently, and she looks at Mansour. As he waves over Davis and Liam, who emerge from the airport doors, Mansour appears more calm and put together here, after all they've suffered, than he did on a daily basis at home. She will never make sense of him.

Small as he is, the promoter puts one arm around Bonnie, one around Mansour, and starts to walk with them some paces away from the others. She is quickly enlivened by the mountains in the distance, a scene she almost missed in the thickness of the dark.

"You're scheduled for Thursday, I know—but could you be available sooner? Why come all the way from Paris for one show?" He smiles that struggling smile again, and Bonnie can see this won't be hard. He is a hustler, and thank God he isn't any good at hiding it.

She looks at Mansour, speaking their silent language. *Wanna do it?* She puts a cigarette between her lips and lights it. He winks, and she knows he's cool. She turns to the man again. Blows smoke. He looks hungry. He needs them as much as they need him, maybe more. He scratches his sweaty neck.

In the open trunk, fumbling for a while, she finds the contract in her briefcase. She sits on the hood of the car with her legs carefully crossed, the wind blowing her stretched Afro around as she marks up the paper by the light of the opening and closing airport doors.

She gives the man the document, blows smoke, fluffing her hair, feeling herself.

"What's this?"

"The terms," she says.

The cheer leaves the man's face. He looks far better without it.

"*Triple?*" he says, looking up from the paper.

She nods sweetly. Mansour's smitten, shaking his head at her gall.

In Bahia, the car winds in steeper and steeper rounds until the vibe splits among the band: half of them screaming, the other half laughing riotously. Bonnie and Mansour are in the laughing half. When they finally step down from the smoking car, when they fall onto the slick cold clay, the cool air quells their dizziness.

Now with a show booked for the day after tomorrow, they wander into the empty festival grounds. At their feet, 400-year-old stones from the torn-down sugar mill are strewn about, marking a path that takes them in a circle. They are told by an attendant with a complexion richer and darker than both of theirs, that the enslaved once toiled here on a plantation so large and notorious that the land likely holds the bones of folks from both of their bloodlines under its ground. Bonnie looks above her head and gasps at the dozens of monkeys sleeping, their bodies clinging to palm trunks like children to mothers. She reaches for Mansour's hand.

The light is dwindling, but the evening feels particularly alive: men work on the stage in a loud and steady rhythm; cicadas in the dense foliage surrounding them make a sound like sizzling oil. The percussionists who will open the festival can be heard practicing in a layered symphony, echoing around the hills.

They approach the stage and she watches him walk the length of it slowly, as if entering a sacred space. He puts both hands on his head and takes in the risers, starting some feet from the stage and then into the distance where the mountains peak. Preparation for the largest crowd he's ever sung for. The largest crowd either of them will have ever seen. He sits on the stage, rests his arms on his knees awestruck.

She looks up, seeing the lights that have been installed by the hundreds, the thousands of black cords swaying in the warm, gentle breeze like vines. She sits on the stage's edge beside him, and protectively he puts an arm in front of her knees. She looks and sees the drop down. Their wide eyes meet: *How. Did. We. Do. This?*

Bonnie wins some battles—the tripled money, more press—but the promoter wins some too. With a plan not to announce Mansour as a replacement until seconds before he goes onstage, the man will get a big audience for a cheaper act, leaving it to Mansour to turn the crowd around.

Bahia does not believe in secrets. Everything the city says and feels and cooks pours in through their hotel shutters; there is no way to make the room quiet.

In the bathroom doorway, Bonnie tries to keep her eyes on the bright teal tiles, desperate to stop her racing mind. Ever since they've entered the hotel suite, she's been battling a silent panic, certain of some vague danger she cannot define. She crouches down on the bathroom floor now, trying to get as small as she feels.

"What's the matter?" he calls calmly from the bedroom. When she doesn't answer, he tells her to come to him, and she does, stopping a

few feet shy of where he sits on the edge of the bed, ashamed of herself
for being how she is

Another woman would be out dancing with him, sparkling with his
sweat, her ass at his pelvis, her shoes long abandoned in the sand of
some beachfront Samba club, dragging him between the giant cars
from the 1950s that crowd the Bahia streets. But they will pass the
night in a hotel suite with half the lights off and a fuzzy jazz station on
the radio because she, despite all they've accomplished to be here, cannot simply feel good.

"You should go out if you want. You're just gonna end up working
if you stay here."

As if he hasn't heard her, he guides her the rest of the way to him by
her wrist. He's looking up at her, speaking with a pencil in his mouth.

"You're always thinking too much," he says, his hands running up
and down her arms as if to warm them. She would climb onto his lap,
but there's sheet music in it.

"I'm frustrated," she guesses wearily, unsure of what exactly she's
feeling. Hoping that maybe he knows. He observes carefully, removing the pencil before diagnosing her. He gets her right most of the
time.

"You're just exhausted," he says at last. He taps the bed beside him.
Instead, she puts the music aside in a heap and pushes him down, falling onto him.

"Hey! Not me. You," he says, smiling up at her.

She lays there, watching him like a pendulum she's waiting to be
hypnotized by. Seeing the shape she's in, he pushes the sheet music
farther away, surrendering the night to her. He removes her glasses
and starts smoothing her braids.

"What are you thinking about so hard?"

He suddenly seems so young. She blinks, but that doesn't change
the softening of his jaw and cheekbones. His eyes a little wider. The

way he might've looked ten years before. And then she knows what she's feeling.

"Are you . . . are you sure she drowned herself?"

"I shouldn't have told you—"

"It could've been an accident."

He shakes his head, just shakes his head, and says nothing.

"How can you be sure?" she asks.

He won't look her in the eyes, keeps his head down, and when he finally speaks again his voice is gone.

"She said goodbye to me."

———

Bonnie's tears fall without sound, a hand to his cheek, caressing it. For a long while, they lie like this, her touching his face, him just watching her, detached and bewildered. Mute, but he is listening. Listening, and holding fast to her, finally tasting freedom as she cries, and cries, and cries for him.

———

Mansour drifts into a soundless sleep, her hand still at his cheek. She plays with his facial hair, petal soft when it's damp like this. The heat has risen with the night and she cannot sleep. She takes her hand from his face and gently pries his fingers apart where they are locked around her waist. When she succeeds at unfastening him, he stirs with a grunt and his eyes pop open, beaming panic for the seconds it takes him to find her in the dark. Then he spreads wider, freeing her body. A breeze rushes along her back and she feels some relief. Farther away now on the large bed, he still faces her, watching her the way he'd been before. He looks, for a moment, like he's awake enough to speak. His puts his own hand under his cheek as if to recreate her touch. He locks eyes with her and, in seconds, he drifts again.

Bonnie leaves him asleep in the suite and begins to wander. She cannot unsee the look he'd given her. First on the street with the promoter, then again before he'd drifted off to sleep. Something reckless that said he belonged to her and didn't care what she did with him. A declaration that they were one. As she considers it this first time, commitment scrapes her insides as it warms them. Feeling loved is nothing like she imagined; it is more glorious, but still a raw and heavy thing.

Her route takes her into a neighborhood preparing for Carnival. The stars are visible, but the people's liveliness generates the warmth of daytime. Tables of dice, old men with young teeth laughing out contact highs. Making room for him, her soul says, *Go lower, get even closer to the ground*, so she climbs down some rocks to a promontory of houses where the air turns salty, signaling the presence of an ocean far below.

She entices the women there: Black, brown, white, all living Black. A thing she knows without knowing. They want to dress her. They want to adorn her as they are adorned. These performers in a larger festival—in Carnival—lean out of their houses with indigo on their hands as dark as the evening itself. Yards of cloth—golden, yellow, red—bridging the dirt ground from neighbor to neighbor.

The royalty of this world are common people, in slips and girdles, in T-shirts and jeans. They try on headwraps and wigs fit for *The Marriage of Figaro* on shack porches. There is chatter, there is drumming, there are bells and whistles blown. There are foreigners, fellow migrants like Bonnie who stand in the doorways of the little houses like tourists, procuring culture, and liquor and intrigue, rather than sleeping away the night. She walks on, yards of finer cloth hang overhead, and some women hold it in their arms. As they stand, they hold it out to her: an offering. And that scent from massaging thread that lived on her hands when she worked at the textile shop swims through this air in waves and waves. At her feet, there is a trail of large bright-white feathers that compromise no part of their brilliance for the night. A trail of feathers that seem to go the length of the world's waist. What dinosaur of a bird made them? Each one reaching from her elbow to her fingertips.

The trail of feathers leads to a dome of a skirt, above which small, fast-moving women stitch by no light at all. Bonnie's eyes trail up the body in their center, a person on stilts or born as tall as the palm nearby. Blue black, this person doesn't separate from the night until they move, beginning to dance, feathers flapping, feathers gaining on the air. Will they fly? Will they really? "Please fly," Bonnie whispers and waits to see.

74.

THE DAY BEFORE Mansour's first performance, they leave their suite and the large clawfoot tub where they've been entangled for hours, scaring off the geckos, breathing in the scent of limes, playing and planning their life together as their skin pruned from the tepid water. It's where he first tells her, not dreamily but with alarming directness, that he wants her to have his children, six daughters. She'd put a hand to his forehead and said that, clearly, he needed some air.

Now, they climb the mountain until their thighs ache, joining the crowd from the rear to see whatever festival act is playing this early afternoon. It is a Mandingue chamber ensemble from Bamako. They are court musicians, and their king, who has flown with them to Brazil (him in first class, them in coach), will meet Bonnie and Mansour later in the catering tent. Their talk, at a corner table in the bustling place, will begin with the king's real estate projects in New York City, a place where he does good business but has never traveled to.

What they tell him about what's happening in Mississippi will reduce his impressive girth and make him lower his shoulders, and over the course of their tale, he will appear, more and more, like an ordinary man. A person to whom the horrors they describe could happen.

Their conversation will carry on until day turns to evening, until Bonnie, from listening to the stories of the king's daily life, will create

a picture of Africa in her mind. A sky that never makes the same picture twice. Clothes that billow, sand that gets swept. People huddled
close. Very close. And she will look to Mansour beside her, and she will
see that he's protecting himself from the king's stories, even as he listens with a gentle smile. And it will occur to her that it is sound that
will open him up. Just as it was for her. *What is the sound that will open
the rest of him up to me?* And she will close her eyes to the smoke of
steak and upslope fog and her soul will answer. *A child.* The answer
will startle her, even frighten her, with the ease and speed with which
it arrives. But she will find that she needs the rest of him, a little more
than she needs to be afraid, so she will wrap her arms around her body,
and she will savor the last moments of belonging only to herself.

———

They are sitting on the grass watching the stage as the music begins.
The chamber ensemble plays a wide assemblage of string instruments
that, to Bonnie, look like museum antiques. That their sound can reach
so far astounds her. There is something close to a guitar among them,
but the body of the instrument is round. The lead singer is a woman.
She walks from one end of the stage to the other, letting the background, the string instruments, answer her dark phrases as if they are
questions. The singer has a voice like a horn: bellowing long and short
notes, long and short notes between listening. And she is listening
more than she sings. She is waiting for all of the rhythms to lock—listening for that syncing that Bonnie can already hear.

———

The Malians play. Mansour looks over his shoulder and sees Bonnie
grooving with closed eyes. The music nourishes her in a place he
thought only he could reach, a place where only she can reach him, a

place within himself he doesn't like to go to alone. Her freedom makes him feel strangely lonely. When the kora player takes over, Bonnie spreads her arms and reaches into the grass, breaking the dirt on either side of him with her hands.

That night, it starts with a taste. A mix of things that makes her push his mouth from hers with a soft hand.

"What does it taste like?"

She tries to describe it: charcoal in chocolate cake batter. The scent of collard greens when they first hit the pan. The aroma from cooking broccoli when you forget to start with garlic and onions.

He gets out of the tub to bring her water.

The water even tastes like the taste.

They stand over the toilet bowl, waiting for her to vomit. Nothing happens.

They go to the bed and sit and wait.

"It's still there?"

She nods.

"Let's just go back to the tub," she says. He says, "No," tells her to rest.

He's doing that thing. Switching from playmate to protector at the quietest whisper of catastrophe. Some days she doesn't mind this. Today, she hates it, tells him she's not a goddamn child.

Child is the word that brings it again, and she rushes to the bathroom, where it still won't come up. She sits on the toilet top, feeling his worry more than her own.

Did she drink the water from the tap?

"No, Mansour."

Did she eat the fruit here without rinsing it?

"No, Mansour."

Did she eat anything that wasn't cooked?

"No, man. Goddamn."

He wakes her in the middle of the night, maybe early morning, she can't tell. She is sweating, her bones heavy.

He's very close to her face, that scent of soap and lightning.

"I think something in here's bothering you," he says.

She tries to speak, but her throat is clogged.

"On y va." *Let's* go, he says.

She groans. "You're outrageous." She rolls over.

She doesn't remember the walk in the dark to the carriage. Only waking once or twice when the waves crash too loudly in the distance, otherwise sleeping hard on his shoulder the whole way to the road. When they reach a higher altitude, her body wakes her, eager for her to witness the narrow wooden carriage that carries her, drawn by a white mare on a winding clay road. A shimmering teal ocean below as the sun rises. Their shadows, somehow, are reflected widely across its expanse, making her and Mansour and the coachman larger than the green islands that are strewn about the water like jade stones. She calls his name to be certain that she isn't dreaming all of this. He looks down at her, and the darkness under his eyes lets her know he hasn't slept.

"La Belle au Bois Dormant." *Sleeping Beauty*, he teases, a toothpick in his mouth, a hand to her cheek. "You could sleep through the end of the world."

Pulling herself up, she clasps the wooden seat in front of her and feels the new weight of her wrists. Both of them, laden with his bracelets. When he reaches toward the sky for a stretch, she notices that his wrists are now bare.

They stop at a yellow house on the hill. Mansour thanks the coachman in Portuguese, shaking hands in that way that is more like a hug, that way she's seen Black boys do in New York. The man comes and goes through the open front door, bringing them things she doesn't take note of, too enamored with their surroundings to care.

Mansour tells her this is their home. She is eager for him to come in and close the door, to be inside with her as she walks the bright-red tiles of the cool ground, taking in the house's stucco walls, the squeal of twin yellow birds in a cage at the corner. The dawn breeze is scented with the sweet foulness of fermenting mangoes. She parts the floor-length checkered curtains with two hands. They are so high up that the boats in the distance seem to be moving through the clouds. "It's like," Bonnie says to Mansour, "God took a paintbrush and blurred the line of the horizon. See?"

75. **LATER THAT EVENING,** after a good rehearsal with Liam and the others, Mansour returns to their house in the hills, still needing a way into his own voice. Music can be that way sometimes. Blocking him from its insides. And no matter the condition of his voice, which is particularly good right now (the softer water, the humidity, easing up on the alcohol), not being able to get inside makes singing all mechanics, no feeling. Artistic apathy. It's the kind of thing that can poison an audience against you after a single phrase. Never mind that it's painful in and of itself to endure. To combat his insecurity, he's turned, as usual, to ornamentation, overarranging his compositions. He can hear Gil in his head warning him not to overdo it: *Stop showing off. You got it, but you gotta trust that you do.*

From the living room, where he should be making sense of the strange transitions between songs, jotting down some final notes on arrangements in these last hours of solitude, he's instead distracted by Bonnie's wheezy snore. He tries working with the bedroom door closed, but it makes no difference. She's loud as hell.

When they'd first arrived in Paris, she was a deep, shy sleeper, shrinking from his touch, a tight ball that didn't seem to even breathe. But tonight, her outstretched limbs circle the king-size bed like the arms of a clock. Now her hair, which has grown past her shoulders, grazes the floor. From the open shutters, the moonlight follows her as closely as his eyes, keeping her spotlighted in its silver glow. He sees his daughters in the bed surrounding her body, sparkling silver limbs flung over one another in the same wild way. Some with her wide nose, others with her mole, and all with that hair she fights with so much.

Turning back to the music, Mansour thinks of what Keifer told him after the band's first showcase for Onyx Records, after Mansour's first transformative experience onstage. The next time they'd rehearsed, he'd become frustrated, got to the brink of quitting altogether because he couldn't get to that feeling again.

"What? You tryna get high?" Keifer laughed. "Mansour, you're not gonna feel that way every time you perform. And chasing that feeling is the fastest way to drive yourself crazy."

"If I can't feel this again then what's the point?"

"Sometimes it's just work, man. Believe me, there's a lot more to life," Keifer had replied.

In Bahia, Mansour has seen more men who resemble Keifer than he ever did in America. At the market, the beaches; in the men who smoke pipes and play claves, who send samba rhythms into the house from either side of the chilly hills. He keeps seeing his aunts in the Brazilian women too. When he called home to confirm that Mama received his wire for the down payment on the estate, she had been all business, chastising him when she heard the longing in his voice on the muffled line.

"Eh, don't get distracted, you're about to be famous." He'd smiled at the phone; she couldn't hide her pride in him.

Lost in his memories, Mansour lets out a sigh, and the small noise bothers Bonnie, who stirs in the bed.

"Mansee," Bonnie mutters now in the dark room, a name for him that came out of her mouth out of nowhere a couple of days ago. "Are you smoking again?"

She lifts her head to see more of him.

"You're gonna be all *raspy*," she says, throwing back her head, as if his grittiness were the most delicious thing in the world, before dropping her face in the pillow again.

On the first night they met, he saw in her what he'd thought he'd never find. Someone with his penchant for manifesting dreams. Someone with a need for a life of wonder. Someone ripped so violently from all roots that they needed the whole world to feel like home.

76. **AN HOUR TO SHOWTIME,** and when Mansour looks up from the stage, the sky corroborates his plan to chill: it's overcast but terrifyingly bright. All day the band has buzzed around him with repetitive questions, but he'd dodged everybody's angst with nods and vague one-word answers. When they wouldn't leave him alone, he hid out in an old slave cabin on the festival grounds, and when the musicians asked Bonnie if she knew where he'd gone, she kept it vague to protect his peace. Laughing, she said that he'd gone back to the plantation.

He just needs them to feel it now, doesn't want to plan it any tighter than it's already been planned. Given the way he and Keifer carried on about the music, he knows he's thrown off the New York musicians with these new liberal instructions, contradicting his reputation as a meticulous composer (or, as Bonnie says, a control freak).

But today, even Bonnie would agree that he is weirdly lax, was late to wake. Then made love to her so good and slow like it was the dead of night and not the most important morning of their lives. Washing her back in the shower, he told her that he'd surrendered the day. He could tell she had enough on her mind without getting too far into his; he could tell that she was half-listening, nodding and pretending to understand what the hell he meant. And now, out on the stage for their run-through, he's still not quite in his body, his mind hovering just above the preshow scene.

The drummer, Davis, has food poisoning, but he is coming into the wings now; he has found a blonde to tend to him. The trumpeter is still unclear on the transitions. He's stopped asking Mansour for clarity because he doesn't understand his answers, but as he walks onstage, he pulls Liam to one side and vents.

"It's just crazy how he hears one thing and can't ever communicate what the hell he means! Play it like this, like that; like what?"

Liam nods, sympathetic, but this many years in, he's used to it.

"And he keeps tellin' me to look at the music. I see the goddamn music, I see the notes, that's not what I'm asking you for, man. Damn."

Bonnie sits on the edge of the stage barefoot, yelling commands at the tech staff with a microphone in hand. They're running the lights, but these aren't the lights he wanted.

The filters finally shift blue. "*Obrigada!*" she lets out, dramatically applauding in the direction of the tech booth. She speaks into the mic to Mansour.

"Is that what you wanted, Mr. Ndoye?"

"Perfeito," he replies with a thumbs-up.

"It took thirty-five people but won't he do it. Hallelujah. Glory in the end," Bonnie jokes on the mic.

"Don't you start," the trumpeter laughs across the stage, making Bonnie laugh louder. She loves having a brother from the States with them.

The new horn section rehearses across the stage. They are perfectly in sync. Crisp. Mansour's notes pop; they enlarge and flow just as he imagined. Mansour is beaming. It's a lifelong dream come true to have musicians who play what's actually on the damn page.

"Hey, you," Bonnie says on the mic, turning back to him.

"Hey," he yells over to her on his mic.

"First smile of the day. I saw that."

"They're fantastic."

"They auditioned for me first. So that's my taste you're appreciating."

"I'm forever in your debt."

"And how would you like to repay me?"

He teases, speaking into the mic with an extra-deep voice—something Don Cornelius-esque. "Mind your manners, Mrs. Ndoye."

"No proposals onstage, please. You'll never live it down," Liam jokes from across the way.

Bonnie is still staring at Mansour. She bites her bottom lip and turns away.

There is a strange sound growing in the distance. An ocean roaring. A thousand monsters hyperventilating. When Mansour leans to the right of the stage, he sees them: the boisterous audience is arriving at the barriers, too many bodies to count. It's the kind of gathering that makes him lose all balance, all sense of time and place. The people are held back by an iron gate like rabid cattle. They've come to dance and are already dancing.

———

To preserve his voice, Mansour doesn't go full out during their last sound check. He sits on a stool in the middle of the stage. But he's making far too many changes this close to showtime. His final-hour ambition always flips Bonnie's stomach: pulling songs, changing rhythms. She disappears to the caterer's tent. There's a host of problems there too, chiefly that everything has pork in it. She speaks to the promoter's assistant.

"Did you read the rider? He can't eat any of this stuff. Can you get me a hotel menu instead, please?"

"Sure, absolutely, ma'am."

She turns away, gagging at the scent of the food. She rushes back to the stage's open air. The breeze works well at first.

A poster of the album cover, scaled for the enormous stage, has just been erected. It lords over the entire event. At this size, all its flaws are exaggerated: the awkward shape of Claudine's left eyeball, the full lips that look misshapen, the chin that is too pointy (she could never do chins). Gaudy, childish, a brazen cry for her mother. And yet it has gone around the world and still, somehow, never reached her. There are copies of the records and posters of it on high tables in the press tent. The image can be seen on the bootlegged T-shirts people are rocking that some Brazilian has made without permission and is selling at the door (one of many battles she doesn't have time to bother with).

She can smell her sweat, realizing that she didn't use deodorant. Brazilian journalists and seasoned music managers are standing around the stage. Hands in pockets. Swirling glasses of brandy. Approaching Mansour with bad jokes like college boys at a party. Older. White. Connected. Among them, Bonnie knows, is an RCA executive. Someone else from Columbia.

One such man had made a pass at her. Earlier that morning, he'd fondled her hand more than shaking it and then gripped it so long and tight that Mansour had put his hand over hers, breaking the man's grip as he stared him in the eye. As they'd chewed gum, not speaking, just staring at the ocean for a moment afterward, she'd clung to him, wanting to tell him about everything that happened before—all of the unwanted attention she'd suffered through for him—but she didn't want to distract him right before the show. These days the balance between manager and girlfriend is critical, and it always leaves her wanting.

Now, as she stands in the wings with the buzz of the crowd building, she worries if a day is coming when she'll have to completely sacrifice one for the other to thrive. Suddenly her throat is full of too many tastes. She vomits. It splatters loudly, a pale and textured map of her mind at her toes.

77. **"OH-OH-OH,** ça va là? Bonnie—" Mansour rushes to the wings, grabbing her before she falls. Two women working the stage approach and one caresses her back while the other speaks to her too loudly in Portuguese. He responds for her, and they begin to usher her to the greenroom. A moment later, he brings water. Squatting before her, he hands her the glass, then grips her knees.

"You're like Aquaman," she jokes, seeing his worry over her and trying to quell it.

"I don't know who that is." He wipes her face, still serious.

"Didn't you ever read comic books?"

"I was too busy listening to Vivaldi," he says and winks.

"Naturally." She rolls her eyes. "And I've been meaning to ask: When did you learn Portuguese?" she says, mimicking his accent.

"I don't sound like that," he says, and having finally made him laugh, she smiles, satisfied.

"Yes, you do—"

"Shh. Stop talking," he says. "Bois."

He's watching her drink the water, waiting for her to get all of it down. She holds eye contact, studying him. The audience roars; the wind blows open the tent. Twenty minutes to showtime. He's shaking at the sound, his nerves, for a moment, turning frazzled. She doesn't mention it but takes his hand.

"Do you think that maybe . . ." He's talking quietly, carefully.

"Hmm?" she says, her mouth full.

"Do you think that maybe you're pregnant?"

Panic crosses her face. "No."

"Have you been . . . pregnant before?"

"Was it not obvious that you were my first?"

He starts to smile. "I got that sense. Yes."

"How?"

"You were . . . as the Americans say . . . biting off a little more than you could chew."

She starts to laugh, burying it behind her hand. He's chuckling too as she pushes him playfully.

"What can I say? That's me." She looks beyond the tent, where the fruits of her enormous ambition can be heard in the sound of the people. Like the crash of the ocean. When she looks back at him, he's staring at her, a little dazed, and she knows that he's thinking the same things about her that she's thinking of herself, seeing her magnificence. She drops her eyes, humbled by the reverence on his face, snapping them both out of it.

"But, listen, I'm making a point at you."

"What point are you making *at* me?" She clowns his English syntax.

He leans closer, says, quietly, in French, "How can you be so sure that you're not pregnant if you've never been pregnant before?"

She shrugs, feigns indifference, plays with his talisman necklace.

He shrugs, imitating her. She smiles. He studies her for a moment, as if assessing something. Then he stands abruptly.

"That's it. Let's get you back to the house."

"No, I gotta be *here*! This is it!"

As if on cue, the audience swells even louder, and he has to speak up to be heard.

"What if it happens again?"

"Can't you find me a bucket?"

He stares.

"Mansee, I'm just kidding. Relax."

78. SHE'LL REMEMBER THAT SHOW most for the way the air grew thin, the dense concentration of bodies for miles.

She'll remember the way the crowd changed after a few songs, from having a good time to trusting Mansour with their souls. The way that fifty thousand bodies could be as silent as one.

She'll remember it for the panting, drenched musicians. A band thrown together in a single weekend from every part of the world, telling its story from Switzerland to Kedougou, from Mississippi to Belgium, from Brooklyn to Brazil, never losing the rhythm.

She'll remember it for the rain that should have washed out the show, for the way the people had shouted, threatening the festival organizers with murder when an early closure of the concert was announced.

She'll remember it for the way that Mansour walked back up to the mic. *Would you like to stay with me?* he'd said, and she watched thousands of bodies jump high, a dark wave that merged with the night sky. The rain was warm, and when she let it touch her tongue, she found it sweet.

She'll remember the moment she came closer, sitting onstage. In the darkness of the backdrop, watching him from behind, trying to imagine what it felt like to do what he did. He only wore jeans, his sculpted back bent forward, one voice filling up the world.

———

She'll remember the way he looked at her when it was over and the audience was roaring. Didn't speak, only looked at her like she had just appeared. A wonder. And how he didn't bow, just paced the stage for twenty minutes of applause, until he jumped down, disappearing among them. The crowd carried him and his song for miles and miles.

79.

WHEN MANSOUR LEFT the stage, he cemented his future as an artist and hers as a manager. The weekend after his second performance, there is a constant stream of calls at their little house on the hill. In the mornings, she walks like a zombie to the living room, takes the phone off the hook to finally get some sleep. In the evenings, she receives all the messages, returns the most important calls, and sits through enough pitches (now she is the one getting pitched) to change their lives forever.

She is surprised by her agitation. Somehow, despite all this good news, she would like to curl back into bed with him and keep life the way it is for a little while longer. Instead of the meetings in Rio she now has to take to close new deals, instead of the trip back to Paris to consider the other artists pursuing her for representation (that was a surprise), she would rather spend the day walking through the market with him, maybe going fishing in the little boat the owner of the house has loaned them. Staying out on the water, hiding from life until dark. To Bonnie's surprise, good things, even great things, brought along fear and joy in equal measure.

She calls him awake from across the room to eat food that has turned
cold since the first time she tried to wake him some hours before. He
sits up in the dark, silent for too long.

"Mansee?"

His head is down, unmoving. He tells her there's someone at the
door. Insists that he's heard a knock. When he yells for her to check,
she goes, though she heard no knocking. When she's just barely out
of sight, he is unable to resist any longer, letting the seizure come
over him.

There is first discussion of a helicopter to take them to the best hospital in Sao Paulo, but after the logistics go in circles, Bonnie hitches
them a ride down to the nearest hotel. In the lobby, loud and barefoot,
patrons gathering to watch her and her Afro, she insists that they get
him somewhere *now*. They make it to a crowded hospital in Bahia
forty minutes later. His Senegalese passport doesn't do much, but her
American one helps them cut through the standing-room-only waiting
room, and the presence of the promoter's assistant (a white Brazilian)
does just as much to get him seen.

Bonnie spends the night and the following morning in his hospital
room, waiting for him to wake. She's offered water and the slimy white
flesh of a cold coconut, but she only eats two morsels before her stomach starts to turn. When he finally wakes, he's complaining of a headache, cursing out the sunlight in Wolof, that language with all the
round notes from his dreams.

"Who the hell are you?" he says with a furrowed brow.

"C'est moi," she says, frightened. "It's me, Mansee."

"Are you my nurse?"

"Oh my God, it's me, Bonnie."

"Bonnie has very distinct features; I need to check to be sure." He starts to lift her skirt; she slaps his hand as hard as she can. He grabs his wrist, reeling in pain from the strength of her slap as he chuckles.

"Merde." He shakes it off.

She's swiping tears from her eyes.

"You should know me by now," he says. "You're so easy. Come here."

"No."

"Come on."

She straddles him. She's looking him over. He, somehow, for all of his melanin, looks pale, but when she touches his forehead, it's surprisingly cool. She takes in the disjointed rhythm of his heart, the way his stomach lifts and drops in a wonky beat.

"You had a seizure."

He nods gently.

"Has this happened before?"

He nods again.

"Since we've been together?"

"Yeah."

"How come I've never seen it happen?"

"I can usually get rid of you. You finally didn't fall for it."

"Are you sick?"

"You could say that."

"Elaborate."

"Your voice is getting deeper," he says, imitating her sultry tone.

"Mansour, I'm serious."

He looks away to the window where one enormous green leaf fills the view, dripping dew.

"I don't know," he says. "It just happens. It's like I'm separated from everything, like I go someplace else."

"Does it hurt?" She puts a hand to his face.

"Not really."

He swipes the single tear from her cheek with his thumb, adjusts her glasses. "Hey. I'm OK. It's just a thing that happens sometimes."

"Then why didn't you tell me?"

"Because," he gestures to her, "women freak out."

"Now I'm being *grouped* with other women—your *harem?* When you were seeing Amal, were you seeing all those girls that hang around her place at the *same time?*." Bonnie's voice is gossipy and light amused. She wants to gloat.

"This is the perfect time for that thing you do." He shrugs, demonstrating. Shrugging. The American shrug: the shoulders up to her ears, has no place in his culture; he's been guessing exactly what it means since they met. He does it again. "Comme ça, n'est ce pas?" *Like that, right?*

She just looks at him with a slight smile, shakes her head. He touches her new and very subtle sideburns, feels again the new heat of her hands, taking in the fullness of her cheeks.

"What?" she says, smiling at his stare.

"I think you're pregnant."

She gets quiet, combing the tassels on his blanket with her fingers, "Stop. I can't . . . I can't think about that."

"Then don't. Let me think about it . . ."

He sits up a little, adjusting her body on his. She's pulling at the fringes on his blanket.

"Bonnie. I need to know. Don't be scared of anything." He kisses her until she turns her head from his mouth, just the slightest turn so that his lips remain on her face, so that her lips graze his face too. She's very quiet.

"Mansee?"

"Hm."

"We're not so good with kids in my family."

"We're the same way," he says. "But maybe you and I can be . . . maybe we can be different."

V.

THE LAST (INDIE) GIGS

The World, 1969

80. **HE TURNS THEM** down the first time, liking things the way they are, but the third time a seasoned manager calls with a full roster of concerts already lined up and a solo record deal with a good label, Bonnie tells Mansour to take it (*Don't be stupid, man*). Well into a warm spring, naked in the low-hanging hammock of a German hostel, they are client and artist no more as he completes the last gigs on the indie circuit from their bookings.

Mansour runs his hand across her body, noting the fairness of her breasts. He gazes at the rest of her, her deeper reddish-brown color from all the months spent in the wings of stages at folk festivals, the rocky sands of Croatian and South American beaches, cabin porches in woodsy parts of Ireland.

She kisses his hand, tells him of tongues being cut out in the Americas if an African language was spoken.

He laughs. "You're lying," he says.

He kisses her back and tells her how Ahmadou Bamba prayed standing on water, how he was found petting the lions that the French sent to kill him.

"That's just folklore," she says.

He remarks, for the first time, that she could be from Senegal. She could be Bambara: the shape of her nose. He touches her. Peule, more likely, with her extended neck and wide doe eyes.

She drags her fingertips down the ridges of his chest, tells him he is such a Southern boy. Could be from Mississippi: the chestnut complexion, the lean body, his quiet way. Maybe NOLA: the full eyebrows, the jet-black soft hair.

"So where is this baby from?" she says, his hand on her stomach, her hand over his.

———

When he leaves for Spain in May, he's rushing. They've both hardly slept, argued through the night about things she can't even remember now. She only remembers that she refused to see him to the door. She watches from the attic window as he packs his things into the car. And then they'd both given in at the last minute, meeting at Mama Eva's front door. He squats down, lifting her shirt to kiss her stomach.

"I remember when you used to kiss *me* like that," she says, tapping the door frame with her finger.

He stands, salutes her with a military hand to his head.

"Seriously?" she chastises from the open front door.

Liam yells from the car. "Would you like to play these games on a day when we're not already late for the only train to Spain?"

Mansour snatches her close with an arm around her waist, puts his forehead to hers, closes his eyes, breathing her in. He pulls his talisman necklace over his head, places it into the palm of her hand and presses it closed.

"Stay sweet," he says.

PART
FIVE

I.

ON LIAM'S SIDE OF TOWN

France, 1970

81. **THERE IS A** retired orderly who believes it's still war-time. The deranged man runs up to happy tourists sitting at wicker tables on the sidewalk and, as they pour their melted chocolate into milk, warns them that German bombs could drop down at any moment, that it's time to hide in the basement shelter underground. As he comes and goes from gigs and every time he returns to his apart-ment window, Liam finds that the man's panic is ever fresh, never dis-sipating. A terror familiar in its endurance, in its relentlessness. Liam relates: he killed a man in America over a year ago, and he is surprised that he has yet to recover.

Life has gone on. Gigs mostly in Paris, teaching guitar privately for kids in the city. Breaking ties with Mansour has been healthy for him. He has committed to keeping his distance: changing his number, stor-ing photographs, finding new venues. But he still sometimes wonders what they could have done together. What they would have done if they had never gone to New York. Or maybe just if that one night with Keifer had never happened.

Last year, the details of the aftermath were relayed in a phone call to his Paris apartment from his uncle in Bay Ridge: the man he shot (the stepson of the incumbent local councilman; a boy born good, only turn-ing wayward at nineteen after an undetected tick bite was left to fester for too long) died within twelve hours of arriving at a Brooklyn hospital. Liam's aunt brought the grieving family lilies in a jar from her backyard, returning every other week to replace the dead lilies with fresh ones. She washed the mourning mother's hair while pretending not to know who truly murdered her son. *I'm tired of lying for you* ... The phone was taken from the aunt by the uncle as she broke into sobs.

Liam's uncle says that he can hear in Liam's voice that he's not doing well. He suggests, then pleads, the antidote to what he's certain is troubling him, to what's *always* troubled him: *I know that you two are like brothers. But you gotta forget him. Please, son. Please.* And then there is silence as Liam puts the landlady's phone back on the hook and walks up the three flights to his apartment, where he still, sometimes, keeps off all the lights.

II.

THE THIRD TRIMESTER

Switzerland, 1969

82. **BONNIE IS SHAKEN** awake by the dishwasher girl sitting at the foot of her bed, offering her a shawl and red prayer beads.

Out of bed and at the top of the staircase, Bonnie looks down on the living room, where the women chant in a loose circle, their bowed heads draped in similar fabric. The smell of fried fish is still trapped in the room, and it mixes with the incense roasting in the center of the floor. The combination makes Bonnie queasy. She doesn't cover her head as they do. She puts the shawl around her shoulders and stands on the staircase with her arms crossed. Bonnie's eyes are blurry and swollen from another day spent on her feet, tending to Mama's guests. Something about the strong scents, about being summoned to pray to their God, is too much; it's where she draws the line. Her mother had always insisted that God was private, personal, quietly inhabiting the unique shape of every individual's form.

In the attic, confined since the bleeding made it impossible to travel and push forward in her search for him, she's turned to praying, in her own way. She prays as she'd seen him pray, hands open, and as she'd seen her mother pray, on her knees. *Please. Please. Send him home.* But her god is drying up. She prays more and more over time, fiddling with the tears in her T-shirt, rubbing her dry eyes, opening them to look around the room where, as usual, nothing divine has happened.

She prays on, broken, her voice swallowing itself until the prayers become a talk with her half-finished glasses of orange juice, the grime on the window. A thing without her heart, and so terribly unliving.

She drops the prayer beads on the steps and turns back toward her room.

Mama calls her out, breaking the chant.

"If you cared for Mansour, you would come! You want to call the police, but you won't pray for his soul," Mama retorts.

"His soul?" Bonnie stares down at Mama from the top step. "You think . . . you think he's dead?"

Mama says nothing.

Bonnie looks next at Marie, who lies in Sokhna's lap, her face buried. She takes in the looks of resignation on the women's faces. Mansour has been gone for five months. They are beginning to mourn.

"It wasn't him in Geneva," Bonnie says, close to tears. "He's not dead."

"Come, come and pray with us," Mama manages.

Bonnie shakes her head, walks slowly back to her room, holding her stomach, grabbing the wall to stay on her feet.

83. ANOTHER MOURNER'S MEAL must be pre-pared, another funeral without a body to bury. Life and its circles. Mama feels the comedy of it, the cruelty of living this a second time. It feels personal. Somebody up there has something serious against her. What lesson did she miss the first time, she wonders, as she stirs and stirs ngalakh until her arm is tired. The peanut drink will not become smooth. She stops stirring.

Someone is digging a hole in the backyard, and they keep hitting rock. She rushes to see who could possibly be in her garden. Since the storm, most of the neighborhood farms are still unattended, and thieves have been known to roam the land, snatching whatever mangled vegetables they can find.

At the window, she sees Bonnie in the yard. The girl has a stomach large enough to carry two babies. Eight months pregnant, and Mansour has been gone for five of them. Mama watches the girl grunt as she digs up the yard of the estate. Mama just watches, saying nothing from the open window. The girl stops in a huff, resting her body on the shovel, weeping like a child just born.

It has all seemed dreamlike. Even as she discussed a memorial ser-vice with Sokhna, even as they made plans to invite neighbors who knew him, even as she went to the pay phone herself and called and called Liam, where there was still no answer. Even as she stayed awake through the night, selecting photos of Mansour, compiling memorabilia, surahs, going as far as contacting her imam in Paris to discuss proceedings, Mama did not register the declaration of his death until this moment, until she sees Bonnie pulling each of his bracelets from her wrists and dropping them into the hole she's dug in the ground. Last to go in the hole is the talisman necklace, and then Mama opens the kitchen's back door.

The girl has crouched on the ground before the hole. Her long hair is matted, uncombed. Mama sees herself in the girl. She sees herself on the day of Kiné's funeral, one woman attempting to hold faith in something that the world no longer believes.

"Bonnie," Mama says, speaking her name for the first time. She feels the strangeness of it, the newness, in her mouth. She's always called her "the girl," worried that she would say her name wrong, never wanting to try. The girl doesn't move from where she squats on the ground. Mama approaches, leans down, taking the bracelets back out from the hole as the girl watches in silence. Mama stops her from conceding his death. Seeing the strong girl break down is a sight Mama cannot bear, is too great a defeat to witness.

"Marie will braid your hair," she says to Bonnie softly. "And then . . . and then you can come down. We will go to the police."

Mama walks back inside, feeling the girl come to life behind her. She knows that as soon as she picks up the phone and calls the police chief, everything she's built could quickly tumble. But Bonnie truly believes that she will see Mansour again, a belief that has never diminished over all these months, and this girl's hope finally gives Mama the strength to risk everything. *Maybe . . . maybe he'll come home.*

The Swiss police search the yard, the house, for clues. One of them interviews the women. Bonnie's interview is the longest. Mama is surprised by her own nervousness but more so by her desire for the women to stay in the room with her. She considers, for the first time, that they are all she has. Some policemen leave, go off to begin interviewing neighbors. This makes Mama nervous; the neighbors are not exactly friends of hers. All the more reason to speak to them, one man says. The women sit still in the living room. They don't know what else to do, so they prepare the policemen a big meal.

Two weeks after the police begin their search, Mansour still has not been found. Mama counts out Bonnie's last wages by the light of the coals that are roasting incense and the flash of the muted evening news. Mama takes her time, the nub of a cigarette between her wide fingers. She slides the francs across the table to the girl. The money is damp and sticky from splashes of palm oil and dishwater. It is more than what she promised when Bonnie asked if she could have her last wages and stop working. Mama goes to the kitchen, and Bonnie looks out of the living room window. The evening looks pleasant enough. The walk to the train would be beautiful, the air warm.

Bonnie's mind starts turning over, her thoughts a record of strange categorical things: colors, numbers, cities. She's felt some fluttering before, but this is different. Her chest contracts, like her heart is being squeezed into a tight ball. And held. It takes opening her mouth wide to feel like air could reach her.

"*Mama!*" she calls, keeling over with a violent pain, the word escaping her mouth before she has time to think. She uses both hands to try to crawl to the staircase and hold on. *Just get to the attic steps*, her mind says. But her legs become useless, and before she can remember her pride, she waits for help.

Mama helps Bonnie to the couch and stands over her, rubbing her enormous stomach with shea butter.

"That's the first time that's happened to me," Bonnie says, staring at her belly. Mama says nothing, keeps rubbing.

"Are there other twins in your family? Besides you and Kiné," she asks Mama, a question she finally feels close enough to ask her.

The question startles Mama. Her sister's name—a sacred thing she hasn't heard spoken by anyone in fifteen years—rolls out of the girl's mouth easily, like it's a name she's said before.

Mama looks down at her, haunted.

"What did Mansour tell you about my sister?" The nutty grease turns warm in Mama's hands as she stretches out Bonnie's skin and pushes her pulsing bones flat, making it easier to breathe.

"He has this dream about her drowning. He has it all the time."

Mama spreads the balm across Bonnie's chest and arms, her stomach and neck. Bonnie looks up at Mama. She has never been close enough to for Bonnie to really see her: to see the subtle scarifications on her cheekbones, the yellow tint to the whites of her eyes, the stark pinkness of her tongue, the unusual thickness and length of her eyelashes, the fact that she is missing a tooth.

"I thought that he'd forgotten her. He was so small . . . ," Mama says.

"You don't forget your mother," Bonnie replies.

Mama leaves her to rest, to await further contractions, but they are still unpredictable, and nothing comes. Bonnie follows Mama to the kitchen and waits in the doorway, standing, saying nothing.

"You can come in, Bonnie." Mama gestures for her to approach. She hands her a large spoon, tells her to spoon out the boiled fish from the large pot. Mama next puts the gund—the tall wooden mortar and pestle—between Bonnie's feet and tells her to pound, to pound softly, while she drops in parsley, garlic, whole black peppercorns. Teaching her to make Kiné's favorite meal: fishballs in tomato sauce. When the pounding has emulsified the herb mixture, Mama spoons it out and sits at the table, mixing it into the fish she's skinned and separated from the bones.

Bonnie knows where the rice is kept. When she reaches, the pain returns, and she grips the doors to stay on her feet. "*Whoo!*"

Mama watches her carefully as Bonnie makes it to the table with the rice. She looks up at Mama with devilish eyes.

"I'm gonna kill him when he comes home," she says, breathing through the pain. Mama chuckles; Bonnie laughs at herself too. The women sit across from each other at the table, sifting the rice for stones.

III.

A BLACK MAN IS A BLACK MAN IS A BLACK MAN IS A BLACK MAN IS A BLACK MAN IS A BLACK MAN IS A BLACK MAN IS A BLACK MAN IS A BLACK MAN . . .

France, 1969

84. **SHE WAS THE TALL** Algerian waitress who walked between the tables in a tight black skirt with a mildewed rag over her shoulder. He, the Black man, had been watching her during her shift. She was staring from the bar while he picked his teeth. And as he stood outside, having one more beer to keep his buzz before getting into the car to leave, she was dumping a tray of ice into the gutter out the side door.

The Black man moved into the alley and pressed her against the stone wall, pulling her apart. When he put his hand between her legs, she bit his neck, spitting out his blood, but, still, he'd overpowered her.

The bouncer intervened too late; he pushed her aside to reach the Black man. He threw him around, corner to corner, until the Black man was too dizzy to stand. He was bloody but thought it was sweat. The swinging front door of the club wouldn't hold him, so he fell backward, feeling his body burn after he hit his head on the old stone ground. He was still well enough to get up and run.

IV.

TO SPARK A FIRE ON THE AIR

Spain, 1969

85. **ON A WOODEN STAGE** constructed the night before, Mansour uses his right foot like a hammer, pounding on the downbeat, setting the music in motion. The Irishman and the other musicians lay down each melody beside him, completing the spell over the infinite pool of dark eyes and olive skin below them. They sway, and scream, and dance. It is May of 1969, and the towns of northern Spain are alive with their music.

Their car gives out, so they borrow an old Fiat and drive through the night to the next town and the town after that. They pick fat black olives out of rich stews and force full cases of cheap spirits into a trunk already crowded with their instruments. They all stay high and famished, terrified that the old car will stop midway between towns like the other had. But it doesn't.

After Barcelona, the tiny towns have no banks, and they worry that their pocket money will run out—and it does. Twice on their way farther north, they barter on the corners of ancient cobblestone blocks with four-minute concerts for dinner and cigarettes. Mansour holds the electric guitar on his lap as he devours roasted lamb and Spanish rice with his hand. Liam watches him form the rice into little balls he throws down his throat.

The Irishman does most of the driving, well into the morning hours, while the rest of the men start into their dreams. Delaying sleep, he drives for as long as he can, eventually pulling off on some side of the road. As he has done before in these past few days, he dreams of death, of a dying man. Sometimes the man has Mansour's face, sometime Keifer's. The scene, always, on the same street where Keifer collapsed. It is a recurring dream that doesn't have an ending.

Some of the roads in northern Spain are shrouded in sparkling rubble and dirt, others lined with privately owned citrus trees. They pass ancient villages where the flat houses match the color of the earth; they row across a brown river to play at a university auditorium with no windows. At the climax of a concert with over a thousand bodies breathing in the same stagnant air, harmonizing with the guitar riff, for the first time onstage, Mansour seizes.

With his collapse, the crowd is still, and Liam and the trumpeter lift Mansour from the stage to the wings. The Irishman, having dreamed thrice now of his death, had not expected him to awake. Liam shakes as they walk out of the venue, grateful to God that the night is pitch-black, that Mansour and the others cannot see the way he cries.

They do not make it to the car quietly. The crowd follows. Theirs is a palpable and wild love that even Liam feels. Among them, Liam notes the Africans. They always find their way to Mansour's shows, even in the most remote European towns. Mansour, whose eyes are still low from the seizure, stares into their faces like a preacher. Even after blacking out onstage, the Irishman can surmise from his manner that the African is giving his people words of encouragement, words from scripture.

But once inside the car, the African's mood darkens. And he again indulges in spirits, picks drunken fights with the other musicians, and eventually curls into a corner in the car and sings himself to sleep.

At the edge of a village town, deep into the night, they pass an old church. Having been possessed by strange dreams for several nights, the Irishman parks the car and goes inside while the other men sleep soundly. Inside the stately old church, the wild winds have opened two of the numerous windows. He kneels in the first pew and as he thinks up words to pray, he hears deep wailing, a guttural cry, carried in by the winds of the otherwise-silent dawn. It is the voice of Mansour.

The Irishman comes out to the car to find Mansour passed out outside, sleeping soundly against the car's back tire. The Irishman shakes him by the shoulders, worried again, until Mansour opens his eyes. He helps Mansour back into the front seat of the car, and they light fresh cigarettes and watch the sunrise in silence.

Mansour and Liam make it home to Paris a day early. Famished after three weeks on the road, they stop at a bar, walking distance from Liam's apartment. Mansour will take the train to Switzerland in the morning. He has gone out to the phone booth to call Bonnie. Liam watches from the foggy bar window as Mansour walks to the corner and just leans against the phone booth's door. His hand is over his mouth, one leg crossed over the other. When he returns, Liam plays along.

"How is she?"

Mansour leans back in his chair, rearranges the glasses of brandy on the table, pulls his hoodie over his head, pushes it off again.

When he speaks, his deep voice has an airy, unsteady sound, as it drifts among the clinking glasses and gruff conversations that surround them.

"Call her for me, just tell her everything's good. She'll believe you. She'll see right through me," he says.

"No, *Mansee*," Liam teases. "The girl's having your kid."

Mansour shakes his head, grabs his face.

"She'll worry. She's such a worrier."

Liam leans closer, but then, protecting his heart, he looks out of the window, whispers his fear with sour breath. "You're getting worse. You have to tell her."

When he raises his eyes, Mansour is glaring at him, a strange look at first like he might weep, but then it hardens into his resting expression. "You have to tell her," Liam says again. Mansour runs his hand over his facial hair and folds his hands on the table. He sits up, staring down at them.

"We were pregnant in Brazil," he says and takes a swig of his drink. Liam is listening. "But we . . . we got into this thing in Germany some weeks later. She'd already told me she wasn't feeling well. One of our worst times. And I was screaming, and she was screaming. I left. Came back really late."

His eyes have welled.

"Anyway she lost it. The first one."

"I'm sorry."

Mansour shakes his head, runs his hands over the table. He reaches into his pocket for a new cigarette. He puts the thing in his mouth, lighting it with a shaky hand. "I'll never let that happen again," he says, and exhales, shaking the fire off of the match, smearing off tears. "I can't tell her what happened to me in Spain."

"You're not gonna tell her about your manager either?"

Mansour focuses on his drink as Liam continues.

"You fired a good man. You had an excellent manager. He was probably the only person who could've kept that seizure onstage out of the press. He saved your career and mine."

"He didn't save me. We built this from the ground." He taps the table twice, leans in. "If it falls apart, we'll build it again. And again." Mansour asserts with defiance.

Liam speaks, "I've never met a motherfucker who'd work his ass off, almost make it big, and then walk away from a major deal. How many chances do you think a man should get to blow up his life? And how many chances should he get to blow up mine?"

Liam throws back his drink and shoves the table forward to make way as he stands. Once he's pulled on his jacket and thrown his bag over his shoulder, he looks once more at Mansour, who looks like he might speak but only rolls his tongue across his teeth as he studies the messy table of empty glasses, planning his next drink.

Liam tugs on his jacket. Calmer, with worry, he says, "Don't get stupid drunk before you get on the train."

Liam turns to leave, and Mansour follows him out to the quiet street, whistling after him.

"Liam!"

Liam turns to see Mansour extending him money. Payment for the last gig. The dark, empty road lies between them.

"Just mail it to me with the rest."

"Mail's slow." Mansour tips his head, extends the money again with a tiny smile. "Come on."

Liam puts his hands in his pockets and rocks on his feet. He eyes the money, needing it, but he won't approach.

"What is this? What's with you?" Mansour says.

Liam won't look at Mansour, watching the street like he's looking for someone. "I'm beginning to feel like . . . I feel like you're getting some kind of pleasure from this."

"From paying you?"

"From screwing me over," he says, looking Mansour in the eye.

"I wrote half those songs you played in Brazil. That should've been double billing! We were a duo!"

"So how come you never said anything?!"

"I shouldn't have to, Mansour."

"When Keifer died, you didn't want anything to do me with me. So I was supposed to just stop gigging because you didn't want to? You dropped off, you fucked up shows, you didn't take my calls—"

"I killed a man. I . . . killed him."

Liam takes two steps back and grips his hair the way he did that night in New York. He's staring at the ground, like the story of the night Keifer died has been etched into the grooves of the pavement. His face is red when he looks up at Mansour, open with a desperate need for forgiveness, and Mansour is paralyzed, staring back at him the same way.

86. MANSOUR RETURNS ALONE to the bar and, a few hours later, during his drunken walk to the train, he is stopped by police. When he resists, he's thrown against the wall. Disoriented, he can't feel anything, but he tastes blood. Three policemen threaten to shoot him in the hundred-year-old cobblestone alley.

Mansour tries not to laugh at their short heights and tiny heads. The sweatiness of their hands and the way it tickles when they grip him. He laughs until they force the barrel of a gun under his chin. Then he feels his body turn to liquid in their hands.

By the time he's handcuffed, wrist to wrist, ankle to ankle in a heavy browning chain that leaves a scent on his body like money, he is laughing out of fear.

When he is alone, in the dark, his swollen arm keeps him from losing consciousness. He was beaten twice and now his limbs feel flammable, like his own touch might ignite him. He keeps his palms flat beside himself on the ground, trying to make a thought, trying to find his bearings. It all happened extremely quickly. His drunkenness and the strength of their blows upon his head had deafened him in one ear and weakened his vision. Their questions for him—if he knew the woman, what time he arrived at the club, how many times had he followed her home—swarmed with the room. His answers, his befuddlement, his screams, his demanding to know who in the hell this woman was and why they suspected him, they did not hear. They did not even seem to see him, their gazes firmly on him but seeing something else entirely. It all struck him as a terrible dream. A dream in which he was not the dreamer.

This is what it feels like to be forced into another man's fate. To disappear into another. And with this thought, the cell begins to breed a terrifying vastness within him. But he breathes into it, and breathes into it, hearing, needing the sound.

ON THE NIGHT SHIFT,
A PRISON GUARD PRAYS ISHA

France, 1969

87. **LIMBS. CROOKED, SCALDED,** sculpted. Some bowed and bushy, others slender on men far too young to be in prison, their flesh still shinier than eyes. Limbs are all he sees. Limbs are how he distinguishes one prisoner from another. Mansour has stopped looking at faces. He's discovered that the face of a fellow prisoner is the prison's most dangerous place, for everyone is a mirror of him. When he sees another man's anger, he finds that he beats the iron slab harder, the sparks growing brighter with the force of his rage, sparks soon so thick and golden that he expects, any day now, to spark a fire on the air. So he keeps, more and more, a new distance from himself, a thing that was easy to do, if you intended it. He knows now why Gil Rodney seldom ever smiled.

Men as stock, as product, as limbs and feet: he feels it when they are sprayed down on the yard, when they are weighted, when they are pulled by their chains, when they are left to perform their rage on one another's bodies—locked in a mess hall and left to fight. He knows why Olu had fought so hard to put him in the choir, had fought so hard to keep him out of the world.

One man commits murder over socks with holes; others war over accents and cities—the kind of Black, the kind of brown, they are; the white men war in another cell block far away. When Mansour participates, the first time in defense, the second time as perpetrator, he knows then that what Keifer had accused Gil of—pulling a gun on him—was the truth. He knows how and why Gil Rodney became two men. And how easy it would be for him to do the same.

He discovers that he must *intend* to remain himself, for Bonnie, and their child, though this is a thing constantly tested. But he makes the decision. So that evening, when an officer strikes him, he strikes back.

88. ISHA IS PRAYED ALOUD, but Ishmael does it

silently. Since he arrived from Tunisia five months ago, he does all five prayers under his breath. It is a practice he is ashamed of but, after the Paris riots, also too frightened to break, even though there are no other guards in this wing on shift. Working the night shift makes monitoring the most sordid section of a prison a little easier. For everyone, both the tortured and the torturer, must sleep. And that brings silence. A void that keeps Ishmael deaf and blind, to whatever really happens here in the waking hours. Things he can smell when he walks the halls, scents of things he has to wash out of his clothes once home but never has to witness.

As he lifts his head from his prayer rug, he hears the verses he was reciting in his mind aloud. His hands vibrate with the sound. An airy, elegant Tajwid rolling across the hall. He imagines himself to be hallucinating. Other guards who worked in solitary have been broken by less: sightings of ghosts, echoes of moans driving them from the wing. But there it is again, the sound growing purer, coming from the cell belonging to the Black man who came in the other night. He'd been cursing out the guards with a bloody face as they'd dragged him in, his accent so sharp and Parisian that Ishmael was shocked when he saw his complexion. It is another shock to him that now his own language, his own holy book, comes again from that man's voice, a man in a body he would never associate with himself, or with God.

Mansour wakes palpitating. So soaked from the effort of lucid dreaming that when he peels off his clothes, darkened and weighted with sweat, and drops them on the cell's concrete floor, they sound like mud. Each morning, when twilight arrives, he incants a spiritual request for freedom and a dream of her. Sweating cold when he comes down, headfirst on the sharp ground that awakens the rash on his forehead, a mark made in childhood from praying in this position.

Nights later, his prayer is finally answered. The dream begins the same way each time: yellow bees the size of apples, slurping sap from mango trees with the purple flowers that prophesy their harvest. He reflects, pondering on the metaphor. Then, Bonnie appears. A vision of her from the back, in bed, the golden waist beads she wears for him showing just above the white sheet at her hips. *Just turn around, Bonnie. Look at me. I'm here, I'm right here.* But she won't turn around.

He begins to fast, for he knows from childhood that the more hunger he endures, the more frequent and vivid his dreams of her will become. He's passing out in the daytime, but at night the dream sharpens: now the moles scattered across her back are visible to him. The only part of her he can see, he counts the moles from every angle: thirty-three, thirty-three, thirty-three, thirty-three, thirty-three, thirty-three, thirty-three . . . But still, she won't turn around.

By the fourth week, he can touch her. He savors this breakthrough by slowing his breath in sleep, hot tears stinging his cheeks. She is so close to real. He knows that his scorching need to pull her toward him is a force that will wake him and end the dream. It feels like choking, suppressing his need for her. Though he does, to preserve the vision. Sliding his fingers down the round moles between her shoulder blades, touching them carefully, reverently, savoring, like he's reading sheet music in braille.

Twilight after twilight, Ishmael listens. Some mornings, the Black man goes for longer than others. Some mornings, his incantations are rhythmless. Pauses in the wrong places. Long silences that drift into snores. Mixing verses from different surahs. Too many gaps, too much slurring. Ishmael starts to listen to the radio, to drown out the man. Afraid he'll hear murmurs, those first hints of insanity—a sound he's been warned that some men in confinement begin to make on the fourth or fifth day. But the Black man makes no such sound. On the fifth day in solitary, judging by the noise from his cell, he is still lucid. Wearier, but still himself.

On the morning of the sixth day, the day before the Black man's last in isolation, the hours pass in silence. Curious, Ishmael ventures to the Black man's cell for the first time. His footsteps are the only sound in the wing, and a pool of white light from the one bulb that does not obey the switchboard blinks down at him. The flash bounces off the floor, the line of cell doors. Nearer, Ishmael hears weak pounding. The pounding strengthens as he approaches. He unlocks and slides open the small window that allows in water and food and smells the Black man's vomit before he can make him out: convulsing in the dark.

For the first time, Ishmael is seeing the prison in daylight. He should have long been gone, but after succeeding, finally, at getting the Black man transferred from solitary to the prison hospital, he is also responsible for taking him back to his old cell in population before he leaves for the day. He could weasel out of it, but he wants to see how all of this will end.

He is standing outside of the prison infirmary's door, listening to the day begin on the floor below him: howls and the rummaging of chains. Doors slamming, men called by numbers in that strange singsong of guards, men pleading in Arabic and heavily accented French. The infirmary door swings open.

Passing Ishmael on his way out, all the prison doctor says is, "You can take him now."

Ishmael enters the dim room; one tiny window is open to a cloud flashing its golden veins, threatening a storm.

In a mere week, from when Ishmael first saw him dragged into solitary to now, the man's weight has dwindled. With a face mostly made of cheekbones and eyes, he is staring Ishmael down, and Ishmael remembers that he is the inmate that assaulted an officer. But when they catch eyes, the Black man nods, the smallest nod. Some kind of thanks? It is too subtle to tell. Ishmael unlocks the handcuff chaining the man to the bed and gestures for the man to put his wrists together before him to be rechained. The Black man sits up, allowing this, studying Ishmael very hard.

"Where are you taking me?" he says, a voice that surprises him in its calmness.

"Your old cell, with the others,"

"Tunisie," the Black man guesses, with a curious glare as Ishmael locks the cuffs in place.

VI.

THE BIRTH BEGINS

Switzerland, 1969

89. **BONNIE AND MARIE** brew ataya. A tea served in rounds. A dilution that progresses from bitter to sweet. They are pouring it from high up in the air, building the froth, when Bonnie tells Marie that for the past several nights, she has felt Mansour sleeping behind her, breathing on her back. Once or twice touching her. But he never speaks, and she awakes every time she turns to face him.

"It was so real," she whispers, leaning on the pantry doorway with crossed arms.

"It's just because the baby's coming. The mind can do all kinds of crazy things," Marie says.

Bonnie looks down at her stomach and molds it into another position, pushing down the part that is closest to her chest.

"You're so wild in there," she says. She takes a glass of tea for herself and waddles out of the kitchen's back door, her back to Marie as she sits on the landing, taking in the mild breeze. Protective of her thoughts. Determined to believe that the dreams are more than dreams.

When Bonnie proposes preparing something for the women, they laugh her out of the kitchen, but Mama humors her.

"Vas y," she says, "but if I get sick . . . I will punish your big-headed daughter," she continues, shaking a spoon at Bonnie.

"How do you know it's a girl?" Bonnie asks, touching her stomach. It has hardened in the last few weeks, a dark line running down the middle. Mama says nothing and smiles, just like Mansour would.

Bonnie comes back down to the kitchen the following morning before anyone is awake. She boils and mashes potatoes with heavy cream and butter and roasted chicken. The women wake up to the smell, crowding the kitchen door at sunrise. She serves the meal as they serve meals, on one platter, spreading the potatoes out from the center and placing the lemon-stuffed bird there in the middle.

Mama tastes first, unsure, chewing carefully. Bonnie avoids her eyes, pretends to be indifferent to her reaction. But Bonnie can tell that she's pleased. It is in the slowness of the swallowing, the subtlest moan. All the women's spoons get louder, racing into the dark meat and gravy. Bonnie sits between Mama and Marie around the platter—the only left arm reaching in for more.

The next morning, the full pot of mixed stock—lamb, vegetable, beef—breaks the middle tray in the old refrigerator. The hinges have been rusting for quite some time, and so, it seems, the shelf finally cracks. Bonnie hears it from the attic—not the thump, but the round, echoing note that the enormous iron pot makes when it hits ground. She drops an arm of laundry onto her bed and runs downstairs to the kitchen, only to get stopped by the stream of golden liquid rushing down the hallway, wrapping itself around her bare feet. She mourns the perfect stock as she washes the peppery aroma from between her toes. She turns sullen when the white peppercorns and stems from thyme and parsley disappear into the yellowing fibers of the old mop. And then she knows that, in spite of herself, she's developed a feeling for Mama's kitchen.

She notices the quiet. There should be music at this hour. Fela these days, but the house instead is eerily silent.

Bonnie turns the corner to the women's bedrooms. The doors are open, the rooms empty. The fans still whirl, spreading the curtains, swirling loose papers and pocket change.

Hours pass and the women do not return, but she presses away her worries and starts to prepare for the evening's dinner service. She sits on the edge of the counter, stopping every so often to stand or adjust her body. No position is comfortable. She seasons the fish, leaving it in a marinade of lemon, white vinegar, and pepper cloves, the way Mama taught her. She prepares the chickens, stuffs the lamb with parsley, and waits. She slices some onions and, unsure of what else to do, goes upstairs to change in case she has to welcome the first guests herself.

The doorbell rings while she's in the bath. It's still early enough that she assumes it's one of the sisters, and she runs downstairs.

Before even a hello, the man asks how many women live in the house and tells her that he is looking for Eva Ndoye.

When she tells him that Mama isn't home, he asks to be seated for lunch. She tells him that they are between services, that they will open for dinner in an hour or two. She gingerly asks him to wait elsewhere and watches from the kitchen's back window as he wanders around the property. She keeps an eye on him as she starts the yassa.

Once the lemons are squeezed, the contractions begin. Her body conquers her, sliding her into the bowl of sliced onions beside her on the stone floor, spreading her leg out into the path of the oil vat. She gets on her knees, crawls until her body changes course. She gets on her back, staring up at the swinging pots, emptying her mind of anything but a plan to cope. She yells, her mind too distracted with pain to call names, but no one is in the house.

90.

IN ZURICH, Sokhna leaves flight school a little early. She's been doing well on her course to get a Swiss pilot's license, breezing through the classroom lessons, but then it came time to enter one of the small student planes. Her cohort was not flying yet, just getting used to the gears. Turning on the ignition. Things she'd done countless times in childhood and expected to be second nature. But as soon as got inside the plane, the cockpit had felt confining, memories of Claude's rich cologne so strong that she'd scrambled to open the door. And it took a while, with her feet hanging out, with her seat belt being off, for her heart rate to settle down.

She moved out a few weeks ago, finding life in Mama's house suddenly unbearable, a constant reminder of Mansour. Now she only goes into Lausanne for work. She knows the other women have not forgotten Mansour, but, in her mind, they have surrendered him. She'd watched the women work in the kitchen all day and night and then turn, after hours, to care for Bonnie. The girl is having a noisy, disruptive pregnancy. She has stopped washing her own clothes and hair. Sokhna resents how the women take to her, fawning over her, pampering her now that Mansour is gone, as if the arrival of a healthy child can somehow replace him.

When Sokhna arrives at the restaurant, a barefoot neighbor is waving her arms, running down the estate's steep hill toward her. The woman's blonde hair obscures her face in the breeze, and it takes Sokhna a moment to process that it is the police chief's wife. The woman takes Sokhna by both hands, catching her breath.

"Your younger sister is at the hospital." The woman exhales, and Sokhna stares, confused. "The baby's coming," she says.

Sokhna sits beside her hospital bed, digesting the nurse's report that Bonnie's vitals are not strong and that the baby will be coming in the next few hours. There's a knock at the door.

Mama is led in by a policeman. Alarmed, Sokhna stands.

"Please, leave us," Sokhna says to the man. When he doesn't move, she repeats, sternly, "Please." He hesitates before leaving quietly, standing outside the door.

When they are alone, Mama says, "He scared Marie something terrible. I don't know why they even pulled her into this."

Mama returns Mansour's bracelets to Bonnie's wrists. Adds some of her own too. After watching her, Sokhna does the same.

Bonnie's eyes are closed, a face like a statue: firm and full of tension. The shades are closed; the room is dim. One machine beeps and blinks in bright colors. The women listen to the girl's breathing. Sokhna looks to Mama.

"Is there someone we should call in America?"

"I don't think so," Mama says.

"No one?" Sokhna whispers, stunned. Mama looks away, takes Bonnie's hand into hers, wonders for the first time if the girl has family. Is there anyone else in the world who loves her?

"This didn't have to happen, Eva," Sokhna whispers. "We didn't have to lose everything."

"We didn't lose," Mama says, exhausted.

"What about the house?"

"They don't want the restaurant. They just want money. Money, or for me to go. I could pay it . . . but . . . I *want* to go home," Mama says. "I forgot that was an option until they tried to threaten me with it. I'm tired Sokhna." She rubs Bonnie's arm. "You manage the restaurant very well," The first compliment after all these years. "It's yours from now on."

Sokhna is speechless.

"Just send me my money every first of the month," Mama continues. "I'm going to build a house. Find a husband."

"You? A man? My word," Sokhna teases.

Mama sucks her teeth. "And call me when she finds him," she says, fully joined with Bonnie's fight. They hear it in her heavy breaths, a reminder of the life she also had to fight for.

"Mama . . . ," Sokhna starts, then goes quiet. Afraid to say what she's thinking.

"She will find him," Mama says, firm. She still hasn't taken her eyes off Bonnie. "And Sokhna, you will call me? Just to talk?"

91. **THE CHILD IS BORN** at 9:16 in the morning. By the time the Swiss midwife enters the room, the birth is already happening, the baby falling into a pile of upturned yellow palms. She is stained on contact with their turmeric-coated hands, worn things calloused by wooden mortars. The women wait for sound.

Falling into the world in pieces (gray baby, placenta, more still). A placenta the color of tamarind, thick as bad gravy, a baby smelling of smoke: the scent of something burning, equal parts earth and chemicals.

Then, finally, a weak wail, a soul that isn't crazy about living in the flesh.

Mama alone on the floor. Hands still upturned, the afterbirth clinging to her fingers like dark egg whites, while the women coo and cry and approach the newborn. The child's cry grows louder when they cry, a child like her mother and father—made of sound.

Mama remains there, hands upturned, silent. Feeling something new and brave within her. Within the body that's never held a child but has given life. These hands that held Mansour in the days after he was born now drip with Bonnie's afterbirth.

Mama looks to where the women she's lived for are cuddled on the bed: Bonnie's golden body, the gray one in her hands, blue and purple women all around. She closes her eyes. Her body moves, already on its way home.

92. **WEEPING BREASTS WAKE** her in the mornings, overflowing. After two weeks, she cannot nurse her child without screaming. A pain that is too much to bear. Her nipples have chafed and bled and scabbed and bled again. And with her breasts more and more engorged, each morning after birth sharper than the last, the air around her bed pokes her like pins. It is 4:00 a.m. and she's stirring flour into goat's milk—trying a little honey, this time, like Mama said, an alternative the child refuses.

They've found a surrogate in the village, a woman who's just had her third baby and has been hearing Bonnie's daughter scream from across the plain. A woman so pale that Bonnie stares in awe at the contrast when her dark daughter latches onto the woman's nipple and settles into bliss. Mama encouraged Bonnie to use a surrogate. The day before she left, she told Bonnie of her two mothers, told her of the beauty there was in trying to love another woman's child and letting her love yours.

Watch. Watch, says the surrogate. *See how I am calm? So, she is calm. See how I am loving? So, she is loving. She can feel you. You are her mother.*

You are her mother. It feels to Bonnie less a given thing and more like a thing that has to be slathered on, like she has to get up in the morning and reapply Mother each day, with will.

The women of the house hear Bonnie's woes. And in it, they hear their own mothers. When Bonnie struggles with concoctions in the kitchen, Sokhna is reminded of her mother's dough. Marie feels her mother in the ways that Bonnie seems trapped—the mark is still on Oumou's ankle from the rope the villagers tied in preparation to sacrifice her for rain.

Bonnie squats now with her back against the wall in the dark room, letting her concoction burn. Deciding just to wait on the surrogate. To surrender to the woman's help. To let her hungry child, in the meantime, cry itself to sleep. And as she watches the goat's milk turn to smoke, she remembers what Mansour once said about compositions. How they are defiant, flighty, impossible to grasp. You could not hold them in your hand. You could never plot and plan a good composition. But still, you had to find a way to trust yourself, while you questioned everything. That is what has rung true about being a mother so far.

VII.

HE CALLS ON A SUNDAY

Switzerland, 1970

93. **ISHMAEL ENSURES HIS** access to medication, albeit a catchall medication, used to treat a range of unrelated conditions in the prison, from schizophrenia to undiagnosed bipolar II. It leaves Mansour drowsier than he'd like to be but more at ease. His body is changing for the worse. He has never relied so heavily on pills, but Ishmael assures him that the pills are no harm to him. So he stops tossing them down the toilet or through the window bars.

Mansour meets his attorney, finally. His first time in the visiting room, a sordid place that is overpowered by smell: a clinical scent that is a welcome departure from feces and mold. He weathers the sight of his worst nightmare all around him—young brown wives and small children visiting jailed fathers—but he's focused. The prospect of real help centers him. He shakes the lawyer's hand and is pleased to hear the man call him by his name and not his number.

They smoke together (a nearly orgasmic sensation after so long) as he begins his story of returning to Paris in the early evening from a Spanish train and then leaving his residency paperwork and passport in a bag in a bar due to drunkenness. A fight with his childhood friend. The only person with him that night, whom he now cannot reach.

At the end, the man is silent, his green eyes darting between the graffiti on the table and Mansour's desperate eyes. With his silence grows a shield until the man seems not cold but more indifferent to him than the prison guards. They, at least, have a definitive feeling about him, even if it is contempt.

"A singer, you say?"

"Yes."

"You said you did all this traveling with your wife?"

"Yes."

"You didn't come up married in the paperwork," the man says, and Mansour stumbles. He'd long been calling her his wife, a habit.

"No, we're not ... we're not formally ..." He's moving his head from side to side.

"I see. How old is she?"

"She's ... twenty-one now."

The man looks at him for a long time. "How come I've never heard of you? And the residency paperwork at the bar—you just left it? You were drunk, you say?"

Mansour puts out his cigarette on the scarred table, and, with the smoke, his hope dissipates. He's met another foe.

"How come I've never heard of you?" the man says again, examining the paperwork with frustration.

"I don't think I make your kind of music," Mansour says finally.

As they talk on, arguing eventually, the lawyer maintains that he should confess. That that might serve him better than denial. The worst, the lawyer warns, is deportation. A real possibility if he's convicted.

"If you confess, there's the possibility that you can be rehabilitated. Maybe get over your ... proclivities. I'm speaking for the judge—we have to think like the judge," the man adds, cutting Mansour off before he can argue with him.

They are both sweating, and Mansour can tell that the man has lost both his nerve and his patience. His knee is bouncing under the table as he speaks. "Because if you don't even seem remorseful, are arrogant even, why would a judge keep someone like that in his country?"

Mansour says that he never wants to see the man again. But the man is his only option, Ishmael reminds him. The trial is Monday; it is Sunday night.

Like everything else in prison, securing a call home requires strategy. But even Ishmael, slipping him extra pills through the bars of his cell, doesn't buy this as the reason why he hasn't called home. As Mansour takes the large blue pills from his palm, Ishmael teases in a whisper. The lights go out in the hall for the night, and the colors that remain cast Ishmael's profile in a deep red.

"You got me bringing you meds, Jean brings you extra soup, you hustle everybody around here, and you can't get a call home? Bullshit. I can get you a call home."

In the middle of the night, as he sneaks into Ishmael's office for the call, Mansour remains conflicted. He's wanted to resolve this on his own, without involving Bonnie. Without torturing her any more than he knows he already has. As he dials the number to Mama's, his fingers stiffen. With Bonnie on his mind, his rage melts and reveals his true feelings. His terror that this is where he'll remain, or he'll be returned to a country he hardly knows. Either way, away from her, for far too long, or forever.

94.

"ALLO?" BONNIE SAYS, her voice deliciously deep with sleepiness.

"Hi." He laughs a little, pure joy, at the sound.

When she hears his voice, she shrieks. A sound so loud and guttural that the baby in her arms starts to wail. She repeats his name, terrified that she's still mistaken. He affirms, each time, his voice full of so much air that he's hardly audible by the end of their exchange. Dizzy, she slides to the ground, straining the phone cord to keep it to her ear. She's rambling, talking over him and herself in shock. "I came downstairs to get some water and I said, 'Who in the hell is calling at this time in the mor—' oh my goodness . . . oh, Mansee . . ." She's catching her breath, and Mansour talks over her:

"Is that the baby? Is that the baby crying?" He's overcome with joy.

"Yes, that's her." She's smearing away tears, giving the child a pacifier. "Mansee. Where are you?"

He sighs. "I'm in prison."

"*Prison?*"

"A woman was assaulted and . . . they think it's me."

"Don't play with me."

"I wish I were."

"Jesus Christ . . ." She's crying.

"I know. I'm . . ." He stops himself, on the verge of breaking down. "Is the baby really OK?"

Bonnie looks down and sees the child sucking on the pacifier peacefully. The sight calms her. "Yeah."

"Is she a little you?" He's grinning, she can hear it. She closes her eyes, taking it in.

"No. She's all you."

"I'm so sorry."

"You're stupid," she laughs, with her eyes still closed, weathering a strange mix of pain and elation that makes it hard to grip the phone. "She's so beautiful, Mansee."

He's silent for a while.

"Hello? Mansee?"

"I'm just . . . I'm seeing her. And you," he says. The helplessness, the silence that follows, drags them back down.

"Did you tell them it wasn't you?"

"Of course."

"Then why can't you come home?"

She's softened him completely; she can hear it in his voice when he speaks again.

"They don't believe me, Bonnie. Or they just really need someone to nail."

She inhales, her body suffering. The A groan that carries through the phone.

"Bonnie. I . . . I'm so sorry," he whispers. "I'm so sorry."

"You have to convince them!"

"I know, I know . . . the lawyer told me I need some documents. I have to tell our story to the judge. To prove who I am and where I was. To show him that this couldn't be me."

"Like the posters, the visa papers?"

"Yes, everything. But you have to bring everything tonight. The trial's in the morning."

"In the morning?"

"It'll be OK. Everything's in the house."

"In the *morning*?"

"You can do this. I trust you, Bonnie. You can do this. OK?"

"OK," she says, focusing.

"Write this down . . ." He lists the documents as quickly as he can before the call must end. She can't tell by the end if he'd finished. But she gathers the gist: his residency paperwork, the visas she'd painstakingly gotten for him from every country where he'd gigged, contracts from the venues—receipts for his train tickets to and from Spain.

With the baby close to her chest, Bonnie hurries down the mansion's long hallways, tripping twice as she races to Sokhna's door. She bangs hard, then throws the door open, panting. Sokhna sits up on her elbows, hardly awake.

"Mansour once told me," Bonnie says breathlessly, "that you fly planes."

95. **BONNIE FOLLOWS SOKHNA** from room to room. They yell back and forth, their voices echoing in the dark, empty house. The sun has yet to rise.

"*He can call a city office and get everything messengered!*"

"*His trial's today and he needs originals!*"

"*Then get the press involved! You know editors at all the major publications—*"

"*We don't have that kind of time, Sokhna!*"

"*I haven't flown in years! I'm not even licensed in Europe yet!*"

"*This is our only option!*"

"*We don't even know if these documents will make a difference!*"

"We gotta try! If you get the plane now, when we find them, we can—"

"Get the plane? I can't just go *get a plane*!"

"What about at the flight school? Don't you have planes there?" Bonnie speaks at a feverish pace. When she comes closer, the heat of her body is palpable. Sokhna staggers back a few steps.

"I can't just take one, Bonnie! We'd need real money to rent it, to even get it off the ground—"

"I have it. I have money. Whatever you need," Bonnie says decisively, alluding to her hardly tapped inheritance.

Sokhna looks at Bonnie, seeing the extreme extent of her sincerity and stupidity. The many faces of Mansour's ex-girlfriends breeze through Sokhna's mind. Introductions to so many well-dressed, reasonable girls, none of them this brazen, this outrageous.

Turns out he'd chosen the right one after all.

"Meet me outside Eva's room," she says.

The dishwasher girl stands guard outside Mama Eva's door, holding the key as tightly as she can, her eyes shut tight in resolve.

"She won't give the key to me," Bonnie says to Sokhna as she arrives.

Sokhna sucks her teeth at the girl.

"Jox ko chabi-bi!" Sokhna is shouting, but the girl stands stiff. When Sokhna begins to wrestle her for it, she fights, running down the hall. Marie slips by while they wrestle, pulls a pin from her hair, and picks the lock to Mama's door open in a single gesture.

"Buh Mama Nyo," the dishwasher girl whines quietly. "Just wait till Mama comes back! She told me not to let anyone in there."

Marie, Bonnie, and Sokhna ignore her and dig through the room's boxes at warp speed.

"See anything that can pass for a residency papers?" Bonnie says.

"This might do something." Sokhna places what looks to be an old birth certificate on the bed.

By the time they find half of the required documents, over two hours have passed. Sokhna tells them that they have to stop here, or they'll never make it to Paris in time. They leave the dishwasher girl at home alone, beginning the two-hour ride to Zurich with the baby in Bonnie's arms.

There's still no light in the sky, and every office at the flight school is closed. There's no one, not even a janitor, to help them access a plane. Sokhna's parked at the back driveway, behind the chained gate. Across from them, behind the metal bars, are all the shiny planes.

"They're *right there*," Bonnie says, with a dreamy longing.

"I think I have a pin big enough for that lock," Marie says. She starts to fumble around her complicated chignon. Bonnie fumbles in her hair too.

"No!" Sokhna looks at both of them with wide eyes. "Absolutely not!"

"Oh, you have bigger ones. Let me see," Marie says to Bonnie, examining the pins in her hair.

"We are not *stealing* a plane. Do you seriously intend to get a man out of prison by breaking the law?!"

Bonnie and Marie exchange a look. They open the car doors, venturing toward the gate. Sokhna almost believes that they might try to fly a plane themselves.

"You won't get that open without a key!" she yells from the front seat, reaching behind her to pick up the baby, who's starting to cry. "Marie, ndax danga àndatul ak sa sago?" Sokhna shouts from the car, asking Marie if she's lost her mind. When the young women pay her no mind, she continues, "Are the following behind this spoiled American girl?"

But Marie remains focused, already working the lock with Bonnie's hairpin. She's patient. It takes twenty minutes, but it finally pops. Sokhna watches as Bonnie and Marie push the gate open slowly, quietly sneaking inside.

Minutes later, Bonnie rushes back to the car, knocking on the window, where Sokhna holds the baby, trying to calm the child as much as herself.

"I know that you don't want to do this, Sokhna. So just tell me what to do and I'll do it. How do I turn the plane on?"

"You'll crash. You'll crash and die, Bonnie. And I'm not raising this child for you."

"So then help us." Bonnie smiles a little. "We found one with the keys inside."

They roll the plane out into the open parking lot and position it for takeoff.

Sokhna opens the door to the small four-seater plane, sits in the driver's seat. She runs her hands over the gears. Checks the fuel. She's getting turned on. This is her place in the world.

"Do you have the documents?" she says.

"Right here," Bonnie replies, touching the bag under the baby's carrier.

Sokhna puts her headphones on, looks to the sky. "Bismillah."

She starts the engine, and the noise makes her want to take her hands from the gears—the fear of commanding the sky again for the first time in decades. She takes off nervously and then, as the plane shakes and tips up into the sky, she is remembering, yearning for the weightlessness; if only she can get to the weightlessness above the clouds, then she knows she can fly this plane.

The sky looks heavy, some warning of snow. At altitude, she takes a dip left—her father's trick to slice the fog and get the plane on her side. *A new plane is like a horse*, he once said. *You have to prove yourself before it fully surrenders*.

Then the weightlessness comes: the lower half of her body hovering, just a bit, above the seat. And it is just as sweet as she remembers. Sokhna thinks of Claude as she goes high, higher than the tiny plane should. She pushes the plane to its capacities (just as he would) to dodge the turbulence around the Swiss Alps. She will not admit to her passengers that she really just wants to see the mountains. This close, as the sun rises, they are frightening in their majesty—enormous navy blue pyramids with a white coating. She dips down, up, and down again, so close that she can see the plane's shadow, a tiny dark mark on the mountains' white peaks. The growing frost on the windows makes a crisping sound as it settles. Turbulence engulfs them, and she yells for Bonnie to cup her hands over the wailing baby's ears to ease the pain.

After a fast hour, the clouds part for Sokhna as she descends into Paris, revealing the city's bright, hopeful lights.

The baby still wails from the pressure in her ears as Sokhna parks at the small private airport that's nearest to the prison. On this Monday, at 9:00 a.m., the private lot is empty. Marie runs across the tarmac, flagging a lone cab by waving her arms as wildly as she can.

———

Eyes follow the three Black women as they enter the administrative building of the prison in their heels and nice coats.

"We would like to see Officer Pié, please," Sokhna says, giving the name of the supervising officer Mansour gave Bonnie on the phone. They are asked to take a seat. The three of them sit on a hard bench in the pristine lobby that looks more like a courthouse than a prison.

"I need to see him," Bonnie says as she stares at his daughter in her arms, seeing his face in her features. Sokhna chupses.

"Sure, you can see him. Marie can break you in. Could find you both a good cell too." For a moment, the three women pause and take each other in, in awe at what they've done.

When Officer Pié emerges from his office, he seems surprised.

"Can I help you?"

Bonnie puts the baby in the bassinet on the floor, preparing to approach him, but Sokhna puts a hand on her shoulder, a silent communication to let her handle this.

"Are you holding a man here named Mansour Ndoye? He has a trial this afternoon."

The man looks perplexed.

"And who are you?"

"We're his relatives. Could we please join you in your office?"

"Only one of you," he says, skeptically. "Follow me."

96. **BONNIE SITS BESIDE** Marie-Antoinette on the hard bench in the lobby. Marie places her hand on top of Bonnie's. Bonnie rests her head on Marie's shoulder.

Hours pass like this, and Bonnie and Marie fall in and out of sleep. The baby is wide awake but occupies herself by gazing at the shoes in the room. She wails now and then to wake her weary mother. Bonnie rocks her a little before dozing off again. She wakes for the last time to the far-away sound of Sokhna's heels crossing the marble floor.

Before she can see him, her body tells her that he's near. That bone-deep warming that moves through her body like a sap. But it is different now. Childbirth, or the span of months without him, has made her body rawer, and the effect is a pang that nearly aches.

When Sokhna finally emerges, Mansour is a few steps behind, and it takes Bonnie a moment to recognize him—with his shaved head and very thin physique. But his stride is the same: that steady unsteadiness that looks like style. He is dressed in civilian's clothes but escorted by a guard. And maybe because of the dreams, strangely it seems that she and Mansour have not been apart for so long. Bonnie runs to him, and he scoops her up from the ground in a single gesture. Holds her tight enough to muffle their voices.

"I should kill you," she whispers, grabbing his face, kissing him. Over his shoulder, she sees the guard staring.

"Can you give us a minute!" she snaps in French. "Jesus."

Mansour laughs a little, wiping his eyes.

"No, he's cool. That's my brother, Ishmael." Ishmael waves at her.

"You find brothers everywhere," she chides as he starts kissing her again. And then, mid-kiss, she sees his attention wander. The baby in the bassinet on the marble floor. She is silent, staring up at them inquisitively.

"Oh yeah," Bonnie says, smiling through the tears. "I should introduce you two."

Her feet back on the floor, she takes his hand and walks him over to his daughter. He approaches reverently, curiously, stooping down.

"And what's your name?" he asks the baby, touching her gingerly, very conscious of her fragility.

"She doesn't have one yet," Bonnie whispers from over his shoulder. She kisses his cheek, her eyes still brimming with tears. "I was waiting for you to come back."

───

It is hours after the trial has been stumped by the victim's conclusion that Mansour was not the perpetrator. She was certain that his was not the face of the man, and the hours of his travels from Spain did enough to prove the rest. When Sokhna lands the plane back in Zurich, Bonnie, Marie, and Mansour watch from the car's back seat as she pleads her case to the supervising janitor. Mansour is kissing Bonnie. He is shoulder to shoulder with Marie, and she cringes at their loud smacking right in her ear.

"OK. Ça suffit. Vous etes déguelasses!" She elbows him in disgust. Bonnie turns to the window as Sokhna gets louder.

"Maybe we should go out there," Bonnie says, rocking the baby nervously.

"Please, she's got this. He has a crush on her," Marie says, smiling, thoroughly entertained.

"Look at him. He can't even focus on what she's saying," Mansour says next, laughing.

They all straighten up as Sokhna marches back to the car in her heels.

She opens the door, dramatically throws her shawl over her shoulder, and sighs, closing herself in.

"You pulled it off, didn't you?" Mansour says, teasing her.

"Mansour Ndoye, bu ma foontoo!" *Don't joke with me!*" Sohkna says and whips around. She points her finger at them, a word for each of the three twenty-somethings: "Don't. Even. Speak."

A lecture follows: ten straight minutes for each of them. Sokhna saves Mansour's for last. It's well into the day now, and the flight-school parking lot is filling with cars.

"How could you lose your residency papers? Eh? Je te parle!" *I'm talking to you!*

Mansour is trying to stay awake. In the back seat, he has one arm around Marie, one around Bonnie, so relieved to be free.

"Why in God's name are you smiling?" Sokhna asks from up front.

"I'm not, I'm not," he says, still smiling.

"In all of your flying around the world, all of your concerts, it didn't occur to you to have your immigration papers in order? What if you didn't have two felons on standby to break into planes for you?!"

Marie's trying not to laugh at the grandeur of Sokhna's delivery. The diction, the performance quality of it, is killing her.

"Tanti, baal ma, j'ai tort. J'ai tort." *Auntie, I'm sorry. I'm completely in the wrong.*

"Non, jamais! Jamais! Mansour, tu devrais avoir honte. Tu nous as rendues *folle! Folles, pendant tous ces mois!* Je te jure, Mansour." *You should be ashamed! You've made all of us crazy for months* . . .

But Mansour's stopped listening. He's kissing Bonnie again, losing himself in it. When Sokhna whips around, he sits back stoically, feigning remorse.

97. **IN THE ATTIC**, where their child doses off while they speak softly of their lucid dreams—the metaphysical encounters between them while he was away—watching her with his child is a new feeling entirely. Something more than pride, it gives him energy, like his spine is being straightened from his crown. And when she leans over and kisses his daughter, her thin braids cascading down, music rushes him: the kind of chords he'd ordinarily have to scrape and pray for. A walking bassline, when Bonnie places the baby in her crib across the room and pulls the sheet up to her shoulders. Cello, violin, viola, when she leans back and rests all her weight on him. A delicious weight. A hard-earned heaviness. No piano. No drums. Her body is fuller now, cymbals, cymbals, a wild snare. Congas. Double bass as he pulls at the strings lacing her dress. *You wore this on purpose*, he whispers, and the air in her breathy giggles conjures woodwinds. The strength, the hunger in his grip, breaks her waist beads. And the beads—a hundred amber sparkles in the dark—flood the bed. Her tongue interrupts his breathless apologies for the beads that cling to his knees, and her thighs, his palms, and her back, her cheeks, and his neck. Desperate not to wake the child, who sleeps far away in the corner of the attic, at first, they are swallowing their sounds, but in their joy, it soon becomes a game, and they are deliberately provoking one another, through playful bites, and thrusts, trying to get the other to be the first to scream in pleasure. She breaks first—a sound darker than laughter, but sweeter than a cry, a sum of what it has felt like to become herself in his absence—and Mansour follows: something just as loud, something just as free.

He wakes, feeling her fingers along the new scar that runs from his left earlobe to the corner of his mouth. When his eyes are open, she whispers to him:

"I don't think I ever want you to tell me what happened in there. Promise?"

He nods. But she keeps her hand at his mouth to stop him from saying anything. Instead, he sucks her finger until she giggles. He's never forgotten what an elder patriarch, one of their Parisian neighbors, told him about the importance of keeping a woman laughing. About its power to get them through anything.

"Stop," she says, though she doesn't pull her hand away.

He laughs sleepily, closing his eyes, drifting off again.

"Mansee?"

"Hm?"

"Baby? Wake up."

His eyes pop open, a seductive glare. "Did you just call me 'baby'? When'd you get so soft?" he teases, pulling her to down to him. She falls beside him again, folding her fingers into his.

"Mansee, get up, man. I need to tell you something."

"Me too."

"What?" she's panicking now.

"It's not like that . . . I want you to take over the deal. I fired my manager."

"I really need to show you something."

It is not that he doesn't remember the house. But it feels foreign, more her home than his as he follows Bonnie down the long corridors. She wears their sleeping daughter on her back, tied to her body with a golden cloth, the way women do back home. And for the first time, he decides he will teach them both his language, wanting to strengthen the gates of their world. He watches the baby, for so long that he breathes in tandem with her. She is already beautiful enough to make him anxious. A startling prettiness more than a baby cute. A darker shade of her mother. He sees himself in her too: her eyes, her mouth, but she pouts in her sleep like her mother. He wants to touch her full cheek. It hangs over the edge of the wrap that encases her. Bonnie has already made the joke that he knew was coming: that she is grateful their daughter has his hair and not hers. It is so strange, that a baby he has made can still be a stranger, someone that he is shy of, someone he wants to impress more than anyone else he has ever known.

The hall's ceiling has been repaired, free of water stains and cracks, and the mildew smell that once filled the rooms has been replaced by a rich turpentine. Instead of the creaking that he remembers, their bare feet are silenced by a long Persian rug that ends at their destination: a door Bonnie opens with a key.

When she grips the knob, she hesitates, turning to him. She's biting her lip, leaning against the door frame, blocking his way inside.

"What?" he says, leaning close, playing along with false seriousness, though he wants to smile. The girl in her will always be adorable to him.

"You said you wanted me to manage you again . . ." She's twisting the edge of his shirt around two fingers.

"Yeah."

"Well, you won't be the only one this time around . . ."

Jealousy, an ugly flutter in his chest.

"Who is it?"

"Musicians."

"OK . . . you're gonna make me guess. Is it more than one?"

"Something like that."

When she opens the door, paper rustles loudly and a breeze spills out from the room along with the first true morning light he's seen in eight months. The sun bathes every corner and floorboard and nook and windowsill in a rich gold. Her handwriting is everywhere. On the walls, spilling over from long posters that hang like scrolls from the ceiling to the wooden floors. There are lists of things, names of places and people. Photographs of musicians with their instruments, mostly in black and white. Men and women of every color pinned to the wall. Records with handwritten labels fill boxes, sit on the steps of ladders. Two phones sit side by side on a messy desk, from which papers have overflown and fallen to the floor. His eyes settle to the right of him, where a portrait fills the wall—it is Bonnie's work, reminiscent of the album cover. An ode to their daughter that startles in its scale and precision. Overcome, he sits on the floor, staring.

When she approaches, her new scent finds him first, a subtle thing she shares with the baby—a smoke with no burning, the smell of hot water. She sits on the ground beside him. Their daughter nurses at her breast, a smacking, greedy suckling. The parents exchange a shy look.

Bonnie feels his yearning, so she guides his hand along the baby's cheek, then her forehead, as she watches something in him unfurl, something hard in him gone with a single touch of his child. And when he looks at her, her eyes are wet with some kind of fear, but freedom too, as she looks around the room.

"I'm different now," she whispers, her gaze asking him if all of her will still fit in his arms. Just as he leans close to kiss her, to say yes, the morning breeze takes flight—a surge of crisp wind that stirs the curtains, that lifts the scrolls, that sends the papers on the desk through the room. As she moves to stand, he puts a hand to her shoulder, telling her not to. She watches as he straightens up, watches as he restores the room.

"I just have one question," he says, the golden light engulfing him.

"Yeah?"

"Are there any men on this roster of yours?" He looks up at the scrolls.

"Just white boys," she says coyly and smiles.

He smiles too, shakes his head. "Is that supposed to make me feel better?"

VIII.

CHER MANSOUR

Senegal, 1970

98. **I DIDN'T KNOW** *what you remembered...* Mama begins the first sentence of her letter, but stops, gets up, leaves the ink and paper on her desk. She ventures out to the marketplace on foot. It is the same marketplace where she'd once left him, willed him not to love her, but had, in the end, turned back. The marketplace seems incredibly small now, too narrow and dense, the tables of wares low to the ground, but the smells of fondé, grilled corn, gedje, and yéet are enlivening.

All of the women working in the market look to be around her age, and Mama moves fast, not quite ready to see a familiar face. Though everything has been shifted around, the bench where she'd told Mansour to wait for her is still where it was back then, albeit blackened with time.

She buys tamarind, peanuts, water by the bag. She's moved into the first floor of a duplex: a pink house not far from Corniche, where she can watch the foreigners march up and down the block of embassies and quell her yearnings for Switzerland. From far away, the life she left in Europe seems richer than it felt while she was living it. However strange, however painful it had been, in reflection, it had excited her, had been a lot of what she'd hoped for.

While Mama Eva sits alone in the top row of the Thiès Movie Theater one Saturday, the correct way to open the letter comes to her. She jots it down on her palm by the light of the big screen:

> *I did not know that we could talk about her. I did not know*
> *that you remembered her. I did not know that we were both*
> *grieving all these years.*

Her thoughts are interrupted by the projectionist moaning from the creaky wooden balcony. His brown teeth rip the lamb from the bone as he devours the meal she'd swapped with him for a private screening of *Doosri Aurat*, the latest Hindi film to come to Senegal.

Later, back home, she continues.

> *Bonnie told me that you dream of her death, all of the time.*
> *Bonnie told me that you think she meant to die.*
> *Do you think—*

Mama springs up from the table with hot hands and a sore throat. She circumambulates the room's center, watching the pen and paper from a safe distance. She watches it like a pot that's boiling over, like a pot where some oil has dripped down the sides and a grease fire has sparked. The letter only has five lines since she's begun, and that is still more than she can take.

She's pulling the bedsheet around her shoulders, though the room is smoldering. Then she goes out to the courtyard and starts another little fire with charcoal. The rag dipped in kerosene is slow to ignite the coals. She feeds in her letter to excite the flame. And waits.

Under the moon, she sits on the tiles, still warm from the daytime, watching the fire crackle, the embers darting loud and bright across the open space. Killed herself? What could he know? He had only been two years old.

Killed herself. *Kiné killed herself.* She tries the sentence in her head.

First it means nothing. A line like the ones in French children's books, where the African child is not yet being taught the meaning of French words, only the way that they relate to each other in a sentence.

But then, against her will, without prompting, vivid memories flood in as if on a chain that is being yanked. Her mind is finding clues, finding evidence, long-buried information that suggests it's true: The wandering off; her frightening quiet;

And then Mama doesn't know what to do with her body. Her arms seem useless, but her legs need to move. She puts out the fire and starts to walk. She hadn't consciously decided to go to the beach, but she realizes, too late, that that's where her body is taking her.

No one goes to the beach at night, so no one is on the road, but a stray cow—a white body with high white horns—moves past her in a peaceful stride that calls her to slow down.

She senses the ocean, that calm it sends through the air, and the sand changes, from the reddish brown of the Sahara to the beige sparkle of the beach. When she arrives, the sign blocking it off, erected after Kiné's disappearance, is long gone. And when she enters, she sees that the tide, after twenty-one years, is still moving. After twenty-one years, it never stopped, not even for a few seconds. An ebb and flow, blind to the death that transformed her life and Mansour's forever. And the sound: How could it be that this sound, after what it took from her, is still so calming? It confounds her, the way of life.

She gathers the sand in her hands. Pushes off her headwrap, the wind thickening her hair. She is not afraid of the water and goes in until it is up to her neck. She buoys. Just her and the moon. Of course, the water is mild and warm today. She goes under. She cannot see anything, only feels that the water gets cooler the deeper she goes. And when she brings up her head, gasping for breath, tasting the sweet night air and the strength of the ocean's brine, she knows, finally, where to begin. Not from death, but from life.

> *Mansour, your mother, Kiné, was tall. She sang well.*
> *She was everything good. We shared one life for as long as*
> *we could. I'm sending you my only photograph of her.*
> *Keep it close.*

Now, every morning, she sucks on tamarind like a lollipop, the shiny black seeds rolling around her bedroom floor like black dice. The shells and skins of sand-roasted peanuts can be seen in the corners. One day soon, she will clean it up. But in starting over and returning home, she feels seventeen again and has no desire to clean her room.

Her neighbor is a herdsman. Peule guys and their prettiness never did much for her, but the aroma of his slow-roasting beef, goat, and lamb at the corner of her block eventually draws her to him and his wares. The first night, without much more than a hello, she buys her meat and goes, but by the fourth night, she is sitting outside with him, learning about the Fouta he came from at the end of 1969 and talking about her kitchen in Europe. He too feels like a foreigner in the city. This and their devotion to good food makes talking to him good and easy. They both want to know why people would ever eat things they don't like, why people would drink a bad brew, when there were things in the world that tasted so good.

Mama doesn't like the boutiques, all of their canned, imported produce. She is accustomed to owning her own farm, tilling her own garden, used to freshness and harvesting. Her upstairs neighbor laughs from her balcony when she sees Mama in the courtyard trying to turn over soil and plant things in the city.

Mansour, when will you and your family come to see me?
I don't live far from the beach. It was your mother's
favorite place.

By her third month in town, Mama gets into a rhythm. Market shopping, the Peule neighbor, then sometimes the two cousins in Pikine who don't ask for any money, just her company. Maybe, one day, she thinks she might take a trip home to Tivaouane.

Mansour, thank you for your letter. I am glad that you've
reached Germany and are preparing for your tour—and that
Bonnie is a Ndoye now. Alhamdulilah. We must have a
wedding here. I am preparing for this year. Yes, this year!
You are a big artist who goes to many countries throughout
the year, so put Senegal—your home—on the list. It will not
be hard. If you do not, your marriage will not be blessed.

I am happy to hear also that the baby is doing well, that she
has adapted to life so easily. Mansour—I know I did things
when you were a child that were difficult to understand. My
sister's shadow was ever-present. But now, in your little one,
there is new light.

Also, do not irritate Bonnie, she called me the other day,
frustrated with you. She is kind, but has a hot head like all

Ndoye women. So be balanced for her. Good wives need peace and quiet. And you by nature are not peaceful, so try sometimes to be quiet.

Sincerely,
Tanti

IX.

BONNIE IS MARRIED

Pennsylvania, 1971

99. **AT FIRST**, it's hard. Onyx Records doesn't have any file for a cover artist on staff named Bonnie King. Claudine calls and calls, getting transferred from office to office, and even when she goes to the New York label in person, the answer is still the same. The poor man at the front desk, who she pressures for access to the head of the label, is undone by the end of her rant. ("She didn't work here, ma'am! Not now, not ever!")

But then she sees Mansour's profile in the *New York Times*.

She reads it on the patio of her Philly brownstone, surrounded by the morning glories in her flower garden (she'd persisted, exposing herself to the scent of soil over several months before getting the courage to kneel in the dirt). She reads quickly, whispering the words under her breath.

> *Ndoye's manager makes the conditions under which I*
> *will be granted this interview unapologetically clear. First,*
> *no questions about his health, and I cannot come to their*
> *home. She prefers that I meet him at a family-owned*
> *restaurant in the Swiss countryside. She cautions to arrive*
> *before sunset, that the path will be pitch-black once*
> *night falls.*

The mansion and its African restaurant have become a
tourist attraction. A reputation bolstered by its new music
venue—a small eighty-seat establishment that is at capacity
on the night I arrive. The waitstaff is made up of young
locals, but in the mutterings of the more esteemed waitresses,
who direct the flow of the room, I hear what I'm told is
Wolof, Ndoye's native tongue.

Among the venue's fleet of waiters, I spot a sweaty Mansour.
He bounces his toddler daughter on his hip.

As we talk, he is the way he seems onstage: warm, eccentric,
brimming with delight. It is Mansour who convinces his
wife-cum-manager, Bonnie Ndoye, to allow me into her
office. When I finally meet her, I would never have put her
with the woman on the phone. She is quiet, gazing up at
him as he and I speak . . .

Claudine stops reading. She turns back to the photograph of
Mansour. He's very handsome. Magnetic, even. A little more rugged
and wild than she would like for Bonnie. (Why did he have to be
half-naked in *every picture* of him onstage?) But he is Bonnie's husband. *Bonnie's husband.* Her daughter is married.

Claudine stands up from the bench, looks over her brick wall at the
scarce traffic this cool morning. She spreads the paper across the patio
table. Keeps reading. He'll be in New York for a weeklong residency
at the Village Vanguard next month.

"Where in Switzerland?" she whispers out loud, perusing the article, searching for more details, until she finds the line in italics: *This*
interview took place at the couple's family restaurant in Lausanne.

Two weeks later, fourteen *Pages Jaunes*—the Swiss yellow pages she sent for—arrive on her stoop. When she opens the door, the postman is doubled over, weighed down by the stacks of paper. He yells over his shoulder that she ought to tip. And as soon as she tracks down the address, two days later, she calls, giving no thought to the time in Switzerland.

"Hello?" Bonnie answers as Marie walks off sleepily, releasing the phone.

She can hear someone swallow.

"Hello?" Bonnie says again. Still no answer.

She chupses (something she's picked up from her African family) and hangs up. By the time she's back in the bedroom, under covers, the phone rings again.

"Mansee . . . Mansee!"

"Mm."

"Get the phone, man."

"I'm dead," he says.

She rolls her eyes, drags herself back to the living room.

"Hello?" She's awake now. Her voice is firm, and clear.

"Hi," the voice says.

"Who is this?"

"Is this Bonnie?"

She hesitates, surprised by the American accent. Nobody has ever called her from home. "Who is this?"

"It's me. It's . . . Claudine."

"Claudine . . . ?" "Then Bonnie gasps. A whisper, "Mama?"

"Yes."

"*Mama?*"

"Yes. It's me."

Bonnie holds the phone close, says nothing, focuses on the pulsing in her temple.

"Are you still there?" Claudine says.

"Yes."

"How are you?" Her mother's voice is smaller, more timid.

"I'm ... I'm fine, Mama," Bonnie says. She exhales, grateful to find herself suddenly numb.

"Grandma died." It's been three years now, but it's all Bonnie can think to say.

"Yes, I ... I heard about Sylvia. I'm sorry that I wasn't there."

They are silent for a moment. Bonnie is frozen. Claudine breaks the silence, speaks quickly.

"Well, the last time we talked, you wanted a house. A brownstone, like the ones in Park Slope. And you won't believe this, but ... I found such a place. A few years ago now. I've been fixing it up, and I ... well it's certainly not a place for just one person ..."

"Mama ... Mama," Bonnie repeats, getting Claudine to quiet down, "I ... I ... I have to go," Bonnie whispers, putting the phone on the hook. She sits there alone in the dark and quiet of the room, a decade of feelings raining down.

All day, Bonnie won't go into the room when the baby is awake. Won't hold her either. Mansour has noticed that she does this sometimes; if the baby is fussy, Bonnie takes it personally. Quick to lose patience, disappearing to town in the name of procuring this or that from the store.

But today, it's different. When he finds her on the couch that evening, she confesses that it was Claudine on the phone in the early hours of the morning.

"She was continuing a conversation we had when I was twelve years old. Talking like it just happened. But she missed it. She missed my whole life!"

Mansour speaks gently. "I think you have to go see her."

Bonnie sits up. "Why?"

"So that she can have all of you," he says, looking toward the baby in the crib across the room. "So we can all start again."

X.

ON THE INSIDE,
EVERYBODY HAS A SOUND

Philadelphia, 1971

100. **THEY LEAVE MARIE** in their sunny suite at the Waldorf Astoria in Manhattan. She has come to see some universities but can't yet shake the party scene. She waves good-bye with her foot, stomach-first on the couch, hungover from a night at a hot New York nightclub. Bonnie had been invited by a rock artist she represents, but they'd sent Marie instead, and she finds them, still snoring face down on either side of their chunky baby girl when she returns. She calls them The Baby Slaves.

This morning, they turn down her offer to watch their mistress for extra cash and take the Amtrak to Philly, baby in tow. It's the one day that Mansour doesn't have any shows or press lined up.

The baby screams the whole train ride down, and they take turns walking her up and down the train car, terrorizing business class. Bonnie says over and over that it's a sign, that they should get off on the next stop and go back to New York, but he wins the argument each time. And just as they step off the train into Philly's sticky summer air, the child falls asleep, dissolving the tension between her parents.

Bonnie watches Philly from the cab window, gripping Mansour's hand tightly, the baby's bassinet balanced between them. His bracelets rattle on her wrist as the car dips in and out of potholes. She grips the seat in front of her with her free hand, trying to steady herself along the bouncy ride.

"Why did you give me all these bracelets anyway? In Brazil."

"Are you familiar with the periodic table?" he asks her.

She's peering at him curiously. "Why are we discussing the periodic table?"

He tugs at each bracelet on her wrist. "Le cuivre, le fer. La vie." *Copper, iron. Life.*

"It seeps into the skin?" she asks, turning the bracelets on her wrist.

She gathers the few on her wrist that are not this. "These are Mama's," she says with a smile.

"Toppatoo na leen bu baax?" *Did she take good care of y'all?*

He asks Bonnie,, looking away, out at the city.

"I told you . . . she really did, Mansee." She replies in English, gently, running a hand over his hair.

He notices the shortness of her breaths, feels the clamminess of her hand. He kisses her forehead, assuaging her fears until the driver interrupts, remarking on the sweetness of their romance.

"You're making me miss my wife."

He is from Lebanon. He knows Mansour's music. He saw Mansour and his band a while ago . . . *in Spain.* An accidental sighting, but he'd loved his performance. Bonnie and Mansour groan at this detail, and the driver perks up, wanting to know what it's all about. But they tell him it's too long of a story, that he wouldn't believe it anyway.

The conversation is a great distraction. Bonnie's full of dread as the street numbers ascend, indicating that they are closing in on their destination. The man invites them to dinner that night, and Bonnie seriously considers switching plans.

He drops them at the corner of the block. "You sure this is it?" he says, as Mansour closes the back door.

It is a sprawling brownstone mansion that takes up half the square block. The other half is taken up by its guesthouse and carriage house. Bonnie stands on the sidewalk, taking it in. It is exactly what she described to her mother as her dream home so many years ago: the lush flower gardens spilling over from both sides of the house, the gargoyles and lions etched on either side of the front steps. They are detailed, down to the gaps in the gargoyles' teeth; one is smiling, the other menacing.

She walks up the marble steps slowly, one by one. The iron knocker, heavy in her hand, is shaped like a bird. She knocks, waits. Hears nothing. She turns around, ready to leave. But Mansour is there, the baby's bassinet in one hand. He shrugs, doing her thing, gives her a wink. She's teary-eyed.

"No one's coming."

As soon as she speaks, she hears rustling with latches and keys. And the large mahogany door opens.

Before her is a smiling, attractive man around her age. She's relieved to have another moment to gather herself.

"You must be Bonnie," he says. "Come inside, please." He steps back, ushering her in with a hand on her back.

And there, down the hall, is the same woman Bonnie was reaching for on the Paris airport tarmac. For a few breaths, she can't move, can't speak. And then the shock gives way to a freedom, from herself, from the twelve years she's been waiting and running, and she feels that jumping over her fear and pride is all of her love bursting out.

———

Her hair is salt and pepper now, as big and long as Bonnie's, but nothing else is different. Even though they are the same height, Claudine seems taller still. Bonnie's trembling, but she manages to walk forward; Claudine is trembling and moving closer too. They rush until they are in each other's arms.

They sit on the floor of the mansion's foyer. Bonnie can see that one of the rooms has been converted into a studio, and her heart is happy that Claudine's love for dance never died. A Japanese tea set emits steam on the tray beside them.

They are in disbelief, digesting the presence of each other, but the sun has already merged their shadows on the hardwood floor.

"Can I tell you a story?" Claudine says.

Bonnie nods. Claudine begins.

Claudine birthed Bonnie alone, at some time in the evening. She'd wailed, her deep bellow swallowed by the glass and bricks between the front door and the entrance to the emergency room. It was only some years after the war, and the local hospitals were still unreliable. No one saw her come in, except for a woman who'd locked herself in the bathroom to drink whiskey, and no one came to help.

The delivery was fast. The child took total possession of her body. Her skin crawled and her spine burned, her legs stretched out before her and unable to move. Claudine was paralyzed. To tame her racing mind, she watched moths brawling at the light bulb above her head, every muscle in her body erect. Bones protruded from the tops of her feet and her neck; every breath was sharp and shallow. She turned hot enough to sweat and then turned cold again, convulsing so deeply that her teeth slammed together, and she nearly swallowed her tongue. She weathered the wave of pain that she desperately hoped would not end in death. In the final contractions, she'd become deaf. The child slid out of her onto the stone floor and didn't cry.

Claudine walked the two blocks home up a windy hill as the sound came back to her ears. Her legs were stiff and heavy, but the cold air helped push her along. Bonnie was swaddled close to her skin, the uncut umbilical cord pressed between them, her beaver coat hardly covering the wetness that still rolled down her legs. Bonnie had purred when they'd gotten out into the cold morning but had fallen asleep by the time they made it into the apartment building. Claudine took the three flights step by step, taking a moment to sit on the cold marble at every landing.

The sun was rising then. The sky started off blue all over, with one line of fire that sent waves of gold in every direction. With bloodstained hands, Claudine lit a fire. She laid the sleeping baby on the kitchen counter and stretched the umbilical cord across the wooden chopping block. She broke it with a dull knife she'd been cutting onions with earlier that day. Onion skins still scattered across the countertop. She tossed the cord and onions into the trash can. She wiped down the child's body with a warm dish towel.

Over the days, before the fire and on the living room couch, she looked at the child's face from different angles. From every angle, with every beam of light the sun made, it was the face of someone she loved. From the left side, Claudine saw Sylvia in the elegance of Bonnie's features, the ease and looseness of their arrangement. The generous nose was that of her own grandmother (Julia); the cheekbones, formed early, mild and round, were her those of her father (Solomon); and the chin somehow looked just like the chin of her best friend (Sophie), a French girl from the ballet troupe, who'd died in her youth.

With every breath she took, Bonnie's small body curled in deeper.

In her deepest sleep, she resembled a snail.

Bonnie would never know these people, but they lived on in her.

"Is there more?" Bonnie asks, breathless.

"There is so much more," Claudine says, and then her tears begin to fall.

"I want to know it all."

"I'll tell it to you." Claudine slides closer, gesturing for her daughter's hands. Bonnie gives them to her. "You tell me your story, and I'll tell you mine."

Bonnie nods, her tears starting again too. She and her mother are truly meeting for the first time.

They can hear Mansour singing to the baby in Wolof, the sound carrying from the dining room across the hall.

"What's her name?" Claudine asks, a little sadly.

"Kiné," Bonnie responds proudly.

Kiné is imitating her father, trying to hit higher and higher notes, her spirited coos echoing loudly around the house.

Mother and grandmother listen.

They beam at the sound.

ACKNOWLEDGMENTS

First to the Source of this book and me. I only pray that you are pleased.

Nene and Baba, thank you, foremost, for teaching me how to pray, sacrificing so that I could dream, and convincing me that the world is truly mine.

Cecelia, Elsie, John, and Quincy: Thank you.

Kumba: What do you say to your life force, to your first friend? To the one who taught me the power of imagination? Remember how we used to dream of worlds together? This book is as much yours as it is mine. It only exists because you believed and kept believing even when I couldn't.

Dr. Linda Wharton, a.k.a. AL: You anchor me, affirm me, sustain me, love on me in ways that have brought me into myself.

Kamau, thank you. You made the call that sparked the completion of this book. I would have given up if you had not proposed those writing sessions. Thank you for the music all these years. And the love.

Vernon and Cynthia Hubbard: You will always be my second parents. I will never forget the way you kept me safe, loved, and affirmed in the place where my writing dreams first started.

Auntie Kathy and Uncle Rasool: Thank you for the journals every birthday. I've filled every single one.

Yaa: Thank you for building with me. Now we can all stand tall as the fab 4! I love you.

Teyimba Jess: Thank you for seeing the merits of this story in its earliest iteration and publishing what would become the first version of its first chapter in the African American Review at JHU Press.

Mariah: You saved this novel twice. The first time with your willingness to take a chance. The second, with your patience as it revealed itself to me. People talk about the work of diversifying publishing, but you're actually doing it. Please keep going, against all odds. You're needed.

Allison, Khalid and the Trellis team: Thank you for breaking barriers and helping this novel find its home

Caolinn: It is uncanny to have your work seen and known so clearly by someone you've never even met in person. From the first time you shared your vision for this novel, it aligned so well with mine that I felt like you were in my head. Thank you for stewarding a different kind of story into the world.

Anne: Your taste! Your sensibility! I have felt so seen by you, and so heard, and so encouraged. Every time I worried if my little word experiments would work, you got it—always got it—and that gave me courage to power through this transformative journey.

Mr. Wesley: You saw the work first. Thank you for launching me into my purpose.

To my favorite teachers: Ellen Krich, Maria Hampton, Dr. Ezekiel Vifansi, Dr. Lisa Wilde, Lonnie Carter, Dan Pulick.

Greg Tate: For affirming me, and for convincing me to write women like the ones I know.

Rashida Ishmail: For hosting my first-ever staged reading in your beautiful apartment. I haven't stopped, and never will.

To the New York theater community, to the friends, supporters, and artists who helped me grow. Thank you.

To the experts who lent their time, resources, network, and kindness to me to make this book the very best it could be: Dr. El Hadj Dieye, Dr. Saliou Dione, Dr. Sylviane Diouf, Jocelyn Dubin, Dr.

Michael Flynn, Dr. Basilien-Gainche, Dr. Serge Slama, Audrey Henry, Alexis Perryman, and Maryse Petasis.

Chloe, Sara, Amelia, and Emily, I deeply admire your cool and calm approach to such a tremendous task! Thank you for all that you do.

Molly Stern: Thank you for daring to innovate in this industry. I am so excited and honored that this book is part of your vision.

SJP: That you are shepherding this into the world is right in line with the theme of dreaming. No one would believe that I was binging *SATC* on Prime in the earliest days of this manuscript. Your reverence for craft, your integrity as an artist, and your love of reading are a gift to us all. Thank you.

And last but not least to my Senegalese family. The dearest love is the love we choose. That is what we have.

ABOUT THE AUTHOR

MAI SENNAAR is a graduate of NYU's Tisch School of the Arts. The Smithsonian Affiliate Museum of the African Diaspora, the Berkeley Art Museum and Pacific Film Archive, and the Classical Theatre of Harlem are among the venues that have presented her plays. Her short film *Wax Lovers' Playlist* premiered at AFI Silver Theatre and Cultural Center and was an Official Selection of the Martha's Vineyard African American Film Festival. She is the book writer for *Carry On!*, a new musical by Broadway composer Diana Wharton-Sennaar and the creative director of the performing arts company MWPLive. *They Dream in Gold* is her first novel. She lives between Baltimore and Dakar.

A BODY IN THE
LIBRARY

Other titles in our
Great Short Stories series
include:

GREAT RACING STORIES

Edited & Introduced by
Dick Francis & John Welcome

CLASSIC LINES
More Great Racing Stories

Edited & Introduced by
Dick Francis & John Welcome

FOOLS, KNAVES & HEROES
Great Political Short Stories

Edited & Introduced by
Jeffrey Archer & Simon Bainbridge

GREAT LAW & ORDER STORIES

Edited & Introduced by
John Mortimer

GREAT SOLDIERS' TALES

Edited & Introduced by
Field Marshal Lord Carver

A BODY IN THE LIBRARY

Classic Tales of Mystery
and Suspense

Edited & Introduced by

Rex Collings

BELLEW PUBLISHING
London

This collection first published in Great Britain
in 1991 by Bellew Publishing Company Limited
7 Southampton Place, London WC1A 2DR

ISBN 0 947792 58 9

Phototypeset by Input Typesetting Ltd, London

Printed and bound in Great Britain by
Billings & Sons Ltd

CONTENTS

ACKNOWLEDGEMENTS

INTRODUCTION

'ELEMENTARY my dear Watson.' No one has been able in the published record of Mr Holmes's cases to discover the place where this was said – yet the statement with marvellous succinctness not only describes the relationship of the two men but also indicates the way in which the great detective tackled his problems. In much the same way the phrases 'a body in the library' and 'the butler did it' accurately represent the ethos of the pre-war detective story; although the number of times when the body was found in the library or in the study, or when it was the butler who had committed the crime are actually very few. It is a fact, however, that Mrs Christie published a full-length novel entitled *The Body in the Library*; in a short foreword to which she wrote:

> 'There are certain clichés belonging to certain types of fiction. The 'bold bad baronet' for melodrama, 'the body in the library' for the detective story. For several years I treasured up the possibility of a suitable 'variation on a well-known theme'. I laid down for myself certain conditions. The library in question must be a highly orthodox and conventional library. The body, on the other hand must be a wildly improbable and highly sensational body. Such were the terms of the problem.'

In that early novel, Miss Marple explains in the last chapter the reasoning that led her to the successful solution of the crime – reasoning it is true that relied a good deal on common sense and intuition.

Miss Marple, today, owing partly to television and the sensitive acting of the admirable Miss Hickson, is one of the best known and admired of fictional detectives; but it was not always so. In his introduction to a collection of short stories in 1927.★ Father Knox dismisses her perfunctorily with this comment on *The Tuesday Night Club*, the short story in which Miss Marple makes, possibly, her first appearance:

> 'Miss Christie goes further; she presents us with a mystery which is solved by the stupidest member of the party, who happens to have special knowledge of the technicalities bearing on the point.'

'Stupidest' is a term neither critics nor policemen would dare today to apply to Miss Jane Marple of St Mary Mead. Father Ronald Knox, not perhaps so successful nor lucid a writer of detective stories as he was a theologian, in his perceptive introduction to the book suggests a personal Decalogue for the would-be writer, which I believe is worth quoting:

> '1. The criminal must be someone mentioned in the early part of the story, but must not be anyone whose thoughts the reader has been allowed to follow.
> 2. All supernatural or preternatural agencies are ruled out as a matter of course.
> 3. Not more than one secret room or passage allowable.
> 4. No hitherto undiscovered poisons may be used, nor any appliance which will need a long scientific explanation at the end.
> 5. No Chinaman must figure in the story.
> 6. No accident must over help the detective nor must he ever have an unaccountable intuition which proves to be right.
> 7. The detective must not himself commit the crime.
> 8. The detective must not light on any clues which are not instantly produced for the inspection of the reader.
> 9. The stupid friend of the detective, the Watson, must not conceal any thoughts which pass through his mind; his intelligence must be slightly, but very slightly, below that of the average reader.
> 10. Twin brothers, and doubles generally, must not appear unless we have been duly prepared for them.

★ *Best Detective Stories*, first series, London 1927. Edited by Father Ronald Knox and H. Harrington. With an introduction by Father Ronald Knox.

This Decalogue is, I suspect, far from exhaustive; no doubt my
reader is all agog to add a few more prohibitions to the list.'

Father Knox is right, certainly sixty years on, our list of do's and
don'ts would, if one were so rash as to compile one, be vastly
different. But we are dealing here with history not current affairs
and the witness of contemporaries can be illumination. Warning
of the danger of writing to an established formula, Father Knox
continues:

'Even the exterior setting of the thing is in danger of becoming
stereotyped. We know, as we sit down to the book, that a foul
murder has almost certainly be done at a country house; that the
butler will have been with the family for sixteen years; that a
young male secretary will have recently been engaged; that the
chauffeur will have gone away for the night to visit his widowed
mother . . . we know that the victim, if this is a man, will have
been killed either in the shrubbery or in his own study, with a
wound in the back of his head.'

Thus, two writers, the successful practitioner Mrs Christie, and the
eminent commentator Father Ronald Knox, commend to us, the
former as a cliché the latter as a stereotype, the formula: *The Body
in the Library (or Study)*. But as I noted earlier the body was not
often found in the library and on those rare occasions when it was,
the butler was seldom responsible for the corpse.

What the quotations do indicate, however, very clearly, is that
the detective story was for many years predominantly a middle-
class taste. The popular press might contain detailed reports of Dr
Crippen's crime, of the brides in the bath case, or even horrific
descriptions of the activities of Jack the Ripper; but the novels
borrowed from *Boots*, that Queen of lending libraries, at twopence
or threepence a time, were not concerned with such lurid occur-
rences, they dealt with the latest adventures of Lord Peter Wimsey,
Mr Fortune, Mr Albert Campion, and Mrs Lestrange Bradley. On
the whole the pattern provided by Sherlock Holmes, the gifted
amateur sleuth, was preferred to that of Wilkie Collins's earlier
professional policemen, Sergeant Cuff and Sergeant Bulmer. The
sleuth was an amateur, a gentleman of private means; even when a
professional policeman, like Ngaio Marsh's Inspector Roderick

Alleyn or Michael Innes's Inspector (today Sir John) Appleby it usually turned out that he was a migrant from a more exalted background. This was a time of civilized crime, Lord Peter emulating A. C. Maclaren and Albert Campion a royal pretender, which lasted until after the Second World War, when it was swept away in the tidal wave of permissiveness and egalitarianism. The gentle, rather muddled, but successful amateur gave way to the hard drinking, swearing, loose living Private Eye more often adept at sleeping with his client than at solving the mystery. The Cold War gave rise to spy stories, and Bond and Smiley (the professional disguised as the amateur) were the new heroes; if they owed anything to the clubland heroes of *The Thirty-Nine Steps* or *The Riddle of the Sands* it was no more than Shakespeare's debt to Holinshed.

Violence, brutality and lashings of uninhibited sex, often of a most recondite nature, characterized many of the new wave novels; the older respectable and above all reliable story seemed dead. Even those that in any way conformed to Father Knox's Decalogue were usually by the bluntness of the language and the unpleasantness of the detective, now either a fornicating Private Eye (often an ex-cop, cop, note how easy it is to fall into the use of unregenerate language) or a gross, belching disillusioned, unlovable and not infrequently corrupt policeman. Bias of Priene centuries ago wrote in the dust at Delphi 'Most men are bad' and it would seem that this was the formula chosen, even if unwittingly, by many of the post-war generation of writers. It was not unusual for the reader to dislike with equal intensity victim, criminal, and detective, and it was no longer possible to be Father Brown, Mr Fortune, or indeed if one were so inclined, Professor Moriarty. The old detective story if not already dead was certainly on its last legs, and put out to grass. Few bookshops if any carried, automatically, the latest Black-and-Yellow Gollancz crime novel; the Green Penguins, for long *sans pareil*, lost their typographical distinction (and some would say their quality). *Boots* closed the branches of its lending libraries.

All was not lost. Mrs Christie still wrought her traditional craft, and the Innes-Crispin school on occasion provided fresh offerings in the old style, as indeed did Gladys Mitchell, Ngaio Marsh, and Margery Allingham. But at this juncture they were a valiant rearguard force, defending the old frontiers rather than establishing new ones – at the airports and main line stations it became well-nigh

impossible to find an old-type green Penguin with which to beguile
the journey, as blockbusters of ever increasing size filled the shelves.
A desert of dreariness, grey men and women in grey clothes and in
grey settings had taken over. Reaction had to take place, the tide
turned, with Clough one could rejoice:

> 'For while the tired waves, vainly breaking
>   Seem here no painful inch to gain
> Far back through creeks and inlets making
>   Comes silent, flooding the main.'

How and when it started is difficult to pinpoint, perhaps television
had something to do with it, perhaps it was the inevitable swing of
the pendulum, the turn of the wheel. Howbeit, the fierce blaze of
the transatlantic comet has passed and its tail is but a fading memory.

There is discernible, too, a return to the cult of the amateur, not
only are the old stories being widely reprinted – the Christies,
the Sayers, the Allinghams, the Marshs, but also those lesser stars
Josephine Tey, Antony Berkeley and Gladys Mitchell. The new
amateurs, experts in their own fields; John Thatcher the urbane
New York banker, Lovejoy the shady antiques dealer, talented and
eminently likeable, Jemima Shore, the not so likeable T.V. person-
ality created by Lady Antonia Fraser and Brother Cadfael, Ellis
Peters's medieval sleuth.

Parallel to the resurgence of the amateur, there has also been a
new group of polished, professional policemen, notably Inspector
Adam Dalgliesh, P. D. James's offering, a poetry loving (and writing) educated man susceptible to females in distress; Inspector Ghote,
Keating's rather tedious Bombay detective, and perhaps my favourite, Ellis Peters's Inspector Felse who shares, at some centuries
removed, certain of Brother Cadfael's characteristics. But today it
is unlikely that amateur or professional will be presented with a
body in the library and, except where Inspector Morse is involved,
a study is as exotic as one of Miss Blandish's orchids – and as rare!

What of this collection? Here are more than a dozen stories, each
complete in itself, which reflect the world in which and for which
they were written. The secure world, the known, above all the
predictable world, the world of Fullers' Walnut Cake, Lyons Corner
Houses where the waitresses wore cap and apron, the world of

Empires and the Orient Express, of world maps splashed with great splotches of red – a world of the known.

> 'The short story' Father Knox says 'must always take an honour-able place in detective fiction; it is the medium which has given us some of the best Holmes literature, and the whole cycle of Father Brown. But it labours under an obvious disadvantage as compared with the full armchair performance. There are three questions which call for solution in any criminal mystery – Who did it? Why did he do it? How did he do it? The short story has sufficient elbow room to deal with the question of method – How did the man come to be murdered when he was sitting alone in a hermetically sealed room? . . . It is far more difficult to create in such a short compass a genuine doubt as to the motive with which the crime was done, or the identity of the criminal. . . .'

These stories then will be strong on method but rather weaker on the exploration of motive, they are really here to be enjoyed, to provide a means of escape to a vanished but not forgotten world. I have not been able to discover a collective noun for such a group of stories as this. But I did find in an early nineteenth century book largely devoted to games and pastimes a word for a collection of butlers – a draught. It would not be inappropriate I think to borrow this term (for who now would keep more than one butler) and apply it to this present collection. Which of the word's several definitions one chooses I leave to the reader's judgment, all I hope is that when they have finished they will have been refreshed.

A BODY IN THE
LIBRARY

LORD CHIZELRIGG'S MISSING FORTUNE

Robert Barr

THE name of the late Lord Chizelrigg never comes to my mind without instantly suggesting that of Mr T. A. Edison. I never saw the late Lord Chizelrigg, and I have met Mr Edison only twice in my life, yet the two men are linked in my memory, and it was a remark the latter once made that in great measure enabled me to solve the mystery which the former had wrapped round his actions.

There is no memorandum at hand to tell me the year in which those two meetings with Edison took place. I received a note from the Italian Ambassador in Paris requesting me to wait upon him at the Embassy. I learned that on the next day a deputation was to set out from the Embassy to one of the chief hotels, there to make a call in state upon the great American inventor, and formally present to him various insignia accompanying certain honours which the King of Italy had conferred upon him. As many Italian nobles of high rank had been invited, and as these dignitaries would not only be robed in the costumes pertaining to their orders, but in many cases would wear jewels of almost inestimable value, my presence was desired in the belief that I might perhaps be able to ward off any attempt on the part of the deft-handed gentry who might possibly make an effort to gain these treasures, and I may add, with perhaps some little self-gratification, no *contretemps* occurred.

Mr Edison, of course, had long before received notification of the hour at which the deputation would wait upon him, but when we entered the large parlour assigned to the inventor, it was evident to me at a glance that the celebrated man had forgotten all about the function. He stood by a bare table, from which the cloth had been jerked and flung into a corner, and upon that table were placed several bits of black and greasy machinery – cog wheels, pulleys, bolts, etc. These seemingly belonged to a French workman who stood on the other side of the table, with one of the parts in his grimy hand. Edison's own hands were not too clean, for he had palpably been examining the material, and conversing with the workman, who wore the ordinary long blouse of an iron craftsman in a small way. I judged him to be a man with a little shop of his own in some back street, who did odd jobs of engineering, assisted perhaps by a skilled helper or two, and a few apprentices. Edison looked sternly towards the door as the solemn procession filed in, and there was a trace of annoyance on his face at the interruption, mixed with a shade of perplexity as to what this gorgeous display all meant. The Italian is as ceremonious as the Spaniard where a function is concerned, and the official who held the ornate box which contained the jewellery resting on a velvet cushion, stepped slowly forward, and came to a stand in front of the bewildered American. Then the Ambassador, in sonorous voice, spoke some gracious words regarding the friendship existing between the United States and Italy, expressed a wish that their rivalry should ever take the form of benefits conferred upon the human race, and instanced the honoured recipient as the most notable example the world had yet produced of a man bestowing blessings upon all nations in the arts of peace. The eloquent Ambassador concluded by saying that, at the command of his Royal master, it was both his duty and his pleasure to present, and so forth and so forth.

Mr Edison, visibly ill at ease, nevertheless made a suitable reply in the fewest possible words, and the *étalage* being thus at an end, the noblemen, headed by their Ambassador, slowly retired, myself forming the tail of the procession. Inwardly I deeply sympathized with the French workman who thus unexpectedly found himself confronted by so much magnificence. He cast one wild look about him, but saw that his retreat was cut off unless he displaced some of these gorgeous grandees. He tried then to shrink into himself, and finally stood helpless like one paralyzed. In spite of Republican institutions, there is deep down in every Frenchman's heart a respect and awe for official pageants, sumptuously staged and costumed as this one was. But he likes to view it from afar, and supported by his fellows, not thrust incongruously into the midst of things, as was the case with this panic-stricken engineer. As I passed out, I cast a glance over my shoulder at the humble artisan content with a profit of a few francs a day, and at the millionaire inventor opposite him. Edison's face, which during the address had been cold and impassive, reminding me vividly of a bust of Napoleon, was now all aglow with enthusiasm as he turned to his humble visitor. He cried joyfully to the workman:

'A minute's demonstration is worth an hour's explanation. I'll call round to-morrow at your shop, about ten o'clock, and show you how to make the thing work.'

I lingered in the hall until the Frenchman came out, then, introducing myself to him, asked the privilege of visiting his shop next day at ten. This was accorded with that courtesy which you will always find among the industrial classes of France, and next day I had the pleasure of meeting Mr Edison. During our conversation I complimented him on his invention of the incandescent electric light, and this was the reply that has ever remained in my memory:

'It was not an invention, but a discovery. We knew what we wanted; a carbonized tissue, which would withstand the electric current in a vacuum for, say, a thousand hours. If no such tissue existed, then the incandescent light, as we know it, was not possible. My assistants started out to find this tissue, and we simply carbonized everything we could lay our hands on, and ran the current through it in a vacuum. At last we struck the right thing, as we were bound to do if we kept on long enough, and if the thing existed. Patience and hard work will overcome any obstacle.'

This belief has been of great assistance to me in my profession. I know the idea is prevalent that a detective arrives at his solutions in a dramatic way through following clues invisible to the ordinary man. This doubtless frequently happens, but, as a general thing, the patience and hard work which Mr Edison commends is a much safer guide. Very often the following of excellent clues had led me to disaster, as was the case with my unfortunate attempt to solve the mystery of the five hundred diamonds.

As I was saying, I never think of the late Lord Chizelrigg without remembering Mr Edison at the same time, and yet the two were very dissimilar. I suppose Lord Chizelrigg was the most useless man that ever lived, while Edison is the opposite.

One day my servant brought into me a card on which was engraved 'Lord Chizelrigg.'

'Show his lordship in,' I said, and there appeared a young man of perhaps twenty-four or twenty-five, well dressed, and of most charming manners, who, nevertheless, began his interview by asking a question such as had never before been addressed to me, and which, if put to a solicitor, or other professional man, would have been answered with some indignation. Indeed, I believe it is a written or unwritten law of the legal profession that the acceptance of such a proposal as Lord Chizelrigg made to me, would if proved, result in the disgrace and ruin of the lawyer.

'Monsieur Valmont,' began Lord Chizelrigg, 'do you ever take up cases on speculation?'

'On speculation, sir? I do not think I understand you.'

His lordship blushed like a girl, and stammered slightly as he attempted an explanation.

'What I mean is, do you accept a case on a contingent fee? That is to say, monsieur – er – well, not to put too fine a point upon it, no results, no pay.'

I replied somewhat severely:

'Such an offer has never been made to me, and I may say at once that I should be compelled to decline it were I favoured with the opportunity. In the cases submitted to me, I devote my time and attention to their solution. I try to deserve success, but I cannot command it, and as in the interim I must live, I am reluctantly compelled to make a charge for my time, at least. I believe the doctor sends in his bill, though the patient dies.'

The young man laughed uneasily, and seemed almost too embarrassed to proceed, but finally he said:

'Your illustration strikes home with greater accuracy than probably you imagined when you uttered it. I have just paid my last penny to the physician who attended my late uncle, Lord Chizelrigg, who died six months ago. I am fully aware that the suggestion I made may seem like a reflection upon your skill, or rather, as implying a doubt regarding it. But I should be grieved, monsieur, if you fell into such an error. I could have come here and commissioned you to undertake some elucidation of the strange situation in which I find myself, and I make no doubt you would have accepted the task if your numerous engagements had permitted.

Then, if you failed, I should have been unable to pay you, for I am practically bankrupt. My whole desire, therefore, was to make an honest beginning, and to let you know exactly how I stand. If you succeed, I shall be a rich man; if you do not succeed, I shall be what I am now, penniless. Have I made it plain now why I began with a question which you had every right to resent?'

'Perfectly plain, my lord, and your candour does you credit.'

I was very much taken with the unassuming manners of the young man, and his evident desire to accept no service under false pretences. When I had finished my sentence the pauper nobleman rose to his feet, and bowed.

'I am very much your debtor, monsieur, for your courtesy in receiving me, and can only beg pardon for occupying your time on a futile quest. I wish you good-morning, monsieur.'

'One moment, my lord,' I rejoined, waving him to his chair again. 'Although I am unprepared to accept a commission on the terms you suggest, I may, nevertheless, be able to offer a hint or two that will prove of service to you. I think I remember the announcement of Lord Chizelrigg's death. He was somewhat eccentric, was he not?'

'Eccentric?' said the young man, with a slight laugh, seating himself again – 'well, *rather!*'

'I vaguely remember that he was accredited with the possession of something like twenty thousand acres of land?'

'Twenty-seven thousand, as a matter of fact,' replied my visitor.

'Have you fallen heir to the lands as well as to the title?'

'Oh, yes; the estate was entailed. The old gentleman could not divert it from me if he would, and I rather suspect that fact must have been the cause of some worry to him.'

'But surely, my lord, a man who owns, as one might say, a principality in this wealthy realm of England, cannot be penniless?'

Again the young man laughed.

'Well, no,' he replied, thrusting his hand in his pocket and bringing to light a few brown coppers, and a white silver piece. 'I possess enough money to buy some food to-night, but not enough to dine at the Hotel Cecil. You see, it is like this. I belong to a somewhat ancient family, various members of whom went the pace, and mortgaged their acres up to the hilt. I could not raise a further penny on my estates were I to try my hardest, because at the time the money was lent, land was much more valuable than it is to-day. Agricultural depression, and all that sort of thing, have, if I may put it so, left me a good many thousands worse off than if I had no land at all. Besides this, during my late uncle's life, Parliament, on his behalf, intervened once or twice, allowing him in the first place to cut valuable timber, and in the second place to sell the pictures of Chizelrigg Chase at Christie's for figures which made one's mouth water.'

'And what became of the money?' I asked, whereupon once more this genial nobleman laughed.

'That is exactly what I came up in the lift to learn if Monsieur Valmont could discover.'

'My lord, you interest me,' I said, quite truly, with an uneasy apprehension that I should take up his case after all, for I liked the young man already. His lack of pretence appealed to me, and that sympathy which is so universal among my countrymen enveloped him, as I may say, quite independent of my own will.

'My uncle,' went on Lord Chizelrigg, 'was somewhat of an anomaly in our family. He must have been a reversal to a very, very ancient type; a type of which we have no record. He was as miserly as his forefathers were prodigal. When he came into the title and estate some twenty years ago, he dismissed the whole retinue of servants, and, indeed, was defendant in several cases at law where retainers of our family brought suit against him for wrongful dismissal, or dismissal without a penny compensation in lieu of notice. I am pleased to say he lost all his cases, and when he pleaded poverty, got permission to sell a certain number of heirlooms, enabling him to make compensation, and giving him something on which to live. These heirlooms at auction sold so unexpectedly well, that my uncle acquired a taste, as it were, of what might be done. He could always prove that the rents went to the mortgagees, and that he had nothing on which to exist, so on several occasions he obtained permission from the courts to cut timber and sell pictures, until he denuded the estate and made an empty barn of the old manor house. He lived like any labourer, occupying himself sometimes as a carpenter, sometimes as a blacksmith; indeed, he made a blacksmith's shop of the library, one of the most noble rooms in Britain, containing thousands of valuable books which again and again he applied for permission to sell, but this privilege was never granted to him. I find on coming into the property that my uncle quite persistently evaded the law, and depleted this superb collection, book by book, surreptitiously through dealers in London. This, of course, would have got him into deep trouble if it had been discovered before his death, but now the valuable volumes are gone, and there is no redress. Many of them are doubtless in America, or in museums and collections of Europe.'

'You wish me to trace them, perhaps?' I interpolated.

'Oh, no; they are past praying for. The old man made tens of thousands by the sale of the timber, and other of thousands by disposing of the pictures. The house is denuded of its fine old furniture, which was immensely valuable, and then the books, as I have said, must have brought in the revenue of a prince, if he got anything like their value, and you may be sure he was shrewd enough to know their worth. Since the last refusal of the courts to allow him further relief, as he termed it, which was some seven years ago, he had quite evidently been disposing of books and furniture by a private sale, in defiance of the law. At that time I was under age, but my guardians opposed his application to the courts, and demanded an account of the moneys already in his hands. The judges upheld the opposition of my guardians, and refused to allow a further spoliation of the estate, but they did not grant the accounting my guardians asked, because the proceeds of the former sales were entirely at the disposal of my uncle, and were sanctioned by the law to permit him to live as befitted his station. If he lived meagrely instead of lavishly, as my guardians contended, that, the judges said, was his affair, and there the matter ended.

'My uncle took a violent dislike to me on account of this opposition to his last application, although, of course, I had nothing whatever to do with the matter. He lived like a hermit, mostly in the library, and was waited upon by an old man and his wife, and these three were the only inhabitants of a mansion that could comfortably house a hundred. He visited nobody, and would allow no one to approach Chizelrigg Chase. In order that all who had the misfortune to have dealing with him should continue to endure trouble after his death, he left what might be called a will, but which rather may be termed a letter to me. Here is a copy of it.

' "MY DEAR TOM, – You will find your fortune between a couple of sheets of paper in the library.

' "Your affectionate uncle,

' "REGINALD MORAN, EARL OF CHIZELRIGG." '

'I should doubt if that were a legal will,' said I.

'It doesn't need to be,' replied the young man with a smile. 'I am next-of-kin, and heir to everything he possessed, although, of course, he might have given his money elsewhere if he had chosen to do so. Why he did not bequeath it to some institution, I do not know. He knew no man personally except his own servants, whom he misused and starved, but, as he told them, he misused and starved himself, so they had no cause to grumble. He said he was treating them like one of the family. I suppose he thought it would cause me more worry and anxiety if he concealed the money and put me on the wrong scent, which I am convinced he has done, than to leave it openly to any person or charity.'

'I need not ask if you have searched the library?'

'Searched it? Why, there never was such a search since the world began!'

'Possibly you put the task into incompetent hands?'

'You are hinting, Monsieur Valmont, that I engaged others until my money was gone, then came to you with a speculative proposal. Let me assure you such is not the case. Incompetent hands, I grant you, but the hands were my own. For the past six months I have lived practically as my uncle lived. I have rummaged that library from floor to ceiling. It was left in a frightful state, littered with old newspapers, accounts, and what-not. Then, of course, there were the books remaining in the library, still a formidable collection.'

'Was your uncle a religious man?'

'I could not say. I surmise not. You see, I was unacquainted with him, and never saw him until after his death. I fancy he was not religious, otherwise he could not have acted as he did. Still, he proved himself a man of such twisted mentality that anything is possible.'

'I knew a case once where an heir who expected a large sum of money was bequeathed a family Bible, which he threw into the fire, learning afterwards, to his dismay, that it contained many thousands of pounds in Bank of England notes, the object of the devisor being to induce the legatee to read the good Book or suffer through the neglect of it.'

'I have searched the Scriptures,' said the youthful earl with a laugh, 'but the benefit has been moral rather than material.'

'Is there any chance that your uncle has deposited his wealth in a bank, and has written a cheque for the amount, leaving it between two leaves of a book?'

'Anything is possible, monsieur, but I think that highly improbable. I have gone through every tome, page by page, and I suspect very few of the volumes have been opened for the last twenty years.'

'How much money do you estimate he accumulated?'

'He must have cleared more than a hundred thousand pounds, but speaking of banking it, I would like to say that my uncle evinced a deep distrust of banks, and never drew a cheque in his life so far as I am aware. All accounts were paid in gold by this old steward, who first brought the receipted bill in to my uncle, and then received the exact amount, after having left the room, and waited until he was rung for, so that he might not learn the repository from which my uncle drew his store. I believe if the money is ever found it will be in gold, and I am very sure that this will was written, if we may call it a will, to put us on the wrong scent.'

'Have you had the library cleared out?'

'Oh, no, it is practically as my uncle left it. I realized that if I were to call in help, it would be well that the new-comer found it undisturbed.'

'You were quite right, my lord. You say you examined all the papers?'

'Yes; so far as that is concerned, the room has been very fairly gone over, but nothing that was in it the day my uncle died has been removed, not even his anvil.'

'His anvil?'

'Yes; I told you he made a blacksmith's shop, as well as bedroom, of the library. It is a huge room, with a great fire-place at one end which formed an excellent forge. He and the steward built the forge in the eastern fire-place, of brick and clay, with their own hands, and erected there a second-hand-blacksmith's bellows.'

'What work did he do at his forge?'

'Oh, anything that was required about the place. He seems to have been a very expert ironworker. He would never buy a new implement for the garden or the house so long as he could get one second-hand, and he never bought anything second-hand while at his forge he might repair what was already in use. He kept an old cob, on which he used to ride through the park, and he always put the shoes on this cob himself, the steward informs me, so he must have understood the use of blacksmith's tools. He made a carpenter's shop of the chief drawing-room and erected a bench there. I think a very useful mechanic was spoiled when my uncle became an earl.'

'You have been living at the Chase since your uncle died?'

'If you call it living, yes. The old steward and his wife have been looking after me, as they looked after my uncle, and, seeing me day after day, coatless and covered with dust, I imagine they think me a second edition of the old man.'

'Does the steward know the money is missing?'

'No; no one knows it but myself. This will was left on the anvil, in an envelope addressed to me.'

'Your statement is exceedingly clear, Lord Chizelrigg, but I confess I don't see much daylight through it. Is there a pleasant country around Chizelrigg Chase?'

'Very; especially at this season of the year. In autumn and winter the house is a little draughty. It needs several thousand pounds to put it in repair.'

'Draughts do not matter in the summer. I have been long enough in England not to share the fear of my countrymen for a *courant d'air*. Is there a spare bed in the manor house, or shall I take down a cot with me, or let us say a hammock?'

'Really,' stammered the earl, blushing again, 'you must not think I detailed all these circumstances in order to influence you to take up what may be a hopeless case. I, of course, am deeply interested, and, therefore, somewhat prone to be carried away when I begin a recital of my uncle's eccentricities. If I receive your permission, I will call on you again in a month or two. To tell you the truth, I borrowed a little money from the old steward, and visited London to see my legal advisers, hoping that in the circumstances I may get permission to sell something that will keep me from starvation. When I spoke of the house being denuded I meant relatively, of course. There are still a good many antiquities which would doubtless bring me in a comfortable sum of money. I have been borne up by the belief that I should find my uncle's gold. Lately, I have been beset by a suspicion that the old gentleman thought the library the only valuable asset left, and for this reason wrote his note, thinking I would be afraid to sell anything from that room. The old rascal must have made a pot of money out of those shelves. The catalogue shows that there was a copy of the first book printed in England by Caxton, and several priceless Shakespeares, as well as many other volumes that a collector would give a small fortune for. All these are gone. I think when I show this to be the case, the authorities cannot refuse me the right to sell something, and, if I get this permission, I shall at once call upon you.'

'Nonsense, Lord Chizelrigg. Put your application in motion, if you like. Meanwhile I beg of you to look upon me as more substantial banker than your old steward. Let us enjoy a good dinner together at the Cecil to-night, if you will do me the honour to be my guest. To-morrow we can leave for Chizelrigg Chase. How far is it?'

'About three hours,' replied the young man, becoming as red as a new Queen Anne villa. 'Reelly, Monsieur Valmont, you overwhelm me with your kindness, but nevertheless I accept your generous offer.'

'Then that's settled. What's the name of the old steward?'

'Higgins.'

'You are certain he has no knowledge of the hiding-place of this treasure?'

'Oh, quite sure. My uncle was not a man to make a confidant of any one, least of all an old babbler like Higgins.'

'Well, I should like to be introduced to Higgins as a benighted foreigner. That will make him despise me and treat me like a child.'

'Oh, I say,' protested the earl, 'I should have thought you'd lived long enough in England to have got out of the notion that we do not appreciate the foreigner. Indeed, we are the only nation in the world that extends a cordial welcome to him, rich or poor.'

'*Certainement*, my lord, I should be deeply disappointed did you not take me at my proper valuation, but I cherish no delusions regarding the contempt with which Higgins will regard me. He will look upon me as a sort of simpleton to whom the Lord had been unkind by not making England my native land. Now, Higgins must be led to believe that I am in his own class; that is, a servant of yours. Higgins and I will gossip over the fire together, should these spring evenings prove chilly, and before two or three weeks are past I shall have learned a great deal about your uncle that you never dreamed of. Higgins will talk more freely with a fellow-servant than with his master, however much he may respect that master, and then, as I am a foreigner, he will babble down to my comprehension, and I shall get details that he never would think of giving to a fellow-countryman.'

The young earl's modesty in such description of his home as he had given me, left me totally unprepared for the grandeur of the mansion, one corner of which he inhabited. It is such a place as you read of in romances of the Middle Ages; not a pinnacled or turreted French château of that period, but a beautiful and substantial stone manor house of a ruddy colour, whose warm hue seemed to add a softness to the severity of its architecture. It is built round an outer and an inner courtyard and could house a thousand, rather than the hundred with which its owner had accredited it. There are many stone-mullioned windows, and one at the end of the library might well have graced a cathedral. This superb residence occupies the centre of a heavily timbered park, and from the lodge at the gates we drove at least a mile and a half under the grandest avenue of old oaks I have ever seen. It seemed incredible that the owner of all this should actually lack the ready money to pay his fare to town!

Old Higgins met us at the station with a somewhat rickety cart, to which was attached the ancient cob that the late earl used to shoe. We entered a noble hall, which probably looked the larger because of the entire absence of any kind of furniture, unless two complete suits of venerable armour which stood on either hand might be considered as furnishing. I laughed aloud when the door was shut, and the sound echoed like the merriment of ghosts from the dim timbered roof above me.

'What are you laughing at?' asked the earl.

'I am laughing to see you put your modern tall hat on that mediæval helmet.'

'Oh, that's it! Well, put yours on the other. I mean no disrespect to the ancestor who wore this suit, but we are short of the harmless, necessary hat-rack, so I put my topper on the antique helmet, and thrust the umbrella (if I have one) in behind here, and down one of his legs. Since I came in possession, a very crafty-looking dealer from London visited me, and attempted to sound me regarding the sale of these suits of armour. I gathered he would give enough money to keep me in new suits, London made, for the rest of my life, but when I endeavoured to find out if he had had commercial dealings with my prophetic uncle, he became frightened and bolted. I imagine that if I had possessed presence of mind enough to have lured him into one of our most uncomfortable dungeons, I might have learned where some of the family treasures went to. Come up these stairs, Monsieur Valmont, and I will show you your room.'

We had lunched on the train coming down, so after a wash in my own room I proceeded at once to inspect the library. It proved, indeed, a most noble apartment, and it had been scandalously used by the old reprobate, its late tenant. There were two huge fire-places, one in the middle of the north wall and the other at the eastern end. In the latter had been erected a rude brick forge, and beside the forge hung a great black bellows, smoky with usage. On a wooden block lay the anvil, and around it rested and rusted several hammers, large and small. At the western end was a glorious window filled with ancient stained glass, which, as I have said, might have adorned a cathedral. Extensive as the collection of books was, the great size of this chamber made it necessary that only the outside wall should be covered with book cases, and even these were divided by tall windows. The opposite wall was blank, with the exception of a picture here and there, and these pictures offered a further insult to the room, for they were cheap prints, mostly coloured lithographs that had appeared in Christmas numbers of London weekly journals, encased in poverty-stricken frames, hanging from nails ruthlessly driven in above them. The floor was covered with a litter of papers, in some places knee-deep, and in the corner farthest from the forge still stood the bed on which the ancient miser had died.

'Looks like a stable, doesn't it?' commented the earl, when I had finished my inspection. 'I am sure the old boy simply filled it up with this rubbish to give me the trouble of examining it. Higgins tells me that up to within a month before he died the room was reasonably clear of all this muck. Of course, it had to be, or the place would have caught fire from the sparks of the forge. The old man made Higgins gather all the papers he could find anywhere about the place, ancient accounts, newspapers, and what not, even to the brown wrapping paper you see, in which parcels came, and commanded him to strew the floor with this litter, because, as he complained, Higgins's boots on the boards made too much noise, and Higgins, who is not in the least of an inquiring mind, accepted this explanation as entirely meeting the case.'

Higgins proved to be a garrulous old fellow, who needed no urging to talk about the late earl; indeed, it was almost impossible to deflect his conversation into any other channel. Twenty years' intimacy with the eccentric nobleman had largely obliterated that sense of deference with which an English servant usually approaches his master. An English underling's idea of nobility is the man who never by any possibility works with his hands. The fact that Lord Chizelrigg had toiled at the carpenter's bench; had mixed cement in the drawing-room; had caused the anvil to ring out till midnight, aroused no admiration in Higgins's mind. In addition to this, the ancient nobleman had been penuriously strict in his examination of accounts, exacting the uttermost farthing, so the humble servitor regarded his memory with supreme contempt. I realized before the drive was finished from the station to Chizelrigg Chase that there was little use of introducing me to Higgins as a foreigner and a fellow-servant. I found myself completely unable to understand what the old fellow said. His dialect was as unknown to me as the Choctaw language would have been, and the young earl was compelled to act as interpreter on the occasions when we set this garrulous talking-machine going.

The new Earl of Chizelrigg, with the enthusiasm of a boy, proclaimed himself my pupil and assistant, and said he would do whatever he was told. His thorough and fruitless search of the library had convinced him that the old man was merely chaffing him, as he put it, by leaving such a letter as he had written. His lordship was certain that the money had been hidden somewhere else; probably buried under one of the trees in the park. Of course this was possible, and represented the usual method by which a stupid person conceals treasure, yet I did not think it probable. All conversations with Higgins showed the earl to have been an extremely suspicious man; suspicious of banks, suspicious even of Bank of England notes, suspicious of every person on earth, not omitting Higgins himself. Therefore, as I told his nephew, the miser would never allow the fortune out of his sight and immediate reach.

From the first the oddity of the forge and anvil being placed in his bedroom struck me as peculiar, and I said to the young man, –

'I'll stake my reputation that forge or anvil, or both, contain the secret. You see, the old gentleman worked sometimes till midnight, for Higgins could hear his hammering. If he used hard coal on the forge the fire would last through the night, and being in continual terror of thieves, as Higgins says, barricading the castle every evening before dark as if it were a fortress, he was bound to place the treasure in the most unlikely spot for a thief to get at it. Now, the coal fire smouldered all night long, and if the gold was in the forge underneath the embers, it would be extremely difficult to get at. A robber rummaging in the dark would burn his fingers in more senses than one. Then, as his lordship kept no less than four loaded revolvers under his pillow, all he had to do, if a thief entered his room was to allow the search to go on until the thief started at the forge, then doubtless, as he had the range with reasonable accuracy night or day, he might sit up in bed and blaze away with revolver after revolver. There were twenty-eight shots that could be fired in about double as many seconds, so you see the robber stood little chance in the face of such a fusillade. I propose that we dismantle the forge.'

Lord Chizelrigg was much taken by my reasoning, and one morning early we cut down the big bellows, tore it open, found it empty, them took brick after brick from the forge with a crowbar, for the old man had builded better than he knew with Portland cement. In fact, when we cleared away the rubbish between the bricks and the core of the furnace we came upon one cube of cement which was as hard as granite. With the aid of Higgins, and a set of rollers and levers, we managed to get this block out into the park, and attempted to crush it with the sledge hammers belonging to the forge, in which we were entirely unsuccessful. The more it resisted our efforts, the more certain we became that the coins would be found within it. As this would not be treasure-trove in the sense that the Government might make a claim upon it, there was no particular necessity for secrecy, so we had up a man from the mines near by with drills and dynamite, who speedily shattered the block into a million pieces, more or less. Alas! there was no trace in its debris of 'pay dirt,' as the western miner puts it. While the dynamite expert was on the spot, we induced him to shatter the anvil as well

as the block of cement, and then the workman, doubtless thinking
the new earl was as insane as the old one had been, shouldered his
tools, and went back to his mine.

The earl reverted to his former opinion that the gold was concealed in the park, while I held even more firmly to my own belief
that the fortune rested in the library.

'It is obvious,' I said to him,' 'that if the treasure is buried outside,
some one must have dug the hole. A man so timorous and so
reticent as your uncle would allow no one to do this but himself.
Higgins maintained the other evening that all picks and spades were
safely locked up by himself each night in the tool-house. The mansion itself was barricaded with such exceeding care that it would
have been difficult for your uncle to get outside even if he wished
to do so. Then such a man as your uncle is described to have been
would continually desire ocular demonstration that his savings were
intact, which would be practically impossible if the gold had found
a grave in the park. I propose now that we abandon violence and
dynamite, and proceed to an intellectual search of the library.'

'Very well,' replied the young earl, 'but as I have already searched
the library very thoroughly, your use of the word "intellectual,"
Monsieur Valmont, is not in accord with your customary politeness.
However, I am with you. 'Tis for you to command, and me to
obey.'

'Pardon me, my lord!' I said, 'I used the word "intellectual" in
contradistinction to the word "dynamite." It had no reference to
your former search. I merely propose that we now abandon the use
of chemical reaction, and employ the much greater force of mental
activity. Did you notice any writing on the margins of the newspapers you examined?'

'No, I did not.'

'Is it possible that there may have been some communication on
the white border of a newspaper?'

'It is, of course, possible.'

'Then will you set yourself to the task of glancing over the margin
of every newspaper, piling them away in another room when your
scrutiny of each is complete? Do not destroy anything, but we must
clear out the library completely. I am interested in the accounts, and
will examine them.'

It was exasperatingly tedious work, but after several days my assistant reported every margin scanned without result, while I had collected each bill and memorandum, classifying them according to date. I could not get rid of a suspicion that the contrary old beast had written instructions for the finding of the treasure on the back of some account, or on the fly-leaf of a book, and as I looked at the thousands of volumes still left in the library, the prospect of such a patient and minute search appalled me. But I remembered Edison's words to the effect that if a thing exists, search, exhaustive enough, will find it. From the mass of accounts I selected several; the rest I placed in another room, alongside the heap of the earl's newspapers.

'Now,' said I to my helper, 'if it pleases you, we will have Higgins in, as I wish some explanation of these accounts.'

'Perhaps I can assist you,' suggested his lordship, drawing up a chair opposite the table on which I had spread the statements. 'I have lived here for six months, and know as much about things as Higgins does. He is so difficult to stop when once he begins to talk. What is the first account you wish further to light upon?'

'To go back thirteen years I find that your uncle bought a second-hand safe in Sheffield. Here is the bill. I consider it necessary to find that safe.'

'Pray forgive me, Monsieur Valmont,' cried the young man, springing to his feet and laughing, 'so heavy an article as a safe should not slip readily from a man's memory, but it did from mine. The safe is empty, and I gave no more thought to it.'

Saying this the earl went to one of the bookcases that stood against the wall, pulled it round as if it were a door, books and all, and displayed the front of an iron safe, the door of which he also drew open, exhibiting the usual empty interior of such a receptacle.

'I came on this,' he said, 'when I took down all these volumes. It appears that there was once a secret door leading from the library into an outside room, which has long since disappeared; the walls are very thick. My uncle doubtless caused this door to be taken off its hinges, and the safe placed in the aperture, the rest of which he then bricked up.'

'Quite so,' said I, endeavouring to conceal my disappointment. 'As this strong box was bought second-hand and not made to order, I suppose there can be no secret crannies in it?'

'It looks like a common or garden safe,' reported my assistant, 'but we'll have it out if you say so.'

'Not just now,' I replied; 'we've had enough of dynamiting to make us feel like housebreakers already.'

'I agree with you. What's the next item on the programme?'

'Your uncle's mania for buying things at second-hand was broken in three instances so far as I have been able to learn from a scrutiny of these accounts. About four years ago he purchased a new book from Denny and Co., the well-known booksellers of the Strand. Denny and Co. deal only in new books. Is there any comparatively new volume in the library?'

'Not one.'

'Are you sure of that?'

'Oh, quite; I searched all the literature in the house. What is the name of the volume he bought?'

'That I cannot decipher. The initial letter looks like "M," but the rest is a mere wavy line. I see, however, that it cost twelve-and-sixpence, while the cost of carriage by parcel post was sixpence, which shows it weighed something under four pounds. This, with the price of the book, induces me to think that it was a scientific work, printed on heavy paper and illustrated.'

'I know nothing of it,' said the earl.

'The third account is for wall paper; twenty-seven rolls of an expensive wall paper, and twenty-seven rolls of a cheap paper, the latter being just half the price of the former. This wall paper seems to have been supplied by a tradesman in the station road in the village of Chizelrigg.'

'There's your wall paper,' cried the youth, waving his hand; 'he was going to paper the whole house, Higgins told me, but got tired after he had finished the library, which took him nearly a year to accomplish, for he worked at it very intermittently, mixing the paste in the boudoir, a pailful at a time as he needed it. It was a scandalous thing to do, for underneath the paper is the most exquisite oak panelling, very plain, but very rich in colour.'

I rose and examined the paper on the wall. It was dark brown, and answered the description of the expensive paper on the bill.

'What became of the cheap paper?' I asked.

'I don't know.'

'I think,' said I, 'we are on the track of the mystery. I believe that paper covers a sliding panel or concealed door.'

'It is very likely,' replied the earl. 'I intended to have the paper off, but I had no money to pay a workman, and I am not so industrious as was my uncle. What is your remaining account?'

'The last also pertains to paper, but comes from a firm in Budge Row, London, E.C. He has had, it seems, a thousand sheets of it, and it appears to have been frightfully expensive. This bill is also illegible, but I take it a thousand sheets were supplied, although of course it may have been a thousand quires, which would be a little more reasonable for the price charged, or a thousand reams, which would be exceedingly cheap.'

'I don't know anything about that. Let's turn on Higgins.'

Higgins knew nothing of this last order of paper either. The wall paper mystery he at once cleared up. Apparently the old earl had discovered by experiment that the heavy, expensive wall paper would not stick to the glossy panelling, so he had purchased a cheaper paper, and had pasted that on first. Higgins said he had gone all over the panelling with a yellowish-white paper, and after that was dry, he pasted over it the more expensive rolls.

'But,' I objected, 'the two papers were bought and delivered at the same time; therefore, he could not have found by experiment that the heavy paper would not stick.'

'I don't think there is much in that,' commented the earl; 'the heavy paper may have been bought first, and found to be unsuitable, and then the coarse, cheap paper bought afterwards. The bill merely shows that the account was sent in on that date. Indeed, as the village of Chizelrigg is but a few miles away, it would have been quite possible for my uncle to have bought the heavy paper in the morning, tried it, and in the afternoon sent for the commoner lot; but in any case, the bill would not have been presented until months after the order, and the two purchases were thus lumped together.'

I was forced to confess that this seemed reasonable.

Now, about the book ordered from Denny's. Did Higgins remember anything regarding it? It came four years ago.

Ah, yes, Higgins did; he remembered it very well indeed. He had come in one morning with the earl's tea, and the old man was sitting up in bed reading this volume with such interest that he was unaware of Higgins's knock, and Higgins himself, being a little hard of hearing, took for granted the command to enter. The earl hastily thrust the book under the pillow, alongside the revolvers, and rated Higgins in a most cruel way for entering the room before getting permission to do so. He had never seen the earl so angry before, and he laid it all to this book. It was after the book had come that the forge had been erected and the anvil bought. Higgins never saw the book again, but one morning, six months before the earl died, Higgins, in raking out the cinders of the forge, found what he supposed was a portion of the book's cover. He believed his master had burnt the volume.

Having dismissed Higgins, I said to the earl:

'The first thing to be done is to enclose this bill to Denny and Co., booksellers, Strand. Tell them you have lost the volume, and ask them to send another. There is likely some one in the shop who can decipher the illegible writing. I am certain the book will give us a clue. Now, I shall write to Braun and Sons, Budge Row. This is evidently a French company; in fact, the name as connected with paper-making runs in my mind, although I cannot at this moment place it. I shall ask them the use of this paper that they furnished to the late earl.'

This was done accordingly, and now, as we thought, until the answers came, we were two men out of work. Yet the next morning, I am pleased to say, and I have always rather plumed myself on the fact, I solved the mystery before replies were received from London. Of course, both the book and the answer of the paper agents, by putting two and two together, would have given us the key.

After breakfast, I strolled somewhat aimlessly into the library, whose floor was now strewn merely with brown wrapping paper, bits of string, and all that. As I shuffled among this with my feet, as if tossing aside dead autumn leaves in a forest path, my attention was suddenly drawn to several squares of paper, unwrinkled, and never used for wrapping. These sheets seemed to me strangely familiar. I picked one of them up, and at once the significance of the name Braun and Sons occurred to me. They are paper makers in France, who produce a smooth, very tough sheet, which, dear as it is, proves infinitely cheap compared with the fine vellum it deposed in a certain branch of industry. In Paris, years before, these sheets had given me the knowledge of how a gang of thieves disposed of their gold without melting it. The paper was used instead of vellum in the rougher processes of manufacturing gold leaf. It stood the constant beating of the hammer nearly as well as the vellum, and here at once there flashed on me the secret of the old man's midnight anvil work. He was transforming his sovereigns into gold-leaf, which must have been of a rude, thick kind, because to produce the gold-leaf of commerce he still needed the vellum as well as a 'crutch' and other machinery, of which we had found no trace.

'My lord,' I called to my assistant; he was at the other end of the room; 'I wish to test a theory on the anvil of your own fresh common sense.'

'Hammer away,' replied the earl, approaching me with his usual good-natured, jocular expression.

'I eliminate the safe from our investigations because it was purchased thirteen years ago, but the buying of the book, of wall covering, of this tough paper from France, all group themselves into a set of incidents occurring within the same month as the purchase of the anvil and the building of the forge; therefore, I think they are related to one another. Here are some sheets of paper he got from Budge Row. Have you ever seen anything like it? Try to tear this sample.'

'It's reasonably tough,' admitted his lordship, fruitlessly endeavouring to grip it apart.

'Yes. It was made in France, and is used in gold beating. Your uncle beat his sovereigns into gold-leaf. You will find that the book from Denny's is a volume on gold beating, and now as I remember that scribbled word which I could not make out, I think the title of the volume is "Metallurgy." It contains, no doubt, a chapter on the manufacture of gold-leaf.'

'I believe you,' said the earl; 'but I don't see that the discovery sets us any further forward. We're now looking for gold-leaf instead of sovereigns.'

'Let's examine this wall paper,' said I.

I placed my knife under a corner of it at the floor, and quite easily ripped off a large section. As Higgins had said, the brown paper was on top, and the coarse, light-coloured paper underneath. But even that came away from the oak panelling as easily as though it hung there from habit, and not because of paste.

'Feel the weight of that,' I cried, handing him the sheet I had torn from the wall.

'By Jove!' said the earl, in a voice almost of awe.

I took it from him, and laid it, face downwards, on the wooden table, threw a little water on the back, and with a knife scraped away the porous white paper. Instantly there gleamed up at us the baleful yellow of the gold. I shrugged my shoulders and spread out my hands. The Earl of Chizelrigg laughed aloud and very heartily.

'You see how it is,' I cried. 'The old man first covered the entire wall with this whitish paper. He heated his sovereigns at the forge and beat them out on the anvil, then completed the process rudely between the sheets of this paper from France. Probably he pasted the gold to the wall as soon as he shut himself in for the night, and covered it over with the more expensive paper before Higgins entered in the morning.'

We found afterwards, however, that he had actually fastened the thick sheets of gold to the wall with carpet tacks.

His lordship netted a trifle over a hundred and twenty-three thousand pounds through my discovery, and I am pleased to pay tribute to the young man's generosity by saying that his voluntary settlement made my bank account swell stout as a City alderman.

THE BULLET

J. J. Bell

'**B**ECAUSE,' said the fair young man, with the well-featured yet scarcely attractive face, 'because you are a millionaire and I am a broken man.' He moved slightly on the chair at the side of the desk; his eyes wavered from those of the man who sat at the desk; his fingers raising the cigarette to his lips trembled.

The dark man, who looked the senior by a dozen years, but who was of the same age as his visitor, leaned forward, his strong hand under his strong chin, his gaze steady, uncompromising. His words were cool and deliberate.

'And you give that as a good reason, Corliss, why I should help you, or rather, continue to help you. Well, such a reason does not appeal to me – certainly not in your case.'

Corliss gave a little jerk, dropped his cigarette, and in the act of recovering it glanced sidelong at the other. 'Why certainly not in my case?' His tone was half timid, half impudent. 'Why should not any rich man help any poor man?'

'We are not talking of any poor man,' returned the dark man, whose name was Chester. 'You and I,' he went on, 'are what we have made ourselves – I, as you say, a millionaire; you, as you have not said, a broken man over and over again.'

'I've never had any luck.'

'You have never deserved it. You have wilfully broken yourself. You have never done an honest day's work. You are a crazy gambler – '

'Pardon me, but have you never gambled?'

'I gamble every day of my life, but I gamble sanely on chances I can see and estimate – not on the form of a horse a hundred miles away, or a card in a pack. But I could overlook your crazy gambing if – ' Chester paused.

'If what?'

'Well, you may as well have it, Corliss, for we shall probably not meet again.' Chester spoke as quietly as ever, but a note of disgust was now in his voice. 'You are a swindler of tradesmen, a deceiver of friends, a trifler with women – and I wish to have no more to do with you. Clear out!'

He flung his hand in the direction of the door and sat back in his chair, his mouth hard, his black eyes implacable.

Corliss was on his feet, his face working; but the unexpectedness of the other's denunciation had checked his usual readiness with words. Hitherto he had regarded Chester as a fortunate fool, who knew all about business and nothing of life – life, that is, as he himself understood it. In the past he had received Chester's benefits without shame, with a gratitude that dwindled as the money was spent, with, indeed, a certain contempt for the man who had believed his story and signed the cheque without question. Nor was there any shame now: only rage of bafflement and terror of a thing that was still hid from the other's knowledge. To himself he was arguing that Chester had 'let him down,' and, all benefits forgot, he hated Chester accordingly.

'Look here,' he said at last, desperately, sweat on his face, 'give me another chance.'

'No! Five times I have set you on your feet; five times you have – not fallen – I can pardon a man's falling – but, open-eyed, cast yourself down. Go!'

With an abrupt movement, Chester turned his attention to the papers on his desk.

'You may yet be sorry for this,' said Corliss, a whine in his voice. 'I'm at the limit.'

Chester gave no sign that he had heard.

At the end of half a minute Corliss, with a bitter look, went slowly to the door. There he halted.

'By the way,' he said, with an odd affectation of ease, 'you may not be aware of it, but as it happens, we are both invited to Richardson's for the week-end.'

'I was not aware that were were both invited,' Chester answered, making pencillings on a margin. 'What about it?'

'I intend to go.'

'Why not?'

'And you?' said Corliss, after a moment.

Chester looked up. 'Don't be an ass, man,' he said, almost good-humouredly. 'In the house of a mutual friend I shall meet you courteously, though not cordially. What has passed in this office has been between ourselves, and shall remain so.'

'You mean that – you won't give me away to Richardson, one of the few friends I have left?'

'That's a question in ethics,' was the dry reply. 'Still I have known you longer than I have known Richardson. I leave Richardson to protect himself – if that be necessary.'

'What do you mean?'

'Your indignation is overdone, Corliss. It suggests to me that you have treated Richardson pretty much as you have treated myself. But that, I repeat, is Richardson's affair. Now you must excuse me. I'm busy.' Chester bent over his papers.

Corliss hesitated, gnawing his underlip. Then he went out.

The time was late autumn, but the afternoon atmosphere of the City was close and oppressive. Business men less industrious, or less keen, than Chester were beginning to leave their offices for the day. Corliss, feeling weak, looked at his watch. Licensed places would not open until nearly half an hour had passed. He took a taxi, giving the man the name of an hotel in the West-end. Arrived in the lounge he ordered a drink to be brought to him the moment the clock said 'Yes!'

In a corner he sat down with his thoughts. They were awful thoughts for a decent young man to have; but Corliss had ceased to be that. The centre around which his thoughts revolved, and now and then madly whirled, was a slip of paper which lay safely – too safely – behind a steel door in the elegantly-appointed office of a certain 'financial agent.' To the 'financial agent' the slip represented five hundred pounds; to Corliss, who had written his name on it, black ruin. Seven days from now the 'financial agent' would request Corliss to pay him the five hundred pounds, and on being disappointed, as he surely would be in Corliss's response, would console himself by applying to Chester, whose name was also on the slip, but who had certainly not put it there.

So Corliss had come, it seemed, to the end of his crooked career. It was inconceivable that the man whose name he had forged, the man from whom he had just been begging the wherewithal to cover the forgery, would condone the crime. Corliss recognized that he had blundered fatally in asking Chester for more money. He perceived too late that his one poor chance had lain in making a full confession.

Desperately he surveyed, as it were, his circle of acquaintances. All were more or less men of substance, for Corliss had never had 'any use' for the poorer sort. But was there one among them in whose purse and patience he could hope once more? Not one – unless, perhaps, Richardson, his host during the approaching week-end. And Richardson was one of those damned uncertain people, open-handed one day, close-fisted the next, grudging half a crown for a taxi in the morning, and in the afternoon spending hundreds of pounds at a sale of old books. Yet there was none other, and if Richardson failed him –

The waiter brought the drink, took payment, and retired. Corliss was parched; there was a hot, dry feeling about his eyes; but he drank in sips, with little pauses between.

Flight? Impossible without money, and in these days of wireless almost vain even with a fortune. There was but one sure way by which man in his situation could evade the tentacles of the Law – but one sure way, and it was a horribly dark way, and the end thereof was – what? In his soul Corliss knew that he would never dare to take it. He might toy with the idea, but the deed was beyond him. He might have the key to the door of escape in his hand, but in the last moment he would surely let the Law snatch it from him.

His thoughts were straying; he whipped them back to concentration on that slip of paper. Seven days – no, it was actually only six days now – six days till Chester, looking at the signature, would say: 'That is not mine; I never wrote it.' And the solitary chance of keeping the signature from the keen eyes of Chester was hidden like a fragile thread twisted into the uncertain humours of Richardson.

Corliss rose and sat down again. Haste might break the fragile thread. Besides, Richardson was not at his own town rooms, but at his place in Oxfordshire, entertaining guests. Out of the question to intrude, either in person or by letter, with such a request upon the man who would be his host forty-eight hours hence! Distracted as he was, Corliss perceived that it would be folly. Moreover, experience had taught him that the most favourable season in which to approach Richardson was the hour following one of Richardson's very elegant little dinners. There was nothing for it but to endure for two nights and two days – perhaps longer. But how to endure on nothing but the strength of a slender possibility? Was there not, after all, something he could do to protect himself from the gulf that would open at Richardson's refusal?

He ordered another drink. In a way it soothed him; his thoughts were fewer and more orderly. He gave less attention to Richardson and more to Chester. His hate for Chester had ceased to boil and bubble; colder and colder it grew; in the end it was still, controlled by its own bitterness and cruelty, the human essence gone out of it. It was no longer his own fate, but Chester's, that hung on the mood of Richardson.

The lounge had filled up, for the hour of dining was at hand, when Corliss got up and proceeded to one of the telephone-boxes in the hall.

'That you, Loftis? Corliss speaking. If you have no plans, come in and dine with me – don't dress – Planet Hotel.'

'Sorry. Too busy.' The tone of the speaker was not very cordial, but Corliss did not seem to notice it.

'Sorry, too, old man. I rather want to have a word with you to-night,' he said. 'Are you in the laboratory?'

'Yes – but I'm afraid I –'

'Look here, Loftis! I'm not a friend in need this time. On the contrary,' Corliss proceeded, almost gaily, 'I'm practically at the end of my difficulties, and shall be starting to repay very shortly.'

'Well, I'm delighted to hear it, Corliss, for your sake as well as my own. If I weren't so awfully rushed here –'

'Can't you leave your devil's brews for an hour?'

'That's just what I can't do. But, I say, I'll be here till midnight –'

'Then I'll look in and smoke one cigarette – say, about ten.'

'Right! Come straight through the garden to the laboratory door. 'Bye.'

Corliss went to his club for dinner, though he was aware that men there were beginning to avoid his company. There was one man, however, whom he wanted to see, and of whom he was not in any way afraid. In the corner of the smoke-room he handed this man a scrap of paper bearing a telephone number.

'At ten precisely,' he said, 'you will get this number and ask for Mr Lester. On being told that there is no Mr Lester, you will pretend to be hearing badly and repeat your question, keeping the subscriber at the 'phone for at least a minute. Then you will apologize for having used the wrong number, and cut off. That's all; but it's important that you do it punctually.'

'I quite understand,' said the other. He had done odder things than this for Corliss. 'Girl, I suppose?'

'Some letters I want to get back,' said Corliss. 'What will you drink?'

The little house-party at Richardson's was a bachelor one. None of the five men, two of them brothers, was particularly keen on Bridge, and the evenings were spent between the billiard-room and the library. Chester was the only guest who respected the host's passion for old books; as the host put it, the poison was already working in Chester, who would surely develop into the greediest of collectors, as certain millionaires had done before him. At any rate, Chester seemed fascinated by the more ancient tomes which were lodged in a small annexe to the library proper, wherein he would ask leave to sit for an hour after the others were gone to bed.

It was Sunday night, and there would be an early start for London in the morning. At dinner, which was just over, Richardson had mentioned that he would be travelling too. Fortune had not been kind to Corliss. Everything seemed to have conspired against his obtaining a moment alone with his host. Now, as a move was being made to the billiard-room, feverish and desperate, he forced himself to whisper his request for an interview.

Without a word, Richardson turned and led the way to the library. Corliss followed, not altogether without hope. Since Friday Richardson had been uniformly amiable; to-night at dinner he had exhibited his most genial side. In the library, however, Corliss experienced a sudden chill.

Richardson shut the door and advanced to the big writing-table. He did not sit, nor invite his guest to do so. His simply stood, waiting. And the moment the nature of Corliss's communication became clear to him, he held up his hand.

'No!' he said, quietly. 'No, Corliss. Spare yourself and me. You will find me in the billiard-room.' He left the library.

Corliss sat down on the nearest chair, and for a while was very still. He did not hate Richardson; perhaps he did not hate Chester just then. He thought only of himself, of his own preservation.

About ten he went to the billiard-room. A game of 'Snooker' had just ended. He was invited to join in a new game, but said he preferred to look on. There were drinks on a side-table; he helped himself lavishly and took a seat in the shadow. He ought, he knew, to have offered to mark, but he also knew that he could not have added the scores correctly. He sat watching the coloured balls on the light-flooded green, saw them disappear, one by one, into pockets, without knowing, or caring, who had made the shot. He did not wish to see the face of the player, lest it should be Chester's. He would fain have retired, but there was a remark he wanted to make, if only he could find a natural opening. Further, he desired to learn whether Chester intended to sit late in the library.

The game ended. They started another. Quietly Corliss helped himself to more brandy, but not so much. He was aiming at self-confidence rather than recklessness.

Presently he became aware that Richardson was standing close to him.

'Would anyone mind,' said Corliss, in a fairly even voice, 'if I raised this window for a few minutes?'

'By all means, Corliss,' the host pleasantly replied. 'Allow me. It's a bit close to-night.' He unfastened and threw up the sash.

Corliss stepped over and peered into the still, dark night. Then he fingered the fastening.

'I suppose this would keep out a burglar, Richardson?' he said, casually.

'Nothing,' Richardson returned, with a laugh, 'will keep out a first-class burglar. The servants fasten the windows at night, but it's a matter of form. We don't bother about burglars here.'

'Still,' put in one of the men, 'yours would be a handy house for the gentry.'

'The library windows, for instance,' remarked Chester.

'Only respectable people like you would want to burgle my library,' said the host, and there was a general laugh. 'I begin to be suspicious of your late sittings, Chester. Monkeying with the window fastenings – eh?'

'That's it!' replied Chester. 'To-night I hope to take impressions of the keys in the doors.'

'You're not going to sit up to-night! Breakfast at seven-thirty, you know.'

'Five hours' sleep satisfies me. With your permission, Richardson, I will have one more –'

'My dear fellow, my house is at your disposal. Do as you will. But I think we ordinary sluggards might turn in at eleven. What do you say?'

The brothers agreed.

'If you will excuse me, Richardson,' said Corliss, 'I'll turn in now. I – I want a long sleep.'

'Good night, Corliss,' said Richardson, sympathetically, thinking he understood. 'You look a bit done up. If you want anything, be sure to ring.'

'Thanks. Good night, everybody.' It was little more than a whisper.

Chester was standing near the door. 'Good night, Corliss,' he said, kindly enough, and seemed about to say more.

But Corliss, without looking up, went out quickly, closing the door. In the hall he paused, listening, then slipped into the library, laid his cigarette-case on the big table, and out again.

He ascended slowly. In his room he turned the key and sat down, breathing heavily. His face was white and wet. Though the room was warmed by a cheery fire, he shivered.

It was not long before he heard Richardson and the brothers come upstairs. Their rooms, as he had taken care to learn, were in the other corridor. Chester's was almost exactly opposite his own.

Presently Richardson came and tapped on the door.

'All right, Corliss?'

'All right, thanks. I've taken some tabloids and expect to be asleep in five minutes. Good night.'

'Good night.' Richardson, who was a little uneasy about his guest, lingered.

Had Corliss opened the door then, things might have turned out differently, but he sat silently cursing the interrupter of his dizzy thoughts, and Richardson went softly away. Corliss heard his door close.

At the end of half an hour Corliss got up. He unlocked the smaller of his suit-cases, which had not come under the valet's inspection, and brought out a long-barrelled air-pistol, powerful but not too noisy at its work; also a cardboard box containing three sharp-nosed bullets and a pair of light forceps. He had travelled two hundred and fifty miles by rail in order to purchase these things, and had taken care to go to the shops on foot, walking with a limp and wearing a wig, a moustache, and tinted glasses.

He placed the pistol and forceps on the table by the bedside. Two of the bullets he slipped into his vest-pocket, from which he took a penknife. Drawing a chair to the table, he proceeded with the smaller blade to score little rifts in the side of the third bullet, turning it round till they numbered about a score. He then cautiously scraped the bullet to remove roughness produced by the first operation, and as cautiously removed the tiny scrapings from the table to the fire, wherein he placed also the empty cardboard box.

And now he was come to the more delicate part of the business. On the table he laid a half-sheet of thick notepaper, and upon it from a tube squeezed a blob of a glycerine preparation. He brought out a small flat wooden box with a close-fitting top, purchased on the evening of his visit to Loftis, the chemist. It contained about half a teaspoonful of a fine white crystalline powder, which he had taken from a squat bottle in the laboratory safe while Loftis was at the telephone. Loftis was a specialist in poisons, and had, not so long ago, pointed out to Corliss the squat bottle as containing one of the deadliest substances known to science.

Corliss now, holding his breath, emptied the powder upon the paper and gave the box to the fire. With a match he mixed powder and glycerine into a thick paste, then burned the match. Taking the scored bullet in the forceps, he rubbed and rolled it in the paste. Finally, having opened the pistol, he, still by means of the forceps, inserted the bullet. For the time being he laid the open weapon on the table and proceeded to burn the half-sheet of note-paper.

Remained the forceps to dispose of. Turning back the rug, he examined the floor. It was a good floor, but not perfect. He found a crevice between planks. With a little effort the forceps went down and out of sight. He replaced the rug, and stood sweating.

When he was steady he closed the pistol, thus compressing the air in the chamber.

He sat down and looked at his watch. Too early! Only eleven-thirty. He must wait for an hour.

He began to shake in a dreadful fashion, and had recourse to a flask. But he must not, he warned himself, overdo the brandy. Huddling over the fire, he waited – waited.

Down in the hall an ancient clock, with a remarkably clear bell, began to toll midnight. At the first stroke Corliss started; at the second he relapsed and took to counting under his breath. Another half-hour to wait. Yet he was afraid of delaying too long. Chester had got to die in any case, but it would be ever so much simpler to kill him in the library. To Corliss's mind, Chester had now become nothing but a dangerous, wicked enemy. Corliss was acting simply to ensure his own preservation. The eyes of Chester must never look upon that slip of paper with his name upon it.

At twenty minutes past twelve Corliss got up. Taking up the pistol, he tested his nerves by presenting it at a small object on the dressing-table. His nerves were not good; the barrel wavered. He took more brandy. In his own case, at least, he knew that there was a point at which alcohol, the wrecker, had a steadying or stiffening influence, if only for the space of a few minutes. For a little while he kept still, and then repeated the test. That was better! One more dose – a very small one – of the spirit –

He removed his slippers, went to the door, switched off the light, and stood listening. Not a sound. Softly he opened the door and listened again. With the pistol tucked under the left wing of his dinner jacket he stepped into the corridor, which was lighted by an orange-tinted bulb. It struck him how providential it was that the stair was a stone one.

He stood in the half-light of the hall. The library was towards the rear of the house on the left; its door stood partly open, allowing a glimpse of an almost dark interior. He stole towards it, saying to himself: 'I have come down for my cigarette-case.'

He managed to enter without touching the door. The library was not so dark after all. The heavy curtains on the door-way of the annexe had not been drawn close; a space of about six inches separated them; and though the lamp within was shaded, a certain amount of illumination escaped into the larger room.

Corliss was conscious of an odour of Turkish tobacco smoke, not stale. There was no sound, and from his halting-place he could see nothing of Chester. He stole farther into the room, keeping away, however, from the curtain.

Suddenly he stopped. Into his view had come a small table, on which was an ash-tray containing a cigarette that appeared to be burning itself away – till a hand appeared and removed it, as it were, from the picture. Presently, through a cloudlet of smoke, the hand came back and replaced the cigarette on the tray.

Corliss took a soft step forward, and saw a hand holding a quarto-size volume bound in ancient-looking parchment. Another step, and he saw Chester, or, at least, Chester's head and shoulders. And at that his nerves threatened to fail, his sight to confound him, for it seemed to him that he was seeing through a window. Chester was seated in a low-backed easy-chair, perfectly still, absorbed in the yellowed page. He was facing the aperture between the curtains. Had he raised his head he would have been looking directly at Corliss.

Corliss, feeling as though he were sinking into a cold vapour, sinking out of sight of his one salvation, made a supreme effort of will, set his teeth, and presented the pistol telling himself for the tenth time that the bullet carried poison to slay a hundred men, that the slightest wound would be swiftly fatal.

'God!' he cried under his breath, and pressed the trigger.

In his ears the mild report sounded as a thunder-clap – but he heard also the sharp crack of an impact not on flesh. Looking not to see what had happened – now half-blind with terror – he turned and darted behind the curtains of one of the deep windows.

He had missed! He must pull himself together and play his part. He had come down for his cigarette-case, and found a burglar in the act of shooting. The burglar had escaped by the window. Corliss turned to undo the fastenings – and paused. Why was there no sound from the annexe?

But even as he listened there came a groan. It was followed by a soft thud – the sound of a body falling a short distance on a thickly carpeted floor.

He had not missed! Corliss revived as one injected with a potent drug: his brain cleared.

A long, long wait – all things silent save his own pulses – and Corliss set to work to open the window. The sash went up without noise, and he looked out into blackness filled with the whisper of rain. He polished the pistol with a bunch of curtain and threw it into the night. The rain, he told himself, would remove any last traces of finger-prints. Also he threw out the two bullets taken from his vest-pocket. The burglar had dropped these things in his flight.

Leaving the window wide, and having rubbed with the curtain the parts he had touched, Corliss crossed the library and peeped into the annexe.

Chester lay sprawled, face down, on the carpet, one arm thrown out, the hand clenched, the other crooked under the head. The wound – it must have been little more than a graze, thought Corliss, for the bullet had starred a tall, narrow, antique mirror which reached from near the floor to the picture-moulding – the wound was not visible. Corliss did not wish to see it. The poison had been quick, as Corliss had expected, but he was puzzled by the fact that the low easy-chair was now with its back to him. It looked as though there had been a brief but violent struggle, yet Corliss had not heard anything of the sort; moreover, the poison ought not to have created any convulsion, but produced a swift paralysis.

But what did it matter? Chester was dead, and his successors woud have to honour his signature, concerning which Corliss had an incontrovertible statement all ready.

Corliss turned away from the sight, which was beginning to strike him as rather pathetic – a millionaire who would never more sign a cheque! His head was now heavy and very hot; his hands were very cold. The sense of triumph was fading fast. The virtue of the alcohol had gone; the vice of it remained. His first idea of rousing the house seemed no longer so clever and cunning. Far safer to go to bed and let the discovery be made in the ordinary course; drug himself so that he should be hard to awaken in the morning.

Yes; he would get to bed. But stop a moment! Had he remembered everything – left no traces? Let him go over it all once more. He found it rather difficult to think coherently.

The third bullet! Would it not be wise to get it out of the way, seeing that it could be so easily secured? In all probability it was lying somewhere in front of the starred mirror. Why leave it for the detectives? Suppose, for instance, that they wanted to consult a poison expert: suppose they went to Loftis – and suppppose Loftis, inspired by the devil, took it into his head to weigh, in one of those delicate balances, the contents of that squat bottle in his safe! And suppose –

He *must* secure the bullet! In a state of panic he pushed between the curtains, fell on his knees, and began to search, his handkerchief held ready in his left hand for the deadly thing, while he supported himself on his right. Working nearer to the mirror, he avoided some glittering splinters, and –

A slight sound, real or fancied, caused him to turn his head in awful fright. Had Chester moved? No! Nothing but imagination! Chester would never move again!

Corliss went on with his search, but now in frantic fashion. A spicule of glass stabbed his palm, lacerating it slightly. He took no notice.

And then a voice said: 'You, Corliss! Well, I'm devilish glad to see you! You were right about burglars after all!' And Chester rose steadily to his feet.

For an instant Corliss, gaping, sat up, then fell forward on his hands.

'Looking for the bullet – eh?' Chester went on. 'Did you see the scoundrel? I can only guess that he fired at my reflection in the mirror, but I thought it wise, in case he came again, to pretend I was done for.' A pause. 'I say, Corliss, what's the matter? Did he hurt you? Let me help you.'

Corliss turned laboriously into a sitting posture. He sat staring at his right hand, which was clenched. Alarmed by his pallor, Chester muttered 'Water' – looked vainly around, darted at the bell, then dashed from the room.

In less than a minute he was back with a tumbler of water. But as he passed between the curtains, Corliss drooped sideways. And at the sight of Corliss's face, Chester stopped short; the glass slipped from his fingers.

Later, in the wounded hand, they found the bullet.

THE YELLOW IMPS

Thomas Burke

I HAVE heard many times (said old Quong) that conscience makes cowards of us all, but I have never had an authenticated case brought to my knowledge. What is undoubtedly true, and each of us can prove it from his own observation, is that conscience can and does make fools of us all. As it did in the tale of the yellow imps, which I have not, I believe, told you before. Indeed, I am sure I have not, because I only thought of it this morning; so I need not employ that disarming stroke of the polite English entertainer and request you to stop me if you have heard it.

(I had never at any time been under the necessity of stopping old Quong. My chief trouble was in starting him and keeping him in progress. The tale of the yellow imps seemed to work itself out like this.)

There was a high wind in London one October evening, and among others who struggled under it was a man in a blue macintosh. It made hats fly and frocks dance. It set the lamplight fluttering as a bird flutters when an alien hand approaches its cage. The pavements were glistening with recent rain, and it made them shiver. The roadways were lakes of ebony and it set broken pieces of the lamplight skating upon them. It whipped columns of chimney smoke into one maelstrom. Only the houses stood rigid before it; they acknowledged it as a man acknowledges a buzzing fly.

But to man himself it was no mere fly: it was unloosed power; and to the man in the blue macintosh, with whom we are concerned, it was destiny. Dead bricks it could not move, but the man in the blue macintosh, symbol of the immortal, was its toy; and it was now driving him, against half his will, to commit the sin that the other half wanted to commit. It first pestered his face, and stung his eyes, and chilled his hands, and filled his heart with its own rage: then it drove him out of his path into Bayswater.

He was faintly aware that he was grateful to the wind. By assuming the function of destiny it made his half-purpose a purpose. He hadn't really meant to turn into that road; he believed that he had meant to go past it; but while he stood at the corner, thinking the thing over, a sudden gust caught him under his macintosh and sent him running some paces down it. When the gust eased he found that he was actually in Leinster Gardens, and that to get out of it he would have to turn and battle again with the wind; and he was tired of battling. Here, clearly, was the hand-push of destiny. Useless to resist that. Being in Leinster Gardens, he felt that he was meant to go on. The affair had been decided for him by the wind. His infirmity of purpose now became upright, and he allowed that wind, which could not move the houses, to whirl him to disaster.

In the lavender dusk the interlocked squares and terraces of Bayswater made a map of the land of nightmare. The lines of tall dark houses looming upward and stretching forward to infinity; the lines of lamps that waited like a frozen guard for a procession that never came; the deep hush; the sudden enclosed spaces of whispering trees, and the insane repetition of terrace upon terrace – all this made this bourgeois quarter the apt setting for a tale of horror. Horror seldom grows among horror; almost always it springs up in the incongruous air of pastoral beauty or urban decorum; but if ever horror should outstrip itself in London, Bayswater should be its setting.

Now that he had got into Leinster Gardens, he began to walk up and down, and for half an hour he went up and down, pad-pad-pad, eye and mind directed to one house. By the disposition of the street lights he was sometimes energy and sometimes reverie. Now, as he crossed the amber radius of the lamplight, he lived as a man; now, as he passed into the interspaces of purple, he was an impalpable organism. That flickering march was a miniature of his life. Pad-pad-pad he went, fixed like a shuttle in a groove of two hundred yards, while all around him beat the life of this city of glittering distances.

At six o'clock he was in the house. He was standing behind a velvet hanging that draped the connecting door of the smoking-room and the study. He was on the study side, and was peering through the opening of the hanging into its dusky depths. He saw a large room strewn with rugs of Daghestan and Kerman and Coulas, and set with appointments that confirmed the rugs. Clearly the study of a rich man of over-opulent tastes. There were deep divan chairs in glowing yellow hide. The dark yellow walls were dressed with Oriental banners and curved weapons. On brackets and tables stood Buddhas and Sivas, large and small. On the mantelshelf and on other shelves were idols with movable heads; with the passing of heavy traffic, their shaven crowns nodded in various rhythms, as at some secret thought. These figures nodding out of the shadows fascinated the man: he had the feeling of being spied upon. Elsewhere were great vases of the Sung and Ming period, the carvings in coral and rock-crystal; and on the desk in the centre of the room, scattered among inkstand and cigar-box and lamp-standard, were a number of small figures and netsukes in old ivory. The dominant note of the room, struck by the rugs and taken up by the wallpaper, the vases, the idols, the chairs and the ivory, was gold; and this note expressed its owner.

At the moment when the man behind the curtain, no longer beaten by the wind, was relaxing in his purpose under the hush and warmth of the room, it received three bursts of light from its electric lamps, and his victim stood within his reach. Gold, or hues verging upon gold, was about his person as well as about his room. There was the hard bronze face, the amber-coloured waistcoat, the amber cigar-holder, the watch-chain, and the russet tie; and as he stood for a second or two by one of the rugs he had the appearance of a golden god in a setting of gold receiving the homage of his nodding priests. That was his last appearance in magnificence, and it was an appearance of four seconds only, for at the fifth second he was on his back across the desk, and the floor was littered with cigars and little ivory figures.

With one spring the man in the macintosh fell upon him. With fingers at throat, he forced the head back and back. But it was an uncalculated spring; it was taken in the moment when resolution was weakening; and there was no certainty behind it. Even with his fingers at that throat he couldn't be sure that he was going to do it. Even in the next few ticks of the clock, when he had in his hand a gold dagger snatched from the desk – even then he wasn't sure that he was going to do it. He could still, if he wished, drop the dagger and take his fingers from the throat, and try to laugh it away as an insane joke, or a rough-and-tumble assault. But he didn't know whether he *did* wish to do that; he didn't know what he wished to do; the room had softened and bewildered him; and he was trying to make a firm decision this way or that when the gold man made it for him.

The gold man wrenched his neck aside, and through closed jaws spluttered one word. On that word down came the dagger into the neck, and down it came again into the side just below the arm. As it was drawn back for a third stroke, and the pressure on the throat a little loosened, the gold man made a death-heave and broke away. They fell, and on the floor, among the litter of ivories, they struggled softly. The vibration set the solemn idols nodding to each other – Look, look, look! There were slow gasps and hot panting. They spluttered. The gold man could make no words, but the blue macintosh was crisp. 'There – that's shut *your* mouth. *You* won't talk much more. How's *that*?'

A third time the dagger came down, this time full into the throat. There was a gurgle, a sigh, and then peace. The blue macintosh got up. It was done. After months of approaching it and retreating from it, of nursing it and dismissing it, it was done. He had tried to frighten himself out of it by visualizing himself as a murderer in the dock and in the condemned cell and on the scaffold. He had tried to laugh himself out of it by imagining himself doing it – a ludicrous picture. He had tried to kill the idea by observing it from the outside as the silly antics of a fool. And now he had done it. Well, he must see about fixing things.

He stood over the body and bent himself to a question-mark, listening. But the great house was silent and still. Nobody had seen him enter, nobody, it seemed, had heard their struggle, and, by familiarity with the man's habits, he knew that nobody would come to the study until the dinner-gong was sounded. He looked down at the body and the blood-stained carpet and ivories, and then at his own clothes. No marks or stains that he could see. The dagger was still in the body, and could stay there; by his precaution of wearing gloves the haft could hold no clue. To assure himself that he had missed no danger-points he made a quick glance round the room, and in the moment of that glance his forehead froze. At every point

of the room was something that grinned and nodded at him. Then
he remembered the idols and laughed. But the moment was useful;
it showed that he hadn't yet come to himself. He must wake up and
be wary. One must be specially wary in matters like this – much
more wary than in his ordinary business. He found himself shaking
a little, and his thoughts had a tendency to stray from the immediate
business. That wouldn't do. His eye caught the glint of a series of
decanters and glasses. Perhaps they would help. He never touched
anything like that when on his regular business; but this was different. It was a new crisis for him, and a little slowing-down of his
nerves might be useful.

He stepped through the litter of ivories and cigars, and opened
the first decanter and poured himself a drunkard's draught. It was
brandy. He drank it in quick sips, neat, keeping his ears tightened
for the tiniest sound. When it was done he found that he was still
trembling, still unable to fix his mind on the best way of meeting
the situation. He turned to the next decanter and took a liberal one
from that – whisky. In a few seconds he felt more at ease. A goods
van went past the house, and the idols, which had recovered from
the vibrations of the struggle, were set nodding again. With fer-
ocious geniality he nodded back at them. One more peg – then he
would be ready for a clean exit. He took it, this time in one gulp;
then went across to the switches and turned off the light.

And here came another spot of panic. The sudden plunge of
darkness gave him the shock of an unexpected plunge downstairs.
He could have screamed. It was so complete a darkness that it came
with a burning pain upon his hot eyes, and in the sudden void of
black he staggered and almost fell. Staring into it, seeking his way
to the window, he could see the projected aureole of his own eyes
just beyond the temples; and as he looked past that glow into the
pit of darkness he saw it filled not with bloody faces or nodding
idols, but with amorphous bodies of fear. The corners of the black
room were breeding grey shadows, and the grey shadows bred
purple shadows, and the purple shadows bred other shadows blacker
even than the blackness of the room. Each shadow was a growth
of new and stronger fear.

Never before had he been afraid, and he did not know how to
handle himself. The knowledge that he was afraid surprised him.
He made a gesture of bewilderment. Putting his hands to his face,

he found that they were damp with sweat, and that his heart was a dynamo. The hostile mixture of brandy and whisky was working, and as the realization of that went slowly into his brain and showed him his danger, instead of sobering him, it made him laugh. He told himself that he was too old a hand to be flustered by accidents. He was drunk. That's what it was – drunk. Just that. Those shadows were whisky and brandy shadows. They weren't there at all. Funny one should feel afraid of nothing just because one had killed a brute.

Still, it would be wise to get away, and to get away as tactfully as he had come. He went to the window, swaying across the rug and turning his ankle on the scattered ivories. In the middle of the room he stopped and listened, wondering whether his drunken self might not have made some noise that his other self had not heard. But the whole house seemed as stark and dumb as the corpse on the floor. Only the ticking of the clock, for sound, and the nodding of the idols, for motion. Nothing else.

He put his gloved fingers to the window, raised it without noise, and looked out. He waited for a lorry to pass; then slid to the sill. He pulled the window down behind him. He reached forward from a kneeling position, and with one hand grasped a gutter-pipe that ran down the front of the house to the area. With the animal grace of a dancer he swung himself clear of the kitchen windows and landed on his toes by the entrance-porch of the next house. Some half-minute he stood there with the air of one waiting for the bell to be answered. This was his method of proving whether an exit had been 'clean.' It seemed that it was. He heard no stir anywhere, and met no curious eyes. With a glance of apparent disappointment he went down the steps and walked casually away. The wind was behind him, as it had been behind him at half-past five.

Once out and free, he was conscious of the wild air, and discovered that in the last half-hour he had not taken one full breath. Breathing was a momentary luxury, and he breathed deep. He filled his lungs with the rushing air, breathing in time with his long steps. He was making for the canal, where he had planned to sink his macintosh and soft hat, and he was almost upon it when his long breathing defeated him. He was feeling once again master of himself and of the occasion when, without warning, earth and sky were twisted into one, and the moon came reeling and crashing through the wind into a chaos of nausea and vomit.

When, some minutes later, he came up from this collapse, he found himself clinging to the railings of Porchester Square. His legs were weak and his ears were buzzing and his eyes were blocked by a picture of the gold man's face as he last saw it when they lay wrestling on the floor. A popular dance-melody came into his head. He tried to drive it away by thinking of other melodies and of conversational phrases, but it came back and danced upon his brain. He began to be afraid that he would sing it or whistle it. That would never do. Mustn't attract attention. Must be careful. With a jerk he pulled himself up, loosened his collar and prepared to walk on.

It was at this moment of moving away that he first became clearly aware of a noise that had been troubling his ear under the dance-melody: a little clittering as of fairy castanets. He looked about him, into the square, along the railings, and then at the pavement, and as he saw how the noise was being made a frozen wire went down his spine. He was nearly a mile from the house in Leinster Gardens, but there they were. They had trotted after him, and they were now trotting round him – the little golden blood-stained netsukes. His brain was still slumbering under the drink, but at this sight it came to a kind of cloudy awakening that deceived him into thinking it was a true awakening. There they were, clearly enough, running around his feet, jumping, curvetting in the frightful contortions of Oriental carpets. They were making arabesques all round him.

He did not attempt to imagine how the thing had happened. It *had* happened; and he was sensible enough to see the danger of the situation. If people passed and saw him like this, they might come and ask awkward questions. Certainly they would remember having seen him with these things all round him; and they would make a guess that he had stolen them and dropped them in running; and they might speak to the next policeman. He must pick them up and hide them. He bent towards them, toppled, and fell on his hands. In that position he groped for them and snatched at them; but in his nervous haste he was clumsy, and they were too quick for him. They dodged and doubled, and danced under and over his hand. Not one could he hold, and meantime they pestered him and leapt about him, and vexed his eyes with their dartings. He felt one of them warm and wet against his cheek.

Well, if he couldn't pick them up he must get away. He had forgotten now about the canal and his macintosh. The important matter was to get away from these blood-stained things, and he clambered up and turned his back on them, and went with a quick lurch through the square. He kept as much out of the light as he could. To deceive them he made two or three crossing and recrossings of the road. In Gloucester Terrace he could see nothing of them, and was applauding himself at having shaken them off, when in Cleveland Square his ear told him that his stratagem had failed. Close behind him came the sound of castanets. Soon they caught up with him and encircled him. He broke through them, and they again encircled him. He kicked at them, but still they made their undisciplined ballet between his feet. Some of them leapt at him in Lilliput anger. The faces of these held the features of the dead man on the floor. He tried to turn back towards the stir and glare of Harrow Road, where he might lose them, but they buzzed and twisted about his knees with the infuriating pester of mosquitoes. For peace he was compelled to go forward.

He went at a half-running pace, and all the time they were with him. They kept about him, before and behind, in a sort of open order. When he ran, they ran; when he trotted, they trotted; and when he kicked at them he kicked only the air. He was sobbing now, striking with arms and legs. As he stumbled on through the lamplit dusk of Craven Road he was aware that the few people who passed looked curiously at him. No wonder. A man being chased by little golden men.

But he was not now so concerned with the figure he cut. He was mainly concerned with dodging these damnable things. They filled him with the crawling horror of necromancy. He felt that they had Satanic powers drawn from all the objects of that room, and from their owner. Whichever way he turned they were with him, sometimes driving him, sometimes impeding him. Some of them settled on his trousers. With inward gasps, he struck them off. Some of them jumped high in the air and pattered elfin clog-dances on the crown of his hat. They played about him with the intimate deviltry of afreets. As they pattered and buzzed, it seemed to him that they called on other little golden things to join them. Coming into a half-lit square, he was met by a new host. He turned right and left, but only when he went straight on did they suspend their pestering. Even at those dark corners where he could not see them he could still hear them and feel them.

He went forward at a shamble, and as he went he thought again of the canal. If he could get there he might elude them. If he could get into the water they couldn't follow him there. He could swim across or stay in the water; they surely couldn't walk on water.

He turned for the canal, but as he turned they made a cloud about him, and he lost his direction. He could only go blindly forward.

Then, as he came out of the square into a side-street, they seemed to turn aside to his right, the whole host of them. He was fighting them with both arms when he saw that there was a clear space on his left, and that they had dropped behind him. Before him he saw an open door and a lighted hall. If he could get in there.

He got in. In the hall a man met him. He addressed the man in whimpering indignation. 'I say – look here – all these things following me. Can't get along the street for them. Perfect pest.'

'Oh? What's the trouble? What things?'

'Those things out there. Little golden men. Followed me from Leinster Gardens. Worsen' mosquitoes. All round one's face.'

'Followed you from Leinster Gardens? Let's have a look at 'em. Here – hold up.'

He swayed, and supported himself with an arm on the wall. 'Ah – all the way from Leinster Gardens.'

'I see. You better sit down a bit. Little golden men, eh? Leinster Gardens? Come and sit down.'

The Inspector led him to a farther room, and spoke to two men in the room. 'Just look after this man. He's a bit faint.' The two men got up, and as one of them caught the Inspector's eye, he closed the door and stood against it. The Inspector went to the telephone at the desk in the hall, and the October gale continued to rush down the street and fill the hall with companies of yellow leaves.

THE ADVENTURE OF CHARLES AUGUSTUS MILVERTON

Sir Arthur Conan Doyle

IT is years since the incidents of which I speak took place, and yet it is with diffidence that I allude to them. For a long time, even with the utmost discretion and reticence, it would have been impossible to make the facts public; but now the principal person concerned is beyond the reach of human law, and with due suppression the story may be told in such fashion as to injure no one. It records an absolutely unique experience in the career both of Mr Sherlock Holmes and of myself. The reader will excuse me if I conceal the date or any other fact by which he might trace the actual occurrence.

We had been out for one of our evening rambles, Holmes and I, and had returned about six o'clock on a cold, frosty winter's evening. As Holmes turned up the lamp the light fell upon a card on the table. He glanced at it, and then, with an ejaculation of disgust, threw it on the floor. I picked it up and read:-

CHARLES AUGUSTUS MILVERTON,
APPLEDORE TOWERS,
HAMPSTEAD.

Agent.

'Who is he?' I asked.
'The worst man in London,' Holmes answered, as he sat down

and stretched his legs before the fire. 'Is anything on the back of the card?'

I turned it over.

'Will call at 6.30. – C. A. M.,' I read.

'Hum! He's about due. Do you feel a creeping, shrinking sensation, Watson, when you stand before the serpents in the Zoo and see the slithery, gliding, venomous creatures, with their deadly eyes and wicked, flattened faces? Well, that's how Milverton impresses me. I've had to do with fifty murderers in my career, but the worst of them never gave me the repulsion which I have for this fellow. And yet I can't get out of doing business with him – indeed, he is here at my invitation.'

'But who is he?'

'I'll tell you, Watson. He is the king of all the blackmailers. Heaven help the man, and still more the woman, whose secret and reputation come into the power of Milverton. With a smiling face and a heart of marble he will squeeze and squeeze until he has drained them dry. The fellow is a genius in his way, and would have made his mark in some more savoury trade. His method is as follows: He allows it to be known that he is prepared to pay very high sums for letters which compromise people of wealth or position. He receives these wares not only from treacherous valets or maids, but frequently from genteel ruffians who have gained the confidence and affection of trusting women. He deals with no niggard hand. I happen to know that he paid seven hundred pounds to a footman for a note two lines in length, and that the ruin of a noble family was the result. Everything which is in the market goes to Milverton, and there are hundreds in this great city who turn white at his name. No one knows where his grip may fall, for he is far too rich and far too cunning to work from hand to mouth. He will hold a card back for years in order to play it at the moment when the stake is best worth winning. I have said that he is the worst man in London, and I would ask you how could one compare the ruffian who in hot blood bludgeons his mate with this man, who methodically and at his leisure tortures the soul and wrings the nerves in order to add to his already swollen money-bags?'

I had seldom heard my friend speak with such intensity of feeling.

'But surely,' said I, 'the fellow must be within the grasp of the law?'

'Technically, no doubt, but practically not. What would it profit a woman, for example, to get him a few months' imprisonment if her own ruin must immediately follow? His victims dare not hit back. If ever he blackmailed an innocent person, then, indeed, we should have him; but he is as cunning as the Evil One. No, no; we must find other ways to fight him.'

'And why is he here?'

'Because an illustrious client has placed her piteous case in my hands. It is the Lady Eva Brackwell, the most beautiful *débutante* of last season. She is to be married in a fortnight to the Earl of Dovercourt. This fiend has several imprudent letters – imprudent, Watson, nothing worse – which were written to an impecunious young squire in the country. They would suffice to break off the match. Milverton will send the letters to the earl unless a large sum of money is paid him. I have been commissioned to meet him, and – to make the best terms I can.'

At that instant there was a clatter and a rattle in the street below. Looking down I saw a stately carriage and pair, the brilliant lamps gleaming on the glossy haunches of the noble chestnuts. A footman opened the door, and a small, stout man in a shaggy astrachan overcoat descended. A minute later he was in the room.

Charles Augustus Milverton was a man of fifty, with a large, intellectual head, a round, plump, hairless face, a perpetual frozen smile, and two keen grey eyes, which gleamed brightly from behind broad, golden-rimmed glasses. There was someting of Mr Pickwick's benevolence in his appearance, marred only by the insincerity of the fixed smile and by the hard glitter of those restless and penetrating eyes. His voice was as smooth and suave as his countenance, as he advanced with a plump little hand extended, murmuring his regret for having missed us at his first visit.

Holmes disregarded the outstretched hand and looked at him with a face of granite. Milverton's smile broadened; he shrugged his shoulders, removed his overcoat, folded it with great deliberation over the back of a chair, and then took a seat.

'This gentleman,' said he, with a wave in my direction. 'Is it discreet? Is it right?'

'Dr Watson is my friend and partner.'

'Very good, Mr Holmes. It is only in your client's interests that I protested. The matter is so very delicate – '

'Dr Watson has already heard of it.'

'Then we can proceed to business. You say that you are acting for Lady Eva. Has she empowered you to accept my terms?'

'What are your terms?'

'Seven thousand pounds.'

'And the alternative?'

'My dear sir, it is painful to me to discuss it; but if the money is not paid on the 14th there certainly will be no marriage on the 18th.' His insufferable smile was more complacent than ever. Holmes thought for a little.

'You appear to me,' he said at last, 'to be taking matters too much for granted. I am, of course, familiar with the contents of these letters. My client will certainly do what I may advise. I shall counsel her to tell her future husband the whole story and to trust to his generosity.'

Milverton chuckled.

'You evidently do not know the earl,' said he.

From the baffled look upon Holmes's face I could clearly see that he did.

'What harm is there in the letters?' he asked.

'They are sprightly – very sprightly,' Milverton answered. 'The lady was a charming correspondent. But I can assure you that the Earl of Dovercourt would fail to appreciate them. However, since you think otherwise, we will let it rest at that. It is purely a matter of business. If you think that it is in the best interests of your client that these letters should be placed in the hands of the earl, then you would indeed be foolish to pay so large a sum of money to regain them.' He rose and seized his astrachan coat.

Holmes was grey with anger and mortification.

'Wait a little,' he said. 'You go too fast. We would certainly make every effort to avoid scandal in so delicate a matter.'

Milverton relapsed into his chair.

'I was sure that you would see it in that light,' he purred.

'At the same time,' Holmes continued, 'Lady Eva is not a wealthy woman. I assure you that two thousand pounds would be a drain upon her resources, and that the sum you name is utterly beyond her power. I beg, therefore, that you will moderate your demands, and that you will return the letters at the price I indicate, which is, I assure you, the highest that you can get.'

Milverton's smile broadened and his eyes twinkled humorously.

'I am aware that what you say is true about the lady's resources,' said he. 'At the same time, you must admit that the occasion of a lady's marriage is a very suitable time for her friends and relatives to make some little effort upon her behalf. They may hesitate as to an acceptable wedding present. Let me assure them that this little bundle of letters would give more joy than all the candelabra and butter-dishes in London.'

'It is impossible,' said Holmes.

'Dear me, dear me, how unfortunate!' cried Milverton, taking out a bulky pocket-book. 'I cannot help thinking that ladies are ill-advised in not making an effort. Look at this!' He held up a little note with a coat-of-arms upon the envelope. 'That belongs to – well, perhaps it is hardly fair to tell the name until to-morrow morning. But at that time it will be in the hands of the lady's husband. And all because she will not find a beggarly sum which she could get in an hour by turning her diamonds into paste. It *is* such a pity. Now, you remember the sudden end of the engagement between the Honourable Miss Miles and Colonel Dorking? Only two days before the wedding there was a paragraph in the *Morning Post* to say that it was all off. And why? It is almost incredible, but the absurd sum of twelve hundred pounds would have settled the whole question. Is it not pitiful? And there I find you, a man of sense, boggling about terms when your client's future and honour are at stake. You surprise me, Mr Holmes.'

'What I say is true,' Holmes answered. 'The money cannot be found. Surely it is better for you to take the substantial sum which I offer than to ruin this woman's career, which can profit you in no way?'

'There you make a mistake, Mr Holmes. An exposure would profit me indirectly to a considerable extent. I have eight or ten similar cases maturing. If it was circulated among them that I had made a severe example of the Lady Eva I should find all of them much more open to reason. You see my point?'

Holmes sprang from his chair.

'Get behind him, Watson. Don't let him out! Now, sir, let us see the contents of that notebook.'

Milverton had glided as quick as a rat to the side of the room, and stood with his back against the wall.

'Mr Holmes, Mr Holmes!' he said. Turning the front of his coat and exhibiting the butt of a large revolver, which projected from the inside pocket. 'I have been expecting you to do something original. This has been done so often, and what good has ever come from it? I assure you that I am armed to the teeth, and I am perfectly prepared to use my weapon, knowing that the law will support me. Besides, your supposition that I would bring the letters here in a notebook is entirely mistaken. I would do nothing so foolish. And now, gentlemen, I have one or two little interviews this evening, and it is a long drive to Hampstead.' He stepped forward, took up his coat, laid his hand on his revolver, and turned to the door. I picked up a chair, but Holmes shook his head, and I laid it down again. With a bow, a smile, and a twinkle Milverton was out of the room, and a few moments after we heard the slam of the carriage door and the rattle of the wheels as he drove away.

Holmes sat motionless by the fire, his hands buried deep in his trouser pockets, his chin sunk upon his breast, his eyes fixed upon the glowing embers. For half an hour he was silent and still. Then, with the gesture of a man who has taken his decision, he sprang to his feet and passed into his bedroom. A little later a rakish young workman with a goatee beard and a swagger lit his clay pipe at the lamp before descending into the street. 'I'll be back some time, Watson,' said he, and vanished into the night. I understood that he had opened his campaign against Charles Augustus Milverton; but I little dreamed the strange shape which that campaign was destined to take.

For some days Holmes came and went at all hours in this attire, but beyond a remark that his time was spent at Hampstead, and that it was not wasted, I knew nothing of what he was doing. At last, however, on a wild, tempestuous evening, when the wind screamed and rattled against the windows, he returned from his last expedition, and, having removed his disguise, he sat before the fire and laughed heartily in his silent, inward fashion.

'You would not call me a marrying man, Watson?'

'No, indeed!'

'You will be interested to hear that I am engaged.'

'My dear fellow! I congrat –'

'To Milverton's housemaid.'

'Good heavens, Holmes!'

'I wanted information, Watson.'

'Surely you have gone too far?'

'It was a most necessary step. I am a plumber with a rising business, Escott by name. I have walked out with her each evening, and I have talked with her. Good heavens, those talks! However, I have got all I wanted. I know Milverton's house as I know the palm of my hand.'

'But the girl, Holmes?'

He shrugged his shoulders.

'You can't help it, my dear Watson. You must play your cards as best you can when such a stake is on the table. However, I rejoice to say that I have a hated rival who will certainly cut me out the instant that my back is turned. What a splendid night it is!'

'You like this weather?'

'It suits my purpose. Watson, I mean to burgle Milverton's house to-night.'

I had a catching of the breath, and my skin went cold at the words, which were slowly uttered in a tone of concentrated resolution. As a flash of lightning in the night shows up in an instant every detail of a wide landscape, so at one glance I seemed to see every possible result of such an action – the detection, the capture, the honoured career ending in irreparable failure and disgrace, my friend himself lying at the mercy of the odious Milverton.

'For Heaven's sake, Holmes, think what you are doing!' I cried.

'My dear fellow, I have given it every consideration. I am never precipitate in my actions, nor would I adopt so energetic and indeed so dangerous a course if any other were possible. Let us look at the matter clearly and fairly. I suppose that you will admit that the action is morally justifiable, though technically criminal. To burgle his house is no more than to forcibly take his pocket-book – an action in which you were prepared to aid me.'

I turned it over in my mind.

'Yes,' I said; 'it is morally justifiable so long as our object is to take no articles save those which are used for an illegal purpose.'

'Exactly. Since it is morally justifiable, I have only to consider the question of personal risk. Surely a gentleman should not lay much stress upon this when a lady is in most desperate need of his help?'

'You will be in such a false position.'

'Well, that is part of the risk. There is no other possible way of regaining these letters. The unfortunate lady had not the money, and there are none of her people in whom she could confide. To-morrow is the last day of grace, and unless we can get the letters to-night this villain will be as good as his word, and will bring about her ruin. I must, therefore, abandon my client to her fate, or I must play this last card. Between ourselves, Watson, it's a sporting duel between this fellow Milverton and me. He had, as you saw, the best of the first exchanges; but my self-respect and my reputation are concerned to fight it to a finish.'

'Well, I don't like it; but I suppose it must be,' said I. 'When do we start?'

'You are not coming.'

'Then you are not going,' said I. 'I give you my word of honour – and I never broke it in my life – that I will take a cab straight to the police-station and give you away unless you let me share this adventure with you.'

'You can't help me.'

'How do you know that? You can't tell what may happen. Anyway, my resolution is taken. Other people besides you have self-respect and even reputations.'

Holmes had looked annoyed, but his brow cleared, and he clapped me on the shoulder.

'Well, well, my dear fellow, be it so. We have shared the same room for some years, and it would be amusing if we ended by sharing the same cell. You know, Watson, I don't mind confessing to you that I have always had an idea that I would have made a highly efficient criminal. This is the chance of my lifetime in that direction. See here!' He took a neat little leather case out of a drawer, and opening it he exhibited a number of shining instruments. 'This is a first-class, up-to-date burgling kit, with nickel-plated jemmy, diamond-tipped glass cutter, adaptable keys, and every modern improvement which the march of civilization demands. Here, too, is my dark lantern. Everything is in order. Have you a pair of silent shoes?'

'I have rubber-soled tennis shoes.'

'Excellent. And a mask?'

'I can make a couple out of black silk.'

'I can see that you have a strong natural turn for this sort of thing.

Very good; do you make the masks. We shall have some cold supper before we start. It is now nine-thirty. At eleven we shall drive as far as Church Row. It is a quarter of an hour's walk from there to Appledore Towers. We shall be at work before midnight. Milverton is a heavy sleeper, and retires punctually at ten-thirty. With any luck we should be back here by two, with the Lady Eva's letters in my pocket.'

Holmes and I put on our dress-clothes, so that we might appear to be two theatre-goers homeward bound. In Oxford Street we picked up a hansom and drove to an address in Hampstead. Here we paid off our cab, and with our greatcoats buttoned up – for it was bitterly cold, and the wind seemed to blow through us – we walked along the edge of the Heath.

'It's a business that needs delicate treatment,' said Holmes. 'These documents are contained in a safe in the fellow's study, and the study is the anteroom of his bedchamber. On the other hand, like all these stout, little men who do themselves well, he is a plethoric sleeper. Agatha – that's my *fiancée* – says it is a joke in the servants' hall that it's impossible to wake the master. He has a secretary who is devoted to his interests, and never budges from the study all day. That's why we are going at night. Then he has a beast of a dog which roams the garden. I met Agatha late the last two evenings and she locks the brute up so as to give me a clear run. This is the house, this big one in its own grounds. Through the gate – now to the right among the laurels. We might put on our masks here, I think. You see, there is not a glimmer of light in any of the windows, and everything is working splendidly.'

With our black silk face-coverings, which turned us into two of the most truculent figures in London, we stole up to the silent, gloomy house. A sort of tiled veranda extended along one side of it, lined by several windows and two doors.

'That's his bedroom,' Holmes whispered. 'This door opens straight into the study. It would suit us best, but it is bolted as well as locked, and we should make too much noise getting in. Come round here. There's a greenhouse which opens into the drawing-room.'

The place was locked, but Holmes removed a circle of glass and turned the key from the inside. An instant afterwards he had closed the door behind us, and we had become felons in the eyes of the

law. The thick warm air of the conservatory and the rich, choking
fragrance of exotic plants took us by the throat. He seized my hand
in the darkness and led me swiftly past banks of shrubs which
brushed against our faces. Holmes had remarkable powers, carefully
cultivated, of seeing in the dark. Still holding my hand in one of
his, he opened a door, and I was vaguely conscious that we had
entered a large room in which a cigar had been smoked not long
before. He felt his way among the furniture, opened another door,
and closed it behind us. Putting out my hand I felt several coats
hanging from the wall, and I understood that I was in a passage.
We passed along it, and Holmes very gently opened a door upon
the right-hand side. Something rushed out at us, and my heart
sprang into my mouth, but I could have laughed when I realized
that it was the cat. A fire was burning in this new room, and again
the air was heavy with tobacco smoke. Holmes entered on tiptoe,
waited for me to follow, and then very gently closed the door. We
were in Milverton's study, and a *portière* at the farther side showed
the entrance to his bedroom.

It was a good fire, and the room was illuminated by it. Near the
door I saw the gleam of an electric switch, but it was unnecessary,
even if it had been safe, to turn it on. At one side of the fireplace
was a heavy curtain, which covered the bay window we had seen
from outside. On the other side was the door which communicated
with the veranda. A desk stood in the centre, with a turning chair
of shining red leather. Opposite was a large bookcase, with a marble
bust of Athene on the top. In the corner between the bookcase and
the wall there stood a tall green safe, the firelight flashing back from
the polished brass knobs upon its face. Holmes stole across and
looked at it. Then he crept to the door of the bedroom, and stood
with slanting head listening intently. No sound came from within.
Meanwhile it had struck me that it would be wise to secure our
retreat through the outer door, so I examined it. To my amazement
it was neither locked nor bolted! I touched Holmes on the arm, and
he turned his masked face in that direction. I saw him start, and he
was evidently as surprised as I.

'I don't like it,' he whispered, putting his lips to my very ear. 'I
can't quite make it out. Anyhow, we have no time to lose.'

'Can I do anything?'

'Yes; stand by the door. If you hear any one come, bolt it on the inside, and we can get away as we came. If they come the other way, we can get through the door if our job is done, or hide behind these window curtains if it is not. Do you understand?'

I nodded and stood by the door. My first feeling of fear had passed away, and I thrilled now with a keener zest than I had ever enjoyed when we were the defenders of the law instead of its defiers. The high object of our mission, the consciousness that it was unselfish and chivalrous, the villainous character of our opponent, all added to the sporting interest of the adventure. Far from feeling guilty, I rejoiced and exulted in our dangers. With a glow of admiration I watched Holmes unrolling his case of instruments and choosing his tool with the calm, scientific accuracy of a surgeon who performs a delicate operation. I knew that the opening of safes was a particular hobby with him, and I understood the joy which it gave him to be confronted with this green and gold monster, the dragon which held in its maw the reputations of many fair ladies. Turning up the cuffs of his dress-coat – he had placed his overcoat on a chair – Holmes laid out two drills, a jemmy, and several skeleton keys. I stood at the centre door with my eyes glancing at each of the others, ready for any emergency; though, indeed, my plans were somewhat vague as to what I should do if we were interrupted. For half an hour Holmes worked with concentrated energy, laying down one tool, picking up another, handling each with the strength and delicacy of the trained mechanic. Finally I heard a click, the broad green door swung open, and inside I had a glimpse of a number of paper packets, each tied, sealed, and inscribed. Holmes picked one out, but it was hard to read by the flickering fire, and he drew out his little dark lantern, for it was too dangerous, with Milverton in the next room, to switch on the electric light. Suddenly I saw him halt, listen intently, and then in an instant he had swung the door of the safe to, picked up his coat, stuffed his tools into the pockets, and darted behind the window curtain, motioning me to do the same.

It was only when I had joined him there that I heard what had alarmed his quicker senses. There was a noise somewhere within the house. A door slammed in the distance. Then a confused, dull murmur broke itself into the measured thud of heavy footsteps rapidly approaching. They were in the passage outside the room. They paused at the door. The door opened. There was a sharp snick as the electric light was turned on. The door closed once more, and the pungent reek of a strong cigar was borne to our nostrils. Then the footsteps continued backwards and forwards, backwards and forwards, within a few yards of us. Finally, there was a creak from a chair, and the footsteps ceased. Then a key clicked in a lock, and I heard the rustle of papers. So far I had not dared to look out, but now I gently parted the division of the curtains in front of me and peeped through. From the pressure of Holmes's shoulder against mine I knew that he was sharing my observations. Right in front of us, and almost within our reach, was the broad, rounded back of Milverton. It was evident that we had entirely miscalculated his movements, that he had never been to his bedroom, but that he had been sitting up in some smoking or billiard room in the farther wing of the house, the windows of which we had not seen. His broad, grizzled head, with its shining patch of baldness, was in the immediate foreground of our vision. He was leaning far back in the red leather chair, his legs outstretched, a long black cigar projecting at an angle from his mouth. He wore a semi-military smoking jacket, claret-coloured, with a black velvet collar. In his hand he held a long legal document, which he was reading in an indolent fashion, blowing rings of tobacco smoke from his lips as he did so. There was no promise of a speedy departure in his composed bearing and his comfortable attitude.

I felt Holmes's hand steal into mine and give me a reassuring shake, as if to say that the situation was within his powers, and that he was easy in his mind. I was not sure whether he had seen what was only too obvious from my position – that the door of the safe was imperfectly closed, and that Milverton might at any moment observe it. In my own mind I had determined that if I were sure, from the rigidity of his gaze, that it had caught his eye, I would at once spring out, throw my greatcoat over his head, pinion him, and leave the rest to Holmes. But Milverton never looked up. He was languidly interested by the papers in his hand, and page after page was turned as he followed the argument of the lawyer. At least, I thought, when he has finished the document and the cigar he will go to his room; but before he had reached the end of either there came a remarkable development which turned our thoughts into quite another channel.

Several times I had observed that Milverton looked at his watch, and once he had risen and sat down again, with a gesture of impatience. The idea, however, that he might have an appointment at so strange an hour never occurred to me until a faint sound reached my ears from the veranda outside. Milverton dropped his papers and sat rigid in his chair. The sound was repeated, and then there came a gentle tap at the door. Milverton rose and opened it.

'Well,' said he curtly, 'you are nearly half an hour late.'

So this was the explanation of the unlocked door and of the nocturnal vigil of Milverton. There was the gentle rustle of a woman's dress. I had closed the slit between the curtains as Milverton's face turned in our direction, but now I ventured very carefully to open it once more. He had resumed his seat, the cigar still projecting at an insolent angle from the corner of his mouth. In front of him, in the full glare of the electric light, there stood a tall, slim, dark woman, a veil over her face, a mantle drawn round her chin. Her breath came quick and fast, and every inch of the lithe figure was quivering with strong emotion.

'Well,' said Milverton, 'you've made me lose a good night's rest, my dear. I hope you'll prove worth it. You couldn't come any other time – eh?'

The woman shook her head.

'Well, if you couldn't you couldn't. If the countess is a hard mistress you have your chance to get level with her now. Bless the girl, what are you shivering about? That's right! Pull yourself together! Now, let us get down to business.' He took a note from the drawer of his desk. 'You say that you have five letters which compromise the Countess d'Albert. You want to sell them. I want to buy them. So far so good. It only remains to fix a price. I should want to inspect the letters, of course. If they are really good specimens – Great heavens, is it you?'

The woman without a word had raised her veil and dropped the mantle from her chin. It was a dark, handsome, clear-cut face which confronted Milverton, a face with a curved nose, strong, dark eyebrows, shading hard, glittering eyes, and a straight, thin-lipped mouth set in a dangerous smile.

'It is I,' she said – 'the woman whose life you have ruined.'

Milverton laughed, but fear vibrated in his voice. 'You were so very obstinate,' said he. 'Why did you drive me to such extremities? I assure you I wouldn't hurt a fly of my own accord, but every man has his business, and what was I to do? I put the price well within your means. You would not pay.'

'So you sent the letters to my husband, and he – the noblest gentleman that ever lived, a man whose boots I was never worthy to lace – he broke his gallant heart and died. You remember that last night when I came through that door I begged and prayed you for mercy, and you laughed in my face as you are trying to laugh now, only your coward heart cannot keep your lips from twitching? Yes; you never thought to see me here again, but it was that night which taught me how I could meet you face to face, and alone. Well, Charles Milverton, what have you to say?'

'Don't imagine that you can bully me,' said he, rising to his feet. 'I have only to raise my voice, and I could call my servants and have you arrested. But I will make allowance for your natural anger. Leave the room at once as you came, and I will say no more.'

The woman stood with her hand buried in her bosom, and the same deadly smile on her thin lips.

'You will ruin no more lives as you ruined mine. You will wring no more hearts as you wrung mine. I will free the world of a poisonous thing. Take that, you hound, and that! – and that! – and that! – and that!'

She had drawn a little gleaming revolver, and emptied barrel after barrel into Milverton's body, the muzzle within two feet of his shirt-front. He shrank away, and then fell forward upon the table, coughing furiously and clawing among the papers. Then he staggered to his feet, received another shot, and rolled upon the floor. 'You've done me,' he cried, and lay still. The woman looked at him intently and ground her heel into his upturned face. She looked again, but there was no sound or movement. I heard a sharp rustle, the night air blew into the heated room, and the avenger was gone.

No interference upon our part could have saved the man from his fate; but as the woman poured bullet after bullet into Milverton's shrinking body, I was about to spring out, when I felt Holmes's cold, strong grasp upon my wrist. I understood the whole argument of that firm, restraining grip – that it was no affair of ours; that justice had overtaken a villain; that we had our own duties and our own objects which were not to be lost sight of. But hardly had the woman rushed from the room when Holmes, with swift, silent steps, was over at the other door. He turned the key in the lock.

At the same instant we heard voices in the house and the sound of hurrying feet. The revolver shots had roused the household. With perfect coolness Holmes slipped across to the safe, filled his two arms with bundles of letters, and poured them all into the fire. Again and again he did it, until the safe was empty. Some one turned the handle and beat upon the outside of the door. Holmes looked swiftly round. The letter which had been the messenger of death for Milverton lay, all mottled with his blood, upon the table. Holmes tossed it in among the blazing papers. Then he drew the key from the outer door, passed through after me, and locked it on the outside. 'This way, Watson,' said he; 'we can scale the garden wall in this direction.'

I could not have believed that an alarm could have spread so swiftly. Looking back, the huge house was one blaze of light. The front door was open, and figures were rushing down the drive. The whole garden was alive with people, and one fellow raised a view-halloa as we emerged from the veranda and followed hard at our heels. Holmes seemed to know the ground perfectly, and he threaded his way swiftly among a plantation of small trees, I close at his heels, and our foremost pursuer panting behind us. It was a six-foot wall which barred our path, but he sprang to the top and over. As I did the same I felt the hand of the man behind me grab at my ankle; but I kicked myself free, and scrambled over a glass-strewn coping. I fell upon my face among some bushes; but Holmes had me on my feet in an instant, and together we dashed away across the huge expanse of Hampstead Heath. We had run two miles, I suppose, before Holmes at last halted and listened intently. All was absolutely silence behind us. We had shaken off our pursuers, and were safe.

We had breakfasted and were smoking our morning pipe, on the day after the remarkable experience which I have recorded, when Mr Lestrade, of Scotland Yard, very solemn and impressive, was ushered into our modest sitting-room.

'Good morning, Mr Holmes,' said he – 'good morning. May I ask if you are very busy just now?'

'Not too busy to listen to you.'

'I thought that, perhaps, if you had nothing particular on hand, you might care to assist us in a most remarkable case which occurred only last night at Hampstead.'

'Dear me!' said Holmes. 'What was that?'

'A murder – a most dramatic and remarkable murder. I know how keen you are upon these things, and I would take it as a great favour if you would step down to Appledore Towers and give us the benefit of your advice. It is no ordinary crime. We have had our eyes upon this Mr Milverton for some time, and, between ourselves, he was a bit of a villain. He is known to have held papers which he used for blackmailing purposes. These papers have all been burned by the murderers. No article of value was taken, as it is probable that the criminals were men of good position, whose sole object was to prevent social exposure.'

'Criminals!' exclaimed Holmes. 'Plural!'

'Yes, there were two of them. They were, as nearly as possible, captured red-handed. We have their footmarks, we have their description; it's ten to one that we trace them. The first fellow was a bit too active, but the second was caught by the under-gardener, and only got away after a struggle. He was a middle-sized, strongly built man – square jaw, thick neck, moustache, a mask over his eyes.'

'That's rather vague,' said Sherlock Holmes. 'Why, it might be a description of Watson!'

'It's true,' said the inspector, with much amusement. 'It might be a description of Watson.'

'Well, I am afraid I can't help you, Lestrade,' said Holmes. 'The fact is that I knew this fellow Milverton, that I considered him one of the most dangerous men in London, and that I think there are certain crimes which the law cannot touch, and which therefore, to some extent, justify private revenge. No, it's no use arguing. I have made up my mind. My sympathies are with the criminals rather than with the victim, and I will not handle this case.'

Holmes had not said one word to me about the tragedy which we had witnessed, but I observed all the morning that he was in the most thoughtful mood, and he gave me the impression, from his vacant eyes and his abstracted manner, of a man who is striving to recall something to his memory. We were in the middle of our lunch, when he suddenly sprang to his feet. 'By Jove, Watson! I've got it!' he cried. 'Take your hat! Come with me!' He hurried at his top speed down Baker Street and along Oxford Street, until we had almost reached Regent Circus. Here on the left hand there stands a shop window filled with photographs of the celebrities and beauties of the day. Holmes's eyes fixed themselves upon one of them, and following his gaze I saw the picture of a regal and stately lady in Court dress, with a high diamond tiara upon her noble head. I looked at that delicately curved nose, at the marked eyebrows, at the straight mouth, and the strong little chin beneath it. Then I caught my breath as I read the time-honoured title of the great nobleman and statesman whose wife she had been. My eyes met those of Holmes, and he put his finger to his lips as we turned away from the window.

PING-PONG

George Allan England

THE coroner's inquest seemed hardly more than a matter of routine. So obvious was the fact that Douglas Powell, the eccentric retired cotton broker, had fallen to his death from one of his library windows on the third floor of his house on West Heights Boulevard that Coroner Drummond would undoubtedly have omitted even the formality of a finding in the matter, had not the law rendered it mandatory.

Assembled in the back room of McCabe's Undertaking Parlours, whither the body had been removed – for Mr Powell was without relatives and Drummond had so ordered – the little gathering spoke in tones as subdued as the dim light from the frosted bulb overhead. The presence of death, weighing upon them all, muted and constrained the spirit of life.

'It seems quite obvious', judged Drummond, joining the tips of his thin fingers and squinting through his glasses, 'that the deceased came to his death through accidental means. His library window was open. The fragment of woollen cloth caught on the blind cord corresponds to the fabric of the coat he wore last night. His body, as you have heard from Mr Shannigan, the milkman, and from Mrs Estill, the housekeeper, was discovered at 6.15 this morning lying in the soft earth of the flower-bed under the window. Mulvey, here,' and he gestured at the officer who, helmet in hand, stood very ill at ease beside the chair in which the coroner was seated, 'has given us a very lucid statement of the manner in which Mrs Estill summoned him, and of how he let the body remain where it was until my arrival. The evidence is self-explanatory and conclusive. If no further facts are forthcoming, I shall render a verdict of accidental death.'

For a moment nobody moved or spoke. Drummond's eyes sought the witnesses, one by one – the housekeeper, pale, tight-lipped, and wary; Shannigan, who knew not where to put his hands and feet; the self-sufficient Mulvey; Dr Edwin Graun, Powell's long-time friend and physician; and last of all Dr Jamison Herrick, the police surgeon.

'Well, gentlemen,' said he, 'are there any further remarks to be made? If not, I will render my verdict.'

The little pause that followed seemed to indicate unanimity of opinion. But before Drummond could take his fountain pen from his pocket, Dr Herrick spoke up.

'Just a minute,' said he, passing a hand over his bald head, as he sat there across the table from the coroner. 'Before you make out the certificate, we should be positive of all the factors involved in this matter. I am still not quite satisfied that Mr Powell's death was caused by the cranial fracture obviously due to his head striking that white-washed boulder at the edge of the flower-bed.'

'You mean there may have been a frature of the cervical vertebrae, as well?' inquired Graun. 'If so, a little further examination will establish that fact. That, or the shock, may have killed him. This, however, is immaterial. The mere details do not matter. Whatever they may be, the prime factor remains that it was the fall which produced death. Am I not right?'

His full-fleshed, rubicund face assumed an inquiring expression. He twirled the little gold cigar cutter at the end of his watch chain, and looked from face to face. All met his gaze save Mrs Estill. Her eyes, lowered and blinking, seemed studying the carpet as if mightily interested in the dull, obscure pattern there.

'Well, am I right, gentlemen, or not?' repeated he.

'I hardly know,' answered the police surgeon. 'What strikes me as peculiar is that the scalp wound shows no sign of bleeding, or at least none commensurate with the injury involved. In fact, the appearance of the wound – if I didn't feel so positive, myself, that the fall caused his death – would suggest to me the idea that Mr Powell had already been dead for some time before having fallen from the window.'

'What's that?' demanded Dr Graun. 'I don't quite follow you. How could he have been dead *before* he fell?'

'That is the puzzling factor in the case,' replied Dr Herrick. 'Until we get it cleared up, I think we ought not to go ahead with the verdict.'

Dr Graun's eyes blinked with a thoughtful expression. For a moment he ceased spinning his cigar cutter. Then, while Drummond peered inquiringly at him, and Mrs Estill's lips moved as if she were mechanically counting the number of pattern repetitions in the carpet, he said:

'In view of the fact that I spent the evening with Mr Powell last night, and that I left him at 11.30, in his usual health and spirits, I confess I'm at a loss to understand just how it all happened. Mrs Estill heard us talking and playing ping-pong – his favourite game, gentlemen, barring chess – up to the time I left. She herself let me out, and chained and locked the front door after me, as she has just now testified. After that, she claims she went directly to bed, although of course there can be no witness to that fact.

'Mr Powell was alive at 11.30. That much we know. The house shows no signs of having been entered. There are no traces of murder. Death must have been caused by the fall. That much we can be sure of by a process of elimination. No other hypothesis will fit the facts. Do any of you gentlemen see any other explanation?'

'I don't for one,' answered the police surgeon, frowning. 'That's what puzzles me so. Because even that won't hold water. If the fall caused Mr Powell's death, how the devil does it happen that he didn't bleed freely from the wound on the head?'

For a moment Graun pondered. Then, looking up, he answered:

'There's just one possible hypothesis that may fit the facts.'

'And what is that?' demanded Herrick.

'Powell may have suffered an attack of heart failure while leaning out of the window – '

'In which case there would undoubtedly have been more bleeding.'

'Not necessarily,' put in the coroner. 'Circulation would have already stopped. I think, on the whole, that's the best explanation we can give. In the circumstances, I'll change my finding to death from natural causes or accident.'

He reached for his pen, opened the death certificate on the table before him, and was about to begin filling it in when Herrick stayed his hand with the remark:

'Hold on a minute, please, if you don't mind. Mrs Estill, after

Dr Graun left, did you hear any sound that might have been caused by anybody entering Mr Powell's library or bedroom? Did anything happen that in any way suggested trouble or violence of any kind?'

'No, sir,' the housekeeper answered with an oblique and nervous look, bobbing her little jet-trimmed bonnet. 'Not a thing, sir.'

'Hear any footsteps, or anything of that kind?'

'In the library, sir? Nothing. That thick carpet deafens everything. It's extra thick, sir.'

Frowning, the police surgeon fixed critical eyes on her.

'Now see here,' he said. 'Tell me just what you did hear last night, if anything.'

'Well, sir, all I heard was the doctor, here, and Mr Powell playing their game and talking, until about half-past eleven. First he'd say something and then the doctor would answer. I could hear the little ping-pong ball go *tack-tack-tack* on the library table. And then maybe it would fall to the floor.'

'How did you know that, Mrs Estill?'

'Why – there'd come a little pause in the game, and then it would go on again. Mr Powell was wonderful fond of that game, God rest him! The kindest man and the best that ever – '

'What else did you hear?' interrupted the surgeon, dryly, while the coroner and Dr Graun studied the woman with close attention. The housekeeper dabbed at her eyes with a moist handkerchief, gave a shrewd look at her inquisitor, and continued:

'At half-past eleven I heard them say good-night, and the doctor went away. After that, everything was quiet, same as usual.'

'Did you enter the library, or see Mr Powell alive, after that time?'

'No, sir. He was always very particular about not being disturbed at night. That was his reading time. He was the best man in the world, sir, and always treated me like a lady, though he was odd in his ways. And I shall miss him – '

'That will do,' interrupted Herrick, in no mood to listen to discursions regarding the character of the deceased. He bent his gaze on the coroner, seeming to peer through him at vacancy beyond. 'This is most peculiar. Direct testimony exists, from two witnesses, that Mr Powell was alive at 11.30, and yet the condition of the body certainly points to the fact that he was dead at that time. Dr Graun, will you kindly give us a few additional details of your call on him, last night?'

'Certainly, with the greatest pleasure,' answered Graun, still whirling his cigar cutter. 'In fact, I'll go over the whole matter again. I arrived about nine – one of my weekly routine calls, such as I've been making for the past eight or ten months. I found him in his usual state of health, barring a noticeable increase in the mitral insufficiency that had been gaining on him, little by little, since last summer; nothing serious, however – nothing that would warrant me in the belief that he was going to be stricken with heart failure so soon.'

'It's odd about heart cases, that way,' put in Herrick. 'You think a man – say with a leaky valve, or whatnot – might live for a year or two, or five; and he drops dead almost at once. Another man you wouldn't give a week to live – everything all shot to pieces – and he survives to bury you. During your call last night, Dr Graun, did you make a stethoscopic examination?'

'I did, as usual,' Graun answered, nodding. 'Mr Powell, of course, was something of a hypochondriac. If it were not for the old rule of *De mortuis nil nisi bonum* – nothing but good about the dead – I suppose I'd have to call him a particularly fussy crank. For the last three years he has never eaten a bite that he hasn't weighed in a little pair of scales. Half his time and attention have been given to pro-teids, calories, enzymes, Bulgarian milk cultures and all that sort of thing. Nobody but a crank would be so interested in a childish game like ping-pong at his age. Every time I called he insisted on playing a game. A good patient; I couldn't refuse – though Lord! how it bored me! You know the type, Herrick, don't you?'

'Yes, I know; but never mind about that, now. You say his condition wasn't such last night as to warrant any presumption of immediate danger?'

'Not that I could see,' answered Graun, while Drummond listened with close attenion and the others watched him anxiously – all save Mrs Estill, who had once more gone back to counting the patterns in the carpet, as if to keep from hearing all those interrogatory questions.

'The only supposition that seems to meet the case is that, after I left him, he must have opened the window to get a breath of fresh air. We'd both been smoking, and the air was somewhat vitiated. He probably took several long breaths, had a syncope – as sometimes happens when an excess of oxygen suddenly enters the blood – fell forward and slid over the sill. That's the only hypothesis I can think of that fits all the known facts.'

A little silence followed, during which the police surgeon rose, clasped his hands behind his back, and began slowly to pace up and down the dim-lit room. Graun continued to whirl the trinket on his watch chain. Suddenly Drummond, the coroner, spoke again.

'Mrs Estill,' he asked, 'how did you know it was 11.30 when the doctor left?'

'The hall clock struck the half-hour, sir, just after I heard the street door close.'

'Did you hear the library window open, at any time during the evening?'

The housekeeper pondered a moment, then nodded affirmation. 'Yes, sir, I did.'

'At what time, please?'

'I can't just say, sir, but I think it was while they were playing their game.'

'Did you hear it shut again?'

'No, sir.'

'Are you sure this was during the course of the game?'

'No, sir, not just exactly sure, but I think so. Still, it may have been afterwards. I don't remember.'

'Surely, it must have been afterwards,' put in Dr Graun. 'I recall very distinctly that the air was close and smoky – recall thinking in a casual way that it would be a good thing to have a little fresh air, but didn't suggest it. That was while we were talking, before we'd started the routine game – the game, I'll confess, that my willingness to play helped me to retain Mr Powell as a patient. Then something else diverted my mind. To my personal knowledge, the window was not opened during my call.'

The coroner pondered a moment, while Herrick stopped his pacing, then put his pen to the certificate of death.

'I think, gentlemen,' said he, 'that we have heard enough. The case is conclusive and self-evident. Any further investigation would be a needless waste of time and energy. I shall give a finding of death by natural causes or accidental means.'

While the others watched him with mute interest, a little inflated by the instinctive sense of dignity we all feel when taking part in official proceedings, Drummond filled in the blank, dried it with a blotter and put it in his pocket. He reached for his hat, on the table before him, and stood up.

'Thank you, gentlemen,' said he. 'I'm glad the case is so obvious – glad there are no painful or embarrassing complications. Thank you, Mrs Estill. Good day.'

Dr Herrick likewise took his hat. The coroner, the surgeon, and the policeman departed with Shannigan, the milkman, leaving Dr Graun with the housekeeper and McCabe, to talk over some further details. Out on the pavement, in the cheerful March sunshine once more, the little group broke up, Herrick touched his hat, gave the coroner a brief good-day and, turning on his heel, departed with his hands thrust far into his overcoat pockets and his deep eyes smouldering.

'A wound that didn't bleed,' he murmured, 'and a doubt concerning the time of a window being opened. H–m!'

Downtown walked Dr Herrick, with the air of a man sunk in deep abstraction. Arriving at the Arcade Building, he took the elevator to the eleventh floor, and entered an office, the door of which bore the name:

T. H. ASHLEY
INVESTIGATIONS

Then, giving his hand to the sharp-faced man who rose to greet him, he asked:

'What's the news, Tom? Busy?'

Ashley was, and said so. Herrick continued:

'I've got a case for you. Something urgent. It's a sticker with beautiful possibilities. If you can unravel it I'll get you a berth in the secret service. Here's a chance for you to win your spurs.'

'What's the idea?' demanded Ashley. 'Sit down, and let's have the facts.'

Herrick told him all he knew. Ashley listened with close attention, especially when Herrick gave the housekeeper's testimony that the ping-pong game had lasted up to the time of Dr Graun's departure.

'That lets Graun out,' said he. 'In other circumstances, since he was the last man to see Powell alive, some suspicion might attach to him.'

'It certainly would,' assented Herrick. 'But his testimony absolutely coincides with hers. He goes clear. If nobody else entered that house, later, we have only two hypotheses – either the housekeeper murdered Powell, or he died a natural death. You must find out whether or not she would have any motive. Have a look at her and at the premises, and see what you make of it. I rather think the old lady hasn't told all she knows. She was a bit uncertain about the time of that window being opened. Another thing, when I first saw her at the house, and she gave her version of being notified of the accident by Shannigan, the milkman, I thought her grief was just a shade exaggerated. Now you know the principal facts. It's up to you. Get busy.'

Ashley put a few questions to the doctor, squinting with narrowed eyes as he tilted back in his chair, hands deep in trouser pockets. Then, nodding, he answered:

'All right, I'm on. Where shall I see you?'

'Headquarters, all morning.'

'Good! I'm not promising anything, of course, but if there's any thread to pick up, I'll do my best to find it.'

Within half an hour he was examining Powell's library, while Mrs Estill, anxious and pale, stood with hands tightly clasped and nervously watched his investigation.

First he took a general survey of the room, then peered down from the window out of which Powell had fallen. With a large magnifying glass he examined the sill. At different angles he studied the thick-piled carpet from the table to the window.

Next he drew down the window blinds, switched on the electric light of the table, and inspected the table itself – a large oak table, still cleared of books and papers as it had been for the game. Finally he asked for the ping-pong set.

Silently Mrs Estill brought it. A certain unwillingness was now manifest in her attitude; an uneasy suspicion of this abrupt, laconic individual intruding on the privacy of the house of death.

'Here's the things, sir,' said she, putting the box on the table. 'Everything's just as it was left last night.'

'Did Mr Powell always put the bats and balls in the box, this way, after playing?' demanded Ashley.

'Why – not always.'

'Did he ever put them back?'

'Sometimes.'

'What share of this property is coming to you now? This house and land?'

The woman's face twitched slightly.

'I – I don't know, sir. How can I know, till the will is read?'

'Ah, of course you can't,' said Ashley. 'Pardon my asking. I needn't detain you any longer. Please be good enough to leave.'

Troubled, she obeyed him. When she was gone, Ashley took from his vest pocket a jeweller's *loupe*, screwed it into his eye, and carrying the two little ping-pong bats over to the window, raised the blinds.

By the clear light of the winter's day he spent several minutes closely studying the handles of the bats. From time to time he grunted, but what the significance of those grunts might be was betrayed by no remark.

This observation finished, he replaced the bats in the box, removed the *loupe* from his eye, and began pacing the heavily carpeted floor. As he walked, he keenly studied the carpet. He moved the table to one side, so that the light from the incandescents should fall unimpeded over the whole expanse of carpeting.

For a minute or two he seemed to discover nothing; but suddenly he stopped, peered down with close attention, and then, kneeling, began to poke with an inquisitive forefinger at the thick velvet-like fabric.

Carefully he extracted something from its tufts, looked at it a moment as he held it between his fingers, then laid it in his palm and once more put the magnifying glass to his eye. With the greatest minuteness he studied the object, through his lens. It was a tiny, curved fragment of thin glass.

'Glass!' he said, frowning. 'H–m! Glass!'

He took from another pocket a small pasteboard box which, when opened, proved to be full of cotton wool. Into the cotton wool he dropped the shard of glass; he closed the box with care, and pocketed it again. Then he got down on his knees by the place where the table had stood, and with his reading glass meticulously examined the place where he had found the shard.

'More glass – powdered! This looks interesting!'

For about five minutes he studied the place. Then, his investigation seemingly at an end, he got up and summoned Mrs Estill.

'Tell me,' he asked, 'how long ago was an electric-light bulb broken here?'

'Broken, sir? Why – I don't know. I don't remember that one was ever broken in this room. There was one in the hall last week, but – '

'You're quite positive no bulb was ever smashed in the library?'

'Yes, sir. Why?'

'All right, Mrs Estill. Thank you very much indeed for your kindness. Good day!'

Leaving her very pale and anxious, he took his departure, with the box containing the ping-pong set. By the grim smile on his lips, one might have suspected that his errand at the house of Powell had not been entirely in vain.

Straight back to his office he proceeded, entered his little laboratory which led out of it, and spent about twenty minutes there. Then he rang up Dr Herrick at police headquarters.

'Doctor,' said he, 'I have a little fresh evidence in the case that will require some expert medical testimony.'

'Fine!' answered Herrick. 'Come along down!'

'All right. But I think I'll need more than a single opinion on the matter. Please have Dr Graun there, too. He knows so much about Mr Powell's habits that he can give us a great deal of valuable information.'

'O.K. I'll have him here by the time you arrive. Got some evidence, have you?'

'I don't know. That depends on what you and Graun say about the indications.'

Dr Graun was already in Herrick's office when Ashley arrived. Graun shook hands with the investigator, and then – sitting down beside the desk – inquired with a smile:

'Well, Mr Ashley, have you any further light to shed on the mystery?'

'That depends,' answered Ashley, opening the ping-pong box. He laid the box on the desk, took out the bats and – while Graun and Herrick watched him with interest – held them up to view.

'First,' said he, 'I have discovered the curious fact that both of these handles show the same type of fingerprints. Perspiring fingers, of course, leave very definite marks.'

'What?' asked Dr Graun, scowling a little. 'What has that got to do with the case?'

'The hands of one and the same individual were last in contact with both these bats,' Ashley explained. 'The texture of the skin as shown by the prints on both is unmistakably the same. In other words, for some reason or other, after the game was finished, either Mr Powell or you, Doctor, must have held both bats for some time.'

'Very likely,' answered Graun, nodding. 'If I remember rightly, I believe I myself put both bats back in the box. But what bearing can that possibly have on the manner in which Mr Powell met his death?'

'The hand prints do not indicate a hasty or casual touch,' said Ashley. 'In fact, both bats seem to have been held for some considerable time by the same person. This is certainly very puzzling. Can you explain it?'

Graun pondered a moment, then shook his head in negation.

'Well, no,' he answered. 'Perhaps you are mistaken.'

Ashley smiled noncommittally, laid the bats down, and produced the little box of cotton wool. This he also opened. From it he shook out a piece of broken glass upon the desk, and pointing to it said:

'Here, gentlemen, is a bit of very thin, curved glass, which I discovered on the carpet near the table.'

'Glass, eh?' queried Herrick. 'Well, where does that fit in?'

'There were also signs that a little powdered glass had been brushed up from the thick carpet,' Ashley continued, as he stood by the desk and looked at both the other men seated. 'The carpet had certainly been brushed. My inference is that somebody stepped on some pieces of thin glass there, and then brushed them up, but was unable to get all the powder up and also overlooked this little piece here.'

'What possible bearing can that have?' put in Graun, puzzled.

'I don't know yet. Mrs Estill informed me that she broke an electric-light bulb in the library, two or three days ago. Probably this glass, here, is a fragment of that bulb.'

'Undoubtedly so,' assented Graun. He picked up the bit of glass and carefully examined it. 'The curve and the thinness strongly suggest such an explanation. Yes, that's what this must have been – part of a bulb. As such, it can't have any possible significance in this case.'

Casually he tossed it in his palm, two or three times, then dropped it into the wastebasket. Ashley picked it out again, without comment, and once more deposited it carefully in the cotton wool.

'Mrs Estill', said he, 'showed some signs of perturbation when I showed it to her. I also asked her whether Mr Powell ever used perfume of any kind. She rather evaded the question. Perfume, of course, often comes in thin vials. This glass, instead of being part of a bulb, may have been part of a vial.'

'Yes, that's so, too,' put in Graun, while the police surgeon, looking from one to the other, and obviously understanding little of what was forward, drummed on the polished surface of the desk with his nails.

'Well, what about all this, anyhow?' demanded he. 'I don't see that we're getting anywhere, Ashley, or that your "new evidence" is worth the powder to blow it.'

Ashley smiled dryly as he made answer.

'The one fact that destroys both possibilities of an incandescent light or a vial of perfume is that my laboratory tests give conclusive evidence that this glass has been in contact with a very highly poisonous substance.'

'What's that you say?' demanded Herrick, sharply, while Graun stared in astonishment. 'What kind of substance? Some liquid?'

'No, a gas. I tested it carefully, before coming here, and discovered that it had been exposed to CO_2 gas. Carbon dioxide, you know.'

'Carbon dioxide?' repeated Herrick. 'Are you sure?'

'Positive! As both you gentlemen know, it is a violent and fatal poison. When inhaled in any quantity, as, for example, from a vial, it produces a spasm of the glottis and immediate death.'

Dr Graun peered from beneath wrinkled brows at Ashley. Some understanding of the matter now seemed to have dawned on him.

'Extraordinary!' murmured he. 'This gives the case a new and decidedly sinister appearance. As things are shaping now, a good working hypothesis might be formed that after my departure last night somebody – under the pretence of having Mr Powell smell a vial said to contain some pleasing odour – caused him to inhale

CO_2. This, of course, would be premeditated murder. Murder in the first degree.'

There came a little silence in the office, for perhaps the space of half a dozen heartbeats. Then, asked Herrick:

'Would Mrs Estill have had any motive?'

'Gentlemen,' answered Graun, reluctantly, but with the air of a man doing his duty, 'there is one fact which I assume you have not been aware of, but which it is imperative for you to know. Do not misunderstand me as bringing any accusation, but merely take the fact for what it is worth, in connection with the others.'

'What fact, Doctor?' asked Herrick anxiously.

'This: that as a friend of some years' standing, Mr Powell several times informed me that he intended to recompense the housekeeper for many years of faithful service by leaving her a half interest in the estate – a matter, probably, of some sixty thousand dollars.'

'Ah, indeed,' said the police surgeon. 'This is getting interesting. I wish we'd had these facts at the inquest. Now we *are* coming on. Lord, what a wonderful proposition science is! So then, you say the old lady was to get half the estate?'

'Correct,' answered Graun, nodding.

'And the other half was to go to – '

'That I don't know. He never told me.'

'All right,' said Herrick. 'It looks as Mrs Estill was guilty, doesn't it? Now then, assuming that she really did do this murder, where the devil could she have got the knowledge or the means to carry it out? Would you judge that her intelligence was sufficient for such an undertaking?'

'Why, as for that,' put in Ashley, 'from even the little conversation I had with her, I analyzed her as a shrewd, canny woman. The matter seems to be clarifying itself, doesn't it?'

'I should say so!' ejaculated Herrick, while Dr Graun sat pondering, with half-closed eyes. Suddenly Graun spoke.

'With even these few data in hand,' said he, 'I think we can make a beginning towards a reconstruction of the crime.'

'More than a beginning,' supplemented Ashley. From the ping-pong box he took out the bats again, and with them the little celluloid balls. Taking a bat in each hand, he stood there looking at the police surgeon.

'You are familiar with this game, Dr Herrick?' asked he.

'Well, yes,' Herrick answered. 'I played it a few times, years ago, when it was all the rage.'

'Very good! Now please close your eyes and listen.'

Puzzled, Herrick obeyed. Ashley dropped a ball on to the hard surface of the desk. As it bounded, he struck it lightly with his right-hand bat. At the next rebound he hit it back again with the left. To and fro he bounced it, varying the rhythm of the strokes a little.

Tick-tack, tick-tack, tick-tack went the ball.

'Tell me, Dr Herrick,' said Ashley, 'as you sit there, without seeing what I am doing, could you by any possibility determine that one man is playing this game, and not two? Listen acutely and let me have your judgment.'

Herrick gave the problem his acute attention, while Graun bent forward with obvious interest and wonderingly observed the little bouncing sphere of celluloid.

'Well?' questioned Ashley. 'What do you say?'

Herrick opened his eyes and looked up questioningly at the investigator, who now stopped batting the ball and replaced it, with both bats, in the box.

'Bless my soul, but that's a curious deception!' he commented. 'I could have sworn two men were playing!'

'So far, so good,' smiled Ashley. 'Remember, Doctor, the finger prints on the bats indicate that they were both held for some time by one and the same individual.'

'I don't see just what you're driving at,' interpolated Graun, not seeming to understand at all.

'Ah, but you will in a minute,' Ashley assured him. 'Suppose we reconstruct the case, something like this. Follow me closely. Suppose that some person as yet unidentified, somebody with an interest in Mr Powell's death, gave him a vial of CO_2 last night to smell. Mr Powell died immediately, dropping the vial from his hand.

'His fall was undoubtedly eased to the floor by the person who murdered him, this person having, of course, been on the watch for just such a contingency. Then the murderer evidently brushed up the bits of broken and powdered glass, but couldn't quite get up all the powder, and also overlooked one tiny bit of glass – the one fragment which I know have in my box of cotton wool.'

'Very ingenious,' said the police surgeon, 'but would any such bizarre explanation hold water?'

'Wait till I have done,' answered the investigator, smiling again. 'The murderer proceeded to continue the ping-pong game and to carry on a pretence of conversation, altering his voice to imitate Mr Powell's. At some time, not determinable, he dragged the body to the window. The marks on the carpet amply prove that fact. He opened the window, slid the body over the sill, and let it drop into the soft earth of the flower-bed.

'All these suppositions, joined to the fact that Mr Powell's wound did not bleed and that the body gave some evidence that death had occurred previous to 11.30 last night, open up the way to some very entertaining speculations, do they not?'

Questioningly his eyes sought those of Dr Graun, who sat there looking at him with the same studious gaze as from the beginning of the conference. Herrick's eyes, too, drawn by a strange and dawning wonder, fixed themselves to Graun.

'Doctor,' asked he in a tense voice, 'what have you got to say about all this?'

'Pardon me,' answered Graun, 'but I think I'll just light a cigar.'

Speaking, he drew from his waistcoat pocket a thin black Havana.

'Please excuse me for not offering you gentlemen a smoke also,' said he with perfect calm, 'but this is the only one I happen to have. It's rather choice, too – something I have cured according to my own particular formula.'

He struck a match, lit the cigar and took three or four long pulls at it, each of which he inhaled deeply into his lungs and then blew forth into thin vapour.

'Very choice indeed,' he remarked. 'Highly valuable as an aid in answering difficult questions.'

His mouth sagged a little as he spoke, and a peculiar, glassy look came into his narrowed eyes.

'Just one or two things more, gentlemen,' said he. 'The will left by Mr Powell names a certain Frank Blaisdell as the joint heir with Mrs Estill. Mr Blaisdell was to turn over 75 per cent of the proceeds to me. He is in no way involved – a mere dummy I assure you. I state this to protect a weak, though an innocent man.'

'Good God! What are you saying?' ejaculated Herrick, starting up. Graun raised a quivering hand.

'Sit down,' he commanded, speaking thickly now and swaying a little in his chair. 'Silence, and listen to me! I have a wife and two children. They deserve your consideration. Don't forget that!'

Over his face a greyish hue was drawing, like a mask. The muscles of his lips were twitching, but he controlled them with a supreme effort.

'Let – let the verdict for Powell stand,' said Graun in a strange voice. 'And write the same for me – heart failure. Then Katherine and the children need never know. This cigar – wonderful, isn't it? The name of the drug in it is – but never mind . . . '

The last words came in hardly more than a whisper. Suddenly Graun slumped forward; his head dropped on his breast. He shuddered slightly and was still.

'For God's sake!' whispered Herrick, his voice tense as a wire. He shook Graun by the shoulder. The doctor's arm fell limp and dangled horribly.

Silence fell in the office.

All at once, turning to Ashley, the police surgeon gulped:

'What – what are we going to do? You've solved the case – you've won your spurs. If – '

'Spurs be damned!' retorted Ashley. 'Think I'd worry about spurs *now*, with that wife and those children to be saved? Heart failure it is in both cases. Just let it go at that.'

THE UNCONSIDERED TRIFLE

Brandon Fleming

THE two men faced each other. Neither spoke for some moments. Wilder, standing with clenched hands, was white and drawn. Ensor leant back in his chair, smoking quietly, his hard eyes fixed on Wilder's strained face.

Ensor spoke first.

'You can take it or leave it,' he said curtly. 'It's all you'll get.'

Wilder did not move. Ensor took up his glass from the small table by his chair and drank.

'Three hundred pounds – and be out of the country in two days. Those are my terms. I shan't alter them by a penny or an hour. Three hundred pounds and freedom – or certainly not less than five years' penal servitude.'

He put his glass down, and sat up impatiently.

'Well, which is it to be?'

Wilder's face whitened.

'*Three hundred* – when I have put more than as many thousands into the business! You have a great idea of fairness, George Ensor!'

'Those are my terms,' Ensor repeated. 'I will not discuss them any further. You can please yourself.'

'You are seizing this opportunity to force me out of the business and keep my capital for yourself,' Wilder exclaimed furiously.

Ensor shrugged his shoulders.

'People must pay for their crimes,' he retorted. 'I consider I am treating you very leniently. You have not only defrauded *me* as your partner, but you have misused – I put it mildly – money entrusted to the firm.'

'Your own dealings with the firm's money have not always been beyond suspicion,' Wilder sneered.

'Possibly not,' Ensor returned easily; 'but I have been wise enough to keep within the law – and you have been unwise enough to go outside it. That is the difference.'

'I have told you,' Wilder said eagerly, 'I will undertake to replace every penny I have taken within six months.'

Ensor rose.

'You have had my answer to that suggestion. I refuse. I will not allow you to have any further connection, directly or indirectly, with the business. You shall not enter the office again. I have given you the choice of two things. You must decide now which you are going to take.'

He turned away, and going to the open French windows, looked out into the dull, close night. Although there was a busy street within a hundred yards, a curious quietness seemed to hang over the garden. Perhaps the great trees all round shut out the sounds of the movement and traffic. The masses of foliage stood out just darker than the sky behind them, unmoving in the still air.

'The rain has stopped,' Ensor said.

He turned back.

'I can only give you another five minutes,' he said. 'Someone is coming to see me at ten.'

'A woman, I suppose?' Wilder retorted.

Ensor smiled unpleasantly.

'It is possible! A very foolish one – who has been almost as unwise in her way as you have been in yours. I am afraid the interview will be a trying one.'

If he had noticed the change that sprang into Wilder's face, the sudden alertness, the narrowing of the eyes, he might have taken warning. But he had gone back to the table and drained his glass. Wilder controlled himself with an effort.

'So that is why your household staff have all been sent out for the evening?' he said slowly. 'To leave you a clear field for your – er – interview with the lady?'

Sudden anger blazed into Ensor's face.

'Please leave my private affairs alone,' he said harshly. 'You have quite enough to do to look after your own.'

Wilder laughed.

'It would be interesting to know her errand – at this time of night,' he said carelessly.

They looked at each other steadily. Ensor was hard and lowering.

'My terms have changed,' he said deliberately. 'They are now *two* hundred, instead of three. You have one minute to make up your mind.'

He turned his back on Wilder, and began to pour himself out another drink. The face of the man behind him was convulsed with an expression of savage hatred. His hands were so tightly clenched that the veins stood out on them like cords. On his left there was a table of Oriental curios.

His fingers closed over the hilt of a long, curved knife. . . .

Ensor drank, and put his glass down. The sound of a movement caused him to turn quickly. He saw Wilder's livid face . . . the knife in his hand.

'You fool!' he cried sharply. 'Put that thing down!'

He drew back, putting out his hands to ward off the blow . . . too late. A dreadful tearing pain . . . he crumpled up, choking, on the floor . . .

Wilder stood still, looking down at the body. His first sensation was one of a curious surprise at what had happened.

Ensor was dead. He, Richard Wilder, had killed him. A murderer. . . .

He passed a hand across his forehead. He was a murderer. He had taken up that ugly curved knife with the deliberate intention of killing Ensor . . . and driven it home with pitiless strength. The knife remained in the wound, the handle jutting out from the huddled figure on the floor. A dark stain was spreading on the carpet.

He drew back. He was rather pleased at his own coolness.

He felt no regret or remorse for what he had done. It was Ensor's own fault. The fool had driven him to it. It served him right for attempting to force him out of his fair share of the business. For a moment he even felt a little proud of this demonstration that he was not to be taken advantage of in such a fashion. Ensor was the only man in the world who had known of his defalcations. There was no one else. And Ensor was dead.

He glanced at the clock on the mantelpiece. It was five minutes to ten. In another five minutes this woman, whoever she was, would come.

He looked round carefully. There were one or two signs of his own presence to be removed. He pushed the chair he had sat upon back to its usual position, and smoothed the cushions. He did not intend to make any mistake. There would be no clue to point to himself. He took out his handkerchief and carefully wiped the handle of the knife without disturbing it. Then he went on quickly to wipe everything else he might have touched.

Putting the handkerchief back into his pocket he made another careful scrutiny of the room. There were many famous cases in which some stupid little point had been overlooked, and had led to detection – something that a child should not have neglected. He would not be caught like that. He was going to be much too careful. There should be no unconsidered trifle, no fatal little slip.

Nothing whatever to suggest that he had been in the room, or in the house. . . .

At the door he stopped for a final glance round. Not a thing there that could point to Richard Wilder. . . . Not one. He took out his handkerchief again and put it over the handle of the door before he opened it. In the dark hall he felt his way to the table and took up his hat. Cautiously opening the front door, he slipped out of the house. For a moment he stood still, listening, his senses almost painfully taut.

Then he crept quickly round by the wall.

The house stood some way back from the road, and was well hidden by trees and a high fence. There was a semi-circular drive from one gate to another. Wilder went round to the garage yard where he had left his car. Standing by it he made certain that no one approaching the house by either of the gates could see it. Then he went on further round to the far corner at the back of the house where he could watch the library windows.

It was a desperate chance, but he did not hesitate. He felt perfectly safe. He was quite sure he had not overlooked the unconsidered trifle.

He saw the girl come round the opposite corner of the house and slip in through the library window. He had expected that. Ensor's manner when he had looked out into the garden after the rain had told him that it had been arranged that the visitor should come that way. He slipped back to the front of the house and hurried down the drive.

He knew there was a police station a few yards round the corner in the main street. He went in and asked for the inspector in charge.

The inspector in charge was consuming a cup of coffee and a sandwich.

'Well, sir, what can I do for you?'

Wilder's manner showed just a sufficient shade of anxiety.

'Inspector, I'm afraid there may be something wrong at Mr Ensor's house round the corner. I had an appointment to call at ten o'clock, but I couldn't make anyone hear. There are no lights in the front, and the whole place seems to be deserted.'

He paused for a moment.

'My name is Wilder. I am Mr Ensor's partner. We had important business to discuss tonight. Will you send someone back with me to investigate?'

The inspector reached for his hat.

'I'll come with you myself, sir. I know Mr Ensor.'

They hurried to the house. The dark shape of it loomed out against the pale sky. There seemed to be something particularly black and sinister about it. The inspector rang and knocked loudly. He opened the letter-box and listened. There was no sound in the house.

'Don't like the look of it,' he muttered.

He rang again.

'What can have happened to the servants?' Wilder whispered. 'There were three of them.'

The inspector turned away from the door.

'I'm going round to the back,' he said. 'There's something wants looking into here.'

They went quietly round the house.

'There's a light in the library,' Wilder said softly. 'The window is open.'

The inspector signed him to silence, and crept noiselessly up to the window. Wilder followed him. They peered round into the room. The body of Ensor was hidden from them by the couch and the armchair he had been sitting on.

The girl was standing at Ensor's desk, rapidly running through the contents of the drawers. It was evident that the knocking at the front door had alarmed her, for she was scattering the papers right and left, pausing once or twice to listen intently. She was wrapped in a dark cloack, and a small black hat framed a face that was strikingly beautiful in spite of its deathly whiteness.

They saw her glance down, shuddering, at something on the floor, her eyes wide with horror. Then the inspector stepped into the room, Wilder behind him.

The girl screamed and shrank back, staring at them terror-stricken.

'What do you want?' she gasped faintly.

Before the inspector could speak a startled shout came from Wilder.

'My God, look there!'

He knelt on the floor.

'It's Ensor!' he cried. 'Stabbed!'

The inspector looked down at the huddled figure, then at the white face of the girl.

'From the look of it,' he returned grimly, 'I should say I want *you*.'

He turned back, and, closing the windows, fastened them securely.

'You stay where you are, young lady,' he ordered. 'Don't move an inch!'

Wilder looked up.

'He's quite dead,' he said slowly. He got up unsteadily. For a moment he seemed to be dazed. 'Poor fellow,' he muttered. 'It's dreadful. . . . '

He turned to the girl.

'In heaven's name, how did you come to do such a terrible thing?'

She came closer to them. There was something very like madness in her eyes.

'I didn't do it!' she cried wildly. 'I never touched him!'

Wilder shrugged his shoulders.

'I am afraid it seems pretty obvious,' he said curtly.

The inspector had been bending over the body. Then he straightened himself, and looked steadily at the girl.

'It's my duty to warn you,' he said stolidly, 'that anything you say may be used in evidence.'

She brought her hands together desperately. Her voice rose almost to a scream.

'I tell you I didn't kill him! I swear I didn't! He was lying there when I came in.'

The inspector took out his notebook.

'You were going through his papers,' he said sharply. 'You aren't denying *that*, I suppose?'

She put a hand on the back of a chair to steady herself. She was shaking pitifully.

'I was looking for something,' she murmured weakly.

'What?'

She was silent.

'You'd better not try to hide anything,' the inspector warned her. 'Your best chance is to tell us the whole truth.'

She leant heavily on the chair.

'I was looking . . . for a letter.'

'That you had written to Mr Ensor?'

It seemed for a moment as if she was going to faint. But she controlled herself with a great effort.

'Yes . . . I wrote it to him.'

Then suddenly she stood upright, flooded with passion, her eyes blazing with fierce anger.

'He forced me to come here tonight,' she cried. 'It was my only chance to get the letter back. He said if I didn't come he'd pass it on to . . . someone else.'

Her voice broke.

'He was wicked and cruel,' she sobbed. 'He didn't care how much unhappiness he brought on other people. I didn't kill him – but I'm glad he's dead!'

Again she faced them defiantly. 'You can do what you like to me!' she cried recklessly. 'I tell you I'm glad he's dead! I'm glad! I'm glad!'

She covered her face with her hands, sobbing wildly.

'Steady on,' the inspector said, not unkindly. 'You'd better not talk like that.'

He turned to Wilder.

'Well, sir, you were his partner – what do you think about it?'

'I can't understand it,' Wilder returned slowly. 'I did not know very much about his private life, but I certainly had no grounds for suspecting such things as this lady suggests. It is a complete surprise to me.'

The inspector closed his notebook, and put it back in his pocket.

'Suppose she was telling the truth, and he really *was* lying there when she came in. . . . '

The girl uncovered her face, looking at him eagerly.

'He was!' she cried. 'I swear to you he was!'

The inspector silenced her.

'Assuming it to be true for the moment, can you, from your knowledge of him, make any suggestion?'

Wilder shook his head.

'I'm afraid I can't,' he said regretfully. 'For her own sake I should be glad to be able to think that it *was* true – but it really seems too plain. Of course, it's *possible*. . . . ' He made a reluctant gesture. 'But as it stands there doesn't seem much room for doubt.'

The girl sank weakly into a chair, and again buried her face in her hands. The inspector stood looking down at her for a moment. Then he went nearer to Wilder.

'You feel satisfied about it yourself?' he asked, in a low tone.

'I am afraid I must be,' Wilder replied. 'I'm sorry for the girl, but it seems a perfectly clear case.'

'I admit it's clear enough,' the Inspector agreed, 'and yet – '

He looked at the girl again.

'I don't like it,' he confessed frankly. 'I can't help feeling there's something deeper in it. I've had a good deal of experience with witnesses, and I believe she's telling the truth. The worst of it is, on the face of it I haven't any option but to arrest her and charge her with the murder.'

Wilder's face expressed genuine anxiety.

'I don't see how you can help it,' he agreed. 'I will give you all the assistance I can in any direction, but on the evidence you have now I am afraid you cannot do anything but take her in charge at once.'

The inspector scratched his head with his pencil.

'I suppose there's a telephone here, sir?'

'It's in the hall,' Wilder replied.

'I wonder if you'd be kind enough,' the inspector suggested softly, 'to ring up the station – Burnwell 439 – and tell Constable Martin to run over to Doctor Singleton's house, and bring him along here at once? I don't want to leave her.'

'Certainly,' Wilder said.

He went out of the room. When he had closed the door behind him, his face was transformed by an expression of savage exultation. In the reaction of the moment he had to check an inclination to laugh out loud. Luck had been with him all the way; luck and his own astuteness. All he had to do was to play his part out.

He felt no pity for the girl, no remorse. All his life he had been supremely selfish, entirely without scruple. He had always been content if the blame for his own misdoings fell on someone else.

The thought that was uppermost in his mind as he took up the telephone receiver was that now the business was all his; his own defalcations could be covered up; he could use or misuse as he wished. . . .

He gave the inspector's message to the police station, and went back to the room.

The girl had fainted when the inspector told her she would be charged with the murder of George Ensor. When Wilder returned the inspector was trying to revive her with whisky from the bottle on the table, but she did not recover until the doctor and the constable arrived.

'We'll leave Martin here with the doctor, and get her to the station,' the inspector said to Wilder. 'I'll have to question her pretty fully. Perhaps you wouldn't mind coming too, in case any questions crop up that you could help us with.'

'Certainly I'll come with you,' Wilder replied. 'I've got my car here. We can run round in it.'

The inspector took the girl's arm, and led her out of the room. She obeyed mechanically, staring out straight in front of her. She seemed to be dazed and weak.

Wilder opened the front door.

'The car is in the yard,' he said. 'Ensor did not like cars to be left in front of the house.'

They went round to the yard. The girl leant heavily on the inspector's arm. She had almost to be lifted into the back of the car, and sank on to the seat as if exhausted. The inspector shut the door on her, and strolled round the front of the car, while Wilder started up the engine.

Suddenly he took his electric torch from his pocket and, stooping down, flashed the light under the car.

Wilder jumped out and came to him quickly.

'What are you doing?' he demanded sharply.

The inspector straightened himself, and put the torch back into his pocket. He looked steadily at Wilder.

'It is nearly an hour, Mr Wilder,' he said quietly, 'Since the rain stopped. It lasted for about three-quarters of an hour.'

'Well?' Wilder said.

The inspector's eyes were fixed on his face.

'It is just over half an hour since you came to the police station.'

'Well?' Wilder said again.

The inspector took a step closer to him.

'The ground under the car is perfectly dry,' he said slowly. 'It was put here before the rain began. When you came to the station and told me that you could not make anyone hear, Mr Wilder, you had been at this house not less than an hour and a quarter. It would be interesting to know what you were doing.'

Wilder's face blanched. For an instant his head swam. He stared at the Inspector, a white horror growing in his face.

The unconsidered trifle. . . .

He stood perfectly still. The inspector's hand closed on his wrist.

'I told you I believed she was speaking the truth. . . . '

He uttered a savage oath, and tried to wrench himself free. He heard the girl scream as the inspector bent him over backwards and pinned him down on the ground.

THE PERFECT CRIME

Ormond Greville

FARMER Greenwood, a big, stout, red-faced man, was in a disputatious mood, and the other men in the billiard room of the Parish Hall, though they never allowed themselves to smile, were thoroughly enjoying the fun. He had had a glass, as the saying is, and had finished a very erratic game of billiards, and now he was expressing his opinions more freely than usual.

'You chaps all think Parson's a saint. Jumping Jehoshaphat! I'll lay he's much like the rest of us, and we aren't saints that I know of – not even you, Dick Burge, not by a long chalk!'

Dick Burge, who was, amongst other things, parish clerk, undertaker and a contractor in a small way, winked at the others and said, 'Don't know as I ever set up to be, Mr Greenwood. But Parson's nigher to being a saint than anyone *I* ever see.' He puffed at his pipe and added, 'And I've seen a lot of men who ought to have been – three bishops, two deans, and a score of archdeacons, canons and suchlike. Lor' bless me, when it becomes a matter of a talk with Saint Peter, they'll have more to explain away than Parson, and you may lay your shirt on that!'

'You're just like a lot of females,' said the farmer contemptuously, 'taken in by a good-looking face. You're like my missus, who talks to me about his health and says he don't eat enough. Why, I've heard her chatter to my Jane about his lovely voice and eyes and his beautiful smile! She says he's like St Paul! Pah! Why, he's as strong as a young horse, and no more like St Paul than I am.'

Joe Harris, the blacksmith and motor-agent, remarked here:

'I never heard that St Paul was as strong as Samson. But what have you got against Parson, anyway, Mr Greenwood?'

Greenwood finished his glass before replying.

'Well,' he said, 'I've not got nothin' agin him, except that ever since he came to Oldthorpe, nine years ago come midsummer, everyone in the parish talks as if he was perfect, and as for the women, they're clean daft about him!'

Dick Burge put in, 'But he never gives any of them a look, for all the eyes they make at him – you'll allow that, although he hasn't a wife to look after him, like you have, Mr Greenwood!'

'Confound the man!' said the farmer, 'I know that. He can't be caught out in anything, drat him, that's what makes me mad. It's not human nature for a man not to smoke, *nor* drink, *nor* swear, *nor* have his bit of fun with the girls, nor do nothin' at all. I've always found that the men who set up to be plaster saints have a secret somewhere! Jumping Jehoshaphat! I'll lay this one's the same. . . . '

But Bill Hackett, who was a retired builder and said to be the warmest man in the village, broke in here, and told Greenwood that he ought to be ashamed of himself.

'That's as may be,' said Greenwood. 'I'm no plaster saint!' and as some reminiscence in proof of that assertion smote him, he began to roll about with laughter.

He then ordered drinks for all of them, still highly amused with his thoughts, the nature of which the others seemed to understand, for one of them observed: 'We all know what you were, Jim Greenwood, in the time of Parson Gregory.'

'Why,' said Joe Harris, 'look at the words you used to rap out.' He proceeded to point out that since Parson Quaile got at him, his favourite oath had taken the place of a much more blasphemous one. This accusation was met by Greenwood with gusts of laughter and the assertion that he didn't mind obliging anyone who was civil, even a parson.

'But he gets you to church,' said Dick Burge.

'When it's too wet to get about the farm,' said Greenwood, and added, 'but I don't deny he can preach. What a gift for talking! It's as good as a play to listen to him.'

And then Bill Hackett interposed by asking Burge whether there would be anything said by the parson at the funeral of Joshua Pook the next day.

They all had known Joshua Pook, who had recently died at his comfortable house in the parish. He was an auctioneer and estate agent, with offices in the Cathedral town, only three or four miles from Oldthorpe.

'I don't know,' replied Burge. 'What could he say about him, anyway, though he was once a sidesman, to be sure?'

And then they proceeded to make comments on Mr Pook, from which it became apparent that they none of them had either liked or respected him, for all the many years he had lived among them. Mr Hackett observed that his reputation for honesty in the town was such that no man trusted him a yard.

'He's no loss to anyone so far as I can see.'

'And I don't think Parson cared for him much,' said Dick Burge. 'I saw them talking a short time ago after Church, and I thought to myself that Parson couldn't abide him.'

And this brought them to the old topic, and they were still discussing it when closing time came, and they all went out into the windy night.

The subject of this discussion, the Reverend George Theophilus Quaile, was peacefully writing in his study at the Oldthorpe Rectory. He had long been engaged on a life of Julian the Apostate, but it was advancing slowly owing to the many demands of his parish on his time. For there was never a more conscientious rector, and it was quite unusual for him to find that he could give two consecutive hours to his history.

The work had been started originally as a kind of sedative. It kept away distressing thoughts: it occupied any spare time before he felt the need of sleep: it helped him to secure peaceful slumber. The interest of the subject had taken possession of his mind, and he sometimes blamed himself for thinking of the complex character and perplexing motives of the Roman Emperor when he ought to have been thinking of his next sermon.

It was a simply furnished room, with a low ceiling, which Quaile could touch with his hand, when he stood upright, for he was over six feet in height. The only remaining work of the builders was a beautiful Queen Anne fireplace. The windows had been converted into Gothic by a clerical disciple of Horace Walpole. The walls were completely covered with books in every sort of binding and every kind of condition. There were a couple of old oars fastened against the cornice, evidence of successes on the Cam twenty years before. Almost the only furniture was a very long, narrow table of oak, littered with books, papers, two heavy inkstands, an ebony ruler, a couple of candlesticks, a lamp and a Bible-box.

A log fire was burning in the grate and there was a pile of logs beside it. The Rector's reputation for strength in the neighbourhood was largely due to the fact that he was accustomed to fell and trim his own trees in a wood which formed part of the glebe, and it was a subject of talk in the parish, not unmixed with pride, that he could wield a woodman's axe as well or better than any professional.

It was nearly midnight when he gave a sigh and rose to his feet. He had finished the important chapter dealing with the massacre of Alexandria, and the behaviour of Julian to Athanasius. He threw a few more logs on the fire, for he still had an hour's work before him on the parish accounts, and, lighting an old pipe, gave himself up to reflection.

Unexpectedly, he found he was happier than he had been since his university days. He had got the parish into something like reasonable order. There were no crying scandals and the poor were decently housed. He had as many offers of assistance and of money as he could do with. The Bishop, a man chary of praise, had been more than complimentary of late. The parish church was crowded on Sundays, and he was accustomed to preach, either there or elsewhere, including the Cathedral, to a rapt congregation. His reputation in the diocese was spotless. Indeed, he could not help knowing that he was talked of by enthusiasts as if he were a saint.

His lips, at this thought, formed a sardonic smile. For the Reverend Theophilus Quaile had not always been a pattern among men. At Cambridge, and for a few years afterwards, he had been more than gay, if not worse. The hedonist had become an ascetic suddenly, as the result of a tragic occurrence which had nearly driven him to suicide; and he was only just able, now, after fifteen years, to think calmly of the terrible incident of the death of Margaret Powell in his rooms after a Covent Garden Ball. He saw her again in the eyes of the mind with all her remarkable loveliness and charm; and he was still filled with love, pity and remorse.

No one could condemn him as severely as he condemned himself. A lifetime of devotion to others could hardly, he thought to himself, atone. The coroner's inquest was still a nightmare in the retrospect, and the bribing of three Press reporters to suppress their copy was a distasteful close to a horrible morning. . . . And then, after some long weeks of misery, when death would have been welcome, he found peace in religion and social service. If this is to be called a conversion, he had experienced it. . . .

And then, some years later, after taking Orders, and after he had become Rector of Oldthorpe, and when he had thought confidently that the past was buried except in his own heart, Joshua Pook came on the scene. He had become an inhabitant of the parish and was accustomed to drive daily into the town to conduct a doubtful, if not a disreputable business as an auctioneer. The Rector, who had heard of his reputation, had tried to avoid him as far as possible: but one day Joshua Pook had sought a private interview, and then a blow had fallen on poor Quaile.

By what seemed a most untoward chance, Pook was a half-brother of Margaret, and he had made it his business to know the whole terrible story. His arrival and settlement in Oldthorpe was not an accident. He was in great straits for money, and partly by appeals to the Rector's feelings, and partly by putting his claim as one for compensation, he had induced him to pay him money. In some strange and illogical way the Rector felt that he was making atonement and expiation.

Once this fatal step was taken the rest was easy. More pressure was brought to bear, and more money was paid. Finally the Rector, who wanted every penny of his income for his parish, struck, and said he would pay no more. Pook then resorted to the open method of blackmail. The story he was in a position to tell was a scandalous one: with his own embellishments it would sound terrible.

The Rector cared little for himself; but his influence in the parish was as necessary to him as life itself. After a struggle, he gave in on the terms of paying an annual sum to Pook. And now Pook was dead, and he was to be buried next day.

The Rector felt that a cloud had been lifted from his brain. The secret was to be buried with the auctioneer. The book was getting on. He loved his work. He felt younger and stronger than he had felt for years.

He sat down at his table, and, taking the ebony ruler, he had just drawn a line along a sheet of foolscap paper when he heard a tap at the window.

He looked up, fancying that it might be caused by the wind; but it was repeated. He went to the window and, drawing back the curtain, opened it. He saw a man dimly made visible by the light of the room.

The man said, 'It's Longhurst, James Longhurst,' and added, 'Mr Pook's clerk.'

'What do you want here at this time of night? Is it something to do with the funeral?'

'Nothing to do with that, at least, not exactly, governor; but it's something private, deadly private, and I've come at this hour to make sure of a private interview.'

The Rector paused. He could not imagine what the man wanted. But late as it was, it might be of importance. He was not a man to feel any fear, or to be swayed by considerations of prudence, so he said: 'Well, I'll let you in, though you might have come earlier.'

And in a few moments he was back in his room, looking at an undersized, rat-like man, with ferrety eyes and ginger hair.

'Sit down,' said the Rector, 'and tell me what I can do for you.'

Longhurst looked round the room, twisting a cloth cap in his hands, as if uncertain how to begin.

'It's perishing cold outside,' he said, looking at the fire.

'Well,' said the Rector, 'warm yourself at the fire and tell me your private business.'

Longhurst went to the fire, which was blazing, and after cramming his cap into a pocket, held his hands to it, looking back over his shoulder towards the Rector.

'Pretty snug here,' he said; 'there isn't such a thing as a drink handy, I suppose?'

'You can have a glass of water,' was the reply. 'I don't drink either beer or spirits myself, and there are, I believe, none in the house.'

'Gosh!' said the man. 'Water? I don't call that a drink.'

'Well,' said the Rector with a smile, 'the sooner you tell me your business, the sooner you will be back home where I suppose there is what you would call a drink. So speak on!'

'It's deadly private, governor! That's why I've walked out at this time of night, unbeknownst to a living soul.'

'The servants have been in bed and asleep for about three hours, and there's no one to listen. Come! What is it about?'

'It's about Josh Pook, whom you're burying tomorrow.'

'Well, what about him?' said the Rector.

'You used to pay him a hundred and fifty a year,' said the man, looking quickly over his left shoulder to see how the Rector would take this statement.

There was a long pause.

'And what has that to do with you?' said the Rector at last.

'I know what you paid it for.'

The blow had fallen, and a number of wholly unpleasant thoughts raced through the Rector's mind.

'Well?' he said.

Longhurst did not at first reply. He seemed to be in doubt as to how to continue the interview. At last he turned round from the fire and said, 'There's nothing extra to be gained by beating about the bush! You've got to continue the annuity to me.'

'Why should I?'

'For the same reason.'

'And what is that?'

'Silence, I guess,' said Longhurst.

The Rector rose to his feet quickly and advanced towards the man who, shrinking back and putting a hand in his pocket, cried out, 'Don't touch me! I've a revolver in my pocket.'

The Rector stopped.

'You worm!' he said. 'Did you think I was going to dirty my hands on you?'

'Now, now,' said the man, 'there's nothing to be gained by that kind of talk. You're up against it and you'd better take it quietly.'

The Rector sat down again.

'Go on,' he said, 'I'm listening.' And taking up the ruler, he began ruling some fresh lines for his accounts.

Longhurst produced from his inside pocket some flimsy paper.

'I found these while turning out a private drawer of Mr Pook's yesterday. They seemed interesting and I read them. Golly! Oh, what a surprise! Scandal about the Reverend Theophilus Quaile! Spicy stuff, too! And all ready for the newspapers. And all about the Reverend Quaile who preaches religion and moral sob-stuff in the Cathedral, and who hobnobs with the Bishop. I've seen him myself. Why, the copy's worth a guinea a line to the *P____ Gazette* or to the *True Briton*! But more to you, governor, a precious sight more!'

The Rector made no reply.

'Come,' said the man, 'I'll read you a bit,' and he proceeded to read a sensational account of the tragedy, full of imaginary conversations and inaccurate detail.

The Rector paused for a moment in his work, holding the ruler tightly in his right hand.

Longhurst went on reading extracts here and there. He came to a description of Margaret, and smacked his lips over it.

'Be quiet!' said the Rector, in a low, emphatic voice.

Longhurst went on with a coarse laugh. The Rector rose to his feet.

'She seems to have been hot stuff,' said Longhurst, 'and I'll bet a monkey you and she . . . '

The sentence was never finished.

The Rector never knew exactly how it happened. The act was instinctive. With the ruler he had struck, as if to fell the man to the earth. He moved his head and received the blow on his temple. He sank down, a heap of dirty clothes.

The Rector stood looking at the body for a long time without touching it.

He then stooped and found with his hand that the heart had ceased to beat. He got a small mirror and placed it before the man's open mouth. There was no sign of moisture on the glass. It was true, then; he had killed the blackmailer.

He felt no regret, but an enormous disquietude. What was to be done?

The Rector was a man with great powers of imagination. As he sat down again at his table, he visualized in a series of scenes – as if he were looking at a film, all that would follow if he straightway informed the police of everything that had happened. He saw the embarrassed village policemen arriving, the sergeant coming later, the questions put to him and his answers, his arrest, his interview with the inspector of police in the town, the inside of the jail! Would they allow him bail? He thought not. And then he saw himself as the principal figure at the inquest, with hundreds of curious people of both sexes staring at him, and he heard his own answers to the pitiless questions put to him by a hatchet-faced counsel, who seemed not to understand his terrible anxiety not to say anything which might tarnish the reputation of Margaret.

His mind made a jump to his trial in the assize court by a small, red-faced judge, before a jury of men (and two women), who looked like half-wits. He heard his conviction for manslaughter; for his mind refused to think of another possibility, and then the sentence of the judge, in solemn tones. The warder touched him on the shoulder and he walked down some stairs to a prison van.

And then he was in prison for an interminable time, with degraded fellow-prisoners, callous warders, and – a curious freak of his mind – a low-church prison chaplain who cordially disliked him, the exact counterpart of the only clergyman with whom the Rector had ever had a quarrel. The chaplain's visits and conversation were almost more than the Rector could bear. . . .

And then he saw himself having a final interview with the governor of the prison, and walking out of the gates. . . .

One or two sympathetic friends came to meet him, but their honest sympathy showed him the depth to which he had fallen. . . . He was given to understand that he had no future as one of the working clergy in England. His only chance was to begin life over again; preferably in the colonies.

The Rector at this point struck the table with the fatal ruler, and exclaimed aloud, 'By Heaven, I will not give up my work here. I would sooner die!'

He turned his gaze to the untidy object between him and the fireplace. The body, the body! The only obstacle! How could it be made to disappear – and disappear for ever?

He drew nearer to it and, turning it over, looked steadily at the weak, futile, vicious face. His imagination pictured for him the man's life. He thought, as he had often thought of others, 'Poor foolish wretch! Perhaps he never in all his life had a single decent friend.' His anger left him and was replaced by his accustomed sympathy for erring mankind.

He paused, and then said in a low, determined tone, 'He must have Christian burial!'

And upon this thought, all things became clear to the priest, and his further acts seemed to follow an inevitable course, as if, indeed, they were those of an automaton guided by an exterior will.

Taking the body in his arms as easily as if it were a child, he walked with it to the front door and let himself out.

The wind had got up, and the many elms in the garden were

moaning in the gale; but it was not raining. He walked to the garage and placed the body in the back of the old car. He covered it with the rug.

He drove out of the door, and then stopped. He shut the door and got from the neighbouring tool-house and potting-shed a spade, a pick, a piece of rope and two sacks.

The churchyard was little more than a hundred yards away. He drove slowly without lights. The lane was completely desolate. He parked the car in a dark lane under some overhanging trees and entered the churchyard.

The wind was still rising and seemed to threaten the stability of the trees, and the clouds, fitfully visible by the light of a setting moon, were scudding across the sky. The Rector took his tools and walked quickly to the side of the newly dug grave destined to receive, in a few hours, the mortal remains of Joshua Pook. It was close to a row of elms, and the place was so dark that, except at moments when the moon gave a faint light, the Rector could scarcely see the ancient and lofty church spire thirty or forty yards away. The sexton had covered the opening with planks, which the Rector removed. He took one, however, and placed it across the middle of the opening, and with its assistance lowered himself into the grave and began to dig.

Fortunately, digging was an occupation to which he was accustomed, or strong as he was, he would soon have been exhausted. As it was, the thought occurred to him, after half an hour's work, that the sexton was not overpaid. For the first time since the fatal interview he smiled.

At one end of the opening he was much troubled with the roots of a tree, and he was glad he had brought the pick. He worked hard, and it did not seem to him very long before he had excavated about two feet of soil. With the aid of the plank he swung himself up. The keen air seemed to go through him, and he wiped his forehead and put on the coat which he had removed.

When he reached the car, he found that the body was beginning to get stiff; but he managed, without much difficulty, to place it at full length beside the grave. He went back for the rope and the stable lantern. He tied the rope under the arms of the body and, standing at one end of the grave, he carefully lowered it down.

Taking the stable lantern he went down himself, untied the rope
and arranged the corpse in its final resting place.

It did not take more than a few minutes to shovel the soil down,
so that the body was covered to the extent of over a foot. He trod
the soil firmly down over it and smoothed it over with the spade.
After a careful examination, by the light of the lantern, he hoisted
himself out, filled the two sacks with excavated soil, and rearranged
the planks and the earth, leaving everything round the grave just as
he had found it. He carried his two sacks to the car.

There was a running stream close to the road side, and there he
emptied his sacks of soil. He drove home very slowly, for he thought
there might be trees down across the road, but he only encountered
some moderate sized branches.

The gale was dropping when he reached the Rectory garage. He
cleaned out the car, replaced the sacks and the rope, and returned
to the house. By the old clock in the hall he noted that it was
quarter-past four. Except for its loud ticking the house was silent,
as silent as the grave. When the trite phrase crossed his mind, he
shuddered.

He entered the sitting-room, where the lamp was still burning;
everything was as he left it, except that there were only a few bright
embers in the hearth. Its familiar appearance gave him a sense of
tightening at the heart; it seemed to him that he had been away a
year and was returning a different man. He tidied up his desk and
carefully wiped the ebony ruler. The hearth-rug showed no signs
of any unusual happening. He removed some dirt from his shoes
and brushed his clothes before going to bed.

He slept a dreamless sleep.

The funeral of Joshua Pook, which took place at midday, attracted
a large congregation. Nearly every adult in the parish came, for the
dead man, though not a favourite, had been a resident among them
for a long time and, moreover, there was curiosity to hear what the
Rector could find to say about him.

He said nothing beyond the words of the service for the burial of
the dead, which he uttered in his magnificent voice and in his usual
impressive manner. The female members of the assembly noticed,
however, that he looked paler and more ascetic than ever; and Mrs
Greenwood and several others wished that they were allowed to

look after him. When he came to the words, 'Thou knowest, O Lord, the secrets of our hearts,' he made an unusual pause. The men present thought that he was reflecting on the guilty secrets of the deceased sinner; but in this they were mistaken. When the coffin was brought to the grave the Rector, standing at the head of it, was noticed to look down into the opening – as if there was something to be seen at the bottom. But, of course, there was nothing! The coffin was lowered down in the customary way. 'Earth to earth, dust to dust, ashes to ashes. . . . '

That night, a little after eleven, Farmer Greenwood, Bill Hackett, Joe Harris and Dick Burge were walking homewards together from the parish room. Their way led past the churchyard, and not very far from the spot where they had attended the burial of Joshua Pook and where there was now an oblong mound of soil. Not unnaturally they looked towards the spot, and to their surprise they saw beside it a kneeling figure. They stopped and gazed, open-mouthed.
'It's the Parson,' said Joe Harris.
'Praying, begad!' said Greenwood.
'Beside the grave of Pook,' said Hackett.
They were silent while they took in the fact; and then they made their respective comments, which were terse.
'Holy Moses!' said Hackett.
'That scalliwag!' said Joe Harris.
'That's why!' said Dick Burge.
'Jumping Jehoshaphat!' said the farmer.
And they walked on, ruminating on the incident.
How were they to know that the Reverend Theophilus Quaile had committed the perfect crime, never to be discovered by man, and was now praying to God for forgiveness?

THE JIGSAW

Leonard R. Gribble

M Y first recollection of the case is sitting at my desk at New Scotland Yard going through a pile of statements in the case of the Countess of B——'s stolen necklace. It was an evening in early autumn, and Trench was lolling back in his well-worn leather chair glooming at the wall. As usual, a cold pipe was between his teeth, and his thumbs were tucked in the arm-holes of his waistcoat. It was invariably his favourite attitude when meditating, and the truth is it rather suited his ponderous bulk. He was a thinker, not an athlete; many a time I have heard him state his belief in personal comfort as an aid to concentrated thought.

I remember that I was reading the first statement made by the second footman on the night of the robbery, when the telephone rang. The call was for Trench, and I passed the instrument to him. He took it and growled, 'Hullo.' The next moment he was sitting upright, a pencil in his right hand, taking down some notes. I heard him say, 'Very good, sir,' and then the receiver clicked in its cradle and he rose.

'We've got to go to Finchley,' he announced as he took his overcoat from the peg. 'Fellow found with his head bashed in, and the locals have found some useful footprints under an open window. Sounds like a case of possibilities.'

I followed him to where his car was parked in Derby Street, and stowed our attaché-case of equipment under the rear seat. He drove rapidly, and within twenty-five minutes of our receiving that telephone call Trench was speaking to the divisional inspector who had hurried from the Finchley station. I walked with them up a curving gravel path leading between high laurel hedges to a dark-fronted house with deep gables and high porch. Only one light burned in the front of the house, that which threw a murky gleam from the hall transom. The divisional man, whose name was Bellowes, took us through the hall to a room opening on to the garden.

'This is the room where he was found by his manservant,' Bellowes explained. 'It's a sort of library and study combined, and he practically lived in it.'

Bookcases lined two walls and a pair of French windows gave on to the garden. On an old fashioned roll-top desk a green-shaded desk-lamp, tilted, threw a wide shaft of light upon the crumpled figure of a man. The body was slumped backward in a chair with a curved back. Blood streaked the pale face, and soaked into one of the man's shoulders. His hair was whitish grey, and his age, at first glance, I should have put at about fifty-five.

'That's the weapon,' went on Bellowes, pointing to a heavy poker lying on the carpet. 'There's hair and blood sticking to the end.'

Trench asked him the usual questions about the man's age and occupation, and Bellowes told him what he had learned from the dead man's servant, which was not much. Mr Stephen Armitage, the dead man, had been in the habit of dining at the early hour of six-thirty. Always he dined alone. That evening when the manservant – his name was the peculiar one of Biffin – cleared the table at about seven o'clock he was given strict instructions to see that his master was not disturbed. Mr Armitage had retired to his study. That was shortly after seven. About quarter past eight the cook found occasion to visit the shed in the garden. She was searching for some kitchen utensil that had been mislaid. On her way she noticed that the French windows were open. She reported this to Biffin, who went into the garden to reconnoitre. Mr Armitage was an artist, and sometimes indulged in personal eccentricities, and Biffin had learned from experience not to intrude; but upon this occasion he had thought it wise to make sure that the windows had been left open purposely. He had received a shock upon tiptoeing to the windows and seeing the blood streaking his master's head. He had immediately 'phoned for the police.

'He's telling the truth?' queried Trench, not pausing in his survey of the room and its contents.

'Not a doubt of it,' returned Bellowes warmly. 'I've questioned the cook and maid also; they know nothing. It looks as though Armitage had a secret assignation with someone who had reason to silence him for ever. That someone came to the windows, was let in, and killing Armitage went out the same way. So the servants know nothing. They certainly know nothing about an appointment their master had made for this evening, and they assure me that no one called in the usual way and was admitted. It's a complete mystery.'

'Why not a burglar?' asked Trench.

'Because of these,' said the divisional man, with a slight air of triumph, removing a towel from his *pièce de résistance*, two stained glasses. 'Even a cranky artist,' he pointed out, 'doesn't sit down and toast a burglar in his own whisky.'

Trench murmured something about that being decidedly unusual, and turned to the desk.

'What's this?' he inquired, pointing.

Bellowes scratched his head, and his frown revealed perplexity.

'A jigsaw puzzle,' he said. 'Probably he amused himself building it up while waiting for his visitor. And that reminds me,' he added more quickly, 'I've measured the footprints outside the window. They are the same prints, coming and leaving, and they lead round to the gravel path. Furthermore, the window catch wasn't forced. It must have been opened from inside. As Armitage wasn't wearing gloves you should get some confirmatory finger-prints.'

Trench nodded. It was plain that Bellowes was one of those efficient divisional men who had risen because he couldn't be kept down.

'That's doubtless true,' said Trench, 'but I'm not so sure about the jigsaw puzzle. A puzzle like that takes time to build, and this one is completed save for two pieces.' He uncurled the fingers of the dead man's left hand, and removed something that had been pressed against the palm. 'And here's one of the missing two pieces.' He placed the curved fragment of coloured cardboard into its proper niche in the puzzle. 'One piece missing now,' he said, 'a face.'

The three of us stood grouped together at the dead man's side, looking down at the jigsaw. It was certainly the strangest and grimmest puzzle of its kind that I had seen. It depicted a murder. A man in khaki uniform was firing a revolver at a grey-haired man who had thrown up a futile arm to protect himself. In a doorway at the end of the picture stood a younger man peering into the room. The one piece missing from the puzzle was the head of the soldier firing the revolver.

I glanced at Trench. His lined face mirrored deep interest. Apparently he had other views than Bellowes, who voiced the gratuitous opinion that it was a damned queer picture for a puzzle, but unimportant unless it contained some fresh finger-prints.

However, we were given no time to debate the relative importance – or otherwise – of the puzzle at that moment, for a uniformed sergeant entered to announce that the photographers had arrived. I made a cursory examination of the room while the finger-print man brushed door-handles and chair-arms, and when the camera-men began flaring their lamps I retired to another room and busied myself with my notebook. Trench spent some time alone in the room with the dead man, and although Bellowes tried his best to get an opinion from him Trench was not in a communicative mood. We examined the footprints, casts were taken, and the servants were questioned. I myself did not like the looks of the man-servant. His eyes were too narrow and his mouth too mobile; but Trench appeared to have no second thoughts about the man. In fact, he seemed preoccupied during most of the time we were making our investigation. Just before we left to return to the Yard I discovered what was on his mind.

'We'll take that jigsaw with us,' he said to me, 'just as it is, built up.'

I thought Bellowes' smile, when he heard this, slightly contemptuous, but the divisional man wisely kept his thoughts to himself.

It was late when we got back to the Yard, and while I set to work building up a report from our notes and the servants' statements Trench sat at his desk, his pipe blowing full blast, his eyes narrowed on the puzzle. I stopped my work when I saw him take a powerful lens from a drawer and closely scrutinize the picture. Trench was not a man to waste time in idle speculation. The jigsaw puzzle had interested him from the first moment he had seen it, and his interest was increasing.

He looked up and met my inquiring glance.

'Come here,' he said.

I stood by his chair, looking at the puzzle.

'What strikes you about it?' he said.

'It's a strange subject for a jigsaw puzzle.'

'What else? Look more closely.'

Suddenly I saw what he meant. 'It's an original painting!' I exclaimed.

Trench smiled.

'Exactly. But it's something more, if I'm not greatly mistaken. It's a painting of an actual scene, of an incident that actually happened.'

'That would be a murder!' I protested.

Trench smiled, tamping the tobacco in the bowl of his pipe with a blunt finger.

'Of course. That's the reason why Armitage was murdered tonight.'

It didn't make sense to me.

'But if that is the case this murder occurred years ago.' I was peering closely through Trench's lens. 'The date on this calendar is 1916.' I pointed to a calendar hanging on a wall of the room in the picture.

'In short,' said Trench, 'we have in front of us a picture of the commission of an unsolved crime – a twofold crime, I should say, robbery and murder. From his position the soldier has been surprised while tackling the door of the safe. To solve tonight's business we shall have to solve, first, this other crime which was committed nearly twenty years ago.'

My surprise at these words must have been mirrored in my face, for Trench laughed.

'What's wrong? Does it sound too fantastic?'

I had a feeling that he was enjoying himself.

'Not only fantastic, but without reason,' I returned, rather hotly, for I felt that Trench was amused by what he considered my obtuseness, and was prepared to defend myself. 'Why should any sane man – and presumably Armitage was sane – paint a picture of a murder, make it into a jigsaw puzzle, and amuse himself by putting it together when he's expecting a visitor who has designs on his life?'

Put like that, it certainly sounded ludicrous. I smiled in my turn. But Trench's reply, uttered in a low, convinced tone, left me with a very different expression on my face.

'Blackmail,' was all he said.

A vague outline of what he meant took shape in my mind. I sat down, waiting for him to continue. He took his time, as though he had first to settle some mental problem to his own satisfaction.

'It's my belief that Armitage was a blackmailer,' he stated. 'The soldier whose face is missing' – he pointed to the gap in the puzzle – 'stole a considerable sum of money, or possibly jewels or bonds, and was interrupted before he could make a getaway. He shot dead the man who interrupted before he could make a getaway. He shot dead the man who interrupted him, not realizing that there was a second witness.' Trench pointed to the figure in the doorway. 'Armitage might have looked like this when he was younger – I can't say, of course,' he added with a thoughtful frown. 'But the chief point about the picture that interests me is the artist's attention to detail. On the glass panel of the door is a name. Reading backwards, I make it out to be "J. Gorrat and Son." The marks underneath are not decipherable, but they might easily stand for the word manufacturer. The pile of straw hats in the far corner decides what J. Gorratt and Son manufactured, and because of that the town where the murder happened.'

He looked at me, and grinned. Trench was pleased with himself.

'Don't you get it?' he asked.

I didn't.

'In 1916,' he said, 'the straw-hat industry still flourished. One town in England is noted – '

'Luton,' I interrupted.

'Right,' he nodded. 'If I'm not wrong the Luton police records will contain the facts about a murder that took place on the night of April 18 – that's the date on the calendar – in 1916 on the premises of J. Gorrat and Son, straw-hat manufacturers. Those facts should be interesting; they might include the name of a man who was murdered tonight in North London.'

He walked to the window and leaned against the wooden sill, while I stared, fascinated, at the jigsaw puzzle.

'As soon as Armitage's bank is opened I'll have his account checked for the past few years,' decided Trench aloud. 'Then I think we'd better take a trip to Bedfordshire.'

I continued to stare at the puzzle. Trench was right. The details the artist had carefully included in the picture told a clear story. The pile of straw hats, the beam of light streaming through the partly open door, the calendar, the black name on the glass panel, the positions of the figures, the expression on the face of the man staring into the revolver barrel – all those details had been included in the picture with one object, to record something that happened on the night of April 18, 1916.

And the reason for the picture, for the jigsaw puzzle? Trench's guess at blackmail was shrewd, yet I had my doubts.

However, those doubts were settled by Trench himself, after he had called upon the manager of the branch of the Midland and Home Counties Bank at which Stephen Armitage had deposited his ready money. A confidential scrutiny of Armitage's account for the past eleven years – the period during which he had banked at that branch – showed that regularly each half-year he had made a deposit of five hundred pounds.

'Someone's been bled to the tune of a thousand a year,' said Trench, 'and last night that someone came to the end of his tether. Either his funds were exhausted or Armitage had made a fresh proposal which he could not meet. A clever fellow Armitage. That jigsaw must have been a terrible hold over the murderer.'

'We found no money at the house,' I pointed out.

'That proves nothing,' said Trench. 'The murderer might – most likely did – bring the money, and after killing Armitage took it away with him. In the circumstances it would have been senseless to have left it. Those payments were always made in cash, never by cheque. Armitage took few chances, and doubtless understood thoroughly the psychology of the man with whom he was dealing.'

'Twenty years at a thousand a year,' I told him, 'is twenty thousand pounds. That's a big sum.'

'The penalty for murder is – big,' smiled Trench, but there was a peculiar twist to his smile.

'What about the finger-prints?' I asked.

Trench shook his head.

'Nothing there to help us. The only prints that were photographed were Armitage's and his servants'. The footprints are another matter, but we've to find our men first. They won't lead us to him. That will.'

He pointed to his attaché-case, in which, carefully wrapped and secured, was the jigsaw puzzle. Trench carried the case under his arm as we went down to his car. I drove, while he sat in the rear, the case flat on his knees. During the fifty-minutes' run to Luton

Trench barely spoke a word. He sat there behind me, his shoulders hunched, thinking and smoking. I had a suspicion that he had not spent much of his few hours from the Yard in sleep.

The local inspector whom we saw at the Luton police-station smiled when Trench voiced his request.

'Not thinking of raising that ghost, are you?' he asked.

'That depends on the ghost,' countered Trench cautiously.

It was obvious that Trench didn't mean to satisfy the other's curiosity, but that was like Trench. He usually kept things to himself until he was sure he was right.

And he was right this time – at least, in the matter of the murder twenty years before. The filed records gave the following facts.

A Mr Josiah Gorrat, a prosperous straw-hat manufacturer of the town, had been shot through the heart at about eleven-fifteen on the night of April 18, 1916. Suspicion had first fallen on his son, home on leave from the front, who was known to have had a violent quarrel with his father on the day before. According to statements made by a warehouseman and a servant in the Gorrat home the quarrel had arisen because of the younger Gorrat's engagement to a young London actress. The servant had heard father and son quarrelling at lunch, and the warehouseman had passed the father's office at the factory and accidentally heard the son say that his father could do his damnedest, but he wasn't giving up the girl. He'd find a way of making money for himself and live his own life.

This statement had appeared rather significant when it was later proved that not only had Josiah Gorrat been killed by a bullet from an Army pattern revolver, but at the time of his murder there were some thirty-three thousand pounds in Treasury notes in his factory safe. The money constituted a bank loan and a Government grant for the purposes of enabling J. Gorrat and Son to install machinery and equipment for the manufacture of military caps and Army 'warms.' The murdered man had been a keen business man, and with the stoppage of raw materials from Belgium and Austria – dye-stuffs and plait, for instance – he had turned to other trade.

The safe had been opened with Josiah Gorrat's own key, which was later found in the safe door. The money was never found.

Things had looked bad for the son. His story was that he was at home in bed at the time of the murder and robbery, and his story remained unconfirmed by the testimony of any other witness at the inquest than a certain Stephen Armitage, who had stated that he had chanced to pass the Gorrat home at about ten minutes past eleven that night and had seen a light in a certain window, which proved to be the window of the son's bedroom. The son stated that he had lain in bed reading a novel until he had fallen asleep. The light was on when he awoke in the morning.

Stephen Armitage had admitted to the coroner that he was a designer employed by Gorrat and Son.

'Very interesting,' vouchsafed Trench when he had finished perusing the record. 'I suppose young Gorrat wasn't arrested because the money wasn't traced to him.'

'I suppose so,' said the local inspector, who could be as cautious as Trench himself, and who certainly knew little more about the case than I did myself.

'Is he living in the town now?' asked Trench.

The other nodded.

'Very much so. But Gorrat, Ltd, don't make straw hats; they manufacture boiler fittings.'

Trench grinned.

'Advancing with the times, eh?'

'Well, advancing, anyway. I understand the firm's prosperous.'

We obtained the firm's address, and drove there after leaving the police-station. Trench's official card procured us immediate entry to the private office of Mr Wilson Gorrat. He was a tall man with a slight stoop, long limbs and eyes that flickered frequently.

'What can I do for you, gentlemen?' he inquired, with what I thought was a nervous twitching of his lean hands. From the first moment I distrusted him, and I am afraid that I was not long in making up my mind that Josiah Gorrat had been shot by his son.

'We are investigating a murder,' announced Trench after we were seated.

Gorrat started.

'A murder!' he repeated, and his hands fumbled clumsily. 'Not – not – '

'Not your father's murder – no,' said Trench, in a tone decidedly less negative than his words.

'Ah!' Wilson Gorrat breathed an uneasy sigh of relief. 'I thought at first – ' He stopped, eyeing us narrowly. 'But you know about *that*!'

The tone was accusatory, and at the same time suspicious.

'Yes, I know the facts that came out at the inquest,' agreed Trench. 'But I am investigating a more recent affair – in fact, a murder that was committed last night.'

'In this town?'

'No, in London.'

'Oh!' There was pause. 'Excuse me, Inspector Trench, but I do not understand how I – '

'The murdered man was a certain Stephen Armitage. I think you will recall the name. He gave evidence at the inquest on your father, Mr Gorrat.'

'Armitage, Armitage – Stephen Armitage!' If Gorrat was acting he was a good actor. His frown of concentrated reflection was convincing. 'Oh, yes, I recall the man now. Wasn't he a designer at the old works? Drew new shapes for women's straw hats, copied Continental models, and that sort of thing. Rather a clever fellow with his brush, and might have gone quite a way if he'd taken painting seriously.'

'That's the man. He gave you a sort of alibi on the night of the crime.'

Gorrat flushed.

'Yes, he saw the light in my window, I believe. But that was hardly an alibi, if I remember. I'd already said that I fell asleep and left the light on – But you say he's been murdered?'

'Yes. I also believe he was a blackmailer.'

Gorrat's eyes opened wide.

'A blackmailer!' he echoed. 'But who was he blackmailing? And, anyway, what has all this to do with me?'

I thought at the time that I detected a trace of defiance in his manner. Trench was as blunt as usual.

'I believe Stephen Armitage had for years been blackmailing the murderer of your father, Mr Gorrat, the man who stole a considerable sum of money from the safe in your father's straw-hat factory.'

Gorrat sat very still, digesting this. At length he said evenly: 'Then you believe that the man who murdered Armitage is the man who murdered my father, Inspector?'

It was difficult to decide whether the sentence was a question or a simple statement. Trench chose to accept it as the former.

'That's what I believe, Mr Gorrat.'

'And why have you come to Luton?'

'To find the murderer,' replied Trench.

Gorrat winced, but squared his shoulders.

'You think I can help you, then?'

'I'm relying upon your help, Mr Gorrat,' said Trench.

I wondered what Trench had in his mind. He was not usually given to playing a cat-and-mouse game with suspects, and it was plain to see that he must suspect Gorrat.

'Very well,' said the manufacturer, with a forced smile. 'I don't see how I can help, but of course you've only to ask – '

Trench had a keen dislike to receiving gratuitous advice and help. He preferred to ask for what he wanted. Probably that was why he interrupted Gorrat just then.

He said, 'I want to know if you have on your staff here, Mr Gorrat, anyone who was on your father's staff at the time he was murdered.'

The reply came without hesitation, 'Yes, Phillips and Elcock. Phillips is workshop foreman, and – '

'Were they in the War?'

'Both of them.'

'And they were in your father's employ at the time – '

'Ah, I see what you're getting at!' exclaimed Gorrat quickly. 'No, actually I believe they were in khaki at the time my father was shot; but as all the staff who enlisted were promised their jobs when they came back it was always considered that, in a sense, they were still members of the staff.'

'I see. They are the only two?'

'On the staff here – yes. My butler, however, was in my father's employ, and Maggie – our cook – was also with the family then.'

'Mr Gorrat,' said Trench, 'I've a request to make.'

'Yes?' inquired the other.

'I'd like to meet Phillips and Elcock, and your butler and cook, at your house this evening – say, about eight, after dinner, if that would be convenient.'

Gorrat was silent for a few moments. His fleshy face puckered as he tried to divine Trench's purpose.

Finally he said, 'Very well,' and as a gesture added, 'Perhaps you and your assistant would join myself and my wife at dinner. We shall be alone.'

I was surprised, I must confess, when Trench accepted this invitation, but as we left the building I saw that the moment was not ripe for asking questions. We lunched, rather late, in the town, and I drove Trench to Bedford, the county town, where he spent a couple of hours with a brisk-looking sergeant pouring over the records at the headquarters of the Beds. and Herts. Regiment. He was still thoughtful when we left.

From then until the hour we were due at the Gorrat home we killed time, and I for one became thoroughly bored. I remained of the same opinion, that Gorrat was faced by too many coincidences to be able to explain them all satisfactorily. The man might have an alibi for the previous evening, but I was confident that we could break it down, and, frankly, the notion of eating at the man's table and making small talk with him did not appeal to me.

On the other hand, Trench's spirits seemed to revive when we called at the fine house on the outskirts of the town which was the Gorrat home, and when we were introduced to Mrs Gorrat, a striking-looking woman, still beautiful and unfaded, he was giving a very good performance of enjoying himself.

The butler's name was Camp. He was a bachelor of sedate mien and slow movement. In fact, his ponderous gait put me in mind of a senile duck. The meal was over before I realized it. Trench chatted throughout with Gorrat and his wife, and I joined in at times, and found the time passing more pleasantly than I had anticipated.

At a quarter to eight we retired with our cigars and coffee, and almost on the stroke of the hour Phillips and Elcock were announced. They came in, deferential in manner, and although Phillips's looks did not impress me – he was a tall, lean man with a calculating eye – Elcock's cheery face and ready smile won my instant approval. From the first I suspected he was a wag among his fellows.

Mrs Gorrat joined us shortly after we had been introduced, and then Camp was sent to bring the cook, a buxom woman in her middle forties, hair severely parted in the centre and greying rapidly. She was a widow, I understood. When all were assembled Trench unpacked the jigsaw. He placed it on a centre table, made sure that it was complete save for the missing face, and asked everyone to look at it.

After that getting a comment from any of them was like extracting a bad tooth. One could almost feel the change in the atmosphere as Trench dropped his easy manner and became the alert detective. He told them what he thought the picture portrayed, and asked them what they had to say on the subject, which proved to be little. Gorrat was like a man in a dream, and the two men from the works frowned and stared suspiciously at everyone in turn, while Camp and the cook looked everywhere except where Mrs Gorrat sat, a look of intense strain and doubt on her face.

Trench, however, was in no whit put out by this cool reception of his theory.

He said, 'Apart from the missing piece of the puzzle, which is the murderer's face, there is one other significant detail in that picture. It is this. *The murderer is firing with his left hand.*'

I could have kicked myself then. It was a point I had overlooked completely in searching for the various details which told a story. But even as Trench made the announcement I had my misgivings. Gorrat was not left-handed; Phillips and Elcock had certainly used their right hands more than their left since they had been in the room; and Camp had served the meal in a correct and orthodox manner. I failed to see what Trench could do, in the circumstances.

I was soon enlightened. He went out of the room and came back with a long brown-paper parcel and another that was flat and square. When the first was unwrapped he produced an air-gun; the other contained a cheap wooden target with series of red and green concentric circles.

In answer to my stare he said, 'I bought them in Bedford.' Turning to our host, he said, 'With your permission, Mr Gorrat, I'd like to try a little experiment.'

Gorrat and his wife were past objecting.

'Go ahead,' muttered the former wonderingly.

'You're all ex-Service men,' said Trench. 'Presumably you all learned how to fire a rifle.' Each man nodded slowly. 'Very well,' continued Trench, 'I'm going to ask you all to fire one slug at this target. I shall compare the results.'

It seemed absurd to me, for, frankly, I could not see what Trench was trying to prove; and I noticed that Gorrat, for one, looked annoyed at the proposal, although he made no protest. Trench set up the target at one end of the room, and placed a chair at the opposite end.

'I want each of you to sit on this chair as you take aim and fire,' he explained.

One by one they came forward, took aim, and pressed the trigger of the air-gun. Each put the rifle to his right shoulder, I observed. But I did not see the results of the shooting. Trench stood alone by the target, and allowed none of us to approach. When the four men had all fired he removed the target and compared the hits. Then he beckoned to the cook, who, looking rather surprised, followed him out of the room.

He was gone a good while this time, and during his absence we all tried to appear as though we were at ease; but, strangely, all of us were affected in some way by Trench's peculiar behaviour. So far as I could see he had proved nothing, had been able to prove nothing, and the others must have felt as I did. Yet there was a tenseness about the atmosphere of that room which we all sensed. Several times I caught Mrs Gorrat casting furtive anxious glances in her husband's direction. The two men from the works sat apart, smoking silently and trying to appear unperturbed by disturbing thoughts. Camp fidgeted, putting a chair straight here, touching an ornament there.

When Trench came back he entered alone. Without a word he walked to the table and did something to the jigsaw puzzle. I went forward and looked over his shoulder.

He had fitted the missing piece of the puzzle in its place! The face of the soldier firing the revolver with his left hand was there before me, and it was strangely familiar. For a second or two I could not place it. Then I knew whose face it was.

They all crowded round, and suddenly there was a sharp cry. The next moment Trench had snapped a pair of handcuffs round the butler's wrists.

'Joseph Camp,' he said, 'I arrest you for the murder of Stephen Armitage, and I warn you that anything you have to say now will be taken down and later used in evidence against you.'

Of course it was all very sudden and dramatic. But that was like Trench. He kept his own counsel to the end of a case, and the result was generally startling. It was after we were back in London and Camp had confessed that Trench explained to me just how he had worked the seeming miracle.

'Largely,' he said, 'it was a question of character. The character of a man who at one time in his life seized an opportunity, but who, finding himself tricked by circumstance, gave up the fight. Joseph Camp had such a character. Nearly twenty years ago, when home on leave, he heard about the money in the factory safe. He planned the robbery, had to murder to keep his identity a secret, and then found himself tricked by a man who, for all I know, may have had designs on the safe himself. Anyway, we can't ask Armitage to explain what he was doing in the factory on that night. But we know he *was* there. The jigsaw picture showed us that much.'

'He was a clever artist,' I said.

'Competent,' amended Trench thoughtfully, 'not clever. But he was a clever blackmailer. He knew Camp's psychology from A to Z. He knew the man would be frightened to do anything with the money save bank it under a false name, probably, so systematically he set himself to bleed him of the lot. That, too, was a quite novel idea. Most blackmailers can't wait. Armitage could. He let his milch-cow provide him with a regular income. Meanwhile the milch-cow settled down to the life of the family butler.'

'Yes, I can understand all that part of it,' I told Trench. 'The human factor that went to create the problem is plain enough now. What I want to know is how you decided that Camp was your man. It looked like a leap in the dark to me.'

Trench chuckled.

'Say, rather, a leap in the dusk. Anyway, I had enough light to see where I was jumping.'

'You mean,' I said, 'that when you left the room with the cook you knew who had murdered Armitage?'

'Not quite – but very nearly. I knew which of the four men who had fired the air-gun was really left-handed.'

'How?'

'Each had used a rifle in the War, remember,' said Trench. 'Therefore firing at such a distance was child's play. They all plugged the centre circle save one – Camp. His shot was bad, inches from the centre, which showed me that when he last fired a rifle he used it in his most natural manner, with the butt against his left shoulder, sighting with his right eye. He was unaccustomed to firing in right-handed fashion. The assumption is obvious. For years Camp had schooled himself to use his right hand in place of his left. In most things he is by now probably ambidextrous. But when it came to firing a gun it was another matter. He had presence of mind enough to put it to his right shoulder, but he couldn't make a reasonably good hit. Oh, by the way, don't ask me where I bought the air-gun and target. I forget the name of the shop, and, anyway, you were watching the car at the time.'

I turned the conversation back into what I considered its rightful channel.

'Why did you need the cook when you went out of the room?' I asked.

'To show me Camp's room. It was dollars to doughnuts that if he was the man we wanted he had kept that jigsaw piece holding the picture of his own face. He had stood Armitage's baiting for years, had lived in dread of the man giving him away in a moment of spite; doubtless every time he thought of that jigsaw puzzle he made up his mind what he'd do next time he visited Armitage. But he didn't do it until a few nights ago. Armitage cowed him, and there was always the jigsaw puzzle, with its significant details, its date and the name of the firm, and its true-to-life faces. He must have temporarily lost his reason while watching Armitage fumbling with the puzzle, and when it was completed he couldn't stand the strain any longer. He picked up the poker and killed his tormenter, the man who had taken a fiendish delight in robbing him and at the same time in silently threatening him with the puzzle. When he saw what he had done he snatched the really tell-tale piece from the puzzle and his money, and left by the way he had come. His shoes have been measured against the casts taken of those footprints. They are an exact fit. Incidentally, getting back to your question, I found the jigsaw piece in Camp's room, hidden in a collar-box. I must say, in a sense, I'm sorry for the man.'

This assertion astounded me. It was not like Trench to feel sympathetic towards murderers.

'Why?' I demanded. 'The man's a thorough crook. Years ago he robbed a safe of over thirty thousand pounds and killed a man – '

'What good did it do him?' countered Trench; and before I could reply supplied his own answer: 'None. That's the first bit of irony. The whole twenty years is studded with it. And you're forgetting one important thing, the Joseph Camp who slew Stephen Armitage in a fit of semi-righteous rage was a vastly different man from the disappointed soldier who planned a robbery and found himself enmeshed in murder and blackmail. I imagine Joseph Camp's had a tough time of it during those twenty years. Had he been caught and got a life sentence the chances are he would now be coming out of gaol, a free man. As it is, he's had his misery, and now he's got to swing after all. That's the last bit of irony. Yes, I'm certainly sorry for the man. The cards have been stacked against him all through the deal.'

I didn't get Trench's meaning.

'How do you mean all through the deal?' I asked.

Trench smiled and began filling his briar.

'Well, it was only chance that the man who robbed the Gorrat safe and killed the father was still living in Luton, and, furthermore, still connected with the Gorrat family. Normally one would have thought he would have been anywhere else, but I've a shrewd idea that Armitage made that a condition of his silence. The local police suspected the son only; that's why Armitage backed up his story of going to sleep with his light on. That was a lie, because Armitage was at the factory, as we know now; he couldn't have been walking past the Gorrat home and he couldn't have seen the light at the time he said he did. With all this in mind, he probably took good care to browbeat the demobbed Camp into going back into the family service. Makes a compact little story, doesn't it?' added Trench lightly.

'It does *now!*' I said, with emphasis.

BY THE SWORD

Selwyn Jepson

ALFRED CAITHNESS stayed on for Christmas for two reasons, quite apart from the cold weather, which he found easier to support at Dingle House than alone in his Baker Street flat. Snow had fallen heavily in the middle of the month and again on Christmas Day. It lay thickly now, with the thermometer showing four degrees of frost, and it hid the lawns of the Dingle gardens and coated the roofs and gables of the old house like icing sugar on a cake.

Although he told himself that the reasons he had stayed were because an old-fashioned Christmas appealed to him and also because his cousin Herbert would undoubtedly lend him two thousand pounds if he handled him right, there was another thing which kept him here.

This, however, he had not yet fully admitted to himself. He only knew that he was in no great hurry to talk to Herbert about the money.

Life was very pleasant at Dingle House, he reflected. Why go out of the way to speed one's own departure?

This morning he sat by the blazing logs in the great stone fireplace of the library and watched Barbara, who was his cousin's wife, sewing at some pink thing which lay like a pool of silken foam in her lap.

The boy, young Robert, who was five and a bit, was marching a regiment of tin soldiers up and down the low, broad window-sill behind her. Every now and then she would turn her head to smile at him and admire some new arrangement of their ranks. Lifeguards on horseback they were, with red coats and silver breast-plates, a gay and gallant company.

'You couldn't have given him anything he would have liked better, Alfred,' she said. 'It's the Caithness in him.'

He nodded, but was more attentive to the graceful poise of her head on the white column of her neck.

'He'll be a soldier like the rest of them,' she added, and sighed.

Her husband was not one, but only because his left leg was two inches shorter than his right, a childhood accident. Alfred, too, was an exception to the family tradition.

'I never cottoned to the idea,' he remarked, following her thought, 'but not because the old story frightened me.'

'You mean that a Caithness always dies by the sword?'

She had been thinking of it a moment before, when she had seen Robert grown to a man and pursuing the career which his ancestors had fulfilled so gloriously.

'It's very queer, though,' Alfred said, 'how many of them have been killed that way.'

He glanced at the crest carved in the limestone of the mantelpiece, a short sword gripped in a mailed hand.

'But in these days soldiering isn't so fashionable,' he added. 'Perhaps your boy will be a legal luminary like his famous father.'

His eyes went back to her, to the helmet of sleek, fair hair and the cream of her temples.

Heaven! How sorry he was for her! Married to Herbert, who was twenty-eight years her senior. A lame, dry-voiced man, consciously enigmatical, proud of his keen logical brain, his freedom from sentiment and the cloying dangers of emotionalism. In other words, the Honourable Mr Justice Caithness, whose judgments in the criminal court were renowned for the clarity of their law and the severity of their consequences.

Small wonder his life was so often threatened! To hear the smug self-righteousness of the man's voice as he condemned some poor devil to penal servitude was enough to arouse any vengeance. If he had had one threatening letter since the last sessions, he must have had a dozen.

Alfred shifted restlessly in his armchair and banged the dottle out of his pipe against the hearth.

What joy could Barbara get out of a husband like that? Precious little. Where was he now, for that matter? Shut away in his study at the other end of the house with his dictionaries, encyclopædias and books of reference, striving to solve Torquemada's crossword puzzle by Wednesday night! That was his weekly excitement, his one relaxation from the administration of justice and the text-book, *Anomalies in Criminal Law*, which he was preparing with young Donaldson's help. (At the thought of Jim Donaldson, Alfred frowned.)

'Left – right – left – right – left!' sang Robert at the window.

'Barbara!' said Alfred, and stopped abruptly.

She looked up and then dropped her eyes quickly. He bit on the empty pipe.

'They are horsemen, dear,' she explained, turning to the boy. 'Only foot-soldiers march in step.'

'These are diff'rent.'

Alfred knew suddenly why he had stayed at Dingle House for Christmas. He went over to Robert and asked him to run along. The boy did not want to. A little disgruntled, he obeyed.

'I'll find the book of engines for Uncle Jim. An' I'll come back presently,' he said at the door.

Alfred closed it on him and crossed to the chair in which the golden head was bent over the silk. She had not commented on his sending the child away and he took heart. Surely she guessed what was coming?

'I've been here ten days now,' he said, searching for words, 'and I've seen how things are – with you and Herbert.'

'Alfred, please – '

But he hurried on. He knew what he wanted to say.

'You can't go on with it! You can't! You're sacrificing your life to an existence in which there is nothing but the dry dust of – of senility to warm your heart. He married you when you were too young to know anything about life. I saw it – I knew you in those days, remember. Your self-seeking, ambitious mother pushed you into his arms when you were little more than a child, because he was a rich and eminent man. Barbara, you are miserably unhappy, tortured, tied to a complacent fossil of a human being who has no more idea of love than – than that piece of wood!'

She had risen and was facing him with harassed eyes. He strode round the chair and tried to take her hands, but she snatched them behind her.

'Look at it honestly, Barbara! You know I'm stating no more

than the truth of the thing. I've got eyes in my head. I've seen
you looking at him, heard your silence when he says something
particularly inane. You're rushing into disaster. Presently you'll
begin to look for an escape and, because the desire is so urgent,
your judgment will be faulty. You'll make a ghastly mistake. Some
casual man will take advantage of your misery – '

'Alfred, stop!'

'I won't stop. You've got to listen to me. I've loved you from
the moment I first saw you, in that church at Herbert's side. Loved
you, Barbara, d'you hear? I have the right to talk to you like this.
I have the right to look after you – to take you away.'

She stared at him with her hands to her cheeks as though she
could not believe what she heard. Dared not, Alfred thought with
a throb of triumph. The words came easily now.

'You must come away with me – you and the boy. You won't
have to give him up. I wouldn't ask that. I can't take you to a
luxurious home but I can give you the warmer things of life, of the
heart. Listen, Barbara. You know how I have felt about you for a
long time. Last summer when I was here, do you remember the
harvesting, when we rode home in the dusk on the top of that great
mound of hay? You guessed then, didn't you, my darling? I held
back because I wasn't sure of you, because I hadn't realized quite
how terribly unhappy you were. You put up a fine show and it
deceived me. But this last week has been different. You haven't
succeeded for a second in making me think you care at all for
Herbert. How could you pretend? He – '

She shivered and broke into the spate of his sentences with low,
broken phrases.

'Even if I don't care for him – even if I don't – does that give you
the right to . . . ? Alfred, he's my husband – and your cousin. I –
I am loyal to him and you must be.'

'Heaven!' he cried. 'What does *he* matter beside you? It's *your* life
– all the years of life and adventure and *being* – in front of you that
count! Barbara!'

He moved closer to her, with his arms open to take her.

'You don't understand – '

Then the door-handle creaked, and he stopped, drew away. Jim
Donaldson came in, his broad figure filling the doorway and his
wide-set blue eyes cheerfully alert.

'Oh, hullo,' he said, and strolled into the room. If he saw Alfred's scowl he ignored it. If he noticed the white, strained face of Barbara Caithness, he showed no sign.

'Cigarettes about?' he asked and stretched his shoulders, for he had been writing solidly since ten. Alfred disliked him cordially. The crispness of his speech, the health and honesty of his eyes, were irritating. This was the sort of man he saw as a danger to Barbara, living under the same roof with her when she was in this state of mind.

He saw the effort with which she picked up her sewing and made pretence of an easy mind. It was the gallant spirit he so admired in her, that, and all the perfection of form and feature which was hers. A woman in a million . . . his woman. Thank heaven he had had the courage to tell her so. It had startled her a bit but in a little she would see the thing more clearly. Damn this fellow Donaldson. Couldn't the oaf see they were wanting to talk to one another? He watched him take possession of an armchair and thrust his feet toward the fire.

'No sign of the thermometer letting up. But it's going to stay bright, thank goodness.'

But he wasn't as dull as he seemed. Alfred saw his quick glance at the girl. She wasn't giving anything away, though.

Just as well, although the world would soon know about it. Herbert last of all – and not before they had gone. It would be a blow to the man's pride, but undoubtedly good for him to discover a flaw in his omnipotence.

Donaldson, who could not be told to 'run along,' looked as though he proposed to sit there until lunch-time. Alfred searched for some excuse to get rid of him or a cue that would enable Barbara to come outside, but unsuccessfully.

The boy returned at this point, burdened with a picture book and determined to engage Uncle Jim's attention. The library seemed crowded and Alfred left it in ill-humour. He wanted to think. The situation had developed almost by itself. He did not find himself surprised now that it had come at last and he had put words to it, but he was aware of a kind of breathlessness. Emotion, of course, and largely a physical one. He was quite experienced enough to realize that.

He went through the lounge toward the wide stairs.

As his footsteps died away, Donaldson sat up straightly in his chair, all his carelessness gone. In its place was anxiety and concern.

'It has come, has it?'

'I'm frightened of him, Jim. I tried to stop him – '

' – but he ranted on. I know. Oh, damn. Why didn't I arrive a bit earlier? Had it been going on long?'

Her distress cut his heart.

'No. But he said dreadful things about – Herbert. He blamed him and – '

'He would. He's jealous, you see, of all that Herbert has which he hasn't. Money – success – fame. That's why he wants you. To have you, to steal you – make you follow him – would convince him of his own power. Power he knows in his heart of hearts, he can never achieve. But you needn't worry. You mustn't! Just yell for me if he starts again.'

'It's difficult, Jim. You see, he knows. I don't mean about you and me, but about my not being happy.'

He went to her and touched her hand, while Robert, realizing with the infallible instinct of his age that his elders were more interested in themselves than in him, went back to his Lifeguards on the window-sill.

Donaldson spoke softly, with gentleness.

'Was it only yesterday we discovered one another? I'm still a little dazed but I'm beginning to think straight. My dear, I shall have to tell Herbert, and go. It's the only thing to do. I'll tell him soon. Tomorrow. I shan't involve you. He'll be fair. You know, sometimes I think he knows already – and understands. That he knew before I myself did. He's odd in that way. More intuitive and sympathetic than people realize.'

She nodded slowly, and her eyes shone mistily as she looked at him.

'Beloved,' he said, 'I shall carry you in my heart to the end of my days.'

They lunched, the four of them, at the refectory table in the dining-room. A pewter bowl of holly in the middle partially hid husband and wife from one another, and Donaldson from Alfred. But Jim had no need to see Alfred's face to sense his triumph. He realized that the man's conceit, born of unconscious inferiority, would never permit him to see that Barbara, far from being pleased by his declaration, had indeed been nauseated and frightened by it.

She had always vaguely despised Alfred, not necessarily because he seemed constitutionally unable to keep any job more than three months, but because it was never, by the remotest chance, his fault that he lost it. 'I told 'em to go to blazes,' or : 'I've got my principles and when a firm does *that* sort of thing – well, I leave them to it.' Then, complaining bitterly that the gods seemed to have picked on him as their perpetual scapegoat, he would 'borrow' some more money from Herbert to carry on with until something turned up.

Sometimes, too, he had said things about women, which in a queer way made one squirm. But for a certain charm, an indefinable quality, which made him an excellent companion when the mood was upon him, she could have hated him thoroughly. She was near to it now. He was complicating things for her at a difficult moment in her life. She was glad Jim was going to confess to Herbert. She would like to be there and face it with him. She loved, and was neither ashamed nor afraid. But Jim was right. He must leave her.

Lunch came to an end and she went up to her room to lie down and escape Alfred. Jim set off for a tramp across the Downs, taking the spaniels. He wanted to think out the future and nerve himself for the ordeal of saying good-bye to Barbara. Life had got to be lived somehow. Whatever happened he must not be long alone with her.

Alfred was also of a mind to consider the future and the practical aspect of the money shortage in view of his decision to take Barbara away now became very clear to him. He must settle it as soon as possible. With the thought of Barbara strengthening his resolve, he followed the limping Herbert from the lunch table to the study.

His spirits were high and a feeling of invincibility stimulated him. Herbert would stump up like a gentleman. He was as certain of it as he had been of anything in his life.

He accepted a cigar and hoped, he said, that he wasn't in the way. 'How's the book going?'

'Very well, Alfred. Donaldson's help is invaluable. An exceedingly astute brain for such a young man. His knowledge of jurisprudence is remarkable. He'll make a great name for himself when he begins practising in earnest. Like few men with large private incomes, he is ambitious. He will be Attorney-General before he has finished.'

'Lucky devil,' Alfred commented. 'I wish I had had a quarter of his chances. I'm only a couple of years older than he is and, if things had been a bit different – gone better for me – I would be doing as well. It's not a comfortable feeling, that.'

Herbert put on a pair of spectacles and turned over a page in a dictionary.

'You indeed seem to have been unfortunate,' he said.

Alfred nodded and glanced at his cousin. The keen, straight face was not unsympathetic. This seemed to be the moment.

'I've been on the wrong tack, that's the whole trouble,' he went on. 'I've always been doing things for other people instead of for myself. Look at that Sugar Beet Exploitation business! Why, in six weeks I'd put the thing on its feet! I suppose I did more to start that company off than anybody else in it. It must have made a profit of a hundred thousand this year. You see if I'm not right when they publish the balance sheet next month! And I would have been on the board but for Murgatroyd. I made a friend of the man and he started some ridiculous gossip about a row I had had in Coventry with the Invicto crowd. He had got it all wrong, of course, but that didn't prevent people listening to him. It got round to me in time, thank goodness. I called him a scandal-mongering liar to his face and walked out. They tried to get me back, of course, but I wouldn't go.

'No, the whole secret of it is that I ought to be my own boss. Herbert, I've got the idea of a lifetime. An export agency business. A one-man business. And with this new fiscal policy gaining ground all the time I'm on to a marvellous thing. New markets will be opening up every day and there's scarcely a firm or organization in this country ready to put home manufacturers in touch with the fresh fields. I could do it and ship their stuff for them on a commission basis – quite a small one. There's a fortune in it!'

'It sounds quite an idea,' said Herbert.

'Lord, I should think it is! But the devil of it is, it will cost money to get it going.'

'These things do.'

'At least a couple of thousand pounds.'

'Yes?'

'Of course I shall be able to pay it back out of profits in a year –
two years.'

Herbert nodded, closed the dictionary and inspected his cigar.

'I'm afraid I shan't be able to help you very much,' he said.

Alfred's eyes moved uneasily. Well, perhaps two thousand was
rather a lot all at once.

'I might manage it with fifteen hundred – – ' he leaned forward.
'It's a great opportunity from the investment point of view. At a
most conservative estimate, the man who puts up the capital would
see twenty or twenty-five per cent return per annum. I've worked
it out, you see.'

Herbert was silent.

'You said yourself that the idea was a good one,' Alfred pointed
out. 'Frankly, Herbert, I was counting on you to see the – – '

Herbert had taken a small notebook out of a drawer in his desk
and Alfred paused uncertainly. What was the fool doing now?

'In the last eight years, Alfred,' he heard him saying, in a quiet,
unemotional tone. 'I have lent you six thousand pounds. I say
"lent," because on each occasion that you have appealed to me you
have spoken of repayment. I do not for a moment suggest that you
have deliberately borrowed from me without intention of paying
me back, but neither do I pretend to you that I regard these sums
as anything but gifts. Indeed, they appear in this record under the
heading of *Monies Given to A.C.*. I have been very glad to help you
and I am making no criticism. But, if I am not mistaken, I made a
point of telling you when we discussed the matter on the fifteenth
of July last that I would be unable to continue these – ah – loans.'

'Yes, but Herbert, this is – – '

'Different, I think you wish to say? I am sorry, but I am unable
to detect in this any intrinsic variation from your previous applications. I regret it exceedingly, Alfred, but, quite definitely and
finally, no! I feel, and have felt for some while, that if you are ever
to be successful it must be based on your own, unaided efforts. To
continue to give you money – I put it bluntly, I am afraid – can
only serve to postpone your chance of doing something worth
while.'

'All right,' Alfred interrupted. 'I quite understand. We'll say no
more about it. As to the six thousand I've already had, I said I
would repay it and I will.'

His voice was quiet. It surprised and had an effect on his cousin, who seemed a little less sure of himself, almost as though he doubted momentarily the wisdom of his course. But his mouth tightened and Alfred, watching him narrowly, knew all hope had gone.

He rose and put half an inch of cigar ash carefully in the ash-tray on the edge of the desk.

'You're a stubborn old thing, Herbert, but don't worry your head about me. I'll manage, I dare say.'

He went out, and closed the door gently.

He did not immediately proceed on his way, however, but stood tensely in the corridor fighting the weakness which attacked his limbs. He told himself that he was calm, unperturbed by the catas-trophe of that blank refusal. He should have foreseen its suddenness and now remain untroubled by its significance. Laugh! Show that you don't care a damn!

But he whispered a little thickly: 'Turned down! The swine turned me down!'

He walked unsteadily along the corridor with his mind confused by a swirl of thoughts. Barbara . . . the money . . . Herbert's stern face, with its eyes full of comprehension hovering in front of him.

His fingers closed tightly. Herbert had everything, hadn't he? All the money. The fate of men in his hands. The fate of Alfred Caith-ness, also. Even of Barbara. And by what right? By what right of God or man? The pale limping devil!

Then, before he reached the end of the corridor, an idea came which banished the shadows of uncertainty as with a bright light.

He stopped and became quite still, holding his breath as though he feared some eavesdropper of his mind.

He would kill Herbert. The money would come to Barbara.

Kill him, but not in this passion of hatred which possessed him now. Kill him quietly, unseen. Kill him in the night, secretly, so that no one could tell by whose hand he had died. The life of the Honourable Mr Justice Caithness had been threatened by many men who believed that he might have punished their sins less savagely. There had been comments in the Press about it and, a little while ago, after the Glastonbury blackmail case, a police guard had been put to watch over him until the fuss quietened down.

The money would come to Barbara.

As the thought took shape and became decision, he realized that only through the death of this man would his own life, so long buried in a morass of inhibition and failure, grow and blossom to fruitfulness.

Barbara, free at last, could come openly to his arms after a little while.

Thank Heaven he had not quarrelled with Herbert just now! Some blessed instinct must have warned him. An omen of success.

He began to think, to plan, and found himself curiously clear-headed and tranquil. The impatience was there and the need to give expression to this dominant desire which had been born in him. But these, far from hampering him, stimulated and enlivened his imagination.

He lay down on the divan in the library and closed his eyes.

First and foremost, he must school himself to appear normal when the others appeared. He must keep from his eyes and voice the excitement of his heart. There must be nothing they could remember afterwards and hold against him when the inquiry came.

Next, it must be a simple crime. The act of a man who is seeking vengeance without much thought for the consequences. An unsubtle, rather brutal murder. . . .

His glance fell on the long Elizabethan dagger hanging with other antique arms on the wall between the windows. He did not get up and inspect it more closely, but he remembered handling it idly years ago. A weighty, dangerous weapon.

It would come readily to the hand of anyone who climbed in by one of the windows. These were very low to the ground. He saw the carpet of snow stretching across the tennis lawn to the drive and the London road. The road itself had been cleared and threaded like a black ribbon between the white hills.

He drew a sudden deep breath, like a swimmer who comes out of the buffeting of heavy waves into smooth water.

At tea he was quiet. This suited both his mood and his tactics. Barbara would expect him to be on tenterhooks because of his declaration this morning. Herbert, knowing him to be disappointed about the money, would not look to him for any great display of cheerfulness. He noticed that Donaldson was rather silent but that was no more than reasonable in a man who had walked nearly ten miles since lunch.

Barbara talked of little things, but with an effort. Alfred thought he knew why and was wrong. Only Donaldson knew.

She, like himself, was seeking the courage to face a grievous parting. They were both dreading and yet welcoming the morrow. Being near each other was heaven, but the agony of the situation was difficult to bear.

Herbert was the only one of them who seemed to be in an entirely normal frame of mind. He was amiable and discursive. He was glad Alfred had decided to be philosophical. There was no reason why he should not pull himself together and make good.

Dusk had fallen before five. By half-past it was almost dark, with the snow outside a vague blur of lightness.

At a quarter-to-seven the dressing-gong sounded and Alfred, once again in the library, heard the others go to their rooms. He had several minutes in which to work. With a little hurrying he could do what he had to do and be changed and in the drawing-room before the rest.

He went swiftly to the window he had chosen and, opening it, stepped carefully out into the snow. The closed curtains would hide him from the eyes of an unlikely invader of the room. He stood for a moment in the darkness and then ran silently in the yielding snow, covering the fifty yards across the lawn and down the drive to the road in less than half-a-minute. He then turned and *walked* back to the window, taking a slightly indirect route.

His reasoning was sound. The traces of a murderer who had come from outside would appear clearly in the snow between the road and the house but not on the road, which was clear. Furthermore they would indicate that he had cautiously approached the scene of his intended crime and, having committed it, had fled quickly away.

In preparing this evidence he was at pains to make sure that the two sets of tracks did not intersect. Were they to do so, it might betray the fact that the running ones had been made before the walking ones. He was taking no chances. That the road was free from snow was a godsend. A car could have stood there, its wheel-marks lost in those of previous and later traffic, while the man was about his job. And, since the footprints passed in and out of the snow at nearly the same spot on the edge of the road, obviously, the detectives would say, a car had been used.

He regained the window, parted the curtains stealthily and stepped across the sill into the room. He closed the window and wiped what little frozen snow there was from the edges and soles of his boots, using a handkerchief which he dropped into the red heart of the fire as he passed it on his way to the door.

They were not his boots, but an old pair at least two sizes larger than his own which he had come upon some nights ago, when he was looking for an extra blanket, at the bottom of a cupboard on the landing outside his bedroom.

He reached his room unseen and, while the boots were drying on the radiator, changed quickly into his dinner jacket. On the way down to the drawing-room he returned them unobserved to their place, confident that they would never be connected with the tracks in the snow and that, even if by some incredible chance they were, there would be no evidence to show that he had ever worn them.

He was reading in the drawing-room when the others came down. Donaldson was more himself and Herbert mellower than his wont. If Barbara was pale, the two younger men had their own and different explanations for it. Herbert, who seldom if ever betrayed his observation, seemed, however, not to have noticed it. He went to his study after dinner, but reappeared within a few minutes in the drawing-room and suggested Bridge.

It was a welcome suggestion and enabled those who heard it to get through what threatened for each of them to be a difficult evening.

The game came to an end after the fifth rubber at about half-past ten, with Alfred the only winner, twenty-seven shillings to the good.

'Luck seems to be in,' he said. A few minutes later he asked Barbara to excuse him and bade them good night.

Herbert nodded very amiably to him as he went and Alfred interpreted a relief that he had made so little fuss. Selfish hypocrite!

He closed the door of his bedroom, got quickly into pyjamas and dressing-gown, lay down under the eiderdown and, switching off the light, composed himself to wait as patiently as he might.

The moment for action was approaching. Herbert, one of those people who seemed to need very little sleep, would follow his invariable custom of reading a book by the library fire for some while after the rest of the household had gone to bed.

Alfred listened to the sounds in the old house and analyzed them as they occurred.

Once during this period he experienced a moment of uncertainty, which was when he heard Barbara pass his door on her way to her room. She stopped and went back to the landing. He thought he heard Donaldson's voice in a subdued key.

He smiled grimly. Was that brilliant young fellow already falling under her spell?

He heard her return after several minutes and noticed that she walked slowly. He resisted the strong impulse to open his door and speak to her, to see her alone for a moment or two and to hold her closely in his arms. The thought of her embrace made him tremble. Time enough in the swiftly-approaching future. Time enough.

She went into her room and the door closed. Donaldson's was too far away in the east wing to be heard, but Alfred detected his heavy tread on the polished oak as he crossed the landing into the passage which led to it.

What had they said to one another? It was an idle, vaguely jealous question. But he comforted himself with the knowledge that, if Donaldson was beginning to get tiresome, he could soon be dealt with when matters had been straightened out. Barbara was too attractive to be allowed any great degree of freedom. When Herbert was out of it, and she –

He forced his attention to the necessities of the present and, after lying there for twenty minutes or so, swung his feet off the bed into a pair of felt-soled slippers.

He made no sound on the stairs and his movements across the darkened lounge towards the library door were no less silent. The thin line of light beneath it reassured him.

He opened it quietly, but without stealth, and closed it without undue noise.

Herbert, stretched out in an armchair with his shoes off looked up from his reading and peered out of the restricted radiance of the reading-lamp on the small table by his side, the only light in the big room.

'It's I – Alfred. I forgot to look out a book before I went up.'

He came within the radiance of light, his hands comfortably in his dressing-gown pockets, as casual a figure of a man as could be imagined.

Herbert eyed him keenly for a moment, seemed about to say something, changed his mind, and remarked:

'You read *An Experiment in Time*, didn't you? Try the third shelf over there, behind the chesterfield. Most of the newer books are there.'

'Thanks.'

Herbert returned to his book after a moment and Alfred moved to the shelf suggested. He was aware of an immense and stifling excitement. He glanced at the rows of books, but without seeing them. He strolled along the shelves, with his back to the man in the chair. He came close to the corner and the windows between which the Elizabethan poinard hung.

He concentrated on a title in front of him. Read it aloud.

'*Life of Machiavelli*, by Villari,' he said. 'Any good?'

'A little solid. The Victorian biographical fashion.' Herbert did not look round.

'H'm.'

Alfred thought, 'Machiavelli, the man of cunning and ingenuity.'

Machiavelli – Machiavelli – The name ran in and out of his brain like a rat scampering in a bundle of hay. Keep still! Keep quiet!

He edged silently to the wall between the windows and lifted down the dagger. His mind slowed and became rational. Only his breathing was a little faster than normal as his grip closed round the hilt.

Murder in theory was now to be murder in fact. For a moment he had to nerve himself for the physical necessity of action. No holding back now!

The back of Herbert's head was visible above the chair. He was deeply engrossed. Alfred's four paces across the strip of carpet which lay between the windows and the fireplace were quite noiseless and Herbert gave no sign of even a subconscious perception of the movement behind him.

But suddenly he spoke.

Alfred, with a tremor of anxiety, came to an abrupt stop within three feet of him, the dagger held out of sight. Then he realized, by the pitch of Herbert's voice, that he thought he was still at the other side of the room. In relief he stepped swiftly backwards to the shelves again.

'What's that?' he asked.

'I said: "Did you get my note?"'

Alfred brought his wits together with an effort.

'Note?'

'I put it on your dressing-table after dinner, before we started Bridge. Never mind. You must have overlooked it.' He glanced round and added: 'Read it when you go up again. And before we close the subject finally, let me impress upon you that I mean every word of it.'

Alfred was glad that he turned back to his book at that moment. He could not believe that his own quivering emotion, a mingling of rage and nervousness which he controlled with every particle of will he possessed, did not show in his face.

'I see,' he said, and felt sure that the thickness of his tone was perceptible. 'I'll remember. Yes. I must have overlooked it. I'll read it when I go up.'

Written evidence that there had been trouble about money between them! Lying about on a dressing-table! That letter must be destroyed the moment he got back to his room. Destroyed beyond all tracing. He knew perfectly well what was in it. Typical of Mr Justice Caithness! A categorical restatement in writing of his refusal to give his unsatisfactory cousin another penny! 'And let me impress upon you that I mean every word of it!'

All right! Savour your power! Savour it well while you have it, cousin Herbert! For you won't have it long!

Alfred moved again across the space of carpet, his mouth like a scar which is nearly healed, thin and mauve with the tenseness of his muscles. He was no longer conscious of hesitation, of physical reluctance. Savage determination burned in him like a fire.

Herbert did not speak this time, attentive to his book. However, a fraction of a second before the knife swept sideways over the armchair, he straightened himself a little, as though some sixth sense had begun to stir, to warn him of the peril which was upon him.

But the small movement availed him nothing. Indeed, it exposed his side and made the blow more certain.

Alfred used all his strength. Far more, actually, than was necessary to reach the heart, driving the slim blade under the ribs at a slightly upward angle.

He whipped back his hand and left the weapon there.

A slight gasp, it could scarcely be called an exclamation, was the only sound with which Death came. The body twisted once and was still. The head lolled down on to the white shirt front.

Alfred stood motionless behind the chair for perhaps three age-long seconds and then held out his hand in the white rays from the reading-lamp and stared at it. It was quite steady.

He looked up and saw the Caithness crest carved in the stone. It glowed redly in the firelight.

Funny. Even Herbert, lame and sedentary all his days, had come to his end by the sword. The aptness of it pleased strangely.

He took the white handkerchief from the dead man's breast pocket and, bending down, rubbed the hilt of the dagger clean of possible finger-prints. He arranged the handkerchief neatly in its pocket again and went to the window.

Kneeling on the wide sill, the curtains closed behind him, he took out a penknife, opened the window with his hand wrapped in the skirt of his dressing-gown and scratched the paint-work of the frame where the latch came, so that it would look as though it had been forced from outside. The garden was dark and silent, and the cold of the snow smote his cheeks.

He shut the penknife and slipped it back into his dressing-gown pocket.

As he did so he heard a short sound in the room. An inexplicable clatter. It brought his breath to a standstill, cutting him to the depths of his being with sharp, agonizing fear.

He slid off the sill on to the floor behind the curtains, his one instinct being to keep low and out of sight. He landed on hands and knees, rather heavily, crouching and in great fright lest he was bulging the bottom of the curtains.

He stayed there, utterly still, with every sense alert to define the slightest noise or movement in the room he could not see.

As the persistent quietness, unbroken after that one sound, reassured him somewhat, he crawled backwards a foot or so, and put his eye to the join of the curtains.

The library was peaceful, and held nothing living. The dead man's legs and his dangling right arm broke the silhouette of the armchair before the fire. They had not moved.

He stole across the room and saw that the book Herbert had been reading had dropped from his knees to the floor and, striking the shaft of a steel poker as it fell, had disturbed it on the stone hearth.

He brushed his lips with a nervous hand and had the presence of mind to leave the light switched on. A man who fled in haste would not wait to turn it off.

He went unhurriedly out of the library.

All had gone according to plan. No one had heard him, no one had seen him.

As he passed through the lounge he was conscious of a smarting sensation in the top of his thumb and sucked it mechanically. He felt a piece of broken skin with his tongue and wondered vaguely how he had done it.

But he was thinking of the letter on the dressing table and the necessity for obliterating it. Burn it? Yes, in the wash-basin. Swill the ashes down the waste pipe. That would do it.

He reached his room and found the letter, lying under his evening-dress collar. Showed how intent he must have been when he was undressing, not to have noticed it.

He tore it open and read it. His hand shook.

Dear Alfred,

   Here it is, but positively I will not be able to do this again. I believe that you honestly want to succeed in this new project and I detect in you a different attitude. I think it is a genuine one.

                                        Good luck
                                        Herbert.

A slip of pink paper, a blue stamp in the corner . . . a cheque for two thousand pounds.

He stared at it like a man in a trance. The unexpectedness of the thing found him without the capacity for adjustment. His mind flickered helplessly like a candle in a wind and it was several moments before it gathered strength and direction.

Herbert had relented. Affection, generosity – heaven knew what – had moved him to alter his decision.

Herbert . . . whom he had killed.

He covered his eyes and swayed a little on his feet. What had he done?

He caught at his uncertain thoughts and strove to order them.

Then, with sudden uprising, resentment came to his aid.

The magnanimous prig! He had given the money, yes! But with a cramped spirit, reflecting that cramped soul!

He was glad he had killed him! *Glad!* He exulted in it.

And he had *not* killed him uselessly.

Had he been allowed to live there would still have remained the problem of Barbara. His death had set her free – free. Nothing stood between them now.

It had had to be. Fate had ordained that he should not see the letter until afterwards.

He would not dream of destroying it. Together with the cheque it removed beforehand any motive the authorities could find should they, by some impossible effort of imagination, suspect him.

He was safer than ever.

He regarded himself carefully in the mirror, and saw nothing in his eyes to suggest knowledge of what he had done, of what had happened downstairs.

He glanced at his wrist-watch. It congratulated him that he had been out of his bedroom exactly nine-and-a-half minutes.

He took off his dressing-gown and slid between the cold sheets.

But he did not sleep.

His deportment the next morning, during the hour of horror which followed the discovery of the murder by a housemaid, was precisely what it should have been. His pallor and shakiness were no more than to be expected. It was he who rang up the police station and, as a relative of the dead man, took upon his shoulders the burden of the affair in those respects which would have caused pain to Barbara.

He welcomed the Superintendent and the Detective-Inspector, and was exceedingly helpful to those individuals in their preliminary investigation. The tracks in the snow, the open window and the fact that Mr Justice Caithness had not infrequently received threatening letters of one kind or another, seemed to indicate the character and motive of the crime as clearly as any overworked policeman could desire.

'We'll get the fellow all right,' said the Detective-Inspector and set about taking measurements and subjecting the library, the window and the snow to an inch by inch examination. The Superintendent departed to make inquiries in the neighbourhood for evidence of suspicious strangers.

Jim Donaldson seemed to be in a queer state, a profound silence. Only Barbara, in those moments when she could drag her mind from the numbness of shock, realized what he was feeling. Life had played him a trick. He had gained his heart's desire in the eleventh hour but he had paid for it dearly.

He saw her alone for a moment during that terrible morning, and said:

'I shall get over it, my dear, but I have an awful sensation, deep in me, that I have cheated somewhere, somehow.'

She shook her head.

'*He* would not think so.'

He took courage at that and saw the sun shining on the snow-burdened trees. Presently it would disappear, magically.

Alfred, grim but professedly interested in the Detective-Inspector's procedure, watched the man at work. He was satisfied that all was going well but he was not blind to the sudden abstraction which came upon the police officer shortly before mid-day.

He saw him find a finger-print, a single one, on the white paint of the window-sill and also (neither of them paid much attention to it at the moment) a toy soldier on the carpet just below it.

'One of young Robert's,' Alfred explained. 'He was playing with them here yesterday. He must have – – '

He stopped.

The Detective-Inspector, who was puzzled by the fact that the print, which was so particularly clear except for an unevenness in the middle and looked like that of a left thumb should be alone in its glory, noticed the sudden pause.

He did not realize that his companion was struggling with a rising, an overwhelming panic, because he had seen that the tiny sword of the Lifeguardsman was bent and that something had dulled the brightness of its point.

'The sword – ' he muttered and, with his forefinger, felt the small place on the pad of his left thumb where the skin was broken. 'Oh my God! By the sword!'

The Detective-Inspector regarded him curiously and said nothing.

He was not unaccustomed to the sight of a guilty man's face.

It was in that moment that he neglected the trend of his inquiry for a less obvious one. And after a little things began to fit in . . . a very curious affair. And then the widow's story.

★   ★   ★

Counsel for the Defence did his best. He asked, was it sensible to suggest that a man should murder the person who had given him so many reasons for gratitude? Two thousand reasons, for example, that very evening?

But the jury thought it might be. Apart from all that, however, they were much impressed by the evidence of the finger-print expert and the doctor, who together were unshakeably convincing on the subject of the prisoner's left thumb. The blood-chemist proved very successfully that the print on the window-sill had not been there more than ten hours when the Inspector found it. The time it had been made corresponded with the time of the murder.

The prisoner displayed no great effort in denying the charge the Crown had brought against him. He listened to the proceedings without emotion, his eyes now and again fixing themselves in an unwavering stare on the smallest of the exhibits ranged on the table in the well of the court. A toy Lifeguard with a broken sword.

It seemed to fascinate him.

He was hanged in May.

SUPERFLUOUS MURDER

Milward Kennedy

As the train came to a standstill and he alighted from his carriage, John Mansbridge was amazed at the steadiness of his nerves. It was long since he had felt so calm and serene. Perhaps it was because he had reached a definite decision, after weeks of agonized doubt and fear. And yet his decision was not absolutely definite. He did not intend his visit to end in his cousin's murder if there was any hitch, however slight, in his careful yet simple plan.

In accordance with the plan, he engaged the ticket collector in conversation about a mythical parcel which he pretended to have left on the platform on the occasion of his last visit, nearly a month ago. Naturally, he could get no news of it, but time enough was occupied to make him leave the station a clear five minutes after the few other passengers who had left the train at Gorse Hill had departed into the night.

'By Jove!' he said to the ticket collector, looking up at the station clock, 'is it as late as that?' My cousin, Mr Felix Mansbridge, will be wondering what has become of me, and it will take me a good three quarters of an hour to walk to his house.'

'All of that, sir, on a night like this,' said the ticket collector, and bade him a good night which was the more cordial for the shilling which was slipped into his hand.

John Mansbridge stepped briskly out of the station and down the country road towards the village. So far, so good. He had clearly established two facts: to wit, the time when he had left the station, and his intention to make his way on foot to his cousin's house.

He walked rapidly to the village and stopped at the 'Four Feathers' to repeat his inquiry about his parcel – there was just a chance, he suggested, that he had left it there. Again he was at pains to establish the time of his visit; it was just on closing time, so he made his drink a short one. To himself he reflected that the whisky would put just the right edge on his judgment.

Then he went on his way, and at the far end of the village called a cheerful good night to the policeman on duty there. He smiled in the darkness to reflect that the police system was an integral part of his plan. In something under an hour's time the constable would be relieved, and his relief came down the lonely hill past Felix's house.

He walked on steadily, treading rather heavily to ensure that the policeman heard him, until he had turned the next corner. Then he took to his heels along the grass at the edge of the road, climbed a gate on the left, and doubled along a cart-track which led back to the other side of the village. He did not follow it to its end, but turned off across a smooth meadow and found his way without difficulty to a tumble-down shed. He pulled the door open and, drawing an electric torch from his pocket, flashed it on the interior before entering. He gave an involuntary sigh of satisfaction – the dust was undisturbed since his last visit; it seemed safe to assume that the presence of the bicycle had not been noticed.

He had taken great pains with that bicycle – bought it second-hand, and yet in good condition, with tyres well worn (so that they left no distinctive tracks) and yet with plenty of life in them. The dealer in the far-away Gloucestershire town who had sold it to him had taken no particular interest in the deal, and its transport to Gorse Hill had been effected by slow and unobtrusive stages – the last of them, to the abandoned shed, under the cover of darkness. The heap of loose sand inside the shed afforded an admirable means of covering up all signs of the use to which its shelter had been put.

He repeated his precautions, steeling himself against a tendency to hustle. The bicycle was carefully lifted out of the shed and leant against the wall; the heap of sand was used to conceal the marks of his feet; the heap itself was artistically arranged. Then he carried the bicycle to the footpath beyond the shed and mounted it.

Dark as the night was, he found it easy to follow the track. Thanks to the drought, it was hard and firm and he made good speed. Not only that, he was confident that there would be few, if any, traces of his passage. The wind at his back also helped him on his course.

Nor did he hear or see a soul; the dogs, even, at the one farmhouse which he passed at some distance on his right, failed, apparently, to detect him. Almost before he realized it, a dark shimmer told him he had reached his first objective, the pond. He dismounted and, wheeling the bicycle, made his way cautiously to the spot which he had previously marked down as suitable to his purpose – where the bank was covered with short, dry stubble and where, he knew, the water was nearly four feet deep up to the very edge.

He knelt and lowered the bicycle silently into the pond. It was a little more difficult than he had expected, but still, his plan worked smoothly. The bicycle certainly had disappeared; it would be invisible in the dirty water and soon would sink deep into the soft mud and slime. So far as he could judge, the surface weeds would not look as though they had been wilfully and rather drastically disturbed. Deliberately he did what he could to improve this impression.

But he could not afford to linger; on the second stage of his journey time was of vital importance. He left the foot-path, skirted the far end of the pond, climbed another gate, and ran across the field beyond it. From the far side he came in sight of his cousin's house. A soft light shone from the windows of the study, but otherwise there was no sign of life. That was as it should be; the married couple who 'did' for Felix were away on holiday and he was being ministered to by a woman from the village who 'came in by the day.'

John Mansbridge hurried on till he reached the gate at the bottom of the garden. Here he forced himself to pause in order to recover his breath. His heart was pounding against his ribs – this he firmly ascribed to his physical efforts and not to excitement.

Very cautiously he pulled out his watch and flashed his torch on its face. Again he sighed, this time not so much in contentment as because Fate seemed to have committed him to the deed. He had 'gained' a good twenty minutes – in other words, he had reached the house some twenty-two minutes before, on the evidence which he had created, it was possible for him to have done so. He was satisfied that he had arrived in entire secrecy, and it had taken him two minutes less than he had allowed.

He opened the gate and closed it behind him so carefully that the latch did not make a sound. He walked swiftly up the path – or rather the grass border – until he came to the lawn. He tiptoed across it towards the windows. They were closed, and the thin red curtains drawn. He leant close to the glass, though careful not to touch it, and with a shock detected the sound of a voice which seemed strange to him. Had all his plan split upon a single rock?

He crept round to the window at the other side. It was open, and though this side was sheltered from the breeze the curtain had blown sufficiently aside to give him a clear view of most of the room. Simultaneously his lips smiled and his heart gave a fierce thump. The 'strange voice' was that of the loudspeaker, delivering a lecture on Babylonian pottery. Apparently it had had the effect of sending Felix to sleep.

He was sitting in an armchair of the 'grandmother' variety; its back was towards the door, so that it was sideways to the window through which John Mansbridge was peering. His bald head was lodged comfortably on a cushion, and his eyes were closed. His thin hands clasped the arms of the chair. He looked ill and tired, and his cousin felt almost sorry for him, till he noticed also the smug little smile on his lips. On a table beside him were a tumbler and a reading-lamp and a paper or two. On a table in the middle of the room stood a tray containing a small whisky decanter, a siphon and a couple more glasses.

Anger welled up in John Mansbridge. How infernally comfortable and smug Felix was! Always so full of advice and patronage, and at the same time as mean as sin.

All very well to 'advise you, my dear John, to settle down to a steady job; give up the night club and melodrama existence.' As if he didn't know perfectly well that if Felix wasn't so infernally afraid of hurting himself and that heart which he pretended was so weak (as a matter of fact, he probably hadn't got such a thing), he'd have been painting the world red himself. Except that he was so mean. Positively hurt him to spend a halfpenny. Always whining about having no money. Damn it, hadn't he, John, seen the old man's will? He knew damned well that Felix had inherited a fat fortune. And when his only living relative asked him for a hundred or two, to help things along, he said he couldn't do it. Paying off debts of his father's.

Damned lie, that's what it was. Enough to make anyone – well – sign the wrong name on a cheque. It ought to teach Felix a lesson, but the chances were that it would lead him to suppose that a lecture on morality was called for. All very fine to be honest when you've got more money than you want, and hate spending any of it. Canting hypocrite, that's all Felix was; piously swearing he was a poor man. 'All I can do, John, is to carry a large insurance on my life. And I had to pay a stiff price for that – it was all I could do to get the company to accept me at all. My heart, you know. Still, I wanted to do what I could for you, and I'm not likely to live long.'

No, he was not likely to live long, but it wouldn't be his heart that finished him off. And when he wrote that note asking his cousin to come and see him one day next week about a 'cheque which he didn't quite understand,' he finally settled his own fate. If the shock of what his cousin said didn't polish him off then and there (which wasn't likely; nothing wrong with his heart at all), then something else would. And John Mansbridge felt almost grateful to his cousin for being so feeble and flabby; he wouldn't put up much of a fight even for his life.

These thoughts, of a kind which had haunted him for weeks, flashed through John Mansbridge's mind in the second or two which he spent at the window. They served to give him fresh strength and determination.

A new thought suddenly struck him. There was Felix, to all appearances fast asleep. If he crept in noiselessly enough, he might be able to finish him off there, in the chair. It would be easy to fake signs of a struggle afterwards. That Indian club hanging in the hall. But suppose Felix woke up and saw him? Well, it would only curtail the interview. True, he would be sorry not to fire off the speech he had rehearsed, but that was a small point. Damn it, he'd have a shot at it.

He crouched on the lawn and cautiously took off his shoes; he tied the laces together for ease in carrying. He slipped on the gloves which were in his pocket and drew out from his ticket-pocket the 'spare' latch-key which he had so successfully purloined when last he was down at Gorse Hill. He crept round to the front door, deposited his shoes on the doorstep and, with infinite precaution, slipped the key into the Yale lock. To his satisfaction the door opened silently. He dared not turn on the hall light, but there was sufficient illumination from the half-open door of the study to show him all that he needed to see.

There was a faint scrape as he withdrew the key. He paused, but no sound came from the study. A second later the front door was safely and securely closed again. He took down an Indian club (not the first, but the one by the door of the dining-room), and tried its weight with a savage grin. Slipping the door-key back into his pocket, he advanced silently into the study.

Felix had not stirred – a nice way to welcome your only cousin! There was his bald head temptingly visible above the back of the chair. John stepped forward and swung the club . . .

That was that. All old scores wiped out. No need to make sure of the result – and no need to look at it. One had done things of the same kind in the War and felt none the worse. Funny what a difference there was, all the same. Still, no time to lose. No use getting sentimental. Find the cheque, that was the first thing. That ought not to be difficult – Felix would be sure to have it at hand, all ready for the interview; probably in the top drawer of the writing-desk. He jumped as he suddenly became conscious that the voice of the Babylonian expert filled the room, and with an oath he switched off the wireless. Now for the cheque.

But there was no forged cheque in the top drawer, and none in any other drawer of the desk. He began to tear envelopes open feverishly; pulled open the cupboard below the bookshelves; even ran up to Felix's bedroom. Where the hell could it be? He looked at his watch and a sick despair seized him. He had only seven minutes left before he must leave the house, and a lot had still to be done.

Good heavens, perhaps it was in Felix's pocket. What a fool not to think of it! Actually he *had* thought of it, but had thrust the idea aside; he didn't want to touch the body. Well, there was no help for it.

In the breast pocket was nothing but a pocket-book. Well, the notes would be useful, anyway. He took them, and thrust the pocket-book roughly back again. Then in the right hand side-pocket of the dinner-jacket his fingers detected an envelope. He pulled it out, and involuntarily gave a whistle of surprise. The envelope was addressed to himself, and the flap stuck down. He ripped it open. The cheque was inside, enclosed, apparently, in a letter. He heaved a sigh of relief, and thrust the envelope into his own pocket. He had meant to destroy the cheque then and there, but his programme must be slightly modified. The change involved only a very small risk.

He put the spare key back in the top drawer of the writing-table, from which he had originally purloined it; he pushed it well to the back amongst some papers in case its loss had been discovered, and in order to suggest that it had been hidden in the drawer all the time. You could not be too careful of details. Then he went to the front door and wedged it carefully open with the door-mat. He went outside and with a stick from the hall smashed a pane of glass in the dining-room window. He thrust in his hand, unlatched the window, and opened it at the bottom. He returned to the house and again shut the front door. This time he brought his shoes in with him.

Hastily he pulled open the sideboard cupboard in the dining-room, seized some spoons and forks, rolled them roughly in a strip of green baize which was in the cupboard, and tossed the package on the table. That was good enough, he thought.

Then back into the study for the last and most unpleasant job.

He lifted his cousin's arm with a reluctant shudder, and turned back the hand of his wrist-watch until it pointed to about five minutes after the time when he, John, had left the pub in the village. He heaved his cousin's body out of the armchair and arranged it as well as he could to suggest that he had been standing by the fireplace when he was struck. He laid the body on its right side; the left arm he stretched roughly across the fender, and made sure that the blow had stopped the watch. He stood up again and surveyed the room. He knocked over a small chair, but decided that otherwise his own search had produced an excellent representation of a struggle. The club he left lying by the fireplace.

He looked at his watch. All was well. He was within his scheduled time again. He put on his shoes, tying the bows neatly, despite the involuntary trembling of his hands, and made his exit from the silent house by way of the open window in the dining-room. His jump carried him clear of the narrow flower-bed below the window, on to the flagged path leading from the gate to the front door. Then he ran round the house, back to the garden gate, across the paddock to the left, and so through a well-worn gap in the hedge, into the lane from the village. At this point it dipped between two hills. He took off and pocketed his gloves and then walked quickly on for about thirty yards up the hill in the direction of the village, keeping to the grass by the roadside. He stopped and drew from his pocket a pipe, tobacco-pouch and a silver match-box. He filled his pipe and struck one of the wax vestas. The wind blew it out at once and he threw it aside. He used three others before his pipe was fairly alight, and then he began to walk slowly back, down the hill towards the house. He walked at the side of the road, and made a point of kicking his shoes on the loose stones. He ought to arrive with dusty shoes, and he was by no means anxious for his second approach to be as silent as his first.

He reached the gate and paused in some anxiety. The relieving constable was due to pass at any moment now. The direction of the wind for the first time became a slight disadvantage. However, he must take no risks. He walked to the front door, rang the bell, waited, and rang again. Then he knocked. After a further interval he walked back towards the gate and listened intently. To his joy, he caught the sound of footsteps. He ran back to the house and shouted, 'Felix! Felix!' in tones of increasing excitement. He heard the footsteps reach the gate and pause. 'Felix! Felix!' he shouted. 'Are you there?'

The gravel scrunched under a pair of heavy boots.

'Anything the matter?' asked a deep, comfortable voice.

'What? Who's that?' John Mansbridge hoped that he had sounded startled.

'Police, sir. What's the trouble?'

John Mansbridge hastily explained his identity.

'This is my cousin's house. Mr Felix Mansbridge.'

'That's right, sir.'

'He asked me to come and see him and stay the night – I do from time to time. Keep a pair of pyjamas here, don't you know, and I've just walked up from the station and, well – I can't make him hear – or anyone else. I know he's expecting me. And – look at that!' The constable had reached the door and, urged by the excited cousin, peered at the open window.

'Half a minute,' he said. 'I'll just have a look –'

'Here, I've got a torch,' said John and produced his from his pocket. The constable took it with a word of thanks. He flashed it on the window and gave a grunt of surprise. He seemed uncertain what to do next.

Mansbridge thumped on the knocker again; then the two men strained their ears – or one of them did.

'I wonder if one of the other windows . . . ' suggested Mansbridge. The constable leapt at the idea and led the way rapidly round the house until he reached the window through which his companion had peered – oh, years ago, it seemed.

'Looks bad, sir,' said the constable. 'We'd best get round to the front again.' Indeed, the study window was too narrow to admit of entrance.

The constable became a man of action. He bade Mansbridge wait by the door while he climbed in by the window, and Mansbridge again reflected with satisfaction that if he had left any traces by either window, the burly constable would have eliminated them pretty completely.

A moment later the door was opened.

'Come in, sir,' the constable whispered hoarsely, 'and wait outside the room where the light is, if you don't mind. I just want to have a look first.'

He walked to the study and half-closed the door behind him. John Mansbridge waited for what seemed an eternity, but in fact was only a few seconds. The constable sized up the situation and returned, switching on the light in the hall. The other man had been fighting to retain control of his nerves, but he was conscious that sweat was pouring down his face. The constable glanced at him with respectful sympathy and muttering, 'Afraid this will be a shock to you, sir,' led the way to the study.

John Mansbridge followed; his return to the horrible scene which he had left only a few minutes before seemed somehow to act as a stimulant to his nerves. His performance of horror and shock was a convincing one, and all the time his inner consciousness was gleefully congratulating him upon it.

'How – how did it happen?' he gasped.

'Ah, queer business,' the constable answered. 'Can't make out what's happened to the room.'

'Yes, but Felix – my cousin?'

'Well, that will have to be seen to,' was the ponderous reply. 'Maybe he smashed himself on the fender there. But it's queer. You see, sir' – he hesitated and then went on – 'it's a case of suicide, seemingly. I found this on the table there, with the glass on it.'

And he held out a sheet of paper, covered with Felix's writing. John stared at it; how in the devil's name had he overlooked the little table? Of course he found the forged cheque before he got as far, but . . .

Through the daze which beset him he read the opening words:

I, Felix Edward Mansbridge, being of sound mind, solemnly declare that I am dying by my own act. I have taken poison . . .

The room and the paper whirled before his eyes. From a distance he heard the constable say, 'I'll just ring up the Station.' Then a 'Hallo,' but addressed, it seemed, not to the Exchange but to himself, and a strong arm lowered him into the very chair where Felix had sat, his bald head just visible –

There was a clink of glass.

'Drink this, sir,' said the constable, holding a tumbler to his lips.

'Now let's see where we are,' the superintendent addressed the sergeant and the constable; the latter was manifestly uneasy at the prominence into which his part in the affair had thrust him.

'First, let's fix the known facts about this man, John Mansbridge's, movements. We know the train he came by and the time he left the station; we know he was in the "Four Feathers" just before closing time, and we know he left it and walked past Robson, who was still on duty, in the direction of his cousin's house. There is no turning off the lane, and it's pretty deserted at night. In fact, I doubt if anyone uses it except you, Longden. And about forty minutes or three quarters of an hour after John Mansbridge left the village, you see two or three matches struck as you come down the hill towards the house. And when you get to the house, you find the man hammering at the door. That correct?'

The sergeant and the constable agreed.

'Right. And I may add that we're pretty sure it *was* Mr John Mansbridge who lit his pipe because he carried a box of wax vestas – not so common these days in country villages – and we found no less than four used matches of the same kind just about the spot where Longden here indicated.'

The constable perked up a little, as if detecting a word of praise for himself.

'All very well and good,' the superintendent continued. 'It certainly looks as if the man walked from the station as he said he was going to. Took just the normal time, and his shoes bear out his story. And I don't see how else he could have got there. We may, of course, find someone who met him in the lane, but I should think that unlikely. So much for that.'

He paused for a moment, as if to arrange his thoughts in order, and then resumed his lecture (as it seemed to be).

'Now let's consider this Felix Mansbridge. It seems a pretty clear case of suicide to me' – the sergeant made as if to interrupt – 'but I admit that isn't what we're supposed to think. What we are supposed to think is this: that someone or other broke into the house, began to steal the silver, was disturbed, caught up that club from the hall, knocked the dead man on the head, after a struggle, and decamped. And the broken watch is to suggest that this happened about five minutes after Mr John Mansbridge left the "Four Feathers" and when, consequently, he couldn't be at his cousin's house. I'm afraid I can't swallow that story.'

'You're sure he was poisoned, then, sir?' asked the sergeant.

'Perfectly. And that's not all. In the first place, though, it's not impossible that he was killed in a struggle, it's surprising – considering that the blow was delivered from behind and from above. Then, secondly, there's his confession of suicide. You see, it pretty well fixes the time.'

'How's that, sir?'

'Why, he talked about taking his departure from the world to Wagner's accompaniment.'

'Crazy,' said the sergeant.

'Not in the way you mean. I've no doubt he was thinking of the wireless. You look up last's night programmes and you'll find a Wagner item, and you'll see why, in my opinion, he only took the poison ten minutes after the time shown by the broken watch. And, finally, there's the wound on the head. You take my word, the doctors will find that it was delivered after the man was dead.'

'But why in the name of –'

'Sheer accident, Sergeant, in my opinion. Result of sticking to a prearranged plan too closely. Whoever used the club believed that Felix Mansbridge was alive – and that means premeditated murder. Why, in the name of whatever you were going to say, should a burglar suddenly stop his burgling to go into the next room and bash in the head of the owner of the house, and then take to his heels, leaving the swag behind? It stands to reason there never was a burglar at all.'

'Then who d'you reckon it was, sir?'

The superintendent shrugged his shoulders.

'Strictly speaking, I suppose we ought to lay hands on a suspicious fugitive, an unknown visitor,' he said, 'but I fancy it would be sheer waste of time. There was only one visitor – the cousin, John Mansbridge.'

'But his alibi, sir.'

'I know. And I don't see how we're to break it. All I can say is that *somehow* he got there long before he met you, Longden. And as we can *prove* that he got there some minutes at least before Longden found him at the door, I don't think his alibi holds water at all. I admit I don't see how he rigged it, but I'm satisfied that it's a fake.'

'You can *prove* it, sir?' the sergeant interposed, in a tone which suggested respectful doubt.

'Certainly. For here's a letter which was found in his pocket. It's addressed to him and dated yesterday. The woman who looked after Mr Felix Mansbridge said he wrote a letter before she left, but as he hadn't got a stamp he said it could wait till next day. I haven't a doubt this is the letter – no letter was found in the house ready for post, and you can see that this envelope was addressed *and* gummed down. And the woman says he put the letter in the side pocket of his dinner jacket – the right side. You'll observe here that if it really was in the right side pocket it would have been a job to take it out as the body lay, on its right side, in front of the fireplace – in other words, it was taken out before the body lay there. That's a small point, perhaps.

'The main thing is the letter itself – addressed to John Mansbridge Esq., and found in John Mansbridge Esquire's pocket. I suggest that he found it after the writer was dead, and probably before his body lay on the hearth rug. For we know that he didn't take the letter while he was in the house with Longden – and therefore he must have done so a good five minutes sooner, and pretty certainly more than that.'

'What's in the letter, sir?' the sergeant inquired.

'A hint of a motive, to put it mildly. It's long; here's the gist of

it. Felix says that he has had no answer to his note, and supposes
that the cousin cannot face him; in other words, he cannot deny the
forging of the cheque. Felix says it is hopeless. His cousin will never
be convinced that he, Felix, is indeed and in truth a poor man – the
large sums mentioned in his father's will were swallowed up by the
unpaid debts. Nor, apparently, does the cousin believe that Felix is
indeed a sick man. So sick, that though he isn't likely to die next
month, the doctors say that he can't live more than a year at the
outside. The forgery is the last straw; he's to have no peace in this
world, so he'll go to the next, and leave his cousin to inherit his life
insurance and what little else there is. And he is not to worry; he
will make it quite clear to the police that it was a case of suicide –
which thanks to a special clause, will not invalidate the insurance
policy. Oh, yes, he encloses the forged cheque in question, which,
he says, he has told the Bank is in order. Points to a motive, eh?
And makes John Mansbridge's character pretty clear. Thorough
wrong 'un.'

There was another pause.

'I see, sir,' the sergeant said slowly. 'And you don't think that
John Mansbridge got in quite innocently and found that letter – say,
five minutes before Longden saw him light his pipe?'

The Superintendent shook his head.

'No, that meeting with Longden, like those calls at the "Four
Feathers" and the station, were all part of the man's plan. The pipe-
lighting was deliberate – he must have been at pains to observe the
exact hour at which Longden walked down that lane. He never
thought that out on the spur of the moment.'

Police Constable Longden cleared his throat.

'If I may be so bold, sir, do you mean to say Mr Felix was dead
before this Mr John came, and that Mr John smashed his head in
not knowing he was dead already?'

'That's it, in a nutshell, Constable. How he got to the house in
time, and how he got in, I don't know. Perhaps he had a duplicate
key, and chucked it away in the grass somewhere. But in my
opinion, however he did it he came down to murder his cousin,
and to the best of his belief till you stuck that confession in his hands
he *had* murdered his cousin.'

'Thank you, sir. Then to all intents and purposes he was a murderer?'

'I haven't a doubt of it.'

'Well, sir,' and the constable wiped his brow, 'that kind of makes things easier. I don't rightly know what you'll do about it, officially like, but I feel easier in me own mind. I can tell you, sir, when I finished with telephoning and found this Mr John Mansbridge dead in the armchair – well, I didn't know whether I was alive or dead meself. Fancy me trying to help him over the shock of seeing his cousin's corpse by giving him a stiff dose of the very same whisky as his cousin had put the poison in. Act of God like, wasn't it sir?'

He spoke hopefully, with no intention of irreverence.

SAXOPHONE SOLO

G. R. Malloch

'I SENT for you this morning, Ego,' said the Assistant-Commissioner, 'because rather a queer case has turned up and it seems to me that perhaps it is more in your line than that of less eccentric members of the force.'

'Many thanks for those kind words, sir,' murmured Ego. 'Am I to understand that one of my esteemed colleagues has fallen down badly over it?'

'Nothing of the sort. But it may involve prolonged inquiries and we can't spare anyone else at present.'

'Again, thank you, sir.'

'Now, look here – I want you to listen seriously. The truth is that this is a very delicate matter and that's why I'm choosing you. It may be a case of murder and it may not; so you will have to tread delicately. On the face of it, it's simply a sudden death from heart failure and that's likely to be the Coroner's verdict. But the local police are not quite easy about it and the Chief Constable of Fordshire has asked us to look into things.'

'I see, sir.'

'The facts, so far as we know them, are that a young man named Wilkins recently inherited from a distant relative a fortune and a house which, strangely enough, is called Wilkins Hall. He spends most of his time in London and Paris and apparently also a good deal of his money. He is not a very pleasant young fellow, I gather, and is so seldom at the Hall that he is scarcely known at all locally. He has one hobby in addition to those you can imagine from what I have said. That is conducting a jazz band, which he formed and pays himself.'

'I know the fellow,' said Ego. 'He persuaded the Public Cave –

that's a dance club, sir, in case you don't know about such places – to let him provide the music there, for a week. It wasn't a bad band, either. He had a wart on his nose, I remember.'

'Is the Public Cave situated in your suburb, by any chance?' countered the Assistant-Commissioner. 'No? Well, as you have seen Mr Wilkins, I needn't describe him or his activities further. It seems that last week he arrived unexpectedly at the Hall. Dinner was prepared for him by the servants – he had kept on his relative's old butler, by the way – but, just before dinner hour, he announced that he was going out. Sort of fellow who didn't consider the servants. Didn't know enough, perhaps. Anyhow, he went out and was not heard to return that night. But next morning a maid found him, or thought she found him, in the library, dead. Lying on a sofa. Doctor was called and he informed police. No injury of any kind. Shoes dirty, clothing dirty and torn in one or two places, apparently been exposed to weather. It was a cold, windy night. A telegram was sent by the police to his only know relative, a man named Baufstein, who was a musician in an orchestra in some London restaurant.

Ego nodded.

'Baufstein – I know him. Malabani's – plays the saxophone in the band there. Best saxophone player I've ever heard. This is interesting, sir.'

'I am glad of that,' said the Assistant-Commissioner, sardonically. 'To get to the end of it, who should turn up but young Mr Wilkins, himself, very much alive. His story is that he had asked Baufstein to come down to the Hall about some matter of importance and that when he didn't turn up, he went back to London to find him. He was actually at Baufstein's lodgings when the police telegram arrived.

'Did he answer it?'

'Yes – here is a copy. *Cannot understand coming immediately, Wilkins.*'

'And who was the corpse?'

'That's the funny thing. It was his cousin Baufstein, the saxophone man. Wilkin's explanation of the affair, which the police have had to accept, is that his cousin came down to see him, got lost in the darkness and the gale that was blowing and arrived at the Hall too late to arouse the servants. So he climbed in through the window, which was open and had apparently been left unfastened, as there was no sign of its having been forced. Then he died, perhaps of heart failure. He wasn't strong and may have been exhausted.'

'Baufstein was a pale, weak-looking fellow, that's true,' said Ego. 'Any sign of a struggle?'

'Not the slightest. He must have just laid down on the sofa and died.'

'Well, sir,' said Ego, assuming an exasperatingly puzzled air, 'that was no crime, was it? Unless, of course, being on enclosed premises for an unlawful purpose, or breaking in, or insulting behaviour. As he was invited, though, it makes things difficult.'

'I have not said, so far, that there was any crime,' said the Assistant-Commissioner, patiently. 'Merely that the local police are not quite easy in their minds.'

'Post mortem?'

'Yes. The result will be disclosed at the inquest tomorrow but I can tell you that nothing suspicious was found and that the doctor adheres to heart failure. He had a weak heart.'

'Did Wilkins stand to inherit anything from his cousin?'

'Nothing but a few pounds and his effects. But it seems that Wilkins had made a will leaving everything to Baufstein. They were both orphans and cousins and it seems that Baufstein had saved Wilkin's life when they were swimming together.'

'And do you really think there is anything to investigate, sir?'

'Myself, I don't think there is; but you know how in these country districts gossip goes about and people get a bad name. They dislike Wilkins down there. For one thing, he's a stranger to them and remains a stranger. Then he's of foreign parentage, like Baufstein, and came into the Wilkins fortune by some marriage of a Wilkins with a Baufstein. They regard him as an interloper. He never subscribes to their charities or takes any interest in local affairs – and there you are! Quite enough to convince the yokels that he must be a villain.'

'What you want me to do, then,' said Ego, 'is to find out whether Wilkins had any secret motive for murdering his cousin. I dare say there are poisons beyond the range of the local doctor.'

'Quite,' said the Assistant-Commissioner, 'but I think the whole thing's a mare's nest. But there are clever criminals about, as you know.'

'Are there, sir?' asked Ego, with an air of deceptive innocence. 'Some are reputed clever but I always think that reputations of all kinds are the most deceiving things imaginable. When I first went to live in our suburb, I was always hearing about a man named Jones, who was reputed to be the best chess player in the district. It wasn't till I had played with him myself and found out that he was a rabbit, that I realized that his reputation was solely due to the fact that every man who had played with him had beaten him. Naturally, they went about telling their wives what a fine player he was. Only human nature, don't you think, sir?'

'Well, well,' said the Assistant-Commissioner, wearily, 'pray, what is the application?'

'It was only that you used the phrase, clever criminal, sir. There was a man sent down the other day, who was described to the reporters by my esteemed colleague, Jenkins, who happened to have caught him, as the cleverest criminal of the age. And in support of this theory, colleague Jenkins gave a list of twenty convictions against the poor man.'

'What of it?'

'Well, I don't know, sir! I'm not a deep thinker, like some gentlemen at the Yard, but it seems to me that twenty convictions are just twenty reasons for supposing that the man was a fool at the game. It's not a very clever criminal who's caught twenty times, is it, sir? Or caught by Jenkins either, for that matter, though perhaps I should not say so.'

'You should not. Loyalty to one's colleagues should be a basic principle of conduct with all officers.'

'Quite so, sir! That's why I reproach myself so severely with having said it. To get out of further temptation, I'd better go back to the case we were discussing.'

'Has any idea suggested itself to you?'

'Only that if there is a crime in this at all, it's too clever a bit of work for a professional. No, it sounds like a first crime – an amateur's crime. The most difficult of all to detect. The Amateur's First Crime! Sounds like the title of a book, does it not, sir?'

'Why an amateur?'

'Because the amateur always goes about his crime much more carefully than your slapdash professional. You see, he's bound to be a student of detective stories. He knows it all, he knows it all!

And he takes such elaborate precautions that he often gets found out by them. On the other hand, he often gets away with it.

> 'Full many a crook is born to work unseen,
> Full many a pious sidesman stoops to steal,
> Full many a crime of purest ray serene,
> The deep unfathomed cellars of London conceal.

'I often amuse myself at home, sir, with literary work – that's a verse from my Scotland Yard Edition of the Poets. It doesn't scan very well yet, but I shall polish it up in time.'

'One hopes so. But obvious though the connection between poetry and crime is, in your case, I think we had better concentrate on crime for the moment. I'm afraid I do not agree with your ideas about the amateur criminal. He is usually a blunderer of the first water.'

'Sometimes, sir, sometimes,' said Ego, ruminatively. 'Of course a man can take too many precautions. That's the amateur's chief weakness. He leaves so many precautions lying around that the sleuth from Scotland Yard positively trips over them. A precaution is a precaution on one side and a clue on the other. You only want to pick it up and look at the underneath side.'

'When will you come to the point?' asked the Assistant-Commissioner, glancing at his wrist-watch. 'Do you want any more information from me?'

'There is one thing you haven't explained, sir, and that is how the servants didn't see that the dead man was a stranger. A minor point, but interesting.'

'As you have seen both Wilkins and Baufstein, that should not require much explanation. Remember that Wilkins was practically a stranger to his servants at the Hall. He and his cousin were as like as two peas, according to the photographs. The butler is a very old man and near-sighted, and the maid had only seen her employer once before.'

'Yes,' agreed Ego. 'Now that I think of it, they were superficially very much the same type – pale-faced, dark-haired young men with side whiskers like mine, loose mouths and long noses. Yes, I see. Have the police been to Baufstein's lodgings?'

'Yes, and they found a letter from Wilkins asking Baufstein down to the Hall on the day he arrived there. They didn't make an exhaustive search. That satisfied them of the truth of Wilkin's story.'

'I see, sir,' said Ego. 'And they both played the saxophone. I don't think there is any murder in this case, sir, but it's a queer story. The saxophone! That sounds like a good line to follow. There's something very human about a saxophone, don't you think, sir? The way it moans and howls and sobs and laughs at you, I mean. You can't imagine a man who plays the saxophone committing a murder. But a drummer, now – I don't know.'

'For Heaven's sake, go away and get down to it,' moaned the Assistant-Commissioner. 'I don't know why I allow you to come in here and waste my time. You never listen to what anyone else has to say and you never do what you're told. Why the authorities allow you so much latitude, I don't know!'

'It's to please the papers, sir. When they're told that I'm with you, they rush off and get out a stop press edition. "The Assistant-Commissioner was in close conference with a high official at the Yard concerning the Smith murder. Startling developments are expected in connection with this case. An arrest may follow at any moment." They like that sort of thing, sir, and it keeps them busy and out of our way.'

'Good morning, Inspector!'

'Good morning, sir, and thank you. I'm sorry about Baufstein. I rather liked the lad. He told me the other day that he'd just finished a new song that he thought a lot of, you know – one of those jazz songs that the band sings and plays. They were fixing up a sort of production ceremony for him at Malabani's, when it was to be announced and played for the first time. But I suppose that's off, now.'

'What has that to do with the case?'

'I don't know, sir; but I'm going to look for the manuscript of that song. Do you know what it was called, sir?'

'No, I don't, and unless it has some bearing on the matter –'

'Oh, but it's a good title, a striking title, sir. What do you think of this?

There's a Good Big Chicken in this Fresh Egg.

Sort of catchy lilt about it. All right, sir, I'm off!'

The door closed hastily on Detective-Inspector Ego.

* * *

Ego arrived at the Wilkins Arms in the capacity of a benevolent-looking gentleman making a little tour through the Home counties in his car. He chatted genially with the landlord, admired the beauties of the local scene, inquired about fishing, and, on learning that fishing was to be had, announced his intention of stopping for a day or two. The landlord was delighted with his guest and, after a little chat in the bar, he accompanied him to the door of the inn to point out the nearest way to the river which Mr Brown wished to inspect.

'Dear me,' said Mr Brown, adjusting his spectacles to get a better view, 'surely something is happening in the village this morning? Where are all those people going?'

'Well, sir, as a matter of fact, there is something happening in the village this morning, as you say. It's the inquest on the young Squire's cousin to-day. Up at the Hall, it's being held. A strange story, it is.'

'Why, of course!' exclaimed Mr Brown. 'I know – I read about it in the papers. Wilkins – so it was here, was it? Funny I should come to this place to-day of all days! Do you know, landlord, I must confess to some curiosity about such things – a morbid taste, perhaps, but these little dramas of the Courts have an interest all their own. Do you think I should be admitted?'

'The public has a right to attend an inquest, sir, so far as I've ever heard. I dare say you would get in all right.'

'Then, do you know, I think I'll just trot up with the crowd and look at the water afterwards.'

He went off in the track of the little group of men, who were mostly jurymen in their best clothes. The iron gates of the park stood open. They passed the lodge, which had a tumbledown appearance, and followed a weedy drive up to the hall. The house had been imposing but was obviously ill-kept and neglected. Everything bore out the idea that young Mr Wilkins must be an infrequent visitor to the estate he had inherited.

When he reached the front of the house, Mr Brown did not immediately follow the jurymen who passed under a high portico into the hall. He diverged from the group and strolled in a leisurely fashion along the weed-grown gravel, surveying the mansion with the interest of a visitor who saw it for the first time. A policeman who was standing near the door watched his movements curiously and to him Mr Brown presently approached, his hands behind his back and benevolence gleaming in the eyes behind the horn-rimmed spectacles.

'This must have been a fine place in its palmy days, constable,' he remarked with a pleasantly mournful smile.

'It was, sir,' said the constable, disarmed of suspicion, as most people were when Ego willed that they should be. 'When the old Squire, uncle of the present one, lived here, it was a very different place. You wouldn't hardly know it, sir.'

'I dare say, I dare say! But young men have different ideas. They're all for a town life, nowadays. They tell me at the inn that you don't see much of the young squire down here.'

'I'd never set eyes on him myself, sir, till this affair cropped up. Why, his own servants hardly know him, they say.'

'Well, it's a melancholy affair, altogether. I suppose it was in one of those rooms we are looking at now that the poor young cousin's body was found?'

'Yes – the library, sir. I'll show you.' And the constable led the way to the left wing of the building and pointed to two long windows which came down to within a few feet of the ground. 'In there he was found, sir. That right-hand window was open, by which he climbed in. You can see the marks on the stone still, if you look, sir.'

Mr Brown looked with interest. The stone was slightly scratched. There were foot-prints on the earth of a neglected bed just below the sill but these were lost in the strip of grass that divided the bed from the gravelled drive. The drive itself, which had not been weeded recently, presented a hard-baked surface that would leave no trace of anyone crossing it.

'I see, I see. The poor young fellow must have found the place locked up. Did he go to the front door, first?'

'Probably, sir, but we couldn't tell that because this gravel is so hard he would make no trace on it. Why, if you've noticed it, sir, even all those cars we've had about the last day or two have scarcely marked it, except where they've braked.'

'So, even if he had arrived in a car himself, you wouldn't have known,' mused the benevolent stranger, at which the constable laughed.

'We'd have found the car, sir, wouldn't we?' he said with a chuckle.

'Bless me, I was forgetting that,' said the visitor ruefully. And, as if to conceal his confusion, he began to walk slowly backwards across the gravel under the pretence of getting a better view of the house. After a few steps, he paused, pulled out a large coloured handkerchief, took off his spectacles and began to polish them. As he replaced them on his nose, he dropped the handkerchief. Looking more confused than ever, he stooped and picked it up and replaced it in his pocket.

'Well, I'm much obliged to you, constable,' he said. 'I think I'll just see if they'll allow me inside. These affairs have a certain attraction for us outsiders – a morbid one, I dare say!'

The constable allowed himself another chuckle at the departing back. A simple sort of gentleman, he allowed. Fancy his not seeing the point about finding the car if there had been one!

The inquest was held in the room adjoining the library, at the door of which stood a policeman. Mr Brown presented himself for admission.

'Not on the jury, are you, sir?'

'No, officer.'

'Are you Press? Because the Squire don't want much publicity about this case.'

'Oh, no! As a matter of fact, I only arrived in the village this morning and having heard the late Mr Baufstein performing in London, I was interested, that's all.'

'That'll be all right, sir,' said the constable, impressed by the genial Mr Brown. 'Take a chair at the back, sir.'

Mr Brown did, and presently the Coroner arrived and the jury was sworn. Having agreed on a foreman, they filed out to view the body, under the guidance of a policeman. The Coroner shuffled his papers, stared at Mr Brown, stared at the ceiling, made a remark in lowered tones to a military looking man who sat beside him, whom Ego guessed to be the Chief Constable – and then yawned. The few villagers who were present, shuffled their feet and coughed. A shaft of sunlight, full of dancing motes, streamed into the room and made a pool of light on the Coroner's table, like a limelight that had just missed the hero of the drama.

Presently the jury returned, looking embarrassed and uncomfortable. The Coroner sat up and began to explain the circumstances of the case they were investigating.

The first witness was the maid who had discovered the body. She had gone into the library at half-past seven to dust the room and had pulled up one blind when she noticed the body lying on the sofa. It looked like her master and she thought it must be he, but he was practically a stranger to her. All the other blinds were down and the place was half-dark. She thought he might be asleep but he looked so queer that she ran at once to tell Arley, the butler. She didn't go near or touch the body.

The butler followed her. He described how the maid had come to him in a state of agitation and he had gone to the library, which was semi-dark. He noticed as he went in that one blind was flapping and that the window behind it was open. He went straight over to the sofa and saw what he took to be his master's body. He was rather short-sighted and had left his spectacles in the pantry in the hurry of the moment. He touched the face and hands. They were quite cold. Knowing that in such cases nothing should be disturbed, he left the room as it was, locked the door, telephoned for the police and asked them to bring the doctor. It was obvious that the person on the sofa was dead.

The local sergeant followed. The butler had told him that his master was dead and he had brought the doctor up to the Hall with him. He described the position of the body, the open window and the marks he had found on the sill of someone climbing through. There was no sign of violence or of a struggle of any kind. Nothing in the room had been disturbed. He had seldom seen the Squire and then only at a distance and it did not occur to him to question the identity of the body when the servants described it as that of their master. It was certainly like him, from what he recollected.

The doctor had little to say. He had never seen Mr Wilkins, who scarcely ever came to the Hall, and he accepted the servants' word that it was their master. He found nothing to suggest foul play and his subsequent examination of the body had confirmed his opinion of death from heart failure, following exhaustion. The heart was in a very bad state and the physical condition of the deceased was extremely bad.

There was a stir in the room when the Coroner called for Mr Wilkins. A constable went out and returned ushering in the young Squire. Even the rubicund Mr Brown sat up with a display of interest as the tall, pale-faced young man in dark clothes took the oath, speaking with a slight lisp, and sat down in the chair, which the Coroner invited him to take while giving his evidence.

Ego recognized him at once. Then he looked again. He had a good memory for faces and he well remembered the night at the Public Cave when young Mr Wilkins had conducted his own jazz band. He seemed unchanged. His dark hair was as carefully brushed back, his brown eyes were as large and ox-like as ever, his suit was as much pulled in at the waist as his dinner-jacket had been on that occasion and there was that funny little wart on the side of his long nose. He seemed to very genuinely sorry about his cousin's death and near to weeping in his emotional way at moments. He gave his evidence quite clearly.

He had expected his cousin the day before. It had been arranged between them some time ago that he was to come down on a visit. He identified the letter found in Baufstein's rooms as his invitation in confirmation of the arrangement. His cousin was thinking of starting a band of his own and wished him to assist in financing it. It was to discuss the matter that the visit had been arranged.

His cousin was a very temperamental, moody man, and had been rather down on his luck recently and had even talked of suicide. When Baufstein did not arrive on the appointed day, he was worried. He had been thinking about it all day and when he was out walking in the afternoon, he had suddenly decided to run up to town and see Baufstein. He knew that Baufstein hated borrowing money from him, although he was perfectly willing to lend it or even give it to him. He was afraid that something might have happened. So, on impulse he had jumped into the London train at Sufftown – he had walked into the market town to make some purchases, intending to take the 'bus back to the village.

He was so preoccupied with the thought of what might have happened to his cousin that he had quite forgotten to telephone the Hall to let the servants know that he would not require dinner. When he reached London, he went straight to his cousin's rooms and was told that he was out. The people didn't know when he would be back. It was too late to return home that night. The last train had gone and he hadn't his car with him.

He knew the people in whose house his cousin lodged very well and they gave him a room for the night. He was there in the morning when the police telegram arrived. He had come down at once and identified the body as that of Mr Baufstein.

His theory was that his cousin, who was in bad health and a queer state of mind had come to the village and wandered about till he was exhausted. Then he had come to the hall and been unable to rouse the servants. He had noticed that one of the library windows was open, climbed in and, perhaps exhausted by the exertion, fallen on the sofa and died. He thought there was no other possible explanation of the facts. Both his cousin and himself were orphans, and so far as he knew, had no living relatives. He had been very much attached to the dead man and had made arrangements for the funeral as soon as the inquest was over.

The last witness was Mrs Walker, the landlady of Mr Baufstein's lodgings in London. She had seen and identified the body. A nicer young man she had seldom known. He was an excellent lodger. She knew Mr Wilkins quite well, he sometimes visited his cousin. She remembered well his arriving and asking for his cousin on the fatal night and his astonishment when she told him that Mr Baufstein had left the house earlier in the day without saying when he would be back. She confirmed the young Squire's story in every particular, down to the arrival of the telegram and his hasty departure.

The Coroner summed up very briefly. It was unfortunate that a painful mistake had arisen over the identification of the body, a very natural mistake on the part of the servants, when one considered all the circumstances and the striking likeness between the two cousins, a likeness that extended itself even to certain facial markings such as a distinctive – er – spot on the nose.

The jury need have no hesitation about their verdict, he thought. The jury promptly returned a verdict of Death from Natural Causes and expressed their sympathy with the young Squire, who, when the Coroner had finally closed the proceedings, invited all concerned to partake of refreshment in the dining-room. Everyone stood up and began to talk and the rubicund Mr Brown made his way out of the house into the sunshine of the park. But he had not gone very far before he was overtaken by the military-looking man who had sat beside the Coroner.

'Well, what do you make of it?' asked that gentleman, without ceremony. He was rewarded with an innocent stare.

'A lovely place, sir,' replied Mr Brown, 'but sadly neglected, sadly neglected!'

'Come off it,' invited the other. 'I'm Saunders, the Chief Constable. I know all about you. You arrived this morning in a two-seater and pretended that you'd come to fish. One of your names is Mr Brown and the other is Inspector Ego.'

'Quite right, sir. But how did you know?'

'Oh, the Assistant-Commissioner told me to look out for a man like a farmer who liked his beer. No offence, no offence, Inspector!'

'Oh, did he?' said Inspector Ego. 'Indeed! Well, well, sir, what things people will say!'

'Of course I haven't told any of my men that you're here,' said the Chief Constable, grinning. 'But what do you think? Is it all straight?'

Ego walked on in silence for some moments before replying.

'Well, sir, on the face of it it's all straight. Not a hole in it anywhere.'

'But,' said the Chief Constable, quickly, 'you feel like me – not quite comfortable about it?'

'Exactly sir, I'm going to try and find out just what it is that makes us feel not quite comfortable. You would oblige me very much if, when you return to your office, you would send a telegram to Mr Brown at the inn asking him to return to London at once on a matter of business. I've an idea that the end of the thread is in London. I'll be back here in a day or two and will keep my room at the inn.'

They parted after a little further conversation.

When Mr Brown reached his room at the inn, he pulled down the blind to make sure that he was not overlooked. Then he extracted from his pocket with great care the coloured handkerchief and unfolded it on the dressing-table, revealing a tuft of discoloured grass with small specks of gravel adhering to the roots. This he examined with a pocket magnifying glass, lifted it to his nose and sniffed at it, and finally wrapped it up in a piece of paper and placed it in his suitcase. A few minutes later he appeared in the dining-room.

Mr Brown enjoyed an excellent lunch and remarked to the landlord that he had met a very pleasant military-looking gentleman at the Hall, whom the landlord had no difficulty in identifying as Colonel Saunders, the Chief Constable of the County.

'Dear me!' said Mr Brown. 'Fancy his talking to me!'

But at that moment the arrival of a telegram interrupted the conversation. The guest read it with a rueful expression and handed it to the landlord. Ten minutes later, he was steering his car out of the yard, promising a speedy return.

Late that evening, the landlady of a dingy lodging-house in Camden Town, answering a ring at the door, found a pleasant-looking gentleman on the doorstep. He smiled, handed her a card and, before she could read it, had stepped into the little hall. Her protest died away as she took in the legend on the card.

'A gentleman from Scotland Yard! Is it about that poor Mr Baufstein?' she asked. 'I thought that was all settled, sir, with the inquest to-day.'

'Why should you imagine it isn't settled?' asked Ego.

The woman's sallow face flushed a little at the question.

'Of course, I heard the verdict down there, sir,' she said. 'But my husband and I were just talking it over, being so interested, and him being with us so long. We thought there couldn't be anything wrong.'

'Well,' said Ego pleasantly, 'I see no reason to question the verdict of Death from Natural Causes.' He watched her narrowly and saw a faint shadow of relief.

'Poor young fellow!' she said. 'Ten years he has been in this house and a pleasanter young man I couldn't have wished for.'

'Quite, quite, ma'am,' said Ego, sympathetically. 'It must have been a shock for you. Now, will you please let me see his room.'

The landlady led the way up one flight of stairs to a pleasant front room. It was shabbily furnished. There was a bed in one corner, a washstand in another, a table in the window, a much-worn armchair and, dominating all, an upright piano. The table was littered with sheets of music and others were stacked against the walls. Behind the door was a chest of drawers.

Ego walked down the room to the windows, looked out, came back to a point where he could see the landlady's face in a mirror, and with his back still to her asked:

'Where is your husband?'

'He's out, sir.' The answer came without hesitation or change of countenance.

'Your husband's name is Walker, changed some years ago from Baufstein, by deed poll. Any relation of the deceased?'

This time there was some agitation in the woman's features.

'No relation at all, sir. That was just chance – though it did decide my husband to take him as a lodger, when he heard the name, being of foreign extraction, himself, there being another young man after the rooms at the time.'

Well, that might be quite true, thought Ego. He tried again, swinging round as he spoke.

'This is where young Baufstein composed his songs and practised his music, I suppose?'

'Yes – he was always at it, sir. We used to say it was lucky we had no other lodgers.'

'Then where is his saxophone?'

The landlady was clearly perturbed.

'I – I don't know, sir. Someone must have taken it away. It used to lie on top of the piano always. The police have been here already, you know, sir.'

'I know – but they didn't take his saxophone. Think – who took it?'

'I – I don't know, sir.'

'Young Mr Wilkins – did he take it, perhaps?'

The woman looked instantly relieved.

'Why, sir, now that you suggest it, I believe he did. Yes, I remember, now. He said his cousin might want it and he wrapped it up. Then, when the telegram came, he took it with him. Yes, that explains it, sir. It was stupid of me not to remember, but I've been very much upset.'

'I see,' said Ego nodding. 'Very natural! Now, ma'am, if you'll just leave me here, I'll have a look round by myself.'

The woman hesitated.

'There – there isn't anything wrong, sir – about the inquest, I mean?'

'Oh, no! But we want to trace any relatives he might have had – that's all!'

When he was alone, Ego examined the contents of the chest of drawers very carefully. In a few minutes he found what he was looking for – a sealed envelope marked: Private, not to be opened. He broke the seals and extracted a few sheets of music in manuscript, headed: 'There's a Good Big Chicken in this Fresh Egg.'

Quite, he thought. This was to remain sealed till the night of its production at Malabani's – he was afraid of some pirate getting hold of it – lots of money in a good song of the kind. So he tucked it away here – and nobody has seen it, but himself.

'Now, I wonder!' mused Detective-Inspector Ego aloud, as he let himself out of the house quietly without calling the landlady. 'Perhaps there is a good big chicken in this egg, after all. If so, it's a distinctly fresh egg to me!'

Next day Ego was an interested spectator of the very elaborate funeral of young Mr Baufstein at a famous cemetery in London. The chief mourner was young Mr Wilkins and if ever the Inspector had seen genuine grief it was printed on the pale face of Mr Wilkins who, when all was over, was assisted into his car with tears streaming unashamedly down his cheeks. Ego watched him unobtrusively with a puzzled look on his rubicund countenance.

'Still,' he mused, as he turned away, 'it would all fit in. So far as one knows they were good friends. I dare say he is very sorry.'

His next visit was to the Union Bank.

'I know that you gentlemen are very particular about not divulging your clients' affairs,' he said deferentially, when he was seated in the manager's room; 'but I want to ask you a question.'

'Well, Inspector,' said the manager, rubbing his chin, 'we don't like being asked questions about customers, that's true. But suppose you tell me, what it is you want to know?'

'The present address of Mr Wilkins of Wilkins Hall, if there is no objection.'

The manager laughed.

'I shouldn't be revealing any secret,' he said, 'if I told you that so far as I know, it is Wilkins Hall.'

'Ah!' said Inspector Ego. 'Thank you.'

He picked up his hat and stick. The manager looked at him curiously.

'Wait a minute, Inspector,' he said after a moment of hesitation. 'Just between ourselves – quite confidentially – what has our young friend been up to?'

The Inspector's face became a blank.

'Has he been up to anything?' he asked.

'Come, come, Inspector,' said the banker. 'I can put two and two together, you know, and it's my business to know all about my customers. And when you come here asking for his address and he –'

'And he what, sir?' asked Ego, as the other paused. 'Come, it's my business to know about your customers, too, isn't it?'

'Well,' said the banker, 'it's curious. This is in strict confidence – but young Mr Wilkins is going to New York, I understand. It was just your inquiry on top of the fact that we're taking out his passport. If he's in any kind of mess, I'd rather like to know.'

'I suppose he's transferring his money to New York, eh?' said Ego. But the banker shook his head.

'I can't answer any questions about his affairs, Inspector – you know that.'

'Of course, of course!' Ego assented. 'I had no business to ask that. And if it will relieve your mind, so far as I know, Mr Wilkins is not in a scrape of any kind. Have you seen him lately?'

'Not since that unfortunate affair of his cousin's death,' said the manager. 'But he has written to us from Wilkins Hall, so I presume he is still there.'

'In that case, I may hope to find him there,' said Ego, as he rose to leave. 'As a matter of fact, I want to see him about a little matter in connection with his late cousin. Nothing to do with him, really,' he added, with a laugh, 'so don't be alarmed. But he may be able to give me some information that I rather want.'

Later that afternoon, the car of the genial Mr Brown purred into the village and the landlord of the Wilkins Arms re-welcomed his guest. In the bar, to which they adjourned after disposing of the car, a melancholy individual in black sat toying with a glass of port. Mr Brown recognized the butler from the hall and at once suggested that he should finish that glass and join himself and the landlord over another, a course to which the butler offered no objection.

'If I am not mistaken,' said the genial visitor, 'I saw you at the inquest the other day.'

The butler nodded gravely.

'A most tragic affair,' pursued Mr Brown. 'I expect that the young Squire is very much cut up about it?'

'Well, sir,' said the butler, 'he is. And to do him justice, much more than I took it he would be. Seems to have made a change in him, it does. He was a stranger to us, you might say, never coming near the place except very seldom and rather offhand with the staff when he did. But a more polite and considerate young gentleman than he's showed himself to be since the death, I wouldn't ask to serve.'

'The funeral was to-day, I believe. Is he home again?' asked Mr Brown.

'Yes, sir. He came straight home again.'

'It must be a lonely place for him, I should say, up there in that big house all by himself with this grief on him,' said the landlord, sympathetically.

'You would think so,' admitted the butler. 'But he has one consolation and that's his music. He always was a one for music. Had his own jazz band, they tell me, in London, as a sort of hobby. And now he shuts himself up in the drawing-room after dinner and plays to himself on the piano and that other instrument called the saxophone, they tell me. A melancholy sort of instrument it sounds to me.'

Mr Brown nodded gravely.

'Music is a great consoler, they say,' he agreed. And after a little further gossip, the conversation was terminated by the departure of the butler to his duties.

Some time after dinner, Mr Brown announced his intention of going for a stroll. He wandered off pensively down the village street, a cigar between his teeth. On the bridge he exchanged a few remarks about the fishing with the smoking rustics gathered there and continued on his way through the falling dusk till he found himself again at the tumbledown gates of the park. There was no one to question his right to enter and he passed through them and up the winding avenue. But when he came near the dark bulk of the old house, he threw his cigar away and lost his air of leisured benevolence. Leaving the open avenue, he skirted the building, sheltering behind the bushes of an overgrown shrubbery.

The Hall stood black and silent against the last gleam of light in the west. It was late and presumably the servants were either in their own quarters or had retired to bed. But on the south face of the building a shaft of light ran out into the darkness.

Mr Brown made his way round cautiously and saw that it came from a large room, evidently a drawing-room, one window of which was open and uncurtained. He stole silently across the expanse of lawn that lay between him and the window, keeping out of the light, and slipping behind a bush, waited, listening for a sound that he expected to hear. Presently someone in the room struck a chord on a piano.

Mr Brown took a sheet of paper from a pocket and unfolded it. From another pocket, he produced a small electric torch and shone it on the paper.

The unseen occupant of the room began to play and as he played, Mr Brown followed with his torch the lines of music on the sheet he held. Presently the piano stopped and after a pause, the notes of a saxophone floated out into the gardens. It was being played very softly almost as if the performer did not want to be overheard. The melody was a strange, attractive thing.

'An excellent foxtrot!' murmured Mr Brown, who was not a very brilliant musician himself and was following a line of the score in front of him with one finger. 'And an excellent and very appropriate title,' he whispered, as he folded up the sheet and returned it to his pocket, along with his torch. Then he walked boldly up to the window and putting his elbows on the sill, called out:

'Mr Wilkins! May I speak to you a moment?'

The music ceased abruptly and the astonished face of the young Squire appeared at the window.

'Who are you?' he demanded in a voice that held both anger and apprehension.

'Come closer, sir,' said Mr Brown. 'It's important.'

Mr Wilkins thrust his face into the opening and, as he did so, Mr Brown made a quick snatch at his nose. When he withdrew his hand, the nose of Mr Wilkins was minus the little wart that had been a prominent feature of its length. And before the other could find words, Mr Brown was climbing into the room. Mr Wilkins retreated before him, his features working agitatedly.

'Detective-Inspector Ego from Scotland Yard,' announced Mr Brown, as he reached the floor. 'Now, Mr Baufstein, you might just sit down quietly and explain it all in a friendly way.'

Next morning, Ego knocked at the Assistant-Commissioner's door.

'Come in!' shouted that gentleman, adding when he recognized his visitor, 'Well, have you solved the Wilkins mystery already?'

'I have, sir,' said Ego, seating himself in front of the writing table.

'What is it – Murder?'

'No, sir. It's a case for the Inland Revenue people.'

'A case for the Inland Revenue people?' echoed the Assistant-Commissioner.

'Yes, sir – a case of impersonation.'

'But what on earth have the Inland Revenue people got to do with a case of impersonation?'

'I'm sending in my report, sir,' said Ego. 'It's a little complicated and I see that you are busy.'

'Shall I be able to understand your report, do you think?' asked the Assistant-Commissioner, doubtfully.

'I hope so, sir,' said Ego, with a lack of conviction in his voice that was annoying. 'I don't see why not, really. But perhaps I had better just give you the outline. The Wilkins case is just what I expected it to be – the Amateur's First Crime. And that's always the most complicated kind of crime, as I said before, sir, if you remember.'

'Look here, we don't want all that over again,' groaned the Assistant-Commissioner. 'Make it snappy, will you?'

'Very good, sir,' responded Ego, settling himself down as comfortably as the hard chair provided for visitors would permit. 'The key to the whole mystery is that these people were Baufsteins.'

'Quite – but it's not very illuminating, so far. Still, I shall do my best to keep that point in mind, Inspector.'

'Thank you, sir. The late Mr Wilkins –'

'But Wilkins is alive!'

'No, sir! That's where the local police went astray. Wilkins is dead. Baufstein reigns in his stead, as the history books say.'

'Then it was a murder?'

'No – a perfectly natural death. But it didn't take place on the sofa at the Hall. It occurred in the Camden Town lodging of young Mr Baufstein. When Wilkins left the Hall that afternoon, he went – presumably by 'bus – to the market town – Sufftown – and there caught the London train. He proceeded to his cousin's lodgings in Camden Town with the object of finding out why Baufstein had not come down to the Hall the day before as arranged.'

'But,' interrupted the Assistant-Commissioner, 'Baufstein was expected on the night on which Wilkins went out, according to the letter wasn't he?'

'According to the letter, as found, he was,' agreed Ego. 'But what our sleuths failed to notice was a very clever alteration of the date made by Mr Baufstein. Of course, they weren't looking for an alteration and the letter as it stood, confirmed Baufstein's story sufficiently.'

'I see,' said the Assistant-Commissioner. 'Go on.'

'Wilkins was subject to heart attacks. He had one and died in his cousin's room. Baufstein called in his aunt and uncle – for although the latter's present name is Walker, it was originally Baufstein – and they held a council. Now, we must remember what these people were, Polish peasants, who had always been poor, originally much poorer than they are now. Eighteen months ago Wilkins had inherited a fortune of quarter-of-a-million from his uncle, by marriage. You can figure out what he had to pay in death duties. It hurt him but it seems that it hurt still more deeply the next heir, young Mr Baufstein.

'I gathered from him that it had always been a grievance to think of all that beautiful money being swept up by the government and he often thought of how deeply the nice fortune would be depleted by a second government raid before it reached him, if his cousin died first. Now, here was Wilkins actually dead and he realized that another big slice of the fortune, not to speak of law costs, would be taken within eighteen months of the first levy. It was too much for him to bear.

'But he might have borne it, had he not been worked upon by his uncle and aunt, who thought it a crime that any of the money should pass out of the family unnecessarily. The idea of the new death duties was a sort of nightmare to all three – giving money away and getting no value for it, as they saw it. Why do it?'

'A damnably callous lot!' commented his listener.

'No, sir. That's quite a wrong idea,' said Ego, earnestly. 'That's just what they were not. Baufstein was very fond of Wilkins and he had saved Wilkin's life, which would make him fonder than ever. A man is always grateful to a man whose life he has saved – but we needn't go into the psychology of that now. Baufstein was heartbroken but that didn't change his nature. It's a popular theory with novelists that grief changes a man's character – but it doesn't. It accentuates it, that's all.

'Well, they did a little quick thinking. They put some of Baufstein's clothes on the body, weeping heartily while they did it. Then they put the body in an old car belonging to the uncle and drove down to the Hall where they arrived about midnight. Nobody heard them arrive and, if anyone had, they had their explanation. Wilkins had been taken ill at Baufstein's rooms and had begged them to take him home. He must have died on the journey – you see?

'They ran very quietly up the drive and as close to the house as they dared. They meant to force a window but found it providentially unfastened. Baufstein climbed in and the uncle carried the body to the window. It was easy, so long as no one heard and they knew that the few servants were in another wing and that there was no dog about the place. Wilkins hated dogs. If a servant had come along, their story was water-tight.'

'How did you guess it?'

'Guess, sir?' Ego looked pained. 'I don't guess things, sir,' he continued reproachfully. 'A clue which assisted me materially was the presence of a small patch of motor oil on the gravel not very far from the window of the room in which the body was found. A car had stood there recently and it was a place quite out of the track of cars coming to the front door or the back premises.'

'I apologize, Inspector.'

'Baufstein and his uncle returned to London as they had come and awaited the inevitable telegram. When it came, Baufstein sent his reply and signed it Wilkins. By this time, he was equipped with a false wart on his nose. He was a clever actor and it was easy for him to play the part of Wilkins in a place where nobody knew Wilkins with any degree of familiarity.

'He arrived wearing the very clothes that the butler had laid out the day before for his master. Nobody called the bluff – no one could. The police had never seen the real Wilkins. His evidence at the inquest was a masterpiece. And he was really overcome with grief. If you had seen him at the funeral, you wouldn't doubt that.'

'But he couldn't keep it up for ever! Somebody was sure to spot him, sooner or later.'

'He didn't have to,' said Ego. 'He had instructed his bank to sell out his securities and transfer the money to New York. He had taken out a passport. Another week or two and Mr Baufstein Wilkins would have been safely away, with an easy conscience. The Hall was to be sold and the proceeds remitted to America. All done by a clever imitation of his cousin's signature. He didn't risk seeing the bank personally. It was no hardship to go to America. He told me last night that he had always regarded New York as his spiritual home and I think he was right.'

'He might easily have got away with it,' mused the Assistant-Commissioner, 'if I hadn't guessed that there was something wrong. Where did he fall down?'

'He fell down through the common human failing of vanity, sir,' said Ego, severely, and his superior blushed.

'Of course the credit is yours, Inspector,' he said, hastily.

'I don't know so much about that, sir,' said Ego thoughtfully. 'It was his, really. You see, he was the composer of that delightful little foxtrot and song, "There's a Good Big Chicken in this Fresh Egg." He forgot to remove that from his room and I found it in a sealed packet. Now, it was ten to one that Wilkins had never heard it, because he was, in a way, a rival jazz merchant and this thing was being kept secret for a production at Malabani's next month. So when I heard Wilkins playing it on the saxophone on the evening of the funeral, I guessed that it wasn't Wilkins.'

'And what did you do?'

'The obvious thing, sir. I pulled the wart off his nose.'

'You pulled the – the – you took a great risk there, Inspector. Suppose that it had been a real wart and that you had been assaulting the real Wilkins! There would have been an action for assault and a scandal that we should have never heard the end of.'

'Quite true, sir,' agreed Ego, penitently, as he rose; 'but in this case it did come off. Though,' he added, as he reached the door, 'perhaps I'd better leave that brilliant touch out of my detailed report. The Commissioner is such a stickler for etiquette!'

THE WASTE-PAPER BASKET

Alan Melville

M RS Pepper suggested Consequences at ten minutes past ten; that awkward time when the party was beginning to show signs of fatigue, when at least three of the guests had been seen to glance slyly down at their wrist watches, when there was still forty minutes to go before the dance music began on the wireless, and the carpet could be rolled back and Jack and Helen allowed to do their celebrated and quite original rumba. So Consequences it was; and for the next half-hour Mrs Pepper found herself meeting the Prime Minister, or Mr George Robey (or, on one occasion, Mr Pepper himself) in a variety of strange localities, such as the back-kitchen sink or the Battersea Power Station. At ten-forty everyone threw their slips of paper into the waste-paper basket and had another drink. And there was another of those dreadful lulls which give any decent-minded hostess a series of severe nightmares. Saved on this occasion by Mr Pepper, who got up from the settee and parked himself in front of the fire.

'I know a game,' said Mr Pepper. 'Just the very thing. Nice and quiet and everything.'

'This is going to be awful,' said Jack. 'I bet someone has to go out of the room and then come in and ask if it's a mineral or –'

'Shut up!' said Mr Pepper. 'It's a test of one's mental powers, really.'

'In that case you had better go out of the room, darling,' said Helen.

'A few years ago, before I retired on my quite inadequate pension,' said Mr Pepper, 'I was mixed up in rather a peculiar murder case –'

'She married a policeman, you know,' said a young man in an armchair. 'Her family made a dreadful fuss about it, but then she always was one to fall for anything in uniform.'

'He wasn't a policeman,' said Mrs Pepper. 'He was a fully-fledged detective-inspector. Weren't you, darling? Go on, dear, and don't pay any attention to them. I'm sure this is going to be very interesting.'

'Thank you, dear,' said Mr Pepper. 'It was the waste-paper basket that reminded me of it, really. In this case I was speaking about, a man was found murdered in his study –'

'Why is it always the study?' asked Helen. 'I've often wondered that.'

'– and the only clues we had to go on were some things we found in the waste-paper basket standing beside his desk. We didn't know anything about the fellow . . . so far as we knew, he was an ordinary, respectable business man in the city.'

'There's no such thing,' said the young man in the armchair.

'Now,' said Mr Pepper. 'I thought it might be rather fun to tell you what we found in the waste-paper basket, and see if you could find out who killed Bernard Haswell – that was the bloke's name – and how they killed him, and why they killed him. Help to make the party go, I mean.'

'You'll make them go all right, darling,' said Helen. 'What about a tune on the gramophone?'

'Of course, if you're not interested . . . '

'Darling, do go on,' said Mrs Pepper. 'We're thrilled.'

'Right. Here's what we found in the waste-paper basket then. Item One – a cheque for five hundred pounds, made out to the murdered man, unsigned and torn up into four pieces. Item Two – a cutting from the personal column of the *Daily Post*. Item Three – a thread or two of pale green silk . . . the kind of thing that might have been torn from a woman's dress –'

'She did it,' announced the young man in the armchair. 'She'd found out that he knew the secret formula which would make Bohemia declare war on Ruritania, and –'

'Quiet, Douglas,' said Mrs Pepper. 'Yes, dear? What else did you find?'

'Nothing. That was all. Now, all you've got to do is to tell me who killed Bernard Haswell.'

'Don't be stupid, constable,' said Helen. 'Jack, isn't there dance music on some of the Continental stations?'

'Of course, if it's really beyond you, I could tell you the whole thing myself,' said Mr Pepper.

'Which is what you've been dying to do all night. Carry on, darling. And remember we're having lunch with mother at one tomorrow, so make it snappy.'

'Right,' said Mr Pepper, and took another sip of his gin-and-tonic.

They telephoned us from Haswell's house (said Mr Pepper) at about eleven fifteen; 213, Lower Ormadale Street was the address: a big, solid house that looked altogether too respectable to be mixed up in anything like a suicide, let alone a murder. A butler fellow showed us to the study. The house was furnished in the heavy old-fashioned style – plenty of horse-hair and mahogany about the place, a very distressing gilt clock in a glass case on the mantelpiece, and at least three flourishing aspidistras in copper pots. Bernard Haswell was lying at his desk, head downwards. He'd had a slight collision with an inkwell when he fell, and there was a good deal of loose ink all over the desk. All over the late Bernard Haswell too, for that matter.

We had the doctor along inside ten minutes, and he dithered about as doctors will, and said, 'H'm' and 'Uh-huh' and 'Yes . . . looks like it,' and made various other non-committal noises. Finally we got out of him (a) that Haswell had been shot through the heart, (b) that death must have been instantaneous, (c) that the shot had been fired quite recently, and (d) that the shot had been fired at pretty close range. Just how recent or how close the doctor wouldn't say, of course, until he'd had another examination of the body. Then we started to have a look around the room.

First of all the desk itself. If there had been any awards for untidiness going, Haswell's desk would have certainly walked away with the first prize for sheer chaos. It was heaped high with every sort and size and shape of paper imaginable – mostly things relating to Haswell's business affairs. And as most of the stuff was going down for the third time in a pool of ink, the desk wasn't exactly looking its best. Watson (one of our men) wanted to make out from this that there'd been a struggle, but we'd come across a good few business men's desks in our day and none of them had been exactly models of tidiness, so we squashed the struggle idea.

The desk was one of the flat-topped variety – not a roller-top affair – and on the other side of it, right opposite Haswell's body, there was a chair drawn up in a way which suggested that there'd been some sort of a conference or cosy little chat going on that morning. We had the chair examined for prints, and had some photographs taken; any amount of prints, too – enough to get the housemaid dismissed on the charge of skipping her dusting for the last ten years or so. Then we found the note.

It was lying on the desk, just to the left of Haswell's head. The ink had escaped it somehow or other, and we could read the writing quite plainly, though the other side was fairly saturated in the ink-flow. The note was written in pencil, and this is what it said:

'This is the last time I'll trouble you in any way. I'm ending it all now. B. H.'

'Well,' said Watson. 'That's that, anyway.'

'Suicide, eh?' said the doctor. 'Well, saves an awful lot of bother. I'll be getting along now, if you don't mind. Cheerio . . . '

We had another look round the room before we had the servants and Mrs Haswell in. The only thing that really interested us was the waste-paper basket. It was lying on its side to the left of the desk. Haswell's arm was dangling down immediately above it, with the revolver still gripped in his left hand. That seemed queer, to begin with . . . it's ten to one that the revolver will drop out of a man's hand after the shot. However . . .

The waste-paper basket was one of those wicker affairs. The first thing we drew out of it was a cheque. Someone had torn it up into four pieces; when we'd fitted the pieces together we found that it was made out to Bernard Haswell. And that it was for the tidy sum of five hundred pounds. And that it was unsigned. We had it examined for prints, and found one complete set – a man's fingerprints. We found out later that they weren't Haswell's, but that didn't get us anywhere.

The next thing to come out of the lucky dip was a news-paper cutting. On the one side was an advertisement for someone's face cream . . . Joan Was Never Asked Out to Dances, Her Face was So Blotchy, Since Using Dawn O'Delight Face Cream, She is Never In at Night, and so on. But on the other side was an extract from the agony column. There were only two genuine agonies in the cutting – all the rest were advertisements disguised as personal notices. One of the two genuine articles was 'Molly – Cm bk drlg all frgvn – Baba.' Which didn't seem to have very much to do with the case in hand. The other was 'H. B. – 500 Renton's Cafe ten twelfth – B. H.' Which did.

And that seemed to be about all, so far as the waste-paper basket was concerned. We handed it over to Watson for another inspection, and after a minute or two he said, 'Hoi!' It was a favourite expression of Watson's, and usually it meant that he thought of something everyone else had thought of three weeks' earlier. But this time he had got hold of something. One of the uprights of the basket's wicker work had been smashed in – and smashed in very recently. And hanging on to the broken piece were two or three threads of pale green silk . . . the sort of thing that might have been torn from a woman's dress.

'You see?' said Watson. 'There *was* a struggle. And the waste-paper basket was upset and this dame stood on it and smashed it in right here. What did I tell you, eh?'

We all told Watson that some day the Commissioner would sack the Big Five and put him in their place, and then we sent for the butler fellow.

He was called Keeton – a big, tall lad with white hair and the foundations of a corporation. Very, very butlerish in bearing. But by far the most important thing about Mr Keeton was the fact that the thumb and forefinger of his right hand had a faint blue stain all over them.

'When did you last see Mr Haswell?'

'This morning, sir, at nine-thirty. He had breakfast in the sitting-room, and left the room while I was clearing away.'

'Was he all right then?'

'He was in perfectly normal health and spirits, sir, if that is what you mean.'

'That's what we meant, Keeton.'

'Yes, sir.'

'Been here long?'

'Three-and-a-half years, sir.'

'And before then . . . ?'

'I was in service in America, sir.'

'Uh-huh . . . '

'I can produce several excellent references, sir, should you desire
to see them.'

We didn't take to Mr Keeton at all.

'You didn't see Mr Haswell after nine-thirty, you say?'

'No, sir.'

'Were you in this room at all this morning?'

'No, sir.'

'Let me see your hand . . . no, the other one, Keeton.'

And Keeton produced his right hand. It was ink all right. There'd
been a pretty feverish attempt to wash it clean, but the stain was
still there.

'How d'you get that ink on your fingers, Keeton?'

'Ink, sir? . . . oh, yes, sir. I was writing a letter in the kitchen,
sir. Before breakfast sir. I was particularly anxious to catch the first
post, sir. The housemaid upset the ink bottle . . . a very careless
girl, sir.'

Not a flicker on the man's face while he said it, either.

'Seems to have been quite an epidemic of ink-slinging this morning. See that, Keeton?'

The butler looked down at the mess on the desk. Some of
Haswell's hair had come adrift from its brilliantine moorings and
got mixed up in the ink. Keeton took a good, long look at the desk.
Then he said, 'A very distressing occurrence, sir. Mr Haswell was
a very kindly gentleman, sir. We shall all miss him, sir.'

'Sure. Got that letter?'

'No, sir. It's posted, sir. As I think I explained to you, sir, I
particularly wished to catch the early collection at ten-fifteen, sir. I
was writing to a cousin of mine in –'

'All right, all right. Had Mr Haswell any visitors during the
morning?'

'None, sir.'

'Uh-huh . . . '

'Would that be all, sir?'

'Yes . . . no, just a minute. Mr Haswell was left handed, wasn't
he?'

'No, sir. The master was right handed, sir.'

'Oh . . . had he any family?'

'One son, sir. At present at college, sir. Would that be all now, sir?'

'That'll do for the present, Keeton. For the present . . . '

'Thank you, sir. Very good, sir. Good-morning, sir.' And drifted out, the perfect butler.

We had the housemaid in next. She was pretty but talkative. Came from a poor but honest family in Bolton; her mother had warned her against coming up to London and getting in with these high-society houses, what with their cocktail parties and their –

'All right, all right. Listen, Rosie . . . had Mr Haswell any visitors this morning?'

'Yes, sir. Gent called round about ten-thirty. Right nice-looking kind of chap he was, an' all. Kind of chap you only see on pictures nowadays, if you understand-like. He –'

'Did he see Mr Haswell?'

'Yes, sir. That's what he came for. Had an appointment, he had.'

'And did Keeton show him in here?'

'No, sir. Keeton was busy down in kitchen, sir. I was doing hall, you see, sir, and when bell rang I just answered it myself, you see, sir. Keeton gets fair mad if he has to trail upstairs, especially if one of us girls happens to be working up here, sir. So I opened the door for him, sir. He didn't give his name, sir, but he said he had an appointment with Mr Haswell. So I told Mr Haswell, and Mr Haswell says "Show him in here." and I showed him in here, and I don't know no more about nothing.'

'You didn't see him leave the house, eh?'

'No, sir. I'd be upstairs by then. Vacuuming.'

'Thanks, Rosie. Oh . . . just one other thing. Was Keeton writing letters in the kitchen this morning, by any chance?'

'I never saw him, sir. But it's more than likely – he's always writing letters. He's got a dame. Lizzie, they call her – she lives in –'

'You didn't see him writing a letter, though?'

'No, sir.'

'You didn't upset the bottle of ink he was using, did you?'

''Course I didn't. What d'you take me for, eh? I've been in this place five years come next Wakes, and you could number the things I've upset – let alone break – on one hand. And that's flat!'

'Okay, Rosie. Was Mrs Haswell in the study during the morning?'

'Yes, sir. I saw her go in about eleven, sir. Just before I heard about Mr Haswell, sir. I was on with the vacuum when she went in – doing stair carpets, sir.'

'You never heard a shot, did you?'

'No, sir. But that blooming vacuum makes more row than a symphony orchestra, sir. I wouldn't hear a bombardment, not with me going all out on the vacuum, sir.'

'Thanks, Rosie. That's all.'

'I'll be seeing you,' said Rosie, and went back to her vacuum.

We went to see Mrs Haswell after that. She was in a pretty bad state. Watson said 'Hoi!' as soon as we went into the sitting-room. We kicked him good and hard in several places, but there was some excuse for the 'Hoi!' Mrs Haswell was wearing a very attractive dress. Pale green in colour.

No, she didn't know anything that might help us; she'd be glad if we could come back later on when she was feeling better; there was really nothing she could tell us at all . . .

'Just one question, if you don't mind, Mrs Haswell . . . we're very sorry to have to bother you, but . . . when did you see your husband last?'

'This morning. At breakfast. He was perfectly all right then. I can't think what made him . . . '

'You . . . you weren't in the study at all during the morning?'

'No . . . I never go into the study. It's . . . it was his room. I don't expect I've been in there for a month.'

'Thanks, Mrs Haswell.'

The doctor sent round his full report that night. Haswell had been killed by a single shot, fired from the revolver which was found in his hand. But the shot had been fired from a distance of at least six feet. In other words, suicide was out. In other words, it was murder.

So then we got busy. First of all with the cheque we'd found torn up in the waste-paper basket. We went round to the branch of the bank where Haswell parked his cash – and he hadn't nearly as much cash as people imagined, we found that out. In fact, we were pretty sure that the bank manager took us for a couple of trustees starting to wind up Haswell's affairs – or for a brace of broker's men. The manager was snuffy to begin with, then cold and polite, and finally quite gushing – and all the time oily. We got out of him that Haswell had cashed four cheques, all for the same amount – five hundred pounds – at various dates during the last two years. Also that the cheques had arrived just when the manager was thinking of inviting Mr Haswell into the back shop for a heart-to-heart talk on the subject of his overdraft. He was a little awkward when we said we'd like to know whose signature was at the bottom of those four cheques, but in the end he told us. Sir Hugo Blair, the politician fellow; none other. (He was Secretary of State for Herrings, or something like that, in the last government.) After that piece of news we thanked the manager politely; he washed his hands several times with invisible soap and showed us to the door – a happy time having been spent by all.

Next the cutting from the personal column. We traced that to the *Daily Post* of two days before. That was the tenth; Haswell was killed on the twelfth. The notice in the personal column, just in case you've forgotten how it went, read: 'H. B. – 500 Renton's Cafe ten twelfth – B. H.' Or, padded out to its full length and taking at least five guesses at its meaning . . . The pleasure of Sir Hugo Blair's company, along with a cheque for five hundred pounds, is requested by Mr Bernard Haswell at Renton's Cafe at ten o'clock on the twelfth instant. Which looked uncomfortably like that dirtiest of crimes – blackmail.

We checked up the cutting, anyway. It had been handed in at the *Post* Fleet Street office on the ninth, by a gentleman who might or might not have answered Haswell's description. One clerk (male) said it was a tall, elderly man with horn-rimmed glasses, and another clerk (female) said it was a short, youngish man with rimless pince-nez. They don't take the names or addresses of anyone paying cash for a personal advertisement unless the answers are to be forwarded or to come to a box number at the office, so we were stuck there.

Finally the bit of dress material that Watson had found. This meant another bout with Mrs Haswell, which turned out to be pretty unpleasant for all concerned. Mrs Haswell fainted twice, and kept yelling for smelling-salts and asking us if this was America and the Third Degree. Then she said she'd write to the papers about the way a grief-stricken widow was put through all this indignity, or else she'd tell her solicitors to take action against us, or possibly she'd do both. After that she fainted again, and when she came round admitted that she had been in the study that morning.

'But it was after he killed himself,' she said. 'I swear it was after they told me – ask the maids – they must have seen me go in . . . '

We told her that Haswell hadn't killed himself; that he'd been murdered.

'Now do you realize how important it is that you tell us the truth, Mrs Haswell?'

'Oh, God – yes. I'll tell you. Keeton came up and told me he'd found him. I rushed down to see. That's all.'

'And how did you upset the waste-paper basket – smashed it, even?'

'I – that's not true – you don't think I killed him do you?'

'At present we don't know who killed him, Mrs Haswell. That's what we're trying to find out. That's why we're asking you these questions.'

'I wanted something out of his desk. I had to get it, before the police – before anyone came. I didn't want anyone to see it. I leaned across the desk – right over him – to pull open the drawer where I knew he kept it . . . I had to stand on the basket to reach it . . . that's all – that's the truth, I swear it's the truth . . . '

'And what was the something you didn't want the police to see, Mrs Haswell?'

'I can't tell you that.'

'You've got to. For your own sake.'

It seemed to be the right cue for another faint, but she didn't take it.

'We weren't married when our son was born. I didn't want him to know . . . '

She was speaking the truth all right. We knew that.

We left her with her nose to the smelling-salts and concentrated on Mr Keeton. We found out a great deal about Mr Keeton. He had a past. Quite an interesting one. He'd never been nearer the United States than a visit to an American talkie at the local cinema. But he had been to quite a number of other places – Dartmoor for three years for burglary, Wormwood Scrubs for two years for the same – a number of quiet places in the country like that. We went over the desk carefully again and came across Haswell's will in one of the pigeon-holes. All his property and estate was left to Mrs Haswell, or in the event of her death, to the son – they wouldn't get much out of it, the way his affairs were in. All his property and estate to them, with the exception of 'five hundred pounds to my butler, James Keeton, if still in my service at the time of my death, and in consideration of many useful services and of a complete understanding between two men who had much in common.' A queer way of putting it, but a motive. Definitely a motive. Things were looking black for Mr Keeton.

We never could do much clear thinking at the office, but there was a place just round the corner that brewed a brand of ale of its own which was guaranteed to work wonders with the grey matter. Whenever we were up against it there was an adjournment to the Pig and Whistle, and we went into session round the table next to the fire. We did this over the Bernard Haswell case: the Chief, Watson, the doctor, and one or two more of us.

'The note's the thing that worries me,' said the Chief. 'Haswell must have intended to commit suicide, leaving a note like that.'

'Chief, I'll wager the last button on my Sunday pair of pants that the shot was fired from at least six feet away,' said the doctor. 'And that wipes out your suicide.' And the doctor ordered another of the same all round.

'The butler's your man,' said Watson. 'You've got everything – motive, past history, ink-stains on his hand, lies about not being in the study – all that. Get along and arrest Mr Keeton, and let's get a decent night's sleep for once.'

'But the notice in the personal column.'

'What about it?'

'There was blackmail mixed up in this somewhere. We've got to get hold of the gentleman who visited Haswell during the morning. What d'you imagine Sir Hugo Blair can have been up to, to part with two thousand pounds to Haswell so easily, eh?'

'No idea,' said Watson. 'But there's one way to find out.'

'How's that?'

'We've kept Haswell's death quiet so far. You've traced this cafe – Renton's – haven't you?'

'Yes. They can't remember ever seeing either Haswell or Blair there before, but they say they have such an enormous clientele that it's impossible to remember two faces out of the multitude. Though personally it looked to me the kind of place where two customers in a month would be a record.'

'Right. Insert an advertisement in to-morrow's *Post* in the personal

column. "H. B. – Renton's Cafe ten to-morrow urgent. – B. H."
Something on those lines. If he's your man, he won't turn up –
knowing that Haswell's dead. If he does turn up, expecting to meet
Haswell, then he isn't your man. It's worth trying, anyway.'

'Elementary, my dear Watson, elementary.'

'Hoi!' said Watson. And once again the remark was justified. The
barmaid turned our way at once.

We took Rosie with us to the cafe. She talked the whole way there,
mostly about a policeman called Basil with whom she'd once walked
out. She did give us one thing worth knowing, though. That was
about Keeton.

'You know he's been a bit of a lad in his day, I suppose?' she
said.

We said we thought as much, but were never quite sure.

'Well, you can't plant anything about this to-do on him, you take
my word for it. He hadn't anything to do with Mr Haswell's death,
and that's straight. He's no saint, but he's not a murderer. Hasn't
got guts.'

She pronounced it 'goots.' We asked her why she was so sure.

'You found out he was in the study that morning, didn't you?
He was, all right – told me so himself, he did. But he was there
same as missus – after it happened, not before. And for same reason
as missus – to get summat out of the road before all you nosey
Parkers started buzzing around.'

'And what was that, Rosie, dear?'

'Don't you "Rosie dear" me, young man. Oh, summat about
summat he'd done some time or another. Mr Haswell kept it – held
it up in front of Keeton's nose whenever he got fresh. Just like him.
I told him he was daft to get hold of it, but he'd made up his mind
that police weren't going to see it.'

'Anything to do with a burglary in Winchmore Hill in 1932, by
any chance?'

'That's right – no, of course not. I don't know what you're getting
at, mister.'

'All right. Keeton needn't have bothered . . . we knew all about
that long ago, darling.'

Renton's Cafe was one of those dingy tea-houses whose very
respectability must have a minus effect on the cash-register. There

was a good deal of lacquer about it, and a curtain of coloured beads at the main entrance and willow-pattern tea-services on the tables. ('One has to have atmosphere,' said Mrs Renton). The waitresses were dressed as geishas, and gave one the impression that they had all been crossed in love sometime towards the end of the last century, and hadn't quite got over it yet. Mrs Renton pointed to a table in the corner with a good deal of mystery. She was enjoying herself; it was the first time anything had happened in the cafe since that girl spilt tomato soup over a regular customer's flannel trousers.

'That's the lad,' said Rosie. 'That's the bloke who called round that morning all right.'

'Thanks dear. Now run along home like a good girl.'

Rosie sat down and ordered tea and buns.

It was the Herrings man all right: Sir Hugo Blair. We recognized him right away from the photographs we'd seen in the newspapers. He got a bit of a shock when we sat down at his table and ordered coffee.

'You're early, Sir Hugo.'

'I – I don't understand. I've arranged to meet –'

'Mr Bernard Haswell?'

'Yes. Are you gentlemen . . . acting for Mr Haswell?'

'In a way, yes.'

He took a sip of coffee, and then tore the wrapping off a chocolate biscuit. He was left-handed.

'Well, gentlemen?'

Watson had the brain wave. We always said he'd send the Big Five round to the Labour Exchange one day.

'Five hundred pounds, Sir Hugo. To-night.'

He stared at us for a minute. Then he took another drink of coffee.

'I may have been a fool once,' he said. 'I'm not a fool at the moment, though. You're nothing but a set of damned crooks. Bernard Haswell doesn't want another penny out of me. *Bernard Haswell's dead.*'

'Dead? How d'you know that?'

He didn't answer.

'I'll tell you how you know. Because you killed him.'

He sat quite still for what seemed a year. Then he said, 'You're perfectly right. I killed him.'

We hadn't really expected that.

'I suppose you want to know how I killed him, and why I did it, and everything about it?' he said. 'Or do you know it already – maybe it would bore you if I told you, eh?'

We started to give him the usual warning about anything he said being used against him, but he cut us short before we'd got half-way through our party piece.

'I shouldn't worry about that,' he said. 'I knew you were detectives the minute you came in here. You can't disguise yourselves, you know. I only came here out of curiosity . . . I knew it didn't matter. I thought yesterday I might get away with it . . . I suppose you always do at the time. But it's different the next day, when you cool down and think it all over . . . you're bound to make mistakes, you know . . . '

He was perfectly calm about it. It seemed all wrong that we were the ones who were perspiring slightly round the collar.

'Leaving the cheque was one mistake – a bad one. And putting the revolver into his left hand – that was another. He was right handed, of course – I'm not. I'm left handed. I suppose that was why it seemed natural for me to put the revolver in his left hand. But the note – I thought at least the note would be all right . . . '

'Just how did you fix that note?'

'He was blackmailing me, you know. He'd been at it for two years. He found out that I – well, never mind. Enough to finish my career, anyway. I'd paid him two thousand pounds already. He made an appointment for the twelfth – Thursday. He wanted another five hundred. I made up my mind he wasn't going to get it. I went to see him at his house, instead of meeting him here in the evening.'

'Yes? Go on.'

'I saw him in the study. He promised that this was to be the last time. He'd promised that before, of course. I said all right, and started to write out the cheque. Then I said I wanted the promise down in writing . . . I think he thought I was mad – a promise meant nothing to that kind of swine, whether in writing or not. I started to dictate the way I wanted the promise worded. Then he saw through the idea, I think. I tore up the cheque, and took out my revolver . . . I made him finish the note all right. I made him write: "This is the last time I'll trouble you in any way. I'm ending it all now. – B. H." You see? . . . a promise to me, but also just the kind of note that a suicide leaves. Then I shot him. My gun had a silencer on it. I'm not sorry – he deserved it, if ever any man did. Then I put the note in front of him, on the desk, and the revolver in his hand. I thought it was all right at the time . . . I see now it was bound to go wrong.'

We all stood up rather sheepishly.

'You'll have to come along with us now, Sir Hugo.'

He put on his coat and hat, smiling all the time.

'I'll come, certainly. But it's a waste of time, I'm afraid. You see I took poison as soon as you came into the cafe.'

He died that night, and the Government very nearly had to resign over the fuss the papers made about it.

Mr Pepper finished his story, and waited patiently for the applause. Jack and Helen were asleep on the settee. The young man had fallen out of the armchair and was playing patience quietly on the carpet. Mrs Pepper blinked and tried to look as though she hadn't been planning to-morrow's lunch.

'Lovely, darling,' said Mrs Pepper. 'Wake up, you two. Now let's have some dance music. Henry, help me pull back the carpet, there's a lamb.'

' . . . and that concludes to-night's programme, ladies and gentle-men,' said the National transmitter *via* the Peppers' portable. 'Good-night, everyone. *Good*-night.'

'Well, anyway,' said Mr Pepper, when everyone had gone, and he and Mrs Pepper were gathering in a record harvest of tumblers and taking them through to the back kitchen. 'Well, anyway, it did help to fill up a lull, didn't it?'

'Darling, it was wonderful,' said Mrs Pepper. 'I'm so glad I married a policeman. It's such a help when one has people in to spend the evening.'

'Anyway, it wasn't so bad,' said Mr Pepper, 'considering I made the whole thing up on the spur of the moment.'

THE MAN WITH THE TWO·LEFT FEET

Valentine Williams

'In crime everything has its explanation, if we only know where to look for it.'

THE MAXIMS OF H. B. TREADGOLD

IT was, as we were to have good reason to recall, one Monday, the 6th of March, when, arriving for breakfast with H. B. Treadgold at his chambers, I found him engrossed in a crime which was widely featured in that morning's newspapers. The affair at Acacia Lodge appeared to me to be no more than a brutal and sordid murder for gain; but you know what old H. B. is for crime, and he rather wearied me by marshalling the facts at full length. I little knew how soon we were both to be drawn into the orbit of the case.

Dr Alexander Reval was a middle-aged foreigner of rather obscure antecedents who, eight months before, had rented a place on the western outskirts of London called Acacia Lodge, a small house standing in its own grounds. A scholar and a recluse, he lived very quietly, dividing his time between his study and the reading-room of the British Museum. Except for a girl typist who had latterly been working for him in the afternoons, he rarely had a visitor. The only other occupant of the house was his elderly housekeeper, Mrs Kelly, who prepared his meals and did all the housework.

On March 4th, a Saturday, Mrs Kelly had received her employer's permission to spend the day with a married niece at Margate. On arriving back at Acacia Lodge about half an hour after midnight, she noticed a light in the study, but since Reval was in the habit of working late, she did not disturb him but went to bed. On descending at seven next morning to dust the study she found the lights still burning and Reval dead at his desk with his head battered in. No weapon was discovered, but the doctors expressed the opinion that he had been killed with some moderately heavy instrument with a cutting edge and set the hour of death at some time between 9 p.m. and midnight of the preceding evening.

The door of a small wall safe in the study, where the dead man was in the habit of keeping comparatively large sums in Bank of England notes, was found open with the key in it and the money gone. Reval had no bank account. His income was derived from an investment in the Funds, and it was proved that a week before, at the half-year, he had presented the coupons in person at the Bank of England and received a sum of £310 in £5 notes. Mrs Kelly deposed that, the day before she went to Margate, Reval had paid her wages and the housekeeping bill with two notes taken from a roll in the safe. The discovery of a parcel of bearer bonds intact in a locked drawer of the desk suggested that the crime was the work of some hurried prowler.

It was not until I reached my office that I learned, to my stupefaction, that young Christopher Kendrick, whom I had known ever since he was a schoolboy, had been arrested for the crime. Roger Kendrick, his father, who was at Cambridge with me, was killed in the war and, his mother dying soon after, the boy was thrown on his own resources. After a brilliant career at our old college, where he specialized in modern languages, he had come to London, where he made a living out of cramming youths for the diplomatic and army interpreterships, a little journalism and other odd jobs.

A singularly beautiful young woman brought me these disturbing tidings: she was waiting on the doorstep when he arrived at nine, my office-boy told me. 'You don't know me, Mr Duckett,' were her first words to me. 'I'm Tatiana O'Rorke. I'm a friend of Kit Kendrick's.'

I glanced appreciatively at her. Black eyes, hair like the raven's wing, ivory skin – the young beggar had taste. 'You might be Russian, in spite of the surname,' I laughed, offering a chair. Kit, a remarkable linguist, had many foreign friends.

'Mummy was Russian, Daddy Irish. I was born in Petrograd. Daddy was in the timber trade there until the Revolution ruined him; they're both dead now. I know Russian well, and I teach it – that's how I first met Kit.' Then, to my horror, she burst into tears. 'Oh, Mr Duckett,' she sobbed, 'I'm in such trouble. Kit's been arrested!'

'What's the young devil been up to now?' I demanded.

She gasped. 'You don't understand. It's for murder – the murder of Dr Reval. Kit had been doing research for him at the British Museum, and last night the police came to his rooms and – and . . . ' A storm of weeping interrupted her.

I was dumbfounded. Kit, this clean-living, cheery young man, accused of such a crime! He had no private means, and I knew that at times he was pretty broke – I had helped him out once or twice myself. But robbery and murder! I put my mind back – I had a vague remembrance of Kit saying he was assisting some foreign writer in his spare time. 'But this is ludicrous!' I exclaimed. 'There must be some mistake!'

She sobbed aloud. 'It's my fault. Kit got me a job with this man – he wanted someone who could take Russian dictation. Dr Reval rises late – it was arranged I should go out to Acacia Lodge three days a week for lunch, and we would sit down to work directly after. I started a fortnight ago. The doctor was all right at first, but then – well, on Thursday, when Kit took me out to dinner, I told him I couldn't go on with it.'

'You mean it was the old story of the amorous employer?'

She nodded. 'It was horrible. Kit was frightfully upset, though he didn't say much then. But the next afternoon – that was Friday – without telling me a word, he went out to Acacia Lodge and saw Reval. What happened between them I don't know; but Mrs Kelly told the police their voices were so loud that she could hear them in the kitchen and that Kit shouted at Reval as he went away: "You try and see her again, and I'll come back and break your neck!"' She sighed. 'You know what a temper Kit has!'

I nodded. 'And this was only two days before the murder?' She could only bow her head. 'And did Reval worry you again?'

She shook her head. 'Kit wouldn't let me go back. But you haven't heard the worst of it. Three of those five-pound notes stolen from the safe . . . '

With a start I caught the implication of her words. 'You don't mean to say . . . '

The tears streamed down once more. 'The police had the numbers from the Bank of England. Kit says he told Reval on Friday he was through working for him and asked to be paid; and Reval gave him those notes. But of course the police don't believe him.'

'Have you seen Kit?'

'I was at his rooms, helping him out on a rush translation job he's doing, when the police took him away. His last words to me were to get hold of you. But I only had your office address.'

'What was he doing on the night of the murder?'

'He has no alibi, if that's what you mean. He says he was out walking all the evening – you know, he likes to walk at night – and didn't get home till nearly two.' She gazed at me piteously. 'You're his only friend, Mr Duckett. You'll help him, won't you?'

It didn't need more than that for me to call up H. B. I took Tatiana round to Savile Row. Her pretty face fell when she saw 'Bowl, Treadgold & Flack, Civil and Military Tailors,' on the old-fashioned window screen. 'A tailor?' she exclaimed, hanging back.

'As good a detective as he's a tailor. And that's the best in London. I'm his lawyer, and I should know!'

Mr Treadgold, a tape about his shoulders, was visible on the threshold of one of the trying-on rooms, where a gaitered bishop was being fitted. He came out presently and led us into his office. He immediately set the little lady at ease. H. B. has a heart of gold, and no appeal by the helpless and unprotected is ever made to him in vain, especially, I might add, when the pleader is a lovely young woman. 'Leave this to us,' he said when he had heard her story. 'If the young man's to be helped, George Duckett and I will help him. *Tristram Shandy* says, "I reverence truth as much as anybody; and when it has slipped us, if a man will but take me by the hand and go quietly and search for it, I'll go to the world's end with him."' He pinched her cheek paternally. 'Chin up and try not to worry, my dear. Run away now; Mr Duckett will let you know when there's any news for you.'

When she had gone he stared at me questioningly. 'Hot youth will kill to avenge a slight, especially where a woman's concerned. But would he have taken the money?'

'Not in a million years!'

He nodded. 'He comes up before the local beak this morning, the paper says. I'll run you down in my car. I don't know this Divisional

Inspector Hodgetts who's in charge of the case, but a word to Manderton at the Yard will take care of that.'

Young Kendrick, whom we saw for a few minutes before the case was called, was high-strung and defiant. Certainly he'd had a violent scene with the deceased, who'd had the nerve to declare that the girl had led him on. But that was on the Friday before the murder, and he didn't see him again. 'I didn't kill him, George, and I don't know who did,' he told me. 'Nor did I steal those notes. I told him I was through with him, and he paid me for my work – three weeks at a fiver a week.'

We questioned him about Reval. Kit was rather vague. He judged the dead man to be a Russian probably a refugee, like most Russians in London – he had never volunteered any information about himself. Kit had been gathering material for him from the files of pre-war Russian newspapers at the Museum for a history of Communism Reval was writing.

'A Bolshevik, was he?' Mr Treadgold wanted to know.
'I can't say. The stuff he dictated to Tatiana was mainly historical, she told me.'

The proceedings in court were brief. Inspector Hodgetts, a brisk, taciturn person, gave evidence of the arrest and requested a week's remand. He was reserved, but not unfriendly when we spoke to him outside. Chief Inspector Manderton had telephoned him: he would be pleased to show us the scene of the crime. If we cared to see the body it was at the local mortuary – the inquest had taken place earlier.

We called first at the mortuary. The deceased was short of stature and corpulent, with a flat nose and fleshy lips. The face was badly mangled. He had received five blows in all, Hodgetts told us, one across the face from the front, four from the back on top of the skull. There were traces of blood in the hall, showing that Reval had first been attacked there – since there were no signs of entry by violence into the house, it was indicated that Reval, who was alone in the place, had himself opened the front door to the murderer.

'In my opinion,' said the inspector, 'Kendrick went for him the moment he got in and Reval made a bolt for it with Kendrick after him. Kendrick finished him off in the study as Reval crouched at the desk, trying to protect his head with his arms. One of the hands is badly slashed.' He showed us the dead man's right hand. Mr Treadgold made no comment and we went on to Acacia Lodge.

Though a section of the high wall surrounding the place bordered on the North Circular Road, with its heavy day and night traffic, Acacia Lodge impressed me as being almost ideally suited for an isolated murder. It had no near neighbours, the entrance, at the side, was from a lane, and a long avenue of poplars effectually screened the unpretentious, one-story villa from the sight and sounds of the outer world.

The study was a dusty, shabby place encumbered with books – in shelves that reached to the ceiling, in stacks on chairs and on the floor – and darkened by heavy curtains. One of the two windows was open and in the chill draught that entered a sooty lilac bush rattled its naked branches against the panes. My gaze centred on the desk, strewn with open books and papers, the chair, with its back to the door, pulled out, as though the occupant of the room had just been called away. There were crimson stains on some of the papers.

Stock still in the centre of the study, Mr Treadgold gazed about him. He picked up a book or two at random, set them down. Glancing at a brass tea-urn, flanked with glasses, that stood on a table against the wall, he said to Hodgetts, 'Russian, was he?'

'Bulgarian,' the other replied. 'Reval wasn't his real name. The name on his passport and the name he's registered with at Bow Street under the Aliens Act is Dimitrieff.'

I saw H. B.'s bushy eyebrows tilt. 'By his features I'd have said he was Russian, with probably a dash of Tartar. His books are Russian, anyway, and that samovar . . . ' He broke off. 'Do you happen to have a photo I could borrow?'

'He had some spare passport photos in his desk. I dare say you could have one of them.' He extracted a photograph from his wallet and handed it across. Sombrely Mr Treadgold studied the fat, rather sensual face, resolute, notwithstanding the pendulous cheeks and double chin, the small, beady eyes. Hodgetts walked to the open window. 'This is where Kendrick escaped,' he said. 'Look, you can see the marks of his feet.'

A number of fresh scratches were clearly visible on the white paint of the sill. 'May one go out?' Mr Treadgold inquired.

'Why not? We're all through.'

It was a drop of only a few feet to the garden. The grounds were a tangle of laurels and rhododendrons, with a tarred path winding its way between towards the surrounding fence. 'Asphalt,' said Mr Treadgold, tapping with his foot. 'That don't tell us much, Inspector!'

'Wait!' replied our escort.

As we approached the wall, forbiddingly high and set with murderous-looking, broken glass all along its top, it became evident, from the succession of cars that went screaming by out of sight behind it, that we were in that part of the grounds bordering on the main road. A bed of shrubs ran along under the wall; in a gap between the bushes two short lengths of planking had been laid down. 'He left a couple of foot-prints,' Hodgetts remarked, pointing at the planks, then, raising his hand to waist-level, 'Those scrapes on the brickwork of the wall are where he shinned over. The glass is splintered, too.' He indicated the broken bottles set in the coping.

He pulled up the planks. 'It rained pretty hard the night of the murder,' he explained, 'and the edges are pretty much washed away. Still . . . '

Two blurred impressions, side by side, were disclosed. Hands on thighs, Mr Treadgold stooped to examine them. 'It's a large foot!' he observed thoughtfully.

'Kendrick stands six foot one,' the inspector reminded him.

My friend nodded. 'He wasn't taking any running jump – see how the balls of the feet sank in! He made quite a pause here.'

'You bet! He was waiting for a lull in the traffic; it's a busy road, by night as well as by day.'

'Dear me!' exclaimed Mr Treadgold suddenly. 'This is really rather odd!'

He dropped to his knees and was peering down at the footmarks. 'Did you examine these prints particularly?' he asked the inspector.

'I measured 'em, if that's what you mean. They correspond approximately to the size of Kendrick's foot. I tried 'em with a pair of his shoes, but it wasn't much good – the outline's too blurred.'

'All the same . . . ' His finger traced the curve of the impression on the right. 'It's none too sharp, but surely the ball of the right foot is on the wrong side?'

The inspector stooped. 'That right foot does look kind of lopsided, I grant you. But Kendrick walks a bit pigeon-toed. It only means he was treading over on that side.'

Squatting on his hunkers, Mr Treadgold scratched his head. 'It's really most extraordinary!' he proclaimed.

'What's extraordinary?' the inspector demanded.

'It sounds crazy, but I can't help thinking that these are the impressions of two left feet.'

Hodgetts laughed good-humouredly. 'Oh, come off it, sir!'

Mr Treadgold stood up and dusted the mud off his trousers. 'Footprints happen to be one of my subjects – I've made a special study of them at the truly admirable institutes of Forensic Medicine at Lyons and Vienna, and I repeat – these are the prints of two left feet.'

The inspector shot me a humourous glance. 'Well, I'll have to make a special trip to Brixton Jail and check up on Kendrick's tootsie-wootsies, I suppose.'

The witticism was lost on our companion. Head down, he had vanished among the bushes. Hodgetts winked at me and tapped his forehead. We heard Mr Treadgold crashing among the laurels, then the sounds grew fainter. He was away for so long that Hodgetts grew impatient. 'I can't hang round here all the afternoon, really,' he declared. A shout interrupted him. Mr Treadgold had stepped out on the path. His face was crimson and in his hand he grasped, wrapped in the folds of his pocket-handkerchief, a bayonet with a long triangular blade. Crumbs of earth adhered to it, and there was a reddish stain where the blade was set in the haft.

'Well, I'll be jiggered!' declared the inspector. His finger pointed to the stain. 'It's the weapon all right. However did you come to find it?'

'I was looking for it,' was the poised reply. 'No weapon was discovered; I therefore argued that the murderer carried it off with him. He left by the window, ergo, he was in a hurry and he kept going until the wall stopped him and he realized that he'd reached the main road. It seemed to me that his first instinct would be to get rid of the instrument of the crime. So I just poked around and there it was, under the nearest bush, thrust up to the hilt in the ground.'

'Neat work,' said Hodgetts. 'Well, this'll hang our young friend. The walls of his digs are draped with stuff like this.'

I started. I remembered that Kit had all his dead father's war souvenirs. 'It's a French bayonet with that long blade,' the detective remarked. 'Well, I'd best be getting back to headquarters with it.'

We parted from him at the house and, after stopping at the nearest call office to telephone, Mr Treadgold drove me back to town. 'The trouble about you, H. B.,' I told him, 'is that your imagination runs away with you. You know, there's really no such thing as a human being with two left feet!'

He stirred from a long silence. 'Nevertheless, I'm right about that pair of prints!'

'He was deliberately confusing the trail, was he? But why two left feet?'

My companion laughed bleakly. 'That, George, is precisely the difficulty.'

'But a man with two left feet – it doesn't make sense!'

He shook his head gloomily. 'It's we who don't make sense. In crime everything has its explanation, if we only know where to look for it.'

Miss O'Rorke was waiting at Mr Treadgold's rooms. She was aghast when, as gently as possible, I told her of the discovery of the bayonet. 'But I know it well,' she faltered. 'It used to lie about the sitting-room. It had a sheath once, but it got lost.' She dropped down on the couch and covered her face with her hands.

It was a facer for both of us. Mr Treadgold said nothing, but the look he cast me was full of meaning. Then the telephone rang. I answered it. It was Hodgetts. 'I'm speaking from young Kendrick's rooms,' he said. 'Your friend Treadgold might like to know that his landlady has identified that bayonet.'

I repeated the message to H. B. and he took the receiver. 'How did she identify it?' he demanded. 'After all, there are thousands of these French war bayonets knocking about.' I don't know what Hodgetts replied, but my friend went on: 'Even if Kendrick's French bayonet is missing, that's scarcely conclusive evidence of his guilt, is it? What does Kendrick himself say?'

He grunted. 'I should be interested to hear,' he remarked and hung up. With a moody air he began to cram his pipe from the tobacco jar on the desk. 'Tell me about Reval,' he said to the girl abruptly. 'Was he Bulgarian or Russian?'

'Russian,' was the listless answer, 'and South Russian, by his accent. From little things he said I gathered he'd been living in Soviet Russia until fairly recently.'

'Was he a Bolshevik?'

'He was a Communist; but he didn't like Stalin. I remember a phrase he dictated to me about Stalin betraying the gospel of Lenin.'

'Did he number a one-legged man among his acquaintances?'

She shook her head. 'I can't tell you. I never met anyone outside of Mrs Kelly at Acacia Lodge – I don't know who his friends were.'

The front door buzzer whirred. A pause and Mr Treadgold's servant announced, 'Mr Leander Leonard.'

A dried-up, prim little man bustled in. 'George,' said my friend, 'this is Mr Leander Leonard, Moscow correspondent of the *London Bulletin* at present on leave in London, and an old customer of ours. Well, Mr Leonard?'

The visitor fiddled with his glasses. 'As I told you on the telephone this afternoon,' he said nervously. 'I'm always anxious to oblige, and I went into action at once.' He wagged his head. 'This is a mighty ticklish business, Mr Treadgold, and if it should come out that I'm in any way involved in it, I can't go back to Russia.'

He cleared his throat. 'I had a word with a Moscow newspaper man now in town who happens to be under an obligation to me. He tells me that the Soviet Embassy are as silent as the tomb about this business and warns me not to approach them. But he gives me to understand that this Reval is in reality a certain Vassily Luboff, one of the Trotsky crowd implicated in the plot against Stalin last year; he'd have been tried and shot like Zinovieff and the rest if he hadn't contrived to flee abroad.'

'Do you know him?'

He shook his head. 'He's not one of the bigwigs, I can tell you that. My friend says he's been living very quietly in the country outside Leningrad for years, never appearing in public, but very active in the underground politics of the U.S.S.R.' He picked up his hat. 'Well, there's the dope, Mr Treadgold. It's a good newspaper story, but I want to keep my job and I'm not going to print it, especially as it doesn't affect young Kendrick's guilt. I make only one request – if you use it, leave me out!' With that he touched his hand to his hat and hurried away.

'I wonder if he's right,' said Mr Treadgold.

'How do you mean?' I questioned.

'About this not affecting young Kendrick's guilt.' With brooding eyes he sat down at the desk and drew a writing block towards him. Tapping his teeth with his gold pencil, he reflected, then wrote a few lines, detached the sheet and held it out to Miss O'Rorke. 'Can you turn that into Russian for me?' he asked her, then, noting the curiosity in my glance, added, 'All right, George, you can read it, if you like.'

I read:

> 'Pity for the one-legged. Russian veteran, who had the misfortune to lose a leg in the war, is anxious to come to the aid of fellow-sufferers of Russian nationality. Any one-legged Russian, whether a war cripple or not, should apply between the hours of 6 and 9 p.m. at Flat 99b, Bury Street, St James's, London, S.W.1.'

With wonder in her dark eyes the girl read this strange announcement. 'If you wish,' she said, and he made room for her at the desk. When she had finished, he took the sheet, covered with Russian writing, from her and sent her away. When she had gone he remained for a long time, puffing at his pipe and staring at the paper in his hand. I was burning to ask him what this bizarre advertisement, for such it seemed to be, signified, but I was prevented by the appearance of Hodgetts, who, pushing his way past Mr Treadgold's manservant, walked in on us. 'Well,' the inspector announced, 'young Kendrick's seen that bayonet and admits that it's similar to the one he had in his rooms.'

'You mean, he's identified that particular bayonet as his?' Mr Treadgold snapped.

The other laughed. 'You can hardly expect that. He claims that he hasn't seen the bayonet for days and suggests that it was stolen from him. But that's poppycock. I thought I'd just tell you.'

Mr Treadgold nodded impassively. 'A drink?' he suggested.

'Thanks, no. My missus is waiting for me to come home to supper.'

The inspector departed. Mr Treadgold looked at his watch. 'I'm thinking of going to Paris on the plane to-night,' he told me. 'That bayonet has a number, you know – all bayonets have – and I'd like to try and trace it . . . '

I shrugged my shoulders. 'What's the good? The only thing we want to know is, who had it last?'

His mouth set obstinately. 'All the same, I believe I'll go to Paris – I shan't be away long. Already the horizon of this crime has widened; we now know that Luboff was a doomed man when he left Russia and I seem to discern the shadow of political strife athwart his murder, like a cloud across the face of the sun.' He picked up the sheet which Tatiana had left with him. 'Will you take this to *The Times* to-morrow and ask them to run it in Russian script at the head of the agony column until further notice?'

'If you like. But, H. B., what's the idea?'

He gave me an enigmatic smile. 'I'm still interested in the chap with the two left feet.'

Next day I executed Mr Treadgold's commission. Tatiana O'Rorke rang up eager for news, but I had none for her. Evening came and I called on my friend at his rooms, only to learn that he was still absent. The following morning the advertisement, looking very exotic in its Russian script, led the agony column in *The Times*. A court case kept me away from the office until after lunch. Jobling, my clerk, handed me a telegram from Mr Treadgold, despatched from Paris that morning, asking me to be at his chambers at 6 p.m. that evening; Jobling said that Tatiana O'Rorke had made repeated efforts to reach me.

Presently she telephoned again. She, too, had received a wire from Mr Treadgold, giving her a rendezvous at Bury Street at six. She had seen the advertisement and wanted to know what it meant, but I assured her I was as much in the dark as she was. Others had seen it, too, she informed me – at lunch at the Medved, a little Russian restaurant near the British Museum where she sometimes went, the Russians were talking of nothing else.

After she had rung off, I remembered that six o'clock that evening was the hour set for the one-legged Russians to put in an appearance at Bury Street. I had a sudden thrill. Old H. B. was not above staging a dramatic surprise on occasion – was he about to unmask the real murderer?

A talkative client made me a few minutes late in arriving at Bury Street. Vestibule and staircase seemed to be full of excited cripples, some on crutches, others with rubbershod sticks. There must have been a score of them – I had no idea there were so many one-legged Russians in London. Upstairs they were already hobbling into the flat. Installed at the desk, with Mr Treadgold standing behind her,

Tatiana O'Rorke was catechising each applicant and handing out Treasury notes – sometimes a pound, sometimes two, as Mr Treadgold directed – from a bundle on the blotter. As she spoke in Russian I could not understand what she said, but, after listening to her for a while, I was aware that the names Reval and Luboff figured in every question.

I drew H. B. away. 'What luck in Paris?'

The blue eyes sparkled. 'I traced the bayonet.'

'No!'

'It's one of a series issued in the year 1917 to the so-called Russian Legion, composed mainly of ex-officers of the Russian Army who, after the collapse of the Russian front, volunteered for service with the French. This particular bayonet, the records show, formed part of the equipment handed out to a certain Boris Valianko, a Russian artillery colonel . . . '

The girl called from the desk. 'Mr Treadgold, one moment, please!'

A shabby man on crutches confronted her. 'He knows Colonel Valianko,' she said. I caught an exasperated exclamation from Mr Treadgold, 'Tchah! It should be his right leg that's missing.' I glanced at the cripple. His left trouser leg dangled about a wooden stump.

Tatiana said, 'His English is very bad. He says that Colonel Valianko publishes a White Russian weekly paper in London.'

The cripple spoke up. 'The Colonel vairy good man, vairy kind to poor Rossyans. You give me monney for him, perhaps – he lose leg like me.'

Mr Treadgold stiffened. 'A one-legged man, too, is he?' he barked. 'Ask him!' he trumpeted to Tatiana as the cripple stared at him uncomprehendingly. 'And let him tell us which of Valianko's legs is missing.'

The girl translated. 'It's the right,' she said. And Mr Treadgold's eyes flashed.

A voice cried, 'What's going on here?'

It was Hodgetts, gazing blankly at the halt and maimed stretching in a line to the hall. 'I wanted a word with you, Mr Treadgold,' he remarked.

But H. B. brushed him aside. 'Not now, damnit, I'm busy.'

The Inspector, however, persisted. 'It's about that bayonet of

Kendrick's – we've found it at his digs. The slavey had carried it down to the cellar to break up coal.'

Mr Treadgold's laugh was a joyous 'Ha!' 'Then stick along, Inspector, and maybe we'll trace the other bayonet,' he cried. He swung to Tatiana. 'Does he know where this Valianko hangs out?'

She repeated the question. 'His printing office is in Font Street, Islington, and he lives above,' she announced.

Mr Treadgold thrust the bundle of notes into her hand. 'Get rid of the rest of these poor devils,' he bade her, 'and tell our one-legged friend he's coming with us.'

Hodgetts had a police car below. We all piled in. At the last moment Tatiana joined us, breathless. The Inspector demurred, but 'You'll want me to interpret!' she cried, and we made room for her.

As we sped northward Mr Treadgold told Hodgetts briefly of his trip to Paris and his success in tracing the owner of the bayonet. The Inspector's face was grim in the light of a passing tram. 'Then this Valianko's our man!' he exclaimed.

But H. B. said nothing.

The printing office, housed in a shabby shop in a shabby back street, was dark when we reached it, but a light burned over the side door and in answer to the inspector's loud knock a clumping footstep resounded from within. An elderly man with a shock of iron grey hair and bristling moustaches opened to us. He wore a ragged brown cardigan and his right leg ended in a wooden stump.

'Colonel Valianko?' said Hodgetts.

'I am he,' was the proud reply in excellent English.

The inspector handed him a card: I saw the Colonel's face change as he glanced at it. 'I want to talk to you,' said Hodgetts.

The other inclined his head and led us into a small office. I noticed that he stared hard at Tatiana. 'I've seen you at the Medved Restaurant in Museum Street,' he observed to her. 'It was you who were Alexander Reval's secretary, isn't it?'

But the inspector struck in. 'I'm an Inspector of Metropolitan Police, and it's my duty to warn you . . . '

The Colonel cut him off. 'It is about the murder of this man, I know . . . '

'Why did you kill him?'

'He didn't,' Mr Treadgold now interposed. 'But I fancy he can tell us who did.' He bent his bushy eyebrows at him. 'Where is the man who wore two of your shoes that night?'

Valianko gazed at him out of gentle eyes for a long time in silence. Then, with a movement of the head, he indicated the upper regions of the house. 'Upstairs,' he said, and in a dull voice added, 'He's dying.' The inspector would have sprung for the staircase, but the Colonel restrained him with his hand. 'Before you go . . . ' he said.

'This man who called himself Reval,' he told us, 'was in reality the infamous Luboff, who, as Chief of the Secret Police at Odessa after the defeat of Denikin's army, put thousands of innocent people to death. Some months ago I printed in my paper a rumour that reached me from Riga to the effect that Luboff, who had fled from Russia to escape arrest, had taken refuge in London. One day last month a poor ragged fellow called to see me. He had papers showing that he had been a captain in the Preobrashensky Regiment of the Imperial Guards. His name was Paul Michailoff. He told me he had come across a copy of my paper with this story about Luboff while working on the docks at Salonika and wanted to know where Luboff was to be found. I said I couldn't tell him – it was just a rumour which we had failed to confirm. Then he went away.'

'When did you see him again?' Mr Treadgold asked.

'Last week. He came to me absolutely destitute and I discovered that, since our last meeting, he had been living in misery in the East End. He had a terrible cough and was half starved, so I gave him a bed. The next day I took him to a Russian restaurant I frequent to buy him a good dinner. We were passing the British Museum when he stopped dead and pointing to a man who was talking to a girl and who looked like a Russian, asked me if I could tell him who it was. The girl was Mademoiselle here – I'd often seen her at the Medved. I had heard from the proprietess of the restaurant that Mademoiselle was secretary to a man called Reval. I told Michailoff this and said that her companion was probably her employer.'

'Did Michailoff tell you the man was Luboff?'

'Not then. But three days later – that's to say, on Saturday, the day of the murder – he did not come home all night and I discovered that my bayonet, the only souvenir of my service with the Russian Legion in France, where I lost my leg, had vanished. Michailoff returned at daybreak, exhausted, half delirious. He told me he had killed this man, Reval, the fiend of Odessa, who years before had caused the death of his mother and sister.'

'And knowing this you said nothing?' Tatiana broke in with dark eyes flashing. 'Are you aware that an innocent man has been accused of the crime?'

Valianko cast down his eyes. 'Michailoff was my comrade and at death's door. I wanted him to die in peace. He would have been dead long before the other came to trial.'

'Well, let's go to him!' cried Hodgetts. But Mr Treadgold said, 'One moment!' He turned to Valianko 'How did he come to be wearing your shoes?'

The Colonel flushed. 'Gentlemen, I am very poor. When Michailoff came to me the second time his feet were bleeding in torn sandals. Another comrade of mine, whose left leg was shattered at the Masurian Lakes, has helped himself to all the right shoes remaining to me from my wardrobe of other days, and the best I could offer Michailoff was two left boots, part of my equipment as an officer. Fortunately, he is a smaller man than I.' He turned to Hodgetts. 'A moment, please, before we go upstairs . . . ' He unlocked a desk and produced a sheaf of bank-notes, which he placed in the inspector's hand. 'The money he took,' he explained. 'Two hundred and eighty pounds in all – you will find it intact.'

In a barely furnished bedroom on the first floor a naked gas jet cast a trembling light on a haggard, unshaven man who tossed on the bed, coughing incessantly. 'Comrade,' said Valianko gently, 'these gentlemen are from the police.'

The man in the bed turned and his sunken eyes sought each of us in turn. 'It is well,' he answered in a hollow voice. 'I shall tell you the truth, for soon I am going to die.' He spoke in fluent English. 'It was I who killed Vassily Luboff, who called himself Alexander Reval. My only sister fell into his hands when he was Chief of the Ogpu at Odessa, and when my mother heard our poor little Nadia's story she took her own life. Afterwards Nadia was shot, with twenty-eight others in the courtyard of the prison.'

His cough cut his breath and Valianko gave him some medicine from a bottle. 'I was with Denikin's army,' he resumed, 'and I only learned of my mother's and my sister's fate when, after Denikin's defeat, I reached Odessa in disguise. I followed Luboff about for weeks, meaning to kill him, but he was too well guarded. Finally,

I was denounced to the police and had to flee. I reached Constanza, then Constantinople and finally Salonika, where, during all these years, I lived as best I could. But I never forgot Luboff.'

His cough racked him again. When he had regained his breath he went on, 'Then the other day I read in my comrade Valianko's paper that Luboff was believed to be in London. Within a fortnight, as fireman on a Greek fruitship, I was on my way here. Colonel Valianko could not tell me where Luboff was to be found, and for weeks I tramped the streets, looking for him, until all my money was gone and I was forced to ask my comrade for food, a bed. And the very next day I saw Luboff.'

'I have told these gentlemen of that meeting,' Valianko interposed.

Michailoff said, 'This time I was resolved he should not escape me. I did not want to get my kind benefactor into trouble, so I told him nothing of my plan. But I ascertained Reval's address from the telephone directory and for three days, with my comrade Valianko's old bayonet, the only weapon I possessed, under my coat, I hung about the house, waiting for the chance to come upon him alone – I was determined to kill him undisturbed. On Saturday morning he left the house as usual and soon after the housekeeper drove away in a taxi.'

His voice was tiring, but he kept on. 'All day I waited. My hopes rose when the housekeeper did not return. At dusk he came back. I watched him enter the house, then, when it was dark, boldly rang the bell. As I had calculated, he opened the door himself. At the sight of him I lost all control of myself. "Have you forgotten Nadia Michailoff?" I shouted, and slashed him across the face with my bayonet. With the blood running down his cheek he tried to slam the door, but I stopped it with my shoulder and pursued him through the hall into his study. "I don't know you! I don't know you!" he kept crying. "I am the brother of Nadia Michailoff, whom you ravished and murdered!" I told him. When he saw my hand go up he crouched down in his chair, trying to protect himself with his hands. But I split his skull for him. I struck him again and again. I . . . '

He broke off, gasping, spent with excitement. 'There was money in the safe,' he murmured. 'I told myself it was part of the loot he had brought out of Russia – I meant to use it to help my comrades here – all poor Russians . . . ' His voice trailed away, the burning eyes closed.

'And so,' I said to Mr Treadgold as I left him at his door that night, 'you were looking for a one-legged man all along?'

He smiled. 'At any rate, from the moment I came upon those two left-foot impressions. As you very aptly reminded me, there's no such thing as a human being with two left feet. I therefore asked myself who's a likely person to own a collection of shoes of the same foot? A one-legged person, obviously.'

'All right. But, having traced that bayonet to Valianko, why didn't you assume that he was the murderer?'

'My dear George, have you forgotten that wall round the grounds at Acacia Lodge, a good fifteen feet high and set with broken glass? Do you really see a man with a wooden leg scaling it? It had to be an able-bodied person: the problem was to discover how he came to leave the impressions of two left feet. Reason found the answer, reason which, as *Tristram Shandy* says, "is half of it sense!"'

Paul Michailoff never came to trial – he died three weeks later. Soon after, Kit and his Tatiana were married, the bridegroom immaculate in a morning-coat from Bowl, Treadgold & Flack, of Savile Row, a wedding present from Mr Treadgold, who insisted on giving the sweet-looking bride away. Colonel Valianko is managing a flower farm at Grasse. Mr Treadgold denies that he had anything to do with this; but some admirer in the South of France is always sending him boxes of fresh flowers.

Valianko's bayonet, fitted in its sheath which Michailoff had left behind in the colonel's house, hangs over Mr Treadgold's fireplace in Bury Street. A small plate affixed to the scabbard reads 'To H. B. T. in sincere admiration from W. S. H.'

Which, seeing that Divisional Inspector William Samuel Hodgetts owed his promotion to inspector to his brilliant elucidation of the Acacia Lodge mystery, I submit is no more than fair.

INQUEST

Loel Yeo

MEMORY is an odd thing. I can always remember to perfection a mass of unimportant details. So many men stretched end on end would encircle the earth; the exact number is 23,549,115. Thirty and a quarter square yards equal one square rod, pole, or perch. These things and many more I never forget. Yet on the occasional days I can snatch to go up to London (and I being a country doctor they are rare enough), I never fail to leave my shopping list behind. It is only as the train pulls out of London that I remember the instruments I meant to buy.

I overtook the Stanton express as it was grumbling out of the station, and flung myself on to somebody's lap. My apologies were accepted. He was elderly and inconspicuous and neat, and I knew I had seen him before, but thought I still knew rice, sago, and pepper to be the chief exports of North Borneo, I couldn't remember where we had met.

People who live the same sort of lives grow to look alike. Thirty years of the same office, the same suburb, the same daily papers, and they end with the same face. Thin and a little anaemic. Eyes the faded blue of much-washed laundry. In summer and winter always a raincoat and an evening paper.

It was a chilly, foggy evening, the typical raw January day which the inconsequence of the English climate always produces in the middle of October; the window-panes were steaming with the heat of the compartment, and I lay back recovering my breath, wondering where I had seen the man opposite me before. A high white collar held his chin erect. He sat upright on the edge of the seat.

Suddenly he coughed. It was more of a mannerism than a cough, you felt it did his throat no good at all. And I remembered that we had last met on the afternoon of the coroner's inquest two years ago at Langley Abbey.

As one noticed little things in the midst of great excitement during the occasional silences in the dining-room on that day, I remember watching the shadow of the elms stretch themselves across the lawn, hearing the cawing of the rooks, and in the room the creaking of the constable's boots and the dry little cough of the solicitor's clerk who gave his unimportant but necessary evidence clearly and concisely.

The only thing about Langley that suggests an Abbey is the stained-glass window of the bathroom, otherwise it is just one of those solid square Georgian houses. Its gardens and park are lovely. I was practically brought up there with the Neville boys, so I know the place backwards. When they were both killed in 1917 old Sir Guy Neville sold it as it stood to John Hentish.

It's funny how the character of a place changes with its owner. Under the Nevilles, Langley had been a friendly house. The park gates stood open and so did the doors and windows of the house itself, muslin curtains swinging gaily in the breeze. There were village *fêtes* in the park, and the Abbey was part of the life and conversation of all the villages round.

With John Hentish there came a change. Sir Guy was asked to inform the county that the future tenants disliked society, and hoped people would not give themselves the trouble of calling. The park gates were shut and stayed shut. The windows were tightly closed and the muslin curtains hung straight and lifeless behind them. The house developed a thin-lipped, austere look. The only people who gave themselves the trouble of calling were the postman and the tradesmen. And gradually Langley Abbey dropped out of the annals and conversation of the county.

As for me, the house that had been so much a part of my life having shut me out, for ten years as I drove over to Maddenly to prescribe for Miss Taunton's varicose veins or dose Master Willie Twinger, I averted my eyes from the park gates as one would passing a friendly dog whose temper has become changed and uncertain. And then one afternoon four years ago I found a message in my consulting room asking me to go up to the Abbey at once.

After that I went there regularly, at least three times a week.

Practically the whole house, I found, presumably through lack of
interest, had been left exactly as it was bought from the Nevilles.
The hall was large and ran the width of the house, that is French
windows opening on to the lawn faced the front door. The floor
had a higher polish than I remembered, and there were fewer lights.
The furniture was ugly but solid, mostly Victorian. Two long tables,
an oak chest, some stiff chairs, and a Burmese gong. There were
several pairs of antlers on the walls, some lithographs of the early
Christian martyrs, Saint Sébastien looking extraordinarily fit and
cheerful with about forty arrows through his body, a twenty-pound
trout Sir Guy had caught in Scotland, and one fairly good tapestry.

Old Hentish had converted what had been Lady Neville's morn-
ing-room into a bedroom and bathroom. Off the bedroom, what
we had known as the drawing-room had been made into a very
beautiful library. Both rooms were large with high ceilings, and had
French windows opening on to the lawn. He lived almost entirely
in this suite and seldom left it.

Hentish, though he had faith in me as a doctor, disliked me as he
consistently disliked everyone. He was, without exception, the most
unpleasant, disagreeable old swine I have ever met. Practically the
only pleasure I ever received in his company was derived from
jabbing the needle into his arm. He soon exhausted the supply of
London nurses, and finally I persuaded Miss Mavey from Maddenly
village to take the post, she having nursed an invalid mother for
fifteen years who could have given even old Hentish points for
unpleasantness. No man, of course, could live long in John Hentish's
condition, for, besides heart-trouble, he had advanced cirrhosis of
the liver, but because death frightened him he listened to me, and
so with electrical treatments, diet, and drugs, his general health
improved.

Some women are eerie. Miss Taunton has been bedridden for years,
yet she's one of those women whose cousin always knew the murdered man's aunt. This time her sister-in-law's maid's niece had
married the son of the overseer of the Hentish Paper Mills in Onta-
rio. Like all women, Miss Taunton had a profound contempt for
detailed accuracy, but fundamentally her facts are always correct.
Hentish, apparently, during the first forty years of his life had spent
seven separate fortunes; the figures are Miss Taunton's. He had been

the most dissolute man in London, also in Buenos Aires, where the standard is higher and competition keener. He was hard, grasping and avid for power; there wasn't a man in his paper mills or his gold mine that wouldn't be glad to see him boiled in oil. 'And that,' said Miss Taunton, impressively, 'I got more or less straight from the lips of his own overseer.'

Miss Taunton's attitude to God is rather that of a proud aunt; she sees all the motives so clearly and is often a jump ahead of the game. When John Hentish's health failed, her attitude was that of one whose advice had been taken, for she was a firm believer in the wages of sin. Her own varicose veins she knew had been sent to test her – take the well-known case of Job – she took them rather as a compliment than otherwise, applauded God's attempt at impartiality, and forgave him frequently.

I never knew whether old Hentish had any affection for his nephew or not. William was his heir and they quarrelled, of course – over money, among other things – but I think more than disapproval he enjoyed the sense of power it gave him to see his nephew flush as he threatened to stop his allowance, which was a generous one. William's specialities were women and horses. I suppose he was good-looking in a dark, sinister sort of way; he had inherited all his uncle's unpleasantness and developed it with some ideas of his own. He used to motor down to Langley occasionally for two or three days at a time.

So life drifted on placidly and uneventfully. Sometimes after I had seen old Hentish I used to wander down to the boathouse, for the lawn sloped down to a lake fringed with red willow, and I would sit there thinking out beautiful unappetising diets for the old man. Then one afternoon my telephone rang. It was Miss Mavey.

'Dr Mellan? Oh, Dr Mellan, will you please come down at once. Mr Hentish is dead!'

John Hentish had died from an overdose of morphia taken in a glass of sal volatile. The inquest was held that same evening in the Abbey dining-room. Mr Duffy, the coroner, sat with Police-constable Perker at the table, the rest of the household at the end of the room. Mr Duffy blew his knose, and the Vapex on his handkerchief mingled with the smell of leather and pickles. He turned a watery eye on Croucher, the butler.

'Is everybody here?'

'Everyone with the exception of Mr William Hentish, sir. He has not yet returned home.'

'Thank you. Call Dr Mellan.'

My testimony did not take long. History of John Hentish's illness, cause of death, etc. Miss Mavey was called next, and under the impression that she was on trial for her life, opened with a magnificent defence, giving seven distinct alibis for the afternoon.

'You say,' the coroner asked her, 'that the morphia with which you sometimes had occasion to inject the deceased in order to relieve intense pain was kept on the top shelf of a medicine cupboard clearly labelled "morphia"?'

'I do,' said Miss Mavey, looking like the Trial of Mary Dugan. 'Anyone else will say the same.'

'The cupboard has a glass door, I understand. The sal volatile and a glass were placed on a small table beneath the cupboard containing the morphia. Is that correct, Miss Mavey?'

Miss Mavey paled, knowing that all she said would be used in evidence against her.

'In a sense, yes.'

'In a sense?'

'A spoon was also kept on the table,' said Miss Mavey, determined to conceal nothing.

'This medicine, this sal volatile, did the deceased take it at regular hours?'

Miss Mavey turned this over. A trap?

'No, sir, only to relieve the pain if it came on sudden,' she said, guardedly.

'When Dr Mellan gave his opinion that death was not due to natural causes, but to an overdose of morphia, you looked in the bathroom. You found the phial, which when you went off duty was in the cupboard and had contained twenty grains of morphia, lying empty on the table beside the sal volatile. Is that correct?'

'Dr Mellan asked me to look when he saw that the morphia had been put in the glass of sal volatile. I touched nothing, I swear it before Almighty God.'

'Was Mr Hentish in the habit of helping himself to this sal volatile?'

'Yes, sir, if there was no one in the room to get it for him.'

'Miss Mavey, are you of the same opinion as Dr Mellan that the morphia could not have been taken accidentally?'

'No.'

'No! Then you think it could have been taken accidentally?'

'Yes. I mean yes I'm of the opinion that no it couldn't have been taken accidentally.'

'That is all. Thank you.'

Miss Mavey, still under the shadow of the scaffold, gave a shuddering sigh, and borrowing the coroner's Vapex, sank on to a chair, inhaling deeply.

Croucher, the butler, was questioned next.

'You say,' said the coroner, 'that on receipt of the telegram this morning, Mr Hentish showed signs of anger?'

'Distinctly, sir.'

'What then?'

'He asked if Mr William was in.'

'Was he?'

'No, sir, he had left in his car at 9.30.'

'What then?'

'He told me to go to hell, sir, and take his blasted nephew with me, sir, but before I went to get Troubridge and Hay on the telephone.'

'His solicitors?'

'Exactly, sir.'

'Then what?'

'He rang and gave me instructions for the car to meet the 1.45 train. His solicitors were sending down a member of the firm.'

'On arrival he was shown straight into the library, I understand?'

'Yes, sir.'

'What then?'

'After about fifteen minutes the library bell rang and Mr Hentish asked me to witness his signature to a new will.'

'After you had signed the will, anything else?'

'The usual instructions to go to hell, sir.'

'Then I understand the house was quiet until 4.30?'

'Yes, sir. The solicitor's gentleman left the library a few moments after I did. There were standing instructions never to disturb Mr Hentish until Miss Mavey woke him at 4.30. To-day the bell pealed violently, and on my entering the library Miss Mavey informed me that Mr Hentish was dead. I remained in the room until the doctor's arrival.'

The solicitor's clerk was called.

'Your firm had instructions from Mr Hentish by telephone this morning, I understand, to draft out a new will?'

'Yes, sir.'

'You were shown into the library on your arrival. What happened?'

'I read Mr Hentish the new draft, which he approved with one alteration. He rang for the butler and we both witnessed the signature.'

'Did it strike you there was anything in Mr Hentish's manner to suggest he contemplated suicide?'

'Difficult to say, sir.'

'And after you had signed the will?'

'I remained with Mr Hentish ten minutes or so. He wished to discuss a matter of income tax. I then left the library and went and sat in the garden until train time, as is my custom.'

'You've been here before, then? On the same errand?'

'Usually, sir.'

'Mr Hentish was in the habit of changing his will?'

'Yes, sir.'

'Often?'

'Seven times in the last ten years, sir.'

There was a silence. The butler was called again.

'I find a memorandum on Mr Hentish's desk, Twiller and Dwight, Thursday at 12. Can you explain this?'

'His tailors, sir. He told me to telephone and have a fitter sent down to-morrow at twelve.'

'When did he give this order?'

'At breakfast, sir.'

'Then as late as the breakfast hour he was obviously not contemplating suicide. Was he in a bad or good mood?'

'Mr Hentish was never exactly sunny-tempered, sir, but he seemed average.'

'It was only after he received the telegram that his mood changed for the worse?'

'Yes, sir.'

'Mr William came down from London last night, you say?'

'Yes, sir.'

'Did he appear on good terms with his uncle?'

'He seemed slightly nervous at dinner, if I may say so, but trying to be pleasant, I thought, sir.'

'You say he hasn't been in all day?'

'Oh yes, sir. He returned this afternoon but went out again.'

'This afternoon! At what time?'

'Well, sir, I noticed his car in the drive when I passed through the hall to witness the signature, sir. That would be about 2.30, and it was still there when Miss Mavey rang, but when I opened the front door to the doctor about fifteen minutes later it had gone.'

In the silence the smell of pickles became sharper. All our chairs creaked. The same idea had suddenly occurred to everybody.

'Did Mr William know of the arrival of the telegram?'

'No, sir, he had already left when it came.'

There was another silence.

'Then he didn't know that Mr Hentish intended changing his will or that Mr – Mr – that his solicitor was sending down a representative?'

'No, sir.'

People are funny, they can see a man every day for twenty years, know his face, mannerisms, idiosyncrasies, but they've only to hear that his wife has left him, that he's shot his mother, and they'll stand for hours waiting for a glimpse of him.

Practically all of us at the inquest had seen Mr William Hentish frequently during the last two years, some longer; and none of us had ever been particularly elated at the sight, yet when the front door banged as Croucher stopped speaking, and footsteps echoed on the polished floor of the hall, all the eyes in the room turned and became fixed on the handle of the mahogany door. There were people in that room to my certain knowledge, notably the butler and myself, whose day ordinarily could be made simply by not seeing Mr William Hentish, yet as his footsteps echoed nearer, the drone of a solitary bluebottle in the room seemed like the roar of an aeroplane in the silence. Our chairs creaked as each of us leant forward and became still.

The footsteps stopped, the handle turned, and our chairs creaked sharply once again.

I don't know exactly what change we all expected to see in William Hentish, but I remember a feeling of vague disappointment as he stood in the doorway looking just the same as when I had last seen him. When he was told of his uncle's death, and the manner of it, he seemed surprised.

I've often wondered why magistrates and coroners ask the questions they do. Mr Duffy knew William Hentish as well as I did, he'd been splashed often enough with mud from his car in the winter in our narrow village street, yet the next fifteen minutes was entirely taken up with proving his identity.

The questions seemed to go on endlessly. William Hentish wore his customary look of not caring much for the smell of those immediately about him, but he gave his answers quietly and without emotion. He said that he had returned soon after lunch, gone straight through the hall on to the lawn to the boathouse. He sat there until the stable clock struck 4.30, then returned to the house, intending to go in and see his uncle, who, he knew, would be awake by then. He didn't go in because when he reached the hall the library door was ajar.

Police-constable Perker, the official recorder at the inquest, was taking down notes in longhand. A hollow moan was his signal that the pace was too much for him and the questions would cease until he caught up. Presently the coroner continued:

'Through the open door you say you heard Miss Mavey telephone Dr Mellan? But why should this stop you from seeing your uncle?'

'I thought he had probably had another attack and wouldn't want to see me just then.'

'I understand you were not here when the telegram arrived.'

'Telegram?'

The coroner turned to Perker. 'Constable, please read out the telegram.'

Police-constable Perker first got his notes up to date, then there was a roll of drums as he cleared his throat.

'Telegram to John Hentish, Langley Abbey, Langley, Norfolk. Subject secretly married to Miriel Demar yesterday two p.m. Duke Street register office. Awaiting instructions. Signed Ross.'

All our eyes were on William Hentish. I think he became a little more rigid and a pulse throbbed in his temple. The cruet-stand on the table rattled like an express train as Constable Perker settled down to his notes again.

'Is this information correct, Mr Hentish?'

'Yes.'

'You were not aware that your uncle had your movements watched?'

'No.'

'You were married secretly, I presume, because you felt Miss Demar would not have been your uncle's choice of a wife for you?'

William Hentish flushed. 'My uncle was a difficult man. He disapproved of whatever he hadn't arranged himself. My wife was a chorus girl. In time he would have come round, he always did.'

'And in the meantime?'

'He would have forbidden me the house for a month or two, I suppose.'

'And cut you off in his will?'

'Probably.'

'Supposing he had died before reinstating you in the will?'

William Hentish smiled.

'That is a remote contingency now.'

There was an angry moan from Constable Perker, who spelt by ear and preferred words that he had heard before.

'You haven't seen this gentleman before, then?'

Mr Duffy pointed out the solicitor's clerk, who coughed discreetly. William Hentish looked at him, then turned back to the coroner.

'Not consciously. Who is he?'

'He was sent down on your uncle's instructions from Troubridge and Hay with the draft of a new will.'

William Hentish turned quickly to the clerk.

'Did my uncle sign it?'

'Yes, sir.'

'May I ask the contents of the new will, the existing one?'

The clerk managed to clear his throat in the form of a question to the coroner, who nodded back an answer.

'Mr Hentish left his entire fortune to cancer research.'

'And the former will? The one he revoked?' the coroner asked.

'Everything to his nephew, William Hentish.'

While the clerk was speaking, William Hentish sat silent, except that a pulse hammered again in his temple. By chance he caught the cook's eye. I saw him start. She was so obviously a woman who hadn't murdered her uncle looking at a man who had murdered his. And I think it was only then that he realized the danger of the case building up against him.

He had known his uncle would disapprove of a marriage which could probably not remain secret long. He had known his uncle's precarious state of health, had often prepared John Hentish's sal volatile for him, and knew about the morphia. He had only to walk into the library from the garden. He would know from experience that his uncle's rage at being disturbed in the middle of the afternoon would be enough to bring on an attack; and as he had often done before, he would get old Hentish some sal volatile from the bathroom, this time with a generous helping of morphia. Perhaps he had stood with curiosity watching his uncle gulp it down, had seen the purple settle under the eyes, then picking up his book, had walked quietly back to the boathouse. Perhaps he had even sat there reading until the stable clock chimed.

The coroner spoke.

'You say, Mr Hentish, that you didn't leave the garden until you heard the clock strike?'

Until then William Hentish had answered the questions put to him abruptly and with an appearance of indifference. Now his answers became more hesitant, and he paused before he spoke. He was already on the defensive. Our chairs creaked as we leant forward for his answer.

'No.'

'You didn't go near the library the whole afternoon?'

'No.'

'But you could have. Without being observed. Isn't that so, Mr Hentish?'

'Yes, I suppose so. But I repeat that I didn't.'

The cook's sniff re-echoed round the room, which had become nearly dark. Our faces were now only a blurred outline, and a cold breeze rustled Constable Perker's notes. The stable clock clanged eight.

'Then we have only your word for it that you sat in the boathouse all afternoon, Mr Hentish?'

'I'm afraid so.'

There was a silence. Suddenly the solicitor's clerk cleared his throat and spoke.

'It is quite true what Mr Hentish says with regard to his movements. I can substantiate that. Directly I left Mr Hentish I went and sat under the cedar tree whilst waiting my train time. I noticed young Mr Hentish sitting in the boathouse smoking. I don't think he saw me, but his statement is correct. He never left there until the stable clock struck.'

Human nature is weird. Instead of a deep sense of thankfulness that a fellow-creature's hands were not stained with the blood of another fellow-creature, I think that everyone in that room, with perhaps the exception of the coroner, who saw a chance of getting home to a hot mustard bath after all, felt aggrieved that William Hentish's hands were not stained with blood. Probably it was because anyone with an eye for drama could see that William Hentish was perfect for the rôle of villain, an aggressive manner, tall, with a black moustache and large white teeth. His hands *should* have been stained with his uncle's blood, he looked better that way, it suited him. Speaking for myself, preferring, as I do, like the rest of mankind, to believe the worst of my fellow-men, I felt that if he had not murdered his uncle, it was simply because he didn't happen to think of it.

After we had recovered from our natural disappointment, Croucher lit the gas brackets, and the questions, innumerable and interminable, began again. The clerk could add nothing, he could only say that he had seen Mr Hentish sitting as he had said in the boathouse the whole afternoon. The butler was called again, so were Miss Mavey, still at bay, and I. The question of the morphia arose.

'Might not Mr Hentish's insistence,' Mr Duffy asked the room in general, 'on the presence of morphia easily accessible, be attributed, apart from its properties in the alleviation of pain, to his possible contemplation of self-destruction?'

Constable Perker put down his pencil.

'That's coming it too hot for me, sir. Can I put it in my own words? You mean, did he pop himself off, sir?'

The questions and answers continued, but the evidence of a completely disinterested witness was too overwhelming, and on a statement from Miss Mavey that the old man had often spoken wholeheartedly in favour of self-slaughter (actually, I think, he was advocating it for her and not for himself), the coroner, as the stable clock clanged nine, brought in a verdict of suicide while of an unsound mind.

I didn't see whether William Hentish spoke to the little clerk in the dining-room or not, but he walked, frowning, across the hall as if it were empty, through the huddled group of servants, past the rest of us without a sign or word; the front door slammed, his motor roared and whined, and he was gone.

The presence of death does strange things to a place. As we stood in a group near the front door, making arrangements for the following day, the hall seemed lifeless and cold, our footsteps and voices had a hollow sound; somehow the windows reminded me of staring, dead black eyes, for the curtains had not been drawn. The gas jet droned and made the shadows of the stag's head and horns flicker and leap jerkily across the ceiling. A steady draught from an open door edged behind the tapestry, bellying it out till a naked old satyr leaned amorously towards Miss Mavey. She stood gazing after William Hentish.

'Think of losing a fortune, all that money wasted on charity!'

She sighed and sneezed. The solicitor's clerk put down his satchel and helped her on with her coat.

'It won't be wasted,' he said, gently.

A car drew up to the door, the coroner looked at his watch and turned to the clerk. 'That will be the car to take you to the station, I think. Thank you for your evidence. We shall need you again, I'm afraid. I'll communicate with you in a day or so.'

The clerk picked up his satchel and coat and hat.

'I shall be at your convenience, sir. Good night, gentlemen.'

The screech of the engine's whistle jerked me awake. I must have dozed for about two hours, because the train was already rattling over the points approaching Cranham Junction. My back was numb from lying so long in one position, huddled in my overcoat. I stretched myself. The clerk was still opposite, sitting stiffly erect, his worn gloves neatly buttoned over his wrists, his satchel by his side. I leant forward.

'You don't remember me?'

'Indeed, yes, sir. It is Dr Mellan. I had the pleasure at the inquest at Langley Abbey.' He coughed. 'The Abbey is still for sale, I understand.'

'Yes. Quite deserted. I often wander over there; I've known the place all my life, you know.'

I yawned.

'So the Hentish fortune went to charity after all. I wonder young William didn't contest the will. He would have had a case – uncertain temper of the old man, suicide while of unsound mind, etc.'

'I suppose he was afraid he might be reaccused of murder, sir. There was only my word for it that he didn't leave the boathouse. My word between him and a certain accusation of murder with strong motives for it.'

'He's gone abroad, they say.'

'To South America, sir. His mother left him a piece of property in the Argentine. He is doing well, I understand, sir. Mr Troubridge, head of my firm, sir, says it has been the making of him.'

'He'd have only gambled the money away if he'd had it. He promised to be as hard and selfish as his uncle was. It's funny – though he altered his will so often, I always thought old Hentish meant his nephew to have the money in the end. I thought he just enjoyed frightening William by disinheriting him.'

'A sense of power, sir?'

'Yes, the idea of doing good always seemed to sicken him. Odd, he loathed humanity, yet he will be remembered as one of its great benefactors. All that money to cancer research . . . '

I leant forward.

'It's curious,' I said, 'that no one has ever noticed that you can't see the boathouse from the cedar tree. The willows screen it from view. I've often wondered if you planned it or whether it was on an impulse.'

The lights flickered as the train rattled through a tunnel. The little clerk coughed.

'Purely impulse, sir. In a small way I am a student of literature, and it has always struck me as curious that it is generally considered the unhappy ending if charity gets the money instead of the dissolute young heir. An alternative to be averted at all costs. The book I am reading now, sir, deals with a missing will. The hero is at the moment lying handcuffed and gagged on a deserted wharf.'

'And the tide is rising?'

'Swiftly, sir. He has three hours till midnight, in which to find a
certain paper, otherwise his aunt's fortune reverts to charity.'

'And he finds it in time?'

'Yes, sir.'

'You'd have ended it differently?'

'Yes, sir.'

There was a silence.

'I've always wanted to know when the idea occurred to you,' I said.

He coughed.

'Mr Hentish's days were obviously numbered, sir. When he was
signing the will I thought what a fine thing it would be if he should
die before a change of heart. Otherwise, I knew I should soon be
down at the Abbey to alter the will again in young Mr Hentish's
favour, and I knew him too well to hope that anyone but himself
and the bookmakers would benefit by the money. Too like his
uncle, sir.'

'I suppose old Hentish started talking about William and got into
a rage at having been deceived over the wedding. That would bring
on one of his attacks.'

'Yes, sir. His face got purple and his lips went white. I stood
watching him, hoping it might be fatal. He told me to go and pour
him out a glass of medicine from the bottle on the table in the
bathroom. The directions were on the bottle, he said. I'm a little
short-sighted, sir; it took me a little while to get my bearings. When
I got my reading glasses on the first thing that caught my eye was
the phial labelled morphia, and while he was yelling at me from the
library I opened the cupboard door, took out the morphia, and
poured it into the glass of medicine. He took the glass from me.
"You damn fool," he said, and drank it down.'

'Swallowed it too quickly to suspect anything, I suppose?'

'He just drew a deep breath, closed his eyes, and leaned back in
the chair. I went into the bathroom and wiped my fingerprints off
everything, which I understand is the correct procedure in murder.
Then I returned to the library, collected my papers and replaced
them in my brief case. Mr Hentish sat perfectly still. I don't know
whether he was breathing or not. When everything was in order I
went out into the hall, closing the library door quietly behind me.
I rang the bell for Mr Croucher, and told him I should remain in

the garden till my train time. "Is the old screw quiet?" he asked me, and I said he was.'

'Did it occur to you that William Hentish might be accused?'

'No, sir; the fact that the will was not in his favour seemed to preclude that. I didn't know he was unaware of my presence at the Abbey, or the reason for it.'

'I suppose you saw him cross the lawn to the boathouse?'

'No, sir, I didn't. I must have been dozing at the time. I took a chance on corroborating his story. It was the least I could do, I thought, sir.'

'Do you never feel a twinge of remorse about it?'

He looked surprised.

'Remorse! The money went to cancer research, sir. Have you read their last report? They've made great strides forward. Remorse! Oh no, sir. I've too great a regard for human life for that.'

The train quivered as the brakes checked the engine's speed, and the clerk peered out of the window. 'This will be my station, I think.' He gathered up the evening paper and his brief case. As the train groaned to a standstill a porter flung the door open and the fog bellied into the carriage.

'Cranham Junction. All change for Kedam, Stukely, Rye, and Wyming. All change,' he chanted. 'Any baggage, sir?'

'No thank you.' He turned to me. 'I've enjoyed our conversation very much, sir. I wish you good night.'

There is no silence more complete than the silence which follows the cessation of machinery. It intensifies all other sounds, the hiss of escaping steam, the clank and rattle of milk cans and the muffled chant of the porter, 'All ch-aa-nn-ge.' Suddenly the engine throbs, there is a jerk and a scraping as the wheels turn. Green lights, red lights, porters, old women, solicitors' clerks, loom large in the mist for a second through the moisture on the window-panes; the scraping of the wheels becomes more rhythmic, takes on a deeper whine; and the train rolls you on beyond them all.